Thoreau Bound

A Utopian Romance
in the
Isles of Greece

a novel by

Michael Pastore

Zorba Press
Ithaca, New York
www.ZorbaPress.com

This is a work of imaginative fiction, which proves that all characters and events depicted in this novel are delightful fabrications in the author's mind.

Published by Zorba Press
http://www.ZorbaPress.com

For more information about this work, visit the Zorba Press web site:
http://zorbapress.com/?page_id=170

... and the book's forthcoming blog:
http://www.ThoreauBound.com/

Release date: 2011 August 28

Paperback edition: 196,108 words
ISBN+10: 0-927379-68-6
ISBN+13: 978-0927379-68-7

Printed and bound in the United States of America.

For sales, permissions, and all other inquiries, please contact Zorba Press by email: books@ZorbaPress.com

Printings: 2011–01020304050607080910111213141516

Fill my hour so that I shall not say ...
"Alas, an hour of my life is gone,"
but rather:
"I have lived an hour!"

— Ralph Waldo Emerson

It doesn't matter what you do in the bedroom
as long as you don't do it in the street
and frighten the horses.

— Mrs. Patrick Campbell

Even stronger than geometry is the intense power of Eros.

— Plato

When love is temperate it is the sweetest thing,
but save me from the other kind.

— Euripides

INTRODUCTION
BY UMBERTO LAMANTINO

Coincidences create confusion, collisions, opportunities. Reading this Report, readers should grasp the distinction between two entities, similar in sound yet thoroughly unrelated. 'Sextopias' is a questionable utopia in the Greek Islands. 'S.E.X.T.O.P.I.A.S.' represents the not-for-profit organization dedicated to the technological expansion, exploration, and enhancement of human sexuality. — U.L.

Report SEXT–2011:
The Myth of Sextopias —
a Paradise of Open Sexuality and Perfect Love

MONTHS AGO, a unique message drifted into my electronic mailbox, a message too ridiculous to bother about, but too urgent to ignore. It stated passionately that somewhere on this much-suffering planet there existed — not in electronic bits and bytes, but real and in the flesh! — the ultimate Utopia of Eros. Its immodest motto brags: 'Abandon all shame, ye who enter here!' A haven for the repressed, a heaven for Casanovas, a pungent taste of the future for enlightened women and men. A panacea for the frigid, the rigid, the prudish, the nudish, the over-the-hill and the limp. A garden of sensuous delights beyond the dreams of all who have described its bliss in images or words — this steaming rock, this lusty land, this playful paradise: Sextopias.

There is no Sextopias, in fact. All the so-called sightings proved to be mere figments; all the urbane legends, fabricated; all the splendid cities nothing more than sleepy villages. Hundreds of rumors about this sensational kingdom came up empty — as empty as the word 'lust' in the uvula of a nun.

Debunking phallocentric phantasms of this kind is the meat and drink of S.E.X.T.O.P.I.A.S. — Society for Ecstatic eXperiments To Observe and Proliferate Imaginatively Advanced Sexuality — formed to study and promote an enlightened electronic-based approach to the practice of sex. More precisely, our expertise comprises three arenas: we expose exaggerated sexual vaunts; we facilitate Internet-mediated sexual relationships between human beings and one another; and we invent new possibilities for sexual relationships between human beings and all types of thinking and feeling machines.

Sexually speaking, the Internet has degenerated into a pointlessly pretentious plexus for peddling puerile porn. Virtual sex — a.k.a. cybersex, netsex, online sex, websex — is a euphemism for the 'M' word, hardly more satisfying than what any schoolboy could accomplish fifty years ago, hidden in his closet with a flashlight and a magazine. Today's self-made sex facing a computer screen encourages passivity, discourages authentic communication, promotes the degradation of women, and increases the awful trauma of isolation and loneliness. Online sex, like Thomas Hobbes's state of nature, is always "solitary, poor, nasty, brutish, and short."

The mission of S.E.X.T.O.P.I.A.S. is clear as tea: Develop an entirely new genre of electronic virtual sex, open source and free for all, one which might genuinely engage the participants in electronic relationships which are at once stimulating, post-human, and indecipherably complex.

We have called our innovations in online sexuality 'LOVES': Long-distance Online Virtual Experimental Sex. It is the studded opinion of our Board of Directors, who generously fund my research, that the non-contact distance-sexing of LOVES has the potential to become the erotic *ne plus ultra*. To the current sex online it adds emotional and intellectual dimensions; to "real sex in the flesh" it adds variety, convenience, and the wish-fulfillments which are unattainable with thy neighbor's wife or the young woman next door.

This new model of vicarious sexual activity could improve the quality of life in untold ways. LOVES will reduce the vast quantities of human misery caused by traditional sexual relationships: stresses, heartaches, obsessions, stalkings, suicides, wars, sappy literature, and other polytypic ramifications. Millions of vulnerable young women would be saved from lives of servile prostitution, as lazy men realize that they can satisfy themselves without stirring from their office-chairs or home-couches. While not completely free of "viruses", LOVES protects its participants from the gamut of sexually transmitted diseases.

Peerless physical satisfactions and avoidance of sexual side-effects are only the beginnings of a brave new world of Eros. Most promising in this realm is our proliferating crop of prime-mates called APEs — Animated Play Erotomaniacs. APEs are computerogenic sex-partners, sensitive and indefatigable, who can be scrutinized with the mere fingering of desktop mice. A related project, CHIMPS (Choosing Hundreds of Internet-Manipulated Pleasurable Satisfactions) is currently steaming in our jungly labs.

Human-And-Human Sex (HAHS), now vaingloriously passé, has yielded to an e-merging breed of sexual amusements. Yet the crux of this Report SEXT-2011 hangs not around the rough beast waiting to be born, but on the old myths waiting to be buried. Stories about sexual utopias — consummate excellence in flesh-to-flesh sexual encounters — have been multiplying and spreading like spammail. With unmatched zealousness, the S.E.X.T.O.P.I.A.S. research staff unmasks these bumptious flams, revealing thousands of these legends to be distorted, exaggerated, perverted, fraudulent, and false.

How do we debunk? Our methodology is a model for all future psychosexual research. First, our Team-A performs a comprehensive search of the Internet's webpages, newsgroups, mailing lists, email banks, social networks, and other repositories of electronically-stored information. Our light-fast scanners then check all print-version references in recent periodicals and books. This yields a database of individuals who claimed to have founded, frolicked, or fornicated in Sextopias the place. Next, these individuals are interviewed by our Team-B, and asked the DCQ (Delta-Cash-Question): "For how much cash, or for what reward, will you change the story which you have just sworn to be true?"

Naturally — as in the cases of UFO sightings and bogus miracles — for the perfect price, everyone was willing to change, embellish or retract their tales. Some told us that they would swear to murdering their mothers for as little as fifty dollars; others would admit to a thousand crimes and sins for a new car, a harem of women, or a six-figure cash advance.

Alas, the course of true investigation never does run smooth. On the last day allotted for phase-one research we discovered one individual who could not be bribed or persuaded to change his Rabelaisian tale. We could find out nothing about him except for this one sentence buried in our files: "A supreme raconteur and charismatic trickster, O. Thoreau is a crazy combination of Casanova, Robin Hood, Tom Jones, Mahatma Gandhi, and Zorba the Greek."

Three-dimensional video (3DV) images revealed the man. These flashy files showed that Thoreau — between 24 and 28 years old — had the body of an athlete: robust, well-muscled and lithe. He was wearing a hat that had been blown around the world; the soles of his walking shoes were worn down to the soles of his feet; and his leather jacket and multi-pocketed pants were obviously second-hand, and perhaps even third-hand or fourth. His simple clothes, his untamed hair, his satyrical expression, his carefree laugh — all made it appear that he had just leaped out of some enchanted forest, pursued by the soft arms and wild laughter of naked nymphs. And indeed, he later told me that through the entire week we spent interviewing together, he had been sleeping outdoors under the stars, in the cold-aired chill of the public park.

Exceedingly handsome, his face reminded me of a vigorous young man depicted in a painting by Raphael. His eyes — remarkable eyes! — gleamed blue as the brightest sapphires, so clear, so radiant, so dazzling they outshined the blinking pixels in the sockets of our Shockwave Sexbots. Someone not in my position, someone unconcerned with outer appearances and more able to speculate about the worlds within, might describe those jewels as the eyes of a man incapable of insincerities or lies. Perhaps this fact about his childlike openness was related to his poverty. For who among us can survive the disorienting dizziness of the world of business without a dozen long-stemmed ruses, a bouquet of expedient fibs, and a gardenful of day-to-day deceits?

For four weeks before meeting, Thoreau and I corresponded with each other by slugmail. His postcards were cheerful and brief. It struck me as ironic that this man, who owned almost no possessions, was the only one of our subjects who could not be influenced or bribed. When we sent him cash to change his story, Thoreau returned the money to us the very next day. His accompanying letter asked me if I had read the writings of another Thoreau, then quoted: "Rather than love, than money, than fame, give me truth."

For a short time I tried to give him Truth, by attempting to show Thoreau the value of our work at S.E.X.T.O.P.I.A.S. I tried to help him mostly for the purpose of proving my far-gone conclusions, but partly out of pity for his predicament. For Thoreau was a man out of sync with his times, a Transcendental leftover, a rootless vagabond, an artist swimming for his life against the mainstream current of popular culture. He was a poor adventurer seduced by his unbending conscience and abandoned by unbounded optimism. He could never accept the reality of the technologized future, which is the inescapable destiny of Man.

Each day, relentlessly, computerized machines grow more important in our workaday and playaday lives. These same machines become increasingly human as we become less so; and modern persons are becoming more and more indistinguishable from these thinking and creating machines. Thoreau tried to fight these forces by being a good visionary and living his own way. But of course, as soon as the fire of his youth fades, these forces will engulf him, the same way they destroyed profounder artist-rebels: exiles and expatriates like Jean-Jacques Rousseau, Henry Thoreau, Herman Melville, Walt Whitman, Fyodor Dostoyevsky, Jack London, D.H. Lawrence, and countless more.

After he refused to be interviewed by videophone, we met face-to-face in my office downtown. Hours and hours passed as we listened and talked together. Soon the interview slipped into a dialogue, then before long most of the talking was coming from me. For this was one of his powers: he spoke with a childlike sincerity that warmed the truth from the souls of other men.

"Listen to me, Thoreau," I said. "Listen and I'll tell you how I saved myself, and how you can save yourself as well. When I was a young man I read the old books, I yearned for the old civilizations, I worshiped the old ways. But I quit those Quixotic quests as I reached for the stars and grasped their hopelessness. Every man, every morning, makes a vital choice: Leap on the stallion of the Future, or die in the dust of the Past."

Leaning forward across my desk, I explained the inevitable future with a winning grin, oiled with vanity, smeared with certitude.

"Once, the one thing needful was facts for the sake of knowledge; now the one thing necessary is data for the sake of fun. That's what we're promising in the new virtual world, Mr. Thoreau: Pleasure. Infinite varieties of pleasure, pleasure with no limits: effortless to create, easy to reproduce, endless to enjoy. Interminable pleasures. Everlasting pleasures. Pleasures that can be repeated without boredom twenty-four hours every day, seven days every week, fifty-two weeks every year for a man's entire lifetime, and perhaps beyond."

I paused to let him swallow these shrewd tidbits. The boast was yet to come.

"For who, Mr. Thoreau, can know and bear the sufferings of this world? On any morning, who can watch our world on his computer screen and then honestly say: 'Our situation is getting better,' or 'This event will not trigger even deeper disasters,' or 'This news gives me hope and joy'?"

My feemail beeped; I ignored it — for the first time — then spoke on.

"A man has only one chance to survive, to endure, to fulfill himself: Escape to the portentous planets in cyberspace. The 21st Century will be spearheaded then molded by this force: the Technologies of Diversion. Men and machines connected to give countless pleasures to men. No one can stop this humanetworked future. Run away and it chases you like a bad conscience, stand against it and it stamps you down. Faster and faster the future flies forward in spite of your fiery scorn."

Attentively, Thoreau listened to my arguments, all the while shaking his picturesque head. He explained to me how and why he disagreed: how the touch of the hand was as vital as the feeling in the heart; and how the artificial pleasures would never move us as intensely as the natural joys. He told me that he believed in Love, and that only by giving Love — not by using hardware, software and sexware — only by giving Love can we transform the world and feel true happiness. He contended that Truth could never be manipulated, as long as a person speaks from her or his most private experiences. He insisted that every word of his story about Sextopias was genuine and real.

I was unmoved by these meaningless remarks, the same smokepuffs found in the pipe dreams of mystic philosophers, in the confessions of Romantic poets, and in the sentimental novels of Charles Dickens, that unhappiest of men.

For five days we continued to discuss our two distinctive worlds, the virtual and the real. With grim determination I strove to make him see how urgently society needed our technological PERVERTS (Precisely Engineered Relationships Via Electronic Romance Towers Simulations).

Lightheartedly, Thoreau entertained me by telling spontaneous tales of his travels, adventures, and most personal affairs.

Truth is a bottomless abyss. Thus, in the interest of this hole Truth, I have painted zebra stripes over the Trojan horse of knowledge. In short, I have been obligated to include Thoreau's story as a soon-to-be-forgotten footnote to my conclusive report. Perhaps a glimpse of our last meeting will help to convince the unconvinced on which side of the fence my reality lies.

"Mr. Thoreau," I addressed him, as we faced each other across my desk. "We now have some compelling business to transact. I trust that an innocuous background video will not distract you."

Using a voice command I activated the ten wall-sized screens that covered the office's ceiling, floor, and honeycomb-designed walls. Split into a dozen large segments, each screen depicted twelve fresh EGGS: Experimental Games Galvanizing Sex. The room filled up with images of naked bodies, bodies of women, bodies perfectly-sculpted, bodies larger than life. But the titillating flicks had no palpable effect upon Thoreau. Until suddenly, discerning the purpose of these images, he laughed out loud.

"Mr. Thoreau," I said. "We utilize these images for sexual experimentation. Most live males find them arousing. These displays are not a joke."

He laughed wildly before telling me what we now call 'Heresy 21':

"Real men don't buy sex."

And then he looked into my eyes and said: "Technology is a stunning woman: first she turns your head, then she twists it off at the neck. The downloaded dumpling cannot take one's hunger away."

The most effective way to manage insightful criticisms is to ignore them. Thoreau was a thorn in my Achilles heel. It was now clear that I could not change his mind by the voice of my reason or by the vice of my authority.

Another voice command reprogrammed the screens, dissolving the sounds and sights of the frisky females. The screens now filled with three-dimensional videos of the major city which surrounded us, image-edited to erase all traces of homeless persons, ugly architecture, advertising-laden billboards, violent crimes, traffic jams, raucous noises, and health-impairing smog.

"It's not our goal, Mr. Thoreau, to eliminate reality. Our new technologies supplement reality. In just the same manner that all the other arts add something to reality, by allowing us to live in our imaginations without risking the tangible dangers of life in the raw."

When we argued about this issue, Thoreau made a thoroughly preposterous claim. He said that his own dreams and creations were more valuable than the dreams and creations which were manufactured for consumers by teams of expert professionals. Teams — with unlimited financial resources — which could harness the cumulative powers and revelations of the Internet, mass psychology, expert systems, and Artificial Intelligence.

"Mr. Thoreau, without being offensive I will be blunt. The stories you have fabricated do not contribute to the S.E.X.T.O.P.I.A.S. vision: a life where computer-generated diversions provide infinite erotic pleasures to mankind. Do you still insist that everything you've told me about your heterogeneous sexual experiences corresponds precisely to what actually occurred?"

Thoreau nodded; I carried on.

"Since you refuse to deny your myths, Thoreau, our official investigation policy requires me to ask: 'Do I have your permission to scan this manuscript of the unlikely tales you've told me, and then add them to my report?'"

Thoreau murmured the word "cosmos."

For a moment I wondered if he had hacked through our security firewalls and discovered our top-secret COSMOS (Complete Operating System for Maximum Onanistic Sensations). After dismissing this notion as absurd, I explained to Thoreau what his options were. He could change his story; or he could acquiesce to having it included in our web database; or he could refuse to allow us to publish his fabulous adventures. If he refused to grant permission, I told him, then I would change his name and summarize his story into one bland, terse, professionally-written paragraph.

On one condition, Thoreau said, he would allow me to publish his erratic tales. His fable, about how he discovered Sextopias, must be reprinted as a whole: nothing could be deleted, expurgated, or changed. Yet one black hole emerged in his starry-eyed honesty: regarding the manuscript he deposited on my desk, he would neither affirm nor deny he was the author of the work.

We disputed these issues for a long while. Primarily I was concerned that his story might fool readers into believing a dangerous untruth: that 'actual reality' could be more nourishing, vitalizing and beneficial than its virtual child.

At last we were able to agree on a mutually-satisfying compromise. Thoreau's narrative would be included in its entirety — without any of his words omitted — but only as a lowly footnote to this significant report.

Thoreau pressed my hand between his hands as warmly as if I were his brother or his dad. When he smiled then said good-bye to my female staff — ten women between the ages of twenty and sixty — the women rushed from their desks to flock around him, then pleaded for his phone number and address. For five days they had been making lovesick eyes at him; and now they moaned when he told them that he had no address, but lived on "the open road!" Two of the women, one young and the other married, fell to his feet and hugged his knees, begging for some way to contact him. How they shrieked with pleasure when he scribbled then handed them the email address of his closest friend! At last, singing like some wild bird, he stepped outside into the sunlight and the cool fresh air.

My indisputable Report SEXT–2011 — the report that you are reading now via this email or webpage or electronic book — offers a conclusion supported by evidence so overwhelming that no reasonable person can deny it. Sextopias — Thoreau's imaginary paradise — does not exist. And indeed, as an upgraded Voltaire might have said: If a sexual paradise did exist then it would have to be disinvented. Like the box of the curious Pandora spewing unknown evils into the innocent Greek world, think of the planetary havoc it would instantly unleash! Who would bother with shopping malls, daytime television, formula novels, packaged foods, driving cars, indoor life, selfishness, drudge work, newspapers — the panoply of unnecessary habits and luxuries that underlie our lives — if we could experience one year, one week, one day — even one moment! — of whole love and wildly fulfilling sex? Clearly, in a short span, the myths we live by would be irrevocably shattered. The entire global economy would collapse like a bad soufflé.

O. Thoreau's "autobiographical adventures" (as he liked to call them) are offered here, for the reasons previously stated, undiluted, unexpurgated, and complete. Simple to find and access, my Report SEXT-2011 will remain embedded on the Web forever. But Thoreau's foolish footnote, submerged in the electronic ocean of exabytes of information, will presently be lost. And perhaps, sooner that you might expect, his story shall be righteously deleted by the unforgiving finger of a censor-moron, puritan or prude.

I trust that any reader with good judgment, any reader who bothers to compare my veracious version against Thoreau's virgin vision, will have no trouble discerning the Falsehoods from the Truth.

Dr. Umberto Lamantino, Executive Director of Research
S.E.X.T.O.P.I.A.S.
Society for Ecstatic eXperiments To
Observe and Proliferate Imaginatively Advanced Sexuality
www.Sextopias.org

1

THE SORROWS OF YOUNG THOREAU

ON A MOST BEAUTIFUL beach in Crete rests the much-suffering Thoreau — handsome as a god, naked as a tiger, silent as a rose.

He sits on a cube-shaped rock, his heart open, his muscles bulging, his head so heavy from deep thoughts that his chin lies on the back of his great right hand. Memories of two faces chain him to the place. Around him, the stars sputter instead of twinkle, and the sky — suspended between night and morning — glows purple as a young man's prose. The sea roars unsatisfied, a great beast breathing an obscene phone call into daybreak's blushing ears. Rushing along the sand, the heartless sea surrounds his ankles, chills his feet, gurgles unsympathetically. Thoreau weeps into the sea as he remembers how he lost two women, the dark-haired Beatrice and the blonde-haired Bliss.

Two birds scream, then strange noises snortle from the beach. Not far from Thoreau is his faithful factotum, Panzano Panettone — faced like a joker, bared like a bone, as gabby as gaggles of geese. A man of great trust and little confidence, he mutters to himself the insult recently received from female lips: "Fat as a whale, smart as a snail!" At this moment he is lying on his side on the white sand, beached helplessly, hands tied behind his back around the trunk of a tall palm tree.

But these puny obstacles cannot discourage Panzano from the prime passion of his life: food. Without hands to hold the precious morsel, with one cheek pressed against the sand, he chews the last scraps of meat from the legbone of a roasted lamb. Between swallows and bites and big-bellied belches, Panzano peers solicitously toward the sounds from his sobbing friend. His kind heart beats the doors of a dilemma: whether to call out to Thoreau, or to continue his much-needed meal. First in musical Italian, then in butchered *Inglese*, he shouts: *"Cosa faresti al posto mio?"* — "What would you do if you were me?"

Darkness raised her skirts to flaunt the bright red treasures of the crack of Dawn. In the flushing light two more human beings, lying midway between Thoreau and Panzano, became increasingly more visible. Two fleshy females slept snugly on a bed of sand. One redhead, one bluehead, both nude. A campfire smoldering beside them, empty wine bottles, and smiles on both sleeping faces insinuated that the night before had been sublime.

A dark bird descended on the beach near Panzano's greasy lips. The bold scavenger cocked its head, screeched joyfully, then snapped its yellow beak around the lamby leg.

"*Furfante! Birbante! Iniquo! Ladro!*" shouted Panzano. "Rogue! Scoundrel! Rascal! Thief!"

Panzano quickly snatched his bony breakfast and a tug of war ensued, bird-beak holding one end of the bone, man-mouth gripping the other.

Poor Thoreau! so deeply swallowed by his own misfortunes he had forgotten he was not the only man on Earth. Plucked from exile by cacophonous swearing and squawks, Thoreau turned around and stared behind him at the outlandish scene. Panzano's mouth attempted to pull the bone away, but the tenacious bird hung on. Another large bird joined the battle, fell soft as a surgeon's scalpel onto Panzano's belly, then pecked a pointed beak against the skin of the glutton's bulging abdomen. Panzano let out a holler, releasing his beloved bone. Having stolen the treasure and demonstrated Nature's superiority to Man, both birds spread their wings then flew upwards into the lightening sky.

"Panzano!" Thoreau shouted. His rivers of tears had changed course, rolling into an ocean of laughter uncontrolled. He jumped off the rock and sauntered to the carcass of his frustrated friend.

"When I first met you, Panzano, I thought, 'Friar Tuck is reincarnated in the amassing body of this amusing man.' And when I got to know you better, when you pelted me with proverbs and platitudes, I said, 'Beneath his Himalayas of fatuous flesh, here is a Sancho Panza, loyal and earthy and wise.' But just now you looked like Rubens's painting about Prometheus, the Titan who stole fire from the gods and gave it to humankind. For this benevolent burglary, Zeus chained him to a rock for six-hundred years."

Panzano tilted up his head to spit out a gob of sand.

"Only six hundred years?" he said, managing to smile despite his lack of comfort. "What's six hundred years to an immortal? Last night felt like it lasted six-hundred years. And as sure as eggs is eggs, if I ever have one more night as lasting as last night, it will be my last last night."

With embarrassing awkwardness, he struggled to raise his massive body to a position kneeling on both knees. His wrists were still tied behind him around the tree trunk, and he discovered that — unable to indulge in his natural habit of waving his expressive arms as he talked — it was unusually difficult to speak. To compensate, with every spoken word, Panzano punctuated each motion of his body and his head with superabounding oomph.

"Gli uomini gli anni che sentono, è le donne quelli che mostrano. Men are as old as they feel, and women as old as they look. Right now I feel not a day younger than six-hundred years. But give me one good meal, just one, and I'll feel twenty-one again."

Thoreau laughed as he started to untie the knotted rope that bound the wrists of his merry friend. But his concentration wavered from the task at hands. His beauty-loving eyes were drawn to the forms of the young women — painted toenails, feet, ankle bracelets, calves, thighs, buttocks, waists, chests, shoulders, necks, hair, faces, mouths, noses, eyes.

Thoreau's eyes opened wide as he realized an old notion for the first time. Inventive minds are always sparked by things divine: the genius of nature, the sincerity of children, the greatness of noble actions, the loveliness of every woman's face and form.

"Why have men wanted to know the future, Panzano, or tried to conquer the future and bring it under their control? Each day clobbers us with unexpected hazards or joyful serendipities. That's half the rapture in life, our great improvisations! The way we meet, with daring and imagination, whatever good and not-good comes."

Thoreau pressed his temples between his palms.

"An hour ago, when I woke up in the sand in the middle of these two young angels, I couldn't remember ever meeting them before, how I got there, or what we'd done. And I still can't remember now."

Groaning and moaning, Panzano sluggishly stood up, then rubbed his back against the trunk of the rough tree.

"Amico intimo, bosom friend," he said. "For seven days, anyone who has watched us would have said: '*Sono pane è cacio*': They are bread and cheese, they are sworn friends. And the way you cared for me like a brother — after those ten wild gypsies robbed me blind and deaf — I never will forget, not until this cauldron of flesh withers to a teacup of tinkling bones.

"Who is Panzano? A barrel of blubber with the body of a bear and the brain of a twittering bird. But Thoreau tells him the craziest things:

Panzano could be an athlete, a hero, an artist, a lover of women *incomparabile,* incomparable!"

He cast a yearning glance at the enchanting female bodies.

"Again and again Thoreau says to Panzano: 'Eat less, love more. Man does not live by bread alone.' ... Yet last night, you spent eight delicious hours sandwiched between those two succulent slices of bread."

Thoreau stretched his arms then scratched his dark-haired head.

"Panzano, what happened last night?"

Panzano rolled his eyes.

"What happened? What did not happen! If I read it in the newspaper I wouldn't believe any of it, not one *parola,* not one word! If I heard it from my papa or the Pope, I could acknowledge not more than half. From you yourself — my warmest friend in this whole cold world — if you swore it to me on a stack of spaghetti, I might consider as much as eight-tenths of the whole. And even if these two eyes of mine, which have known me since the day I was born, even if these two eyes saw what they saw last night, I would probably say only ninety percent could be true."

Thoreau picked up a chunk of bread littered on the sand, brushed it clean, then tore it in half and stuffed a piece into his mouth. Before resuming the work of loosening the ropes, he placed the other piece into Panzano's maw.

"The whole story, Panzano. Tell me."

One gulp and the bread was gone.

"*Grazie mille,* thanks a million! The good bread, she soaks up the gravy of my tears, and now the story can be told."

Panzano sighed.

"For one day and one night you sleeped and got no sleep with the woman who calls herself Bliss. *Guarda che bomba,* what a beauty! Some great artist — no, a magician! — painted the sun's gold-yellow in her hair, then jeweled her eyes with emerald-green!"

Two teardrops filled his bloodshot eyes then trickled down his ruddy cheeks.

"May the Fates bless her and protect her wherever she is right now! After she left, like a grandmother, a *nonna,* you were crazy with *preoccupazione,* with worry. Sunup to sundown you ran up, you ran down, you ran all around these hills. But when a man's conscience chases him, where can he run to, where can he hide? Whichever way you turn, your *pizzolo* is always in front of you, looking up at you into your eyes."

The face of Panzano appeared puzzled by his own words, but he carried on nevertheless.

"Bliss! *Un bel pezzo di carne,* a beautiful piece of flesh! Thoreau's head was trying to forget her, but his heart shouted: "Never forget!" Last night when you came back, I said: '*Sta' calmo,* Thoreau, *sta' calmo* — keep calm, keep calm. *Quello che è fatto è fatto* — what's done cannot be undone.'"

For a long moment Panzano looked up at the sky.

"*Che tristezza* — how sad! Your heart was so heavy, like a sack of watermelons, you fell down on this sand and cried, cried like a baby without a milky breast. And then your friend and biggest fan, Panzano Panettone — the person you have cheered a dozen dozen times — decided he would do for you what you have done for him: he would give your heart engorgement. He would cook for you *una vera cena italiana,* a real Italian dinner. A meal so *delizioso,* delicious, that you would forget every woman in the universe, except the mother that bores you."

Thoreau's glance scanned the sandy beach.

"I don't see any traces of a sumptuous dinner, Panzano. Did the vultures get it?"

"*Che peccato* — what a pity!" Panzano said. "The missing dinner was born last evening, in the center of the town, when I am walking out of the *mercato,* the market, happy as a mouse in a cheese factory, hungry as a lion with false teeth. Both of these stout arms were filled with bags of groceries, enough to feed every *bona roba* in *Venezia* — every prostitute in Venice. But Fate stuck her middle finger up my *narice,* my nostril, then boogered my plans."

He glanced at the sleeping figures and he sighed.

"Yes, the vultures got all the food! When these two ladies — the ones you call angels — saw me walking they laughed at me, they shouted: 'You make a *terremoto,* an earthquake, every time you take a step!' And when I smiled at these two ladies, they tweaked my nose then pickled my pocket."

"They pickled your pocket?" said Thoreau. "Did they get your cucumber?"

"They got nothing but a square of candy the size your fingernail. The ladies looked hungry enough, so I spat on my hands and brushed back my hair then said: 'Fair maidens, do not be shy. Come with me and help me to cook, and I'll give you a chocolate bar fit for a princess, and a dinner feast fit for a queen.' ... I was like the little pig in the story, safe in his brick house until he opens the front door and invites a wolf-in-disguise to warm herself by his happy fire."

Again Panzano glanced at the two women, and then shook his head.

"When I offered them the chocolate bars they called me a *pervertito,* pervert! And then they cackled like chickens and scurried away like little deers. I spent one hour in the wine store, talking with the owner who had lived for five years in my native town of Rome. I didn't see the two angels as I left that store: I supposed they deserted me to find more prosperous paunches to pinch. But the minute after I got back here to our sunny campsite I found that the shady ladies had followed me all the way home."

Panzano's eyes glistened with promised joy as he recounted the climax of his hopes.

"It was them but it was not them; it was the same ladies but like ladies they no longer looked. They had painted their eyelids silver and their lips red; they had bathed in deodorant; and the dresses they were wearing were cut so low and so short that the both of them together wouldn't give you enough material to wrap up a *rigatoni.* 'Panzano, you dog drooling by the kitchen table,' I said to myself. 'What did you do to deserve all this?' My stomach filled with the moths, my tongue was got by the cats, my throat felt dry as toast, my hands twitched like lobsters in the boiling pot."

More great sighs fell from the man of more great size.

"I handed the ladies some cooking utensils and asked them to boil my potatoes and mash my spuds. Just then — too bad for me, too good for you — they saw you sleeping and they screamed. They threw down the spatulas, they banged my bottom with a frying pan, they jumped up and down, they clapped their hands. They ran to you and ran their fingers across your face, then shouted *'Bello! Bello! Bello!'* — Handsome! Handsome! Handsome! — and *'Non è un sogno!'* — Isn't he a dream!"

Thoreau flashed an admiring glance at his slumbering admirers.

"In Europe they call this a healthy appreciation of beauty. And in America they call this sexual harassment. Go on, Panzano. Go on."

"You were sleeping and the ladies tried to wake you. They tried to wake you in ways which I would be ashamed to describe in front of a *suora* — how do you call them? — those women in the *monastero,* monastery, who dress like penguins, pray all morning, play bingo each afternoon, and ring their bells every night."

"They are called nuns, Panzano: they give up the earthly pleasures to search for ones divine. And if we meet these devout women, who sacrifice themselves to serve others, be assured that our hearts will be unburdened and that our luck will change. And now tell me what happened as I slept."

Panzano shrugged his sandy shoulders.

"The ladies tried to wake you with every trick in the books. And they tried a lot more that wasn't in the books, because if the stuff they were doing would be printed in the books, then every day millions more people would be reading books. They tried, but you would not wake up. The ever-ready Thoreau had had very little sleep for almost two days and one night, and he extended no interest in the ladies and their giddy games."

Thoreau's glances, straying to the bodies of the unclad nymphs, returned to the rope around Panzano's wrists.

"The poison of grief exhausted me," said Thoreau. "I hope I didn't hurt the ladies' feelings with anything I said or did. Or failed to do. What happened then?"

"Had you seen it you would have been proud of them for their persistence: they would not give up. The ladies cut off your clothes with a *temperino,* a penknife. They covered your body with so much *olio d'oliva,* olive oil, I thought they planned to eat you as the salad. And when you didn't rise up they rubbed you with whiskey then scrubbed you with wine."

Thoreau shook his head but could not remember anything at all.

"And after I'd been rubbed and scrubbed?"

"They told Panzano to close off his eyes and take off his clothes. And I said to myself: 'Panzano, at last your minute has come!' I thought they wanted to amuse themselves with me like the well-dressed ladies of Milano."

He laughed good-naturedly.

"But Fate stuck her fist in my *focaccia.* Instead, one of the good ladies took off her rope belt, then the other excellent lady used that belt to tie me to this tree. For the first few moments I nourished the vain hope that my breadloaf would be baked in their ovens. When they laughed at me what did I learn? No matter how big a fool is a man, he can always make himself a bigger one. After the ladies roped me, they threw all our clothes into the fire, my clothes, your clothes — "

Thoreau slapped his thigh.

"Not again! Panzano, I can't seem to stop women from taking my clothes. It must be my destiny to become a professional nudist. I'll give you the sweat off my back, friend, but don't bother to ask me for the shirt."

Panzano was too busy telling to slow down to hear.

" — they even burned their own clothes, lord knows why. And then the most whoreable thing happened. *È roba da far rizzare I capelli* — it's enough to make your hair stand on end."

Fogs of sorrow drifted over Panzano's chubby face.

"They ate all the food and drank all the wine."

"They left nothing for us at all?" asked Thoreau.

"Nothing but a few bones and a few beans. And then they started laughing and wouldn't stop laughing, and — forgive me a thousand times, *amico* — they forced me to watch while they took your advantage."

The long look that Thoreau poured at the sleeping women was filled with a mixture of compassion and disbelief.

"And what did they do when they had my advantage?"

"They played with it *focosamente*."

"*Focosamente, focosamente*," murmured Thoreau. "Ah, passionately."

"Passionately, that's what it was, all right! The ladies they were very very good. But you! You were *superbo*, superb! *Quante storie!* — what a performance! *Sei stato una bomba!* — you were like a dynamite! You should win an Acomedy Award. But me, only a *spettatore*, a spectator. Dreams are so easy, life is so hard."

"What do you mean, friend?"

Panzano closed his eyes.

"You enjoyed a night with everything and you remember nothing. And I enjoyed nothing and remember everything. So which one of us was dreaming, eh?"

Thoreau smiled a smile both sour and sweet.

"Panzano," he said. "Have you seen my books?"

The Buddha-bellied man nodded gravely.

"I was the last man to see them alive. These supine ladies burned them all. They threw them into the fire then danced around the flames."

To this most unfortunate news Thoreau responded coolly.

"And may I assume that you did your best to save the world's great literature, the sacred vessels of those deepest feelings, thoughts and deeds which show us how to love life and freedom, and how we can become more fearless, more individual, more wholly alive?"

Panzano took a moment to ponder the question and the reply.

"I did my best to save the food, I did my best to save the books, I did my best to kiss the girls, but my best is never good enough! I have a hundred wishes and only one regret."

"What's that, Panzano?"

"I regret that I was not born somebody else. But what good would that do me? If I was somebody else, that somebody would want to be somebody else."

When Thoreau untied the rope that bound his friend, his clear eyes surveyed the campsite. Sunrise, sea, sand, rocks, a smoking campfire, wine bottles, a strand of belt-rope, one fat naked Panzano rubbing his wrists, two Rubenesque women sleeping *au naturel,* and nothing else at all except the sounds of waves and sea birds crying overhead.

Thoreau knelt down beside the sleeping beauties. He touched their hair and cheeks. He watched their chests rise as they breathed. Ever-so-gently he stroked their foreheads with his hands. As he studied their faces he sang them a quiet song, and his voice was the soft sounds of sea-shells whispering the sea's sensuous secrets across those innocent ears. Panzano was thinking that his friend handled the lascivious ladies with more kindness than they deserved, but Thoreau knew that no man ever treats a woman with tenderness enough.

"We are all angels when we sleep," said Thoreau.

"Angels," replied Panzano, "with devilish dreams."

Thoreau's lips pressed two kisses against the soft and sleeping lips.

Then he tore his gaze away from the young women and stood up. As he turned to his friend his smile collapsed, his face tensed with lovesick anguish.

"And the woman who calls herself Bliss?" he asked, in a voice that tried not to tremble but trembled still. "Did she get on the boat yesterday morning?"

Tears poured from Panzano's eyes.

"Blissetta, Blissetta! *Superdonna,* superwoman! *Perfetta donna,* perfect woman! No, more than perfect. She is the goddess *Venere,* Venus, worshiped by the stupido *Cupido,* Panzano!"

The large man wiped his eyes with the back of his hairy forearm.

"It broka my heart it was so sad, like that opera of Puccini Verdi. The way you told her it was too dangerous to drive her *bicicletta* around the *mondo,* the world, all alone. And the way she told you to either travel with her, or '*Chiudi il becco!* — Shut your mouth!' and '*Vaffanculo!* — Fuck off!'"

Thoreau recalled his frustration when he could find no solution to their problem: he wanted to travel west, she wanted to see the East. And she insisted that with him or without him East she would go.

Four eyes wept like waterfalls. Thoreau flung his arm around the broad shoulders of his tearful friend.

"When you last saw her, did she say anything about me?"

Panzano's face, reflecting his emotions, was always the perfect mirror of his imperfect mind. Now it showed that he was weighing whether or not to pierce his idol with a stinging truth.

"She said ... Blissetta said ... "

"Tell me, Panzano. I can take it."

Nodding and sniffing, Panzano restrained his overwhelming urge to weep.

"She said that she would never forget two things. The way she got you up, and the way you let her down."

Once more, a thunderstorm of tears rained from the cloudy eyes of these good men.

"Thoreau," said Panzano, between spasms of sobs. "If you had any clothes on, and I had any clothes on, then like a *bambino,* a baby — or maybe like a *bamboccio,* a plump child — I would hug you and cry on your shoulder until I forget everything and fall asleep."

Thoreau looked up in the direction of the nearby town. His head was throbbing and his sinuses were clogged, but his hearing stayed presciently clear. From the dock one mile away came the low blast of a foghorn, which signaled the impending departure of a boat.

A boat! The clear sound inspired an idea that brought vitality to Thoreau's dejected face. He ran to his rock, the throne-shaped rock where each morning he would sit to watch the sunrise. He pushed the heavy rock aside, dug a few inches down into the sand, then pulled out a clear plastic bag.

"Panzano," Thoreau said, as he pulled open the bag. "Whenever I smell trouble or perfume, I conceal the absolute necessities. Except for cash, here we have everything we need. Yesterday at dawn, while Bliss was swimming, I stuffed all your money, and all my money, into her bicycle's pannier bags. And I know that we both wish we could have given more."

"A hundred and a hundred hundred times more!" Panzano shouted.

Thoreau tossed two items from the bag to the hands of his famished friend.

"For Panzano: *passaporto* and food. With this can of fermented soybeans you can fend off starvation for twenty-four hours at least."

He pulled out the remaining items from the clear plastic bag.

"For Thoreau: *passaporto*, Swiss army knife, jar of dehydrated yogurt tablets, roll of phosphorescent-yellow duct tape — the roll you sold me when we first met a week ago — stub of pencil, two notebooks."

To this bare-bones survival kit, Thoreau added the belt-rope strand that had tied Panzano to the tree. He smiled his bright smile, and then playfully slapped his hand against Panzano's shoulder.

"*Coraggio,* courage, Panzano! *Andiamo,* let's go!"

The round man shook his head and vigorously waved his hands. From experience he was certain that nobody could move him from a spot unless he wanted to be moved.

"Where can we go, Thoreau? *Dove,* where? We have no food, we have no money, we have no shoes, we have no clothes. We're too old for nursery schools and too young for hell, and no other places will take us in."

Thoreau smiled as he recalled the words of a wise man: 'There are no obstacles, only in the heart.' Friendship means more than having fun together. To be a true friend is to always tell the truth, and to help your friend find courage to do the almost-impossible things that must be done.

"Friend," said Thoreau, soothingly, "listen to the plan. We are two strong men, men blessed with freedom and everything we need — everything except the perfect women and the perfect world. Our task is to lunge forward from the safety of the ordinary to seek extraordinary paths. This is what we must do: dash to the dock, catch this morning's boat, then sail from the playgrounds of Crete to the battlegrounds of the Turkish coast. Whether the gods like it or not, we're going to find that incomparably beautiful young woman who calls herself Bliss. And when we find her we will explain to her how foolish and dangerous it is to do what she wants to do. Do you understand what I'm saying, Panzano?"

"I understand more than you think, Thoreau. When I studied the English language the teacher read to us an American poem: 'Two roads diverged in a wooden eye.' After six months trying to figure it out, I wrote an essay and explained how it finally made sense: whenever a silly poet does something reckless, he winds up falling on his face."

Panzano looked with pride at the face of his wild friend. Once again he admired Thoreau's resourcefulness, the way he had saved their basic necessities from the claws of the dangerous dames. But Thoreau's plan seemed preposterous. The scheme resembled Panzano's hopeless attitude about his own opportunities for sexual encounters with comely women. Sex sucks: the first step is too embarrassing, the act itself is too perilous, and the chance for success is too remote. He crossed his arms against his chest.

"*Impossibile,* impossible! My friend, you know how tight-up the Greeks are about the nudity in the public places. Without a tent to cover it, this fat body is not fit to be seen by the naked balls of the eyes. The Greeks have laws, Thoreau! For ten years we would rot in some stinkhola of a jail! Look around, *amico,* there is nothing, not a bag or a bandanna to cover our personal parts."

Impatiently, the boat's foghorn resounded once again.

"There's no time to twiddle your twaddle, Panzano! Let's go!"

The sun's bottom edge just slipped up over the watery horizon, and Thoreau stared at the great ball which gave light and life to all living beings. Afire with red-gold glows, the sky flashed a brilliant smile.

Panzano was not now smiling.

"Thoreau, I cannot board a boat undressed like this. All the signs in town say: 'No shirt, no shoes, no service.' Even when I squeeze this elephant body of mine into a bathing suit, I could be fined for blocking the highway, indecent sexposure, uglificating the landscape, and impersonating an endangered species."

Thoreau snatched his Swiss knife then pulled open the large blade. Fear flushed on Panzano's face! He raised both arms straight up above his head, recalling that he had met Thoreau merely seven days ago. He had worshiped him like an older brother; he had found in this friend a relief from his loneliness and a mentor about the dreary and confusing roads of life. But how well did he really know this impulsive adventurer, O. Thoreau? ... Beads of sweat gathered on Panzano's wrinkled brow.

"Thoreau, *amico,* friend! Put down the knife! *Non è il momento di scherazre!* This is no time for jokes!"

Thoreau held the roll of duct tape and pulled out a long strip from the roll. He cut it off with the knife blade, then stuck the tape's end onto Panzano's flesh, a good distance below the navel.

"Did you know, Panzano, that bikinis were invented in ancient Rome? Keep your hands up and spin around like a revolving door."

The three-hundred-pound ballerina turned himself in circles as Thoreau pressed the skin of Panzano's thighs and crotch with just the barest amount of neon-yellow tape to cover that small but distinguishing feature that marked Panzano as a male.

A wide-eyed Panzano grabbed his beachball belly and pressed it firmly with both hands, attempting to peer over the bend of his macaroni-loving gut. Had he succeeded he would have seen that slender strips of tape had been shaped into a bright yellow codpiece, that pendulous pouch protruding from the pants of 15th- and 16th-Century troubadours. Denied this vision, he explored the scant garment with his fingers.

"*Per amor di Dio!* For God's sake!" Panzano shouted, grasping his short hair with his hands. "*Sospensorio! Conchiglia!* My pepperoni is wrapped up like a mummy in a tomb! Thoreau, what happens when my bladder bloats like a gourd of *vino,* when I have to — how do you say it in *Inglese?* — when I have to relive myself?"

Thoreau spun a similar piece of apparel for his own perfectly-shaped body, covering the groin region with the smallest possible amount of the all-purpose tape. Sandals were fabricated by winding more bands of tape around their four bare feet. With the last yard-long strip of tape encircling his steel-strong stomach muscles, Thoreau attached the plastic bag containing his passport, rope strand, pencil, notebooks, and knife. He faced his companion, then grasped both hands around the giant shoulders.

"Panzano, listen. I'll get to the boat first and make sure they don't leave without you. What does a man need to be happy? He needs to take chances, so he can find his love and make his dreams alive. All your life, this is the adventure you've been waiting for."

"Thoreau, " said Panzano with a groan, "this is *pazzo,* crazy! How will we ever find her? Bliss is one whole day ahead of us, she knows where she's going, her *bicicletta* is very fast. I have only one slow brain, one fat belly and two flat feet."

Having made his decision, Thoreau had no more need for questions or for doubts. Already he was sprinting across the sand to the black asphalt road. Panzano stood watching the graceful runner, repeating to himself again and again, "*È un' occasione unica* — it's the chance of a lifetime."

While Panzano screwed up his courage, Thoreau dashed along the road then sprinted through the center of the town. Four times along the way, he reached out — never breaking stride — and ripped four paper posters off four telephone poles. He passed the outdoor cafés where the old Greek men, twirling worry beads around their fingers, shouted at him their motto: *"Seega! Seega!"* — "Go carefully, by degrees!" He nodded to the men, sprinted past the smells of garlic and burning lamb from dockside restaurants, then stepped onto the wooden plank connecting concrete dock to boat. With his Greek language skill and his bright-eyed charm, he persuaded the captain's assistant that the journey would be far more enjoyable if the boat would delay its departure and wait for his humorous friend.

Twenty minutes later Panzano was spotted jogging toward the boat, moving slowly, breathing quickly, drenched in sweat, grimacing with the unshakable determination that nothing would stop him from reaching his goal. He was carrying his passport and soybeans in his left hand, and when he passed the center of town, he ignored the hoots and hollers from the Greek gaffers in the cafés. With his blimpy belly, his revealing costume, his boyish face and close-cropped hair, Panzano resembled a stupendous baby dressed in a glowing plastic diaper. In the honest light of morning he looked like a colossal infant, but in the dimmer evening light he might have been mistaken for a pregnant sumo-wrestler wearing golden slippers and a yellow-hot chastity belt. Passengers on the vessel greeted the sight of this spectacular arrival with a roaring cheer. Panzano stepped onto the boat, raised his acknowledging hand, then smiled at the clapping accolade.

"Vogliate perdonare il mio ritardo," he humbly said. "My apologies for being late."

A curious crowd of about one-hundred persons — more than half of them women — gathered excitedly around the two barely-dressed men. Amused by Panzano these women gaped on the verge of laughter; enchanted by Thoreau they stared adoringly on the verge of love. They admired his body, they enjoyed his face, they smiled at the kind fire in his brilliant eyes. Some of these women desired him to quench their hearty lust. Others needed a sympathetic friend to talk with. And others prayed that he might be the one at last to cure their heartfelt loneliness. Depending on their courage, age, and circumstances, each woman imagined in Thoreau the perfect lover, the perfect brother, or the perfect son.

Thoreau scanned the crowd and looked into the eyes of scores of women, including a dozen nuns. He smiled back at every pair of glowing eyes that smiled. He knew what they wanted from him, and he was sorry for the little he could give. He felt compassion for the way all women and men lived on the stalest crumbs of future hopes and dreams. And he understood how he would treat each woman here: with sympathy, with reverence, with a brother's unconditional good will. A pure Platonic friendship which to some of the women would be a heartbreaking disappointment, and to others would be a thrilling victory.

A woman who had opened her blouse to breast-feed her baby — a lucky baby who would never starve, thought Thoreau — stood up and shouted to the young man.

"Are you married?"

This supreme question silenced the horde of women in the audience — all ripe to hear the answer — who soon cheered wildly after Thoreau held up ten fingers without one ring. More questions spurted from the prying audience: What are your names? Where are you from? Where are you going? Where are you sleeping tonight? Have you eaten anything today? Do you have a sweetheart? If you do, are you in love with her?"

The need for action — the rush to reach the boat — had distracted and absorbed Thoreau's keen mind. Now that there was nothing urgent to be done, he remembered the woman he had learned so much from, admired so deeply and lost so soon. Staring at the sea, envisioning her rising from the waters, he cried for the flowers of his future that would be born to blush unseen. The handsome young man wept like an old god, now powerless, just-booted from the fun-filled Mount Olympus, forced to retire to that tedious rest-home known as Earth.

Watching Thoreau, many of the women wept as well. His bared heart made him even more attractive, for every woman knows that a man who cries is a man who feels, a man who needs, a man who cares. Thoreau wanted to apologize for his outbursts. He tried to say some words, but instead of speaking his great body shivered as fat tears sparkled on his well-tanned cheeks. Romantic heartbreak is a colossal misery, far too great to be expressed in such minuscule vessels as words — though thousands and thousands of cheap novels have tried.

From the crowd a child came forth, and did in deed what all the women only dared in thought. The child hugged Thoreau and kissed his forehead. Then she raised her skirt-hem and wiped the teardrops from his good-looking face.

In one deep breath Thoreau recovered his fearless confidence. He breathed slowly, he breathed deeply, he kissed the child then thanked her for her hug and kiss. His ends, he reminded himself again, would have the best chances to be accomplished if he acted with cheerfulness and calm.

A loud grumble roared from the stomach of Panzano. Ever since Thoreau had mentioned that the small rectangular can of beans could keep a man from starving for twenty-four hours, Panzano had doubted the truth of that implausible nutritional fact. And now he could not wait nearly that long to find out. He twisted the metal key, ripped open the can, then filled his mouth with the salty soybeans.

Murmurs flowed through the crowd and a few moments later the women passed food to Panzano and Thoreau. One man thanked the donors as the other attacked the spoils. Bread, goat cheese, and fruits were now disappearing as quickly and magically as they had appeared.

The ship's assistant captain, dressed in a wrinkled sailing uniform, raised his left hand. The watch on his wrist gleamed under the morning sunlight with such a bright flash that many passengers shielded their eyes with their hands. He announced that the captain had been delayed, and the boat would not be leaving for another three hours at least.

"Tell us your story!" one woman shouted to Thoreau. "Tell us! Tell us everything!" echoed other voices. "Why should a manly face like yours be overcome with tears?"

Thoreau popped two figs into his mouth, then untaped the bag of paraphernalia from around his waist. He grasped the blue notebook and the red notebook, mused for a moment, returned the blue book to the bag, then looked up at the eager crowd. Before speaking, he glanced down at the inked spots on his fingernails which were used to mark the passing of the weeks.

"If I've counted the moons right then today is the first day of April," said Thoreau. "The story starts six months ago, at the beginning of October, on this coast of Crete."

Panzano, who for a long time to come would be filling his paunch with food, stopped for just a blink to shout, *"Adesso viene il bello* — now comes the best bit!" — then continued his binge unabashed.

These story-loving Greeks! Smiling, Thoreau glanced at the faces of the ecstasy of women, who spread their tender sighs and opened wider their delighted smiles. He turned to the first page of the book and then began to read aloud. One voice entranced two hundred eyes and ears. The men listened, hoping for practical advice. The men heard the words, but the women listened deeper yet. The story transported them like music, like a passionate song about the mysteries, the struggles, and the sweet joys in this brief life.

2
GODDESSES HAVE GLOWING EYES

I FIRST MET HER AT THE METEORA — the 'rocks in mid-air' — in the loveliest valley in Greece. The raw beauty of this Meteora can hardly be described. Wondrous stone formations, shaped like strong arms, burst from the earth then reach up to grasp the rapture of the infinite.

"What a perfect place for a paradise!" I murmured, admiring again the mountains, valley, vista, pillars of protuberant stone. But even this colossal rock garden was not immune to the machine. The self-revealing silence shattered as a squad of jet planes roared over the monasteries, and everything below them trembled under supersonic booms. Out from the doorway of a stone outhouse darted a monk wearing a black robe down to his ankles and a white beard almost as long as the robe. He flung a tomato into the morning sky, and then — holding a racy paperback romance novel in his left hand — he shook his fist and swore vociferously at the passing planes.

It was at that moment, as I was laughing at the lively monk, that I first met her — the most ravishing, elegant, heavenly, earthy, feminine, passionate woman in the Milky Way.

We were approaching each other by walking on the same road, about fifty yards apart. Barefooted she walked with the confident posture of a dancer. Her white silk chiton — the Greek predecessor of the Roman toga — revealed the body of an athlete that had strength, vitality, and grace.

When I looked up at her dark-haired head I realized that she had been studying me, and as we walked closer to each other I could see her face beaming smiles into my surrendered eyes. She was wearing a straw hat — a good idea, because everyone who enters Greece for the first time underestimates three things: the heat of the Greek sun, the light of the Greek sky, the warmth of the Greek heart. The sun-heat makes you weary, dreamy, idle; the sky-light lets you see how beautiful the world can be; and the heart-kindness fills your soul with gusts of courage that transforms your life.

As she walked, her hands swept across the air, gestures that accompanied her honeyed voice reciting a passage from Plato.

"And who is Love? ... On the birthday of Aphrodite, Zeus gave a feast for the gods, and the god Plenty was one of the guests. When the feast ended, a goddess named Poverty came around to the back doors to beg. Plenty, having drank too much nectar, fell asleep in the garden of Zeus, and Poverty decided to improve her circumstances by lying down beside him and making a child. So on that night, on the birthday of Aphrodite, Love was born, the child of Plenty and Poverty. And as his parentage is, so also are his fortunes. In the first place he is always poor, and anything but tender and fair, as the many imagine him to be. He is rough and squalid, and has no shoes, nor a house to dwell in; on the bare earth exposed he lies under the open heavens, in the streets, or at the doors of houses, taking his rest; and like his mother he is always in distress. Like his father too, whom he also partly resembles, he is constantly plotting against the beautiful and good; he is bold, enterprising, strong, a mighty hunter, alertly weaving some intrigue or other, keen in the pursuit of wisdom, fertile in resources; a philosopher at all times, terrible as a sophist, deceiver, enchanter."

How beautifully her broad breasts bounced beneath that braless bedgown! As we closened and then walked past each other, the woman coyly removed her hat from her head and held it to conceal her chest. And as she moved this way she nodded with the most enchanting smile. Still in motion, still with gazes locked together, the woman handed me a small package. Her skin felt charged with warmth as we touched fingertips.

Passing her, I took ten steps more — as if this chance encounter had become a duel, a duel in which the woman held all the best weapons: the man was defending himself with a hairpin, and the woman attacking with King Arthur's sword.

I stopped walking suddenly and then I turned around. The woman had stopped seconds ago, at the point we passed each other, and there she stood still gazing at me, smiling all the time. And when I looked into her face and eyes she smiled more brightly, and my new life began that very moment, trembling with fearless happiness.

I heard the thunder of an engine, I saw a pink bus drive up beside her, and then the woman turned around, walked a few hip-swaying paces, climbed the bus's steps without looking back, and vanished from my sight.

That wordless encounter left me with two souvenirs: a memory of her smile and eyes, and a chunk of goat cheese — the gift that she passed into my hand. I searched the gift for her name and address, but I could find nothing at all except one strange word handwritten on the paper wrapped around the cheese: WANDERBORE.

One fleeting meeting is all it takes to magically advance your life. I promised myself that I would find this woman. This new fiery purpose — not the noblest but not the worst — renewed my spirit with a joyful energy.

3
Confessions of A Shy Librarian

HOURS LATER I was sitting at a round wooden table inside the Kalam-baklava Kafe. That morning I had asked dozens of Greeks and tourists about WANDERBORE and a pink bus — everyone knew nothing and said less. I had no clues, no grasp of the native language, no vast library of electronic resources to begin the search. Sudden sounds made me forget WANDERBORE — a little scream, a bump, shoes shuffling, an exaggerated gasp. A stack of paperback books tumbled on top of me; a young woman fell into my arms. Although less gorgeous than the goddess from the Meteora, this woman I had rescued was good-looking in her own way. Her long red hair ponytailed behind her head; her clear face looked intelligent; her legs were slender and not skinny; and her zaftig chest had been bounded by a T-shirt with the words: 'Librarians Know Where To Find It'.

"You're American," I said, breaking the silence.

"How did you know?" she replied.

"I could tell by your accident. My name is Thoreau."

"Odysseus Thoreau," the woman said. "I'm Victoria, Victoria Stumble. I'm so sorry my books met you before I did — knocking a man unconscious is not the best way to get him to notice you. Are you noticing me now?"

Victoria had been gazing at me the way most women gazed at me: with that potent admixture of like and lust and fear and curiosity and admiration, and the promise of undying love.

"Are you feeling OK, Victoria? Your cheeks look rutabaga-red."

"The gorgeous scenery," she said, sighing, "always affects me like this. Did anyone ever tell you that you are the sexiest man on Earth?"

I carried Victoria to a seat at the other side of my table then gathered up her dozen fallen books. Her glowing eyes made me smile.

"We share a love for the world's best literature," I said. "What kind of librarian are you?"

"I specialize in the ancient Greek and Roman classics, and researching the Internet. In less than ten seconds, I can find anything in the world except a good man."

"Women can't find good men, Victoria. You have to find an ordinary man, and then teach him how to be a good one."

"That's depressing," she replied. "Because for every hundred men you find, you get fifty sexist sports-nuts and fifty nifty nerds. My sister says that you have to kiss a thousand frogs before you meet one toad. And if you finally find a man who will talk to you for five minutes without staring at your chest then putting his grimy hands on you, what happens then? I read it on a sundial near the Acropolis: 'Love makes time pass, and then Time makes love pass.'"

"Victoria," I said. "All roads lead to romance. Let me buy you lunch and we can talk about rekindling your optimism and your belief in love. A Meteoran nun told me that this little restaurant has the world's greatest vegetable soup."

"The nun told you that?" Victoria said, moving her chair closer to mine. "Don't you know never to believe one word a woman says when she's in bed with you?"

I liked this young woman: she was funny and clever, and her eyes sparkled with a gentle fire.

"In bed," I said, "is the only place and time when I believe what a woman says. There's a song about that paradox:

"'She only tells the true replies —
When lonely in my bed she lies.'"

Vicki blushed like a nectarine. The old-woman café-owner — who worked as the lone waitress and cook — put two cups and one pitcher of water onto our table, along with a plateful of free appetizers. With the help of a small dictionary, I placed an order in English then in Greek.

"I would like two soups without meat — *Tha eethela dio soopas horees monos meatee.*"

The face of the old proprietress relaxed into a smile then burst into riotous laughter, laughter that sounded like a henhouse crowded with cackling birds.

"You've just ordered two soups without a single nose," Vicki gently explained. "Which sounds like my sister's definition of Love: 'Two minds without a single thought.'"

"Did you want your soup with the nose?" I asked, turning the pages of the dictionary.

"Do you mind if I try?" said Victoria. And then she ordered two soups *hortofagos* — vegetarian — with a yogurt-cucumber-dill dip named *tzadziki* and some fresh *psomee mavro,* the flavorful dark bread.

"Your Greek is perfect," I said.

"The rest of me is great too ... but nobody knows it yet."

"You mean that you've never — "

"I've never."

The young woman sighed. "Victoria is Victorian. The reference librarian that no man ever referred. No young Caesar has ever shouted: *'Veni, vidi, vici,* Vicki!'"

The old woman-chef arrived and cheered up the table with hot soup, cold *tzadziki* and fresh-baked bread. Victoria stared at me with two hungry eyes.

"So where in Greece have you already been?" I asked.

"I flew to Athens then got the train to Thessaloniki," she said. "From there I disguised myself as a man and visited Mount Athos. Then I climbed Mount Olympus, and after that I took the bus here to the Meteora."

"That's an amazing coincidence, Victoria! Except for Athens, in that same order, I've been to those very same — "

I now understood what I should have understood sooner; as usual, the female grasped things long before the male. Victoria slid her chair beside my chair, touched my hand, then pressed her knee into my thigh.

"I fell in love with you, Thoreau, when I first saw you at the youth hostel. I've been following you around, hoping that you would talk to me. I worshiped you too much to start the conversation, so I thought that I could get some attention if I dropped a load of books on top of your ignoring head. Will you blame the goddess of Love and forgive the humble me?"

Another woman had fallen in love with the mere looks of me, without getting to know my essence: my passion for freedom; my love of nature, books, and solitude; my quest for a simpler life; my rebellious inner self; my often-foolish faith in women, men, and Love.

"I forgive you, Victoria," I said. "If it's love, true love, then all's fair. But don't young women these days realize that it could be dangerous to follow strange men? How do you know that I'm a gentle man, and not some sickopath who would beat you then bury your bones in a forest, or fill your heart with promises in order to empty the life savings in your bank account?"

Gingerly, Victoria touched my forearm with her warm hand.

"I've been watching you, Thoreau. I watched you with the sex-crazed Danish woman, with the busty German girl, with the prim Dutch school-teacher, and with those three silly sisters from the Australian coast. Every one of those lusting women threw their bodies at you like hurricanes. You could have sexploited them all, but you treated each one with sincerity and with respect."

"And an extraordinary man like me can't even qualify for a credit card. Tell me more, Victoria."

She reached out and wrapped her fingers around my hand.

"One night outside the Thessaloniki hostel there was a full moon, and an old man on the street playing love tunes on his violin. That night I loved you so much I felt like I was going to explode. I put a white-chocolate heart under your pillow —"

"It was you!"

"—and I watched you all night while you were sleeping, and I held your hand and whispered how much I was in love with you. And while you slept I told you about my dreams, and in the morning when the sunlight fell into the room I kissed your cheek and left, happy that I had spent the night gazing at the most beautiful man alive."

"And now you trust me, Victoria?"

"I know that you would never hurt me, you would never hurt any woman. I would bet every book in the NYPL that you are a real man."

Victoria burst into tears as she squeezed my hand.

"Oh, dammit, I knew this would happen. I'm so shy and I can't believe I did that, and that I'm going to ask you this."

"I'm listening, Vicki. My grandfather used to say, 'It's no shame to ask, and no calamity to be refused.'"

The young woman's face grew redder; she shook with nervous excitement; her chest heaved as she breathed a deep and calming breath.

"Thoreau, I have to be back for work in New York City in just seven days. If a girl like me, a girl not that great looking — "

"Objection, Vicki. Beauty is in the arms of who be hold her — "

She squeezed my hand as if she were gripping a rope that would save her life.

"... a girl who thinks too much and acts too little, a girl sexually inexperienced but passionate and eager to learn ... If a girl like me somehow found the courage to invite you to my hotel room — don't say 'no' until I finish, please, Thoreau — "

"I'm listening, Victoria."

"Invite you back to my hotel room for lovemaking — lovemaking without commitment and without emotional involvement — would you break, shatter, and destroy my heart by telling me that you didn't want a physical relationship, but just wanted to be friends?"

All women have the amazing ability to ask questions that rattle a man's soul.

"I don't know, Vicki," I said. "The best relationships begin with friendship. Sex as a first course is rarely as delicious and nourishing as sex for dessert."

"But what if," she said excitedly, "there's not enough time to start with friendship? Is it against the law in Greece to eat dessert first?"

"Vicki, a sexual relationship inevitably leads to an emotional one. And if the sex is great, then the emotional attachment can get very sticky and hard to unglue. Relationships are not games: there are no rules, no referees, no commitment to good sportsmanship. Breaking up is painful. People get hurt."

"I promise I won't hurt you!" said Victoria.

"That's what they all tell me," I said. "Listen. When I was younger and foolisher, I was too naive to appreciate the overpowering connection between sexuality and love. Every week I woke up in a different bed. And I broke enough hearts to learn one thing: I don't want to break them any more."

"But suppose," said Victoria, "a young woman wants her heart broken?"

"Why would she want that?"

"Because it's so much better to have some experiences, than to be neglected, lonely, and ignored!"

Woe to the man who cannot improvise when the emotional logic of a woman pulverizes his most reasonable arguments. I spoke as gently as I could speak.

"Then someone who cares about this woman might advise her to think this way: Transform your loneliness into solitude. Instead of getting involved with the wrong men, keep both eyes open and wait. When you have nobody to love, then do the next best thing: be some sort of artist and create something radiantly sincere."

Her face quivered as if one wrong word from me would make her weep.

"Does all that mean," she said, "that you don't want to sleep with me?"

"Victoria," I said, leading her to a six-foot mirror on the wall. "Let's start by getting the facts straight. Women always underestimate their own magnificence. Ladies and gentleman of the jury, what do we see here? ... Eyes, sparkling and alert; hair, soft and flowing; lips succulent as plums; breasts sensuous and irresistible; waist to hips ratio the perfect seven to ten. The jury's verdict is unanimous: 'This woman is found guilty of being beautiful!'"

We sat down again, Victoria weeping at the praise. The old Greek woman who owned the café — and did all the cooking and cleaning — approached us like a handmaiden of the love-god Eros. Onto the table she placed a glass filled with colorful wildflowers, then she plunked down a plateful of free desserts. She strolled away humming and smiling, as she recalled her blissful days as a girl of sixteen, in love for the first time.

"Vicki, I'm not ignoring your question, but I have a question for you and for your professional expertise. Do you happen to know anything about something named WANDERBORE?"

The young woman stared at me with two lovely eyes, deep as the evening sky, filled with the twin stars of hope and desire. She wiped those lovestruck eyes with a cloth napkin, then picked up a square-shaped piece of cake.

"WANDERBORE?" she said. "If the right man asked, I might know a few things about that."

I touched her hand.

"It sounds as if this is some sort of mysterious secret."

Victoria looked around to make certain that nobody was listening; except for the old Greek proprietress, there was no one but the two of us inside the café. She leaned forward and spoke in a hushed voice.

"WANDERBORE," she whispered, "is a secret society for members of the feminine sex only."

Again she glanced around the room, and then spoke quietly.

"Every year they hold a conference that draws thousands of women from all around the world. I had planned to attend a workshop there on Saturday, but I can stay only for one day."

"And where is there?" I asked.

"I couldn't tell you that precisely," she said. "The exact location is never revealed until the day before. And I took an oath of secrecy never to talk about WANDERBORE with oppressors of women. And you are considered a woman-oppressor, since you are a m-a-n."

"But suppose," I asked, placing a friendly hand on her shoulder, "suppose that I wouldn't tell anyone else whatever you told me. And suppose that I am not an enemy of women, but that I am a real man, the one man in every million men, the most honest and best friend — and the most tenderly passionate lover — that any woman could ever hope to enjoy?"

I stood up, placed my hands on the back of her shoulders then massaged them with firm gentleness.

As the lonely woman relaxed her head, the hands pressed more deeply into zones of the neglected body, and then the fingers roved beyond the shoulders to make the woman sigh with joy. The old woman café-owner laughed like an exotic bird, then brought us two glasses of pomegranate juice, and a foil-wrapped condom on a plate.

I picked up the protective device, then smiled at the ribald sketch of naked Aphrodite on the wrapper. With a glance at the café-owner I improvised a silly song.

"This modern Cupid —
 Unlike Cupid quondams —
 Knowing men are stupid
 Gives out rubber condoms."

Victoria stood up, placed her hands on my shoulders, looked into my eyes.

"Thoreau, this is the moment I've been dreading and dreaming of. Are you going to break my heart by sleeping with me then leaving me the next day, or break my heart a thousand times more by touching-me-not and then telling me that we should just be friends?"

"Vicki," I said. "You've heard of Percy Bysshe Shelley?"

"Romantic poet," she replied, "born in 1792, husband of the Mary Shelley who wrote *Frankenstein*. After he died at age 30, Mary never stopped loving him; she kept his heart inside a jar on her writing desk."

"That's the one. Percy wrote a poem *Love's Philosophy* ... "

"The fountains mingle with the river
  And the rivers with the Ocean,
The winds of Heaven mix for ever
  With a sweet emotion;
Nothing in the world is single;
  All things by a law divine
In one spirit meet and mingle.
  Why not I with thine? —

"See the mountains kiss high Heaven
  And the waves clasp one another;
No sister-flower would be forgiven
  If it disdained its brother;
And the sunlight clasps the earth
  And the moonbeams kiss the sea:
What is all this sweet work worth
  If thou kiss not me?"

Vicki burst into disappointed tears.

"I knew it was hopeless for a girl like me to get a man like you. When I was a teenager the bottle always spun past me, and when we played 'five minutes in heaven' I went into the closet and the boys left me there alone! ... I'll get married to some dork I don't like, and in nine years I'll be a wrinklepuss like my mom. Oh, I wish my life was more like what I read in books! But no god magically appears to fly you through the danger to the prize. No goddess whispers secrets of courage and wisdom to your desperate ears. No lovers walk into the sunset holding hands. ... Yet being in love with you, Thoreau, gave me beautiful courage for one moment, and I tried my best, didn't I, dearest?"

I handed her a bandanna to wipe the flowing tears.

"Vicki, my hoary grandfather sat on his porch, pointed to women passing, and told me: 'Falling in love is like catching a cold: there's no known cure; it's usually all over in seven to fourteen days; and the best thing you can do for it is to get in bed.'"

At last she grasped the meaning of the grandfatherly wisdom and Shelley's seductive verse. Vicki screamed, strangled me with hugs, then placed her index finger through one of my beltloops.

"Let's go, love!" she cried.

"Your tent or mine?"

"To my virgin den of love. I took a room above this restaurant. This lucky librarian is going to research you like you've never been researched before. And after she's stripped your binding, flipped your pages and made notes in all your margins, she'll make love to you all night until your brains fall out!"

"Vicki, are you sure that's what you'd like? Without brains, I would be a vacuous consumer of products and information, useful merely for drudge labor and sexual intercourse. A reproductive organ on legs, a tool for your most superficial whims, a cheerfully-obedient robot, an unreflecting sex machine."

Victoria nodded.

"The perfect man!"

"What about the food?" I said. "We'll run faster and hump higher if we eat something."

"I can live on love and water," said Victoria.

And then she spoke in Greek to the old-woman café-owner, who quickly packaged our dolmades me humus (grape leaves stuffed with hummus) in a flowerpot. The beaming old woman got a 20-Euro note, and the beaming young woman got carried away in my arms up a steep stairway to her unlocked door.

The sparsely-furnished room reminded me of the unadorned Greek landscape: it contained everything necessary and nothing superfluous. Inside Victoria's room above the café, clothes littered the floor, bodies rested on the bed, laughter lightened the stark hotel. She was twenty-one, she told me, and she had never before been made-love-to by a woman or a man.

"I'm crazy about you, Thoreau," she said. "I wish I could describe how marvelous you make me feel."

"The way you were screaming, Vicki, gave me a few hints. Maybe the ancient Greeks were right when they asserted that every woman enjoys the sexual experience ten times as much as any man."

"Thoreau, I just had a great idea! Suppose I change my plans? I don't need to attend that WANDERBORE conference to learn how to protect myself from predatory men. If a man gets fresh with me, I'll just kick him below the belt."

No man can hear that once without a wince.

"That will send him a subtle message. ... Should I start wearing that titanium-plated underpants that's advertised in the fashion magazines?"

"That's for the creeps, that doesn't apply to you, Thoreau."

She kissed my forehead and then spoke excitedly. "Listen, here's the climax of my great idea. ... Can we stay here for a week together? And when the week's over I'll go back to New York. You don't have to fall in love with me — just make love to me and let me be in love with you!"

"Vicki, do you mean we should stay here a whole week and do nothing but—"

She stroked my cheek, she jumped out of bed onto her knees, she clasped her arms around my muscular thighs.

"I'll crawl on the ground and beg! I'll wash your grungy feet and kiss your bifurcated calves! I'll pay for the hotel! I'll cook for you! I'll coddle your molly! I'll do anything it takes to hear your bloomin' 'Yes, yes, yes'!"

"Vicki, listen. Stand up then sit here beside me ... that's better. I don't want you to beg me, or cook for me, or serve me like a mother. I want a woman who can be my friend and lover with complete equality. Genuine love is a woman and a man living together in an equal partnership. I've dreamed that dream, but I've never been able to find it. The women I meet desire to be nothing but my master or my slave."

Victoria threw off her robe, lay back on the bed, placed her hands behind her head, then thrust out her breasts as far forward as they would go.

"I can do that!" she eagerly exclaimed. "I can be the best friend and the perfect partner. She eats the fat, he eats the lean, combined they lick the platter clean! ... And I know all about the women who shocked their cultures by proclaiming that exploiting the fair sex is unfair: Long live Mary Wollstonecraft! Victoria Woodhull! Aphra Behn!"

I glanced at her, restrained myself from laughing out loud at the beauty of her enthusiasm, and then I spoke in a thoughtful tone.

"We could split expenses fifty-fifty, we could cook for each other, we could share ideas about the classic books, we could — "

"Oh my god!" she shouted. "Is that the magic 'yes'?"

"I'll stay the week with you, Victoria. And in the rare moments when you let me rest, will you teach me to speak and to write the Greek language?"

Victoria joyfully screamed.

"In six days I'll have you writing Greek like Plato and speaking like Socrates! You'll be an expert in language, and I'll be an expert in this!" She jumped on me like a young puppy, then thanked me with a passionate young kiss.

Two days later, when we opened the Greek-language book for the first time, Victoria squeezed my hand.

"I'm going to be very strong on the day when we say *andio* — good-bye — to each other," she said. "No tears from these eyes, and I won't beg you to make me any promises. We'll be friends, and I'll be grateful for the friendship."

"Vicki, you're wonderful. You know, if a genie appeared from a cloud of smoke to offer me three wishes, I'd tell him to get back into his lamp — I have everything I want. And I want you to always remember that you are a beautiful, desirable woman, and that any man who isn't happy with you doesn't deserve the lint in your belly button or the wax in your ears."

She sat up on the bed, stuck a pillow behind her head, then touched my arm.

"I'm so happy right now! Thoreau, do you know that I'd do anything in the world for you? ... I know what you need: WANDERBORE! Intuition tells me that you want to find a very special woman there. My love for you is so unselfish I'll tell you everything I know."

"It's a woman, that's true, Vicki. But it's much more. You see, I think the world's gone mad by idolizing money, things, technology, violence, and entertainment. I'm searching for a way back — a quixotic quest, I know! — to a simpler, sincerer, more creative, and more spontaneous way to live my life."

She kissed me as if she understood.

"And this woman can help you to find that glorious new life?"

"I don't know."

"I trust you better than I trust my best friend, Thoreau. Whatever needs to be done I'll do it, if it will do you good."

For that perfect expression of friendship, I stroked the woman's hair.

"Thanks, Vicki. But if you tell me about that group of men-haters called WANDERBORE, then you'll be breaking your promise not to tell."

She smiled.

"But I won't be breaking any promises if you guess it right."

Foreplay can be hard work, but it is always a labor of love. As my naked hands massaged the woman's nakeder breasts, Victoria billed and cooed like a plague of attorneys locked inside a pigeon cage.

"WANDERBORE ... I'm in love with you so much! ... Ahhh, don't stop, Thoreau! ... the conference ... oooohhhh .... is hidden ... "

"Is the WANDERBORE conference in the hills beside Mount Athos?" I asked.

"Mmmmm ... lower, lower ... "

"Or the marbled temples in Athens?"

"OOOOOh ... lower ... lower ... "

"In Santorini, the volcanic isle?"

Between ecstasies of pleasure and electric shrieks the woman squeezed around the man her legs and arms and hands then shouted:

"There, there, there! .... you've got it now ... "

And together we screamed:

"In Crete!"

4
BIKRESS, BIKRESS BURNING BRIGHT!

CRETE! THIS LARGEST of Greece's 1,400 isles is a land that knows slavery and freedom, where teenagers from Athens were once sacrificed to the labyrinth of the Minotaur, and Minoans built history's most peaceable society by letting women rule their world.

Crete! For a week I had been hiking around the edges of the island, living outdoors, sleeping on the sand, eating whatever I could forage, beg, or find. Time — the time of hurry, worry, clocks, schedules, dates, and deadlines — time had no meaning in this natural way of life. But I might have guessed it was the first days of October, the time of harvest, reaping, celebration, ripeness, all.

In the morning the sun bullied the stars away, the skies dazzled, the sea kicked in with laughs from the rollicking waves. In those early October mornings I would lie on a bed of sand and discover not the *thought* for the day — as if one thought was enough! — but the *theme* for the day, that would give meaning and focus to my wanderings. In Greece I had made one astonishing discovery. For hours and hours every day I experienced a deep joy, a feeling of marvelous aliveness I called "the fire."

The sages say: "Be open and all things come."

Whenever I felt this fire inside, whatever I needed would come to meet me on my path. Money, not yet; but all the other great necessities would come. When I needed food, some kind old man would give me bread; when I felt lonely, some far kinder young woman — a tourist, never a native Greek — would welcome me to share her sacred bed. It all worked because my face was handsome, my needs were simple, my sincerity was genuine, my spirit was strong enough to sacrifice the so-called luxuries. I could live without water for a day, without food for a week, without a woman for umpteen nights.

Jung and Hesse had called this notion 'synchronicity', a meaningful coincidence in time. No one should ever be so laughably foolish as to attempt this wish-come-true philosophy in the middle of a major city. Hoping for synchronicity in what has been grossly misnamed 'the real world' — in the heartless megalopolises — would guarantee you nothing but a hard park bench, a relishless hot-dog from a garbage can, or a sleepless night in the local jail. Here, inside this less complicated Greek world, life is lived with more freedom and spontaneity, and therefore the traveler finds more chances for adventures and serendipities. In traveling, as in real estate, location is the most important fact. With the right mind, the hungry bag-man in Manhattan is a holy wanderer in Greece.

A sea gull glided lazily above me as my mind soared with a vision of the Meteora woman who had touched my fingertips. The light, the sea, this perfect morning and that woman's glowing face set fire to my soul. I threw off all my clothing — T-shirt and shorts — then tied a bandanna into the shape of a hat to cover my head from the sun. Is it not written that every dawn shall bring forth a nude day? The sky was growing lighter but it was still early enough for a clothes-free frolic — no native Greeks would be awake until the sun stood two hands higher than the skyline above the sea. I ran across the dry sand to the wet sand and my feet splashed the foamy sea-toes along the water's edge. Naked as a peach I danced the *hasapiko,* learned from many watchings of the film *Zorba the Greek.* Dancing up and down the beach, barefooted in the wet sand, chasing the tide out and in again, stepping faster and faster, singing and shouting, leaping wild leaps into the air.

Something hit my head. I reached down to the sand and found a small green apple. Looking up I realized that the apple had been thrown at me by a person standing near the road.

A woman! A woman I had never seen before but would have loved to see again! A well-endowed woman with sun-blonde hair! A powerful Amazon standing beside a bicycle, first laughing, then smiling as she looked openly into my eyes. One glance and I knew her type. She wore home-made shorts cut at the middle of her thighs, and a loose-fitting cotton T-shirt, all on top of a body so strong and shapely that it made women envy and men drool. She was a child of the new counterculture, with a fresh face that loved the outdoors, and the worlds she felt at home in were green, vegetarian, progressive, feminist, sexually liberated and emotionally unattached. Every woman was her sister; every living being was her friend; yet she always mistrusted and often maligned the one group that dominated all the others: that immature species known as the human male. The young woman stood still for a few moments, calmly gathering her long golden hair into a ponytail.

Would she be a song of innocence, or a dirge of experience? Except for *The Tyger*, I'd neglected the poems of Blake. Blake saw a tigress and her dread face made him shudder; I saw a bikress and her body made me sing: *The Phallus* —

"Phallus! Phallus dangling loose!
Man is such a lazy creature
He would never rise to reproduce
If he did not possess this feature."

Had she hit me with the apple to get my attention, or hit me to express her hatred of happy men? Determined to find out, I jumped into my shorts then dashed in her direction. The bikress leaped onto her saddle then pedaled slowly, with her arms folded across the T-shirt topping her mountainous chest. Like Aesop's hare toying with the tortoise, she pedaled with arrogant nonchalance. Forward I charged to the asphalt road, and with the utmost efforts I sprinted closer to her bike. For an instant — almost close enough to grab her bike rack — I felt a wisp of hope. Too late! In one motion the woman bent down arching her back, placed both hands on the handlebars, churned her legs, then accelerated forward with heartbreaking velocity and deerlike grace. Swiftly the woman rode forward and never looked back. As her figure grew smaller my eyes could do nothing but admire the flowing form of her strong back, slender waist, rounded buttocks, dancer's thighs.

He who chases two doves catches neither. Before this race I had been heading in the opposite direction to search for clues about the woman from WANDERBORE. Now there was a choice: should I go west to find the dark-haired woman from the Meteora, or east after the blonde woman on the bike?

'Our main business is not to see what lies dimly in the distance, but to do what lies clearly at hand.' ... Wisdom from Thomas Carlyle. Pursuing the impossible — an impractical ideal, or a fairy-tale kingdom, or a perfect love — is often a fearful excuse for avoiding the struggle to live the tangible life here and now within your grasp. But the whole problem is that we can never know what is possible, or impossible, until we try with all our might.

5
THE BEAUTY OF WOMEN
TWEAKS THE INNER PEACE OF MEN

WHAT IS BEAUTY? For Plato, Beauty is a soft, smooth, slippery thing, which easily slides in and permeates our souls. For Emerson, Beauty holds something immeasurable and divine, hiding all wisdom and power in its calm sky. For Keats it is a joy forever; for Plotinus it shows us spiritual light. Gazing up the empty road where Beauty biked away, a simpler definition drifted home. Beauty is just the right amount in just the right places.

Beauty had tagged me then run away. In my mind she left her body, a blazing vision brilliant as the red-gold morning sky. I ran from the roadside then plunged into the cool sea for a brief swim. Returning to the beach I dried my body with a T-shirt, capped my head with the bandanna, then slipped both legs into sand-covered shorts. I picked up a book about Greek grammar and literature, then — as I did every morning of the journey — I studied the beautiful language of the Greeks.

Swarms of beachflies wanted my skin for breakfast; I waved to scatter them away. My morning muses spoke to me.

"There's something very simple I don't understand at all. When today began, the splendid sunrise made the world look like Utopia, and the moment I awakened I was lighted with the brilliance of the day: serenity, quiet joy, thankfulness for all the gifts from the new dawn. I felt whole, I felt complete. I understood the self-sufficient Whitman who sang 'I am good fortune,' — he had his worlds within, he needed nothing more."

The sky's lone clouds hung in the air above me like billowy breasts.

"What is the secret of that attraction between a certain woman and a certain man, what Goethe called the 'elective affinities'? ... From nowhere a ravishing woman appears and in seconds everything is changed! When Woman appears she plucks me from my private peace. How many days, how many golden moments will be lost in thinking about her? Now the perfect sunrise is not colorful enough. Freedom forgets its sweetness. Self-reliance loses its manly charm. Instead of appreciating the ripe moments in this here and now, the Garden of Desire tempts the man with the serpents of longing and regret."

I laughed out loud, then wondered:"Should a man stop chasing women? Or should he run after them faster every time?"

Into one large rucksack I crammed everything I owned: a tent, a blanket, notebooks, empty food containers, assorted travel gear, and my equipment for mental survival — one hardback and more than fifty paperback books. From a water bottle, I drank one long swig of water then picked up a seashell and flipped it high into the air.

"Let's let luck select the path today. Heads and I'll go west for WANDERBORE, or tails I'll travel east for the bosom on the bike."

The shell fell onto the sand with its pearly-bottom up. I would look for the bikress by walking on the road to the nearest tourist-infested town.

The ball-of-sun now sat six fingers over the horizon and it was time to dress for work. I threw on my cleanest dirty T-shirt, donned a pair of shorts ('Real men don't wear underwear'), blister-proofed the feet with grimy socks, then added two high-mileage sneakers, each one with more holes than a Swiss cheese used for target practice. A dash of elegance was added to this attire by tying two cloth bandannas around my neck, one yellow and one black.

Tossing the seventy-pound canvas sack into the air, I spun around, raised my arms, slipped them through the straps, then let the bundle fall thumping against a strong muscular back. Three water bottles, attached to parachute cord and duct-tape sheaths, were tied around my waist for easy access. Packing's last step is a quick scan around the sand to make sure that nothing would be left behind — no garb, garbage or gear.

Had my plan been to walk close to the sea, I could have dined on sea urchins and seaweed — with no impact on my meager financial resources. But inescapable is the first law learned by every loverlad: Romance costs money and trouble and time. Today, since I was heading for the town, I stuffed my left pocket with just enough Euros to buy a yogurt and a bread. My right pocket carried a threadbare wallet containing a dozen colorful but phony dollars, play-money swiped from one of my childhood board games. Any gun-toting thieves who approached me would be rewarded with these bogus bills.

I removed the hat that had been covering the "NO" on the corner of a wooden sign that said: 'NO CAMPING.' This white all-cotton hat

— reversibly black on the inside for escaping from bedrooms at night — served as a portable survival kit. For a man like me — overrefined, hypercivilized, pampered by the ease of city living — without the implements atop this hat it would have been impossible to live the arduous nomadic life. Our ingenious humanoid ancestors survived by making tools from bones, antlers, stones, wood, obsidian and flint. My needs were far greater and my tools were more complex.

To hold the survival gear, I had perforated the hat with dozens of sewn-on grommets, then filled the grommets with metal O-rings, plastic springclips, strong twine and safety pins. As I checked these to make sure they were secure, I improvised a poem in the manner of Walt Whitman. Free verse to celebrate these small but all-important items which made it possible for me to live without credit cards and with laughably little cash.

Song of My Stuff

O multi-tooled Swiss knife! O pencil and small paper pad!
The roll of duct-tape stronger than steel, sticking-loyal like a camerado,
The matches waterproof'd, the water-purifying tablets of deadly iodine,
The string, fishhooks, compass, candle, flashlight the size of a pen,
The toothbrush which scours these teeth thirty-two,
The plastic jar fill'd with baking soda, for toothpaste and fashioning
    scones,
The emergency rations, hi-protein hi-calorie, two cans of fermented soy-
    beans,
The soap bar that touches me places which only a lover would touch,
The sunscreen cream, small bottl'd, to cover each inch of this manly flesh,
Is this then a condom, polyurethane wrapp'd in foil? My son, it is siz'd
    extra large!
Enough! Enough! Enough!

If I parodied the wise Whitman, it was only because I loved his heartspun words. Whitman, whose literary power came from the most intimate contact with all Nature, once sang, "Now I see the secret of making the best persons. It is to live outdoors, and sleep in the open air."

I glanced back at the sky's long streaks of goldeny-red light. I felt so moved, so full of thankfulness. This new day would be completely free.

Free and all my own, to lose or to win, to waste or to make glorious, to fill with routine drudgeries or with all the fiery encounters I could make and find.

Nomading depends on knowing what to carry, where to sleep, and when to leave. So I left the serenity of the beach and — hoping to meet the goddess-woman — afoot and lightheaded I took to the open road. Compared with the soft sand, the black asphalt felt hard under my feet. As always, for safety, I would walk on the side of the road against the flow of traffic, since so often my mind would wander out of the present moment, into uselessly joyous philosophical flights. The road — which sometimes snuggled close to the seashore and othertimes swung far away — led toward the town of Agios Nikolodeonos, a well-known tourist destination on Crete's northeastern coast.

Walking felt wonderful, and synchronicity struck soon. Two age-rounded Greek women, dressed in widow-black, were walking toward me on the dirt-covered shoulder along the opposite side of the road. Wondering if the custom in Greece was "Once a widow, always a widow," I could not resist greeting them with shouts and a cheerful smile.

"*Kalimera! Kalimera!* Good morning! Good morning!"

"*Toureesta* say *kalimera!*" one of the two replied. Both women erupted into cackling laughs then waved their hands to ask me to come near. From their straw baskets they handed me two long loaves of fresh bread. They wished me *"Kalo taxeedee!* Happy Treep!", and then reached up to pinch my cheeks.

I tied one bread to each side of the hat and continued walking. A late-model car drove past, then backed up to a stop. The family inside handed me a plastic bag containing one large chunk of feta cheese, a bunch of grapes, a bag of black olives, and one bottle of Cretan wine. I pressed the driver's hand between my hands and thanked him and his family twice, in the English language and in the Greek. Then I cut some string from my survival hat, tied it into clever knots, and attached the plastic bag of food onto my rucksack.

These small gifts, how much they meant to me! One month ago, in September, I saw a magazine photograph of the Meteora amidst a mountainous region in northern Greece too breathtaking to portray in words. A few days later I walked over the border into Greece with little more than a strong body, a powerful sense of humor, and a pitiful fortune of one-hundred Bedlamerican bucks. My plan had been plain: Stay until the cash ran out, then fly back home. I imagined that my budget could keep me going for a week; two weeks at most.

Courage makes its own luck, and wins unexpected victories. Thanks to camping outdoors, eating sparsely, and the generosity of strangers sharing food — living in Greece cost less than two dollars a day. When the money seemed to be holding — and the Bedlamerican dollar gained slightly on the Euro — I decided to stay, to keep traveling in this magical country until I had absolutely nothing left. Not a Euro or a dollar or a drachma or a dime. Thus, in addition to their precious smiles, these kind people who fed me had given me a priceless gift: Time. Each batch of food they shared would grant me one more day, one more day in this Greek paradise. And how many men have ever dared to imagine that paradise could be so simple and so near?

The fiery Sun, like a blacksmith's heavy hammer, beat down beat down beat down on the hiker's head. According to the road markers, I had walked 20 Greek kilometers, about 12 Bedlamerican miles. Except for a few quick breaks — to dab on sunscreen cream, to empty pebbles from the sneakers, to sip that greatest of all necessities: pure water — without interruption I walked.

I passed an indistinguishably-dead animal on the road; three bent-over Greek grandmothers; and a child crying, alone in a field, separated from me by a barbed-wire fence. For a moment I considered helping the howling child. Immediately, the razor-sharp points on the barbed wire won the argument for caution and not getting involved. The rewards seemed too little and the risks too great. One accident or injury, then instantly the entire journey would be destroyed. For without health and strength, no man can live alone in the wilderness, the life of a beast and a god. Far better — my cowardly self convinced me — to gracefully retreat and let things be. Zen Master Daibi advised: "What comes is not to be avoided, what goes is not to be followed."

I stepped up to the fence, shouted to the child, then tossed all my food over the top: breads, cheese, and fruits. Last, and with great pangs of regret, I tossed the green apple, the head-plunking gift from the free-wheeling woman on the bike.

Technology is a stunning woman: first she turns your head, then she twists it off at the neck. In general, I disliked the way technology separates the human user from his body, from Nature, from real experience. Walking is the healthiest and most rewarding way to travel. But after more hours of walking, a beat-up van pulled over and stopped beside me, and on a hunch I took a hitch.

Two bumper stickers on the van said: *'Freikörperkultur,'* and 'Not everyone who wanders is lost.' The driver, a young German woman, conspicuously braless, wore a T-shirt that declared: 'Men's promises are lies postponed.' Her frayed cut-off shorts — which could not have been a centimeter shorter — had been designed to display her smooth, tanned, shapely legs. Her hair looked as blonde as the sun, her eyes gleamed blue as today's clear sky. She told me little about herself except that her name was Karin, she was twenty-four, she had been lonely in Germany and now she was lonely in Greece. She apologized for being in a lousy mood; she insisted that she wouldn't tell why. Then she plied me with dozens of questions, and seemed surprised when my answers made her laugh. She beamed when I teased her about the German word *'Taube'*, which does not differentiate between the English birds 'pigeon' and 'dove'.

One half hour later when she stopped the van to drop me off, she touched my cheek then blushed as she squeezed my hand good-bye.

"Karin," I said, standing on the road and looking at her sitting in the van. "If you can't tell a pigeon from a dove — a train station poop-bomber from the beloved bird of lasting peace — then how can you determine which hitchhikers are dangerous and which are safe?"

"I have a good intuition in my head," she said. "And a good gun under the driver's seat."

She lit a cigarette then blew a cloud of smoke around my face.

"Don't you like women from Europe?" she asked.

"European women are smart and sexy," I said. "If only someone would invent a European woman who didn't smoke. Smokers get diseases and then they die."

"You plan to live forever?" she replied.

And then Karin handed me a paper where she had written her name, her permanent address in Munich, and her vacation address in Crete. Her alluring smile left me wondering if — all through our conversation — she had been hinting for me to ask her for a date. Why didn't I? ... It was her cigarettes that repelled me, and my past experiences with the women who smoked them. But now that I let her go I would never know if my bland politeness had avoided a slap in the face, or missed the opportunity to make a friend.

6
THREE WOMEN MADE HAPPY BY THOREAU

WHAT SUBLIME MADNESS INSPIRES A MAN to venture into kingdoms new and risky and unknown? When do the sensible strands of Reason tie him to the beaten tracks? ... Once again I recalled the oraculous words of my grizzled grandfather: "Never Lose hope, never stop trying, never give up! Keep on plunging — and everything will go down the drain."

After Karin dropped me off in the center of the town of Agios Nikolodeonos, I continued walking two kilometers to the public beach. The brunt of the tourist season had ended less than a week ago, on the last September day. The beach now, at this time in the evenings, would be empty except for the sea birds and the garbage left by the off-season tourists in the afternoon. Exploring this littered beach, I soon discovered the ideal place to camp. It was a flat ledge on a hillside, sitting between the beach and the road above. Nature had concealed this place from the road by a wall of trees, and hidden it from beach-goers by waist-high shrubs along the ledge's edge. The perfection of this campsite consisted in the fact that from this perch you could peer through the shrubbery and see most of the beach but not be seen. The top of my tent was lower than the shrubs, so the tent could be left standing, and the gear could be stashed here, well-hidden from wanderers and thieves. To avoid being discovered, only one precaution would be required: never let anyone on the beach below see me coming or going through the bushes on this ledge. Which simply meant that between the hours of 10 a.m. and 6 p.m., when people populated the beach, I should enter and leave this campsite by sliding down or climbing up the goat trail from the road above.

The philosopher Zeno of Citium (not to be confused with Zeno of Elea, that maker of the space-and-time paradox 'Achilles and the Tortoise') taught in Athens at a school named *Stoa Poecile:* and thus his students and disciples were called Stoics. Little remains from his writings, but there is this gem: "The goal of life is living in agreement with nature."

As I unpacked my tent I realized again how Nature and Human Beings were meant to be in harmony, and how well the Great Mother provided for her ungrateful kids. On sand or on dirt, I could poke the tent pegs into the ground; here on this rocky ledge where tent pegs could not penetrate, the lines could be secured by tying them around readily-available heavy stones. Nature the great teacher once again reminding a man: Necessity can find a way.

The tent was quickly erected and sticks were laid for a fire inside a ring of rocks. I ate one of the cans of soybeans then drank two cups of water, then jotted down a note to replenish this stock during the next days. After brushing all thirty-two teeth — the three surfaces of each tooth ten times — I looked out at the sunset. Wishful reasoning made me believe that if the woman I'd been seeking appreciated beauty, then sooner or later she would find this gorgeous beach.

For six days and six nights I enjoyed this quiet paradise. The great goal was to meet the woman on the bike, but the time was not wasted in mere waiting and passive hope. In the mornings I avoided the avalanche of sunbathers by hiking through the nearby hills and scavenging lemons, carob pods, and fresh leaves of mint and sage. During the afternoons, I strolled up and down the beach, looking for one face and only one. The aroma of fresh sea-air was smothered under the stench of tanning lotions, perfumy deodorants, and the burning miasma of grilled meats. I never saw the inside of a restaurant. I was buying the basics from the local pushcart vendors, feasting on no more than two Euros per day. Breakfast consisted of water and fresh-squeezed lemon juice served in a cup made from a coconut shell. Lunch was one yogurt and half a kilo of grapes. Snacks were the chewy pulp inside the carob pods. Dinners were stews of lentils, rice, onions, tomatoes, herbs, and garlic cooked in a pot over an open fire.

The jewels of those days were the nights, the great October nights! In the nights I sang and danced like a wild god on a fresh new Earth. When there was no more energy for singing or dancing, I sat and listened — to wind, water, humming insects, silence — listening as I watched the nightstars dazzling the dark unending sky.

Glorious nights! ... And yet these flashes of joy mingled with thunderous solitude. At times I felt profound loneliness, the same feelings of isolation that had plagued me in my own land. What did I have in common with these tourists who had devoted their lives to consuming, shopping, drinking, drugging, gambling, and watching TV? What good is personal

enlightenment, if everyone around you leads lives of boisterous desperation: lives uncreative, predictable, solemn, anguished and devoid of joy?

A rising ridge bordered the beach, and the dirt path along the ridge
sloped steeply upward toward the top of a small hill. Moving slowly up
this path came a line of three enormous bundles of dead branches and
dry sticks. Underneath these bundles there were three skinny women,
older than trees, dressed in widow-black, hunched over like the Greek
letter gamma as they plodded up the hillside slower than snails dragging
their shells. Spectators watching from the beach were amazed because
the bundles looked larger and heavier than the women who carried
them on top of their bent-over backs.

During the past week, every evening I had watched these overburdened
women but I had never seen them right. Like olive trees and rocks, they
were merely part of the fixed landscape. Suddenly my eyes grew young
and the old women sprang to life. They became real for me, part of my
extended family.

The stick-covered women were creeping up the hillside when a volleyball player, a European businessman, shook his fist and shouted at
them: "Go grannies!". On the sand-made volleyball court, the team of
his associates snickered at the gibe as they watched the women struggle
underneath their onerous loads.

Age understands age. And age respects age. A white-haired tourist approached the businessman then slapped his bottom with her cane.

"Shame on you, you brute!" she cried. "Shame, shame, shame! Why
don't you help these women instead of mocking them!"

He turned around, facing her with his beerblubber gut that spilled over
the waistband of puke-green shorts. All mouth and belly, no heart or
brains. Now his face appeared offended, and as he defended an action
that was indefensible he rattled his finger at the elderly woman who had
dressed him down.

"Old girl," the crude man said. "Old girl, if you help these peasant
women today, then tomorrow what will they do without you? Their
labors make them strong and their hard work allows them to survive.
This is the natural law of survival of the fittest that no man should tam-
per with. And even if you do choose to interfere: how could you decide
which one of the three to help, and which ones to leave to their eternal
labors? Suffering is everywhere."

Stupidity is always ready with a bad excuse. The rich and powerful invent philosophies to justify the ways that they ignore — or trample and exploit — the poor and weak. Loving actions are the only hope to teach the heartless, and the only remedy to help the heartful ones in need.

I climbed the hill of sand and then bounded to the path in front of the old grandmothers. Shouting "One-two-three thou art free!", I snatched the bundles from their backs, then piled them one-two-three on top of my powerful outstretched arms.

The old women shrieked. Confused, their wrinkled chicken-faces turned left then right, then scanned the empty air above them; and when they spotted me they screamed. The first moments, chaotic and comical, soon calmed as the women realized that I was helping them, not stealing their precious firewood. The old women clutched my knees with feather-light arms, they stroked my ribs with bony fingers, they cried out with oaths of joy. On the beach, the European audience broke into applause and cheers.

Up the hilly path I walked in giant strides, carrying three piles of wood. The three ancient women — with bent backs and kerchief-covered heads — walked slowly behind me, chattering like happy young girls.

7
THE FIVE APPLES OF HOPE

EVERY GREAT ADVENTURE BEGINS when the hero meets a character who possesses powers, skills, or knowledge that are unusual, magical, divine. These women trailing behind me had lived, I suspected, nearly three hundred years. Three centuries! Who could imagine what secrets their venerable minds contained? ...With a kiss from the goddess of Good Luck, the three good sisters might share some of these mysteries with a young apprentice. Hopefully, my Greek-language skills would prove good enough to make my questions comprehensible and their answers clear.

Our destination, the home of these three sisters, was an old stone cottage on the hilltop. Arriving there, I lay down the piles of wood, then asked the old women if there was something more that I could do to help.

"My son, my son, my son!" shouted the oldest woman. Her eyes glowed into my eyes with the tenderest affection. Taking my hands, she looked slowly and carefully at each one, turning them over once and again, feeling the fingers and calluses, circling my wrists, then pressing the heels of my palms and rubbing them between her bony fingers and her thumbs. When this healing massage had finished, she gestured — by waving her own hands before her mouth — to ask if I wanted to eat. Before I could reply she pulled my wrist and led me toward the cottage door.

"*Pos seleneh?*" the old woman said.

The Greek language spoken on Crete was pronounced a bit differently than the words spoken in Athens and on the mainland. Still it was close enough to understand that she had asked: What is your name?

"Thoreau," said I, pointing to myself. Then pointing to the three women, I asked "*Pos seleneh?*"

The eldest crone told me that her sisters were named Freedom and Destiny, and that her own name was Hope.

"*Katalavehees?*" she asked.

I smiled to hear these three portentous names. Although I could hard-

ly envision this old gal springing eternal in the human breast, I nodded
and told the grandmotherly woman, *"Katalavehno."* I understand.

"Perimeneteh," Hope told me. Wait. She then walked to a wooden cage
beside the cottage. Opening the cage's door, Hope picked up a white
dove, and then caressed it with the utmost gentleness. After speaking to
her pet as if it understood, she tossed the bird into the air and watched
it fly away. Hope repeated this enigmatic rite four more times with the
four remaining birds.

As the old woman pushed open her creaky front door, three garter
snakes slithered along the ground before me, then a large owl flew out
and lodged in the branches of the nearest tree. Sounds of snorting and
footsteps followed, until six clean swine shuffled out the door. Pressing
their snouts against my thighs, the hogs scrupulously sniffed me, shook
their heads, then rumbled lethargically away.

Inside the cottage, Hope and her sisters prattled as they prepared a
meal. There was nothing for me to do except admire the simplicity of
this uncluttered dwelling. It contained a large wooden table for dining,
four wooden chairs, and one more table for cutting food. The walls were
decked with cooking utensils, tools, knives, old photographs. Bunches
of garlic, dried peppers, sage, and other fragrant herbs dangled from
the ceiling on knotted strings. A raised wooden platform, covered with
handmade blankets, lay in the corner to serve as a couch and a bed.

A strange fireplace sat in the center of the cottage. It was made of a
round flat stone buried in the cottage's dirt floor, with four chest-high
stone pillars around the edges of this stone, which somehow supported a
brick chimney above. In the middle of the flat stone, raised by rocks, lay
an enormous iron cauldron — a cauldron big enough to boil or bathe a
large pig or a small man.

"Hope," I said, as the three women buzzed around me at the dining
table. "Are you and your sisters always in such a good mood, or are you
happy to have company tonight?"

"My son, my son is here!" came the answer. And then came the food.
There was a wooden bowl filled with five withered figs; one wedge of
cheese; a bunch of leeks twice as large as any I had ever seen; dark bread
harder than a boulder; and a huge glass of what I took to be water from
the well. The cottage, which lacked electric power, was poorly lighted,
so I unfastened the candle from my hat, lit the wick, dropped a few
waxdrops onto the table, then pressed the candle's bottom on top of the

drops of wax. Now I could clearly see the full array of molds that deco-rated this primeval cheese.

The burning candle shed a new light on many things. On the floor beside me sat a metal bowl, half-filled with water, containing three tired mice swimming for their lives. The veined hand of Destiny pulled them out by their tails, offered them to me, then tossed them safely to the floor when I refused.

With the Swiss knife I stripped the cheese of blue-green mold. Instant-ly, the old woman Freedom snatched the cuttings from the table and thrust those moldy slices into her toothless mouth. That signaled the be-ginning of this pauper's feast, and the women ate voraciously — not like old women at all — with good talk and good appetite and good cheer.

Now would be the perfect time to ask about a secret remedy.

"Eho mia megali meati," I slowly said. Meaning: "I have a big nose." ... With help from my pocket dictionary, I told them how this nose was constantly clogged by sinus blockage. The sinus cavities, I explained by gesticulations, were thin as a pencil point. Then I asked if they could show me how to make a remedy from herbs that would enlarge my tiny sinuses.

Their six hands fluttered though the air like pigeons' wings as each of the old women replied: *"Dhen katalavehno,"* — I do not understand.

My words missed the target and left the sisters thoroughly confused. Now I tried to communicate in gestures only. I placed my hand on the nose then moved the hand outward, imaginarily stretching my snout. I would have no relief, I explained, until the passages in this organ could be enlarged. The women babbled too fast for me to follow; then so much laughter erupted from their old cracked lips that I laughed too, happy that at last they understood.

"Eat, eat, my dear son", said the life-giving Hope. She could help me, she was sure, she said — but first I must eat because I would need all my power. I tried the figs but they were rubbery as bicycle tires; the leeks were flavorless; and despite strong teeth and tools I could not make a scratch or a dent in the rocky bread. The cheese chunk tasted so salty and bitter and dry it scratched its way down the throat then dropped into my stomach with a burning plunk.

Voices, singing voices, grew louder and louder outside the cottage. The old women smiled to one another as they watched my bewildered face. Through the doorway walked five young women all dark-haired and beautiful, dressed in gowns diaphanous and white, each cradling one apple between her lovely hands. I noticed that I was now perspiring profusely, and to calm myself I chewed another piece of pungent cheese, then took a deep swig of the clear liquid in the cup.

"No, no, no" I softly said.

Too late, too late I understood! I had just poured *rachee* — the Greek vodka — *rachee* and much too much *rachee* down my salted throat.

"Hope," I said, trying to concentrate on speaking the right words in Greek. My body felt heavy, my head felt light, my strong legs quivered as they forgot their strength. The walls and all the smiling faces were spinning and spinning in circles wild.

"I don't drink beverages with alcohol," I said to the oldest face. I stood up and clutched the heavy table for support. "It's a genetic thing. The smallest drop of liquor knocks me out."

"*Taxero*, my son," nodded the good-hearted Hope. "*Taxero*."

I staggered toward the corner of the room, trying to remember the meaning of that familiar word. The five young dark-haired women, so lithe and lovely, swirled laughingly around me, hands holding their firm apples, calling me to take a bite. As I closed my eyes and sank down on the bed, the word *taxero* — "I know it" — fell softly into my bedazzled brain.

"He's awake!" a Greek voice whispered.

"He's strong! He's handsome! He's perfect! Look at his eyes!" murmured other cheery voices.

Slowly I woke up, first with my ears, hearing the sounds of cymbal-crashing thunder and the laughing and talking of voices from the women in the room. The chill of the night air against my skin told me that during my deep sleep all my clothes had been removed. My recently-reeking body now smelled clean like fresh mint: either I had just been bathed, or I had been scrubbed with sponges like no man had ever been scrubbed before.

When I opened my eyes I saw that my candle had burned down to nothing but a glob of wax. Candles, a dozen taller and fatter candles placed throughout the cottage, lit the room with just the right amount of light for an evening of crime or romance. Beneath the cauldron raged a wood-fed fire. Around this fire all the women had gathered, the three crones in their black dresses, and the five young women, who still held their apples but had shed their clothes. A flash of lightning illuminated the room for just an instant, and the beauty of these women was so great that it filled my eyes with tears. Tears which I immediately wiped away so that I could see more of the beauty.

A blast of thunder shook the cottage and the women shrieked. Holding long wooden spoons over the cauldron, the old women chanted as they mixed their mysterious brew. I heard — and carefully made mental note of — all the components of this elixir: *"skordo"* (garlic), *"angouree"* (cucumber), *"karota"* (carrots), *"eleea"* (olive); *"kremitheea"* (onions); *"meela"* (apples); *"seeka"* (figs); *"alatee"* (salt); *"peeperee"* (pepper); along with a dozen spices including *"faskomeeleea"* (sage); *"aneethos"* (dill); *"baseelees"* (basil); and *"theemaree"* (thyme). I watched as these ingredients were thrown, poured, or sprinkled into the steaming broth.

Now, curiously, a vegetable that looked like a horseradish root was being carved into the shape of a phallus, large and erect. Then the oldest of the old danced around the cauldron singing:

"Curse Hope, the goddess-bitch,
  So much she promises, so little gives.

"Freedom is the prize, all seek to win —
  But who has understood freedom within?

"Love Destiny, when her you cease to fight
  Her dearest charms she yields to you tonight."

Amidst the melodious blend of laughing from many voices, the women old and young passed around the horseradish phallus. After caressing it fondly — or fondling it with a caress — each woman plucked one of their hairs and tied it around the tip. At last, this enormous vegetable came back to Hope who first kissed it, and then tossed it into the bubbling pot.

Destiny and Freedom spooned out samples of the soup. They added garlic and olive oil, tasted it again, then smacked their lips together as they nodded they were satisfied. Hope tasted a spoonful, agreed with her sisters, then glanced at my eyes and waved her fingers telling me that I should come.

Another bolt of lightning flashed. A thunderous roar again made the cottage tremble and the women shriek. I stood up, and since one large phallus had already been thrown into the boiling brew, I wrapped a blanket around my waist.

"Thoreau," said Hope, "come here."

Her voice was not the voice of an old woman: there was something musical about it, some power in the voice that moved me because it felt so fresh, so honest, so sincere.

"My son, my son, listen," said the old woman tenderly. "There are five apples, five great gifts in this brief life. Right now, there is one that you must choose."

The sisters Destiny and Freedom raised four arm-sized candles, then lit them by touching wicks with candles that already burned. Now everything in the one-room cottage became clearly visible by the candles' lambent light.

In a circle around me stood the five young naked women. After admiring, one by one, their splendid shapes and unique charms, I noticed that each one of their apples looked distinctively different. Again, Hope spoke to me soothingly.

"The first apple," said the wise woman, "is the apple of Joy and Innocence."

Small and green, it reminded me of the crabapples that, in my wild young days, I had thrown with so much enthusiasm at my best friends. Looking closer, I noticed that this apple was the same variety as the one I had picked up on the road then flung over the fence to the ungrateful kids. The young woman who held this fruit smiled a smile radiant with joy, and looked up at me with trusting eyes.

"The second fruit," said Hope, "is the apple of Sex and Foolishness."

This fruit was red and ripe, and the young woman who held it had sensuous lips and the fullest breasts. She gazed at me with curiosity, with passion, and with so much pure desire that I sighed, and tightened the blanket around my waist.

Hope carried on.

"Next is the greatest temptation of all: the apple of Wealth and Suffering."

A full-bodied woman, who looked like she had just stepped from an Italian painting, clutched this golden-yellow fruit. Her body appeared warm and confident and irresistibly attractive: what man could refuse her charms? But her eyes looked cold, as if she never could be satisfied.

And her glance seemed to pierce straight through me, instead of resting on the deeps of my eyes.

"Look now, my son," said Hope, "at the rarest fruit of all: the apple of Love and Danger."

This reddest and largest of all the apples was held by a woman whose eyes, like a blue flame, burned with freedom and strength. In an aura of pure kindness, her face revealed a woman of depth, and humor, and uncompromising truth. What would it feel like, I wondered, to be loved by a woman like this?

"Behold, at last," said the old woman, "the reward and the price of old age: the apple of Wisdom and Loneliness."

This fruit appeared drier and just the slightest bit less shiny than the other ones. The woman who offered it had two streaks of gray running through her fine black hair. The ripened beauty and poise of this woman gripped me, and I stared at her reverently, captivated and entranced.

So beautiful, they were all so beautiful! I desired them all! I wanted Joy but not the innocence that kept her unaware. Likewise, I desired Sex without foolishness; Wealth without suffering; Love without danger; Wisdom without loneliness. Years of experience might teach me to embrace the whole of life. But now, in the full folly of my fiery youth, I wished for all life's blessings, unadulterated with the inescapable misfortunes.

Hope stroked my cheek with her roughly-callused hand.

"Only one, Thoreau," said the old woman. "Choose only one! The one that smiles at you, the one you're ready for. And whenever you place that apple in your mouth, you must remember to swallow every bite and eat up everything: skin, pulp, stem, core and all the seeds. *Katalavehees?* Do you understand?"

I nodded that I understood. Then I reached out for the apple of Joy and Innocence, but the sister Freedom touched my arm and whispered, "You can never go back to that!" And when I stretched to take the apple of Wisdom and Loneliness, the sister Destiny touched my shoulder then said: "For her, you're too impulsive and too young!"

Hope dipped a ladle into the cauldron, blew on the steam, poured its soupy liquid into a mug, then blew on it once again.

"Drink this," she said. "It will help you, my good son. Drink."

I took the cup from her hands, blew on the hot broth, then drank a deep drink from the steaming cup. As the soup warmed me I felt my courage rise. I remembered the woman at the Meteora. I reached toward the apple of Love and Danger.

Suddenly, my arm — feeling awkward and heavy like a thick tree-branch — drops down to my side. Head spins. Heart pounds. Body staggers backward onto the soft bed. Another flash of brilliant lightning, a crash of thunder, shrieks from the women, whelps from the swine. The door of the cottage flings open and the wind blows candles out, filling the room with darkness. I struggle against Sleep, but the old god is too strong and savvy to let me resist. A woman's naked body presses mine. I remember two things before yielding. The last piece of apple in my mouth tastes so crisp, so juicy and so sweet. And the first woman in the bed feels so soft, so eager and so warm.

Early the next morning I was awakened by light from the smiling sun, and a raucous rooster squawking cock-a-doodle-doos. Gone were the five stunning women who had enchanted me the night before. The fire beneath the cauldron had ceased burning; the embers beneath the cauldron were glowing red. Two of the three old sisters, still wearing their black dresses, lay sleeping in the corner of the cottage on a mound of straw. Watching me with ancient yellow eyes, the big-headed owl sat like a stoic philosopher, claws wrapped around his broomstick perch. Under the kitchen table, huddled together, lay six snoring swine.

Which one of the five apples had I consumed? One thing I remembered clearly about last night: how I reached toward the apple of Love, and how the elegant woman who held this apple had watched me with her sympathetic face.

In walked Hope, carrying my clothes: T-shirt, shorts, socks and holey sneakers. Like my body, the clothing had been washed minty and clean. I dressed quickly. Strange to say, I felt no embarrassment at being nude in front of this woman, who had treated me like a grandson or a son.

Hope rubbed spearmint leaves between her hands to make a pot of tea. I touched her shoulder.

"I must ask you about last night," I said. "Was I dreaming or was I awake? Which apple did I choose?"

The woman placed her freckled hands around my sun-tanned cheeks.

"Son, son, son. How young you are!"

And then the old woman sang:

"Bitter? Sweet? A curse or blessing?
Every breeze of Fate is passing.
Sweet or bitter, now and ever —
Nothing earthly lasts forever."

Words of a seer, ambiguous and vast, full of as many meanings as the seeds inside a pomegranate fruit. Words that could hurl a thinking man down to the bottomless pits of despair, or up to the loftiest peaks of inspiration!

"My son, my good son," said Hope, stroking my cheek. "I want you to have this for your beautiful strong hands."

From a pocket in her apron she retrieved a pair of leather gloves. The gloves looked indestructible; the fit was just right; and I smiled when I realized that to make them for me she had stayed awake and worked all through the night.

Almost too moved to speak, I managed to thank her and promise I would visit her again. Hope said good-bye with an embrace, then she would not let me leave until I gathered one more gift. This present was a boulder-hard loaf of *psomee mavro* — a dark Greek bread.

I stood on this hilltop and watched the sunrise light the sand, the trees, the skyline with glowing golds and reds. The whole world this morning looked like the love-light in a woman's eyes.

"What a morning!" I shouted. "I feel renewed, on fire, invincible! Ready to wrangle with the gods and tangle with the goddesses!"

In Greek tragedies, what they call *hubris* — the arrogance and insolence that gods display but men cannot — always initiates a long and tragic fall from privileged heights. Fearing nothing and singing all the way, I ran down the hillside, stripped off my clothes, then dove headfirst into the mind-dark sea.

8
A Raucous Rendezvous

THE LIFE OF A TRAVELER is islands of ecstasy, surrounded by vast seas of cold, hunger, and loneliness. The great problem is how to find the islands and survive the disenchanting seas. How? ... Timing the secret is. There is a precise moment to enter — in traveling, in sex, in relationships — and a precise moment to pull out.

'Twas time to venture from my beachside paradise. The cooking fire was easily rekindled by first stirring the embers, then adding oxygen by fanning the smouldering wood-coals with an open book. A pot half-filled with water was placed on top of two rocks over the burning embers then a stone-hard bread dropped into the water-filled pot. The two-pound tent was dismantled then shaken out — to remove stones, dirt, insects, sand — and then folded up into its pillow-sized pouch. While sipping the stale-bread soup I studied Herodotus and the beautiful language of the Greeks.

I picked up the ring of rocks around the campfire then placed them into the towering shape of a cairn, ready to use again the next time I returned to this friendly home. With a square of cardboard I swept the fire ashes into a bag, then restored the campsite to its pristine state. I wrote some lines in my journal-book, then closed the book and glanced up at the light-blue sky.

How many nights I'd dreamed about a new journey, a new love, and a new life! Youth should not be measured in years, but by inner freedom and energy: the great feeling that your life is open, spontaneous, ripe with thrilling possibilities.

After buying bread and olives from a cheerful man behind a wooden pushcart, I traveled by walking and hitching, and long before noon I found myself standing before the fearsome fence. The same fence where, one week ago, I had failed to help a crying child. The chain-link fence, standing ten feet high, was topped with another three-foot section of rusty rolls of barbed wire. Designed, no doubt, to prevent wild creatures

— especially Travelers — from harvesting the lemons, carob pods, and black olives that had fallen in these orchards in the early Fall. My eyes traced a path beyond the fence, up the hillside lush with yellow-flowered gorse and dried wildflowers and tall stalks of wheatlike grass.

On the top of a small hill, watching me intently, stood a lone child. A barefooted little girl who looked no more than eight years old. Her dress was a torn rag, her face was shy and dirty, her hair had never met or parted with a brush. Cautiously, the child watched me as she wept. Pearls of water poured from her wide-open eyes and streaked her two tanned cheeks.

In shouts of Greek then in English, then by miming with my left hand, I spoke to the forsaken girl.

"Are you hungry?"

The child, like a frightened fawn, scurried ziggedy-zaggedy-zoggedy down the hillside. About ten yards away, despite the fence between us, it was clear she would come no closer. There she stood silently, staring at me with the loneliest dark-brown eyes, eyes that flickered innocence, curiosity, mistrust. Again, accompanied by gestures, I shouted to this child.

"I have food here, good food. Are you hungry?"

The child stood frozen, gaze gripping my gaze, as if she were waiting for something I could not give. As we studied each other the grass rustled and a smudge-faced boy-child, half the size of his sister, ran near then hid behind her tattered dress. Grabbing a handful of lemons, I lobbed them over the fencetop. Before the lemons hit the ground, the tall grasses hissed and swayed as more children ran down the hill and gathered around the little girl.

A flock of small children — I counted thirteen of them — ages two through six, assembled near the girl-child. Some wore shredded clothes, others wore nothing but their olive-colored skin and impish smiles. They rubbed their tummies, they picked their noses, they driveled from their mouths, they stared at me with lonely tea-dark eyes. Quiet as animals, gaping, wondering: Who is this handsome hero and what will he now do? Desperate looks and hopeful faces transformed me from a self-forgiving miser into a self-forgetting saint.

Over the fence I tossed two lovely loaves of bread — loaves like the arms of the love goddess — which bounded to a stop six inches from the girl-child's feet. She stood still staring at me with her two deep-seeing eyes. Next I wrapped my olives inside a paper bag, threw it over the fence, and watched the bag spin fitfully before it fell not far from the breads. I slipped the bottle of wine through the fence and rolled it in their direction — poor kids had poor parents who could drink or sell the wine.

A cloud of dust blew across the children who stood still like stone statues, children without laughter and without tears. At last, the pretty girl-child stepped forward, still gazing at me with dark eyes immense. Reaching down, she picked up a bread loaf, eyed it with worldly scorn, then violently threw it to the dirt.

"*Paras! Paras! Paras!*" she shouted at me in Greek, holding out her tiny palms and rubbing her thumbs against her first two fingers. Buzzing like wasps, the horde of little children imitated her greasy gestures and grasping words.

It took me a moment to take it in. The children had hollered the three words the whole world worshiped: Money! Money! Money!

Respect the magnificent intelligence of children, but do not let that fool you into thinking that at every moment a child knows what he genuinely needs. A nod from my head and a wave from my hands signaled to the kids that they should pick up the nourishing food.

The girl stepped back, glared into my eyes, pointed at my face, stamped her feet, gyrated her pelvis à la Elvis. She spit like a sailor who'd swallowed a horsefly, and then she shook her fist and swore with the same scabrous Greek idioms I'd last heard at a taverna in Piraeus.

Immediately the other dozen children followed their leader. Before I had a chance to turn my back they hooted nasty names, razzed with pink tongues, waved their hands in unthinkable gestures, then turned to display more moons than the planet Neptune.

My great-grandfather had once told me how he survived the years during America's Great Depression. He reminded himself of the words that his own grandfather once passed on to him: "When you don't know what to do — sing!"

So I sang to the children an improvised song.

"Who taught you that insulting way,
to mock poor wand'ring singers?
Act more like kids from USA —
they raise their middle fingers!"

While the singing carried on the children ceased making obscene gestures, but the moment I finished they pelted me with pebbles and handfuls of sand. Clutching the fence and shaking the metal so it rattled and jangled, I pretended to climb. The waifs shrieked, sprinted up the hillside, pissed me good-bye with one last demonstration of lunar exposures, then vanished over the shrub-covered crest.

Hunger kicked me in the belly. The life-giving food scattered on the sandy dirt of the hillside made it appear as if some surrealistic prankster had tossed a bomb at the middle of a painting of a still life.

Vigorously I shook the fence, as if it would be possible to tear it down. Was it worth the risks of climbing over this rusty barbed wire? A boy I knew once slashed his thigh on the claws of a sharp fence, and the terrible white scar — which looked like an enormous albino slug — made all the girls scream and run away. And the older brother of Henry David Thoreau cut himself while fence-climbing, caught a tetanus infection, then died at the age of twenty-six — my present age exact.

Instantaneously, a day can be made interesting by acts of courage: the choices and chances we make and take. Yet it is always wise to stop to ask: Is it gloriously noble, or incomparably stupid, to fight battles you have no chance to win?

There were two options only: to climb or not climb. It was not possible to compromise by sitting on the fence. A few mornings ago I had read a Greek word, which is pronounced '*Apofaseezo!*'. Simply and manfully it means, "Decide!"

Thoughts from my favorite thinkers gave me courage. The blazing words of La Fontaine: 'Man is so made that whenever anything fires his soul, impossibilities vanish.' And Seneca: 'It is not because things are difficult that we do not dare; it is because we do not dare that things are difficult.' And the terribly lonely Vincent van Gogh: 'What would life be if we had no courage to attempt anything?' And Nietzsche, the ever-misunderstood: 'If a man has a *why* to live, he can conquer any *how*.' And my great teacher, Kazantzakis: 'Go forth nevertheless, seek! What if the hunt is better than the prey?'

Whenever you decide to do a foolish deed, do it with the utmost intelligence and skill. Calmly now, I looked at every possibility. The chain-link fence, ten-feet high, had along its top an additional three-foot-long section of metal bars, pointing toward the sky, bent forward at an angle of 45 degrees. These bars were perpendicularly crossed by strips of rusty, razor-sharp barbed wire. Because of the barbs and the bent angle of these bars, getting in appeared improbable. Getting out would be even more difficult than that.

After studying the defense to find a weakness, I opened the rucksack, pulled out a blanket, cut it with my knife into ten squares, then wrapped them around my arms, forearms, thighs, legs and sneakers. Then I tied the blanket-strips tight around my limbs with pieces of strong twine. The clownish costume was completed by slipping both hands into Hope's gift, the new leather gloves.

To prevent my book-stuffed rucksack from being stolen, I picked it up and heaved it over the fence. The native Greeks, I had been told, would never steal. But Greece was rich with sticky-fingered tourists; and professional itinerant thieves who traveled in vans instead of caravans; and tribes of atavistic hippies who believed that "Property is theft" then proved their faith by stealing everything in sight.

The plan was clear: cross the barrier without getting hurt, feed the children or recover the food, then find a way out again. Covered with blankets and concentrating with all my power, I climbed up the fence, placed a sneaker on the wire between two sharp barbs, waited a moment for the wind to die, leaped over the fencetop, flew for a few seconds like a giant chicken, then landed on two sneakers on the soft dirt below.

Ah, life on the other side! Eureka! Somehow — perhaps thanks to its tough outer skin — the apple from the bikress had survived. I picked up the apple — dirt-covered but intact — then used the bottom of my T-shirt to polish it. Success made me sing an opera-like rendition of a silly song, where I assumed both parts, one baritone to call and the other tenor to respond.

> "Who knows not wine, ...Who knows not wine,
> Women and song, ... Women and song,
> Remains a fool, ... Remains a fool,
> His whole life long! ... His whole life long!
> I know not wine, ... He knows not wine,
> Nor women's rule — ... Nor women's rule —
> Therefore am I, ... Therefore he is,
> A singing fool! ... A singing fool!"

The music — if one could call it that — made the hills come alive with the footsteps and weepings of the little gypsy-girl and her childish companions. Artful performers, they rubbed their baby-fat bellies and cried their crocodile tears. I waved to the urchins, held up my hands, then rubbed my fingers against my thumbs.

"You want *paras, paras, paras?*" I shouted.

Predictably, the children stopped crying to coyly nod their heads. Turning my back on the little ones, I picked up two-dozen pebbles and small stones, then concealed them inside two closed fists.

"*Paras!* Here is *paras!*" I yelled, tossing the stones high in the air. And then I shouted to the wind: "The world is too much with us! Getting and spending we lay waste our powers!"

Shivering with excitement, the children ran to the stones, picked them up, peered at them with groans of disappointment, and then with Achillean wrath flung them down into the dirt.

I raised the precious apple then threw it to the thirteen kids. At first they griped, then hunger and curiosity conquered their foolish pride. The oldest little girl snatched it from the ground, took one bite, then passed it to the hands and mouths of other children, until nothing of the small green fruit remained.

Smiling a great smile and then screaming out the shout of a friendly monster, I rushed at the bewildered kids. It took them a mere moment to see and understand. Life delights in life. They shrieked then laughed then scrambled up the hillside. In seven strides I caught the biggest little girl, raised her up, then swung her light body and her laughing face around and around and around through the happy air. All twelve of her companions swarmed around the giant man. One by one, each child laughed wildly as he or she was lifted up and whirled joyfully around. After a number of rounds of this game, we walked up the hill together. I sang a cheerful gypsy song and watched the children's eyes light and their lips move as they learned the chorus then slowly sang along. Like ducklings they followed me, clutching tightly to my hands and to the bottom of my T-shirt. One of the small boys handed me my bottle of wine, then smiled proudly when I thanked him and rubbed my hand over the greasy top of his tangled hair.

I placed a finger above my lips.

"Shhhh!" I said to my wide-eyed companions. And then I whispered to them, "Do you hear that?"

Quietly, the children and the man stepped up to the very top of the tall hill. With deep and mirthful eyes, I gazed down at the other side.

There are times when Life is just, and even more than just: like a loving woman, she gives far more than she receives. Selflessly I'd made the pack of children happy, and now it would be my turn to be delighted, transported, ravishingly surprised.

9
BEAUTIES AND THE BEAST

"THE MUCH-SHIPWRECKED ODYSSEUS, blown from one beautiful woman to another, nakedly washed ashore onto the island of Scheria — possibly Corfu or Crete — owning nothing but the tales of his adventures and his cunning mind. Though bespattered with crud and sea-salt he transformed his fortunes, by supplicating the lovely Nausicaa, princess of the isle."

Just before we reached the hilltop I had heard the carefree melodies of women's voices. Their blithe shouts turned my mind to that light scene in Homer's *Odyssey,* where the exhausted hero, sleeping under an olive tree, is awakened by the voices of the princess and her maidservants playing on the shore.

I now stood on the hillock and looked down. Patches of cotton plants lay spread out like small carpets over the rugged hills. In the center of the cotton fields, on a dirt path, sat an old blue-and-white Volkswagen van with a wooden cart hitched to its rear. In the field I counted ten women, who were just now leaving their cotton-picking work, readying for lunch, gathering together to sit in a circle on the fertile earth. An exhilarating sight! The pastoral background of a Millet painting, filled — not with the hulking bodies of sturdy peasant wives — with voluptuous young women from the canvases of Titian and Rubens and Gauguin and Raphael.

The lithe bodies stopped moving. Fear, that terrible swift sword, chopped down the vine of trust. Talking ceased. When the women noticed a fire-eyed stranger — wild-haired like a beast, head crowned with a junkfilled cap, hands hidden in leather gloves, and limbs wrapped in shreds of blankets — they could not decide whether to fall on the ground and giggle, or to scream and to run for their lives.

Frozen, like women in a painting, they studied me. To conceal the treacherous beauty of her hair, each woman squeezed both hands around the neck-knot of the kerchief on her head. But not before I saw the wisps of hair all raven-black. What wild wonders lay before me? A tribe of

Gypsy sisters hiding hair as black as the darkest nights. With one exception. The toughest-looking of these maids — her hair uncovered and almond-brown — examined me with far more surprise than fear.

Remember Odysseus, persecuted by the gods, who survived and thrived by his own courage, strength, and abilities on land and sea. One shrewd skill saved his life many times: his ends were consummated, his friends carved out of strangers, by his bold and crafty way with words.

My hand grasped the bottle and raised it high. Smiling as if I had just found friends, I opened my arms wide and shouted to the ten beauties below.

"Princesses of this fluffy kingdom. May your lips enjoy this sweet red wine the way my eyes imbibe the nectar of your loveliness."

Nine kerchiefed heads turned to the woman with almond-brown hair.

"Come," she yelled to me, in a gruff voice, nodding and waving her hand. And after I had sprinted down the hill, she said: "Katerina is my name."

"I am called Thoreau, and I bring you a gift of this wine. Do you want it, or do you not want it? ... Decide."

Katerina looked at me up, looked at me down, and then smiled without showing her teeth.

"We weel take your wine."

Cheers rang from mellifluous voices as I handed her the bottle. I would soon learn that the nine dark-haired women spoke two languages: Greek, and the Gypsy tongue known as Romany. The brown-haired woman who had accepted my gift knew both these languages, and sometimes spoke to me in English, accented and mispronounced, but easy enough to understand.

Katerina glanced behind me to find out if I had come with companions; and then she examined the bottle, surprised that it had never been opened before. When she spoke this time, her voice sounded not soft, but appreciably less harsh.

"For the wine, thank you."

A strong woman around thirty years old, Katerina was obviously the leader of this wandering troupe. Her green eyes, exquisitely gleaming, spoke of a character that had suffered much then turned her sufferings to strength. She was fiercely attractive in every way, save for the small burn-scars that streaked her cheeks, her temples, and the skin around her eyes. Shooing away the children like cats, she asked me to sit down and share their meal.

I pulled off the strips of blanket, then freed my hands from the gloves. I looked around and smiled at the pleasant company of women. Bright-colored kerchiefs circled their fresh, well-tanned faces. Strong from work and from living outside, their shapely bodies were veiled under long cotton dresses, each one tied around the waist with a white sash. Their bare feet, smudged by dirt and dust, seemed powerful and lively, filled with the strength of the earth they continuously touched. Not one of the women looked older than twenty-five or younger than seventeen. Their youthful smiles, cheerful and relaxed, were the smiles of children who had not yet been wounded by the world's cold violence and bottom-less greed.

The women eyed me with rapacious curiosity while Katerina pointed to every one and introduced me to their names. Meli, Romantza, Thalia, Cinarella, Fenella, Floure, Kisaiya, Mizella and Narilla. All these maid-ens were breathtakingly lovely, but three captured the heart of my atten-tion. Thalia, the youngest, just eighteen, charmed me with a kind of shy-ness that hinted at deep feelings and original thoughts. Romantza, who looked twenty-one, had great breasts and a perfectly proportioned body, and her eyes sparked with a fire that never knew fear. And Meli (a Greek word for honey), maybe twenty-four, had such a captivating beauty — beauty of body, face, and spirit — that my glance flew at her again and again, though I did my best not to stare.

A raspy voice barked from the bowels of the beat-up van.

"Get back to work you lazy whores!"

"You ugly pig!" Katerina yelled back. "We've got to eat to work!"

My broad smile wanted to burst into a coarse laugh.

"Katerina," I asked. "Who is that?"

Katerina shook her head as she stuck her hands onto her hips.

"Meesus Capeetaleest."

I could not resist peeking inside the van. My two eyebrows jumped al-most off my forehead. On a bed of soft pillows lay a short woman weigh-ing no less than three hundred pounds. Under her cartilaginous snout sat a downy mustache, rotten teeth, and a bearded triple-chin. A metal whistle, hung on a leather cord, dangled from her elephantine neck. In-describably repulsive, she mindlessly shoved cheeses and chocolates and cakes into her flabby face. The van itself nearly overflowed with baskets, crates and sacks of food.

I admired this poor Gypsy woman, Katerina. Her words were flavored with humor and defiance, without the least pinch of envy or despair.

"Last summer," she said, "the van ran into a ditch and Meesus Capeetaleest was stuck in the mountains here for three days. Nobody in town missed her. Three days without anything to stuff into that pig belly! For her it was worse than torture. So now, what does she do? She makes her truck into a market. Sometimes she sells food to tourists for ten times the normal price. Always, she drives around with enough food to stuff into her fat body for three weeks."

The circle of women rang with hearty laughter. As we laughed and glanced into one another's eyes, another scene increased our mirth. The thirteen children slowly approached. They grunted, giggled, grimaced and groaned as they walked toward us, all struggling together, carrying my weighty rucksack between their determined arms. They dropped the sack, picked it up, then dropped and raised it many times. At last, with heroic smiles, they let the sack fall onto the ground beside my feet. To thank them I made funny faces, poked their bellies, then snapped my fingers on the tips of every dirt-smudged nose. The laughing children skipped back up the hill, found hiding places behind bushes, then spied on us from afar.

Katerina spread a cloth on the ground then set out the food for lunch. Ten dates, a bag of olives, a jug of water, and four small loaves of bread — for hard-working laborers under the beating sun, a scanty meal! I would not let myself eat very much from their limited supplies. I took off my hat, unfastened the Swiss knife, uncorked the bottle of wine, then passed it to the gypsy leader's hands. While Katerina raised the bottle then swallowed the first drink, Romantza kneeled down beside me, her dark eyes burning with a playful gleam. Once, twice, and three times, Romantza ran her warm hands up and down my arms, my shoulders and my chest. Had she ever seen a man before? She looked at me with a puzzled gaze.

"Thoreau is so strong!" she shouted like a child.

"Thanks to a regimen," I answered, "of long walking, an all-natural vegetarian diet, and the best of the world's literature. And a lifestyle free from the psycho-saturated fats of television, consumerism, and self-created stress."

Raising then bending my right arm, I flexed the biceps muscles so that they bulged up proudly from the muscular triceps below.

"Watch out for her, Thoreau," said Katerina, as all the other women laughed. "Romantza pretends to be stupid but she is very clever. You never know next what she will say or do."

Romantza stuck out her tongue at Katerina, then smiled at me.

"Where do you keep your money?" she asked.

Prying questions can be answered with prying questions.

"Why do you want to know, Romantza?"

Her impish eyes blazed at the sound of her name.

"I want to know if you are rich!"

Katerina and all the women laughed riotously at Romantza's brashness, and I laughed too, before I replied.

"In my own country, Romantza, I am very poor. But here in Greece I have become rich."

Romantza grabbed my rucksack, then gazed at me with pleading eyes until I nodded yes. With great energy, she untied the knotted rope that kept the rucksack closed, pulled opened the sack, then dumped out all the contents. One by one she raised each item — tent, sweater, rain jacket, long pants, hand spade, plastic containers, extra batteries, notebooks, and the seemingly endless supply of books and books and books. She held up the compact tent.

"In your country, Thoreau," asked Romantza, "how much does this cost?"

And each time she held something up, I translated the amount of dollars into Euros. Astonished oaths and oohs and aahs poured from Romantza's ruby lips. Soon I would learn why. How much these women were paid depended upon how much they could harvest. On the average, for all their intense physical labors — from before sunup to long after sundown — each woman earned less than three Euros per day. The price of my camping gear, very small by Bedlamerican standards, made it seem as if I was as wealthy as a Cretan King.

"That's enough, Romantza," Katerina said sharply. "We don't want money from him."

Then, to Romantza and the others, Katerina spoke one sentence more, something in the Gypsy lingo that I could not comprehend. Words that made the women blush like roses and smile like flowers blossoming.

Lightly I touched her shoulder.

"Katerina. What did you say?"

Katerina instantly removed my hand from her shoulder, then smiled into my eyes.

"It's from a Gypsy story, Thoreau. The cow wants the bull not the bell."

Before I could interpret this amusingly cryptic remark, a more compelling question jumped from mind to mouth.

"Katerina, this friendly tribe of yours has children and women. Where are the men?"

First she shook her head, then sighed, then with both hands pushed her hair back from her forehead.

"The children, they come with Meesus Capeetaleest. She takes them from the working mothers in town. Lazy weetch! She gets food and money for watching them all day."

"And the men?" I asked. "Where are the men?"

Katerina turned her back to me and faced the women. She opened her expressive arms, then shouted something that sounded like an ancient curse.

"The men! He wants to know 'where are the men?'"

This question was met with laughter uproarious, so much so that their boisterous laughter made me laugh. Asked again, Katerina shook her head and told me nothing more. I could only guess. This wandering tribe of Gypsies had done what every woman had dreamed of doing, at least once in her lifetime. They had found a way to live by separating from the brutal and deceiving world of men.

When the roaring laughter settled into scattered titters, I glanced at the gorgeous Meli, who seemed to be gladly awaiting my gaze.

"Thoreau, excuse me," Meli said. And her soft voice purred like a cat scratched behind the ears. "Are you married?"

I paused, looked at this wondrous woman, then held up a ringless hand.

"No. Not married."

"Maybe soon?" said Meli, with an intriguing smile.

I nodded.

"What good is a life without shocks and surprises? Maybe soon, Meli, I will be married."

This reply brought cheers and claps of hands and clamorous laughter more. Sighing then smiling, the gentle Meli lowered her entrancing eyes.

Lunch — the meager ration of dates, bread, olives, wine — was quickly eaten up. I swallowed a thumb-sized chunk of bread, then stood up to leave. All the dark eyes peered at me with hope and disappointment, then turned for help to Katerina.

"Tho-reau," she said, slowly pronouncing the name. "Thoreau, if you want, you can work with us. We can pay you and give you food. You weel stay?"

Romantza clasped her hands together. Thalia stood still, graceful as a deer. Meli, holding her breath, melted me with a glance then tried to look unconcerned.

Would it be a bad thing, I wondered, to be taken in by these lovely women? Why not live and work with them for the next few hours, and learn some things about their rare and mysterious ways? I had planned a quiet evening by the sea, looking at the water and the stars, reading from the *Divine Comedy* of Dante. But plans that cannot change are useless plans. Dante's nine circles of Hell would rage whether or not I joined their blistering realms. Today, tomorrow, and a thousand tomorrows — Beatrice will still be waiting faithfully in *Paradiso*. Art stands still forever as Life flies by.

I put on my hat, shook my head as if to say 'No', then pretended to depart by taking a few steps toward the hilltop. Then I stopped, turned around and faced the women, and tossed my hat high into the air.

"Katerina," I said, still shaking my head. "I ... weel ... stay!"

A shouting cheer welcomed this announcement. Meli rushed to me as if she planned to thank me with a hug. Stopping suddenly, she smiled, then stepped back and thanked me instead with sparks from her dark-brown eyes.

The plucky Romantza did not believe in wasting opportunities or time.

Facing me, she lowered the top of her dress to expose both naked shoulders.

"Thoreau," said Romantza, "I have so many bug bites. Feel these bumps."

Katerina smacked the backside of the flirting siren.

"Slow down, Romantza," Katerina said.

Romantza covered her shoulders, shook her hips as she walked a few steps away, then glanced back at me provocatively.

"The quiet bird," she said "does not get the worm."

"Romantza," said Meli, "The proud bird does not get caught."

These two beauties began shouting at each other until Katerina stepped between. From her pocket she pulled out a red piece of fruit.

"We will settle this right now," Katerina said. She held up the pomegranate. "Thoreau. Here are nine good women. Give this pomegranate to the one you like."

"I like all of them Katerina," I said. "And I like you, as well."

Katerina tossed me the pomegranate then waved her hands.

"Give this pomegranate to the one you like the most."

In the mind-heavy Western world, concepts such as Love and Lust are researched, abstracted, debated, debunked, divided and defined until they shrivel up, lose their vitality, and turn completely meaningless. In the intuitive society of Gypsies, Love and Lust are whole and primal elements, as indisputable as the Sun, instantly recognized by one swift glance.

I reached for the knife on my hat. Katerina deftly snatched it from my hand.

"No, Thoreau! You can't cut it up and give out slices. The one you like the most gets a whole pomegranate. Here, I will help you to decide."

Gypsies can peek into the future with a dozen different techniques. They read tea leaves, they listen to the night sounds, they look at flocks of birds. Katerina pulled a handful of dried pomegranate seeds from her skirt pocket, and then placed them into my right hand and closed my fingers around the seeds. Before she could foretell my splendid nights ahead, the pack of children rushed to her and tugged her skirt. In loud wails they reminded us that now was the time for their afternoon snack. Katerina gave them a paper bag filled with small apples, firm and green.

The bumps between Romantza's shoulders, the melodramatic fight between the two feisty women, and these seeds that would influence my destiny — three sweet sights that dulled my genius, when they distracted my attention from the most important things. And what is this genius in us that fires the creative mind? Nothing more — and nothing less — than the ability to see the obvious and ordinary in a wholly new and thoroughly personal way.

"Katerina," I said, trying to hide my excitement. "Those small apples. Where did you get them?"

"Early this morning," Katerina said, "a woman discovered us here. A strong woman with a bicycle, looking for some kind of work. 'Why not work with us?' I asked. But when I told her how much money we were paid, she crossed her arms and shook her head. She told us that we were getting cheated. She said we should quit working or go on strike. 'And eat what?' I told her. 'The rocks and the dirt?' ... The woman understood.

She said she would go to the South coast to find work. If work there was good, with better pay, she would come back and find us and tell us more. Just before she left, she gave us this bag of apples for the children. She had a strange name — I remember now. Bliss."

Katerina nodded her head, as if the visitor had left her with not just a gift but with a good impression.

"The South coast of Crete," I murmured. But Katerina interrupted my mental wandering as she stared down at the red-stained seeds on my palm. At first I suspected some kind of scheme designed to influence my behavior, but soon it was clear from her eyes that Katerina trusted these readings the same way a scientist relies on her data, or a bibliomaniac believes in his beloved books.

"I see your future, Thoreau, right here in your own hands. A strange path, filled with many detours, many difficulties. A long healthy life with much travel. Many friends, but your caring about these friends — because they do stupid things — will bring you much sadness in the heart. All your life, you will give away your money to the poor. ... Here, see these seeds? They are a bird-monster trying to eat you, and when you kill this monster you will be free. And these seeds here? A thousand women will want your body and your love — some beautiful, some not so beautiful. See this? You will leave a woman who loves you and you will seek a great treasure, and then give that treasure to someone who needs it even more than you. And with the giving of that gift, a new life will begin for you. Now give me your other hand."

Katerina counted ten pomegranate seeds on my left palm.

"See these seeds," she said. "They are my girls and me."

She stared, then moved the seeds, then stared again in disbelief. She cursed in the Gypsy lingo, then with her hand she swiped the seeds off my palm to send them scattering across the ground.

"What do these stupid omens know, eh? Only old grandmothers believe these things! Let's get back to the pomegranate, Thoreau. Or else, till the minute you leave, all nine of my girls will be bickering and fighting like dogs over a nice chunk of meat. Give the pomegranate to the one you like the best."

Odysseus once called himself "the man who is ready for any event." I could wriggle free from this trap, I was sure, if only I could borrow a bit of time to think.

"Come here, everyone," I said to the women, in my best and clearest

Greek. "Sit down close to me. Not that close, Romantza."

Romantza pouted, then moved two inches back. I carried on.

"In just a few minutes, I promise, I'll quench your curiosity and tell you who I like the best. But first let me tell you a story about a handsome young man named Paris, who lived not far from here in hills like these. Many years ago, on Mount Gargarus, the highest peak of the tallest mountain in Crete, a mortal man named Paris was forced to choose between three women divine. Three goddesses — Hera, Athena and Aphrodite — had asked Zeus, lord of all the gods, to decide which one of them was the most beautiful.

"After many close encounters with women, Zeus was wise enough to grasp that if he himself made this choice, he would make at least two enemies for the remainder of his immortal life. So Zeus delegated this task to Paris. The son of Troy's King Priam, Paris had been living a simple life, frolicking with the nymph Oenone, and herding cattle or sheep in the hills of Crete."

Smiling eyes from the audience of women encouraged the bard to tell more.

"One morning, Hermes, Zeus's messenger, broke the news to Paris that he must choose the loveliest, by awarding her the golden apple. Immediately, the three goddesses flew to Paris and stood before him, unclothed and nakedly divine."

At this stunning revelation, first Romantza, then all the other women, removed their head kerchiefs and let their long dark hair flow down down down over their round shoulders, curving backs, and ample chests.

I had read this myth many times. But only now — the moment when the glorious beauty of the women was revealed by their splendid hair — did I fully appreciate Paris's predicament.

"Where was I? ... Oh yes. The naked goddesses asked the lucky mortal to select the fairest of them all. Each goddess promised a great gift to Paris if she were to become his choice. Hera, Zeus's wife, offered to make him the richest man who ever lived. Athena, goddess of wisdom and war, would reinvent him into the handsomest and wisest of men, and give him victories in all his battles.

"It was Aphrodite, the goddess of Beauty and Love and Desire, who promised what this man wanted most. For a wife, Aphrodite would give to Paris the now-legendary Helen of Sparta-Troy, the most desirable woman in the ancient world. ... Now, everyone, please close your eyes and I'll tell you the end of the tale."

The ten mouths continued smiling and the twenty eyelids promptly closed.

"Unable to resist this bribe, Paris presented the golden apple to Aphrodite. With her help, he abducted and married the already-married Helen, and sparked a ten-year war between the Trojans and the Greeks. Poor Paris! Once happy as a humble herder, he scarcely knew one moment of peace after his fateful choice.

"Now I will walk around the circle, and place a pomegranate in front of the one woman I like the best. Don't be angry at me. Don't forget, you insisted that I should choose. And keep your eyes closed until I say it's time to open them."

The goddess Athena had whispered a plan into my eager ears. Quickly I stepped to the van with the snoring Meesus Capeetaleest, and I removed the basket filled with dozens of her reddest fruits. I placed a pomegranate in front of each gypsy woman, then stood back to watch their faces, then asked them to open their eyes. First came the shouts of joy. Then came the groans and then the laughs, as the fair women realized how they'd been fooled and praised at the same time. Katerina looked most surprised to see a pomegranate sitting before her. Touching the scars on her face, she sat silently, as if she had been deeply moved.

"Teras! ... Plastra lesti!"

A fright-filled scream! That first Greek word meant: 'a monster'. And later Katerina told me that *"Plastra lesti!"* is gypsy lingo for: "Run for your life!"

We turned toward the terrified face of young Thalia, who was pointing to a rock ten feet away. On the rock sat a sun-worshiping lizard, large and hideous, with a scaly crown and yellow eyes. The women huddled together. Katerina picked up a stick and shook it at the beast.

Gently, along with a nod that asked her not to move, I placed my hand around Katerina's arm. The creature flapped its tail as it stared at the dusty van. Its eyes amazed me. Primordial eyes, wide-open, bulging, yellow like the mildest flowers and the wildest fires. I tilted my head toward the sounds of snoring from the van.

"Don't be afraid," I told the women. "He's just looking for a mate."

Then I sang the unanswerable question from Mozart's opera 'The Marriage of Figaro'.

"Voi, che sapete, che cosa è amor? Tell me, you who know, what is this

thing, love?"

The lusting reptile raised his head and lunged forward with two brisk steps. The women shrieked. The lizard wiggled its red tongue at us, then slithered down the rock and ran away.

Katerina threw down the stick. She yelled to the women then shook her head.

"Not all."

"Not all what, Katerina?" I asked.

"Not all monsters are men."

When the pandemonium of laughing subsided, we ate the pomegranates and then attacked the work.

10
MARRY ME!

MY MIND and all my energies were now focused on one tangible goal: plucking. Plucking cotton fibers was simple for these nimble-fingered women, but it took me a while to catch on. The sharp thorns on the cotton plant sliced my fingers and made them bleed. Meli, standing close to me, showed me how to work more deftly: "See it with your fingers, not with your eyes," she said. After bandaging my scratches, she insisted that I wear my leather gloves. In glove, inspired, and newly educated, I worked with astounding speed, using my athlete's endurance to fill up baskets and baskets of cottony tufts.

The Mediterranean sun made me the hero of the day. On this afternoon the temperature soared higher than one hundred Fahrenheited degrees. The ten women, perspiring like wet sponges, were forced to take frequent breaks, sipping water under the shade of the olive trees. I laughed at the heat. Since childhood, the slightest tinge of cold weather would make me shiver, but the highest heat and humidity never bothered me at all.

The joy of work outdoors! To move the body. To be outside under the open sky. To smell the flowers and breathe beside the trees. To see with awe the ever-changing light. And when my beautiful companions began to sing — ah, working and singing together! — for an eternity of hours my heart was carried into an Arcadia, a pastoral paradise on Earth beyond heavenly dreams. The voices, *a capella,* sang high like happy birds, and low like melancholy moanings of the wind. Their saddest tune, an old folk song of Crete, reminded me of homelessness and home. The women sang:

"I do not envy others for their vineyards and their gardens,
I envy only those with a home, who can stay in one place
And most I envy those who have sisters and cousins
To grieve with them and rejoice with them
And to help each other when troubles come."

Dusk was now breaking. The sun, bold as a man's hand, slipped itself halfway over the breast of the highest hills. We carried the baskets of cotton fibers and quickly loaded them into the cart behind the van. Meesus Capeetaleest counted the baskets, argued with Katerina, then stuffed a roll of Euros into Katerina's hand. Katerina stepped in front of me and held out a thick wad of bills.

"Thoreau," she said. "You worked like four. You must take theess."

I shook my head and placed both hands behind my back.

"No, Katerina. I don't want it."

Four times she patted her sly hand against my bronzed left cheek.

"If you weel not take it, Thoreau," she said coolly, "then you weel eat it!"

Katerina returned to the van to haggle with Meesus C. After many loud words, they traded Euros for a loaf of bread, a chunk of feta and a bag of oranges.

Light of the sunset faded slowly into evening's shades of dark. Some of the women arranged the cotton-plant stalks as kindling for a fire; others spread cloths and set out the dinner food. Bread, olives, figs. This time, in addition, there would be one orange for each worker, and the small chunk of feta cheese. Good food — food to be thankful for — but in a quantity too small to feed eleven hungry mouths.

When his friends or fellow human beings are hungry, what good man will shut his heart and do nothing to assist? ... I took off my hat and removed my Greek grandmother's Euros, and two of the Bedlamerican twenties. I found Katerina behind an olive tree, carving a dead-wood stick into a fork.

"Katerina, please, can we talk for a minute? Help me, Katerina. I want to buy food from Meesus Capeetaleest. But I'll get gypped unless you do the bargaining."

Then I explained to Katerina how many Euros were the equivalent of my two twenty-dollar bills. Katerina took the Euros and dollars and waved them in front of Meesus Capeetaleest.

Katerina winked at me, then stuck her head into the van and yelled at the woman whose greed was even greater than her girth.

"You beetch!" screamed Katerina. "How can you cheat this good man!"

"Katerina, Katerina!" said Meesus C. "If I get stuck, you will bring food to me? You won't forget me in the hills?"

"Be fair now," said Katerina, "and I won't forget you."

When the war of words was finished, Katerina called me to help carry the prize. There were generous amounts of yogurts and cheeses. Baskets of fruits and vegetables. Sacks of lentils and rice. Jars of honey and spices. Boxes of breads and cakes. Two gallon-sized cans of olive oil. And eleven bottles of wine. Unnoticed by Meesus C — who was counting and re-counting her pile of paper cash — the foresighted Katerina slyly slipped an hourglass into a crate of lemons, then handed the crate to me to carry off.

The greedy woman blew into her whistle three times — her bloated face grew redder with each exhausting blow. Had she noticed that Katerina swiped the timepiece? ... No, those whistles were the warning that brought all the children screaming and running to the van. Ceremoniously I said farewell to each boy and girl: I lifted him high into the air, whispered a funny secret into her small ear, told him to be good to all the other children, then hugged her and kissed her good-bye.

"Will you play with us tomorrow?" asked the little girl with bright eyes. A wonderful or terrible question, depending on which way the answer blows.

"Tomorrow, no," I said. With children, a grownup must always be sincere. "But I will look for you," I said, smiling, "when I come back here, many days from today."

With children, a grownup must always give a spark of hope.

The whistle blew again. The kids scrambled into the cart attached to the van, then they rolled their bodies in the soft cotton fibers. Rumbling and roaring, the van drove down the dirt-covered path. Huge eyes looked back at me, small hands waved, and grateful voices shouted out good-byes.

Now the setting sun — Apollo, the god of reason and order — knocked off for the rest of the day. Night-goddesses, filled with a primitive boldness, devoured the last morsels of fading light. Cicadas hummed; the air cooled slightly; the red-hot planet Venus flickered in the evening sky. The Gypsy women, renewed by the sensuous night and the prospect of a satisfying meal, like little children came alive. Their voices and their movements glowed with passion, vitality, enthusiasm, delight. Scurrying all around me, the women made a fire for cooking, arranged branches for a bonfire, and expertly prepared the orgy of revitalizing food.

"Katerina," I said. "What can I do to help?"

Katerina picked up one of my books and tossed it at me.

"Stay out of the way, Thoreau!" she said, with a mischievous smile.

"Now, you do nothing, you rest. Later we weel need you very much."

I have never liked to be waited on — I want to relate with every human being as an equal, not better and not worse. This time, I would let the women serve me. My principles would yield to the prominent exception. The women were taking joy in the process of making me a marvelous meal.

I took off my sneakers and socks then sat down beneath the branches of an olive tree. The cicadas were sounding louder. The sky shone with a magically romantic purple-blue. Fireflies flashed their glowing tails. I opened my book by Dante, but I could not concentrate hard enough to enter *Paradiso*. Compared to the reality around, the paper and ink seemed so lifeless and so dry.

Meli walked by, stopped, gently pressed her bare foot onto the top of my foot, then without looking back walked on. Barely a moment later a humming Romantza approached me from behind, pulled my earlobe, then ran away after she had pressed her foot on mine.

Up came the moon and the cicadas hummed louder still. The ten women and the one man sat on the ground together in a tight circle. A feast of food was served, warm and fresh, in hand-carved wooden bowls. Katerina pressed the mouth of a wine bottle against her lips and then swallowed a deep drink. She wiped her mouth with her arm, then poked her fingers into my shoulder.

"Thoreau. Why you don't drink your wine?"

"I can't drink, Katerina. One drink, and like a baby I fall asleep."

"Wine makes you sleep? That's no good. What makes you awake?"

Before answering I paused. These women had trusted me, laughed with me, treated me like a friend. They deserved the truth and the whole truth.

"What keeps me awake? Many things. The simple elements that renew every man. Good food, good nights, good music, and good love."

Katerina shouted something and in less than a minute, four more bowls of rice-vegetable stew and a hill of fruits were set before me. Long after everyone else had finished, I was still plowing through the fields of food.

What a perfect perfect night! The radiant faces of the women shined under the moonlight. An invigorating chill tingled the sweet October air.

Whirring music from the cicadas grew louder and louder as the night flew on. The world of men in the cities was filled with strife, but here in the hills, amidst this empire of women, I had discovered a sanctuary of friendship, trust, cheerfulness, peace. Shyness had now been banished from our kingdom: all the women smiled at me with brilliant eyes.

On my left sat Romantza and Meli; on my right, Katerina, brushing Thalia's soft dark hair. The women gazed at me as if they were now waiting for my tale.

"This is the magic night," I said. "A night like this happens once, only once, every 6,209 days. These insects we're hearing are mistakenly called 'seventeen-year locusts'. But that's not the right name. They're not related to the locusts that destroy. They are cicadas. In the Orient, and in ancient Greece, cicadas were kept like nightingales, so the people could enjoy their songs."

The whirring sounds grew louder, faster, and more passionate.

"Imagine existing underground for seventeen years, then suddenly rising to see and feel the wondrous beauty of a night like this! The cicadas live for about one week. One week to live, to eat, to grow, to love, to breed, to die. Rubbing their hind legs, the males make this music to attract females to the long-awaited night of bugly love."

Something about this factual description made the women laugh and laugh. Katerina tied Thalia's hair into a long ponytail, then kissed the young woman's forehead.

"They wait seventeen years to mate," said Katerina, glancing at Thalia then glancing back at me.

The fire blazed up and suddenly I was feeling too warm. Near me, three of the women were feeding the bright bonfire from a tall stack of branches and dried shrubs they had gathered in piles nearby. I slid backwards on my bottom to escape the expanding smoke and the rising heat.

Romantza whispered a question into Katerina's ear, and when the Gypsy leader laughed and nodded yes, the women jumped up with a joyful shout. Katerina kneeled behind me, pressed her knees against the bottom of my back, then combed my knotty hair. She spoke in a whisper like a breeze rustling the leaves.

"No man has ever seen this, Thoreau. And no other man will ever see it."

I imagined that these rites would reveal, with a Gypsy accent, the classic secret ceremony, a symbolic play representing the resurrection of a goddess.

"I'm honored, Katerina," I said. "I've read many books about these kinds of sacred rites. Every October in Athens, in the good old days of Aristophanes, a festival called the Thesmophoria was held — for women only — to worship the Earth-goddess Demeter."

It would not be necessary, I thought, to mention the Maenads who tore the limbs off voyeuristic men; or the Dionysian orgies at Delphi; or the wild nights of licentious revel that were celebrated in many states in Greece. Katerina tugged my hair with the comb, then laughed, then pulled my left earlobe.

"What are you now thinking, Thoreau? Eh?"

She greased my head with olive oil and mint leaves, then rubbed her fingers though my curly hair. Some of the women had raised their instruments, and the song of the cicadas was now joined by drum beats and the piping from a flute. Seven women appeared, then danced around the flickering bonfire. Now and then they would stop, bend down as if to pray, then throw a bunch of sticks into the growing blaze. The women were chanting in the exotic-sounding Gypsy language that I could not understand but loved to hear. I turned my head to Katerina.

"What does it mean?" I asked. And the dancing and chanting continued while the queen of the Gypsies explained.

"Goddess of the Earth, Goddess of the fires
The more sticks she devours, the more sticks she desires."

The moon and the man watched captivated as the night filled with a frenzy of piping and chanting and dance. The bonfire raged higher, as if its sole desire was to swallow the moon and all the stars. Cicadas vigorously sang. The once-cool air grew warmer all the time. The pipe-player entered the scene carrying a basket, then sprinkled flowers on top of the dancers' heads. For a moment, the sprightly dancers vanished from my sight. The spectacle upcoming roused my masculine curiosity.

When the players reappeared, they came as a circle of six women — bright and naked as the full moon — barely covered by their long dark hair. Arms raised like branches, they mimed the roles of trees in a magic forest. Hidden inside these woods stood another woman, also unclothed, her slender body draped with night-black hair that flowed from head to waist. This would be the young Thalia, who fell gently to the ground and pretended to fall asleep.

"Watch theess very carefully, Thoreau," Katerina advised.

"Katerina," I said, knowing that the next words would make her smile. "Men can be exceptionally dense, and I am an exceptional man. But telling a man to watch carefully when naked women are dancing, is like telling —"

"Shut up your mouth and open your eyes, Thoreau!" Katerina replied.

Sleeping Thalia tosses and turns, obviously disturbed by her daring dreams. Drums beat steadily as a pipe plays a sensuous strain. The tree-women dance in place, waving their branches-arms. They point to Thalia, who wakes, runs to each tree, stares at it with awe, then slowly caresses the trees with her elegant hands. Swaying like willows, the trees begin a lascivious dance. Frightened, Thalia tries to escape. She runs, but each step leads her deeper and deeper into the labyrinthine woods. The dance of dancers grows faster and more seductive. Thalia covers her ears. Sounds from the pipe call to her desires. She follows the music, escapes the reaching hands of the trees, and breaks free from the forest's bounds. Thalia laughs in relief, then — O fateful gaze! — looks back at the enticing trees. Thalia's backward glance makes the tree-women scream, and liberates them from their roots.

Ten times, these gorgeous nymphs chased Thalia around the fire.

Was it my imagination? Or the delusion produced from the rare experience of enjoying a colossal meal? ... Each time they danced by, the bodies of the women seemed to grow more lively and lovely, more passionate, more savagely robust.

Catching her at last, her companions lifted Thalia by her arms and legs, then carried her around the crackling fire. Every time around they would pretend to throw the young woman into the bonfire's heart. And each time that they stopped, they moved her closer and closer to the wiggling fingers of the fire.

"Katerina," I said, "they're getting too close to the fire."

Katerina pulled my right earlobe.

"That's the point, Thoreau," she said. She placed a hand on my shoulder and whispered into my ear. "Only the sky-god can save her now. The sky-god disguises himself as a man. A strong handsome man who fears nothing in the earth or sky."

My mouth fell open. I looked at Katerina. Calmly nodding, she looked back at me. I ran into the horde of laughing dancers, grabbed the naked Thalia, then carried her in my arms away from the burning flames.

Katerina slipped a blanket around Thalia, who sipped water then peacefully smiled. The dancers and musicians gathered around her. They kissed Thalia on her cheeks and forehead, they twittered like birds, and then they told her about the oldest and most secret Gypsy ways.

I lay back on the ground and looked up at the sky. Were the stars laughing at me? I had asked that question a thousand times. I could never tell before and I could not tell now. This life, and the women in this life, are mysteries that no man can ever understand. The human mind is never large enough to grasp the human soul. But to understand is not always necessary. All men need to do with women is to appreciate, to love, to give.

"Chich-chich. Chich-chich-chich. Chich-chich. Chich-chich-chich. Chich-chich."

I was trying to imitate the sounds of the cicadas, whose whirring music crescendoed from loud to almost deafening. The women, now dressed, had calmed down — I ingenuously imagined — after the releasing power of the dance. They had gathered around Thalia and they were talking and laughing with great energy. Blankets were piled on top of blankets, then covered with dried flower petals and the soft leaves of sage. Small wooden cups were filled with olive oil. Using my knife, Katerina cut lemons in half and waved them at the women, who giggled and shrieked as she spoke.

Between the fluctuating cries of the cicadas I heard Romantza shouting:

"I want to be the first!"

Some kind of disagreement started, which Katerina resolved by spinning an empty wine bottle, then giving each woman a number from one to nine. The cicadas' songs were drowned beneath a wild roar of womanly laughter. Again I looked up at the stars. The air filled up with the fragrant and stimulating aroma of rose water. The quiet Meli was kneeling at my side.

"Thoreau," she said, tapping my hand with her fingertips. "Are you listening? I want to ask you something."

"Yes, Meli."

She squeezed my hand between her hands.

"Marry me for one night. Will you?"

I sat up. In Meli's comely face I saw the purest most rapturous love.

"Meli," I said, not knowing what next to say. I squeezed her hand. "I like you, Meli. I care about you very much. But what about the others? They will be hurt in their hearts if I chose only you."

Meli turned her head and shouted something to her sisters, who rushed to me with bouncing titters and steady eyes.

"Marry me, Thoreau!" shouted Romantza.

"Marry me!" shouted Thalia.

And the six other women demanded the same.

Katerina, holding her sides as she laughed, stepped through the excited crowd, but not soon enough to keep Romantza from wrapping me inside her arms.

"You gave pomegranates to all of us!" shouted Romantza. "You said you liked us all! Remember?"

Romantza's lightning outburst was followed by a laughing storm.

"Katerina," I said. "Meli, Romantza, Thalia, everyone. ... Men and women are not the same but they are equal. ... I think it's best if just one man and one woman play these love-games together. ... Too many women at once with one man cannot be fully satisfying for the women."

Katerina kissed the air and held up the hourglass.

"Thoreau, we know that. One man, one woman. One woman, one hour. *Katalavehees?*"

I screamed. As loudly and lustily as ten thousand insects in the fields. The women howled with laughter at my astonished face. Katerina faced her family.

"He understands now," she said.

She turned to me and waved her hands.

"Thoreau," said Katerina. "Do you want, or do you not want? Decide!"

11
Panzano Explains
Why The Rooster Crows At Dawn

Tucked in the harbor at Agios Nikolodeonos, and kissed by the morning light, the old boat rocked with laughter. The story of my misfortunes had amazed and amused the entire audience. Everyone had laughed and cried, everyone except for one fun-hating nun, who pushed her way through the crowd and then rammed into Panzano, knocking him off his crate.

Built like a bell and filled with unimaginable flab, when she walked she waddled, when she walked backwards she beeped. Like a drilling woodpecker, she poked her fingers against my bare chest. Her furrowed face frowned from an ancient slow-moving epoch, but harsh words flew from her tongue at supersonic speeds.

"I am Mother Zitella Whackanzakis," she rapidly said. "These are my chaste nuns, and each one is a verified virgin who has never stood under a street lamp, and never understood a man! Today is the first time they have left our monastery, and we are traveling to an art museum on the reverent island of Rhodes. You and your sagas of love and desire must not lead these angels astray!"

Three times the Mother-nun clapped her warty hands. Immediately eleven nuns stepped out from the crowd, and then stood in a straight line shoulder-to-shoulder behind her. Hoods and veils obscured the better parts of their faces; and their white habits with blue crosses on the front, all identical, made height the only method for telling them apart. Mother-nun introduced her brood by calling out their names, and as each name resounded, the nun stepped forward and curtsied modestly.

"This is Forza ... Donnabella ... Volutta ... Scherza ... Agevolezza ... Impetuosamenta ... Anima ... Celerita ... Bria ... Voleggianda ... and Dolcezza. ... Dolcezza!"

The last-named nun, too shy to move, stood on her spot until the other ten sisters stepped backwards to place her in the front. When she realized she was standing all alone, Dolcezza ran and hid behind Mother

Whackanzakis's substantial posterior.

Panzano stood up on wobbly legs and uncertain feet. He shook his head as his fingers groped his scalp to feel two swelling bumps.

"An oak is not cut down," he said, "by a single blow from an axe. But I wish that that nun-Mother would have given me one bowl of cooked oatmeal instead of these two raw eggs."

A rooster chasing a flock of chickens scurried across the boat's wooden deck. Mother-nun snatched the male bird and thrust him into Panzano's hands.

"This bird must not chase the chickens with improper attentions," she shouted. "And you and your friend must not tell stories that set fire to the hearts of my innocent nuns!"

The rooster screeched stridently, as if he wanted to get back to his business. Panzano placed him on the deck, and the bird rushed to the nearest chicken female and jumped on top of her back. Mother-nun screeched and then commanded her eleven nuns — who had taken vows of poverty, chastity, obedience — to cover their eyes with their hands.

Panzano shook his head.

"Dear Mother," he said. "Like soup and garlic, these stories can only do you good. Listen with both ears open, and you will be warned against things that could happen, and entertained by the things that actually did."

The crowd laughed as the rooster strutted proudly, then jumped into the arms of his friend Panzano, who placed the bird on top of his head "to hatch my eggs," he said. A loud belch bellowed from Panzano's bottomless belly.

"'*Vaso vuoto suona meglio*'," he said. "'An empty vessel makes the loudest sounds'. And it's truer than true what they say in Tuscany: '*La fame muta le fave in mandole*' — 'hunger makes the bean taste like an almond.'"

Panzano patted his round stomach.

"If only I had some nourishment to wake me up, I could tell you the story of why the rooster crows every morning at dawn."

A generous crowd soon supplied this gluttonous Aesop with beans and almonds and a large crock of wildflower honey, which Panzano greeted by dipping his hand into the pot then licking the honey-covered palm. Mother and her eleven nuns, and the rest of the audience, crowded closer to Panzano, then sat down on the deck.

"It started with Aphrodite," he said, "the irresistible goddess of love.

Zeus her father had forced her to marry a lame and ugly inventor named Hephaestus. Yes, to his wife and to women he was unappealing, but to the gods he was worth his weight in lemon-strawberry *sgroppino.* So clever was Hephaestus that he once forged female robots out of gold — they could talk, and move, and cook, and help him with every aspect of his work. But that did not solve his problem: he worked too much and ignored his sexy wife. Whenever Hephaestus left home for his workshop, Aphrodite gladly flew into the arms of Ares, the powerful god of war."

Mother-nun shouted, and then ordered her eleven girls to cover their ears with their hands. Panzano sipped a steaming brew from a small ceramic cup.

"Greek coffee," he said, smacking his lips. "It is so thick that you drink it and you eat it. ... What was I telling you about?"

The nun named Volutta spoke out.

"Hephaestus was so busy working in his shop," she said, "that he didn't notice how his wife Aphrodite was working with Ares in bed."

"Thank you," said Panzano. "Now Ares had a servant named Alektryonas, renowned for four reasons: he rarely slept, he could smell things far away, and his eyesight and hearing were especially keen. Ares assigned Alektryonas to stand guard outside the bedroom and warn the lovers just before Helios — the Sun-god Apollo — would rise every morning above the sea. But one morning Alektryonas fell asleep. Apollo rose and spotted the dalliance, then ran to tell Hephaestus right away. The inventor used his skills to weave an invisible net, stronger than steel, which he attached to Aphrodite's bed. The next morning, when Ares and Aphrodite embraced, their wild thrashings brought the net around them, and they were trapped, naked and unable to move. Hephaestus called all the gods to come to witness the fine site, but instead of being outraged, they laughed, and enjoyed seeing Aphrodite in the nudie. At last, when the lovers were released, Ares transformed his servant Alektryonas into a rooster. As punishment for his lapse, his job forevermore would be to crow every dawn when the sun rose, to wake up the world's lovers, and give them a chance to run home."

Mother Whackanzakis screamed, flailed her arms, suddenly charged at the storyteller with surprising speed. Panzano was saved from a thrashing only because the nuns grabbed her robe and begged her to forgive. A shrill ship's whistle blew. The boat's assistant captain raised his left hand — his wristwatch gleamed in the sunlight — and then announced that the boat would not depart on time. He advised all passengers to amuse themselves with conversation and reading, food and drink, stories and songs.

Panzano dipped a chunk of bread into the honey pot.

"Whatever we have to face we will need a good meal," he said. "And the slower you move, the farther you travel. So have patience and pass the pasta. *'Il mondo è di chi ha pazienza* — the world belongs to the man who is patient.'"

Mother Whackanzakis and her eleven nuns pulled long needles and wool balls from beneath their robes and then began to knit. The audience applauded to thank Panzano for his story. And then the crowd cheered after a woman's voice shouted joyfully:

"Thoreau, dear Thoreau! Tell us more of your wonderful tales."

12

THE NIGHT OF THE LOCUSTS: HOW TEN AMOROUS GYPSY-WOMEN RUIN MY PLANS FOR A QUIET EVENING

IS A LIFE OF ADVENTURE still possible in our disintegrating modern world? Or is the Hero a relic to be observed — a few minutes per week — on the walls of the musty museums, or in the pages of books obsolete?

Katerina raised my hand and pressed it firmly underneath the dress of Meli, and rubbed my hand on Meli's trembling breasts.

"That's what we call stacking the deck a bit, Katerina," I said.

I stood up, trying to win a little time. I removed my hand from the woman's body, but the hand still tingled and felt like it was burning up. I wiped the sweat beads from my cheeks and temples. The breasts felt so warm, so soft, so intellectually stimulating. It was very, very, very difficult to think.

"What about babies?" I said. "You don't want nine little Thoreaus in diapers following you around these hills, do you?"

Katerina held up the lemon halves and a cup of olive oil. I recalled having read studies that claimed that as a contraceptive, olive oil and the lemon had never failed.

"Do I get a cup of tea with that lemon?" I asked.

"Thoreau," Katerina insisted. "No jokes now. There is not time for jokes. Night is a woman: she likes men to wait for her, and she does not like to wait."

I noticed the hourglass and then realized that my window for procrastination was slamming closed.

"Ah, the hourglass!" I said. "Shaped like a woman. The symbol of love, and the symbol of harmonious sexual union. Open to each other, each lover at the same time gives and receives."

Tired of talking, Katerina thrust her hands to her hips then glared into my eyes.

"Thoreau! Shut up and decide!"

To refuse, would be to slap these fine women with the cruelest of insults. Would they think that they were worthless, ugly, and unlovable? Would their oily love for me turn rancid? Would they curse me and despise me for the next ten thousand days? And would their opinion of the male species, which had already reached rock-bottom, blast down even deeper and lower through the rocks? ... What I really wanted was a prolonged sexual relationship with one woman who loved me and who I deeply loved. On the other hand, if I survived this night, my consciousness would be expanded, my erotic inhibitions would dissolve forever, and my sexual horizons would be enormously enlarged.

I kissed Meli, then kissed Romantza, then kissed Thalia, then kissed six other pairs of luscious lips. Such joy was there, in those glowing hills of Crete, that moment in the night I smiled and shouted "Yes!"

"And you, Katerina?" I said with a hearty laugh. "For one unforgettable hour tonight, do you want to be my wife? ... Decide!"

The answer hit me as soon as the question was complete. Katerina slapped my cheek.

"You are funny, Thoreau," she said, with a friendly smile. "Just be good to my girls. That's all that matters to me."

Katerina rubbed my body with olive oil, rose water and scented herbs. I was led to the pile of blankets, strewn with flowers and soft leaves, which would serve as the marriage-bed. The cicadas turned up their volume and were now whirring passionately, like thunderous applause from the all-powerful gods.

Lovingly, slowly, tenderly, the stars swirled in the sky and the great night passed. By the time the moon fell and the black sky turned purple deep, nine bodies, one by one, had shared my polygamous bed. Nine bodies, a thousand kisses and caresses, and nine times nine ecstatic screams. At the end of each and every hour, when the last grain of sand had trickled through the hourglass, Katerina came to gently separate the entangled lovers. First the two bodies would be unglued. Next — as the just-loved woman grasped my hand with all her power and murmured to me all the joys her heart contained — Katerina would cut a lock from my bushy hair. Finally, Katerina pried our hands apart, and pressed my lock of hair into the woman's lonely hand. At last, after each hour-long spell of erotic play, and each tearful separation, Katerina cleaned my face and body with damp cloths, then whispered advice to the next new bride.

For the last time, Katerina wiped my forehead, then squeezed my hand between her hands.

"You gave them so much happiness, Thoreau. So much wonderful happiness. And you, eh? You had a good time, too! What do you say, Thoreau?"

We laughed together. I sat up beside her.

"But what did you say to make them laugh, Thoreau? They were all laughing and they wouldn't tell me why."

"What did I say? Each woman is beautiful in her own way, so to each woman I say something unique."

Katerina's face inched closer to my face as she lowered her shining green eyes.

"What would you have said to me?"

"The truth. I would have said the truth, with a humorous slant. You are the beautiful queen of all the goddesses. I am the sky-god who wants to sleep with you. But you refuse me, because you cannot realize how beautiful you are. So I change myself into a rooster, a billy-goat, a male-lion, and a bull."

Katerina laughed as I crowed, bleated, snorted, roared. She kissed my hand, grasped that hand that had been kissed, and then led my hand across her scar-crossed face. I stroked her hair with a touch that spoke — far more sincerely than words — how truly beautiful she was.

"Katerina, tell me. What do you wish for?"

"That my girls live a long and happy life. That someday we will find a house and a garden and stay in one place. That men will stop telling all their lies to women. And that men will always believe the lies that women have to tell to men."

She gripped my hand and placed it against her cheek.

"One more thing — don't laugh at me now. I wish that this morning will last a hundred years. What do you wish for, Thoreau?"

Once more I touched her hair.

"For now, I'm in paradise, and in paradise only a fool makes a wish. For later — can you blame me for being hungry? — one ripe banana would hit the spot."

Katerina's face, usually calm as the rocks now looked as shaky as the sea.

"Thoreau, hear me. Life is a gypsy with two quick hands: one that gives and one that takes away. You weel ... understand us?"

I looked deep into her eyes that swelled with tears.

"Understand?" I asked.

Did she mean, 'know' them, or 'forgive' them? But then in one terrible flash I understood. I understood everything. A wave of sadness washed over me and left me chilled. Old Hope's words rushed to the rescue: "Nothing earthly lasts forever."

In a few sharp moments I recovered myself. The unbearable sorrows of young Thoreau were routed by the incomparable joys of the night.

"Katerina, I think I understand. But tell me exactly what you mean."

"A bird must be a bird," she said. She stroked my forehead, stared into the night-sky, then sang softly from a Cretan song.

> "Not the flowers in the warmest Spring
> Not the sky, not the earth, not the sea,
> Not the scent of the rose, not the birds who sing —
> Nothing is beautiful unless you are free."

When she stopped singing, my fingertips touched lightly her quivering lips.

"Katerina, I understand."

She wiped her face. She too, had conquered a sorrow and had now recovered herself completely. She sat up straight and proud.

"I am better now," the woman said. "Sky-god: did you lie like a man when you said that I was beautiful?"

"I said you that you are very beautiful. And I swear it to my brother stars."

Katerina threw off her dress, laughed wildly, pushed me down onto the blanketed bed, then jumped on top. Her warm breasts pressed themselves impatiently against my chest.

"And you want to marry me," she asked, "for one whole hour?"

"I do. Till dawn do us part."

She grabbed my limp love-organ, shaking it back and forth, like a rubber stick.

"And is there any lightning left in the thunderbolts of the great sky-god?"

Before I could laugh or answer she passionately kissed my lips.

"Ah, good!" the woman cried. "There is still some lightning."

I flipped the hourglass so that the sand began a-flowing, but Katerina stopped Time by turning the hourglass onto its side. My hands rubbed their way up and down the curves of her smooth legs, her firm bottom, her strong back, her round shoulders, her tremulous breasts.

"Katerina," I said. "There's not enough time for talking, I know. But there is one more thing I want to tell you."

I wiggled my tongue at her like a lizard, then licked her lips, then tenderly seized her attention with a kiss. She remembered the lizard on the rock and we laughed and laughed about the beast, and her opinion that not all monsters are men.

Katerina's hand stroked my face. Her eyes were bright and her voice spoke with a new tenderness.

"Tell me, Thoreau," she whispered.

The woman's shoulders felt soft between my firm and gentle hands. I kissed the tips of her perfect breasts, then whispered into her ear.

"Not all."

"Not all what, Thoreau?"

"Not all men are monsters."

The cicadas were still singing their wild songs of undying love. Lesser stars had faded, but bright Venus faithfully glowed. The morning sky, the sky unending, covered the new lovers with kisses of fabulous light.

13
How Nudism Becomes Thoreau, and How Thoreau Becomes A Nudist

THE GODS ON MOUNT OLYMPUS LOVE to make troubles for a man, then laugh uncontrollably as they watch him squirm.

When I started to wake up I was lying on my back, eyes closed, mouth smiling, hands locked together behind my head. Memories, sweeter than grapes in honey, swirled through my exhausted body and rejuvenated soul. Night of rapture, morning of tenderness! Naked bodies, warm skins, ridiculous positions, ticklish touches, luscious lips, titillating tongues, rapt faces, glowing eyes, secret whispers, astonishing requests! All these had gushed and mingled between the wildest outcries and the most passionate screams.

"Women," I murmured, "are the only hope to save the world. These liberated women have liberated me."

The morning's sunshine massaged my skin in sensual caresses. The deep smile on my face declared that the happiness it manifested would live for longer than I could guess. I remembered something that Katerina had told me a few hours before.

"You know, Thoreau," said Katerina, as her lips brushed against my cheek, "that the girls and I wander everywhere on Kreetee. Last summer we saw ruins. Stone temples, marble columns, painted urns, a statue of a naked god, Apollo. Now, all the girls are laughing and saying: 'Thoreau looks like the statue!' Without your clothes, you know, you are more handsome than that god. Why do you hide yourself underneath those rags? You say that you care about women? Then give them the joy of something nice to see. Starting today, for our husband Thoreau, no more ugly clothes!"

I laughed at Katerina's raw advice. What breezy sayings bubble from a woman's lips! What windy promises babble from a man's!

Weary eyelids, shut and stuck together, did not want to open, did not want me to leave the touching memories behind. Too soon, they seemed to say, to rise and face the day. As more sultry memories drifted through my unsuspecting mind, a warm tongue began to lick my face. Meli? Romantza? Thalia? Katerina? Which one had dared return to steal more joy than her allotted hour? ... I reached out to stroke the head of my angel unknown.

Foul-smelling breath — a rare blend of old sneakers and decomposing snails — swamped my twitching nostrils. My hand — that groped to find offending lips and planned to seal them with a kiss — brushed against a thick-haired head and then a beard.

Fright! For a moment I visualized Meesus Capeetaleest, the horrifying woman in the van. Then some relief, as my fingers failed to find the flabby triple-chin, and curled instead around a bony horn. The creature bleated three times, then uttered a loud whining cry of "Baaaaaaaaaah!" A coarse nose snuggled against my nose. Again and again my cheeks were licked by a slobbering tongue. My eyelids — each one felt as heavy as a wooden door — forced themselves to open up.

The head and eyes of a huge he-goat were studying me, staring with a curious and gentle gaze. I had long believed in the rights of animals, in vegetarianism, in the equality of all species — humans should respect all living beings. And last night, my sexual horizons had been expanded by a pack of Gypsy women for whom sex was a natural enjoyment, and nothing is ever "bad" or "wrong" as long as there is agreement between eleven consenting adults. Yet despite this universal compassion and freer sexual mores, at he-goats I drew the line.

Bleating profusely, the friendly beast scampered away to hide behind the nearest tree. My nude body sprang up stiffly from the rocky ground. The dying bonfire beside me smoldered and smoked. Laceless sneakers stood adjacent to my bare feet. The spectacular hills and valleys all around, which last night rang with reckless laughter, now sat as silent as the senseless stones.

Nothing! All gone! Everyone and everything no more! The women who swore they would love me forever. The blankets that had been our marriage bed. The feast of food. And all my clothing, books, and gear. Vanished. Evaporated. A tear in History's unseeing eyes. Gone, gone, gone!

A tugging in the much-used area below my waist captured my attention, and I recalled a 12th-Century horror — during the gelded age of Abelard — then remembered the groinly-popular Bedlamerican ritual where revengeful women severed male penes then served them under glass. Rolling my eyes up to the blue sky, I slowly unrolled the eyes, then hesitantly glanced down. Tied with the sneakerlaces — and now dangling drolly around my extended love-organ — hung one large, mushy, black-skinned, rotten banana. My love-organ looked embarrassed but perfectly intact.

I stepped into the beat-up sneakers, untied the knots in the laces, then disengaged myself from the overripe banana. Running to the top of the empty hill, I cupped my hands around my mouth then shouted with all my might.

"Katerina!" I yelled, surveying the barren lands and shaking the crescent-shaped fruit. "Katerina! Katerina! Katerina!"

Not even an empty echo bothered to reply. A breeze from the south blew cool whispers through the silvery olive leaves. The belly-laughing bleatings of the goat were the only answers to my hopeless cries.

With the plastic-covered tip of a sneakerlace, I pierced one small hole through the crow-black banana skin. I gripped the fruit like a flute with both hands, pressed my lips to the hole, squeezed the banana, then sucked the fermented liquidy mush. After the meal, I preserved the banana peel by folding it into a sun cap, tying it securely to my head. If nothing else edible turned up by nightfall, the vitamin-rich peel could be eaten raw, or — with luck and a cooking pot — boiled and consumed as a savory soup.

In his young manhood, Russian writer Maxim Gorky talked to the rats in his room. Gorky wrote that these discussions saved him from going mad with loneliness. In my darkest and brightest moments I talked to the sky and the trees.

"Where to go now? Wherever the wildest adventures await. To the south coast of Crete, to find the woman on the bike!

"The island of Crete is shaped like a donkey lying on his back. From the head in the West to the hoofs in the East, it stretches two-hundred-and-sixty kilometers, or one-hundred-and-sixty miles. From North to South, this slender island changes size, from as buxomly as sixty kilometers, to as wasp-waisted as fourteen. Starting from here on this spot, the most direct way to reach the south coast is to walk straight south through the Eastern edges of Mount Dikti. I'm about thirty kilometers, or less than nineteen miles, away. There are eight hours of light to walk by, if I want to reach that coast before dark tonight.

"And why? Why carry my carcass across these crusty crags of Crete? To follow Beauty. Somewhere on this rock-covered island a beautiful woman is traveling alone. A woman who needs the kind of help that can be given only by an oddball like me."

I apologized to the olive tree beside me, then broke off a leafy olive branch. What man can stand to be belittled? My genitalia would need to be protected from the burning glares of the sun and the disparaging stares of any prigs, pre-teens, or perverts who happened to be passing by.

Walking in Nature provides three blessings: health in the body, joy in the heart, clear thinking in the mind. Briskly I hiked along a small trail heading directly south. Above me, a lone cloud sat motionless, relaxing in the perfectly blue sky. Green hills lay covered with tall dry grasses; trees stood like giant sprigs of parsley; bushes of velvet-leafed sage smelled sweet. Here and there I found orchards whose ripe fruits had been picked clean. The early-afternoon sun did its scorching best to bake me, but although a rare blend of genes had made me unable to drink alcohol, I was impervious to measurable heat.

"Let's think back for a minute, Thoreau. What have you learned from your experiences? ... That it's possible, at the same time, to have nothing and to have everything. Right now, I have the same amount of possessions as any man who has been divorced ten times. And I hope that Katerina sells all my precious junk, and then buys food or shoes or clothes for all her sisters and for herself, too. I wish with all my heart I could have helped them more."

I shook my head, then inhaled a mighty breath then slowly let it out.

"And I wish they could have trusted me, and let me help them more."

I laughed out loud.

"Can you imagine how they laughed and laughed when they tied me to that decayed banana! Why did they deceive me? Not to be cruel. No, never, impossible! They wanted to make me laugh. And they wanted me to laugh and to remember them. How do I know that? At the end of our love-games, each woman — even Katerina, as tough-shelled as she pretended to be — each woman looked pleadingly into my eyes and whispered: 'Don't forget me, Thoreau! Promise a thousand times you won't forget me! Swear it, love! Swear it! Promise me!'

"They know many things, those women of the earth. They know that every person lives two lives: the real life in this world, and the life lived in the memory of the people who love us with all their heart. And whenever the second life flickers and fades — when there's nobody in the world to think of us! — then the first one loses every sparkle of its joyfulness."

For miles and miles I talked to myself while walking, watching the blue sky, enjoying the scents of the mountain herbs and the clear fresh air. My eyes, which had observed too much of the city's blinding ugliness, now enjoyed sights wondrous and primitive, brightening my mind with aperçus. Hills and hills covered with free-flowing grasses, stretching farther than the mind could see. Stone houses on the hilltops with smoke arising from their chimney stacks. Flocks of sheep and lone goats chewing olive leaves. Hawks soaring above, mice scurrying below, birds of many species, large and small. But no sounds or sightings of human beings, no women, no children, no men.

And then a man at last, ahead on the narrow dirt path. I saw, approaching in my direction, an old man walking beside an old donkey. Except for four small pouches, the beast had no saddlebags or blankets, and the man looked even more nude than his beast. Examining this man, who appeared so thoroughly unmodern, I had momentarily forgotten that I myself was naked as a Jain. Quickly I clutched my leafy olive branch, then raised it waist-high enough so that someone scrutinizing my pelvic region would have barely noticed the tom a-peeping through the brush.

The old man nodded then stopped his ass. The Cretan-style cap on his head looked as black as the hood of Death; his beardless and wrinkled face wore a white mustache, white as the foam of the life-giving sea. His eyes and smile reflected a depth of patience that I had never before seen, the calm of a man who was supremely rich with worlds and worlds and worlds of Time.

"*Kalispera,*" he said.

"*Kalispera,*" I replied. "Good afternoon."

From his donkey he untied one of the pouches, then tossed it to me — a bag of almond nuts.

"Take them all," he said. "You look like you could eat a stack of pancakes from the toes to the tatas of Aphrodite."

He looked me over, tilting his head from side to side.

"Your hair has been chopped like poor Samson. I cannot tell what country has born you, because I notice that you are not wearing clothes.

Did you know that you can learn much about a man's personality by the way he dresses himself up?"

I smiled at the old man.

"What can you tell about my personality?"

He looked at me with great intensity.

"You love material possessions too little, or you love women too much. ... Now, try to forget about women for a few moments, and take your choice between my water and my wine. "

The spring water I drank from his guerba tasted pure at first, and then tingled with a sweet tang. The old man gestured to say I should drink more.

"Hermes," he said, "our god of luck, music, eloquence and the patron of travelers and rogues — Hermes will guide you today. Yet Hermes or no Hermes, you will need this to battle our Greek sun. Put out your hands."

From another guerba he poured olive oil into my cupped hands, then instructed me to rub it all over my body as a sunscreen. And then his hand rubbed the tree beside him with the greatest tenderness, as if he were caressing a woman in his bed.

"Don't thank me for the oil," he said, "thank our olive trees. Do you hear that banging in the next village? ...That is the sound of men and women striking the olive trunk, so that the olives fall into nets on the ground. That's the way they gathered olives eight-thousand years ago — at the beginning of civilization on Crete — and the way that many of us still do it today. These trees can live and bear fruit for one-thousand or even fifteen-hundred years. Whenever I eat an olive from these trees, I feel humble and thankful and proud."

He looked at me and laughed.

"Poo pahss?" he asked. "Where are you going?"

"To the south coast," I replied in Greek. "To the town of Tymros. Can I find any work there?"

"No," the old man answered, slightly raising his head.

In Athens the word 'no' is pronounced *'oh-hee'*, but all through Crete — where the influence of Woman is everywhere — the natives make 'no' female, and say: *'oh-shee.'*

"You want work?" the old man asked. "Go to Dembacchae, where work will find you. And if work doesn't find you there, do not despair. There are better things than work that may discover you. Come, I can show you the shortest way."

The ancient one stared at me then smiled.

"You speak good Greek," he said. "And you have courage. Your eyes are the eyes of a *pallikári*."

A *'palikar'* was a Greek soldier in the years 1821 to 1828, during Greece's great war of independence from Turkey. To be called a *'pallikári'* is to be given the highest praise, because the word means 'a true man, both brave and strong, who can endure hardships and pain'.

As we walked he hummed softly. When I looked at the vigorous old man, there was one question I could not resist.

"You have enormous energy and joy," I said. "Yet you look poor in material things, and you are — forgive me for saying it — past the prime of life. Can you tell me your secret? What keeps you alive and well and full of fire?"

"Past my prime?" he loudly said. He raised his eyebrows as he laughed. "Don't believe that, my boy! I will be past my prime starting from the day I'm on the other side of this grass we're walking on. You want to know my secret? That can be learned, but it cannot be taught. "

At a fork in the road we stopped walking.

"What can I do to learn it?"

"It is simple. You need to work — work like a hundred men! — to make your dreams alive. This road travels to Tymros, where you can sleep under a blanket of stars, then to Dembacchae, where you can ask for work."

"What's your name?" I asked.

"I have many names," he said, with a great smile.

I started to say 'thank you' — for the water, oil, almonds, directions, advice, and for his calm cheerfulness — but the old man shook his hand.

"There is no need to thank me," he said. "I have always believed that one of the most beautiful qualities of the human soul is the generosity of a stranger to another human being in need."

He placed his hand over his heart.

"Good journeys to you. We will meet again."

I waved good-bye then walked down the hillside. Soon after that parting — as if his blessings had given me some luck — I found exactly what I needed: one empty glass bottle, and two trees rich with thirty lemons and dozens of carob pods. I tried to imagine how many billions of bags, plastic and paper, littered my native Bedlamerica. I laughed as I realized that I had fallen to the lowest caste: a bagman without a bag. So I carried my newfound possessions — almonds, bottle, carob pods, lemons — with both arms pressed firmly against my stomach and my chest.

Again I thought of the serene old man, his story, and his gift of the meaningful almonds. Something about the encounter had moved me deeply. The almond tree, in some parts of the world, was a symbol of beauty and revival. That old man had discovered how to live one of life's greatest secrets. A kind of wisdom best explained in a passage from Kazantzakis's novel *Zorba the Greek*. The all-too-human Zorba asks a bent old man, aged ninety, why he is planting an almond tree, since he would never live long enough to see the tree bear fruit. The old man answers that he lives as if he is never going to die. Zorba replies that he lives as if he were going to die this minute. And then he wonders which one of them was right.

After walking many steps and hours, I smelled the sea-air, then soon arrived at the beach on the coastal town of Tymros. The black sand there, soft and fine, would tomorrow be overrun with tourists. Yet tonight the beach lay empty and pristine. I jumped into the sea water for a quick bath. Then I shelled some of the carob pods, removed the hard oval seeds, and chewed on the soft and tasty filling inside. I devoured three whole lemons: tangy skins, nutritious pectins, bitter fruits inside.

Waves rushing against the shore resounded like a breathing giant. Cicadas sang their wild love songs. The full moon hung low in the dark night-sky. The stars greeted me with twinkling smiles. Under the beaming moonlight, using smooth flat stones, I built a knee-high wall to shield me from the chilling winds. Behind the stone wall I placed my pile of carob pods and lemons, then I pressed the glass soda-bottle, bottom-down, into the sand. The wind would rush across the open top of the bottle, make the sounds of a frightening moan, and scare away the beach rodents who desired to steal my stash of food.

I lay down on the comfortable sand bed then talked to the night sky.

"Today was a good day. And look at the moon and the stars! — it's another perfect night. The full moon reminds me of the light in a woman's eyes, as she gazes at the man she loves."

I heard a dog barking in the distance so I spoke aloud more softly; it might be foolish to make noise, but I wanted to hear myself speak.

"How can it be that we live more and learn more in one deep hour than we do in long uneventful years? What mysteries we glean through one passionate night! What lessons we learn from nature and women who touch us! The beauty and the tenderness they are! Each night under the stars, every night with a good woman, a man becomes more human — I mean more sincere, more gentle and more kind."

The sea whispered as it licked the sand.

"The gypsy women, the bikress, and the woman from the Meteora: Where are they tonight? ... Hungry like I am, or stuffing their bellies with food? Thinking of me with longing, or laughing in the arms of other lucky men? ... None of that matters, Thoreau. All that matters is that they're alive and safe."

Before I fell asleep on the black sand, I smiled at the words of Masahide:

My storehouse burned down —
nothing obscures the view
of the bright moon.

14
THE TREASURES OF TYMROS —
HE WHO INSULTS MY PANTS INSULTS TRASH

ONE MAN'S GARBAGE is another man's gold. I woke to the splashings of the waves against the seashore, snorings from a great god in the sea. The dawning sky gleamed with long-winged sea gulls soaring freely. The birds looked free, yet their wild bird-cries pierced my ears with the profoundest gloom.

"Dollars damn me!" shouted Herman Melville, when the income from his novels suddenly dried up. Melville — and Whitman and Thoreau — could not solve the first problem of creative persons: how to get a living without losing a life. Is there a remedy for this impoverishing plight? Keep on creating and do not lose heart. Laughter transforms our unavoidable Fate into a merry Destiny.

Naked as a gull, I ran across the dark-sanded beach, covering my crotch with the leafy olive branch. My destination, my marvelous treasure chest, was the beach's lone garbage can. The can, which sat in the sand near a row of beachside restaurants and shops, was filled every evening by departing beachgoers and emptied only once a week by the laid-back Greeks.

Reaching my hands into this slimepit of food and debris, I pulled out a T-shirt, a broken kite attached to a ball of twine, and more than a dozen squeeze-bottles partly filled with the lotion known as sunscreen spf-100. The diamond-shaped kite had been painted with the words: 'WANDER-BORE OctoberFast'; and the less arcane T-shirt said: 'You're Ugly and Your Mother Dresses You Funny.'

In ten seconds garbage was transformed to garb. I washed the T-shirt in the ocean water, wrung it out, and then fashioned it into a comfortable pair of shorts. Holding the T-shirt upside down, I stepped each leg into an armhole, then tied the extra material so that it fit snugly against my waist.

The invention of these outlandishly stylish T-shorts reminded me of the poet Shelley. My books, my deeds, my loves, my passionate inner life might one day blaze up in the flames of fame, then soonafter be ashed and forgotten in the eternal sleep of ignorance. Perhaps the electronic encyclopedias of the future will recognize me with this one sentence: "The gymnomaniac O. Thoreau first invented T-shorts on the coast of Crete."

Now dressed in a manner befitting a literary artist on a planet that ignored the most genuine in literary arts, I faced the sea and shouted to the waves. First Percy Bysshe Shelley's version showing the briefness of fame, then my parody exposing the fame of briefs.

"Ozymandias of Egypt ...

> I met a traveller from an antique land
> Who said: Two vast and trunkless legs of stone
> Stand in the desert. Near them, on the sand
> Half sunk, a shatter'd visage lies, whose frown
> And wrinkled lip and sneer of cold command
> Tell that its sculptor well those passions read
> Which yet survive, stamp'd on these lifeless things,
> The hand that mock'd them and the heart that fed;
> And on the pedestal these words appear:
> 'My name is Ozymandias, king of kings:
> Look on my works ye Mighty and despair!"
> Nothing beside remains. Round the decay
> Of that colossal wreck, boundless and bare,
> The lone and level sands stretch far away."

The waves surged in, covered the sand, then rushed away as I continued shouting to the sea.

"Cozymandias of Crete ...

> I met a traveller from an antic land
> Who said: Two fast and trunkless legs of cotton
> Stand on the beach. In them, on the sand
> Half hunk, the torso of a naked man decries, gotten
> From the rusted lip and sewer of the garbage can
> Tell that its tailor well those fashions scorned

Which yet survive, stamp'd on his derrière
The man that hocked them and the heart that mourned;
And on the pedicel these words appear:
'My name is Cozymandias, Lear of leers,
Look on my shorts, ye Mighty, undies pair!'
Nothing bedside remains. Round the 'lastic waist
Of that colossal dreck, boundless and bare,
The lone and level bands stretch far abased."

Back at the campsite, I laid my newfound prizes onto the sand. By squeezing and pouring, I combined the many bottles of sunscreen lotion into three large full bottles. Thrilled to have scrounged such a versatile resource as a ball of twine, I began to experiment by tying different kinds of knots. By the end of the morning I had made a strong string-bag, large enough to carry all my possessions, attached to two shoulder straps created from more of the braided twine.

This work complete, I strolled up the now-peopled beach, one eye looking for luck and the other for opportunity. I met a 60-year-old woman, a professor, with a sack of paperbacks; she offered to trade me the whole bag for one long kiss (which her sister photographed); and then I sold the books to other tourists for thirty Euros. Afterwards, stalking the narrow streets of Tymros, I found, in a neglected alley, a grocery store ignored by tourists and patronized by native Cretans. Impressed by the fair prices, I filled a large paper bag with peanuts and a smaller one with figs. One toothbrush, a dark bread, a container of yogurt, and two plastic bottles of bottled water were added to my stock. I was budgeting again; I would shrink the stomach, stretch the dollars, and make the money last for seven days. Thus, the total purchase had been carefully calculated to cost ones-eventh of my current wealth.

I avoided the bars and dance clubs; for entertainment I walked along the shore. That afternoon and evening more than two dozen women approached me — women young, my age, middle-aged, too middle-aged, too old, not old enough — all eyes burning with loneliness and hope. Hidden in these inner flames were the complex needs for friendship, mothering, love, and healthy lust. Some women broke the ice by asking for directions, or for suggestions where to eat. Others, less bashful, asked me to join them for a swim, a board game, a walk, a run, a drink, a meal, a round of cards. The good-hearted and the shameless offered to buy me clothing, or invited me to share their beds. Tactfully, I responded 'no thank you,' without hurting those delicate feelings or breaking those fragile hearts. I explained that tomorrow I would have a long journey on foot, so tonight I needed to prepare by bedding early and getting a good night's rest. Each woman left satisfied enough when she dropped a scrap of paper — with my email and address — into her pocket, cleavage, or purse.

So despite many offers I slept alone. In the morning I unbuilt the stone wall, ate breakfast, then began the Dembacchae-bound hike. I had learned from some natives that the trek from Tymros to Dembacchae lasted about 84 kilometers, or 52 miles.

The gods had not yet finished playing with my fortune. I walked all day; the miles passed quickly; long before dark I saw a sign: 'Dembacchae 40 kilometers'. As I stopped before the sign, two huge pink busses drove by me, displaying words on the side that I had seen before: 'WANDERBORE OctoberFast Dembacchae,' and a new message that I had not yet seen: 'No woman is free as long as one woman remains a slave.'

The busses slowed down, then rolled backwards, then stopped in front of me. The door of one of the busses opened, chilling my skin with an icy blast of air-conditioned air. Then came the scent of orange blossoms, followed by two girls dressed or undressed in bath towels wrapped around the middle of their bouncing breasts. One was blonde-haired and another was brunette, well-developed for their young teenaged years. With great enthusiasm they ran to me, jumping to a stop.

For the longest while the girls inspected me, giggled and sighed, and uttered not one word. After their long stares — which seemed like endless stares to Heaven — I broke the silence with a friendly greeting and a smile.

"My name is Thoreau," I began.

"Becca!" said the dark-haired girl.

"Julie!" said the brunette. "We're eighteen, really!"

With a smile I shook my head.

"Eighteen all together, that makes you each nine years old, the age of Beatrice when Dante fell in love with her."

"We're really thirteen," said Julie, sadly.

Then Becca brightened up and added: "The age of Juliet beloved by Romeo!"

They continued to explore me with their intelligent eyes. The brunette whispered to her friend: "I told you he was American!", and the blonde replied "If I'm dreaming, don't wake me up!" Then they returned to their program of silence, sighs, and stares.

Their good manners and good cheer made me laugh.

"Becca, Julie ... Is there something that you wanted to ask me or tell me?"

Julie sighed compassionately as she clasped her hands.

"Are you hung?"

From the mouths of babes. The accent was English from merry old Eng.

"Come again?" came my reply.

"Hung," said she. "You know, hungry?"

My head nodded.

"Hungry as a horse."

Becca bit her bottom lip then tugged on the top of her towel.

"My mother wants to know," she said, without the least blush of shyness, "if you are offended by female frontal nudity."

This nude question — especially when asked by two precocious and impressionable girls — was one of those deep questions that could not be answered carelessly. It required a full minute of intense cogitation, along with a leap of faith into the deep molasses-vat of Truth.

15
LADY LOVERLY'S CHATTER

"WHO THEN CREATED THIS UNSPEAKABLE POWER, this most versatile of all the tools, this source of vast destruction, this fountain of immeasurable creativity, this dreamer of things unattainable, this schemer of designing deeds, this cause and solution to humankind's predicaments, this path to earthly heavens, this laundry-chute to bottomless hells — the human mind?"

There are philosophers as well as blockheads who claim that thinking is not necessary for a happy life, then prove their claims by every thoughtless thing they say and do. I had always believed that the human mind is a precision instrument. True, men should not think too solemnly or think too much — we should cultivate our bodies, our senses, our intuitions, and all the powers of our inner life. But whenever the need to think arises, I thought, let us think deeply and think well.

The two young women, Julie the blonde and Becca the brunette, stood draped in towels, eagerly awaiting my reply. Suddenly I noticed the obvious: the girls had been staring at me with a lovestruck gaze. I tightened the knot around my T-shorts, then stuck both hands against my hips.

"I'll answer your question in just a moment, girls. But first, will you tell me what is this thing called 'WANDERBORE OctoberFast'?"

"WANDERBORE," said Julie. "Women Allied for Nudism, Dance, Eros, Romance, Biodiversity, Orgasms, and Renewable Energy."

"It's mostly about the self-liberating effects of nudism, vegetarianism, and sustainable living," said Becca. "It's a kind of spiritual goulash. There's a lot of ancient Greek literature and Romanticism, and nature-worship and ecology, all mixed together into a transcendental goop."

Julie sighed.

"My aunt says that these kinds of organizations spring up when ten thousand women can't find even one good man."

"The OctoberFast is our yearly conference in Crete," added Becca. "It finished last week, and now some of us are staying longer to tour the island. Mother says that we won't stop looking until we find a perfect paradise."

I nodded. I wanted to learn more about this group, but I realized it would be unfair to continue to postpone the reply that they had asked for minutes ago.

"What was that double-edged subject that you had wanted me to comment on?"

Becca repeated the question, slowly and patiently.

"Are you offended by female frontal nudity?"

I scratched my head.

"That depends completely on the frontal nudity of the female."

After whispering to each other, the girls nodded their heads, then Becca reached out to me with her closed hands.

"My mother said that if you answered anything other than the word 'yes', then we could give you this."

Becca's hands were loaded with paper money, a stack of Euros. Without touching or counting it, I shook my head from side to side.

"Tell your kind mother that I said thank you for the offer, but I rarely accept money from friends. And I never-ever take money from women, even if the women are the friends. Men have exploited women for ten thousand years. The end of that war will be engendered only when 21st-Century male-and-female relationships are free from the manacles that money manifests."

The girls looked disappointed until I explained a bit more.

"Now and then I do accept temporary loans of food or other necessities, if and only if the getting and the giving of the gifts gives to the giver the gift of unforgettable joy. Did you get all that?"

The girls nodded their smiling heads. Gazing at me dreamily, they burst into fits of giggles, then turned to their pink bus and scurried up the steps.

The light in the sky grew brighter as out from the pink bus walked a woman wearing Greek-style sandals, and an Oriental robe made of colorful silk. She was one of those women whose trim figure and flawless skin made it impossible for men to tell her age. She carried herself with the posture and poise of a benevolent queen, the quintessence of intelligence, elegance, and charm.

The woman! All at once I realized that this was the splendid woman from the Meteora — even more beautiful now than before — and I felt lighter, and radiant, and filled with the warmest glow. The woman held out her lovely hand.

"Chaire, Mr. Thoreau," she said. "I am Lady Beatrice Loverly, founder and president of WANDERBORE. And I am delighted to meet you in the flesh."

Chaire — pronounced something akin to "heh-reh" — is the beautiful word of greeting or parting, spoken by the ancient Greeks. It contains many meanings: 'hello', 'welcome', 'good-bye', 'rejoice', and 'be of good cheer'.

I squeezed Lady Loverly's hand and started to release it, but she would not let me go.

"You know my name somehow, Lady Loverly?"

"The girls haven't stopped talking about you since they kept you under surveillance for twelve hours in Tymros."

"I see. Thanks for your offer to assist me. Right now I have everything I need."

"That's what I call 'polite nonsense', Mr. Thoreau," she cheerfully replied. "At the least, you could use a good backpack, and better walking shoes, I'm sure."

"Mother!" shouted Becca. "Don't be so intrusive!"

The girls had returned and resumed the game of staring at me with awestruck admiration. Lady Loverly lightly laughed.

"My daughter and her friend have cultivated a titanic crush on you, Mr. Thoreau."

"I've noticed," I answered. "But we all know what happened to the Titanic."

Lady Loverly laughed lightly before she quipped: "It hit a large, hard, protruding object, and then it sank."

Again I tried to pull my hand away; the woman held on tight.

"Mr. Thoreau, in your opinion, what prodigious powers caused this meeting between you and the members of WANDERBORE?"

I now realized that I liked this woman immensely, everything about her, not just her perfect body and face. Intelligent and kind, she spoke to me with a deep respect that ignored my poverty and lack of clothes. Before answering, I smiled, conscious of the warm touch of the woman's hand.

"The winds of serendipity blew me to your busses."

Lady Loverly clapped her hands.

"Then perhaps love's tempests will keep you at our lips."

She turned to her daughter and niece and said to them: "You were right, girls, his eyes are quite extraordinary."

The horn of the pink bus beep-beep-beeped.

"Mr. Thoreau, do you plan to remain in Crete for the next forty-eight hours?"

"I would like that," I said.

"Marvelous!" said Lady Loverly. The much-touching woman once again touched me, this time wrapping her warm hand around my strong forearm.

"Mr. Thoreau, at this divine moment, these two pink busses contain the ninety-nine female members from the British contingent of an internationally-connected Non-Governmental Organization known as WANDERBORE. We are now traveling to the Gorge of Samaria in Western Crete for a day of nude hiking and sight-seeing. Would you like to be our guest and join us? The bus is full but we can squeeze you in. And don't believe what your stuffy American author has written: 'Beware of enterprises that require no clothes.'"

When the diamond on her wedding ring poked my arm, my grandfather's morsels of morals made me stop and think. When I was young I had heard him tell my father: "If you want to get along with your neighbor, keep your hands out of two places: his pockets and his wife's pants."

Beatrice Loverly was the perfect diamond with one fantastic flaw: she had a husband.

"Thank you but no thank you," I said. "Today I had planned to walk to Dembacchae and then look for work."

"Dembacchae!" the woman cried. "How marvelous! A Greek friend of mine has a home in that town. Tomorrow night I will be meeting with him for dinner, and for discussing next year's WANDERBORE events. Why don't you join us there?"

"I wouldn't want to be in the way of your meeting," I said.

Both hands of Lady Loverly now clasped my imprisoned arm.

"But you wouldn't be in the way, I assure you," she said. "In fact, a male perspective might be good for a change."

"Are men allowed to join this WANDERBORE group?" I asked.

"Lots of men would like to join us for all the wrong reasons, Mr. Thoreau," Loverly replied. "But WANDERBORE women are always reaching out for upstanding male members. Come to dinner tomorrow, Mr. Thoreau. It would be such a pleasure to have you."

I could not remember if it was Plato or Aristotle who pointed out that although dinner with a married woman is often the first step to adultery, it is not adultery itself.

"If I'm still in the neighborhood tomorrow evening," I said, "then I'll meet you for dinner at the house of your friend."

Lady Loverly squeezed my arm to hear it, and the two girls screamed with joy. Becca, her daughter, who had been following the conversation word-by-word, handed me a small cinnamon bun, with a business card sticking out the top. The card had been inscribed with Lady Loverly's address in England, to which Becca had added the Dembacchae address.

"Mr. Thoreau," said Lady Loverly, "may I assume that in your lifestyle which *carpes* the *diem* and *dulces* the *far niente,* and takes no thought for the morrow, and spins not neither does it toil — that you have neither desire nor need to keep track of the days of the week?"

"If you did assume that, Ms. Loverly, you'd be making a correct assumption."

"Very good," she said. "Then please accept this humble gift from proud *moi.*"

"Mother had it made just for you!" shouted Becca.

The gift was a white scarf made of silk, decorated in the center with the figures of a handsome man and a voluptuous woman fused in a passionate embrace. The words sewn along the top said: 'What many women cannot give, one woman can.'

Loverly tied the scarf around my left wrist.

"Now, Mr. Thoreau," she said. "Today this is on your left wrist, and tomorrow when you rise — hopefully alone — you can move this scarf to your right wrist. And that shall help you to remember your dinner meeting with me that night."

With the utmost caution I accepted gifts from women, because too often the gifts have strings attached, and the receiver of the gifts becomes a puppet on those strings. But this scarf that Lady Loverly created was given so freely and wholeheartedly that there was no question whether or not to accept.

"Thank you very much, Lady Loverly. I'll think of you whenever I touch this silk. But I don't own a bath towel or a robe or even a shirt right now. Will I offend anyone at the dinner if I wear only these stopgap T-shirt shorts?"

"I assure you, Mr. Thoreau, that will be more than enough. Come now, Rebecca and Juliette. We must let this modern Odysseus continue his resplendent journey. He's been long enough delayed by you two Calypsos. Ask Mr. Thoreau if he will be kind enough to present you with a kiss good-bye. So that if you never meet with him again, that kiss will abide deathlessly inside your shattered hearts, thereby condemning you to a lifetime of unrequited misery."

The two girls burst into megagiggles, then closed their eyes and puckered their red unlipsticked lips. Like a brother, I kissed the two foreheads. But the girls remained motionless, lips puckered and eyes closed.

"We may never see him again!" cried Becca.

"We'll wait to get kissed properly!" Julie shouted.

"Come now girls, don't be intrusive," said Lady Loverly. "Remember 'Freedom, not license', dears. Say thank you to Mr. Thoreau. Instead of spying, had you introduced yourselves like proper young ladies, your lips today might have tingled with a scintillating tale to tell. As it now stands, you've both received far more than you deserved."

Lady Loverly squeezed my hand.

"Tell me one thing more, Mr. Thoreau. Is it true that the morning we met at the Meteora, you became profoundly interested in me, and you followed me here to Crete by making inquiries about the pink vehicle?"

With a smile I remembered the passionate librarian.

"She was very pink when I made inquiries about her," I replied.

"I understand perfectly, Mr. Thoreau," said Lady Loverly. "It will be wonderful to see you and get to know you better in Dembacchae tomorrow night. ... Young ladies, advance to the chariot!"

The giggling girls disappeared through the bus's doorway. Lady Loverly lingered behind and surprised me with an alluring glance.

"Mr. Thoreau," she said. "I'm afraid that the nights will be getting rather too cold for sleeping out-of-doors alone. May I give you my kimono?"

With a casual smile, the well-built woman untied the silk sash around her waist, then started to remove her robe. I reached out and held her hands.

"Not now, Lady Loverly. I'm sure something will turn up. The next time you make a kind offer like this one, I promise I won't turn you down."

"I'm thrilled to hear that, Mr. Thoreau. I'm very much looking forward to holding you — "

She paused, flashed a smile, then re-tied the sash around her robe.

" — to that promise. *Chaire*."

Sprightly as a doe she dashed up the steps of the WANDERBORE pink bus. The bus's door closed, horns honked four times, then both busses drove slowly up the road. I looked up at the back window of the bus. Two tragicomic faces, streaming with teenaged tears, were blowing kisses to me, while four flurrying hands waved fond good-byes.

Watching this moving farewell, I failed to notice a Greek mutt who, in one poetic motion, leaped into the air, opened his maw, then chomped-and-swallowed the sticky cinnamon bun along with the card containing Lady Loverly's addresses.

I hiked for the rest of the evening, then slept that night in a field on top of soft nets designed to catch fallen olives. The next morning I walked for hours until I crossed the town's border, past a sign that said 'Welcome to Dembacchae'. I was royally greeted by blaring noise, speeding traffic, and a rumbling garbage truck that reeked like the breath of a goat. The main streets were packed with people instead of cars: Luck had dropped me in Dembacchae on the one day of every seven that was known as 'market day'. On this day, scores of traveling vendors would truck into the town and then set up an outdoor market for their wares. Along the streetsides, tables and flatbed trucks were covered and filled with fruits, vegetables, spices, seeds, tools, knives, plates, old clothing, cheap jewelry, useless gadgets, and thousands of pieces of shoddy junk.

Near the square in the center of town I found the Taverna Dembacchae. Famous to everyone within a radius of two miles, the taverna claimed to house — under one convenient rooftop — a Minoan-style brothel on the second floor, a veterinarian, the mayor's office, and a restaurant that featured native booze and snacks. I pressed my nose against the glass window then peered inside.

"This is it," to myself I said. "I wonder if the back room houses the butchershop, the bakery, the candlestick makery, and the olive oil factory as well. Here we have your basic time-proof Cretan tavern, open only to male natives from this small town. Cretans from other towns are not trusted; Greeks from the mainland are not tolerated; and tourists are worse than pariahs, forbidden to enter this unholy shrine. What kind of men do you find behind these kinds of bars? ... Barbarians. "

With a deep breath I girded my testicles by tightening the knot around the T-shorts, assumed the face of the *pallikári,* then pressed my hand against the heavy wooden door.

16
REAL MEN DON'T BUY SEX

A UNIQUE AROMA wafted through the doorway of the noisy tavern. This scent of garlic-spiced lentils reminded me of a story I had scrawled into the pages of my blue notebook, the notebook in which I was collecting quotes, lines, and passages — wisdom about how to live wisely and intensely — from the world's great books. The story — *Why Diogenes Ate Lentils?* — was written by Plutarch (C.E. 46–120), the Greek biographer and philosopher.

> A sycophant advised the philosopher Diogenes:
> "If you would only learn to flatter King Alexander, then
>   you would not need to eat lentils."
> Whereby the wise Diogenes replied:
> "If you would only learn to eat lentils, then you would not
>   need to flatter Alexander."

What does this anecdote mean? ... How many radiant opportunities are lost — and how much divine fire is extinguished — whenever we abandon the dirt path of simplicity, to lick the superhighway of the insincere?

Standing outside the door of the taverna, I'd been thinking about these questions when my meanderings were drowned by volleys of thunderous shouts. Near me, a funny-looking man was bellowing *"Sockey Amerikanos! Ekato!"* as he held up a white sweatsock, trying to convince the crowd of onlookers that his needless merchandise would radically improve their lives.

I pushed open the heavy door then entered the dimly-lit Taverna Dembacchae. A strange world! Aromas of fresh bread and strong coffee. Ennui so thick you could spread it on your toast. Stone walls decorated with photographs of Greek soldiers, and maps from both World Wars. Ten square-shaped wooden tables, each one surrounded by four wooden chairs. The chairs held the retired or unemployed males of Dembacchae, all grey-haired or white-haired or bald, all drinking little cups of coffee and nibbling on *passatempo,* the salty roasted pumpkin seeds. Years ago, many of these men had been heroes in the war; now they were sitting idly, with nothing in the world to do. Time stagnated and the taverna had become a tomb.

One surreal flash of vitality appeared. A teenaged boy, face cratered with pimples — holding a knife in one hand and a fish-net bag in the other — chased a street cat around and around the taverna. When I opened the door of the café, the cat scrambled outside to light and safety.

The taverna rang with shouts of *"Po, po, po!"* as I stepped up to the bar. Loosely translated into English, that means "What have we here!" The talking first increased in volume then dropped to a murmuring hush. No face smiled. Dark eyes — eighty dark eyes — knifed me with hostile glares. A fog of silence. Quiet so complete I heard the rattlings of the black worry beads twirling click-click-click around the calloused fingers of the bitter old men.

I had saved some coins from my trip to the grocery store in Tymros, and now I tossed them nonchalantly onto the bar's countertop. The bartender, stirring a coffee, spoke to me without raising his eyes.

"Sixty Euros per hour, not including drinks, condoms, taxes, and dessert. Do you want Medusa, Stheno, or Euryale?"

I had been prepared for the worst but when it happened I felt unprepared. Here in this taverna, so close to the exploitation of women, anger gripped me. Somehow, I conquered the anger and replied with calm.

"Real men don't buy sex."

Laughter at my remark spewed from the voices of the old men. Another puritanical American, they must have thought, straight out of the film about the Greek prostitute who never worked one day of the weekends.

"Ena café, one coffee," I said to the aproned bartender. Had I ordered tea I would have been laughed out of the *taverna.* Had I not spoken in Greek, I would have been thrown out before the coins stopped jingling. And maybe, or maybe not, they would have opened the door before they tossed me through.

After drying some glasses with a towel, the bartender served me the coffee without sugar or respect. He slammed down the small white cup with such force it made a spoon jump up then fall off the counter. I sipped the syrupy coffee, nodded my head with approval, then licked my lips.

"Nero, parakalo." Water, please. "It should have come with the coffee."

The clear glass of water was served by slamming it hatefully down. This time a fork leaped up and flew over the edge. The brawny bartender flung my coins at the floor behind me, then leaned toward me with a menacing scowl.

"*Tee thelees?*" he asked, in a tone belligerent. What do you want?

"*To deemarkos,*" I told him in Greek. The mayor.

The mayor, from his table close to the bar, slid his chair back then stood up and approached me with a cautious stare. It was clear from his expression that he now faced an awkward dilemma. He did not want the trouble of a confrontation, and he did not want to appear weak in front of his faultfinding friends. Directly, I looked into the mayor's eyes.

"*Thelo douleea,*" I said. "I want work."

This was a lie spoken to cover my assumption, and to obtain the information I desired. Since the wages were pitifully low, it made no sense for Bedlamericans to seek employment in countries such as Greece.

The mayor looked relieved to learn that I had come on business, and not to invade the sacred grounds of Dembacchae's favorite brothel. He inspected my bulging muscles, then gripped his vice-strong hand around my shoulder.

"Not today," he replied. "In two weeks, yes. Come back. You look strong."

As the mayor turned away, I touched the shoulder of his tweed jacket.

"Excuse me," I said. "In two weeks will there be work only for a man, or will there be work for a woman, too?"

The mayor raised his head just an inch, the Cretan gesture that meant 'no'.

"*Oshee,*" he said. "No. Never. There is never work for a woman. Not with all our men out of work. The only work for a woman is — "

With the fingers of his left hand he formed the shape of a holey 'O', then he used the pointer finger on his right hand to poke in, then out, then in again, through the hole's middle. An ancient gesture for the ancient work that someday will be seen as slavery.

The mayor's now-friendly hand slapped me across the shoulder, and then the old men in the taverna roared with chauvinistic shouts and hooligan guffaws. I swallowed the water in the glass in one long gulp.

"*Effhareesto,* thank you," I told the mayor.

"*Parakalo,*" said the mayor, with half a bow, pronouncing each syllable slowly and distinctly. "You are very strong. You speak good Greek. Come back in two weeks if you like to work."

All heads in the taverna turned around then whistled and yelled as a woman entered, carrying a mop, a bucket, a sponge and a bucketful of rags. She ignored their shouts and laughter, bent down on her hands and knees, then scrubbed the wooden floor. Her hair shined like red fire. Strengthened and shaped by constant labor, the woman had a broad back and powerful buttocks and legs, which made her look appealingly feminine, despite her shabby dress.

The mayor grinned at me, glanced at the woman, then again made the motion of the finger penetrating through the hole. More raucous laughter surged from the childish old men. The rough hand of the narrow-minded mayor playfully slapped my shoulder blade. Shouts and cackles resounded when one old man grabbed a sponge from the cleaning woman's bucket, and then a dozen men threw that sponge to one another, around and around the room.

The laughter stopped as if it had been turned off with a switch as I reached up then intercepted the flying object with my left hand. I walked to the woman — who had been sitting on her knees watching the men taunt her with this game — and then I handed her the sponge. The woman stood up, looked into my eyes, then rubbed her hand against my cheek.

"*Effhareesto,* thank you," she said. "You know, for years I thought: What does it matter if they laugh at me and make their dirty gestures behind my back? ... But it matters now. I don't know why."

She picked up her bucket and cleaning supplies, threw the wet sponge onto the mayor's shirt, then proudly walked out the door.

Shouts of "*Sockey Amerikanos!*" invaded my ears when I stepped through the café's doorway to the brighter world outside. My tongue licked some coffee grounds stuck between my two front teeth.

"Out of clues," I murmured. "No chance here for women to find honest work. The bikress could be anywhere on the 3,235 square miles of Crete."

Honesty and self-disclosure are liberating things. After speaking those disappointed words, I felt two sparks of intuition flash. Firstly, I sensed that I was being watched. And secondly, despite today's unpleasant setback, I felt that more opportunities would quickly open up. A great happiness filled me. I turned around, slowly, then peered across the crowded street.

Someone had been staring at me, it was true. I looked into the face of a bearded man, dressed in ripped dungarees and a checkered shirt smeared with grimy stains. Measured in years, he looked twice my age; but in spirit he seemed as full of energy as the liveliest young man. I felt gripped by this man's eyes, eyes that glowed like a child at play, a man in love, a woman gazing at her child. The old man who had greeted me in the mountains had emanated serenity, tranquility, Olympian calm. This man, standing across the street, lit up the day with his fiery smile. The smile of an enlightened being who had climbed the tree of earthly sorrow, risked his fortune to slay invincible dragons, and now watched over our world from a higher realm, graced with inner freedom, and the rapture of being alive.

As this man smiled at me, the joyous words of Whitman floated through my mind: "And I or you pocketless of a dime may purchase the pick of the earth."

Two times a loud horn beeped. The man with the great smile turned around, hoisted a garbage can, then hurled its contents into the back-end of a pick-up truck. Now the garbage truck drove slowly forward through the mass of shoppers, with Greek *bouzouki* music blaring from a radio tied to its side. The smiling man sang along, danced up to the next garbage can, slipped his arm around the can as if she were his danc-ing partner, and then — in perfect rhythm with the lively music — shook his backside as he tossed the garbage into the truck's rear end. The truck drove further on and the garbage man followed, dancing all the way. Shaking his whole body — feet, legs, hips, hands, arms, shoulders, head — he strolled to the next can, raised it high then heaved the garbage, all the while dipping and skipping in time to the spirited musical beat. A New Age observer might have thusly described the scene: "A cosmic oneness rippled through the music, the dancer, the garbage, and the dance."

The joyful garbage man danced out of sight. I strolled through the crowded street, looking at the vendors and the vendables on both sides. Bizarre characters were easy to meet in this bazaar. Again I heard the shouting of a man's voice, unamplified by electronic means, yet so loud it resounded many decibels above the din. The demagogue-vendor now jumped up onto a tabletop and furiously shouted *Ekato! Ekato! Ekato!* — the Greek words for a hundred. The voice was loud and the man behind the voice was ostentatious. Though eyebrows alone do not make the philosopher, thick black bushes of Nietzschean eyebrows sprouted lushly across the sockmonger's wrinkled brow. His gargoyley face looked like a failed experiment concocted in an underfunded laboratory, a mixed-up mixture of the faces of all the Marx Brothers combined. To sell his schlock he waved his arms with violent flurries, like a political fanatic, screaming zealously for a new independence for Crete.

My attention was stolen by a stiller smaller voice. The voice of an old Greek woman, dressed in the standard black Cretan-widow dress.

"*Ella, ella! Oreesteh!*" she shouted. Here, here! Come here!

The toothless woman nodded, then waved her hand at me to come and see.

"Meester! Meester! Lookie-lookie! Goot goot!"

She was standing behind a table covered with garlic, olives, potatoes, squash, melons, tomatoes, apples, and pears. On both sides of this woman there lay ten more tables, and behind each table one old woman at the helm. Each of these old women attempted to sell the harvest from her backyard garden. Each woman eyed me, as they eyed all tourists, with the utmost of mercenary hopes. All looked the same — the women, their placid faces, their clothing, their stout or stick-thin bodies underneath, their stock of vegetables and fruits.

The one table which looked different attracted me. This table was filled with produce that ranged from unappetizing to inedible, all dried up and immeasurably old. The vegetables could have easily been mistaken for prehistoric fossils; the fruits were overripe for anything but satire. The woman behind this table was more withered and shriveled than the vegetables she tried so unsuccessfully to sell. Her body was thin as a string bean, her hair horseradish-white, her face furrowed like baked potato skins. Her gummy mouth, which still harbored a friendly smile, had not felt a tooth since long before the happy day I had been born. The other old women were grandmothers or great-grandmothers, but this good woman had been both of these, and looked one generation older than the oldest of the rest.

I picked up a handful of her greenish-yellow beans, brushed off the dust and scratched off some mold, then asked her how much they would cost. The ancient woman stood up from her chair, walked slowly around the side of her table and clutched my strong hand. She pressed her bony finger against my palm, held out a coin, and then made a straight stroke for the number one.

"One lepton?" I asked. "Only one lepton?"

The brittle old woman nodded yes. The lepton, a Greek denomination no longer in use, was worth one hundredth of a drachma, and a drachma less than one hundredth of a Euro. So one Euro would buy far more than ten thousand lepta, if a lepton could anywhere be found.

Suddenly, like songs of morning birds, I heard a warbling melody deep from my inner voice. The voice that thrust my life into adventures, sometimes leading to the most glorious of summits, and other times misleading to the most embarrassing of pits. Now I knew what needed to be done. I took out my entire fortune of paper Euros and then placed them into the ancient woman's hand.

For a moment she looked confused, but soon she understood. Tears poured from her neglected eyes. A dozen times she kissed my hands. And in between the kisses cried: "Thank you! Thank you! On your head the light of Greece will shine!"

The ten other old women at the nearby tables rushed to me and thanked me with the same degree of warmth as if I had given the money to them.

Tears flowed; the women clasped my hands. Some reached up to stroke my cheeks; others kissed my shoulder; one woman dropped down and hugged me around the knees.

"You are a good man," the youngest of these old women said. "The gods will bless you!"

Tears filled my eyes, but I did not want these women to see my tears. Greenish-yellow beans in hand, I turned around and found a mule a-munching on my vegetables. His head had been covered by a familiar-looking paperback of the poems of the poet Dante. My eyes opened even wider at another observation, remarkably obvious the moment after it had been observed. The mule had been wearing my survival hat on top of his asinine head! Two holes had been cut through the hat to let the mule ears stick through. When I pulled it off his head he snatched the hat firmly between his jaws.

Lo, behold, remember! Greece is the rocky land of miracles and light! Once again an enchantingly-formed female delivered me good luck. I did not need to battle with the legendary stubbornness of the mule. My tool-covered hat was set free by the softest voice.

"*Oshee*, Dante, *Oshee*."

A young Greek woman, strikingly attractive, clasped her soft fingers around my hand. Her bashful nod explained that she wanted me to cease striving and to follow her. Holding hands, we walked together through the crowd, as throngs of people parted, like magic, to let this slender woman pass. She led me across the main street, through a maze of smaller streets, and finally to a series of even smaller alleyways.

At last we arrived at a large garden that circled a small stone house. The house had no door except a blanket hung from the top beam of the door frame. Still holding my hand, with her free hand the young woman pushed the blanket aside, then stepped through the mysterious doorway.

"*Ella mazee,*" she said softly. "Come with me."

For the first time since we had met, this modest dark-eyed beauty dared to look deeply into my eyes. She smiled, lowered her trusting eyes, then raised my hand to her rose-soft lips. With lovely tenderness she kissed my palm.

"What's your name?" I asked.

"*Eereenee,*" she shyly replied.

Irene — the Greek word for, and the Greek goddess of that much-desired treasure: peace.

Tugging my arm, Irene stepped through the doorway into the stone house. I stopped for an instant, then smiled at this adventure unforseen. Who but a fool would fail to follow after the gentle way of Peace? I let her take me by the hand, across the threshold to the strange inside.

17
WHEREIN THOREAU IS CAPTIVATED
BY THE SNAKE GODDESS
AND A MARVELOUS STONE HOUSE

"THE SNAKE GODDESS OF CRETE! Her bare breasts dare men to advance, while each hand raises a serpent venomous to frighten all comers away."

The captivating young Irene had led me by the hand into the living room of this one-story house made of white stone. Inside, on opposite sides of the doorway — as if to discourage the occupants from wanting to escape — stood two six-feet-tall pieces of sculpture carved from wood. One of these wooden guards was an unclad Priapus, ugly-faced and smiling beneath the beard. His head had been wreathed with olive leaves, and his large curved phallus stood upward and erect. Presiding on the doorway's left stood a wooden image of the Snake Goddess. Her bodice lay open in the center to display two proud breasts; her flounced skirt seemed to be made for peeling off one layer at a time; the bodies of serpents encircled her outstretched arms; and her hands were holding the serpents about six inches below the heads — hooded heads with protruding tongues that pointed at the goddess's rubied eyes.

I read the inscription on the base underneath the sculpture's feet: this wood-carved female heroine had been modeled from an original figurine created on Crete more than three-thousand six-hundred years ago. But it's rude to read with a woman in the room. Clamoring for attention, Irene pulled my hand and led me across the room to a soft couch. She tugged my arm downward until I willingly sat down; she took off my string-made backpack and my sneakers; she reached up and placed a hand on my improvised shorts. Before she could remove them I brushed her soft hair with my hand, then raised her hand and kissed her fingertips.

"*Oshee, Irenaki mou.* No, my little Irene," I said. "It took me many embarrassing hours to find these, and I'm not taking them off so soon."

Irene stuck out her tongue at me, then pouted and folded her arms.

She stood as tall as my chin, her body was slender, her legs athletic, her breasts the size of grapefruits, her hair dark as a plum, her eyes like olives, her lips red even without lipstick, and her happy face was made to smile. Her pout vanished; she brightened up and told me *"Pereemene-teh!"* (Wait!). Without the slightest blush of shyness she removed her dress. Naked as a nymph and singing like a Muse she ran into the bedroom, leaving me alone to examine the inside of this remarkable house.

I was now sitting in the sparsely-furnished living room. A large room with a wooden floor, it felt spaciously immense. The room contained only two small rugs, many pillows, one couch, and a glass terrarium pervaded with garden snakes, snakes foot-long and finger-thin. No walls, doorways, or partitions separated the living room from the combined kitchen and dining room which lay to my far right. This eating space was filled with cupboards and countertops, earthen jugs and metal containers, two wooden tables (one round, one rectangular) and ten wood chairs. The kitchen wall — covered with well-used pots, pans, knives, and sundry utensils — shimmered with natural vitality. And the three remaining walls in the living room were spectacles that dazzled the mind and the eyes.

The wall behind me, situated opposite the blanket-covered doorway, had been blessed with an exquisite likeness of Raphael's painting *School of Athens*. This majestic work shows us a marble-white building without a ceiling, packed with more than fifty persons, mostly men but some women and children, all talking, reading, writing, or lost in lofty thoughts. Relaxed and studying, the venerable body of Diogenes sprawls on marbled steps. Behind and above him in the center of the picture, dressed in bright tunics — the Greeks called this clothing 'chitons' — walk the powerful forms of Aristotle and Plato. The handsome student holds his right arm in front of him to point to experience and the world, while the noble-looking teacher, with his hand raised, declares that Truth lies somewhere up above.

The wall opposite the kitchen wall, to the left of where I was sitting, had been painted with another famous work of art. This picture, *Shepherds in Arcadia* by Nicolas Poussin, is set amidst a beautiful background landscape in the heart of Greece. It shows three young men and one young woman, reading the inscription on the front of a stone tomb. The words they read are: *Et in Arcadia Ego* — Latin language that means: "Even in Arcadia, I am present."

The "I", of course, refers to Death, although the shepherds in the painting are so happy and innocent they can hardly imagine this grim fate.

The last picture lay on the wall that was divided in half by the blanket-covered doorway, behind the sculpture of the god Priapus. The artist, I believed, was Adolphe-William Bouguereau, and the painting was titled *Nymphs and Satyr.* It depicts a seated, bearded, and muscular satyr, being pulled by four full-bodied, naked, and smiling nymphs. The satyr is a creature with a human head and torso, embellished with a goat's ears, horns, and legs. In this painting, the reluctant satyr does not want to go wherever in the woods — and for whatever purpose — these four young nymphs so cheerfully want to take him.

On the other side of the doorway, beside and behind the statue of the Snake Goddess, the white wall had been painted at the top with this title:

Is Paradise a dream?

... and below this title were four literary passages in red letters, written by an artistic hand.

One life: a little gleam of time
between two eternities;
No second chance forevermore.
—Thomas Carlyle

Not in Utopia, — subterranean fields, —
Or some secreted island, Heaven knows where!
But in the very world, which is the world
Of all of us, — the place where, in the end,
We find our happiness, or not at all!
—William Wordsworth

Paint your paradise and walk in.
—Nikos Kazantzakis

After the fashion of thy people, thou hast wandered from one place to another, until thou art happy and content in none.
—Ralph Waldo Emerson

Taken together, all the words and pictures seemed to hint at some kind of paradise long-sought and far away. They symbolized a warning, or an inspiration, to everyone who somehow seeks these luminous imagined worlds.

For the moment there was no chance to make sense from these enigmatic scenes. Irene returned from the bedroom, smiling full of light like the radiant Greek sky. She was now wearing red lipstick and dark eyeshadow, and dressed exactly like the goddess of the snakes. Her hair was pinned up, golden bracelets bangled around her wrists, and her Minoan-style dress lay open in front to display two melon-shaped naked breasts. Irene placed a wreath of olive leaves around my head, then opened the glass top of the terrarium and snatched two snakes. She took my hand then led me in front of the carving of Priapus, so close that I moved forward one step to avoid being poked from the rear.

The costumed Irene stood across from me, and assumed the sculpture's pose, poise, and cool expression so well that I laughed at her immortal face, and at the eternally recurring beauty of the four out-thrusting breasts. With snakes wriggling in each hand, Irene smiled at me as if she too were about to laugh.

"The Snake Goddess is ready," she said.

I imitated Priapus, with his body raised on the balls of his feet, his head cocked downward to wonder at his ever-upstanding instrument, his right hand on his hip, and his left arm bent in the air with the palm open to the sky as if to say: "What's the difference?" or "Why not?" Then I turned my eyes from the statues to the statuesque Irene.

"*Dhen katalavehno,* I don't understand. Irene, what should the god Priapus do now?"

Gazing at this innocent young beauty, I suspected what was required of me, but it would be foolish not to inquire to make sure. Irene glanced at me for a long instant. Before resuming her bright smile, she flashed an expression that spoke: you've just asked the stupidest question that any man has ever asked.

For a split-second the Raphael painting stole my attention. My eyes followed the up-pointing finger of Plato, to a spot on the high white ceiling where, in black letters, one word had been painted: Kosmos.

Irene stamped her foot to recapture my gaze.

"Let's play!" she shouted happily. Again she looked at me with her wide-open eyes and her light smile. While the snakes wriggled in her hands, Irene stood still like the proud sculpture and waited for the live Priapus to begin.

By now I had guessed how the game was supposed to proceed. Before I could make the first move, we heard the sound of cheerful singing approaching the entrance of the house.

18
O Kosmos!

KOSMOS IS A MARVELOUS GREEK word, ripe with hidden meanings that uncover wondrous things. According to the dictionaries, kosmos signifies "world, people, and humankind". Nikos Kazantzakis, writing in his autobiography, tells us that kosmos is "harmony." Walt Whitman used the word to describe himself, and to identify himself with the kosmos that to him meant: "the universe as a harmoniously ordered system". And Ralph Emerson revealed another resplendent facet of this heavenly word when he essayed: "The Greeks called the world kosmos, beauty."

The deep-voiced chanting from the world outside grew louder and louder. The blanket that served as a door slid aside, and then into the room danced a gargantuan man singing with radiant joy. This good gray singer had a lush gray beard, a thick mustache, a full head of intractable hair. His smile looked young but later he told me that, chronologically speaking, he was midway between fifty and sixty years. Earthy is the one word which best described him, yet streaks of whitening hair implied a head that had been touched by the dreamy clouds. His whole being emanated Courage, Justice, and Wisdom — every Greek virtue except Temperance.

I laughed at the destiny that no man can defy: two men who are bound to meet will meet. Just before he stepped through the blanketed doorway, I had recognized the voice. And now, the lemon rinds sticking to his jacket were a telltale sign. The singer, dancer, passionate human being in the room was the same man whose songs had lit up the Dembacchae streets. The garbage man!

Irene rushed to him and stood on her tiptoes to kiss his bearded cheek. He tossed his cap over his shoulder, then glanced back to watch it land precisely on the sculpture's upturned phallic tip.

Irene, glowing with enthusiasm, tugged on the singer's shirt sleeve, and shouted to get his attention.

"Thoreau is here! Thoreau is here!"

But the singer grew so enraptured in his song — a song with words mixed in English and in Greek — he continued singing as he danced around the room.

"I love you! *S'agapo!*
Do you know, do you want to know
How much *s'agapo!*
Eleftheros! I am free!
It doesn't matter, it's more a comedy
If you don't love me!"

The young woman broke the singing spell by more shouting, and by wrapping her arms around the smiling singing man.

"Uncle Kosmos! Thoreau is here! Thoreau is here!"

Uncle Kosmos glanced at me then hugged Irene.

"I see. Did you welcome him like a member of the family?"

Irene jumped up and down, unconcerned about her bare and bouncing chest.

"He called me *Irenaki mou!* My little Irene!"

The girl's enthusiasm made Kosmos smile.

"He likes you already, Irene."

"Uncle Kosmos, you said that he would be very smart. But he doesn't even know how to play Snake Goddess!"

Infinite patience and endless calm poured from the older man's eyes.

"You can teach him, Irene. He'll learn very fast. But he'll do much better in your games if his stomach isn't growling. Did you remember the hospitality we've learned from Homer? What have you given our guest to eat? He looks hungrier than a swarm of moths in a colony of nudists."

Irene's eyes widened as she shouted, "Oh! I forgot!", and then she ran to the kitchen to get food.

Still smiling, the garbage man approached me, stopped for an instant, then hugged me like a brother he had not seen in seven years.

"I am called Kosmos, as you've just heard. Welcome, Thoreau! To meet you makes my heart dance like the flowers on the hills of Kreetee, when the warm winds make them sway and blossom in the Spring. We have been expecting you, you know. What took you so long?"

Were these words the rantings of a madman or the greetings of a saint? I could not yet tell. But I'd learned at least one lesson on my travels: Whatever the question is, the best way to answer is to mix one dash of humor with every pinch of truth.

"I would have come sooner, Kosmos, but I didn't have a thing to wear."
Kosmos laughed.

"I've heard about that too, Thoreau. From an old man with a donkey in the hills. But the olive branch would have been enough!"

Again he burst out laughing, then returned my sincere expression with one equally sincere. A crash exploded from the kitchen. In ran Irene.

"Uncle Kosmos! I broke a cup!"

Kosmos waved his arm.

"Break another one, Irene, for good luck. No, break two more, one for each of us!"

Two more crashes exploded from the kitchen world. Minutes later, Irene returned carrying a tray laden with — in addition to food — her bare breasts that rested on the top of the tray. The breasts stayed up as the tray was placed down on the floor before me, covered with grapes, pears, assorted fruits, nuts, cucumbers, tomatoes, cheeses, olives, and breads.

I sat down on the colorful carpet then wiped my hands on my T-shirt shorts.

"Kosmos, tell me this. Many people on this island call me Thoreau before I've met them. How did you know my name?"

"Start eating, Thoreau, and I'll show you."

Kosmos vanished into one of the two back rooms, then straightaway returned. He dropped my long-lost backpack onto the floor beside the tray of food.

"A few days ago," Kosmos began, "a peddler set up a table covered with this pack and more than fifty books. The classics of world literature, and all the sublime Greek writers: Homer, Sophocles, Aristophanes, Plato, Thucydides, Plutarch, Vincenzo Cornaro, Cavafy, Seferis, Sikelianos, Ritsos, Elytis. And four volumes by my dearest Kazantzakis — for me the sublimest of all — whose words pluck my heart from my chest then send it flying through the bright Greek sky in ecstasy."

The eyes of Kosmos glowed with reverence.

"'Great books?' myself said to me. 'Where on the whole South Coast of Crete can you find great books?' The peddler claimed that he had bought the whole lot from a mysterious woman — a gypsy with a body like a movie actress — who must have been recently widowed because she covered her face with a black veil. The peddler sold some of the socks to his crazy cousin, but nobody was interested in the rest of the useless books or junk. So I traded all your worldly goods for the native currency around here — one bottle of fine Cretan wine. The books are now gracing the bookshelves in my library, where you are welcome to sleep tonight."

Kosmos glanced approvingly at Irene, then looked again into my eyes.

"But tonight, I don't think you'll find time for any reading."

The cunning man squeezed half a lemon into my cup of water and the other half into his own.

"Take the books now, or leave them here. Leave them until you find a place on Kreetee that stimulates you so much you want to stop wandering and settle in. How did I know your name, Thoreau? I found your passport inside this rare book among your books."

Kosmos tossed a book at me, my hardbound copy of *Zorba the Greek*. Before my journey, I had hollowed out the book to use it as a safe, to keep passport and cash hidden from robbers and thieves. That it should all come back to me, thanks to the shrewdness and honesty of a garbage man, seemed more than a coincidence.

"You know a lot, Kosmos," I said, "but how did you know I would pass through this town of yours?"

"Thoreau, most men live by three things: money, hopes, and fears. My gods are more primitive. I live by love, intuitions, dreams. Yesterday, a flash of intuition whispered that I would meet someone unique, a man with great humor and energy. A few minutes after the flash, a letter arrived. From an old man who refuses to grow old, who wrote to tell me that a naked traveler with a great heart was walking to Dembacchae."

"You have connections all over Crete, Kosmos?"

"Not everywhere, but in many places, yes, I have good friends. My best connections are with my father, a man who worships olive trees, and lives in the mountains like a sage from ancient days."

Irene, who had been staring at me during this entire conversation, hummed quietly, then sat down behind me and vigorously brushed my hair. Each time she stroked the brush her rosy breastbuds brushed softly against my back.

Kosmos observed my reddening face and laughed at my embarrassment. I filled my mouth with bunches of plump purple grapes.

"Irene is full of surprises, Kosmos."

"Surprises, and shocks, too — we can thank her mother for that."

He glanced at the young woman. "Irene, your new friend Thoreau — or should we call him Priapus? — would like some oranges. They will perk him up. Will you please go to the backyard and find some for us? Thank you, little dove."

Happy to serve the two men she loved in different ways, the young woman ran to the backyard. Kosmos sat down on the carpet, eager for a serious session of listening and talk.

"It's time to tell you about Irene, Thoreau. She is my daughter; she is eighteen years old; I love her more than I can say."

"But she calls you 'Uncle'?"

"That is a one of the many games we play. All the teenagers in this town call me that. Irene says that she'll call me father when her mother and I live together again under one roof."

"Do you and Irene's mother see each other?" I asked.

"What a question! Every Friday night Irene's mother sleeps with me here or at her house, and then on Saturday mornings we have breakfast, and we talk. And then I read aloud to her from my collection of marvelous books. Around noon every Saturday we separate, because after a few hours together we will start to fight. She's a good woman — I've never met one better — but our twenty years together have proved that we are two stubborn people who are incompatible."

"And Irene lives here with you?" I asked.

Kosmos smiled.

"Irene lives here with me when her mother is working, and she lives at her mother's house when her mother is home. Sometimes, when I have a woman here to stay the night, Irene stays at the house of her grandmother, or one of her friends. Unfortunately or fortunately — I've often wondered which — the women in my life change more often than you change your socks."

He shook his head, laughing at his own predicament.

"Until today, I've been the only man in Irene's life. A father to her, not a lover, if that's what you're wondering about. Irene resembles the girl in that tempestuous comic play by Shakespeare. Except for the deformed slave, the only man Miranda knew was her father, Prospero. One day she meets the shipwrecked Ferdinand, becomes enraptured by his good looks, and at first sight falls in love with him. Love at first sight! It sounds ridiculous, but young women do that all the time. ... And so do old men."

"Kosmos, I'm surprised that a Greek garbage man in a one-mule town knows Shakespeare."

"I know all the writers and artists worth knowing, Thoreau. That's my

business. Writers — like Shakespeare and Homer and Goethe and Kazantzakis — point the way to new worlds. They show me possibilities
in life, in living, that I alone would otherwise have never even dared to
dream."

Kosmos broke a chunk of feta cheese in half, handed the larger part to
me, then placed his morsel on top of a slice of pear.

"Ah, it's so good to talk like this! Later, Thoreau, we'll speak about writers and books. But now, if you don't mind, I must finish telling you about
Irene. She has just had a birthday that marked eighteen years. She is still
childlike, still innocent. That doesn't mean she's stupid, Thoreau! She can
do math as well as any girl or boy her age; and I taught her to speak and
to write our Greek language, and English too, the second language of the
world. Every day I instruct Irene about those dead things that the world
esteems — facts! — those poisoned darts that blast the gods out of the
creative sky. And every night I give her a real education: I tell her stories
and fables and myths. As you can see, her favorite way to play is to act
them out. Today she is the Snake Goddess, yesterday she was Nausicaa.
Tonight, who knows who she'll want to be?"

Two thoughts at that moment took hold of me: there is no need to keep
secrets from this man; and no need to refrain from asking about him
about his secrets.

"Kosmos, you impress me as the kind of man who likes to ask — and to
be asked — the questions that are the deepest and most personal."

Kosmos laughed heartily at this.

"Thoreau, you are too polite. What good are the superficial questions?
Ask anything you want. If I have it, I will give it. If I know it, I will tell it.
If I don't know it, then together we can find out."

I swallowed the salty feta cheese, then paused, then looked up at Kosmos, who had guessed my question long before I asked.

"Kosmos, I'm curious why you don't seem to mind at all if I sleep with
your daughter Irene."

Kosmos laughed again, then moved closer to me, his wild eyes searching the depths of my curious eyes.

"Why should I mind, Thoreau? Freedom is my life. Freedom absolute.
And along with freedom, the complete responsibility that saves us from
hurting others and from destroying our own selves. This freedom is so
precious — what kind of man would I be if I wanted it only for myself?
Freedom is for everyone. Even if I love the other persons — and espe-

cially if I love them! — I must let them be free."

Kosmos observed my face, and knew his words had failed to penetrate. He slapped his hand against my side then gripped my skin above the ribs.

"The more you free yourself, the more you'll understand, Thoreau. You're Bedlamerican, you can't escape from that. You try very hard not to behave like one, but your bones will be buried in your country, and your country is buried in your bones. Your priggish culture ties you to the rock. And every morning the vulture swoops down and claws your skin, sticks his beak into your side and then breakfasts on your bitter liver."

I nodded, amazed to discover that this man could see into my soul as easily as I could scan a line of verse. "I've been fighting that culture and that vulture," I confessed, "and writhing on that cold rock for all my adult life."

"Bravo, Thoreau! You are winning that fight, my boy! That is clear. But you have to realize that you live surrounded by an artificial world that is desperately starving for real life. Love is one goddess of that real life; Nature is another. And Sex is one goddess more, the most complicated of them all, because whenever she's in the mood she swallows up the other two."

Kosmos glanced upward as if he were searching for words which, any moment now, might be falling from the all-wise sky.

"A free man — the kind of man you want to be — walks on a tightrope high above the circus spectators. Fall to the right, and he plummets into the fires of the puritan morality, stoked by the sex-haters who hate sex because they despise themselves and hate their life. ... Fall to the left, and you dive into the pit of the future: 'Sex technologismo'. Isolated and passionless, it caters to immature men who pleasure themselves by using women at a distance. The strange pre-scripted voices over a telephone wire; the flat photographs in magazines; the untouchable images on tele- visions and computer screens. Some people call that sex, Thoreau. But for me, that compares to real sex the same way as eating a piece of card- board compares to eating a home-cooked feast."

A shadow passed over his light face, and for a brief moment the face filled up with care. When he continued speaking the words fell out in deeper and more pensive tones.

"Years ago I laughed at all this! This morality that wants to kill everyone who won't agree with it; this bizarrely-isolating technological substitution for real-live companionship and sex. But one day, Thoreau, I stopped laughing. Because this new world of stupidity is coming here, here to Greece and here to Kreetee. The Greeks should be teaching the West how to live and how to love — love persons, love freedom, love life. But we, too, are succumbing to the mass foolishness. Instead of teaching the West, instead of fighting to preserve what is good and right in our culture, we are imitating every one of your self-destructive practices and ways."

His care-covered face, weary from these anxious reflections, came home to its natural smiles. I decided to test him with a formidable question. I had read much, but never before had I heard this question answered thoroughly.

"Tell me, Kosmos, because as Socrates and Plato knew, it's easier to refute a thousand fleeting falsehoods than to discover one eternal truth. To a free man, what would the world of sex be like?"

Kosmos answered instantly, without needing even a split second to ponder his reply.

"Sex is a mystery! A mystery we must surrender to. A mystery that each individual must explore until he or she understands."

"And after we understand?" I asked. "At the end of our exploring?"

Kosmos laughed.

"Keep on exploring more! Real learning is a donkey with two heads — he always wants to eat more, and he has no end. But pity those poor creatures you call 'academics': headless donkeys with two rear ends. Nothing new ever goes in, and all the time the same old hash of you-knowwhat plops out."

I laughed at his analogies, almost forgetting to return to the essential theme. When Irene's voice began to sing a soft soprano melody, I remembered the issue that had set my curiosity aflame.

"And you still think, Kosmos, that a man like me should explore the endless depths of your beautiful daughter?"

Kosmos nodded yes.

"Thoreau, you have no money, and little desire to get any, and that lack of ambition can be either a blessed virtue or a fatal vice. But your biggest problem and your greatest quality is that you make everything more complicated than it needs to be. Sex is such a simple thing! Two bodies for a time being one, a whisper of joy between two persons who desire.

And you want to strangle it with your rights and wrongs and overcivi-lized moralities! Sex between you and Irene is an affair between you and Irene. It shouldn't bother anyone else and it doesn't bother me."

Kosmos sliced a red pomegranate then tossed one half of it onto my lap.

"You must sleep with Irene, Thoreau. I not only approve, I will cel-ebrate the day! I can see — by the way you walk, by the way you talk, by the way you blush when my daughter touches you — "

At this remark, Kosmos jabbed me in the ribs, then laughed playfully.

" ... I can see that your sexual experience has been very limited, very closed. From your end, a week of nights with my daughter — or maybe a month or two of nights — would liberate you. For the both of you it would be the best university in the world. Irene's future is in your hands. If her first sexual experience is tender and filled with love, then imagine, for the next thirty years, what a wonderful sex life she could enjoy! How could you deprive a young woman of all those nights of bliss?"

He bit his half of the pomegranate.

"Thoreau, listen to me. You are a god, we are all goddesses and gods. And the secret of the goddesses and gods is that they always do what they passionately want to do. Some people wait their whole lives to real-ize this. Others never learn at all."

19
THE HEART OF KOSMOS

TO LIVE THE NATURAL LIFE IS NEARLY IMPOSSIBLE amidst this hyper-modern age. Indoor living is too expensive: a man buys a house and exchanges the heart of his life for a 30-year mortgage, or rents his dreams by slave-working to pay his rents. Outdoor living is too unsafe: no mad nomad can drink chemically-polluted waters; and the sunrays which once gave vitamin-D and joy, now — thanks to a thinning ozone layer — cause skin-burning cankerous moles.

Sex, in an artificial culture, has a hard time being natural. For a moment it seemed that human sexuality was ripping off two-thousand years of church-dictated chains. But the *virgin intacta* becomes a *vagina dentata,* and a yawning abyss of new dangers swallow our chances for toothsome erotic liberation. About 650 years ago when the Crusaders returned from Asia, they brought the Black Plague to Europe, which decimated its population by one-third. Today a potentially more devastating epidemic threatens: HIV/AIDS. In the mere twenty years between 1980 and 2000, almost 50 million cases of HIV/AIDS have been reported, resulting in 14 million deaths worldwide.

Thus, I had reservations — medical, ethical and practical — about Kosmos's philosophy of complete sexual freedom. It may still be true that "A little knowledge is a dangerous thing." But in today's planetary culture spinning in a frenzy of frazzled facts, the greatest threat to survival and to the quality of life is the *bete noir* of Voltaire: ignorance.

Grasping a pitcher of water I refilled Kosmos's drinking glass and then my own.

"Kosmos, what good is freedom without love and knowledge? What does Irene actually know about the intimate relations between women and men?"

Kosmos waved his hand and snatched a horsefly in mid-air, then opened the fist and let the fly fly flightily away.

"Thoreau, I am still trying to explain to you that you think too much. And when people think too much then all they can do is worry and complain. You're like the American tourist who traveled to the nude beach on the island of Ios. All day, surrounded by topless women, he turned his head left, right, everywhere to look at the bouncing breasts. And after twenty-four hours in that paradise of pulchritude, what words of thanks do you think he uttered to the ears of gods? ... Nothing! He griped and he complained about the neck strain!"

"Kosmos, I'll buy a railway ticket and take the neck strain to Athens if you dodge my question one more time. Does Irene know how babies are made? How men lie to women to lie with them? And how sexual activity involves the risk of a sexually transmitted disease?"

The Greek gods were not perfect, not reasonable, not omnipotent — and these flaws were the secrets of their great charm. There were so many godlike qualities about Kosmos the man. But even this tender knight had a chink in his armor. After hearing the question, Kosmos started sweating like a toilet tank. He removed a bright cloth from the pocket of his jeans, then wiped the perspiration from the furrows of his child-burdened brow.

"Thoreau, I can't hide it, you've guessed it right! Irene knows as much about the birds and the bees as the birds and the bees know about Irene. I haven't told her anything, Thoreau. To say these things requires the right time and the right words. I tried to tell her — believe me, and give me the *Odyssey* to swear on! But I am an impulsive man and a blunt man, and if Kreetee was filled with a hundred Kosmos's, then all put together they would not have enough patience and tact for something as delicate as this! Every time I sat down with her to say something, Irene looked up at me with her baby-lamb eyes, and I melted like *granita lemoniou* in July."

He gripped his beard with both hands, a gesture he would always make whenever he was grappling with a difficult idea.

"What could I do, Thoreau? I kept asking myself: 'Can I be the one to spoil her joy and innocence?' You see, Thoreau, Irene still lives in the blissful world of childhood. Before the grownup world storms in, let her live there and play there for as long as she can stay."

Kosmos laughed as he patted my cheek three times.

"So make love with Irene, Thoreau! What are you afraid of? Something is holding you back, and if you can cut that rope, you'll save yourself. And if you save your own self, then someday you might be able to help others to do the same."

Was Kosmos right? Or were his ultra-liberal sexual ideas perfect for

Kosmos but not for everyone, and not ideal for me?

"Irene is a wonderful young woman, Kosmos, and I enjoy her company. But as a sex partner for me, she is too young."

Kosmos shook his head.

"And there, my friend Thoreau, is that constipated prig inside you, talking as if there is a right and a wrong in sex! There is no right and no wrong, as long as the two partners — or however many are involved — as long as the participants willingly agree."

Tempted was I, but not totally convinced.

"Give me a little time, Kosmos, to think about these things. Until I'm sure, I'll stick with my old ways. And now you've made me curious about something. With your permissively broad-minded ideas, aren't you afraid that Irene will get involved with one of the younger or older men here in town? She's heartbreakingly attractive, and she's at the age where falling in love is the only important thing in life."

Kosmos threw two figs into his mouth.

"In this town, Thoreau, Irene is as safe from the lechers as a ninety-nine-year-old widow with a face like a wild boar. Every male in Dembacchae knows that if they put one finger on my Irene, I'll skewer his hams and barbecue his beans."

I laughed and raised my hands.

"But wait, Kosmos! What was all that sexual freedom business you were just blathering about! I thought I heard you say that sexplay is a private matter between Irene and her partner."

Kosmos pointed two fingers at me then edged his face closer to mine.

"If you are her partner, Thoreau, then it's between Irene and her partner. But if it's anyone else, then I cut off his *souvlaki* and feed it to the fish! You laugh about that? Good! I'm laughing too! I can't help thinking that way, Thoreau. I was born a Greek, and Greek men can be hard as marble and crueler than the widow-making sea. For eighteen years she has been my daughter. Do you understand?"

He didn't wait a blink for my reply.

"Of course you don't understand, you're too young! Your eyes are saying that all this is unreasonable. Do you know the first thing I do when I wake up each day? I thank the goddesses that Life is not managed by that conscientious taskmaster, Reason! Live by Reason — cut off all your intuitions, passions, feelings — and what will your life be? Boring, predictable, unfulfilled! Every morning at exactly six o'clock you'll walk your dog around the park carrying a plastic bag in your hand, and every time the dog shits on the grass you'll bend down and say "Good poopsie" then scoop up the dung and carry it all the way home!"

He opened his arms and laughed.

"Was it Reason that led you to Greece in the first place, Thoreau? And why did you come to Kreetee, and to my doorstep? Did you follow Reason, or did you follow something else, or someone else? Something deeper and wiser than Reason can ever be. *Katalavehees,* my friend?"

Kosmos picked up a pile of grapes then stuffed his mouth with the whole bunch. He gulped a glass of water with the slice of lemon floating on the top, then he chewed the lemon slice, and swallowed it — rind, pulp and seeds.

"Already, Thoreau, I'm wearing you out with the talk! Would you like to relax a little? There are two more rooms in this house that you haven't seen, a bedroom and a library. You can rest there now, if you like."

"I'm not tired Kosmos. And your talk isn't wearing me out. It's profoundly alive, and it speaks to me like a great book. Only it's better than a book, because I can ask questions about the things I don't agree with or don't understand."

"Good! We will talk more. For now, I wonder if you would care to see more of the people of Dembacchae. If you just know Kosmos and the town's taverna, then you might think that the whole town is made of lunatics and male chauvinists. I have some special work to do for the next few hours. Come with me, or stay, whatever you like."

I drank the lemon-water then stood up.

"Let's go then, Kosmos. And if you'll let me, maybe I can help you with your special work."

Kosmos led me to his library, my bedroom for the night, a large sunny room with a wooden floor, one couch, a desk and chair, and shelves and shelves of books. Books in the shelves, books on the desk, books on the chairs, books in high piles from the floor: thousands of volumes in all. Mostly paperbacks, they were written in more than ten different languages, about half nonfiction and the other half novels, poetry, autobiography, and plays.

We washed our hands and faces, then I threw on a T-shirt and my only pair of shorts, and a gift from Kosmos: a pair of his thick black-cotton socks. As we rinsed some dishes and picked up shards of broken cups, we laughed about my hat on the head of the mule. I thanked Kosmos for washing my clothes.

"Thank Irene," said Kosmos. "I asked her to wash them before they stunk so bad they would crawl out of the bag like her snakes."

I threw a handful of dishwater at him.

"And if a garbage man says that my clothes reeked," I said, "then who can argue with that?"

Irene burst through the doorway, skipping and singing, carrying a dozen oranges inside a pouch she had made by raising the front hem of her dress. She placed the oranges in a wooden bowl, insisted that she must come with us, then started to run through the doorway. Kosmos called her back.

"Irene, little bird who makes me sing. Please cover your chest with a shirt."

"Why, Uncle Kosmos? It's not cold outside."

He nodded and looked into her eyes.

"You could wear one of Thoreau's shirts, Irene."

Delighted, Irene ran into the library, rummaged through my pile of worldly goods, selected my last remaining T-shirt, ran back to us, dropped the T-shirt over her head, then kissed the cheek of Kosmos and kissed my cheek. Singing and skipping, she ran to the sunny outside. When she met Kosmos's dog Zorba she stroked him with her hands, and spoke to him as if he were a boy changed magically into a beast.

During the next hours I realized that this man Kosmos was a hero, an enlightened individual who used his intelligence and love to improve the world immediately around him. What were his great secrets? ... He lived for others; and he never postponed living, he lived today and now. Perhaps he truly believed that each hour we are alive is a paradise, each situation can be transformed, each moment can be the most intense moment we have ever lived.

We walked to a humble grocery store owned by friends of Kosmos. Here he bought a small hill of food, which the three of us carried, each of our hands holding one or two full plastic bags.

"The garbage collecting, that is for money only," he said. "Until I find my Paradise — or it finds me — this is the real work."

The real work comprised his weekly visits with elderly persons who had been forgotten, and with teenagers who had been ignored. At one house he left a bag of food for a poor old man; at another house he fixed a toilet and moved newspapers away from the wood stove; at a third he made arrangements to drive a woman to a doctor's appointment later in the week, then pick up her medicine; at a fourth house, he simply said hello to a woman living alone, and promised to return soon to talk and drink tea. Each day he would visit others — men, women, children, and even animals — the old, the sick, the orphans, the poor and the alone.

"This unique man," I thought, "has no greed, no need of the things that money buys, and not one selfish impulse in his entire soul. And he has no fear of any human being. Maybe that fearless kindness is the whole key."

As we were walking homeward and I was thinking about these ideas, a dark-haired boy, breathing fast, ran up to Kosmos and shouted *"Ella! Grigora!"* — Come! Quickly! We ran and followed the boy to the sounds of angry shouts blaring from a seedy-looking tavern.

Inside, we saw a foreign tourist with tattooed arms — a tall muscular Dutchman in his mid-twenties — standing at the bar holding a large hunting knife. Facing him stood two Greek brothers, about the same height and age as the foreigner, each holding in their hands a weapon just-made from a broken beer bottle, edged with jagged glass. A woman with a large chest and a low-cut dress that advertised it, sat smoking on a bar stool behind the Greeks. The argument had erupted when this woman — a German, and the girlfriend of one of the Greeks — had asked the Dutchman for a light for her cigarette.

Now, the three men involved in the altercation were shaking their weapons and shouting at one another, their faces flushed red from booze and rage. So much alcohol and anger it seemed inevitable that the drama had to finish in a bloody fight.

Kosmos said to the Dutchman, in the Dutch language, "Excuse my back," as he placed his bag of groceries onto a bar stool. He stepped between the three men, then faced the two angry Greeks. One of these Greek brothers, named Costas, waved the glass bottle and shouted hoarsely like a man whose clothes were on fire, as the sides of his mouth dripped with salivary foam.

"Get out, Kosmos! This is not your fight!"

I took a step to stand beside my friend but I stopped immediately, as Kosmos warned me to stay back with a brusque swish of his hand. Smiling as cheerfully as if he had been strolling through a field of wildflowers, Kosmos spoke to Costas in a deep and soothing voice.

"You're right, Costas. It's not my fight. But I am wondering, and I ask you to wonder with me: Is this fight yours? ... Think about it, my friend. Fighting is serious business. A real man, a *pallikári,* will fight if there is no other choice, but first he does everything he can to make the peace."

Costas was not so easily persuaded by nonviolent words. Consumed by flames of hate, he spat on the ground then waved his arms.

"Get out or you'll get hurt, Kosmos!" Costas shouted. "You should have seen the way that *malaka* looked at my girlfriend's tits!"

The smile on the face of Kosmos changed to the forgiving look of a father teaching a lesson to his son.

"Costas, look at her," said Kosmos. "Your girlfriend, she has nice tits, right? As long as other men don't touch them, why don't you like other men to look? If other men did not look, it would mean that she was ugly. As ugly as the girlfriend I had last week. Remember that one? Nobody looked at her tits. Even I didn't look at her tits, and if I would have looked I couldn't have found them without a road map and a magnifying glass."

The patrons in the bar burst out laughing, and the brother of Costas started to snicker. But Costas would not back down.

"I'm going to cut out his fuckeeng Dutch tongue!"

Kosmos's voice remained the voice of the father who had dealt with many heated arguments between little boys. The voice that was fair to all sides, calm in any storm of insults, confident enough to speak his truth, trusting enough to let the young minds grow by making decisions for themselves. He reached inside the grocery bag and pulled out a large bottle.

"See this, Costas," Kosmos said, turning the bottle in his hand. "This is the best wine in all of Kreetee. Not like the crap you get here at this cheap bar. This wine is the very best."

Kosmos slammed the bottle onto the countertop, looked into the eyes of Costas, stepped closer to the raging young man, then spoke unyielding words with all of his usual good cheer.

"Now listen, Costas. Young men on Kreetee are too smart to fight with women or with old men, do you know why? Because they know that if they kick your ass then you're disgraced, and if you kick their ass then people think you're a coward and wonder why you don't fight men your own age. You can't win, see? So right now, you and me can fight until we kill we each other, or we can drink this wine. Decide."

The silence that lasted a moment felt like it lasted a week. First, Costas's brother put down his weapon. Then the Dutchman sheathed his knife. At last, Costas threw his jagged bottle against a wall.

Kosmos opened his bag and passed out wine bottles so everyone could drink. He filled his glass then stood up on a stool.

"To all ten thousand tourist dames
 Who've shared my burning bed!
 And to the dozen smarter names —
 Who've chosen other men instead!"

He winked to the Dutchman, then smiled to Costas and his girl.

"To your health and long life!" Kosmos shouted. *"Yassas!"*

"Yassas!" shouted voices from the crowd.

An old man, a friend of Kosmos, was sitting at a table near the door. Kosmos bent down and whispered into his friend's ear.

"Georgios, do me a favor. Keep an eye on these little boys to make sure things don't flare up again. If you need anything, send a kid to find me. I'll be rambling around town for a while, then at the artist's apartment, then at home."

Georgios casually nodded, then Kosmos stepped outside the bar and took a deep breath.

"Shit, that was close, Thoreau. Don't try that yourself, unless you have a deep rapport with the guy holding the jagged glass. I've known Costas since he was three years old. Let's go now, before I think about how close I was to getting this body, that gives me so much pleasure, sliced up in twenty-four pieces like a plastic-wrapped bread. We've got more work to do."

We visited the apartment of an old woman who was giving violin lessons to a teenaged girl: Kosmos placed a wad of Euros on her table, to pay for the lessons and a new bow. We passed a restaurant filled with a dozen teenagers standing in front of pay-per-play video games, and all the players laughed when Kosmos opened the door then shouted: "Look outward, children! Life is here, outside!"

A pack of twelve teenaged boys with sticks in their hands ran near us, chasing a cat with a string on its tail. Kosmos shouted to them and they approached him.

"Want to chase cats or play soccer?" he said. When soccer was unanimously chosen, Kosmos gave them the tools. "You guys lost your balls again? ... There's a soccer ball in my truck, front seat, but don't mess with my papers there. Goal posts are in my backyard: take them and put them up in the schoolyard. If I can't come and play tonight, then I'll see you guys on Saturday afternoon."

As we strolled along the empty back streets, a sixteen-year-old boy walked past us, with hands in his pocket and his head dejectedly tucked down. Kosmos wrapped his arm around the boy's shoulder.

"Yiannis," he said. "Don't you say hello to your friend, eh? ... Listen, I've been hearing stories about you and that nice girl, Galatea. You know that I won't tell you what to do, I will just tell you what life will do to you if you keep on doing what you're doing. See this rock? When I was your age, this rock had more brains then me. I would go out with any girl, it didn't matter who it was. All the time I was telling the girls that I loved them, but to my friends I was saying: 'I like her ass, but I don't like her.' ... Look inside the girl, not just what's on the outside, do you understand? Don't kiss her unless you like what's on the inside, too. ... I'll see you Friday afternoon at my house for the art class. *Endaxi?* OK."

We walked to the bakery where Kosmos bought breads for dinner and a bouquet of flowers, then walked to the school and sat down on a bench there, and watched the boys and girls play soccer. There were no referees, and no adults involved to organize, and the children played not to win but for the pure joy of the game. Kosmos looked tired now, and he shook his head and laughed.

"I'm like that kid at the leaking dike, trying to stick his fingers in all the holes to keep the water from flooding the town! All day I'm putting fires out. But sometimes I wonder: what is anyone doing to snuff out the causes of these fires? ... Somebody needs to bring Truth back into Art, Thoreau. Or else these kids, and kids everywhere, will never have a chance for a good life. Art was invented to show the Truth in the world, to tell the Truth in one man's heart. But when Art can't find a respectable place, she puts on her low-cut red dress and she stands whistling on the corners of the streets. Art today is made for money, and money-covered Art is the highway to the murder of Truth, the decay of Culture and the extinction of Art."

He gripped my shoulder with his hand.

"Thoreau, listen to me. If some pompous, self-deluded fool ever gives you the chance to choose — between the naked truth and the decked-out shams — remember how we talked today, and remember the eyes of these children that need our honesty. And then pick the Truth above Money and stand with that Truth, even if it means you'll wind up cold, and hungry, and unpopular, and the loneliest man on Earth. ... There's not much time, Thoreau! If our artists can't find courage to take the honest path, then we might as well build another Cretan labyrinth, and throw the kids inside, and let the Minotaur eat up them up."

He shouted "Bravo! Bravo!" to the boys and girls playing, and then stood up.

"Now I can ask for your help with something, Thoreau. Take Irene to the beach and play with her. If I'm lucky, I'll be home in a few hours. And if not, in a few minutes. There's an attractive thirty-year-old French woman who has invited me to see her paintings. She'd probably enjoy your company, but I'd rather work with her alone. Thank you, Thoreau."

When Kosmos had left us, I looked up at the sky's peaceful light and then down at the carefree smile of Irene.

"Irene, let's take the food home. After that, you can show me the beach, and then we can play anything you want to play."

Irene screamed with joy. "We can play Snake Goddess!"

Fifteen minutes later we were walking on the beach and holding hands. Irene smiled sweetly into my deep-seeing eyes. Once again, she assumed the posture of the Snake Goddess, and assigned me to play the role of Priapus, that upstanding reject of the gods.

"I'll do my best, Irene. But I know only a little bit about this minor deity named Priapus. Aphrodite was his mother, and no one is sure whether his father was Adonis or Dionysus. He was the god of procreation, god of the gardens and the vines. He once caused a stir when he got drunk and tried to violate the virgin-goddess Hestia, but before he could molest her, an ass braying woke the sleeping goddess, and Priapus ran terrified away. A kind of national village idiot to the ancient Greeks, Priapus stands for obscene humor, thanks to his comical phallus, always-ready and ever-erect. This state of permanent erection was a subtle curse from Hera — wife of Zeus — to show her disapproval of the promiscuity of Aphrodite. Priapus's ugly face reflected the morals of the Greeks, who were far from prudes, but believed that sexual excess interfered with the functioning of an orderly society. These days, many statues of Priapus are used as grotesque scarecrows, to guard the gardens and to hold the hollowed gourds."

Irene's face revealed that she had understood only a small part of that description. I placed my hands on both hips.

"Irene, did you know that Priapus was a gardener who loved to prune pear trees? And you know, sometimes the goddesses cast a spell on him. And because of this spell, every time he sees a Snake Goddess, he thinks she is a pear tree and he wants to prune her — " Priapus opened and closed his arms like a pruning tool's great jaws. " — with these sharp shears!"

Irene screamed happily and ran laughing up the beach. For the next hours I chased her — over the sand, up and down the hillsides, in the water, through the lemon orchards — catching her and swinging her around, then letting her go, and chasing her again and again. Now and then I tickled her, or pretended to throw her into the waves, or let her ride on my back or shoulders. It was in this lighthearted way — Irene laughing wildly as I ran with her on my shouldertops — that we arrived back at the house of Kosmos. Kosmos was standing in the kitchen wearing an apron, holding a wooden spoon, and when he saw us he shouted with joy.

"Irene! Thoreau! I'm so glad to see you both!"

He stood watching us with paternal pride. "Irene, you look especially lovely this evening. And Thoreau, thank you ten thousand times for taking care of my little girl. Whenever I see Irene laughing that way, then the gods envy my happiness."

He threw me a bunched-up cloth which opened up to be an apron.

"I have a feeling you like to cook, Thoreau."

"I love to cook. How did you know? But I want to ask you something, Kosmos. Is what I've seen today typical of your life every day?"

Kosmos smiled as he stirred the soup.

"My life is helping people. I can't change the way I am. Yes, every day I do two hours with the garbage work; then make a round to see my old white-haired friends; and every week I play soccer and give art lessons, and I talk with the troubled teenaged girls and boys. After my social work, I come back here to build things out of wood or stone, or to make music, or to read or paint, or sing to my garden to help the vegetables and flowers grow."

He threw a handful of spices into the pot, then licked a soup sample from his wooden spoon.

"And every day I give lessons to Irene. But the truth is, I learn more from her — about how to live with simple honesty and joy — than I can teach from all my stories and books. And every night I share dinner with friends or interesting travelers. Or with tourist women, the ones who don't mind sleeping with a man older than their dads. And there's a secret project I'm working on — something that means everything to me — but already I've hinted too much about that."

I noticed that he hadn't faced me once since I'd returned home with Irene.

"Kosmos, did you enjoy the paintings of your female friend from France?"

He laughed as he turned his head then pointed to the red mark on his cheek where he'd been slapped.

"Win a few, lose a few," he said, with a disappointed sigh. "Although as I get older I'm finding that I'm losing a lot more than I'm winning. That Frenchwoman really did have paintings to show me. But when I tried to show her some strokes and the brush I use ... "

He rubbed his aching cheek, then turned down the fire beneath the kettle.

"Now come into the living room, Thoreau, I want to ask you something important. But first, get rid of that funny hat. It's making me laugh too much, and this is serious."

I tossed the tool-covered hat so that it flew across the room and landed on top of Kosmos's hat, on top of the phallus of Priapus.

"Bravo, Thoreau. Now listen well. There is something I must ask you."

Kosmos had placed his calloused hands on my shoulders and stood facing me at arm's length. He spoke slowly and deliberately, as if he were discovering — or re-appreciating — the ideas just now for the first time.

"I believe this," said Kosmos, in his deep voice. "And I must know if you believe it too. 'Money is nothing, Persons are everything.'"

A smile seemed to grow inside me from the depths of my hidden soul. Over the past years I had poured through hundreds of books to try to understand the most meaningful way to live my life. And the essence of wisdom had been epitomized inside these six simple words.

"You are quiet, Thoreau. Do you agree?"

"Yes," I said, nodding. "I agree. I've never heard anything that I agree with more."

Kosmos bear-hugged me then stood back and looked at me again.

"Good! No, good is not good enough, this is wonderful! I knew it the instant I saw your worthless clothing and your priceless books! Now, from my side at least, we are brothers. If you need anything, or want anything, anything at all ... "

With an expression on his face that I did not completely understand, he cocked his head toward the kitchen where Irene was standing. Kosmos sensed my confusion and continued to explain.

"If you need anything at all, then ask me before you think about it twice. And if I need anything, then I will ask you. Like brothers! Good, yes? Now I will tell you, Thoreau, what your eyes say you are thinking. You are thinking: 'This is madness! Two men meet for the first time, and they swear loyalty and brotherhood forever!' I agree, madness it is! But is there a greater madness a man can live by? If there is tell me now, and I'll be the first to dive in!"

Kosmos pressed his right hand against his shirt over his heart.

"But I swear to you, Thoreau, I will never ask you for money. Never! And I will never let you give money to me. And for the next fifty years when we will be friends and brothers, I will only ask one thing from you, and it will be such a small thing that when you hear it you will laugh like thunder. What do you say now? Shall we be brothers? Do you agree to that, too?"

Fools fear to tread where angels jump right in. I placed my hand on his strong shoulder.

"I agree, Kosmos. I agree with my whole heart."

He offered his large open hand and together we shook hands, each hand impressed and inspired by the other's powerful grip.

"Ah!" Kosmos shouted. "This is a day! This is a day of days! Now, to seal our agreement, to celebrate this rare moment, we must drink. I have another bottle of the best wine on Kreetee. This wine here is the real stuff, not like that junk I gave away at the bar."

Grasping the penis of Priapus, he pulled it outward. This opened a drawer in the god's midsection, and Kosmos took out a bottle of wine. He filled up two glasses, raised his glass, and then clinked it against mine.

"*Athanatos*. That means 'deathless', Thoreau. May our friendship last forever, and may we both live twice as long as that! And a thousand years after we die, may the memory of our friendship and our brotherhood be sung throughout these hills of Kreetee!"

He drank then I drank a large glass of the thick sweet wine.

"*Athanatos!*" I said. "May our friendship last forever, and our young spirits last a day longer than that. And now, Kosmos, listen and don't take offense. I have a rare medical condition called vinose intolerance. Our friendship may last a long time, but whenever I drink wine, even the best, I — ”

In the middle of the sentence I fell asleep.

Two hours later, when I awoke, the room was filled with the powerful aromas of onion soup and garlic bread. I was surprised but not astonished to discover that I was lying on the couch and covered with a fishnet large enough to hold a shark.

Moments after I opened my eyes, Irene — dressed in a skimpy white tunic — shouted: "He's awake!", then lifted the net and leaped on top of me into my arms.

"Thoreau, why is Priapus so big and you are so small?" she asked.

"How do you know that?" I answered.

"I peeked while you were sleeping," she said with a smile. "Is there something wrong with that? Is the human body a thing of beauty?"

"It is a thing of beauty," I answered.

"And is every part of the body beautiful?"

I was trapped in the logical meshes of this lovely Socrates.

"Yes, Irene. Every part of the body is beautiful."

"Am I beautiful?" she asked.

"Very beautiful."

"Thoreau, will you rape me now?"

"Rape you? Oh god!" I shouted. "Kosmos! Kosmos!"

Then I understood: To the pure all things are pure.

"Irene, what do you mean?"

"You know, silly. Take off all my clothes and kiss me. Just like in the story. Aphrodite is in bed with Ares — they're not wearing any clothes — and her hubby Hephaestus catches and traps them by throwing an unbreakable net on top of them both!" Irene cuddled even closer against me.

"Kosmos!" I shouted again.

Kosmos appeared, dressed as Zeus, the adopted father of Aphrodite, holding in his hand a shining thunderbolt made of cardboard that had been covered by aluminum foil.

"Thoreau," said Kosmos, laughing and holding his belly, "are you enjoying yourself?"

"I'm captivated, Kosmos. I'm sure I would never get this kind of authentic Greek experience if I were spending my nights in the Herakleion Heelton."

Kosmos laughed more, and patted the net against my cheek.

"My friend, just wait. This is only the beginning."

"Thoreau," Irene said, "I want to sleep with you! It will be fun!"

This naive young woman, uninformed about sexual relations, envisioned a night of lying in bed together, talking, laughing, exchanging the most innocent kisses, tickles, and tales.

"Kosmos," I said, sitting up, but still covered by the net. "You've told Irene all the myths. Now it's time to tell her some facts. The so-called facts of life."

"Right now?" Kosmos said.

I answered with the most common expression on Crete.

"*Yeeatee oshee?* Why not?"

Kosmos took a deep breath, then took Irene's hand in his hand.

"Irene, stop looking into Thoreau's eyes for a minute. This is important."

"I love looking at his eyes. They look like the diamonds of sunlight dancing on the sea. What is it that you want to teach me, Uncle Zeus?"

Looking tense, Kosmos cleared his throat, paused, then suddenly looked relieved.

"Thoreau has something very very important to tell you! And I am certain that he will explain it in the style of Kazantzakis: clear, interesting, alive, sensual, filled with stories that touch the heart of all."

Irene beamed.

"What is it, Thoreau? I mean, Ares."

I glared at Kosmos.

"Kosmos, my Greek-speaking is not bad, but it's not perfect enough to risk something this difficult and this important."

"Thoreau, forgive me," Kosmos said. "I'm not good at these kinds of things. With words, as with women, I can be clumsy and lose my way. As you have heard, I have very healthy and very outrageous opinions about this business of love-play. I think one thing, and I do another thing. Won't that confuse her completely? And I have nothing of what you call 'morals,' which is just what children need until they grow wise and responsible enough for the joyous burden of complete freedom. Despite my best intentions, I would corrupt her, Thoreau. I am sure that you can explain these mysteries in a better way."

"Kosmos," I said firmly. "You are her father. The person above all who she admires and trusts."

Kosmos waved his hands.

"That's exactly why I should not tell her! If I do, she'll never look at me again in the same way."

Irene hung her arms around my neck, kissed my forehead, then began to sweetly sing.

"Ares, Ares, Ares! Aphrodite is in love with Ares! Hephaestus is going to catch us, and we don't care!"

"What are we going to do, Kosmos?" I asked.

"Ah! I know!" he said. "There are times in life — too many times, I swear! — when a man needs a woman, and nothing but a woman will do. We need a woman to tell her!"

"You're right, Kosmos. But it has to be the right woman. A woman who is warm, gentle, intelligent, experienced, eloquent, sensitive, and wise."

At that crucial moment, a most feminine voice rang through the doorway.

"Ding-dong!" chanted the singsong voice.

Kosmos looked at me. I looked at Kosmos. Together we said:

"Saved by the belle."

The saving voice sang once again.

"Hellololoooloooooo! Is anyone at home sweet home?"

Kosmos stared at the doorway and his eyes lit up, as if he had been pierced by the arrow of a spectacular idea.

"Luck follows us everywhere, Thoreau! Do you know why? Because Luck loves men who risk everything for what they really want. We live dangerously, we let our days be unpredictable, we're not afraid to fail. One day we're noshing ambrosia and schmoozing with the goddesses, the next day we're hungry and penniless, stuck in a dunghill up to our necks. The gods love that! They love to watch men struggle with all their cunning. And the goddesses, disguised as mortal women, bring help whenever we need them most."

The whole Kosmos seemed charged with a new energy and a new youth.

"Capture two pigeons with one bean! That's what we're going to do tonight, Thoreau, if things work out. We'll get a tutoress for a young girl, and some love lessons for an old man, too!"

He slapped my shoulder.

"You know, Thoreau, they say it would be better if a man were born old and then grew younger every day, instead of the other way around. Even for Zorba, old age is a disgrace, a monster he fights every minute of his life. When you're young you're a lion, you can do anything you want! Then suddenly — I swear it happens in an instant, all at once! — one morning you wake up and you're an old man. You're a sheep tied to a tree hoping to get through one more day without getting your head cut off! How can any man survive a fall like that!"

With both hands he tugged his greying beard.

"But there's one thing about old age that the books don't tell you. When a young man sleeps with a beautiful young woman he doesn't appreciate it enough. But when an old man sleeps with a young woman he desires, and when he uses every trick he knows to make that woman squeal with the sublimest ecstasy — ah! The joy of that! The joy of that! It makes up a thousand times for the hell of getting old!"

He pressed his hands together as if he were about to pray.

"I'm feeling lucky tonight, Thoreau. What do you think?"

I wasn't completely clear about Kosmos's schemes, but I knew that before long I would find out.

"My grandfather, Kosmos, used to tell me something every Sunday when I visited: 'Every woman has a key.'"

The melodious voice from the doorway sang again.

"We're coming in, Kosmos! *Chaire!*"

Like brothers, flashing smiles into each other's eyes, Kosmos and I clasped our happy hands.

20
A Night of Whine, Women, and Song

"If every woman has a key ... the locksmith is the life for me!"

Kosmos, seized by a mad joy, sang out in his deeply-resonating voice.

Lady Loverly, followed by her friend, raised the blanket and passed through the doorway, then listened to the made-up song with teeth-gleaming smiles. Loverly kissed the cheek of Kosmos as he sang. Her lips lingered as she kissed my cheek, and at last she handed me a gift-wrapped box.

"This is a small present from Becca and Juliette, Mr. Thoreau," she said. "You're looking wonderful, dear! We've all missed you terribly. We worry about you living outdoors as you do, exposed to the savage elements — the cold, the rain, the winds, the birds of the air, the beasts of the fields, and all the other women in the world."

Lady Loverly gave gifts to Kosmos and Irene, then introduced them to her friend Prudence, the treasurer of WANDERBORE. As soon as these three began talking, Lady Loverly flitted back to me, gripped the sash of her kimono, turned her back, then showed me her profile.

"Mr. Thoreau," she said, "you don't look like a man who so quickly forgets something he promises. And if you do forget, then I'll be even quicker to remind you."

Recalling what she meant I stepped up behind her, paused to look at her dark hair pinned up like a pumpernickel-challah bread, then removed her silk kimono. Lady Loverly swirled around with a divinely-knowing smile.

A white silk gown hugged her body, revealing the woman's sinuous dimensions. Slits on both sides, from hem to waist, exhibited her shapely legs and thighs. Like honeydew melons, her breasts dazzled from her décolletage, squirming and juggling, ingeniously designed to stupefy each woman-loving man.

Entranced by this storybook sight, Irene ran to Lady Loverly. With her childlike eyes opened wide, Irene pointed her finger at the majestic woman, so excited that she could hardly speak.

"You're ... you're ... you're ... Aphrodite!" Irene shouted at last.

Lady Loverly stroked Irene's shining hair.

"Yes, dear child," she gently replied. "Every woman, even a liberated woman, glows like Aphrodite when she finds a man she can love and desire with her whole heart and her whole soul."

Kosmos and I carried his round wooden table from the kitchen into the living room, and all five of us sat down after Lady Loverly covered the tabletop with her presents of breads and fruits and healthy drinks.

Kosmos shook his grey-haired head.

"Welcome to the Café Olympus," he said, with a twinkling smile. He turned to Lady Loverly then scolded her with his most cheerful voice.

"Beatrice, I told you there was no need to bring anything."

"Wouldn't this be the worst of all possible worlds, Kosmos," Lady Loverly answered, "if we women did everything that men told us to do?"

Kosmos — I could read his Zorbatic mind — was about to say, "That depends on who's doing the telling!" But as he opened his mouth he changed his mind, realized that she was right, then smiled and nodded to agree.

The open mind of Kosmos, reflected in his face, was easy to read by any observer as keen as Lady Loverly. She glanced at Kosmos, gleaned something more, then looked to her left at Prudence, her dear friend.

Prudence was thirty-two, the same age as Loverly, but while Beatrice looked ten years younger, Prudence looked ten years older or even a bit more. Beatrice looked lively and radiant, Prudence appeared dull and bovine. Her mass of brown hair had been compressed into a stale bun, better suited for a spinster twice her age. Her skin had the bland color of uncooked tofu, and the mole on her left cheek would have terrified a small child. She was plump in all the wrong places; and her face, though not unfriendly, was not a face that a man would enjoy waking up to in the morning — or any other part of the day. Her burlappy brown dress — drooping down like a potato sack and covering every inch of flesh from neck to anklebones — might have been stamped with the letters "ten bushels" or "two-hundred pounds". As the hard-working treasurer and events coordinator for WANDERBORE, she had spent too many hours worrying over the account book's figures, and not enough time tending to her own.

Prudence pulled a pencil from her hair bun.

"Shall we get business out of the way, Kosmos?" she began. "For next year's WANDERBORE events in Crete, we will require food for twelve-hundred women for seven days."

I smiled to learn that Kosmos would be acting as the catering liaison for this affair. As usual, he was donating his time, and he would gain not one Euro of profit for his work. He assured the women that he would provide more than enough of the healthiest food and drink available on Crete.

Prudence scribbled some notes into a notebook.

"You don't require a contract from us, or a deposit, Kosmos?"

Kosmos laughed as he waved his arms.

"I say I will get food for you, I will get food for you. You say you will pay me, you will pay me. In a moment we'll drink to our mutual good fortune. The wine is our contract, and all the deposit that I require are your smiles."

Prudence tapped her pencil against her pad.

"It seems like a rather large number to feed, Kosmos. You're certain that you can pull it off?"

Kosmos had been staring at the chest area of Prudence's sack-dress as if he could see right through.

"My dear, for years I have been pulling it off. And for a charitable case like yours, I will move mountains."

At that moment a lightning bug alighted in the valley between Lady Loverly's grand breasts. After watching the bug shine on then off then on, Irene ever-so-carefully scooped it up inside a cardboard matchbox.

"It will be happier outside," said the gentle Irene. "Uncle Kosmos says that we can't kill anything, not even a bug, because every living thing is important. Every living thing helps something, and every living thing depends on something else."

Lady Loverly placed her warm hand on my forearm, then smiled to Irene.

"That's very thoughtful of you, dear child," she said. "And who do you depend on, Mr. Thoreau?"

Distracted by the roundness of her breasts, I first glanced at Lady Loverly's hand on my arm, then I looked up into her radiant eyes.

"Right now? For Facts I depend on Prudence. For Truth, I depend on Kosmos. For Goodness, I depend on Irene. And for Beauty, I depend on you, Lady Loverly."

The eyes of Lady Loverly looked happily surprised. "Be careful how you flatter a woman, Mr. Thoreau. If she disbelieves you, she will think you are a liar. And if she believes you, she will think that you are trying to get something from her. In either case, dear boy, she may fall hopelessly in love with you."

"Is that such a bad thing?" I asked.

"For the woman it is a catastrophe," said Lady Loverly, heaving a great sigh. "Unless the man desires to surrender his heart with the same intensity that he desires to conquer her body."

Kosmos laughed at this exchange. Rather than attempt to interpret the hidden meanings underlying her remarks, I slyly changed the subject.

"How was your trip to Samaria Gorge, Lady Loverly?

She gripped my arm tighter.

"You change the subject so deftly, dear. Actually, the local authorities tried to discourage one-hundred women from hiking while wearing nothing but socks and shoes. They arrested us, but they wouldn't take us to the station without any clothes. So we all wound up wrapped in the official towels that said: 'Tourist Police.' It made a hilarious group photo, but we never completed the hike."

Prudence was not amused. The Tourist Police had spoiled her outing and she would never forgive them.

"Those dreadful people have no appreciation of the human body! And no sense of humor! None at all!"

Prudence slid her notebook into her handbag. Kosmos stared at her then nodded, then turned to Irene.

"Irene, would you like to have a photograph of Thoreau, and Prudence, and Aphrodite? If you like, you can eat dinner at your mother's tonight, then visit the widow Yentagabpolis. Borrow that camera I loaned her thirteen years ago."

Irene, thrilled at this idea, ran outside after she kissed Kosmos on the left cheek, me on the right cheek, Prudence on the forehead, and Lady Loverly on the lips. Kosmos followed her with his eyes, then turned to Lady Loverly and spoke to her slowly, with more than a twinge of anxiousness in his strong voice.

"Beatrice, we need your help," he began. "Thoreau and I agree that it's time for Irene to learn some things about — how shall I say it — about how to make the great transition from girlhood to womanhood."

Raising her eyebrows, Lady Loverly smiled at Kosmos, and continued to stroke my forearm with her hand.

"Are you trying to say," she began," that you would like for me, with the utmost of poetic feeling, to instruct the young woman in all aspects of sexuality, including structure and functions of the sex organs, basic activities, evaluating relationships, male psychology and that hot-air balloon known as the male ego, self-defenses physical and emotional, strategies for seduction, enjoying pleasures, reducing perils, and managing exhilarating hopes and crushingly disappointing aftermaths?"

Kosmos nodded. "That would get her off to a good start."

Playfully, Lady Loverly pinched my cheek.

"Tell me, Kosmos," she said. "Why don't you teach her? Or why don't you ask Irene if she would like to take lovemaking lessons from our good Thoreau?"

Kosmos swallowed more wine as his mind groped for just the right words. As he answered, his arms and hands came alive, waving through the air in front of him, sometimes flying swiftly like two bold eagles, othertimes moving gently like two soft doves.

"Not me, Beatrice," said Kosmos. "I am too liberated. What's right for Kosmos is not right for everyone. Teaching by example is the only way to teach. And if I can't teach her by example, then I can't teach her at all."

He pointed to me and wagged his finger.

"And as for Thoreau, he's a good man, but he's not the right one for the job. Sexwise, he is too inhibited. Too restrained. Too ethical. He needs to learn how to loosen up, how to cut the rope that binds him to his old-fashioned ideas. The sex problem is ripping him in two. His conscience pulls him West, his desires pull him East. A most dangerous crisis in a young man's life: too old to like his conscience, and too young to trust his desires. Thoreau thirsts for freedom, but he knows he's not quite ready for the necessary responsibility that leads the free man from the gutter to the stars. He's so close to Paradise he can reach out and touch it: but because he does not dare to seize it, that Paradise could be a billion miles away. All because he does not dare!"

Lady Loverly smiled at these revelations, staring at me all the while, as if she were trying to determine which, if any, of these penetrating words were true.

"Perhaps, Kosmos, you underestimate our remarkable Thoreau," said Lady Loverly. "His heart is in the right place, he's gentle to women and children, and he's thoroughly sincere. And that's all he needs to make his way, through oceans and deserts and starry nights, and all the traps we wily women lay."

Beatrice smiled brightly, like the sun and all her sister stars.

"In any case," she said, "of course I will be pleased to accept this tremendous task of teaching your daughter the incomparable arts of love. I have time to begin later tonight, if Irene is willing."

Kosmos clapped his hands together and breathed a loud sigh of relief.

"She will be willing," he said. "Thank you, Beatrice. Thank you."

Prudence, who had all-the-while been humming to herself, now pointed to the image on the wall that had divided her attention.

"Hopefully more willing than that satyr in the painting," she said.

Lady Loverly cocked her head as her eyes opened at an embarrassing discovery. Her comely face flushed red.

"Look, Prue! Doesn't the satyr in the painting resemble our handsome Thoreau! ... No, I am mistaken, it can't be him at all. If it were Thoreau, then we would see the entire forest of nymphs tugging at him, not merely four."

At these remarks, Prudence and Loverly exploded into fits of giggles, falling into each others arms as they laughed and laughed. Kosmos stood up, circled the table, slapped my shoulder, then led me into the kitchen.

"Come on, Thoreau, it's getting hot in here. Help me with the soup."

Kosmos swirled the kitchen knife like a Samurai warrior, and side-by-side we chopped bulbs of garlic then dropped the pungent slices into the simmering soup. He sang for a few moments, glanced at me, then decided to unburden himself of secrets so weighty he could no longer carry them alone.

"Thoreau, there are some things about you that I can't understand at all! You've hardly looked at her all evening. What a knockout that woman is! She's driving me insane! I can't keep my eyes off her! Imagine what a Raphael would do with a woman like that! Sensuous. Savage. Uninhibited. Beneath that calm mountainous exterior, a volcano ready at any moment to erupt. My pistachios are trembling like two eggs rolling around inside a pot of boiling water. If I don't go to bed with her tonight, I'm going to explode. I'll have to find a sheep, do the job seven times with the woolly beast, and wake up the whole neighborhood with squeals and bleats. Go back and join them, Thoreau. I can finish here ... Thoreau?"

"Kosmos?"

"I was joking about the sheep. Where could I find a sheep at this time in the evening? ... But I was serious about everything else."

The roguish saint Kosmos was on fire once again. He danced back into the dining room, carrying a tray with breads, cheeses, and steaming bowls of his special garlic soup. As he served us he danced around the table, singing wildly, like a man en route to the bedroom of his mistress for a night of indescribable love. An improvised song burst from the lips of Kosmos, as he placed the first bowl in front of Lady Loverly.

"There was a lad loved by a lass,
   O troll-dee roll-dee ray-o!
   But he was such a stupid ass — "

A bowl of soup from the hand of Kosmos was slammed down onto the table in front of me.

"With her he would not play-ay-o,
   With her he would not play-o."

It was hard to tell which essence aired more powerfully: the scent of steamy insinuations or the aroma from the spicy garlic soup.

"What's that tune, Kosmos?" I asked.

"It's an old English folk ballad, Mr. Thoreau," said Lady Loverly. "Sing more for us, Kosmos."

Kosmos nodded and sang on.

"The just-filled gods cut off his rod
   And flung it to the tay-ay-ble — "

Here and now, onto the center of the table, Kosmos placed his great creation: a two-foot tall sculpture of a phallus. It had been shaped from a heap of *taramosálata*— a paté of smoked cod's roe blended with garlic, lemon juice, cold water and olive oil.

"I call this work of art," said Kosmos, 'A Prick of Remorse.'"

The women laughed riotously.

"Was Thoreau your model for this masterpiece?" Loverly inquired. "And if yes, who was the fortunate woman who helped him to pose with such poise?"

Kosmos answered with a smile and then continued his song.

"And now the lad eats hay and nods
   Inside a donkey's stay-ay-ble.
   Inside a donkey's stay-ble."

"Kosmos," I said. "You can't leave us hanging like this. I hope there's a happy ending to this song."

"There is, Thoreau," Kosmos said. "But only for those who are free."

And more he sang.

"Another lass so fair came by — "

Here, Kosmos placed a plate of Greek hors d'oeuvres onto the table in front of Prudence.

"Another lad so trim — "

Now he set down a plate of savory delicacies in front of the place where he would be sitting.

"He merely winked his smiling eye
  And down she lay with him — troll-dee-ray-hee!
  And down-own she lay-ay with him."

We applauded the song as Kosmos filled three goblets with the thick Cretan wine — and one goblet, mine, with thick Cretan apple cider. He raised his glass.

"First," said Kosmos, "let us give some drops of this drink to the gods who have blessed us with freedom and friendship and health."

We all followed Kosmos's example as he spilled a few droplets of drink from his goblet into a wooden bowl.

"Drink with us, O gods. And be quick about it, or else I'll forget about you, and guzzle it all down myself!"

Kosmos placed his arm around my shoulder.

"And now," the great seducer continued, "let us praise Lady Loverly and Prudence. The halls of Olympus darkened when these two beauties flew to Earth, to brighten our table with their burning charms."

The women laughed, and their laughter encouraged the man, who had learned from his heroic Greek ancestors to be a lyre with two strings: to be a doer of deeds, and a speaker of words.

"Tonight I speak with your voices, O Muses wise! Don't wait for paradise: live and work to make a paradise out of the muck on earth. Don't search for truth: listen to your heart. Don't fret about goodness: treat each living being tenderly. Don't circle the globe for imagined beauty: reach out and touch the real beauteous globes that are here at hand."

Lady Loverly and Prudence applauded this *double entente,* then filled their plates with food. With wine flowing, women laughing, food on the table — that looked like it had walked out of a cookbook specializing in aphrodisiac delights — the room was beginning to feel somewhat un-comfortable for an eligible young man.

Kosmos sensed my uneasiness. Compassionately, he looked at me.

"Is there something wrong, Thoreau?"

"I'm not homophobic, Kosmos," I said. "But I'm having trouble eating with that phallus standing on the table four inches from my nose. For me, sex is something private. An activity that a man and woman share together with the hearts open but the doors closed. When I'm in bed with a woman I don't want to eat pie, and when I'm eating dinner I don't want to look up at a giant penis."

Kosmos laughed and slapped his hand onto the heavy table.

"You see? Once again, the cold hand of conscience wraps itself around the hot phallus of desire. Which one is stronger? Does the hand freeze the phallus, or does the phallus burn the hand? ... Thoreau, I promise you one thing. If I take away this *taramosálata* sculpture, it won't stop you from thinking about sex. So tell me, my troubled friend — what solution to this problem do you propose? I make you a gift of this mouth-watering appetizer, to do with whatever you please."

All creativity comes in two basic flavors: seeing something new, or seeing something ordinary in a new way. Six lips were smiling and six eyes were watching me as I stood up.

"A Greek legend, Kosmos, says that the first drinking cup was molded on the breast of Helen of Troy. And if a cup can be molded on a breast, then versa vice."

I drank the cider in my goblet, turned it upside-down, then pressed this goblet on top of the *taromosálata* penis, transforming its shape into a woman's breast.

"Bravo, Thoreau!" shouted Kosmos, clapping his hands. "You make me laugh like no man has made me laugh before!"

He refilled all the glasses then raised his own.

"May every meal we eat be blessed by beautiful and cheerful company like this. And may we wolf down everything in front of us, and laugh like lions roaring, because when Aphrodite on Olympus hears laughter and sees good appetites, she sends Eros to shoot us full of arrows, and make us wild with love."

A table overflowing with splendid things to eat is not the place for shyness. For the next minutes I forgot the friends around me and dove headfirst into the sea of food. Prudence cupped her hand and whispered into the ear of Lady Loverly.

"Look at that poor starved young American!" she said. "He hasn't had a good meal in as long as I haven't had a good male."

Lady Loverly tapped my shoulder.

"Mr. Thoreau ... Mr. Thoreau. I apologize for interrupting your feeding session at the climax of its unbridled frenzy. But dear boy, mere quantity will never satisfy you. Yin and yang desire to merge harmoniously, in every individual, in every relationship, and in every belly. You must have a balanced meal. Shall we share this succulent dessert? ... Don't be shy, dearest, you won't be expelled from Paradise if you consume my fruit."

She split a pomegranate in half, then placed one half into her mouth and the other half into mine. I chewed the seeds and sucked the tart red juice.

"The apple and the pomegranate are the two fruits of paradise and love," she said. "The names of the paradises in Greek and Arthurian mythology — Elysium and Avalon — both mean 'apple land'. At the other end, Persephone, Queen of the Underworld, could not be released from that hell because she ate pomegranate seeds, symbols of both fertility and death. ... Mr. Thoreau, when you were a little boy did any little girl ever place a buttercup flower beneath your chin, pretending to determine if you liked butter?"

"My chin turned yellow every time," I said.

"There's a similar superstition about pomegranates," she said. And with a mellifluous mezzo-soprano voice the woman sang:

"If his tongue is turning red, then he wants your burning bed!"

The man-savvy woman grasped my bottom lip. "Stick out your tongue, Thoreau," she said, "and show the world how much you desire me."

The tongue outstuck was colored so deep red-purple from the pomegranate seeds, that Kosmos and the women laughed like they would never cease.

Lady Loverly carried my hand to her lips and kissed it gently.

"Mr. Thoreau, I'm so sorry! Your poor embarrassed face is redder than your tongue! You look like a hero in a Greek tragedy, mocked by irony, plagued by prophecies, berated by the chorus, then clobbered by the cudgel of a stunning discovery about his dubious life in the past. Whatever it is, dear one, you can lighten the burden by sharing it with your friends. Wholehearted self-discolosure is the first steep step to free yourself from the fatuous fingers of the Fates."

"I want to confess something, Lady Loverly," I said, "because a pound of honesty today saves a ton of heartbreak tomorrow."

"Go ahead, Thoreau," she said. "Pound me with your honesty. And call me Beatrice, please."

Still red-faced and burning with embarrassment, I looked at her bright face.

"Lady Loverly ... Beatrice ... Since the day we met at the Meteora, I imagined that you were a perfect woman, and I have been searching for you all over Crete."

"Is that all?" said Kosmos. "That's what made your face redder than my best wine? Tell us something more embarrassing than that, Thoreau!"

"Kosmos," said Lady Loverly, "let the dear boy idolize me if he wishes to make that mistake. Don't we all believe in perfect love? The Italian poet Dante met his Beatrice when he was only nine years old. He didn't see her for another nine years after that, and from that moment until she died he exchanged with her hardly a dozen words. With nothing more than those brief encounters, he loved her so devotedly that he gave the remainder of his life to making poems that glorified her goodness. Her glance made him a poet, and his words made her immortal. And no powers in the world can transform persons in that way, except the magic of all-embracing Love."

The warm consoling arm of Lady Loverly fell lightly around my shoulders.

"And now that poor Thoreau has bared his soul and confessed his secret passion, he needs our unconditional approval and support."

Lady Loverly hugged me, pressing the side of my head against her gleaming breasts. Kosmos, his face red with envy, glanced at Prudence, then glared back at me, then stood up.

"Young Werther," said Kosmos, with a twist of irritation in his voice. "I mean, young Thoreau. Tear yourself away from paradise and help me with the coffee."

In the kitchen, I loaded a tray with a bowl of dark honey, a pitcher of milk, and fresh pastries oozing with honey and almonds. Kosmos poured Greek coffee grounds into four small cups, filled the cups with boiling water — equal parts of water and coffee was his formula — then vigorously stirred.

"What a beauty!" Kosmos said, gripping my shoulder. "Did you see the look she gave me? I could sit and watch her for a hundred years! What do you think she'll look like when she lets her hair down?"

"About the same as she looked before, Kosmos, with more hair."

"You know what's really driving me wild about her?"

"Tell me, Kosmos."

"That mole on her left cheek."

A smile skipped across my lips. I looked back, laughed out loud, then whispered to my friend.

"It's not Lady Loverly! You're in lust with Prudence?"

"Shhhh!" said Kosmos, placing his hand over my lips. "Yes, of course it's Prudence! She wants me, Thoreau. She looks at this old face and sees the young handsome man inside. More than anything else, that's what makes a woman beautiful — when her eyes look at an ordinary man and see the hero and the god!"

Kosmos glanced again at the woman he desired.

"Right now, my friend, you see the beauty on the outside and forget about what really matters underneath. In thirty years — when your hair gets grey as dust, your teeth drop out like high school seniors, and the women stop falling at your feet like olives in October — only then will you understand what I'm talking about."

As he glanced back at the women an immense smile filled his face.

"What quality does a fifty-five year-old man like me look for in a woman? Just one: that she's willing! That's all I need to make the both of us happy for one eternal night."

Kosmos more tightly gripped my arm.

"Thoreau, you're an interesting character because you're so complex. Mostly I see through you like glass, sometimes like a mirror, and other times, I don't understand you at all."

"What don't you understand?"

"You won't hurt the wing of a repulsive fly, but you will break the heart of a beautiful woman!"

"Kosmos, what do you mean?"

"Look at her!" I glanced at the dining room table.

"Which her?"

"Beatrice Loverly," said Kosmos. "She's madly in love with you! If you winked once, then before you could raise your eyelid she would follow you straight to your bed!"

"I don't believe that, Kosmos," I said. "If I make a pass at her, she'll think I'm like most other men — a slimeball."

"Imagine, Thoreau, what it would be like to make love with a woman in love with you like that! ... You can't imagine because you're too young. And when I was your age I also lacked that same romantic imagination."

Like a baker kneading dough I shook my hands at Kosmos.

"Wait, Kosmos, all this is nonsense! She's treating me like a mother would treat her son. Or like an older sister taking care of a younger brother."

A blast of laughter exploded from Kosmos's mouth. Tears rolled down his cheeks and dripped into one of the coffee cups.

"Thoreau, Thoreau! If I could have your youth and my experience! I'd knock down Zeus, take over his throne on Mount Olympus, then make love with every goddess in the skies and every woman on the Earth! Forgive me, please, Thoreau. When I laugh at you, I laugh at me when I was your age. *Katalavehees,* my friend?"

He faced me and placed both hands on my shoulders, the posture he would take whenever he wanted to tell me something of the utmost importance. He glanced back into the living room, then peered into my eyes.

"Beatrice Loverly could sleep with any man she wanted on two islands — England or Kreetee. But she wants only one man, and he's standing in this kitchen, and he's not me."

I shook my head.

"Kosmos, listen. I respect you, believe me. But are you right every time? Am I supposed to believe you when your ideas and intuitions defy logic and deny common sense? Lady Loverly can't be in love with me."

"Why not?" said Kosmos, placing both hands on his hips. "Why not?"

"She can't be in love with me for three reasons: she's married, she has a daughter, and although we've met three times we've spent less than an hour together."

This remark triggered thunderous laughter from Kosmos, and more streamlets of tears. When he calmed down he looked at me and — as he had done many times — patted my beardless cheek with his calloused hand.

"Love strikes a woman faster than a lightning flash! In sixty minutes, she could have fallen in love with you thirty-six hundred times! And about that silly business of marriage! A woman does not stop being a woman simply because she bands her finger with a silver ring. Thoreau, you'd better go with Lady Loverly instead of Irene, so she can explain the facts of love to you. Or you'd better go back and read Tolstoy more carefully, and ask yourself why Anna Karénina threw herself under a train."

Again, I shook my hands and head.

"And Kosmos, you think that Prudence — Prudence, as cold as a dog's nose and as stiff as a road-killed cat — Prudence wants to go to bed with you? She's an iceberg in a frozen sea."

He threw open his arms. "And Kosmos is the sun! I will melt her."

"How do you plan to do it?" I asked.

"Thoreau, you know that the goddess Aphrodite loves to laugh. Make a woman laugh in the morning, and she'll be warming your bed in the afternoon. I will make Prudence laugh like she has never laughed, then love like she has never loved."

I knew that Kosmos demanded of me one thing only: that I always say what I was thinking, and never spare his feelings and try to be polite.

"Seduction is never that easy, Kosmos. Almost never."

"You don't believe it? Come with me and we will see."

Kosmos whistled as we carried the coffee and desserts into the dining room. He set them down in front of the two women, who greeted their men, and their desserts, with the sphinxiest of smiles.

21
PANZANO TELLS THE HEARTBREAKING SAGA
OF THE LION STRUCK BY LOVE

WARMED BY THE APRIL MORNING SUN, the boat stuck at Agios Nikolode-onos seemed to be in no hurry to venture from the port.

Twelve nuns-a-knitting, and a hundred-odd passengers, had forgotten all about their destinations. Far away, calling seductively as Homer's sirens, those dreamy islands sparkled gemlike in the sea, promising adventure and romance. But, as the proverb claims, 'It is better to travel hopefully than to arrive.' For the divine experience guaranteed in the brochures proved to be no more than packaged tours, over-refined foods, needless luxuries, and a bill-for-it-all that stabbed the heart with more false passion and perfidy than the right hand of Macbeth.

Yet there was natural beauty on these islands, too, and for the simple heart that beauty felt more than enough. These island hillsides, like the coasts of Crete, welcomed their visitors with white stone houses colored by Greek-blue shutters and doors. I thought of those houses as I glanced at the eleven nuns covered in white-and-blue frocks, standing together calmly, chastely, unspeakably innocent. Their protectress, the Mother-nun — who served her god by censoring truths, forbidding freedom, and hating men — reminded me of a mountain, an island, an undiscovered country fraught with dangers that no guidebook dared describe. No man would return unscathed if his hands caressed those untouched shoulders, or his feet planted themselves near her widespread unpolluted shores.

That Mother-nun — with her age-marked face, yellowed teeth and wisp of a dark mustache — glared at me as she knitted. I answered with a smile, then stood up to stretch and find a cool glass of water to drink. The tallest nun, named Donnabella, anticipated my desires, and handed the water to me in a clear glass. She bowed before me and then turned to face my plump friend.

"Panzano," she said, loud enough for all to hear. "Do you chase women for love or for other things? Have you ever been in love?"

The well-rounded man stood up and then rubbed his belly.

"I am large," he said, "but about Love and those other things I know little. Love is the most dangerous game, because the game plays the man. Love turns every man — young and old, poor and rich, shrewd and stupid — into a slobbering fool."

The nun named Forza stepped forward and waved her arms as she spoke.

"And now, Panzano, you are going to tell us that you know a wise story which proves how your philosophy is true. And that your mind will empty its words to us only when that always-hungry Muse who lives inside your belly gets fed!"

The crowd laughed as Panzano slapped his gut.

"The way I can smell a dinner four hours before it's cooked, this nun can read my thoughts!" he said. "Yes, I can tell you a story that my grandmother told me: 'The Lion Struck By Love'. "

With astonishing agility, Panzano hopped on one foot and danced a bit from a lively Italian dance called the *saltarello.* As he danced briskly he sang:

"And if you want the man to tell—
With breads and cheeses feed him well."

The generosity of the native Greeks — and vacationing tourists — has been recorded many times by thankful travelers, and exploited many more times by lazy vagabonds. Fresh breads and white balls of feta cheese were delivered to Panzano, while beside his tape-wrapped feet one kind woman placed a wooden bowl, which quickly filled up with coins and paper cash. Panzano's eyes filled with tears as he offered his hard-begged food to me. One minute later he began to eat the lion's share, and to tell the lion's tale.

"Nowadays," said Panzano, grasping food with one hand and gesturing with the other, "Mother Nature is a neglected hag. But twenty-five hundred years ago she was a svelte-looking woman, worshiped by men and women everywhere in Greece. In those days men could speak and understand the language of animals and birds. So one day a hunting lion saw a young shepherdess walking with her flock, and he forgot about the sheep and fell instantly in love. He combed his mane, he licked himself clean, and then he found her father and asked him for permission to marry the lovely girl."

Panzano sighed.

"Luckily, this father was a smart biscuit. He knew that even though it would be fatal to take a ferocious lion into his family, it would be far more dangerous to deny the lion's request.

"'My daughter is soft,' he said to the king of cats. 'Let's clip your claws, so that every time you hug her you won't scratch her to shreds.'

"The lion permitted the girl's father to trim his claws, and as soon as this pedicure was finished, the man said to the beast: 'And now we must do something about your sharp teeth. When you can kiss without biting off my daughter's lips, imagine how much more pleasant your kisses will be.'

"The lion imagined this happiness, while the father filed down every sharp molar, incisor, and fang.

"'Now at last,' said the girl's father to the lion, 'we must find out if you have courage. Not only the courage to get married, but courage to defend your bride from anyone who dares to bother her at work or home.'

"Then the shrewd father whistled, and his pack of guard dogs rushed to his side, and then attacked the lovesick lion. Without claws or teeth he stood as helpless as a kitten, and the only way he could defend himself was to run for his life and to hide in a forest far away. In the end the poor beast was left with nothing: not one kiss of love, not one flake of common sense, not one shred of his former strength. That's what Love does to every man and beast, and that is why I flee like a housefly whenever Love buzzes near my careful head."

As the audience laughed and applauded Panzano's story, the shy nun named Dolcezza brought him a kerchief filled with cookies — treats, she explained, that she had baked at the nunnery last night.

"I know these sweet things," Panzano said. "These heart-shaped cookies, baked on holidays to honor holy men, were first called 'Saints' hearts'. And they were served as snacks at the monastery, at the time the evening bells were ringing. And this ringing din made it impossible to hear, so that the name 'Saints' hearts' soon became misunderstood, and they were mistakenly called 'sand tarts'. And that's what they're called to this day."

Panzano devoured the cookie in one bite.

"Many young women," he said, "have started as angels in heaven, and ended up as tarts on the sandy beach."

Sharp-eared Mother Whackanzakis screamed then dashed for Panzano, who tripped over his own feet trying to escape. Again the nuns restrained their Mother-nun, and Panzano stood up slowly, feeling on his scalp for fresh-made lumps.

Dolcezza asked Panzano to sit down on his crate, and when he complied — first checking that Mother-nun was securely held by her daughters — then Dolcezza gently dabbed his head with a damp cloth.

"*Socorro non viene mai tardi*," he said. "Help that comes is never too late."

He looked up into Dolcezza's sparkling eyes.

"*Corpo di Bacco!* Good Heavens!" shouted Panzano. "For the first time I understand the noble lion!" ... And then he slowly murmured: "*Poca favilla gran fiamma seconda!* From one small spark a roaring fire rose!"

Speechless, Panzano stared a-dreaming at the dark eyes of the pretty nun.

The captain's assistant raised his left hand; his wristwatch gleamed, and he announced regretfully that the boat was not yet ready to depart. Except for Dolcezza, eleven nuns continued knitting. Again, the impassioned voice of a female passenger asked Thoreau to tell more stories to the crowd.

And everyone listened attentively, for they knew that what happened to the heroes and heroines might one day happen to them.

22
Who Seduces Who ?

In the year 1933, sigmund freud — who smoked as many as twenty cigars per day — concluded a book with the confession that he could not find a solution to the great enigma: What do women want? ... More than five hundred years earlier, Chaucer's Canterbury character, the Wife of Bath, answered that very question, by telling how men should behave in the same four words: Do what women want!

This thought tingled my neurons and tickled my funconscious mind as I watched Kosmos, curious about the strategies and tactics he would use to accomplish his erotic aim. He set the four small white coffee cups onto the table, winked at me, glanced at Bea, smiled at Prudence, then spoke to us of the murky waters of coffee and desire.

"In Turkey they have a saying: 'Coffee should be dark as night, hot as hell, sweet as love.'"

Kosmos sipped the coffee, licked his lips, smiled with a self-approving nod.

"Perfect. And in Kreetee we have a bawdy song: 'Love is as sweet as coffee, when a Greek man stirs his spoon!' ... The Turks know the secret of making perfect coffee, and the Greeks know the secret of making perfect love."

The face of Prudence wrinkled like a prune.

"Goddess spare us!" she cried out. "In the entire nation of Greece, is there even one man who doesn't bluster about how great he is in bed? The Greek women tell a different story. They say, when it comes to lovemaking, the Greek men are all sizzle and no steak, all flustered and no custard, all bleat and no meat."

Politely, Lady Loverly suppressed a smile, as she stirred one teaspoon of honey into her coffee cup.

"Tell us this, Kosmos," she said. "Why were you two gentleman laughing so riotously in the kitchen a few minutes ago?"

Kosmos, who always found a quick reply, answered without missing a beat.

"Why were we laughing? Because, Beatrice, Thoreau was telling me how indescribably beautiful you are."

Lady Loverly beamed.

"Do tell us more, Mr. Thoreau! Describe the indescribable — isn't that what poets are for? Let me play Roxanne to your Cyrano. Improvise! Fantasize! Rhapsodize!"

I glanced at Kosmos, telling him with my eyes that I would repay him tit-for-tat for his work as my unauthorized matchmaker. I lit the candle on the table then raised my goblet.

"To the beauty of candlelight, and the greater beauty of what this candlelight shines upon."

Lady Loverly sighed. "Is that all, Mr. Thoreau? Every woman deserves at least fifteen minutes of flame, not merely fifteen words."

Kosmos, a consummate artist of the impromptu, jumped in to help. And his help was like shouting "Catch this!" to a man sinking in quicksand — then throwing an anvil, an anchor, and a bowling ball.

"Is that all?" said Kosmos. "Of course that is not all! Thoreau was telling me that you, Beatrice Loverly, have more and better curves than —"

Kosmos winked at me as he waited for me to round off the sentence with witty words of praise. I looked at the lovely lady.

"She has better and more curves than a textbook of Euclidean geometry."

Loverly laughed. "I'm sure I've never before been compared to a mathematics textbook, Mr. Thoreau. Please go on."

Mark Twain was right when he wrote: "Praise, like gold, derives its value due to its scarcity."

I studied this gorgeous woman, surprised that she'd been pleased by my simple words. Then I recalled that years ago, a beautiful woman with long slender legs had told me that she had never been asked for a date, because all the men she met naturally assumed they had no chance with her. We treat beautiful women and handsome men differently than we treat the less-gifted physically endowed. But it might be better for everyone involved if we treated the beautiful persons just the same as if they were not so good-looking, and we treated the ordinary persons as if they were as lovely as the goddesses and gods.

Kosmos, who had been enjoying himself immensely, glanced at Lady Loverly, then spoke again.

"Thoreau," he said. "tell us about the skin on her body."

I looked at the skin on her body.

"Softer, smoother, creamier than yogurt from Vrisses."

"Her eyes?" asked Kosmos.

"Was it that thief Prometheus?" I asked. "Who plucked two stars from the skies of night!"

"Her nose?"

"The perfect size, the perfect place, the center of a perfect face."

"Her lips?"

"Sweeter than Hymettus honey."

"Her teeth?"

"Oysters in the Sea of Crete would brag to have them as their pearls."

"Her hair?"

"What magic calls me in its curls? Surprise! — When her hair falls, I rise!"

"Her arms?"

"Venus de Milo has none better."

"Her legs?"

"Smooth roads with no stop signs, meeting in paradise."

"Her breasts?" said Kosmos, just about to burst with laughter.

"Her breasts are the peaks of Mount Parnassus. Spend one night there and either you become divinely inspired, or you go mad."

"Bravo, Thoreaukritos!" shouted Kosmos, applauding with his mighty hands. "Bravo and bravissimo!"

Lady Loverly seized my hand. She wiped two tears from her sparkling eyes.

"That was so charming, Mr. Thoreau! Thank you so much, really. And here I had been worrying if there was something you didn't like about my breasts. You've hardly glanced at them all evening."

"I was trying to be polite, Beatrice," I said. "If I let myself go, then you'd be spending all evening fishing my eyeballs out of your cleavage."

"My dear boy," Loverly answered. "Don't you believe in setting a good example? If all men in history had been as polite to all women in a similar manner, then the human species would have died out two million years ago."

Prudence twirled a carrot stick between her fingers, then brushed it like lipstick across her lips.

"Imagine," she said. "We'd all be swinging in banana trees today."

Prudence, like the sister I'd never had, placed her free hand onto my shoulder. Her eyes, which had been staring at me, flickered with a pyrotechnic gleam. An unabashed admiration which at times means love, at times means lust, at times means a potent cocktail of these two unwieldy powers. In the eyes of a woman we desire, that ready gleam is the promise of enjoyment. In the eyes of a woman with less appeal, that same gleam is the guarantee of grief.

Carrying my cider-filled goblet, I walked around the table to stand behind Kosmos, then patted his grey-bearded cheek.

"Prudence," I said. "While Kosmos and I were laughing in the kitchen, what were you and Lady Loverly whispering about?"

"Something my mother told me, Thoreau," Prudence replied. "It takes a woman less time to decide which man she likes, than it takes her to decide which dress to wear for dinner."

Despite her ordinary appearance — sitting beside Lady Loverly, only one woman in ten thousand would not look ordinary — I at last recognized a certain likable vitality in Prudence. Now it would be her turn to be complimented, flattered, and praised.

"A tale half-finished is a tale untold," I said. "Moments ago, in that cosmic kitchen, where so many schemes are concocted and ideas are brewed, the body of Lady Loverly was not the only topic of our praise. Kosmos praised Prudence to Pluto and beyond. He told me how your darting glances made him quiver, and how he would be thrilled to glance your quiver with his darts. In fact, for you alone he composed a song."

"Bravo, Kosmos!" shouted Lady Loverly. "Let her play Eurydice to your Orpheus. Extemporize! Dramatize! Satirize! ... But don't look back!"

The eyes of Kosmos, as he stared at Prudence, glowed first with the cool glance of Apollo, then with Dionysus's fiery leer. He sipped some coffee, laughed and shook his head.

"Thank you for reminding me, Thoreau," he said, with a playful smile. "Just give me a moment to make — I mean, remember something about it."

After another gulp of coffee, Kosmos began the risqué song slowly, then finished with a crescendoing flourish.

"It is called, 'The Archers'," he said.

"Sweet maid, thou art the target just —
 Of the burning arrow of my lust.
 Bold sir, how swiftly through the skies —
 The target to the arrow flies!"

I laughed at this rare bard of the air. Lady Loverly was the first to realize that this tune could be sung harmoniously as a round — a rhythmical canon where each part enters in unison at equal intervals of time. We sang a few choruses, each of us starting one line after the other, my baritone voice followed by Lady Loverly's mezzo-soprano, then Prudence's alto pursued by Kosmos's bass behind.

This fine performance, transforming doggerel into delightful song, was concluded with our laughter and applause. And now Prudence, still gazing with a dangerous glimmer at the two men, undid the bun of her brown hair and let it drop down past her shoulders. A woman who lets down her hair after dinner is more dangerous than a Western gunfighter pulling out his pistol at high noon.

"Kosmos," said Prudence. "All the while you were singing that adolescent jingle you were staring blatantly at my chest. Might I infer that your song is hinting at some posterior motive that might be called disgusting?"

Roused by the woman's hair and the prospect of a deep conversation, Kosmos leaned forward on the edge of his chair.

"What do you call disgusting, Prudence? The fact that a man finds you sexually attractive? Or the fact that a man has the courage to candidly express that feeling?"

Prudence leaned forward. Her eyes smoldered with feminist fire.

"What I find disgusting is the fact that you look at me as a woman to be utilized for sex, and not as a whole human being. Do you imagine that any intelligent woman would be seduced by those silly words?"

Kosmos snatched her twirling carrot stick, stuck it into a bowl of dip, then handed it back to her.

"Of course not," Kosmos said. "I imagine that any intelligent woman would understand the poem as a go-ahead signal, a welcome mat that says she could successfully seduce the man who sang those words."

Prudence stood up. Now she was shouting.

"What impudent blither-blather! How dare you insult every woman by insinuating that in the jungle of sex, women are the ferocious predators!"

Kosmos wagged his head. "The jungle of sex! I like that. But dear Prudence, I was not insinuating anything, I was simply stating a truth compressed into a pleasant song. Women chase men for many reasons: for love, to get children, for financial security, and for sex. These are well-known facts."

Prudence's reply, crisper than stale crackers, would have dried the throat of almost any man.

"Any man who believes those so-called facts," she said sharply, "is an oppressor of women who seeks to increase his power!"

Kosmos replied straightaway.

"Any woman who disbelieves them is lying to herself about her own needs and desires."

Prudence removed her glasses then slipped them into a flower-covered case.

"Ah, now I can see your lovely eyes!" said Kosmos. "Men don't make passes at girls who wear glasses."

Prudence shook her fist at Kosmos.

"And girls don't get crushes on men with big tushes."

In between these two antagonists I softly stepped.

"Look, what a bizarre coincidence! We've all finished our tiny cups of coffees at the same time. Was it a Greek philosopher, or a college entrance exam, that said: 'Car motors is to heavy-duty oil as good conversation is to strong coffee.'? ... Kosmos, can you help me in the kitchen for a moment?"

We gathered the empty cups then stepped into the kitchen. I placed my hand on his shoulder.

"Kosmos, you once told me 'You can say anything to anyone, as long as you say it cheerfully.' Do you remember?"

"I remember."

"Well," I said, smiling. "How goes the war, Casanova?"

"Read his autobiography, Thoreau. All twelve volumes. No man makes the right moves with women all the time. But at least —"

He glanced at me then poked his finger into my ribs.

" — at least some men have pistachios enough to try."

We returned to the dining table. I set down the coffee while Kosmos picked up the debate.

"Where were we?" Kosmos asked.

Prudence, with her ring-covered hand, brushed her long hair back behind her neck.

"We were swirling in the vortex of a vicious disagreement. I was telling you that men seduce women."

Kosmos slapped his hands against the table.

"And I was saying that you have everything bass ackwards. The women seduce the men!"

"That is a myth," shouted Prudence, "perpetrated by power-seeking males!"

"Kosmos," I said, trying to lighten the mood of things. "It looks to me like you've met your match."

Kosmos waved his arm.

"Thoreau," he replied, "you are always wondering how to keep the fire alive in a relationship. And now I will tell you: 'When you meet your match, strike her.' ... That is a matchless metaphor: as you know, I would never hit a woman, even if she hit me first."

Prudence grabbed her purse and stood up as if to leave.

"Where are you going, my beauty!" Kosmos shouted. "One hour under the spell of my lovemaking, and you will clutch me in your tentacles like an octopus sticking to the rocks!"

"I understand you now!" shrieked Prudence. "You're the kind of barbarian who thinks a man should never put a foot in the kitchen, and a woman should never get her feet out of the bedroom!"

Kosmos laughed.

"A man like me should spend more time in the kitchen. A woman like you should spend more time in the bedroom. Then you will understand all men, and especially men like me."

Prudence clenched her fists.

"A woman is more than an animal in heat!"

Kosmos opened his arms.

"A woman is a very hot animal, Prudence. And whenever the animal in a person is denied, that person can never discover life's higher and deeper things."

"You are an impossible man!"

"You are an irresistible woman! All evening you flirt with me. And the minute I respond, you react with the innocent behavior calculated to fuel my flames, and to make me desire you one thousand times more! At last, you deny the first stubborn fact of muliebrity — a woman will do anything to snare her man!"

Prudence stamped her foot.

"Flirting with you! Mr. Kosmos that is utterly ridiculous! In what way was I flirting?"

Kosmos leaned forward. The tip of his nose and the nosetip of Prudence were so close together that the wing of a damselfly could not have squeezed between.

"You were flirting in a dozen ways. The way you didn't look at me. The way you ignored me to stare at Thoreau. The way you laughed at my jokes. The way you tap-tap-tapped your foot under the table. The way your hair slid down your shoulders like a falling dress. The way you ate that cucumber. The way you admired that painting of the satyr. The way you licked your lips when you drank your wine. The way your fingers twirled that slice of carrot. Sometimes a carrot stick is more than just a carrot stick."

Prudence screamed, stamped her foot, threw a glass, and then exhibited other symptoms of tempestuous behavior that indicated she was having — as the English-speaking Greeks called it — 'a sheet-feet'. At last, when the emotional tornado untwisted into a full-blown storm, she smushed her dip-covered carrot stick between the two largest wrinkles on her admirer's furrowed forehead.

"Mister Kosmos. You are a vile man. An odious man. A contemptible man. A despicable man. An abhorrent man. A devious man. A detestable man. A loathsome man. An offensive man. A repulsive man. An abominable man. A nauseating man. And I don't like you at all!"

The bearded man's eyes gleamed as he laughed a roaring laugh.

"That explains why it feels so easy to be with you, Prudence. With you, I have no lofty expectations to live up to!"

"Oh!" Prudence shouted. "I am fumigating! ... Mr. Kosmos, you are living proof of the radical feminist credo: 'From the neck down, all men are animals. And from the neck up, all men are idiots!'"

Kosmos digested this skewed world-view with his typical exasperating calm.

"My dear Prudence, why should a woman hate all men because of what a few bad men have done?"

"Mr. Kosmos, a barrel of rotten apples with a few good seeds in it is still a barrel of rotten apples."

"Tell the truth," said Kosmos. "You hate me because I am a man."

"Never!" shouted Prudence. "I hate men because of men like you."

Kosmos, who had thoroughly studied Aristotle's *Rhetoric*, knew that the effective sales pitch always concluded with a call for action.

"Prudence," Kosmos pleaded. "Share one night with me. One wild inspired night! You have nothing to lose but your virginity. And you will wake up so inflated with love, that never again will you hate any man, or any human being on this new sweet earth."

"You are a sex maniac!" Prudence screamed.

"No, dear Prudence," said Kosmos coolly. "I am not a sex maniac, I am a love maniac. I love beauty, I love women, I love sex. If there were more men like me then the war between the sexes would be over in five minutes, because women and men would surrender in each other's arms."

"Oh, what egomania!" Prudence shouted. "Mr. Kosmos, you have a condition known to the medical establishment as satyriasis. I should have known it when I saw that *taramosálata* phallus. That was an abomination!"

Kosmos laughed. "That was an autobiographical work of art! A thing of beauty to enjoy forever."

"If you were my husband, Kosmos, I'd give you poison!"

"Prudence, if you were my wife, I'd take it."

At this repartee, Lady Loverly scurried to the doorway then slipped under the blanket to the cool outside. A slight nod from the head of Kosmos told me to follow. When I found her, Lady Loverly was leaning against a wall of Kosmos's stone house, laughing like the muse of comedy.

"Aren't they just wonderful together," she said, laughing and laughing more.

"The quintessential blind date," I said, admiring how beautiful she looked as she laughed. "But Beatrice, do you think we should intervene in the battle between Prudence and the Kosmic forces? Or at least try to distract them by talking about some neutral theme."

She smiled knowingly.

"My dear Mr. Thoreau. It is not just your handsome face and virile body that women are attracted to, it is your simple goodness. If only those lovely eyes of yours could see when a woman and a man want to be alone together."

The blanket swung back and a shouting Prudence rushed out of the house.

"That absolute idiot! That mindless chauvinist! That heartless Don Juan!"

One moment later, Kosmos burst through the doorway, carrying the tools of the seducer's trade: in his left hand a flower and a guitar, in his right hand a box of chocolates and a bottle of the finest Cretan wine.

23
AH, LOVE, LET US BE TRUE

THE MORE WE LIVE, THE MORE WE LEARN that few things in life are indispensable. But there is one phrase which every tourist and traveler to the land of Greece must learn by heart: *"Dhen eena teepota! Dhen eena teepota!"* It means, literally: "It's nothing! It's nothing!" And whenever a Greek man shouts this phrase to you — when your luggage is late, your hotel room is cold, your bill is incorrect, or his hand is creeping up your thigh — then by a strange admixture of language and culture, you can be positively certain that this two-faced phrase now means: "It's something, it's something!"

In the garden, Prudence had sat down underneath a tree with orange blossoms, and Kosmos — shouting *"Dhen eena teepota!"* — followed her then sat down beside. Near the feuding lovebirds beneath the tree, Irene lay on the grass, a camera in her hand, sleeping deeply like a perfect child.

Lady Loverly touched my arm.

"Mr. Thoreau," she said. "Shall we butter two bread slices with one knife? If we take Irene back to my hotel room, I can begin her sentimental education, and we can leave Prudence and Kosmos to conclude their quarrel by either reviling each other, or uniting in sexual bliss."

Lady Loverly ran back into the house to get her purse, while I approached Kosmos to tell him we were leaving with Irene. Prudence and Kosmos — the irresistible object and the immovable farce — were still sitting under the orange tree. Kosmos smiled unconcerned as Prudence swore at him, as Englishwomen do, with a "Bloody!" this and a "Bloody!" that and a "Bloody!" other thing.

But Kosmos was a fire, and anything thrown at the fire — the kindest words, the coldest apathy, or even the most severe abuse — all served to feed the flames. The charismatic man strummed his guitar and chanted in his dreadful imitation of a Britishly-accented voice.

"Your vanity is ridiculous, your conduct an outrage, and your presence in my garden is utterly absurd."

How could he have known, I wondered — what genre of genius is this? — that this irreverent line, from the great play by Oscar Wilde, would calm the woman down?

"Can you be serious for just a moment, Kosmos?" Prudence said, separating her hair in the middle, and tying it into two pigtails.

Kosmos observed this preening gesture with sparks of fascination glimmering from his delighted eyes.

"I can be serious for a moment, Prudence. But not much longer than that."

Prudence shook a handful of chubby fingers at him.

"I never meant to say, Kosmos, that your opinions were immoral or obscene. I'm trying to explain that your ideas are irresponsible. If practiced they would lead to unhappiness and anarchy."

Loudly did the voice of Kosmos laugh.

"More unhappiness and anarchy than we have now?" he said. "I can't believe that, not at all. Give freedom a chance, dear one, and let's see if freedom makes the world better or makes the world worse."

Kosmos opened the box of chocolates, placed it in front of Prudence, then spoke to her in a serious tone.

"Prudence, love, think about this: Could our problem be that you are intrigued by me, you are attracted to me, you even like me a little bit — but you're not accustomed to my style? ... Most men will lie to you and deceive you just to get into your bed. Men who are nothing will say anything. Not Kosmos, never! He will never tell you a lie. He will tell you that he likes your mind, your spirit, and he wants to explore your body for one sweet night. Then if you like him, and he likes you, the program can continue — one day at a time — until the magic fades. 'Enter and leave freely,' is my motto: that was the sign that Tolstoy placed over the door of his school for peasant kids. With Kosmos, you get no improbable promises, no insincere flattery, no — how do the crude Americans say it — no shit from the bull."

Again I smiled as I discovered a new reason to admire this bold man: he always spoke his truth, he spoke it cheerfully, he never wasted a care about how others would respond. And speaking his truth was even more important to him than winning this woman he so ardently desired.

Kosmos now looked relaxed, imperturbable, serene — as if he had played these kinds of games a thousand times before. He reminded me of a fisherman sitting calmly in the boat as the fish hovered near the bait. He would always do his best, and thus there was nothing to fear and nothing to worry about, not now and not evermore. He knew that only two things could happen: either the fish would never bite, or the fish had been hooked from the very start.

He had been concentrating his whole attentions on Prudence, but suddenly he sensed my presence and he turned to me.

"Ah, Thoreau! You're leaving to take Irene back with Beatrice. You can take my truck — it's a twelve-kilometer drive along a sinuous asphalt road — or you can walk the three kilometers along the beach. My crystal ball tells me that you will choose to walk, enjoy a brilliant dialogue with Beatrice, and then you'll stupidly refuse her offer to stay overnight in the spare bed in her hotel room. Then you will walk back to this garden, torn by the war between the great free man inside you, and your enslaving conscience. Curse that pipsqueaking judge a thousand times!"

Affectionately, Kosmos slapped my shoulder.

"Tonight you'll sleep in my library. Move the books around, it doesn't matter where they go. Tomorrow morning we must talk. I have a story to tell you. A very personal story. A story that will stay with you and change your life. And mine too, I hope. Nine o'clock tomorrow morning. Meet me in the kitchen for breakfast."

He glanced at Prudence then smacked his lips.

"No, let's make that eleven o'clock for what you call brunch. Is all this good for you, my friend?"

"I'll be there, Kosmos. But methinks this lady doth protest just the right amount. It looks like the great Kosmos, the Bard of Dembacchae, will be free at nine tomorrow morning. And I'll even bet that you'll be free twelve hours earlier than that."

He winked at me with a gleaming eye.

"The loser of the bet, Thoreau, can make brunch for the three of us."

He said goodnight and clasped my hand warmly between his two strong hands. Then he turned to the woman who — by all appearances — hated his garrulous guts.

"Ah, Prudence! How my proud prod prayed to propagate this preponderated prude! Green is the moon with envy when she beams on Prue! Thus shamed, she hides her beaming face behind the clouds. And the gods will shake their thunderbolts and shout: 'Hermes, is this your prank? This loveliest of all the moons has fallen to the Earth!'"

Prudence listened, all the while shaking her pig-tailed head and shimmering her pig-headed tail.

"You are incorrigible, Kosmos! Stop staring at me that way! Can't you look at me without leering at my chest?"

Talking is not the only way to answer questions. Kosmos started strumming and singing another of his ad-libbed songs.

> "A frisky cat looked at a Queen,
> O troll-dee roll-dee ray-o! ...
> The fairest sight he'd ever seen,
> In many-a many-a day-o!"

"Will you please shut up and listen!" Prudence shouted above the song. Exasperated, she sat down on a stone bench. "Why are you laughing now, Kosmos?"

"Because all this is so funny, my dear sweet Prude!" he said. "Don't you see why we're a perfect match? You can stay calm for almost as long as I can stay serious."

And Kosmos continued to strum and to sing more verses of improvised songs.

Under the orange tree I whispered to Irene.

"Irene?"

"Who is it?" she replied, her eyes still dreamily closed.

"Irenaki mou."

"Thoreau!"

"No. It's Pegasus, your wonderful winged horse. Would you like a ride?"

Much closer to sleep than wake, three times she nodded her pretty head.

A bustle of growls and a blur of fur, and then I saw Zorba the mutt run past me, chased by a female dog named Bouboulina.

"Mr. Thoreau! Yoo-hoo boo-hoo, Mr. Thoreau!"

The blithe voice of Lady Loverly had been calling. I found her sitting on the ground, alone and appearing lonely, faraway gazing into the evening sky.

"I'm so sorry, dear," she said. Her eyes, failing to look into mine for the first time, faced the golden-red sunset. "I need to ask you for assistance. I'm afraid I've fallen over a root and turned my ankle."

"Which one, Beatrice?"

"The left one, I suppose."

The house of Kosmos had no refrigerator and no ice: he insisted his food must be fresh. Instead of icing the ankle I did the next best thing. I grabbed my T-shirt at the neck collar, ripped it off my chest, tore it into rectangular rags, then wrapped the cloth strips around Beatrice's left ankle. Then I placed Irene on my back in the piggyback position, asked her if she could hold on, and after she said "Yes, forever!" I returned to the passenger next.

"Beatrice, I know that you and Irene are going to become great friends. And I don't want to come between you two, but — "

Lady Loverly screamed delightedly, then laughed like a young girl, as I raised her into the air and carried her in my outstretched arms.

In this way we traveled like some mythical three-headed beast, Irene on my back and Beatrice in my arms, her arms circled tightly around my neck. I strode through the small streets of the town and found the dirt road leading to the beach. From a house nearby, two dogs barked and growled, and Irene tightened her grip around me, then whispered that she had always had been afraid of large dogs. The dogs barked again, sounding even more vicious, and just when I assured Irene that I would protect her, we heard the sound of two loud whistles, presumably from the owner of the dogs. The fearful noises ceased and the night again was filled with silence and the stars.

How tenderly the night embraced us as we walked on the soft sand! The moon shined brightly, the cicadas sang, the girl breathed like a warm breeze, the woman laughed like murmurs from the sea. Lady Loverly and I talked about so many things — art, books, music, Greece, England, vegetarianism, the suffering in the world, the rapture of being alive.

To catch my full attention, to bring me from the world of ideas back to the present moment, the woman squeezed her arms around my neck.

"Thoreau, do you know that man?"

"Which man, Beatrice?"

"That elderly man with a donkey who just walked by us," she said. "He smiled to you and waved as if he were your best friend."

Gazing at Beatrice, I had turned around too late to see the wise old man.

"That must have been Kosmos's father," I said. "We met recently in an olive grove."

Lady Loverly laughed at this.

"What were you thinking about so intensely, dear?"

"About Kosmos's living room walls, and about the chance for Paradise on Earth," I said.

"Paradise," echoed Lady Loverly, pressing against me. "Paradise, dear one, could be closer, much closer, than you imagine."

Here the sandy shoreline curved into the shape of a smile and for a long stretch — maybe the length of three city blocks — the lights from the towns at the two ends of the beach disappeared from view. And everywhere along the lips of this smile, the whole world looked exquisitely beautiful: nothing man-made could be seen, only sand, water, moon, stars in the night sky.

For many steps we traveled silently, listening with great attention to the night's inspired sounds.

"You're smiling at something, Thoreau," said Lady Loverly. "Is it because tonight is the most wonderful night of your life?"

At this suggestion I smiled more.

"I was thinking of a line from Emerson. 'Though we travel the world over to find the beautiful, we must carry it with us or we find it not.'"

"Thoreau, dear, is that line an objective quote or a personal compliment?"

"It is both, Beatrice. And I wonder what the fiery Emerson would have written had he known you and your triple beauty: beauty of body, mind, and heart. There's a radiance inside you — a glowing that's childlike and magical, and gives joy to everyone you meet."

Wiping her eyes, the woman turned her head away. In trying to say just the right thing, perhaps I had said just the wrong thing.

"Are you getting tired, Beatrice? Does your ankle hurt very much?"

Twice she shook her head, and her soft hair brushed against my chest. Filled with two tears and a thousand stars, the eyes of the woman gazed into my eyes.

"The sea is calm tonight," she said.

And smiling, I answered, looking at the sea.

"The tide is full, the moon lies fair Upon the straits."

"Continue, Thoreau, please," she said. "I didn't imagine that you would know our Matthew Arnold."

As the sea sang beside us, we continued to recite from the poem *Dover Beach*. Together we spoke the last stanza of the poem.

"Ah, love, let us be true

To one another! for the world, which seems
To lie before us like a land of dreams,
So various, so beautiful, so new,
Hath really neither joy, nor love, nor light,
Nor certitude, nor peace, nor help for pain;
And we are here as on a darkling plain
Swept with confused alarms of struggle and flight,
Where ignorant armies clash by night."

"Somewhere along his journey," said Beatrice, "dear Matthew lost his youthful optimism, and then ended his poem with five lines of disillusionment. How strange that we lose contact with our land of dreams! I wonder ... "

The woman squeezed her arms around me just a bit more tightly.

"You wondered?" I said.

"How passionately I would hold on to it, if I could ever find that beautiful new world."

"You can rewrite the last lines of Arnold's poem, Beatrice."

"Dear love, I've rewritten it a dozen times. And it never comes out right. I'll never be able to do it until I believe again in happy endings. ... Oh dear, we can't be here already but we are."

We arrived at Lady Loverly's seaside hotel which sat in the nearest town west of Dembacchae. Usually during this off-season time the hotel would be empty, but now its luxurious rooms were filled with WANDERBORE members, relaxing after their conference. The chairwoman of this conference rested in my arms; her newest admirer hugged my back. Under these cheerful burdens I climbed three stair-flights to the fourth floor. After Loverly directed me to the door of her hotel room, I released the lady and set down Irene.

"Irene," I said. You'll stay overnight tonight with Aphrodite. Do you like that idea?"

Eyes closed, she nodded yes, then hugged me and kissed my cheek.

"Ares," she said. "Will you play with me tomorrow?"

"When I'm done talking with Kosmos, Irene. Some time before dinner, we can play whatever you want to play."

Lady Loverly swung her arm around Irene's shoulders, led her through the doorway, and then spoke to her with motherly affection.

"We'll take good care of you here, Irene dearest. My daughter Rebecca and her friend Juliette will be your sisters tonight. Dear Thoreau, can you wait for a moment? I have something I must give you."

The porch outside the room provided a marvelous view of the sea. I was looking at the rolling waves when Lady Loverly returned, quietly closing the door behind her. She had changed from her low-cut evening dress into a boldly diaphanous nightgown. The soft curls of her long black hair, recently unpinned, fell shiningly to just above her waist.

"This is for you, Thoreau," the woman said. "Some fruits and nuts and drinks to replenish the calories you've expended in carrying us here. Don't you dare refuse it out of pride. Would Odysseus have reached home safely without help from the queen of the Scherians, or without continual attention from his benefactress Athena? ... Bright-eyed Athena and bright-eyed Thoreau. Tell me what you're thinking, love."

When a gorgeous woman charms us, how quickly we forget about the beauty of the sea. And how quickly we forget everything else. Lady Loverly looked so stunningly gorgeous that all I could do was admire and silently stare.

At last I had to speak and break the spell.

"You look like ... a goddess that saves the lives of heroes," I said. "Or a princess with a perfect heart, searching for a fairy tale."

The woman, raising both hands, captured her hair and brushed it behind her head, revealing her veiled breasts and her glowing face.

"And suppose the goddess invited her hero to stay the night in the extra bed in her hotel room?"

The footloose words of Kosmos came back to kick me in the pants.

"Not tonight, Beatrice, I have a heartache. To be honest, I think I'm becoming a little too much attracted to you. And in a moment of weakness I might make advances to you that we would both regret."

"A moment of weakness or of wisdom, Thoreau? If a man finds a woman beautiful and he doesn't make advances, then what can he do but regress? ... I can read your heart, love. Your eyes say you want to stay here with me tonight, if only you understood how much! For deceiving yourself I forgive you, since soon you shall forgive me for deceiving you. Think of the poor princess you've mentioned! Perhaps at last she has found a prince, but a sliver of ice in his heart has turned his love for her into the coldest apathy."

"Ice!" I shouted. "We were going to put ice on your ankle, to reduce the swelling and the pain. How is your ankle feeling, Lady Loverly?"

"Which ankle, dear?"

"The one you injured."

"Which one was that?"

"The left one, you supposed."

Tears burst from the woman's eyes as she covered her face. Her voluptuous body shook under shivering weeps. As I watched her crying I remembered something I had heard from Kosmos. The gods know everything except three things: how to change the fated future, how to change the stone-carved past, and how to stop a woman's tears. Between the bursts of sobs poor Lady Loverly confessed.

"My dear Thoreau, I have a terrible thing to tell you! ... I'm so ashamed! ... Earlier this evening I gleaned that you and I might never see each other again. Never! Can you understand what that means, dearest? Two stars in the long dark night, the sky's only lights, finding each other at last — then separating into eternal darkness! ... So I pretended to be injured. What woman would not deceive you to be carried in your arms? ... Oh, I've never done a thing like this before! I feel dreadful about it now. You're so trusting, dear one. The persons we care about, and the persons who care about us, deserve nothing less than our honesty, perfect and complete. And now, even if you do forgive me — "

With her nightgown the woman wiped her eyes.

" — never again will you trust me as before! Never!"

Tears gushed out and more sobs shook this loveliest of forms. I watched her, helplessly, until another goddess whispered words into my ears.

"Beatrice, there's no need to be upset. There's all the difference in the world between the malevolent deception of Machiavelli, and the admirable ingenuity of Odysseus. You're like the Greek goddesses — they never tell lies, except when they are making love or making war."

Beatrice sniffled.

"But aren't the goddesses always making love or war?"

"That's what goddesses are for," I said, smiling. "And gods are for compassion, so I forgive you now and evermore. And I trust you completely. The ankle misadventure was a game and we both enjoyed it. No harm's been done. The only thing that matters to me is that you're not really hurt."

These sympathetic sentences caused another outbreak of streaming tears.

"You're so good, and you're so good to me, Thoreau. I'm so fortunate to know you. Never again will I deceive you. I swear it."

With these words of thanks, Lady Loverly gazed into my eyes, her eyes glowing serene with rapture and gratitude and bliss. Another glow in the sky, half as bright as her eyes, made me shout with joy.

"Look, Beatrice! A shooting star! Make a wish before it vanishes."

The burning head and tail of this resplendent meteor streaked across the night sky then wholly disappeared.

"In our corner of England, Thoreau, if you want your wish to come true, you have to tell the wish to the first person you see. I wished, Thoreau, that you get whatever you just wished for."

"And I wished, Beatrice, that you get whatever you just wished for. That doesn't leave us with very much, does it?"

We laughed and laughed together at this waste of precious wishes. And then from inside the hotel room we heard a call from a sleepy voice.

"Mother," shouted Becca, "are you coming in? We need you! Irene has never heard of a vagina!"

"Oh, dear," the woman sighed. "Mother! In the entire twenty volumes of the unabridged Oxford English dictionary, 'Mother' is most wonderfully rewarding and terribly responsible of all the words."

"Beatrice," I said. "I'm not very good at saying goodnights or goodbyes."

"Then I'll teach you, Thoreau. First, you place your hands on my shoulders and say 'Dear Beatrice, with your hair unleashed you look so beautiful I can't resist kissing you goodnight. To do otherwise would deny your loveliness.' And then you step closer to me, and let yourself fall forward towards my lips. But just as you're about to kiss me, I place my hands in front of me and stop you. Like a proper Englishwoman, I gently but firmly push you away. I remind you that I'm a married woman, older than you by six years. Then, as we shake hands with the epitome of chilled politeness, we say goodnight."

To the letter, I followed the instructions and I spoke the words. But when I leaned towards her, instead of pushing me away, Lady Loverly let me fall forward and my lips touched ever-so lightly against her lips.

"Don't you ever dare kiss me like that!" shouted Lady Loverly.

Then the woman wrapped her arms around my neck and whispered: "Kiss me like this!"

Beatrice pressed her body against my body, crushed her lips against my lips, then kissed me slowly, sensually, with feverish passion and rapturous tenderness. She rubbed her breasts against my chest, then gently chewed my lip, then stepped back and pushed opened her door.

"I hope that the next time we meet, Mr. Thoreau," she said, with a winsome smile, "you will do a much better job of controlling your impetuous passion."

She placed her hand over her heart and aimed her dark-eyed glance into my eyes.

"Odysseus, will you play with me tomorrow?" she asked.

"We can — "

"Play whatever I want to play!"

"We can take a walk tomorrow night, Beatrice."

"I love to hear you say my name."

"Beatrice."

"Love?"

"*Kaleeneekta,* Beatrice. Goodnight."

Before she disappeared behind the door, Beatrice raised my hand to her lips, nipped it with her teeth, blessed my fingers with three kisses, then said goodnight with a wildly tender glance from her enticing eyes.

The moon shined bright as I walked back along the sandy beach. The thrilling sounds of night were lost beneath a blaring introspection.

"What is right? ... How could I hurt another man, by making love with his sacred wife? ... It could destroy the relationship. It could wipe out years of commitment, burning those years into ashes of bitter regrets. I've always been amazed how other people, how other women mostly, forgive their husbands for these betrayals of trust."

I lay down on the sand, looked up at the sky, listened to the stirring sounds all-trembling in the night. My lips still burned with the forbidden kiss.

"But suppose Lady Loverly's husband doesn't love her anymore? And suppose he has a dozen other women and a closetful of clandestine affairs? Then should the woman-wife do the same? Of course she should. ... But even if her husband doesn't betray, even if he's perfect — why should I deprive this woman of her happiness with me? Is real happiness a common thing in this brief life, so common that a man can close his eyes and let it go? What man is rich enough for that? ... "

Many footsteps later, carrying the bag of food from Lady Loverly, I returned to the garden of Kosmos and nearly walked into the body of Prudence. Naked as a nymph — her long brown hair flowing behind her,

her face aglow, her wild laughter ringing through the night — Prudence chased Kosmos across the garden grass. Not Prudence the prude: this was a new woman, a woman reborn, transformed by three great ecstasies: laughter, lust, and love.

Kosmos, too, looked like a different man. Naked and laughing, his round white belly and his large untanned buttocks shined under the moonlight like three more moons. He too, transformed by happiness, had grown young again through the kosmic dance of love. Now and again the man would stop moving to let the woman catch him and embrace him. The upcoming lovers would hug, then kiss, then sing to each other, then whisper secret things, then begin again the game of running and chasing and laughing through this sweetest night.

Once more my eyes turned to the night sky, glad to see the winking stars. After watching these stars I walked into Kosmos's library, made a pillow by stuffing clothes into my pillow case, then lay down on the floor amidst the books. Screams of joy and laughter, ringing from the garden, made me smile.

Seekers and dreamers, never despair, clues to life's secrets are everywhere. The classic books, all the lovely landscapes and living things, and the great stars forever in the sky at night. And wild men like Kosmos who love life so much, they dare to follow their deepest voice. And glorious women like Beatrice and Prudence, who teach us foolish men by offering us everything — their bodies, their minds, their hearts all flowingover with the radiance of love.

Men, poor men! How dense we are! ... Why can't we learn from women — each day anew! — to see, to touch, to feel, to understand?

24
No Man Can Serve Two Mistresses

"The night, october wildness, moon like a lemon pie, lovers' laughter spreading a daffiness wail over the immortal nakedness of geese. Many are the joys of this world — women, women with fruit, women with ideas. But to slide your feet into new sneakers, lacing them up and murmuring the number of each eyelet, is to my mind the joy most apt to transport the body of man into paradise."

It was just one hour before midnight when I woke up, dreaming of a memorable passage by Kazantzakis. I counted the eleven dongs from a nearby church steeple; I tried not to listen to the raucous mirth bellowing from the bedroom beside. I lit a candle, then unwrapped the gift that Lady Loverly had given earlier this evening. The gift was a new pair of sneakers and a new pair of socks: they fit perfectly, they felt marvelous, they inspired me to daring feats.

During the hour while I had slept, my erotic dilemma was solved unconsciously. Nature conquered conscience once again. I grasped that I had nothing to give Beatrice Loverly except my whole self, my laughter, my fiery love. Now I knew what needed to be done. I would get up immediately, walk across the beach to the hotel, knock on Beatrice's door, then ask if I had correctly interpreted her subtle hints that she wanted me to share her bed. If she said yes, then I would give her a night she would never in a hundred years forget.

Would she say 'Yes!'? Perhaps I had mistranslated the language of the heart: the woman's eyes, her smiles, her touches, her voice's tenderness. For each woman is unique: some women flirt with men who mean less than nothing to them, and other women hide their feelings from men they passionately love. And the only way to find out how she felt about me would be to quit playing games and simply ask.

The walls of Cretan homes were thin, and the singing voice of Kosmos scratched the night.

"Have some more *krassi*, m'lassie ..."

The lassie laughed and kissed Kosmos like a plunger in a toilet bowl.

"Shhhh!" Prudence loudly whispered, giggling between the words of the reprimand. "Be quiet, Kosmos, you'll wake Thoreau."

I had known many love-filled nights where quiet was required, and many nights where we could scream and freely shout. And I loved more the nights when man and woman played with shoutings and with screams.

"I'm awake, you lovebirds," I said. "Don't worry about making noise. Kosmos, I'm going for a walk. If things don't work out, I'll drown my sorrows with a swim, come back in a couple of hours, then sleep on the grass outside."

Kosmos shouted back and his voice rang with humor and good cheer.

"Where could you be going at this time of night, Thoreau?"

His laugh was like a roar, and as he tickled Prudence, she laughed as well.

"Say hello to Beatrice from us. And if you need some love lessons, come and watch us for a while, and learn how the heir of Zeus makes love to the most beautiful woman on Earth!"

I heard the sounds of another plunging kiss, more loud whispers, then the lust-drunk voice of Kosmos calling to me again.

"Thoreau! Whatever time you get back, we'll still be going at it!" Kosmos shouted. "And I'll be ten years younger when you return!"

I threw on a sweatshirt and a pair of shorts. Mere moments later, Kosmos was snoring — snoring like an old goat bleating — and poor Prudence lay swearing at him, and then shouting: "Kosmos, wake up! We've just started! You promised me a hundred orgasms! Wake up, Kosmos! Wake up!"

I grabbed the scarf gift from Beatrice, tied it around my right wrist, then stepped outside to the quiet of the cooling night.

Excitedly I walked along the town's dirt streets. Dogs barked in the distance, cicadas chirped nearby, dark clouds wrapped a veil around the feminine face of the moon. The thrill of going to the woman you adore! All I could think about was the woman, touching the woman, how she would first be shy and enchanting, how her eyes would tell me how much she loved me and desired me, how quickly we would leap the wall between friendship and intimacy, how she would then laugh and grow bolder, and then at last be lost to me completely, carried away — again! again! again! again! — by undulating waves of pleasure we would receive and give.

My newly-sneakered feet carried me to the end of the road and the beginning of the sandy beach. The barking of the dogs grew louder here. This was the double-edged freedom of country living: no police to harass you, and no police to protect you. Calmly and quickly I prepared for the unseen beasts. I pulled off my sweatshirt then wrapped it into a ball in my left fist. The dogs barked again — louder, nearer, more savagely. Then the owner's whistle came, the danger ended, the barks grew fainter and the dogs ran home.

I walked along the sand thinking about Beatrice. The night wanted to be peaceful, but soon it was startled by a reek of perfume and the sultry voice of a woman in distress. When I looked up in the direction of the voice I saw a scene from a myth or a fairy tale.

Between the sea foam and the sea sand a woman was walking — not walking, staggering — along the water's edge. Her right hand carried a wine bottle and her left hand held a flower on a long stem. No blouse concealed the plentiful treasures on her chest, and a splash of moon-shine gleamed across her sweetly swaying breasts. From the waist down she was covered with gaudy golden pants, pants so tight they looked like they'd been sprayed on to her legs. Her long red hair, wet from the sea-water, stretched down to the sacred temple beneath her curvaceous hips. From the back she resembled an Aphrodite being born from a seashell; or a sea-nymph praying for the new dawn; or a virgin mermaid search-ing for her two-legged lover on the land. But viewed from the front the lines on her face, like the rings inside a tree trunk, showed her age to be just a footstep over the hill of forty. Had she been younger she would have been a ravishing beauty; even now, even older, even drunk — even after whatever hard life had brought her here — she remained well-built, good-looking, provocatively brash, and as sexy as sexy could be.

The woman walked in the knee-high water and sang a medley of mot-ley song lines in a strangely seductive voice.

"Get me to the church ... s'agapo ... j'taime ... buy you a mockin' bird ... get me to the goddamn church on time!"

She stopped walking, teetered, tittered, shouted at the tattered man.

"Is that you, Ligeia?"

I stepped just close enough to the woman to smell the breath on her wine.

"My name is Thoreau. And your name, sea goddess?"

The woman shook her head. Still clutching bottle and flower, she held up the bottoms of her breasts.

"Goddess my assidopolis! Call me Siren. If you get too close to me I'll eat you, I'll beat you, I'll dash your ship against my rocks!"

She drank a gulp from the wine bottle then stared at me curiously.

"Every man who sees me wants to fuck me. Are you a man?"

She staggered two steps towards me then lost her balance as she reached out to grab my arm. I caught hold of her before she fell.

"I'm a man. And I'm in love with a wonderful woman."

The siren nodded.

"I'm in love, too. That son of a bitch!"

She tied strands of my hair around the long stem of her flower.

"That's for you for being nice to me tonight."

With Mediterranean passion she kissed my lips.

"And that's for when you saved my sponge."

Ah! From the Dembacchae tavern, this lusty siren was the cleaning maid!

"You look cold," I said. "Put this on."

She took my sweatshirt, but instead of putting it over her chest she tied it around her waist.

"When your ass is cold, your whole body is cold," she said. Then she placed her right hand on my shoulder as her left hand patted my cheek.

"You wouldn't know it to look at me, but I have a grown daughter. She is eighteen years young. She is so good and so beautiful, and I love her more than I love myself."

Having had very little experience with intoxicated women, I could think of nothing better to do than to ask a practical question.

"Is her father helping you to support her?"

She stuck her nose against my nose then patted my shoulder as she spoke.

"That son of a mongrel, he can barely support himself and all his one-night friends! He can go to hell, and then all the deceiving men in the world can follow him straight down! Except you. You're too handsome and too nice. You stay here in the land of the living and take care of all the lonely women. Why don't you kiss me? I bet you won't kiss me because I'm drunk."

I listened to her with my whole heart, and each moment I looked at her and listened, the woman seemed to grow younger and more attractive.

"If I drown, they'll all be sorry," she said. "Instead of wishing they were screwing me they'll have nothing to do all day but jingle their worry beads and beat their *souvlakis*. You know what? If a man like you would really kiss me then maybe I wouldn't need to drink anymore. Did you ever think of that?"

She wiped her hair from her face then looked at me up, down and up again.

"Hera and Zeus, you're good-looking! I won't be around forever, you know: I'm almost twenty-nine. Make a pass at me already. What are you waiting for, Easter? You can hide your eggs in my basket anytime. Why don't you try to kiss me? Either I'll turn into a princess, or you'll turn into a frog."

I kissed her forehead and the woman laughed.

"Don't think I'm going to kiss you just because I let you fuck me. You know that the man I'm in love with, the father of my girl, thinks I'm good enough to sleep with once a week, but not good enough to marry."

The free-spirited woman fell into the water onto her knees. When she stood up she announced "I'm going for a swim," then right away fell down again.

I knelt down, raised her up, then lifted her in my outstretched arms.

"Listen, mermaid," I said. "In my country we have a saying: 'Friends don't let friends dive drunk.' ... I know someone who can help you and I'm taking you to his house. Kosmos is his name. He'll give you a good meal, let you sleep on his couch, listen to your troubles then make you laugh when he narrates the troubles of his own. Whether you like him or hate him for it, he'll tell you what you need to hear. And whatever is bothering you, he'll help you to fix it and make it better. Trust me for a while, will you?"

The woman laughed, then beat my backside with the wine bottle. With sharp fingernails she scratched my chest — not quite deep enough to make me bleed — then threw her arms around my neck. She seemed calmed by the sense in my words, the sincerity in my voice, the strength in my supporting arms. Carrying her relaxed body, I walked out of the shallow water onto the dry sand.

She pressed her chest against my chest.

"Hey, Heracles, you want good luck? Rub my boobs and you'll get good luck! Ha-ha-ha-ha!"

I walked on with the woman in my arms. Her honesty made me smile, her sensuality made me wonder, her earthy vitality made me laugh out loud.

"Here," she said, waving the bottle before my lips. "I'm going to call you Adam because you look like that painting by Angelomichael. Adam, have a drink. It's on me."

I shook my head and told her, "I don't drink."

She poured the last ounces of wine onto my head then rubbed my hair.

"The drink was on me, and now the drink is on you. Hey, listen, I like you. I mean it. You're not like the other pigdogs who think they're men. You care about me. I know what I can do for you. This is the way a woman says thanks to a man. You like *purro?*"

Purro, I slowly remembered, is the Greek word for cigar. I shook my head.

"I don't smoke."

A spree of resounding laughter burst from the woman's wine-soaked lips. Reaching into the pocket of her glimmering pants, she pulled out a cigar then stuffed it into the waistband of my shorts.

"Here's one for you, and when we get to your friend's house tell him I want to give him one, too."

Her wine-soaked tongue licked the inside of my right ear.

"You don't like the drink, you don't like the smoke. But you like the women, yes?"

"I like all women and I'm in love with one of them."

"Does she love you?" the woman asked.

"I don't know."

Playfully she slapped my cheek.

"You don't know! Why you don't know? There's one way to find out: Make her jealous! Put some lipstick on your collar — where is your damn collar? ... Oh, it's around my waist."

My chest — like the cupboard of the old woman in the nursery rhyme — was completely bare. With lipsticked lips as red as raspberries, the woman kissed me ten times on my neck and cheek and chest.

"There! If she sees you with another woman and she stays calm, then you know she doesn't give a fig about you, she's glad to get rid of you. But if she gets mad, then she's yours. The madder she gets, the more she loves you."

The woman stared at my face once again.

"Goddamnit! Life dies, then you're a bitch! Why didn't I meet a man like you when I was twenty-one? What fun we would have had together! There's a man in my life now but he doesn't know it. Goddamn him, I've been sleeping with him more than twenty years and he won't marry me! And I'm still in love with that garbage-rat! When Cupid shoots a woman with a real love-arrow it never comes out."

The moonlight lit her face, her naked shoulders, her flabbergasting breasts. I studied the sparkling reflections in this woman's eyes.

"Tell me something," I asked. "Did you ever tell the father of your daughter that you were in love with him?"

The woman in my arms laughed.

"You don't know the secret of being a woman, do you? She may have all the best-looking equipment, but if a woman needs words to tell a man she loves him, then she's not much of a woman at all."

The tough-talking woman began to cry. And this surprised me. I had read books about many subjects, about all the mysteries of the universe, about all the ideas that the greatest thinkers had ever dared to dream. Yet never had I discovered any words of wisdom about this one subject: how to respond to a woman's genuine tears.

I handed her the scarf-gift that Beatrice had given me. After wiping her eyes with that silk cloth, she tied it around her neck.

"Goddamn it! I'm a woman, aren't I? Why doesn't anybody ever treat me like a woman? Do you like my boobs?"

"You have lovely boobs," I said. "You have the best boobs in Greece."

"They're all natural, nothing plastic in there. Here, feel them. Then you'll know if I'm a liar, and you'll get good luck, too."

Throughout the whole journey the intoxicated woman talked this way. As quickly as I could walk, I carried her over the dirt streets and through the small alleyways to the haven of Kosmos.

When I arrived outside the doorway, all the lights were lit. The sounds of laughter from one man and many women rang heartily from inside the cheerful house. Still carrying the half-naked woman, I pushed aside the doorway's blanket and softly stepped inside.

As I watched the faces gathered around the table, I thought: "So many of my days have been lived wandering, alone, or with people who never feel or think about the deeper things in life. But here in this simple house are true friends who I care about, and care about me, and whenever we are together we share the profoundest of all the joys."

Around the table I saw the friendly heads of Kosmos, Prudence, Beatrice Loverly, Becca her daughter, and Julie, her daughter's friend. My gaze was drawn to the face of Beatrice: in that moment how perfectly beautiful she looked! How could it be that no painter had ever captured that kind of living beauty, and no painting could move me with even a fragment of that much force? I stared at her radiant face with fascinated reverence, with breathtaking awe. Moments like these — glorious! magical! ripe with ecstasy! — were the moments that the mystics lived for, moments that the greatest poets had sought to feel and then immortalize in words sublime. Yet even the electrifying words of these great poets faded to nothing beside real beauty in the flesh.

Kosmos filled everyone's glasses with tea or apple cider, then passed around a plate of cakes.

"Tell me, Beatrice," he said. "How did it go with Irene's first lesson in *ars amore,* the art of love?"

Lady Loverly answered with a beaming smile.

"It went smashingly, Kosmos. I told her: 'Irene, babies are made this way. The man inserts his penis into the woman's vagina.' ... Irene sat silently, then her face lit up with astonishment, and then she shouted — tell us what you said, Irene dear."

Irene stood up and told us "I said: 'Ewwwww! I'm not going to do it that way! Do you have to do it that way!'"

Everyone laughed, including the delighted Irene, who — dressed in white shorts and a white peasant shirt — was kissed on the cheek then hugged with one arm by Lady Loverly, her compassionate mentor.

"So you see, Kosmos," Beatrice said, "at that point I realized that it would be best to proceed with these lessons slowly. Very slowly. Because it's not too little knowledge which is the dangerous thing, it's too much knowledge too quickly that confuses us, and makes us disoriented, hurried, forgetful and afraid."

With her left hand that bore a silver ring, Beatrice brushed her hair from her eyes.

"And after we talked a little more about the theory of sexual activity, then we — Julie, Becca, Irene and I — began chatting about the practice. We were all perishing with curiosity to find out what was happening or not happening between you and Prudence! We knew that underneath those accountant's glasses there was a tigress waiting to devour some lucky man — and we wondered if that lucky man could manage her!

And the four of us women missed the company of Mr. Thoreau so much, so very much, that we decided to come back and visit your happy house."

"This is so much fun, Mother!" shouted Becca. "I can't wait until he sees the pomegranates!"

"Mr. Kosmos," asked Julie. "When do you think Thoreau will be coming back?"

The question fell unheard. Still laughing from the story about Irene, Kosmos called her *"papaki"* — duckling —as he kissed her forehead. He looked tenderly into her luminous eyes, and together they laughed more.

Suddenly he sensed that more warm bodies filled his house, and as he looked up at his doorway he met my gaze with his smiling eyes. But the instant he saw the woman in my arms his face dropped in the middle of a laugh. There ensued a brief fierce battle inside his colossal heart. When the battle had finished, general Kosmos had been demoted to a private; and although he had lost his warm cheer he quickly recovered his cool poise.

"Thoreau, my boy!" Kosmos yelled. And the table of women turned their heads and shouted joyous welcomings. The three youngest women — Julie, Becca, Irene — ran to me and kissed my cheek. They explained how they had found a grocer who opened his store at night, just so they could bring me four baskets filled with a hundred pomegranates, symbols of love and desire.

In his scheming brain, Kosmos had already worked out how he would save the evening from catastrophe. He had envisioned three different scenarios; at last he decided that he would bring into light all the darkest imaginings that lurked in the women's minds. Tell the truth and keep skating. And this plan seemed to his mind the best.

"Zeus and his thousand consorts, Thoreau! What the hell happened to you? You smell like fifty-cent wine, your hair's meshed with a wilted flower, your chest is scratched, your torso's smeared with lipstick, your legs dripping with wet sand. You look like the last man on Earth, lost at sea, shipwrecked on an island, just escaped from the foreplayground of a hundred savage Amazons."

The women around the table laughed, and Kosmos continued his narration.

"And you've brought us a present named Penelope, may the gods have pity and protect me from her smiles and guiles and wiles! If Shakespeare had known her, then that shrew Katharina would have tamed her husband Petruchio, and walked him through the Padua dogpark on a very short leash."

Penelope started to say something but Kosmos jumped in.

"In Crete we have a saying: The cup drinks the first wine; the second wine you drink; and the third wine drinks you. How many have you had, Penelope?"

"I lost count after the fourth," she said.

The face of Prudence looked mesmerized, as if she'd been reading a mystery novel and had just now reached the chilling denouement. Prudence stood up, slapped her hands onto her hips, then addressed Kosmos in a sweetly irritated voice.

"Kosmos, love," she said, glaring at Penelope. "Do you know this woman?"

Kosmos calmly replied.

"Of course I know this woman, Prudence," he said. "I am a man, and this woman is known by all the men in Dembacchae, and half the men in Crete. Her name is Penelope and she is the mother of my daughter. For the past twenty years, we have spent every Friday night together: what man could resist a woman with a body like that? And then on Saturday mornings we talk, and I read to her from the best books. At noon she goes home, and on Saturday nights she gets drunk and makes herself wild like this. On Sundays and for the rest of the week she is a hard-working woman, and as perfect a mother to my daughter as any man could ever dream for."

Prudence crossed her arms and tapped her foot against the floor. Kosmos placed his right hand over the left side of his chest.

"Dear Prudence, listen with both ears and you'll hear the truth. I know what you're wondering. I swear on all my books that Penelope to me is like a sister. You think, everyone here thinks, that Kosmos has a nice disposition? Whenever I'm in the same room as Penelope, just count to five-Thessaloniki — and then I turn into a monster, and we're fighting like Turkey and Greece. I would rather live with one hundred Xantippes than one Penelope! So you see, Prudence, one day Penelope and I put our brains together, and we agreed on an ingenious compromise. Unless one of us cancels the rendezvous in advance, we stay together Friday nights and Saturday mornings, and then we part at noon. And let me tell you, that's more than enough time! Any longer than that and we'd be murdering each other like tragic heroes in Sophocles."

Kosmos, studying the skeptical face of Prudence, gleaned that his two lovers could not be peaceably together in the same place.

"Let's get Penelope a tall mug of coffee," he said. "We'll sober her up, then send her home for a good night's rest."

Lady Loverly looked hot as the chowder and cool as the New England clam.

"Puck is here," she said, "that merry wanderer of the night! Mr. Thoreau, why don't you and your new friend sit down here and drink something hot or cold with us?"

I had been so astonished to see Beatrice here that I forgot to explain how and why I'd come to be holding half-naked Penelope so intimately inside my arms. But how to explain it and be believed? There was the rub.

Lady Loverly spoke again.

"You'll be pleased to learn that we've been making splendid progress with Irene's sexual education. And we have been curious about your own, this evening, Mr. Thoreau. Would you like to tell us about it?"

I let go of Penelope and when she stood up on wobbly legs she nodded her head at me then pointed her finger at Lady Loverly.

"You nosy bitch!" shouted Penelope. "Adam and me have been rolling in the sand together!"

She tried to kiss my mouth, but gently I pushed her body back from mine. Penelope gripped my shoulder.

"And he liked me so much he paid me by giving me this."

The drunkenly loose-tongued woman raised Lady Loverly's scarf then twirled it in her hand around and around and around.

Beatrice stood up. Even wearing a humble T-shirt she looked ravishing. The words on her T-shirt caught my eyes:

'Stare at my breasts ecologically —
Enjoy the view, but leave the landscape untouched.'

Lady Loverly was not afraid of truth. As she told me what she was thinking, her words were spoken in a cheerful tone and an ever-present smile.

"Ah, so now we know your *modus operandi*, Mr. Odizziness Thoreau. To seduce a woman you make up a name and then you get her drunk. Or should we call you Adam, the first man, a tortured man because for less than twenty-four hours he knew paradise then lost it when he acted like a fool?"

Books about nature will explain that, on a dark night, if you shine a bright light into the eyes of a rabbit, that rabbit will be stunned, unable to run away. The thorough disorientation keeps him frozen motionless on the same spot. ... Mystified by Beatrice's beauty, dumbfounded by the tall tales Penelope had told about me, and confused about the meaning of Lady Loverly's cool response — why hadn't she reacted jealously? — I was now too overwhelmed to speak. Love was the light that made me mute.

Penelope had no trouble dispelling the solemn silence that poisoned the evening air. She glanced at Lady Loverly then back to me.

"Is that your girlfriend?" Penelope asked.

"Not yet," I murmured. "And the chances are diminishing very fast."

"She's too good for you!" Penelope said. "She's a lady. If she wasn't a lady she would have pulled all my hair out by now and I'd be bald. That wouldn't be the first time I was bald by a lady. But for your girlfriend, Adam, you don't need a lady. You need a woman of the earth like me. Hey, baby, tell my good friend Kosmos about the *purro* that will make him purr."

My bone-deep sincerity pulled me straight down into the trap.

"Penelope wanted to thank me so she gave me a *purro,* and she said that she wanted to give one to you too, Kosmos."

Kosmos picked up a cigar-sized burning candle. Using broad gestures, he placed the candle into then out of his mouth like a cigar. Thus, dramatically, he explained to my awestruck eyes that a *purro,* in the beautiful language of the Greeks, was a slang word for what tenderer mouths have called 'fellatio.'

I reached into my waistband to show the real cigar. But there was no cigar, it had fallen long ago onto the Dembacchae streets.

Lady Loverly looked tranquil and composed as a sonnet about enduring love.

"Isn't this all something out of a book by D.H. Lawrence?" she said, smiling. "Kosmos, will you pass me some of that honey-walnut baklava? A large helping, please. There's no longer any need to count calories and watch my figure."

Penelope flung her arms around my neck.

"I have my dessert right here!" she said. Before I could squirm away she kissed my cheek.

"Adam, are you one of those cunt-teasers? You've kissed me, now you have to go to bed with me again. Make it as good as the last time! Give me a thousand organisms!"

Beatrice looked deep and furious into my eyes.

"Isn't it wonderful, in this advanced era of the Twenty-first Century, that all of us are all such psychosexually liberated human beings! We can sit here and eat cake and watch imperturbably — without getting the least bit upset — as an inebriated vamp throws her body shamelessly at the man we hoped we would be fortunate enough to throw our bodies at! You see, Becca, Julie, and Irene, how every moment in our lives is an opportunity for learning. And note well, young ladies, that even an educated woman can grasp valuable lessons from a woman with far less education and good breeding."

Penelope, again, pecked a kiss against my reluctant cheek.

"I'm all for good breeding!" she shouted.

Slowly, Beatrice sipped her tea.

"Young ladies, would you leave us alone for a few minutes. I have something very private to discuss with the very public Mister Thoreau. You may first say goodnight to your knight in tarnished armor."

Immediately, Becca, Julie, and Irene jumped out of their seats. They yelled "Goodnight, Thoreau! See you tomorrow! We'll dream about you!" and then they dashed through the doorway with blushes on their faces and giggles on their lips.

Beatrice placed her teacup on the table then walked slowly across the room until she faced my face. From Penelope's hand she snatched the silk scarf. She took a deep breath, she tied the scarf around my neck, she slapped me sharply on the left cheek. Wonderfully did her eyes flash.

"Mister Thoreau!" she cried out. "I'm so angry at you I could slap you!"

"Beatrice," I said. "Give me just five minutes to explain."

"You made me believe that you cared about me!" she shouted.

"Beatrice," I said.

"You gazed into my eyes and shared my dreams!"

"Beatrice, let's — "

"I hate you!" shouted the woman.

"Bea!"

"I never want to see you again. Never! Never! Never!"

And as soon as she cried that final word — the word we often say and rarely mean — Beatrice vanished through the doorway like a fierce wind.

In a moment her daughter Becca came back, eyes reddened and wet with tears.

"You broke my mother's heart!" shouted Becca. And she slapped me across the cheek.

Then in walked Julie, also teary-eyed.

"You broke my best friend's mother's heart!" she shouted as she slapped.

And at last in walked Irene, whose tears had fallen so copiously that they had soaked her blouse.

"You broke my Aunt Bea's heart!" she said.

But when she reached up to slap me her hand changed its mind, and instead of hitting me she sighed and sobbed then turned and ran beneath the blanket and out into the night.

Hurricane Penelope had yet not finished wreaking blusters of destruction on the shores of her washed-up men. Penelope turned her Medusan gaze to Kosmos and then, swaying her hips, walked to the table where Kosmos was now sitting beside Prudence. She jumped onto his lap, flung her arms around his neck then kissed his lips.

"You singing goat-turd," she began. "For twenty years I've been stupid enough to be in love with you! You're the father of my daughter, and every week I wash your goddamn clothes and socks. Marry me and I'll make an honest man out of you!"

Kosmos held her affectionately but shook his head.

"Us, married!" he shouted. "Penelope, you know that we fight too much. And here is something you may not know: legally I cannot marry you. I am married already. In Athens I have two wives."

Penelope, thoroughly unruffled, rose from the lap of Kosmos, and then walked toward the kitchen to get a cup of strong Greek coffee. Prudence stood up, screamed like a wild bird, then ran to the bedroom to gather up her clothes. Kosmos let out a groan toasted with disappointment and buttered with grief.

"Thoreau, tell me something. Why does a little iota of truth get so many people so pissed off? Why is it so dangerous to speak your mind? In every culture we find proverbs such as: 'Tell the truth with one foot in the stirrup!' and 'Tell the truth in the form of a joke!'"

Kosmos pointed his head toward the bedroom then shouted to Prudence in a warm but tired voice.

"Prudence, *dhen eena teepota*: it's nothing! No problem! Don't make Othello's blunder and ruin a good relationship from unfounded jealousy based on faulty facts. If you had asked me if I were married, I would have told you, but you never asked."

Prudence, who had heard enough and more than enough, returned fully dressed, with a face that looked like it had been chiseled out of ice.

"You have two wives in Athens, and one lover in your kitchen. And another one on her way out of your life forever!"

Prudence approached me then slapped my busy cheek "For betraying Beatrice!" she said.

She returned to her ex-lover.

"This is for being a perfect ass!" she cried. And before she departed she raised her fist then punched Kosmos above his right eye.

Kosmos downed another glass of the wine of forgetfulness. Penelope smiled at the man she loved.

"Some women get upset over the littlest things. Darling, did she hurt you?"

And as she rushed toward Kosmos to try to help, Penelope slipped and fell forward and her open palm accidentally smacked him underneath the eye left.

2 5
THE FATEFUL PENELOPE

"ONCE UPON A TIME THERE LIVED a king's son. His castle was filled with beautiful books: he owned more books than all the princes in all the other kingdoms of the world combined. Every morning he would open his books and read about everything that had ever happened in the world, and study the exquisite pictures. He could find out information about every country, every culture, every custom, every clime. But his books contained not one word about this subject: where to find the Garden of Paradise. And this was the one thing that he thought about every day and every night."

Early next morning I woke up to the aroma of Greek coffee — so powerful it made my nose twitch — and the sounds of two voices bickering, like lovers playfully teasing each other before their bouts of love. When I stepped into the living room, I found Kosmos lying on the couch. His whole face — except for two eyeballs and a beard — was covered with a healing paste made from crushed garlic, olive oil and herbs. On a chair beside him sat Penelope, who had just begun to read from a book of tales by Hans Christian Andersen. She would read a few words, then lift her eyes over the top edge of the book, glance at her listener with the tenderest feminine fondness, then continue to read more.

Kosmos had been pretending to ignore these glances, as well as the enticing body of the reader, and instead he stared with intense concentration at his paintings which brightened the walls.

"*Kalimera,* Thoreau, good morning!" shouted Kosmos, without turning his head to me. "For twenty years I've been reading to Penelope, and now for the first time she's reading to me. Maybe that change will turn our luck around today — your luck and my luck, I mean. What do you think?"

Penelope swatted his bulging belly with the book.

"When I'm around," she said, "why do you need luck?"

Dressed in a nothing but a plunging neckline and a short silk bathrobe tied loosely at her waist, Penelope beckoned me with her sly eyes and her undulating hand.

"Come here, Thoreau, and let me look at you close up. I won't seduce you in front of Kosmos, I promise. Kosmos, get the hell out of here for an hour so me and Thoreau can take care of some personal business."

Kosmos laughed and waved at me to come near.

"Don't be afraid of her, Thoreau. She talks like a man-eating tigress, but she's as shy as a baby duck. She won't put a finger on you — unless you make the first move."

Penelope grasped my chin with her right hand and her robe — as she knew it would — slipped open invitingly.

"This Thoreau that you have discovered, Kosmos, is the most beautiful man in Greece. If I weren't in love with an old garbage man, then I'd teach him a few new tricks."

Kosmos sat up.

"Before you teach him anything, Penelope, you'd better apologize to Thoreau for last night. In one sweet blow you ruined the greatest love of his life."

"What do you mean?" the woman said. "Last night I went for a walk on the beach then — "

The events of the previous evening jumped suddenly into her morning mind.

"Ah! I'm such a bitch sometimes!" she cried. "First, my handsome Mr. Thoreau, I will fix your breakfast. Then I will fix your life!"

Penelope kissed my cheek then set the breakfast table with coffee, tea, yogurt, fruit, and puddles of honey over thick slices of dark bread.

Kosmos thanked her for taking care of breakfast and his swollen face. Slowly, he climbed off the couch and walked to the kitchen sink. Using a shoehorn, he scraped the garlic paste from his face into a salad bowl, rinsed his face and hands, then placed the salad bowl onto the kitchen table next to the *tzadziki.* Then he gazed into a mirror on the wall. Examining his blackened eyes, he shook his head and laughed heartily at his own reflection.

"Last night when I peered into this mirror I asked myself: How the hell did that bearded raccoon get into the house? Then I wondered if any saint once said: 'If a woman socks you in your right eye, turn and offer her your left.' The age-old formula for ending all violence in this world: Turn the other eye!"

He poured some olive oil onto his hair, rubbed it around with both hands, then combed the hair straight back.

"The main problem with being fifty-five years old," he said, "is that some nights you feel like twenty-five inside."

"What's wrong with that, Kosmos?" I asked.

"When I feel like twenty-five," he said, "then I act like twenty-five. And for the entire week after I act like twenty-five, I feel like eighty-five. I pay seven times over for my folly of one night."

The telephone rang and Penelope rushed to pick it up. Kosmos opened his mouth to talk but it was not necessary.

"I know, I know, Kosmos," Penelope said. "If it's a man, you're not home. If it's a woman, you're dead. If it's a young woman, she should come over at nine o'clock tonight."

She picked up the phone receiver.

"Ela, Hello. ... No, I've never heard of a Kosmos. ... *Parakalo."*

She stepped into her gold pants.

"Some lawyer from Athens," she said.

Staring at the mirror, Penelope brushed her hair, and then with two deft swipes she painted lipstick across her luscious lips. From a hook on the wall she grabbed the keys to Kosmos's garbage truck. Penelope hugged Kosmos, whispered some soft words to him, then winked at me and pinched my cheek.

"Don't worry, Thoreau! For you, I will fix everything."

Her eyes gleamed with a noble purpose as she hurried toward the doorway.

"Penelope!" yelled Kosmos. "You can't leave without eating something."

The woman Penelope blew kisses to her men, shoved a piece of toast into her mouth, and then — swaying spellbinding buttocks and shaking hypnotic hips — she ran underneath the doorway's blanket to the great outside.

Kosmos watched the woman with hungry eyes. He sighed, then he smiled his ever-joyful smile, and at last he spoke to me in a voice simmering with warm feelings.

"She tries hard and she never gives up," he said. "But she's more likely to make things a lot worse before she makes things better. Sometimes I call her Penelopandora: she's curious about everything, she's all action, and she never looks ahead. Maybe the reason that Penelope and I never got together permanently is because she works all the time, and I spend half my life avoiding work. Avoiding work so that I can live and do my art."

I placed my hand on his shoulder.

"You care about her very much, don't you Kosmos?"

Kosmos buttered a slice of bread then looked at me with a glance that seemed to wonder how I had guessed this secret.

"Penelope? I care about her and I admire her too, Thoreau. She lives for her daughter and for her old parents: she doesn't have very much money, and she gives everything she has to them. Penelope is a smart woman with two stupid habits: one is named booze and the other is named Kosmos."

Down his throat he poured the entire contents of the syrupy coffee cup.

"You know," he added, "I've always wondered this: if Jesus had lived longer, would he have married Mary Magdalene?"

He looked up at me as if he wanted to talk more about Penelope; instead he shook his head and continued to eat silently. His ears were aimed at his garden filled with whistling, twittering, and warbling birds.

"I'd like to have a whole lifetime of mornings to listen to the birds," he said. "Do you know how primitive music began? The poets — "

Jarringly, the telephone rang; Kosmos answered it by saying: *"Ela."*

Soon he was shouting at the phone, waving his arms, until at last he slammed down the receiver and stood up.

"Problem, Kosmos?"

"Dhen eena teepota: it's nothing. No problem. *Pame,* Thoreau, let's go! Before the world floods in and finishes me off as an artist and as a human being, I want to tell you about my dreams of sex and paradise."

Kosmos took one long last look at the pictures he had painted on his walls, then covered his eyes with a pair of sunglasses.

"You know, Thoreau," he said, "Art is a road, not the destination. Art is great when it sends you to life, when it helps you to live your life with more sincerity, aliveness, tenderness. One old lady who takes care of her neighbors is worth ten thousand Grecian urns. But until we all learn how to fill our hearts with love, we'll need to fill our homes with art."

He grabbed two pomegranates then raised the blanket on his doorway.

"Art is the earthen vessel that transmits divine fire from man to man. But if you don't take that fire and go directly to life — if the painting of a man starving moves you to buy the print but not quite enough to send you rushing outside and handing food to the hungry families in your own neighborhood — then you're a passive observer, not an active participant: you've missed the whole point of Art. You become the fool in that Zen story, the schlemiel who worships the pointing finger instead of seeing the glorious moon."

The early morning felt enchanting: the sky glowed red-gold, and the wild sea roared with the music of goddesses and gods. In silence we walked though the town's still streets. As soon as we stepped onto the sandy beach, two dogs barked and snarled, then Kosmos began his tale.

26
THE KOSMOSUTRA

"FOR ME IN SEX, as for Ivan Karamazov in morality, everything is permitted. The old gods have retired with full pensions, and the new gods are human: the new women and the new men."

Walking beside me along the seashore, enjoying the play of the morning light and the vast view of the sky, Kosmos revealed his hard-won philosophy of life, lust, lovemaking, and love.

"Listen, Thoreau," he said. "A handful of years after you were born, something called 'the sexual revolution' swept across your country with the fervor of a withered hag pushing a dilapidated straw broom. Like most revolutions, the new tyrants who came to power were more ruthless than the previous tyrants they dethroned. What was the motto of this so-called revolution? 'If it feels good, do it.' That's a philosophy for a 5-year-old child, but not for post-adolescent women and men. It was freedom without responsibility, lust without love, diversion without happiness, snatching without giving, equality without individuality, knowledge without wisdom. The age-old formula for a lousy life."

He breathed the fresh air with a smile of satisfaction the way a connoisseur inhales the bouquet of a fine wine.

"Of course, when the fireworks had ended — when the effusive brouhaha fizzled into little more than beer and smirks — then we heard endless talk-talk-talk-talk-talk and nothing significantly changed. What went wrong? And why? ... The liberated women imitated the worst characteristics of the men who once oppressed them. The women became aggressive, domineering, greedy, shallow, superficial, isolated, obsessed with their own orgasms, cautious about commitments, casual about sex encounters. And the men? Men stayed about the same: just as confused and oblivious as they ever were. Most men today think that a women's movement happens whenever a mistress flicks on her vibrator, or a wife scurries from the kitchen to the TV-room to bring them a hot sandwich and a cold drink."

He stopped walking, looked down at a hole in the sand, dug out a razor clam, then put the creature back under the sand.

"Yes, the New Men of this New Age are disappointing duds just like the old. And what happened to the new crop of erotic Superwomen we were promised? The new woman we were told, by basking in her own explosive sexuality, would make herself the ultimate self-pleasuring sex machine. She's popping out of her pajamas with insatiable lust, but god help the poor man who looks on this woman as an object for extraordinary sex! I've heard stories — maybe from the goddess Rumor who exaggerates everything — and the stories are so bizarre I don't know whether or not to believe. They tell me that in America — the nation founded on free expression — that if you dare to whistle at a woman to show you think she's desirable, then a horde of ferocious females attack you like a pack of hunting dogs. They sue you, or throw you into jail or expel you from the university — all for the sin of communicating your honest appreciation of the fabulous feminine form!"

Kosmos waved his hand at the soaring sea gulls.

"When I was living in Rome — I was a sailor like Sinbad, and traveled round the world seven times — I saw how things could be. There was a husband walking along the street with his wife and two daughters, one eighteen and the other a few years older, and all three women were good-looking and proud to be. A drunk man staggered down the street, passed them, turned his head, examined the backs of the women, and then he shouted: 'Nice ass!' ... The wife said: 'He was talking to me!' and each of the daughters echoed 'He was talking to me!' — then the husband and three women burst out laughing, and everyone around them laughed with them as they walked on. ... What kind of world do we want, Thoreau? A world of free speech, free laughing, and free minds? Or a world of ten million lawsuits where all our natural desires are punished for being religious sins or secular crimes?"

"And you, Kosmos?" I asked. "What were you doing all those years while the cliterati were reading sex manuals, searching for the perfect 'O'?"

Kosmos laughed.

"What was I doing? The same thing I am always doing. I am working out my own salvation with diligence. Because I knew then and know now that freedom can never be given to you, as Kazantzakis says, like a cake dropped into your mouth. You have to work for your freedom and earn it for yourself. I burned my jockstrap twenty years before the feminists set their bras on fire. I had already begun beating the conundrums of women, love and sex."

I looked at him with a smile.

"Your own personal version of the 'Kosmosutra?'"

Kosmos slapped my shoulder.

"Yes, that's not a bad name for it. Not a bad name at all. Because Vatsyayana, the author of the provocative *Kamasutra* written 1600 years ago, understood sex the way I understand it. Sex cannot be isolated: sex is intimately connected with the other essential realms of life. To liberate himself, the Hindu needed to practice and perfect his life in three spheres. *Dharma* concerned religion and morals; *Artha* focused on material prosperity; and the realm of *Kama* satisfied pleasure and sexual love. All three realms were necessary and vital for the realization of the whole man. Today, each male needs to find the balance: too little attention to *kama* — love and sex — is just as fatal as too much."

Kosmos stopped walking and I stopped beside him. We looked out at the endless sea.

"How did you begin your erotic self-education, Kosmos?"

His eyes gleamed like the morning light.

"Forty years ago, when I was fifteen years old, I was a shy and bumbling adolescent. In those days, Thoreau, I was terrified of women, all women: women near, far, gorgeous, hideous, young, old, middle-aged. Because women had something I wanted, they had power over me: with a wink that said yes or no they could transport me to a sexual paradise or keep me in my lonely hell. You can laugh all you want to, Thoreau! Whenever I stood beside a beautiful young woman I was too shy to look at her and too nervous to speak. And once when I tried to light a girl's cigarette with a match, my hand was shaking so much that I singed the tip of her nose.

"For a whole year I was miserable. Every night I dreamed about rescuing the girls and getting rewarded with passionate kisses; every morning I daydreamed about transforming myself into a crazy combination of Zeus, Zorba and Casanova, a virile virtuoso in the art of erotic love.

"But the road from dreams to deeds is seven thousand miles. You could have filled up a vacuum cleaner, in just one week, with the dust I had collected on my longing phallus! My mother worried about me because I lost weight and enthusiasm. She made me go to confession one Sunday at the local church, and the priest asked me: "Have you stopped touching your private parts, Kosmos?" ... So I answered the question with a question: "Have you, father?" ... With a stick in his hand, a bible in his pocket, and murder in his eyes, the priest chased me out of the church. That started me questioning the powers that be: eventually I realized that the powers that be be because they are the powers that pay. What good is a government or a religion if its high and low muckamucks persecute a man for saying what he thinks?

"I was telling you about my education at the University of Love. I might have stayed trapped inside my shell, I might have remained a daydreamer all my life, if it wasn't for a schmuck who lived in a village nearby. His name was Marcos, he was one year older than me. He bragged about everything, and if he was half as good as he said he was, he would have been Prometheus, Heracles, and Odysseus combined. Well, one day, this Marcos character was boasting and he got me furious. I felt like your beautiful-minded Emerson when he wrote: 'It takes a good indignation to bring out all one's powers.' I was sitting with a bunch of friends when Marcos approached me. He flicked my nose with his fingertip and jeered: 'How are you doing with the girls, Kosmos? I'll tell you how: this whole month and not even one Dutch fuck!'

"You have never smoked, Thoreau, so you might not know that a 'Dutch fuck' means lighting one cigarette by touching it to the tip of another one already lit. That remark fried my fritters all right, but I didn't show anything. I was burning inside, but fighting about it couldn't make things better. Instead, I became determined to find out the secret, to change myself, to learn, to solve my problem and transform my dull life into a real adventure."

Kosmos laughed at the memory of his young self. From his pocket he pulled out a small mirror, gazed at his aging face, then returned the mirror to its place. We continued walking and he talked on.

"How did I start my self-education? With books, of course. My uncle had a fairly large library and I started there. The poetry of Ovid, the dialogues of Aretino, the *Kamasutra,* and a few Oriental manuals. Books took me as far as books can take a man. But one morning I realized that I needed experience. And soon after that I met three amazing human beings: an old woman, a stick woman, and a dead woman. They taught me that everything important about love can be epitomized by thinking 'FIE!' — Foresight, Insight, and Excite!"

He began to hum an old Cretan folk tune and shuffle his feet across the beach. Would his joy carry him away into the heavens of songs and dances, or could he resist temptation and continue to impart his tale?

"Tell me more, Kosmos!" I said. "Dance later and talk now!"

"All right, Thoreau, I'll keep going for as long as it gives you joy to hear. I told you it was that idiot Marcos who got me mad enough to change my life. What writer said: 'Love thy enemies, because thy enemies are part of your destiny'? ... Well, one afternoon Marcos came to me and blustered that he would be sleeping with a girl named Angelika — the one girl I was secretly in love with more than I loved anyone else! They were to meet at the local cemetery when the twelve church bells resounded at midnight that night. My beautiful Angelika screwing that scumbag! — the notion made me insane. I did the logical thing for a young madman: I resolved to hide in the cemetery, kill him if he showed up with her, force myself on Angelika, then end my worthless life by jumping into the sea."

He shook his head in disgust.

"That evening, everything felt out of joint. At dinner, I was too nervous to eat anything. Even my father — who had always been radiant and joyful at our dinner table — seemed unusually solemn. After the meal he told me to take his antique urn to his brother's house, then ask his brother to fill it with his best wine. This urn we are talking about was thousands of years old. It was painted black and etched all around with a picture of the lithest and most beautiful Cretan maiden you could ever imagine. My father had found it years ago when he had been digging a foundation for an outhouse near Gortys. Ever-so-carefully I carried this treasure to my uncle's house; my uncle hugged me then filled it up with wine. When I got back home my father took the urn from me and held it his powerful hands.

"'Start counting!' he commanded. And I began 'Ena, dia ...' — one, two — but as soon as I did my father released his grip and the priceless urn fell to the ground and smashed.

"When he glared at me his eyes blazed like the Crete sun on an August afternoon. 'Now remember son, and never forget,' he told me. 'Remember how easy it is to destroy something that can never be replaced.'

"And saying that, he walked out of the house then walked toward the mountains. He walked all night, and he didn't return until the morning next.

"When my father left I looked over my shoulder, then sharpened my fishing knife. Like a zombie I walked toward the cemetery to kill my rival or to be killed. On the way I passed the house of the oldest woman in the village. Her name was Kara. She stood in her doorway dressed in black, skinnier than a skeleton, older than olive trees, uglier than greed. But beneath her wrinkled skin she was kindly and wise with a hundred years of experience. As I waved to her her eyes peered back at me like two torches in the darkest night.

"Kosmos, come here and help me," she called. It was four hours until midnight and I had lots of time. I chopped some wood for her then filled her lamps with oil. Kara set the table with cakes and made a cup of hot coffee for me, commenting that the drink would help me to stay awake. By candlelight we ate and drank and talked.

"I told her that I admired her kitchen: simple, stark, filled with flowers and flowering plants. 'I wanted to tell you about them,' old Kara said. 'There are only four varieties of flowers: some bloom for one night, some for one season, some for a year and some for a lifetime. *Katalavehees?* Do you understand?' ... And she showed me examples of each kind.

"And suddenly she smiled a toothless grin then said to me: 'You're in love, boy, aren't you?' She cut a flower from a stem and told me to place it in my shirt pocket, against my heart, for luck in love. 'And you believe, young Kosmos, that this angel you worship from afar is the flower of all womanhood?'

"I know that you've already guessed the secret, Thoreau. What she was saying about flowers was true about women, too! Some for a night, some for a season, some for year, some for a life!

"Between my fingertips I twirled the flower stem. 'How can I tell,' I asked Kara, 'which of the four varieties is which?'

"Kara curled her withered forefinger at me, then with her bony fingers she gripped my arm. When I moved close to her her old dry lips brushed my earlobe and she whispered the answer into my ear.

"'Go one step at a time, Kosmos' she said, 'and you'll still reach the mountaintop. I cannot teach you how to tell the difference. But I can tell you what the difference is. The woman for a night wants your money; the woman for a season wants your body; the woman for a year wants you to cure her loneliness; and the woman for a lifetime wants to make you happy. When you find the last type, give up all the rest.'

"Well, by the time I left old Kara I was certain that she knew that things were going badly with me. I stumbled through the main gate of the cemetery then sat down on a grave with my back against a tombstone. I had everything planned out in advance. If Marcos didn't have a knife with him, then I would not take an unfair advantage: we would fight with bare hands and feet. You see, Thoreau, why I could never be effective as a bad-guy? For me, the means are always more important than the ends!

"The bell rang twelve times. Soon after, I heard footsteps and voices approaching the cemetery. Marcos! He appeared walking with a young woman but I couldn't see who she was because her scarf covered her head and the sides of her face. I tightened my fist around the handle of the knife.

"At that moment I smelled the flower given to me by old Kara. In one swift flash I understood!

"'Marcos, come here!' I shouted. Shocked to hear a voice, when Marcos saw me he knew the score. He jumped out of his shoes, he screamed, he trembled like cold dog. And when I pulled out my knife he wet his pants then fell down to his knees.

"I laughed and shouted at him. 'Marcos, stand up like a man! I came here to kill you but I just realized how stupid it is to fight about a woman. And how stupid it is to fight about anything at all. Let's stop this nonsense and shake hands! May your spring never run dry, may your lips be ever wet with wine, and may your bed be always filled with a hundred maidens, and may not one of them be your mother, your sisters or your wives!'

"With a twitching mouth and a sweating forehead, Marcos reached up and gripped my hand. A smile broke over my face when I observed that the young woman beside him was not my angel, not my Angelika. Once again I felt a flash of inspiration, I knew what needed to be done."

For a few steps, Kosmos and I walked silently on the soft sand. These images from his past, from so very long ago, had stayed alive in his keen mind. The trick was to let his unconscious take over so that he could talk about these experiences freely — so that his unique listener would see and feel these things the way the teller saw and felt them: with passionate intensity.

"My feet carried me to the house of Angelika. In that Indian manual of erotic love, the *Kamasutra*, they talk about a charm a lover can use to sneak into the house of his beloved without making a noise and waking the rest of the family. I didn't have much charm then, but luck was with me. On bare feet I managed to step through the house and get to Angelika's bedroom unheard, unsmelled, unseen.

"As I opened the door to her room she gripped her nightgown at the neck then sat up in her bed and whispered, 'Who is it?'

"I answered: 'It's Kosmos. I'm in love with you, Angelika. Do you love me even a little bit?'

"I was certain she would say yes, because the courage it took to enter her bedroom deserved at least a little bit of love. But damn her and bless her — for forty years women have shocked me and surprised me! Angelika explained that she was in love with Michaelis: a 15-year-old bookworm with thick glasses and pimples on his face. It took all my self-control to keep from laughing out loud and waking up the entire household.

"In the semi-darkness I could see the outlines of her body and her face. And suddenly all her beauty faded, all the beauty that had been created by my imagination and my loving gaze. 'Here, Angelika,' I told her, 'take this flower and give it to your Michaelis. I don't love you anymore and I'll never bother you again! You're not even a woman for a night!'

"You see, Thoreau, old Kara was right: there are four kinds of women: women for a night, for a season, for a year, for a lifetime. And the first great secret is Foresight. When you meet a woman you have to figure out exactly which type of woman she is for you. If you mix them up then you're as helpless as a skewered lamb.

"That was the last time I saw Angelika until ten years later, when she weighed two-hundred and forty pounds, and she looked like an angel that no wings could carry, an angel who had eaten up all heaven's hoards of angelhair pasta and angelfood cake! Anyway, when the bells struck one that night I was strolling homeward and I passed old Kara's house. Her lamps were still burning so I walked inside to tell her how she had saved my life.

"'How can I thank you, Kara?' I asked. 'There's no need for that, Kosmos,' she said. Then after a moment, 'Well, there is one thing you could do. Take this letter to my daughter in Nikolodeonos. Tell her I'm not going to live forever.' Then she kissed me with her old lips and gave me some food for my trip.

"In a few hours I had matured twenty years. And that was only the beginning! The next morning I packed a sack with bread, cheese, olives, figs, blankets, my knife, and a few hundred drachs. I met Kara's daughter, a stick woman who lived on the top of a hill with her two sisters and five doves. There I learned 'Insight', and a lot more. And a week later, on the once-sacred island of Delos, a dead woman introduced me to the sacred mysteries of sex."

"A dead woman? Do you mean that she was no-pulse dead, or merely deadened in her capacity to be happy, to enjoy sex and to love life?"

"Someday, Thoreau — when you're ready but not a moment before — I'll tell you about that."

"Kosmos, what was the heart of your education?"

"I had learned how to learn: how to seek and find the knowledge of the self. We can learn something essential from every encounter, every person, every moment, every unselfish act."

A sea breeze blew across our faces. I looked at my friend's perplexing smile.

"I've often wondered, Kosmos, if enlightenment is worth the price. In every generation, a small number of individuals find some kind of liberation. They grow one within themselves and with the Mind of the universe, then immediately thereafter they clash ferociously against the foolish world. Truth and Love blind the masses with their light. Socrates is hemlocked. Jesus is crucified. Abelard is castrated. Thomas More is beheaded. Rousseau forced to live like a vagabond. Blake deemed a madman by his contemporaries. Walt Whitman, for his sublime poems, is called 'a pig rooting among garbage'. Dostoyevsky is hounded by the dogs of poverty. Gandhi is assassinated. Wilhelm Reich dies in prison for his harmless Orgone box. D.H. Lawrence's most beautiful books are banned."

"I know that problem very well, Thoreau," said Kosmos. "There is one solution."

I looked at him to make certain he was being serious, and his eyes said clearly it was so.

"Kosmos, I can't even imagine what that solution could be."

He looked up and smiled at the Greek light.

"A place."

"A place? ... What kind of place, Kosmos, are you thinking of?"

"A place of complete freedom for the flourishing of sex and love."

"You've seen a paradise like that?" I asked.

"Let me tell you all about it, my boy. If you want to know, if you'll open your mind for a moment, then I'll open up my heart and sing."

27
THE DREAM OF SEXTOPIAS

"LOVE AND SEX ARE THE ANSWERS, whatever the questions are! Is it Happiness we desire? Health? Freedom? ... Then our personal relations, our politics, our economics, our arts, our education — every facet of our lives must turn around the twin suns of Sex and Love."

As Kosmos uttered these words we sauntered past a pole sticking in the sand, holding a wooden sign inscribed in English which warned:

THE NUDISM AND THE BATHING IS FORBIDDING.

Smiling at the near-perfect translation, I questioned Kosmos about the stupendous difference between his thrilling theory and the world's priggish practice.

"But where, Kosmos, where in this great galaxy could a woman or a man live the way you have envisioned? Where could a human being enjoy perfect freedom to explore and experience her-and-his powerful impulses, sexual and compassionate?"

Those questions were the very questions that Kosmos had been waiting for.

"Answer me this, Thoreau. Do you believe the proven fact that lightning can strike more than once in the same place? And the old maxim of old geologists: 'What happened once could happen again?'"

"I believe that, Kosmos. Lightning hits the Empire State Building more than one thousand times each year. History repeats itself in recurring cycles. Every year, the same trashy books litter the best-seller lists. Bad habits formed in youth haunt a man throughout his lifetime."

Kosmos nodded.

"Sex and love join two bodies into one being — so let me combine your questions and ask: 'Where can men and women live as if life and love were one?' ... Assuming I can prove that places like this have existed in the past, would you then agree that Utopias are not impossible?"

I nodded.

"The love of truth, Kosmocrates, would force me to agree to that."

Briefly, I told Kosmos what I knew about the dark and bright Utopias in literature and myth. Dreamers have been inspired and lullabied to sleep by Plato's *Timaeus* and *Republic*; More's *Utopia*; Bacon's *New Atlantis*; Campanella's *The City of The Sun*; Rabelais' tale *The Abbey of Theleme*; Fénelon's *Voyage en Solente*; Cabot's *Voyage to Icaria*; Lytton's *The Coming Race*; Hawthorne's *Blythdale Romance*; Melville's *Typee, Omoo,* and *Mardi*; Bellamy's *Looking Backward*; Morris's *News From Nowhere*; Butler's *Erewhon* and *Erewhon Revisited*; Graves's *Seven Days in New Crete*; Huxley's *Brave New World* and *Island*.

But none of these fictions were what he had in mind. Kosmos looked up with great appreciation at the sky's good light. He waved his arms at me.

"This is all very important, Thoreau. You know how much great literature means to me. We need these magnificent visions, the best that has been thought and said. But great ideas are just the first small step. 'Give me the bagels, darling, and you can keep the holes.'"

His homespun philosophy made me laugh and think.

"And you insist, Kosmos, that this polluted planet Earth — in every age, it seems, about to burst from too-much suffering — has at times known carefree paradises in-the-flesh?"

Kosmos clapped his hands together.

"Of course!" he said. "In the glorious history of Greece we can find five recorded Utopias. I'll call them Utopias, but what I mean, simply, is advanced cities or cultures or places where creative men and women could live freely and thrive.

"Fifty-five hundred years ago — who knows when for sure? — here on Kreetee, we find the beginnings of the Minoan civilization, named for the legendary King Minos, the divine son of Europa and Zeus. The son grew up to imitate his philandering father: Minos slept around so much that his wife — foolish woman! — misused her magic powers, which caused Minos to ejaculate serpents, scorpions, and deadly insects instead of sperm. Crete flourished, nonetheless. Women maintained at least as much equality as men: Cretan women proudly bare their breasts, the snake goddesses dominate the hen-pecked bull-gods, nude priestesses shake down the fruits from the trees, and Nature is worshiped everywhere. Games are glamorized instead of war. At the *taurokatharpsia* — the bull-games — graceful gymnasts grasped the bull by the horns, and after the bull threw these athletes into the air, the youths somer-saulted toward the sky, then landed on their feet on the bull's back, or on the ground beyond. During these games no bull is ever killed. Pluck, prosperity and peace pervaded the island's ninety cities, and made Crete into our first paradise.

"Then came the Age of Heroes, when Homer humanized the goddess-es and gods. Here we find stories that signify the best that human be-ings can attain: Passionate and faithful love between one woman and one man; tender affection between the father and the son; the loyalest friend-ships; the most remarkable acts of courage and ingenuity. It wasn't all honey and cakes: there was treachery, jealousy, murder in those times, too. But a sense of justice and goodness prevailed. And the Greeks were not cursed with a mania for introspection: they looked outward and they lived like children — energetic, playful, good-humored and sincere.

"The third great place in Hellenic history was the island of Lesbos, where Sappho came to birth around 612 B.C.E. Socrates called her 'the Beautiful'. Plato crowned her immortally as 'the Tenth Muse'. Plutarch described her words as being 'mingled with flames'. For criticizing tyran-ny she was banished by a tyrant; when she returned to her native Lesbos she established a school for girls which taught poetry, music, and dance. Most of her fiery poems were burned sixteen hundred years later by the Church; only fragments remain. Her style was radiantly natural, and her subject was the passionate, breathtaking, body-trembling love she felt for her female friends.

"The next slice of paradise was initiated by the philosopher-mathema-tician Pythagoras, born thirty years after Sappho on the island of Samos. Unhappy with Samosian politics, Pythagoras gathered disciples and founded a community of vegetarian-mystics on the heel of the boot of Italy in a town named Croton. Eventually, the citizens of Croton burned down his school, and he moved his entourage to another Italian city. Why did those citizens slash and burn? We do not know. So many of Pythagoras's theories and practices were revolutionary: Women were admitted to his community on the same criteria as men; and all property was equally shared. Pythagoras taught that there were three varieties of men in the world, just like the varieties of men in the Olympic Games. The lowest kind were those that came to buy and sell; the middle were the athletes who participated; and the highest were the spectators. His ideal person was the man or woman who spent time contemplating the great mysteries. A radical idea! And one which greatly influenced the citizens of Athens, who believed that a man must be free because he needed his leisure time for the highest human activity: to learn and to cultivate his mind.

"And the fifth recorded paradise, as I'm sure you've guessed, is the Golden Age of Greece, which began with a great military victory in 480 B.C.E. These Greeks in Athens loved freedom, Thoreau, even if they didn't extend that same freedom to their colonies and women and slaves. Yet twenty-four hundred years ago they knew what life was for: their vision demanded that we develop all our faculties and become whole men: men of action, lovers of Beauty and Art, and thinkers devoted to knowledge and wisdom and truth. Pericles was their devoted leader. Phidias the sculptor oversaw the making of the Acropolis. Two garrulous gadflies, Socrates and young Plato, stung the Athenians in the backside of their morals and their minds. Athens's literary artists included Aeschylus, Sophocles, Euripides, and the bawdy Aristophanes. How could a city of barely fifty-thousand persons, during a stretch of merely eighty years, create a civilization that would influence every aspect of Western life for thousands of years hence? Imagine, my friend, how we could transform our own world, if we were given one whole century of peace. How we could live today, if all the money pissed away for making wars was used instead to make small cities that are noble, and beautiful, and good!"

Kosmos tossed some bread and suet onto the sand. A flock of sea gulls, squawking excitedly, soared to the food and began eating voraciously.

"Five places, Thoreau, in the past five thousand years. Not much to speak of after that: but doesn't that make you stop and wonder why? ... One morning — after my first night of lovemaking with Penelope — I wondered; and after wondering awhile I fell asleep then woke up with an amazing idea! I realized all at once that there was a sixth place. Another Paradise, alive right now and living right here on Crete! I called it 'Sextopias'."

"Where is it, Kosmos?"

Like the clear sky his eyes were glowing as he explained.

"Where is this Paradise, you ask? Wouldn't we like to know! Wherever it is it's hidden well. Disguised so that reporters and developers and tourists can't find it and tear it down! What I realized that morning, Thoreau, is that the dream of an earthly paradise is the dream of every human soul. And after Athens surrendered to Sparta in 404 B.C.E., then all the visionaries and paradise-makers realized this: Deception is necessary in order to survive. Everything beautiful and true and good and original in this world lives precariously, in danger every moment of their lovely lives."

My mind said it was impossible, but my heart wanted to believe.

"Can an old husband keep his young wife faithful, Kosmos? You can't lock up a whole city with a chastity belt, or paint the peacock's feathers black. What could the elders of a good-place do to keep their land and members secret and safe?"

"Another good question, Thoreau! But here's the answer: If it is necessary, it can be done. How? Cut down on the glitter and the hype. Dress your gods in holey shoes, hand-me-downs and dungarees. Dispose of the golden treasures that tempt invading armies. Outlaw the luxuries that bring in the wrong varieties of women and men. The Zen Master Sozan said it: 'Hide your good deeds and keep your functioning a secret. Look like a simpleton or fool.'"

I had never seen a Greek sky that shined more blue and radiant, than the sky that covered us that morning as we sauntered on the sand.

"Then where on Crete is your paradise, Kosmos?" I asked. "Where is this last Sextopias?"

We stopped walking as we reached the beginning of that stretch of beach that looked incomparably lovely and pristine. Like a father, Kosmos grasped my shoulder with his heavy and calloused hand.

"Damn it, Thoreau!" he shouted cheerfully. "For twenty years I've been asking that! One thing I know: the paradise would be situated in an inspiring place. Have you seen what is called our Meteora, the rocks-in-mid-air, set in the center of Greece, in the most beautiful valley in the world? Today, there are roads so wide you can drive a bus up to the peaks. For the benefit of tourists there are two sets of walking trails leading up the slopes to the monasteries: the easy paths marked with wooden signs depicting bent-over old men, and the steep paths marked by signs etched with miniature mountain goats. But hundreds of years ago the monks who built these monasteries wanted complete safety from persecution. In those days, the one and only way to travel up and down was to be raised and lowered like a fish inside a rope-net bag.

"Here in Crete, even today, there are some unspoiled spots — and no man alive, except my father, knows this island better than I know it. Countless times I've asked myself: Where would a wise man place a paradise on Crete? ... If I were king of Sextopias, I might place it in the mountains where Zeus was born; or hide it in the little Cretan village where my father grew up as a boy. Or I would make it right here on this divine stretch of beach that I call my *kaliparalea,* which in Greek means 'beautiful seashore'. But I've hiked there and walked here on five thousand mornings, and never found even one shard of evidence."

We continued walking along this stretch of beach, where nothing manmade could be seen or heard, only the perfect natural loveliness of light, sky, sea, birds, cicadas, rocks, sand.

"Tell me, Kosmos," I asked. "What's it like, this Sextopian paradise you believe in?"

"What a question!" he shouted. "Sometimes I think that if we knew precisely what we were looking for, we could find it easily tonight!"

He placed his arm around my shoulder as he laughed.

"You hear the word 'Sextopias' and what do you think of right away? Some kind of ultimate erotic fantasy, a feast of female flesh, a harem of succulent women ever-ready to satisfy insatiable erotic whims.

"Ah, but it wouldn't be like that at all! It would be better than that! Because — as I've told you before and I'll tell you again — most people in the modern world live vicariously. They don't dare to feel deeply, they don't love deeply, they don't think for themselves, they don't create, they don't experience life firsthand. Buying, instead of Being, is our culture's most devilish god.

"What would my Sextopias be like? Too good to imagine! I can tell you two things only: about the men and women, and about the enlightened education there.

"The men would be strong yet gentle. Violence would be abolished from this kingdom, and 'to be a man' would mean to solve problems creatively with a compassionate mind, and to devote your energies to living and working for peacefulness in all activities and all relations. And the women, the women! Women — with their profound gentleness and subtle intuitions — would be the great teachers and leaders in this place. The ideal woman — who I call 'The Nubile Savage' — is passionate and tender, sensuous and innocent, active and serene. As lusty an animal as Penelope and as gentle a rose as my Irene.

"Education is the whole key to my paradise. Because humankind is the only species that has freed itself from the tyranny of instincts. With the right education, we can shape the environment that creates us, the environment that raises us to gods or reduces us to slaves. By loving and learning we can become almost any kind of splendid person that we dare to be!"

He picked up a seashell and placed it against his ear.

"I know that the paradise is here, somewhere on Kreetee. I'm certain of it! My dreams tell me it's true, and I always believe my dreams. Yet still, in more than twenty years of seeking and wandering, I've never found a trace of it. I've accomplished so much in my life except that one great thing."

Then he handed the seashell to me and said:

"There's too much noise in the modern world, Thoreau. We can't hear what our own hearts whisper, and we forget our dreams."

Kosmos grew livelier, danced and leaped for a few steps, then he threw his arms around my shoulders and gripped me like a papa bear.

"Thoreau, the moment I met you I knew that in some way you would be the one to help me find my place."

He dragged me into the sea and for many minutes we wrestled in the shallow water and on the soft wet sand. Exhausted but still laughing, he stood up, brushed the sand off the back of my shirt, then brushed it from his own.

"But all this fantasy about the paradise Sextopias is for old farts like me! Young people don't need a paradise: a young man's paradise is the goddess Love. Without love, you have nothing; with Love, what more do you need? ... You need a whole lot more, but fortunately you're too young to notice it! And right now the Love-goddess manifests herself in the flawless face and the bounteous body of Beatrice Loverly. If we can't find my paradise this morning, Thoreau, then let's go forward and grab hold of yours."

We continued walking along the coast until we arrived at the hotel where Beatrice stayed. Near Beatrice's room we were greeted by the old maid — who was part-owner of the hotel — a woman holding a broom in one hand and a bunch of withered flowers in the other. Kosmos had known her for many years; her name was Ligeia. She was not fat, she was immense; she was not old, she was outmoded; she was not ugly, she was hideous. Her neck looked like the leg of an elephant; her hair like a snaggle of snakes; and her teeth resembled white-and-black piano keys — keys that had been banged around a lot but never really played.

Ligeia told us that Beatrice Loverly, along with Prudence and the two girls, had — earlier that morning — "to England gone home."

"Gone home!" I shouted. The words dropped from my mouth and fell like two boulders that dragged me beneath the earth.

Kosmos felt my sharp disappointment in addition to his own. For years he had treasured a close friendship with Lady Loverly; and now he was sorry that Prudence had left before he had a chance to heal their quarrel. With both hands he grabbed his hair.

"Did she leave a note?" he asked. "A forwarding address, or a few kind words to soothe the annihilated heart of a lovestruck young American?"

Ligeia nodded.

"Yes," she said placidly. "There is a note."

Kosmos waited but Ligeia stood motionless as a mountain, gawkily grinning, and never produced the note. The old woman shot him with a syrupy gaze, thick enough to make him realize that capital-T trouble was already boiling in the pot. Kosmos reached into his pocket then pulled out a wad of Euros.

"Can we see the note?" he asked.

The woman shook her hands and head to thoroughly refuse the cash.

"Mrs. Loverly explained to me," she said in her slow Greek, "that these days, information is a valuable commodity. She said that we women need to learn one lesson above all: how to select the right men. And she made me swear — on my copy of my favorite bodice-ripping love saga: *At A Picnic In Italy I Found Rome-Ants* —that I would give her note to nobody. Nobody but the right man."

Kosmos had already guessed the appalling answer, but still with a match-tip of flickering hope he asked.

"And who is the right man?"

The woman sighed a Mona Lisa sigh. She handed one red pomegranate to me, and one red pomegranate to Kosmos.

"The right man? ... The first man who sleeps with me."

Kosmos and I eyeballed each other, each wondering how we had survived this long in a society of women so much wiser and more cunning than we men. The huge woman shrugged her shoulders then opened the door of the bedroom.

"Wait!" shouted Kosmos. "What would you — "

Ligeia shook her broom.

"I know you, Kosmos!" she scolded. "Don't try to bargain with me for anything else! Not for money, not for lambs, not for silk stockings, not even for your best cheap wine in Crete. If one of you handsome men wants the note, then get undressed and get into that bed."

"First give us the note," said Kosmos.

"First get into bed!" said the wizened maid. "When you pay in advance you never get good work."

Kosmos placed his hands against his hips.

"Suppose there is no note!" he said defiantly.

Ligeia reached into her cleavage — which could have held all the love letters of Heloise and Abelard. She pulled out a sheet of paper which she tore twice, ripping the note into three parts. One of those three pieces she placed into my hands. Without looking back she plodded into the room, slammed the door, and pulled the shutters closed. Then, with her fat fingers, she opened those shutters just an inch, enough to peer at us through the crack with one inquisitively-bloodshot eye.

With a horrified expression, Kosmos watched her watching eye. Then he placed his hand on my shoulder.

"We're advancing in our quest to find the perfect woman," he said. "Just a few minutes ago, everything looked bleak and hopeless. Now there is hope!"

"Hopelessness is sometimes better, Kosmos," I replied.

Kosmos smiled, shaking his head to disagree.

"You think, my friend, that we're screwed as a prude in the nude?"

"I think, Kosmos, we're as stuck as a duck in the muck."

"The gods are laughing at us, Thoreau! You know they say that the Greek sailors mistook those sea mammals, the manatees, for the enchanting Sirens; and in some parts of the world the fisherman would mate with those odd-shaped manatees when women were hard to find. Given the choice, I'm not sure I wouldn't pick a manatee right now. But my father once taught me something I've never forgotten: 'When you have no choice, at least be brave!'"

The decision lasted one eternal minute of mental agony. Kosmos tossed his pomegranate to me. Then he laughed as he unbuttoned and removed his shirt.

"Never let it be said that Kosmos committed Zorba's one unforgivable sin! When a woman calls Kosmos to her bed, no matter who the woman is, he goes! Sometimes a little more slowly than other times, but still he goes! ... Thoreau, kiss the kaboodle of the goddesses and give thanks for the lucky day we met! Do you know what the Greek Genius is? When everybody else sees darkness at the end of darkness, the Greek Genius finds a light."

Taking one deep breath, and then two more, he pushed open the room's heavy door, then turned his face to me and smiled.

"This will take just a minute, Thoreau. I've been through worse, almost. Once I was in the navy in an airplane, thousands of feet in the air. I'd been brooding about a woman again and not paying attention to what I was doing. When I jumped out of the plane, I realized immediately that I had strapped my food pack onto my back instead of my parachute."

"What did you do then, Kosmos?"

"I remembered Hector's words from the *Iliad* about 'uncompromising courage'. As I plummeted downward I took out a chunk of cheese and ate it in mid-air, then washed it down with a swig of wine. I promised myself that, if I should live, from then on I would live with the good sense of a goddess and the recklessness of an immortal god. I landed feet-first in the Aegean Sea and got picked up by a fisherwoman and her three blonde-haired daughters. And the moment we looked into one another's eyes, we fished no more from the boat that day."

Confidently he strided through the doorway. But almost immediately he staggered backwards, a beaten man.

"Zeus and Hera!" he shouted, coughing and gasping. "Her breath would melt a spoon!"

Before returning to the boudoir he tore off some leaves from a eucalyptus tree, chewed a few, then saved a handful for the mouth of Ligeia. He pulled up the shutters so that light would fill the room and he could see what he was doing, then he removed his pants to reveal a puny pretumescent putz. The old maid pointed to his instrument, shook her head, rocked her massive body, then laughed hysterically.

"What did you expect, you old basilisk!" Kosmos shouted. "What the hell was your last husband, a donkey?"

I opened the door just a crack and shouted through.

"Kosmos, do you need anything?"

"Just three things, Thoreau," he said. "A blindfold, my last meal, and words of wisdom to keep my courage up."

Again a shriek of shrilly laughter burst from the throat of the hilarious hag. At least, I said softly to myself, one out of two of them would be having a merry time. More laughing blasted from the woman's lips, laughing so loud it could be heard from here to Herakleion.

28
Love Lessons

"True love is like a fairy tale, a tortuous road from 'Once Upon A Time' to 'Happily Ever After.' ... But woe to the society whose stories are hopeless and bleak! What if Beauty had not looked deeper than skin deep into her Beast? If the Heimlich maneuver had not thrust the poisoned apple from Snow White's swollen throat? If the three bears had taken Goldilocks to court? If Prince Charming had lost faith to find a foot with perfect fit? If those lethargic lips of Sleeping Beauty would have remained unosculated, and the poor girl condemned to a half-life of eternal snores?"

After supplying Kosmos with clear water and vague words, I examined the fragment of Bea Loverly's note. The sheet had been ripped both vertically and horizontally; the handwriting looked as well-formed as calligraphy; the poem had been written on thick parchment paper designed to last longer than Love itself. Holding the twice-torn page, I read the words aloud.

> She loved!
> As the sunset cries
> Eros breaks her
> Love

Thick tears plunked from my eyes. I positioned myself over a potted plant, so that the tears would water the plant and not be wasted. For I knew that most sorrow on the Earth was wasted, yet at times it might be possible to transform the greatest sorrows into courage, action, and inner strength.

How had I managed to hurt so deep the woman I loved so much? I might have stood for hours staring at the sea, watering the plants with tears, dreaming of a world of make-believe built on a love that might have been.

But these devitalizing reflections were suspended by the racket from the old maid's bedroom. Frustrated about his failure to rise to the challenge and perform, the impotent Kosmos cursed and swore a dozen dozen times.

"Oh, horrid vulturism of earth! from which not the mightiest whale is free. ... And of all these things, the albino whale was the symbol."

And each Kosmic outburst tickled the lucky Ligeia, whose shrilly shrieks of laughter shook the shutters, shivered the sheets, and shrank the simmering schlong.

I stepped down the hotel's stairs then wandered — aimlessly, hopelessly, mindlessly — through the streets of the small coastal town.

Kosmos was still swearing and Ligeia still laughing when I returned to find that no progress at all had been made in their preposterous carnal quest. Through the shutters I could see two masses of blubbery flesh. My sense of aesthetic appreciation steered my gaze toward the adjacent room — the room once occupied by the divine presence of Beatrice Loverly. With the door open wide, I could not resist the temptation to step inside.

Here I was startled to discover a woman sitting with her legs crossed on one of the two beds. With flawless posture she sipped coffee from a paper cup as she flipped through pages of a magazine. Her familiar-looking silk kimono had been pinned up to six inches below her waist, revealing two tanned thighs, thighs powerful, shapely, sensual.

"Surprised to see me here, Thoreau?" she asked.

"Penelope!"

Penelope invited me to sit beside her by patting her hand against the covers on the bed.

"Beatrice and I had a long talk this morning. I explained how I like to stretch the truth a little bit, how you and me had never made sex together, and how my foolproof jealousy test proved what a fool I am! We apologized to each other, and then we promised to be sisters and the best of friends. Pen pals for now, because early this morning she discovered that she had urgent business to get back to. And since this room was already paid for through the rest of the week, she told me to take it and to enjoy myself. She gave me some of her clothes, too, and left some of her daughter's clothes for my daughter. And she didn't forget you, she never will! Come here."

I glanced up at a corner of the ceiling — where an insect struggled helplessly in the web of a spider — then I sat down on the bed beside Penelope. She raised my hand then guided it inside the kimono between the two volcanic islands of her breasts. After playing for a moment with the bait, I fished out a folded paper sheet.

"It's a poem for you from Beatrice," Penelope said. "A copy of the one she left with Ligeia. Just in case Kosmos didn't have the guts to get it."

"The same note?" I asked.

The woman's warm hand gripped the top of the my muscular thigh.

"The very same note."

My smile grew like a mushroom on a rainy day. I shook my head.

"Then Kosmos doesn't need to go through all that — "

Penelope's whole body shook as she laughed and laughed.

"A good joke, yes? Prudence came up with the idea! Don't you think our pal Kosmos deserves it for being a triple rat? Two wives in Athens! Arrgh! He has two black eyes right now, and I wish he had a hundred eyes like that giant monster who was turned into a peacock. A hundred eyes so that I could blacken every one!"

She squeezed my arm with a touch that begged for more attention.

"You think we should tell him, Thoreau? I know you do. But who is wise enough to meddle in the private business between a woman and a man? Let Ligeia have a little fun for the first time in twenty years, let Kosmos enjoy the pleasure of doing a good deed for you, and let Prudence relish the story of her ice-cold revenge."

Penelope's face brightened the moment I nodded my head to agree. Slowly — after a deep breath — I unfolded the message from Beatrice. The paper held three four-line poems — or one three-stanza poem of twelve lines. The words I had read earlier had been a piece of the first poem which had been torn near the middle. The entire version of that first stanza said this:

> She loved! She loves him better!
> As the sunset cries to dawn
> Eros breaks her heart!
> And yet, her Love lives on and on.

I hated to cry, and one thing I hated worse than crying was crying in front of a woman I liked. 'Give your joy to others, keep your sadness to yourself,' was my motto. I did my best to hold back the rush of tears.

"Is that what strength a woman is, Penelope? A man destroys a woman's love and she responds by loving more."

Penelope placed her arm around my shoulders and gently stroked my hair.

"Don't be fooled, Thoreau. All women aren't saints, and even the saints among us aren't saints all the time. Break a woman's heart before she's finished with you — sometimes no but sometimes yes — and she'd rather see you boiled alive in olive oil than see you in the arms of the ugliest hag on earth."

"But the poem says she still loves him."

Penelope nodded.

"Because she still has hopes that her love will tame him and win him back."

Now — as often was the case when women explained the ways of women to me — I wound up at the end of the explanation even more confused.

"But Penelope, she left me without saying one word of a good-bye."

"Then trust her," said Penelope, "and believe she had a good reason for doing it that way. Listen, Thoreau. Every time Love grabs you, you risk hurting and being hurt. Eros shoots you in the heart with a poisoned arrow, he doesn't smack you in the face with a cherry pie."

The note in my hand, the hope amidst the heartbreak, the warmth and softness of the woman near helped to free me from the chilling clutch of loneliness. I looked into this woman's eyes and saw my own small face reflected in her earth-brown eyes. Was it possible to learn from my experiences, I wondered, or again and again, would each relationship begin with the best hopes then end with the worst dejection?

Penelope looked at the light in my eyes, sighed twice, and understood what I was thinking. She seized my right hand then laid it against the skin above her quickly-beating heart. The gesture closened the bond between us, and quickened my own heart's beat.

"I can teach you, Thoreau," she said, "if you repeat after me. But don't say it unless you mean it. An oath with the teeth only won't help you at all."

"I mean it already, Penelope, I swear it! Before I wound another woman's heart I'll live in a shack on the tallest mountaintop, thousands of miles away from civilization, without the latest modern inconveniences, without computers or electricity or flush toilets or gift-catalogs, with nothing but one cup for water, one book, one knife, one quick-release loincloth, and one hundred concupiscent concubines."

She pinched my cheek, then rocked me in her robust arms. The rhyme she sang rang with a melody that vaguely resembled the theme from the ditty 'Yankee Doodle.'

> "A woman's body like a bed,
>   how little takes to make it!
> A woman's heart like gingerbread,
>   how little takes to break it!"

I sang along until Penelope kissed my forehead. She placed my hand on her lap, and her hand on mine, then asked me to repeat, line by line, her sympathetic oath.

> "I swear to Aphrodite and to all the other gods — "
> "I swear to Aphrodite and to all the other gods — "
> "... that whenever a woman loves me —"
> "... that whenever a woman loves me —"
> "... I will treasure the pleasure of her love and treat her tenderly."
> "... I will treasure the pleasure of her love and treat her tenderly."

Penelope beamed like a little girl throwing a lei around the neck of a little boy.

"Now that you're no longer a menace to the republic of women, you can meet the most beautiful Greek woman in Greece. She's almost ready! Don't move!"

At first I hoped that Beatrice would appear, but Penelope had said Greek woman, and — thinking of Ligeia and one Englishwoman's revenge — I prepared for the best or the worst.

With one hand holding her kimono closed, Penelope sprang off the bed then ran into the bathroom. She returned glowing with pride, squeezing the hand of a young woman whose natural beauty caused me to stare with reverence and awe. The familiar face had been adorned beneath red lipstick and black eye shadow; the long hair flowed with the softest curls; the curves of the body had been accentuated under a revealing dress that acted like a spring-trap on the animal in man. I stood up.

"*Hero poli,* pleased to meet you," I said. "Are you a dream of perfect loveliness, or does this vision have a name?"

The young woman ran into my arms then poured a long sweet kiss into my thirsty lips.

"Thoreau, silly, it's Irene! But you and only you can call me 'Love.'"

Before I could respond Irene kissed my lips even more passionately, then pressed her nose against my nose.

"I love you, I love you, I love you!" she said like a song. "Do you know the first moment I fell in love with you? It was when you brushed my hair with your hand then kissed my fingers and looked into my eyes. You looked into my eyes as if I were the most beautiful woman in Greece."

Her eyes glowed, she smiled a perfect smile, she kissed my face ten times more then stared at me as if each moment looking in my eyes was worth a thousand years of bliss.

Penelope, laughing and touching her daughter's shoulder, held up a nightgown shorter than a haiku.

"Irene, dearest. There's more to love than words and stares and sighs. Go into the other room and make sure that we don't make the baby. Then put this nightie on and come right back. Today we'll teach this know-it-all Thoreau the difference between a night with anywoman, and a night with a woman in love."

Irene tore herself from my arms, grabbed the nightgown, then ran like a nymph into the next room. At Penelope's urging, I read the second stanza of Bea Loverly's note.

> When burning Love chills then goes sour
> Stop and think and weep one hour.
> Then sooner than this hour's done —
> Go find another loving one.

Penelope resumed her place beside me then she pushed me onto the bed.

"You're not going to let us down, are you Thoreau? Don't you Americans have a saying: 'Make love while the sun shines.'? "

"It's not love, it's hay."

"Hey, Thoreau!" she said as she tickled my ribs. And when I placed my hands there to protect the ribs she reached down and pulled down my shorts.

"A big boy like you," she said, "should not be ashamed of his body. You need to relax and loosen up. An ounce of perversion is worth a pound of liqueur."

"It's prevention and cure," I said.

"Sex is good for everything, I know," replied Penelope. "Take off your undershorts and let's find out if you're a man or a moose."

"Penelope, it's not a moose it's a mouse."

"Moose, mouse? First let me see it," she said, "then I'll be the one to decide."

My mind flew to a kingdom of never-thought ideas. I was twenty-six, the girl eighteen: How young is too young to make love? Beatrice's poem seemed to heartily approve; Kosmos had been urging it from the first day; Penelope was acting more like a brothel madam than a mother; and whether or not Irene was an adult she was certainly consenting. But if I did decide to make love with the young woman then it must not be a handout dispensed from pity, it must be a gift given and received with superabundant joy.

It was difficult to know what was right, but simple to realize what I wanted. When my mind returned from these meditations to the surreal scene around me, I discovered that I was sitting naked on the bed, basking in the shine of Penelope's sunny gaze. More joy! The spritely Irene burst into the bedroom dressed in a nightgown flimsier than a bad excuse. For a radiant minute she laughed and sang and danced around the room. Giggling with glee she suddenly leaped on top of me, kissing again and again, until she sat upright beside me on the bed.

Through the walls next door we heard a raucous gurgling shout from Kosmos:

"He who escapes a mortal danger loves life with a new intensity!"

A new intensity! Every moment of our lives we wish to recapture the enthusiasm we felt in childhood: in our sublimest moments we crave adventure, we nurture nature, we savor sex, we love being in love.

I looked at Irene and saw her with new eyes.

And the moment I smiled at her and touched her hand, tears of happiness drizzled down her cheeks. She sang for me, with so much passion, a song from Sappho, one of her favorite songs.

"The moon has set and the Pleiades turned
 The hours passing by
 And midnight come, and midnight spurned

Alone, alone I lie.

"The moon has set and the Pleiades tossed
 The hours passing on
 And midnight come, and midnight lost
 Alone I lie, alone.
 And midnight come, and midnight lost
 Alone I lie, alone."

From Ligeia's bedroom next door the shrieks of laughter ceased, and all who listened heard the sound of a door swing open then smack against a wall. Penelope heard it, and in less than an instant she threw off her robe and jumped her bare body into my athletic arms.

"Kiss me," she whispered, "if you believe in Love!" — and then she kissed me on the lips as if I was about to leave for war.

As the kiss continued Kosmos strolled in, examined the naked kissers, then laughed his loudest laugh.

"What's this?" he shouted cheerfully. "A meeting of the Nudists Society? I tried being a nudist once, but it wasn't any fun: I couldn't play strip poker, I had no place to hide my ace, and all the women looked down on me and knew what I was thinking about them."

His hair disheveled, his brow beaded with sweat, his face reddened, his towel wrapped around his protruding belly: Kosmos looked like he had just finished running a marathon's twenty-seventh mile. He smiled to the playacting lovers, stepped into the kitchen then returned with three important items.

"Flashlight," he said, holding it up to show us. "I need it, but don't ask why! A large bottle of mouthwash, but a dozen barrels wouldn't be enough! And of course, the Swiss army knife of seducers: a jug of wine. To make love with young women you need to get them drunk; to make love with old women you need to get yourself drunk."

As he stepped toward the door he said: "There's an old Cretan proverb, Thoreau, don't forget it. 'Where you fail, return; where you succeed, depart.'"

Penelope released me, cursed at Kosmos, then threw a pillow at him which he caught with his free hand. Then the fiery woman leaped from the bed and pounced at Kosmos with such speed and ferocity that the quickest tigress in the jungle would have bowed and admired.

"Damn you, Kosmos!" screamed Penelope. "How can you stand there and watch while I'm kissing another man! Don't you care about me, about us, even a little bit?"

Tears streamed from her eyes as she shouted and pounded his chest with both her fists. Without a flinch, Kosmos stood solidly and took the punches. When she had finished hitting with her hands she hit him with a hundred angry words. He looked at her with the utmost sympathy; he spoke to her with all the kindness of the earth and all the sincerity of the clearest skies.

"I know what you're doing, Penelope. Those games don't work with me. And some men don't show their jealously, even though they might be falling apart inside."

Penelope was crying now, and Kosmos — after putting down the flashlight, mouthwash, and wine — becalmed her with a warm embrace. He knew by intuition precisely what to do and say. He let her head fall onto his shoulder, he danced with her around the room, he sang to her another of his made-up songs.

> "You can eat my Gorgonzola
> You can drink my wine, by Jove!
> Let me row my sore gondola
> Through your sweet tunnel of love!"

Through her tears Penelope began to laugh.

"Good luck, Captain Kosmos," she said. "Next door you can't even raise your oar."

He kissed her forehead.

"Don't joke too much about that situation, Penelope!" said Kosmos, smiling. "You know, lots of times the gods make true the very things we ridicule or fear!"

Penelope stroked his hair.

"You're deathly afraid to marry me, you three-timer!" she told him. "Why don't your gods do something about that!"

"Thoreau," said Kosmos. "We can all learn something important from women like Penelope. She can sweet-talk the strawberries out of the shortcake and charm the honey out of the baklava."

To say thanks for the way he had complimented her she rewarded him with a feverish kiss, then together they fell laughing-laughing-laughing onto the adjacent bed.

As I observed the sparks between Penelope and Kosmos, they reminded me of those love-novels where the readers realize that the hero and heroine were made for each other, and everyone in the world can see it clearly except the stubborn He and She. Irene, her mouth as wide open as her eyes, stared bedward at the Kosmo-Penelopedic activities she had never observed before. She had learned some lessons from Beatrice, and now her mother was showing her more. I found the precious piece of paper, then I read the last stanza of Bea Loverly's poem.

> One lust night of wild adoring!
> One last light the stars dare speak,
> Two lost lovers cease exploring
> Find the darkling paradise they seek.

The darkling paradise! ... I felt the seed of an amazing idea sprouting, but it slipped away when my hand was tugged by the gentle hand of Irene.

"Thoreau, please take off my nightgown. Aunt Bea said that I should let you undress me. She said that the only time men like to pick up clothes is when they're on the body of a good-looking girl."

In a moment, the shy young goddess stood before me in her splendid nakedness, and the sight made me sigh with joy. Deeply moved by my appreciation, Irene stroked my cheek to thank me for the admiring stares.

"Thoreau," she said. "Tell me how beautiful I am."

For this woman's beauty there were no sufficient words. But half the job of a poet and a novelist is to describe those things that words cannot describe.

"Irene," I said, truly astonished at her loveliness. "If all the olives in the world could speak they could not say how beautiful you are."

She sat up and kissed me; she bathed my body with those same admiring glances that I showered upon hers. Believing at last she was desired, admired and beloved, the young woman glowed with her own new power. She trusted a man; to him alone would she open the full flower of her body and soul.

"Rub my body with this olive oil," she said. "All over, please. I've never done this before but don't worry, it's one-hundred percent cold-pressed extra virgin oil."

I poured the oil onto my fingers then rubbed her body with the oil. The woman had charm, warmth, effervescence: these things touched me and made me feel more tender, more sincere, more true. Irene hummed, trembled, purred.

"Aunt Bea said that every lovemaking session should begin with a massage. And she said that because I'm inexperienced you wouldn't be sure if we should sleep together, but if I gave you the LMT — the Loverly Magic Touch — then you wouldn't be able to resist me."

One long minute later I shouted under a spasm of rapture too marvelous to imagine and too intense to be described. Looking at the proud Irene I wondered how she accomplished it. It seemed impossible that someone new to lovemaking could give so much pleasure to a partner the first time. How could a novice, who had learned how the chess pieces moved in the morning, play so well that in the evening she would demolish the world champion of chess? Ah, but chess was a war, a quest for individual supremacy, a fierce psychological battle. Whereas lovemaking, like love — pursued in the best spirit — brings us closer together as each member of the partnership strives unselfishly to grow.

"Irene!" I said, à la Dickens, with great expectations. "What else did Aunt Beatrice teach you?"

Irene kissed my lusting lips.

"She taught me what to do if a man in bed does nasty things that I don't want him to do. The LSS: the Loverly Scrotum Scratch."

And before I could respond to the obvious consequences of this remarkable remark, Irene unleashed her fingernails then demonstrated the self-defense which she had so adeptly learned.

Within seconds the mighty had fallen; parts that previously pulsed in pleasure now throbbed in palpitating agony. Like a rushing subway train I screamed. I rolled off the bed, tried to smile at Lady Loverly's long-distance vengeance, then pressed my hands around my throbbing pouch. I had felt more pain than this once in my life: while carelessly zipping up my fly I had caught my nipper-nopper (as my grandfather called it) in the teeth of the zipper. A torturous experience which is the male equivalent of the pains of childbirth.

Penelope jumped to the rescue: she poured wine onto the wounded region and then dabbed it gently with a soft sponge.

"My god! If she keeps that up we'll have to send for the village mourners to chant the dirges. She'll murder the poor boy if I don't teach her what to do!"

Holding a towel around his belly with one hand and a first-aid kit in the other hand, Kosmos examined my magic wand.

"*Dhen eena teepota,* it's nothing!" he declared. "Just a little love scratch, a superficial wound. No blood shed, nothing severed, no parts to sew back on, no beans out of the pod. So the dowry does not need to be re-funded."

Forgivingly, Kosmos kissed Irene's forehead, then he slapped my shoulder with great affection.

"I've got to get back to the trenches. Good luck, Thoreau. If you need anything —," he winked as he stepped backwards through the doorway "— just holler."

A statuesque Irene stood over me, hands prayfully folded, waiting for the moment of judgment. At last she could no longer wait.

"I'm so sorry, Thoreau!" she said, biting the offending fingernails. "Do you still love me?"

I stood up sooner than I might have done had I been alone, with no women to impress.

"For a few seconds I stopped thinking about you, Irene, but I never stopped loving you."

She screamed with joy then threw her arms around my neck and then kissed me a dozen times and hugged me with all her might.

The lovers were separated by Penelope.

"Irene, you'll choke him to death!" she cried. "Sit down and listen up. Thoreau, forget about your sexual uphangs and pay attention. Touch her in a way that says, without words, how much you care about her."

Yangly I touched, touched, touched, and touched; yinly Irene smiled, moaned, melted, and sighed. But Penelope was far from satisfied.

"What the hell do you think you're doing, Thoreau!" she shouted. "That's the breast of a woman, not the udder of a goat!"

I released the breast then sat on both my hands. Penelope shook her head.

"Irene!"

"Yes, mother!"

"Imagine that you are the snake, a python, in the first Garden of Paradise. The python can crush animals much larger than itself, but it only gets its crushing strength when it secures its tail around a tree. Go ahead now."

"I don't see any trees in the room, Mother," Irene cried.

"Embrace Thoreau's tree!" Penelope yelled. "It's right under your nose!"

Irene looked blankly, and Penelope continued shouting at her until the flustered young woman burst into tears.

I stood up, walked across the room, put my hand around the doorknob then pulled opened the door.

"Penelope," I said. "Don't take this personally, but this isn't working out. One of us needs to leave."

Penelope strode to the doorway, faced me, poked her finger into my chest.

"What's the matter with your memory, Thoreau! Now you threaten to abandon us, and ten minutes ago you promised to treasure her love and treat her tenderly! And besides, who made you the king? There are three people involved here. Let's take a vote."

I voted for Penelope to leave; Penelope cast an opposing vote; and then Irene, saying "She's my mother!" also voted for everyone to remain.

"Ha!" shouted Penelope. "One vote says I leave and you stay, two votes say that everybody stays. A two-to-one landslide. Do you believe in democracy and equal rights for women, Thoreau? Then kiss my cheeks, kiss Irene's lips, and go stand up next to the bed!"

I closed the door, kissed the cheeks and lips, then strolled back and stood beside the bed. Penelope, from her purse, removed a thumb-sized container of dark-red lipstick. After studying me for a minute — tilting her head this way then that way like an artist — she drew red lines all over my powerful body, dividing the body into segments like a carcass of fresh beef. There was chuck, ribs, shank, brisket, plate, flank, loin (tenderloin and porterhouse), sirloin, rump, round, brains, ears, lips — and tree.

Into each of my segments Penelope wrote a number, so that she could continue her instructions to Irene with paint-by-number accuracy. Penelope shouted advice like: "Irene, hands on one! Lips on four! Legs around fourteen!"

The lesson continued and Penelope, now armed with an accurate map of the territory, commanded like a general marching her troops to the climax of a rousing victory.

"Irene, dearest," she would say, again and again, "he's beautiful, we know, but concentrate on what you're doing. Always concentrate."

I admired Penelope's original mind almost as much as Irene's original body. But after the third assault I peered down at my subdivided self, and then I shook my head.

"Penelope!" I said. "I'll never forget you for this. I'm a whole man, not an animal hanging in a butcher shop. Am I going to be made love to, or eaten alive?"

"Thoreau!" Penelope replied. "I can see that you've never had sexmaking with a woman who knows what she's doing. Made love to or eaten alive? What a question! You know what the answer to that is? It's five simple words. An old wise woman in Paris told me, and now I'm telling it to you."

She stroked my cheek affectionately, then squeezed my lips together with her hand.

"Be beautiful and shut up!"

29
Decline and Fall of the Kosmos

Whoever wrote the latin proverb *"Post coitum omne animal triste est"* — "After sexual intercourse every animal is sad" — must have been doing it all wrong. Blazing with my enthusiasm and aroused by my god within, the women in my embrace quaked with rapture, quivered with awe, quibbled with devotion, trembled with thankfulness. And afterwards they would have re-written the dusty proverb to say: "After intercourse every animal wants more."

Feelings like these had deeply moved Irene! This new-woman, ever wandering the worlds between realities and dreams, had dived headfirst into the fishy sea of sex. I marveled at her curiosity, her spontaneity, her youthful poise. Unspoiled by fierce neurotic notions or by false romantic hopes, she abandons herself wholeheartedly to this enchanted realm. She is a child playing games, an artist splashing paint against a canvas, a kitten wrestling in the fond embrace of brother cat. Sex for her is not sacred, not ordinary, not obscene: sex is natural and playful and fun. Her sex is a gift and her love is present. She kisses the joy as it flies. She clings to her sweetheart but never with the plodding desperation of a turtle trapped under its shell. She enjoys each moment happy as a lovebird in a nest of love.

The sky was greying and a breeze cooled the air with the invigorating scent of rain. Irene, Penelope, and I — now as close as friends can be — held hands as we strolled back toward Dembacchae along the deserted beach. The lovely evening listened to us talking and praising one another by singing simple songs. Now and again Irene kissed me and whispered sweet lovethings to my ear, while Penelope eyed me with the glance of a fond big sister, stroking my forehead and my hair. Each time the wind gusted it blew open the women's robes. We laughed at the naughty wind, and at the beauty of our bodies, and at the joy of every living being on our earth.

Soon we reached that scenic stretch of seashore that Kosmos had always called 'my *kaliparalea*'. As we walked across this beach the warm winds whispered and the pagan voices sang. The same sweet thought tempted all the minds: how lovely, lovely, lovely it would be to lay down here on sandy beds to touch bodies, smile eyes, and play at love! ... We walked on; we ignored the sacred voices; we trembled with regrets as winds blew once again, a cooler breeze that scattered all desires.

Over this playful piece of beach we passed; we walked more; and at last we saw the first houses on the hilltops on the outskirts of the town. Quickly, with the lusty wind pushing behind our backs, we walked over the sand then through Dembacchae's deserted streets. We remembered one more member of our family; we would find him now and share our joy.

In the garden of Kosmos, sitting alone behind a wooden table, we found the man. He had a tear on his cheek, a carrot in his mouth, a one-page letter in his calloused hands. And when he noticed his three sacred friends holding hands as we entered his garden, his face unwrinkled from a grimace to a smile. He placed the letter on the tabletop, then he waved to us to gather near. Shaking his head, he spurted an embarrassed laugh like a man who'd fallen on the ice and landed on his well-padded backside.

"Beeg fuckeeng problems!" he murmured. Kosmos stared into the clouding sky and two huge tears dripped from his wild eyes into the jungle of his beard.

"Nothing really matters in a man's life except three things: his house, his women, his vitality. If you're having problems with only one of these, then sing and give thanks for your blessings. Trouble with all three all at once? Then you're like a lamb on the chopping block: all you can do is bleat and pray for help. At this auspicious moment I've been cursed with two of these colossal problems. There might be a way out, but right now I don't see a way."

He shook his head, took a deep breath, slammed his fist against the tabletop.

"Learn something from my folly, Thoreau. Don't wait too long to start to free yourself. Begin today, begin right now! It's easier to escape from the lioness's lair than from her clutches, and it's easier to escape from her clutches than from her jaws."

I glanced down at the ominous envelope.

"You've just received a letter with bad news, Kosmos? Tell us every-thing. And don't gild the manure or sugar-coat the sour truth."

Kosmos drummed his fingers on the table, wondering whether he should tell. Older women and men, Kosmos believed, should not bur-den young persons with their own troubles or the troubles of the world. Let youth be a time for play, for learning, and for happiness! Yet at last he decided to hide nothing. His family — Thoreau, Penelope, Irene — were strong enough: his honesty and loving care had nurtured them and made them strong. Briefly they would share and feel his pain, then they would forget and find their joys again.

He asked us to sit around the table, and then he raised his hands to signal we should all hold hands.

"Tomorrow and tomorrow and tomorrow," he began — and he pro-nounced the words slowly as if his meandering pace could postpone the real event and make tomorrow never come. "Tomorrow I am leaving to live for a while in 'the big olive.'"

"The big olive?" I said. And I grasped the meaning the instant my question escaped.

"Athens," Kosmos replied. "That's where my two wives are living. To-morrow morning I will be officially arrested then taken to Athens's finest jail. This house and all my possessions will be confiscated then sold to pay, to pay — how do you say the word in English? In Greek it is pro-nounced 'ameevee'."

"Compensation!" said Irene.

"Thank you, dear child. To pay compensation for the mental anguish I inflicted on my two obnoxious wives."

He looked up at the swelling clouds, glanced at our fearful eyes, then swallowed the last drops of bouzo from his glass.

"Another Don Juan caught by the silent statue and dragged down to the hell he deserves. The hell he made for himself when he charged through life like a young bull, thinking about nothing at all except his own selfish pleasures. His arrogant motto: 'Breed and feed, what more do you need?'"

Penelope stepped behind the seated Kosmos, untied his shoelaces, then clasped her arms around his broad shoulders.

"I won't let that heartless statue take you!" she shouted. "I'll pull you up, the stone demon will pull you down, then I'll kick him where it hurts and send him tumbling down to hell with nothing in his hands except your holey shoes! And then, thanks to that struggle, you'll be all stretched out and taller and more handsome, too!"

Kosmos laughed at this fable while Penelope took a deep breath and filled herself with resignation.

"Don't worry, I'm leaving now," she said. "It's not Friday night, I know. If I stay five minutes longer then we'll start fighting like spiders and wasps. Thoreau and Irene will cheer you up."

Smiling, Kosmos rubbed his hand along her forearm then squeezed her hand.

"Stay here with us, will you Penelope? I'll make a nice dinner for everyone, and after dinner we'll tuck these young lovebirds under the covers in the bedroom. And then — if you're willing and I'm able — Penelope and Kosmos will make love like the immortal Olympians, outside in the raging thunderstorm."

Joyful Penelope! There are words, and there are words, words, words. The instant that Kosmos had asked her to stay she squeezed him in a great embrace. Her eyes danced with delicious delight from a time and a place long ago, half-forgotten, far away.

"No!" she shouted.

"No?" Kosmos disappointedly replied.

"No! You cook for me every week. It's my turn now to cook for you. You'll need to save all your strength for me for tonight."

As tears streamed down her cheeks, the triumphant woman looked up across the table at the lover of Irene.

"All this is thanks to you, Thoreau," she said. "When you arrived, he saw his own reflection in your eyes, he found a friend to share his secrets, he remembered the best of his young self."

This tender moment was interrupted — as so many tender moments are — by rumblings from the too-much-with-us world. First came the pittering patters of footsteps; soon afterwards four flat-footed messengers arrived.

Dressed like bellhops, they had come to Kosmos to deliver — from the notorious Judge Skleerokardos — a singing telegram. The tallest of them blew into a pitchpipe, then they began their message in a four-part *a capella* harmony.

"J is for the Jerk in all your guises
  A for Athens summons you: 'Appear!'
  IL is for ILlegal enterprises

BI is for the BIgamy, oh dear! (oh dear!)
R is for Rejecting your appeal, unheard,
D is for the Demijohns of tears
Put them all together they spell JAILBIRD
The only bird you'll see for twenty years!
— Ten for each wife ... —
The lonely bird you'll be for twenty years!"

Yelling "Bravo! Bravo!", Kosmos applauded then reached into his pocket to find some coins. But a furious Penelope, swinging a corn broom, swore at the messengers then chased them out of the yard. Then she took Irene's hand, and mother and daughter scurried toward the kitchen inside the house.

Kosmos's gaze followed their bouncing bodies with the smile of an artist studying a masterpiece. He asked to see my wisdom-book; and after I retrieved it Kosmos began to read aloud the quintessence of my literary studies, the most interesting passages from the greatest authors, heroes, artists, philosophers.

"Do you know why we need books, Thoreau? Books remind us to be ourselves: to be fearless, to be noble, to live on fire. A simple idea, but without it we can't be happy, we can't do anything worth doing. It's strange, isn't it, how often we forget the most important things."

The soul of Kosmos was a Spring of joy. At times, the plights of friends or strangers could stop it up for a few minutes, but the joy always burst through and ever stronger than before. He closed the book, kissed its cover, then spoke aloud, as much to himself as to me.

"Why are we sitting out here gabbing and farting like a couple of tired old men? Is this really my last night in Crete for the next twenty years? Come on then, wake up, Kosmos! Wake up, Thoreau! Contact, contact, touch, touch, touch! Bust out of your selfish shells and connect with the people in front of your eyes! ... I don't need a chubby little baby with wings to shoot love-arrows at innocent women: my whole body is a love-arrow. And everyone I touch feels warm, then laughs with me and falls a little more in love with life!"

He rushed though his blanketed doorway and made the women laugh when, supercharged with ardor, he waved his arms and shouted the inspired words of Maurice Maeterlinck.

"If you knew that you would die tonight, or merely that you would have to go away and never return, would you, looking on women and things for the last time, see them in the same light that you have previously seen them? Or would you love now as you never yet have loved? ... Eh, eh? ... Or would you love now as you never yet have loved!"

Kosmos hugged the back of Penelope, and the woman — so moved! — turned around to face him and wiped tears from the cheeks beneath her sparkling eyes.

"How can we get any cooking done?" she said, laughing as she cried.

The man's hands kneaded the top of her shoulders then creeped down to the woman's chest.

"Penelope, did I ever tell you how divine you look when you're sleeping and the first gold rays of Saturday morning sunshine light your face? And did you know that in the evenings, when the candlelight flickers and you're talking to me, I don't hear anything you're saying because all I can think about is how beautiful you are?"

As a blind man feeling a beloved face, his hands caressed her generous breasts.

"Thoreau, my boy!" he shouted. "Don't waste that magnificent voice of yours: sing something! Sing something suitable for this eternal moment which will never come again! Sing us a story about how it happens that unenlightened men want to make war against the whole world, but the beauty of women turns them into love-slaves, changes their battle-plans, and saves their foolish lives."

With my body being undressed and massaged sensually by the warm hands of Irene, I could not concentrate on the task of composing something original. Instead, I barely managed to remember two stanzas from Byron's unfinished satiric poem, *Don Juan.* I chanted the passages exuberantly, with all my histrionic power.

> "Fill high the bowl with Samian wine!
> Our virgins dance beneath the shade —
> I see their glorious black eyes shine;
> But gazing on each glowing maid,
> My own the burning tear-drop laves,
> To think such breasts must suckle slaves."

> "A long, long kiss, a kiss of youth and love,
> And beauty, all concentrating like rays

Into one focus, kindled from above;
Where heart, and soul, and sense in concert move,
And the blood's lava, and the pulse a blaze,
Each kiss a heart-quake, — for a kiss's strength,
I think it must be reckon'd by its length."

Kosmos gently kissed his woman and Penelope responded by pressing a long hot kiss against the man's flattering lips.

"Zeus and Hera!" shouted Kosmos. "That kiss could melt an iceberg!" He stroked her hair.

"Penelope," Kosmos said, his eyes smiling into her smiling eyes. "Did I ever tell you how, because I can see the present so clearly, I can foresee the future?"

After a nod and a gesture from Penelope, Irene remembered to run into the bathroom and arrange to protect herself from pregnancy. Penelope slid her hands down her man's body then expertly removed his pants. Hoarse with desire for the woman, Kosmos could barely murmur to his friend: "Sing us our future, Thoreau. Sing!"

And just before Irene returned and laid her naked body over mine, I chanted a prognosticating song.

"The four lovers forgot the food:
A feast of lovemaking ensued.
Even the gods, with all their might,
Envied the mortals' long sweet night.

"Soon after the envy the gods unleash their wrath!
Voyeurs and destroyers of all who cross their path.
Now we must fight these gods who meddle from the mist —
For nights with you and perfect love like this!"

I woke up to the sizzle and the smell of pancakes in a frying pan. Time in the mind had completely disappeared. Outside, a crow cawed, and the morning skies seemed unable to decide whether to rise forward to the lightening dawn, or rush back to the darkness of the night. Inside, the living room glowed with warm candlelight, and the timeless peace that only women bring. Irene lay sleeping in my strong arms. Forty, fifty, sixty times she had climbed the screaming peaks of ecstasy. Through the night she had chirped like a parakeet, cooed like a dove, swore like a parrot, gobbled like a turkey, moaned like an owl, warbled like a nightingale. Now her fine lips smiled like the canary who just swallowed the cat.

Penelope set the table with four plates and four cloth napkins as she tried to recall on which side of the plate she should place the spoons and knives, and which side gets the forks.

Meanwhile, Kosmos, standing near the wrapped-together bodies of me and Irene, had been sketching our pictures on a white drawing pad. When I asked to see the steamy scenes, Kosmos explained that it was not yet ready. Penelope interrupted by asking me to carry the half-asleep Irene to her dining-room chair. Around the table our hearts were one as we looked at one another and joined hands.

With his left hand Kosmos squeezed Penelope's hand, and his right hand gently held Irene's.

"It is fashionable in books these days," he began, "to be cynical about love, ironic about life, skeptical about even the faintest possibility of happiness. The miserable intellectuals — who get paid to think and write, which is why they do both so badly — say that every man is alienated, families are always in conflict, and the dining table is the bloody battleground. How much nonsense is written in the modern books! For thousands of years even the humblest peasants on Crete have known this: There is no greater joy than to gather with your family for a meal."

Sleepy-eyed Irene climbed onto my lap, called me her 'beautiful baby', then fed me as if I were one. Penelope jumped onto the lap of the man she admired and loved.

"Here, my god of garbage," she said to Kosmos. "Try a bit of this and a bite of that."

Kosmos tasted the samples then smiled with great delight.

"What do you call this food for men favored by the goddesses?" he asked.

"Greek love-pancakes," answered Penelope. "Oozing inside with figs and walnuts and feta cheese."

"And this miracle of taste?" said Kosmos.

"That's popeyed salad," she replied. "Spinach and sweet peas in olive oil."

Kosmos licked his lips.

"For Thoreau, fill up an urn, and for me, a whole barrel! Penelope, I didn't know that you could cook like this!"

She pinched his ruddy cheek.

"There are lots of things about me that you do not know."

She giggled like a fairy hiding in the woods.

"Here," she said. "Have more."

The temptress waved a large plate of the food near his face, but when he leaned forward to bite it, she pulled it away from his mouth then laughed and laughed. Penelope melted in his arms, kissed him lasciviously, and then whispered: "One more time, lover, just one more time! Take the food later and take me now."

Poor Kosmos! Worn out from his earlier fiasco with the maid Ligeia and his delightfully-sleepless night with Penelope, the ravenous man wanted to eat a large meal, immediately and undisturbed.

"Penelope," he said, beginning to lose his humor and his calm. "I am not named Tantalus, I am Kosmos. In the last twenty-four hours I have satisfied two insatiable women. And right now I am very very hungry."

Still straddling his lap with her naked thighs she teased him again with the receding food. Instead of the pancakes she fed him her succulent lips.

"Penelope," he said, shaking his head. "There are a few times in a man's life — maybe twice every fifty-five years — when he would rather eat than make love with a woman like you. Did you hear those six bells? If we eat now, we can have another hour this morning to worship Aphrodite by playing her favorite games."

Penelope stood up then grabbed his beard like a kitchen sponge.

"It's our last morning together!" she cried out. "You want food more than me? Here, Casserolenova! Eat this!"

She smushed a chunk of feta cheese onto his face, then decorated the hair on his chest with the oily trimmings of spinach and peas.

"Penelope," he pleaded. "Why should you get mad at me for saying what I think? Will that encourage honesty in our relationship?"

Tears in her eyes, Penelope stood up then thrust her hands against her shapely hips unclad.

"You remind me of that donkey in the Greek fable. He jumped up on top of a rock and started braying: 'I'm an ass! I'm an ass!' He told the truth, it's true, but that didn't turn him into a stallion! He was still an ass, no matter how much he admitted to the truth. ... Do you know what your problem is, my dear Kosmos? You believe that honesty excuses everything!"

Kosmos filled his plate with piles of popeyed salad and Greek pancakes.

"But we must have honesty, my dear Penelope, or we have nothing at all. Let's see how a real man holds up under the heavy hammer of truth."

Stuffing his mouth with food, Kosmos turned his face toward me.

"Thoreau, last night — after many hours of intimate activities too wild to be imagined and too glorious to be described — Penelope and I were talking and we agreed on this: Today you and I should change women."

"Change women?" I shouted. I gripped my arms protectively around my half-awake Irene.

Kosmos swallowed some food then waved his hands as he replied.

"Thoreau, am I speaking English, or am I speaking Gondi, the Dravidian language of the Gonds? I said change women and that's exactly what I mean. I am now with Penelope, and you are with Irene. Now I will take Irene with me and you will take good care of Penelope. Without the least bit of reservations, Penelope is agreed. And Irene? Irene has the heart of a child with the body of a woman. She will resist at first, but it's all for her own good. Someday she'll realize this, and then bless us with her deepest gratitude."

The morning light, winning its battle against the darkness, slipped its glowing fingers though the glassless windows of the stone house. I reflected on this proposition then shook my head to disagree. Irene opened her eyes, smiled at me, then showered my cheeks with delicious kisses.

Before this experiment with truth and morals could carry on, our ears were pierced by desperate shouts of "Kosmos! Kosmos! Kosmos!" screaming from the hectic world outside.

Coolly, Kosmos filled up four mugs with apple cider, one for himself and one for each of his three companions.

"Ladies," Kosmos said, addressing Irene and Penelope. "I can see the future now as clearly as the breasts on your chests. Put something on to cover your splendid bodies. We are about to entertain a frantic guest."

Laughing out loud, he held up a fifth cider-filled mug toward his doorway just as a burly Greek man dashed into the garden like a bull stung by a bumblebee.

30
CHANGE IS GOOD

PENELOPE RAISED her arms then covered her tremendous breasts by draping them under a white T-shirt, a gift from Lady Loverly which in large red letters said:

> Problems, problems, days and nights
> If what you hold has balls or bytes.

Concentrating intensely, Kosmos regarded the woman's form. Beauty always inspires. A brilliant new idea bedazzled his inventive mind.

"You know, Thoreau, when Pericles — the Greek version of your Thomas Jefferson — ruled Athens, the finest prostitutes in his city were never despised, they were honored and adored. What was the greatest danger to the stability of Athenian society? ... Adultery. And the solution to adultery? Prostitution. Whoredom relieves boredom: it preserves the family while satisfying the wandering lusts of men."

Kosmos sipped the cider then carried on.

"How could an amorous man recognize our Hellenic harlots? Large wooden phalluses, even bigger than my own monster, protruded from the doors of the ancient brothels. As for the objects of desire themselves, many of the women wore sandals, carved on the bottoms so that they impressed letters on the dirt paths that spelled two words: 'Follow me.'"

Glancing at Penelope, Kosmos took a deep breath then sighed.

"Have you noticed the way Penelope walks, without even thinking about walking, and the effect this motion has on men like me? From every pore of her luscious body — legs, thighs, hips, cheeks, back, shoulders — Penelope shouts 'Follow me!' every time she moves. Where did she learn to walk and talk like that, so full of meanings without any words! Maybe there's a whore in every good woman, and a good woman in every whore. ... But Penelope is not a prostitute — she sleeps with men who love her and men she loves. Explain it all to me, Thoreau, this mysterious power called desire! It rules even the gods. And in this whole world, what man and which woman is immune?"

He laughed at his own wild thoughts.

"But here I go again, getting distracted by the first good-looking body that passes by, and never getting anything accomplished. We were discussing, my dear old-fashioned Thoreau, the subject of changing women. I will take Irene and you will take Penelope. Change is good, Thoreau. Change rejuvenates a man: it forces us to be alert, to think fresh, to solve new problems creatively."

"Kosmos! Kosmos! It's not too late!"

I wrapped a blanket around Irene at the same moment that a stout guest ran through the blanket-doorway and into the living room. Rakis was his name and he was built like Heracles. His height and his broad shoulders filled up the room, and suddenly the spacious dwelling seemed to shrink to dollhouse size. Bearing the body, neck, and head of a hardworking laborer — sailor, builder, miner, wrestler, piano-mover — this brute man had eyes that strangely glimmered with the depths of human misery.

He carried three suitcases in one hand and a fistful of Euros in the other. Ignoring the curvaceous Penelope and the slender Irene, he ran unswervingly to Kosmos. Rakis had a plan. Talking faster than an auctioneer and waving his arms like a drowning man, he explained how Kosmos could hide for a few weeks in Rakis's wine cellar, then escape from Crete and live disguised as a shepherd in a small mountain village in the region of mainland Greece known as Arcadia.

Kosmos glanced affectionately at the face of his feverish friend.

"*Seega, seega*, Rakis! Drink the wine of courage, and then the deadliest Medusa looks like a lovely young maid! ... Maybe this predicament means the end of the old decaying world, and the beginning of a new and greater one. Change is good. What did you bring us besides your loyal self?"

Rakis placed everything he was holding onto the wooden table, then looked down at Kosmos solemnly.

"Here's a few bags for you," Rakis said, "to pack the necessities, so we can leave at noon before the bastards come and take you off. Here's all my money, but if you need more I can sell my truck and get you twice as much."

Thoreau admired this man who, without hesitating one instant, gave everything he owned to help his friend. Rakis unwrapped a large handkerchief.

"And here's our breakfast for the road. One dozen eggs, freshly poached."

Kosmos shook one of the eggs.

"The eggs don't feel like they've been cooked, Rakis."

"I said they were poached," Rakis explained. "I stole them from the monastery henhouse this morning before dawn."

Kosmos laughed.

"Sit down across from me, Rakis. Sit down, relax, and share some food with us. Shake hands with my friend Thoreau, but don't crush his knuckles like you crushed mine when we first met."

With two nods and a quick 'Kalimera, kalimera', Rakis first greeted Penelope and Irene. Then, staring suspiciously, Rakis grasped my hand with a mighty grip. I gripped back, smiling, wondering if the pun "It's a pressure to meet you" could be effectively translated from English into Greek. Kosmos ended the contest by separating the two clutched hands, and then he spoke to his huge friend.

"You were saying, Rakis, that I should hide out in a wine cellar then run away and live with animals. It's tempting, I admit that. A painter named Gauguin escaped from Paris to paradise then never looked back. But let's look ahead for a moment and ask ourselves questions as clear as our Greek light. What would happen to my integrity? What would happen to your wine? And what rough beasts would roam the hills of Arcady, with heads like the wily Kosmos and bodies like the woolly sheep?"

The face of Rakis paled as he realized that Kosmos had no wish to sneak away and save himself. Kosmos reached up and slapped the giant's shoulder.

"I can't change my way of living. Like Socrates, I need to do what the god inside me advises me to do. Your eyes, dear Rakis, are asking me this question: Why should the great Kosmos follow and fall for our foolish Greek law? Why? ... Because if you say that one man can break the law he chooses, then everyone might break any law they choose. And then there would be anarchy, a state where strong men strangulate the weak, rich men pulverize the poor, ignoramuses ignite the wise, fanatic men fustigate the free. Right now in our so-called democracy we have more than enough of that. Mere anarchy unleashed upon the world would make it worse one thousand times."

Sadly, Rakis nodded to say he understood. Penelope and Irene watched Kosmos with silent admiration. I did not want to interfere, but I could not prevent myself from speaking out.

"I don't agree, Kosmos. I don't agree at all. What if the laws themselves are unjust? What if the leaders of the lands are tyrants who command us to do destructive things? ... Then, not compliance but defiance is the noble and courageous way. ... You treat women with the utmost reverence: I can't believe that you caused mental anguish to any woman or to any living being. And even if you did, why should the courts take your house and all your possessions for something like that? How would that heal the pain of your exasperated ex-wives? Is money a remedy for mental anguish? Can the rooted sorrows of a mind diseased be plucked by the frigid fingers of cold cash?"

Kosmos tugged his beard and thought about these things for a long minute before he spoke.

"No, I've never caused those women any mental anguish, nothing that I know about. They were selfish, unhappy overconsumers before they met me, and they'll be selfish, unhappy overconsumers until the day they diet. While I lived with both my wives I was infatuated like a schoolboy, and I served them as if they were the queens of Greece. Then it all fell apart in one instant: both times it happened the very same way. The wife demanded me to do something in a voice-tone that rattled with contempt. I looked at the strange woman, the scams fell from my eyes, and a god inside me shouted: 'Stand up like a man!' ... One squabble later, I threw everything I owned into a paper bag and I walked out. ... Imagine how Socrates would have argued my defense: 'Women of Athens: you swear that Kosmos is a lump of donkey dreck? In that case, by abandoning you he granted you the biggest favor in the world! Don't punish him for that good deed, give him a generous reward!'"

His smile revealed that, by thinking out loud, he had just discovered an immense idea. From a drawer built-in to the wooden table, he picked up a screwdriver and a mallet, then tossed them to his friend.

"Rakis!" he shouted.

"Boss?" Rakis replied.

"Take the toilet and leave those assholes nothing but the turds!"

Kosmos grasped my shoulders.

"Zeus, throw a thunderbolt and fry my flam! You're right, Thoreau! If money eases mental anguish, then why are most rich people so shallow and so miserable? If the courts of Greece believe that Kosmos is a danger to the society of decent women, then they should lock Kosmos in a jail cell with hordes of indecent women. What the hell does money have to do with it? To take away the things a man has worked his whole life for — house, garden, art, precious books — that is a punishment that does not fit the crime."

Quickly he turned to Penelope but as he tried to begin to talk with her she waved her arms and interrupted.

"Look at his eyes, it's that gleam again!" she shouted. "He's getting another one of his mad ideas. And now he's going to beg me to forgive him for postponing our last sexmaking together, postponing it for twenty years! Ah! If a smart woman falls in love with a complete idiot, does that mean she's stupid, too?"

Her anger vanished as quickly as it had flared. As Penelope gazed at the man she loved, her eyes filled with tears and shined with tenderness and pride.

"Go ahead, my dearest Kosmos! You're off the hook. Whatever your scheme is you'd better eat something now then get moving. The sooner one starts, the sooner one finishes."

Kosmos smiled at the woman and moved closer to hug her, but she pushed him away then covered the table with plates piled high with food.

Kosmos sat down, and while his left hand stuck a fork into a pancake, his right hand plucked the pencil from behind his ear and began writing on a paper scrap.

"Rakis," said Kosmos, with his mouth full. "Feel strong?"

Rakis flexed his muscles and puffed out his mighty chest, then answered in a fractured Greek nursery rhyme:

"Strong as a mountain, strong as a ram, strong as the dingledong of Zeus I am!"

Kosmos thrice punched his fist against Rakis's boulderous shoulder, then shook the sting out his hand.

"That's what I love to hear. Fill up a plate for yourself, Rakis. When you're finished dining, go and find our friend Georgios, then bring your trucks and come back here."

Rakis, who lived for these kinds of spontaneous adventures, desired to get started right away. Using his hand and forearm he swept some food off the table into one of his suitcases, then hurried off.

"Can I help you with anything, Kosmos?" I asked.

"Help me? I can't do it without you, Thoreau. The first thing you can help me with is finishing this sublime breakfast. Good food, good mood!

Eat as if you're about to be locked inside a bedroom with Irene, Penelope, and Beatrice for one thousand and one nights!"

"What for, Kosmos? What mischief are you up to now?"

Kosmos smiled with his eyes.

"We are going to strengthen the Greek legal system and ensure that the unwritten laws of this great country equally protect the just, the lust, the indecent and the innocent. The law is too old and too stiff, it needs need some exercise. The law should never be broken, but bending it will do us all some good. And of course, there is an unwritten law which we will cheerfully obey."

"Which law?" I wondered, as I studied the glow on his courageous face.

Kosmos grabbed a handful of salad and shoveled it into his mouth.

"The one that states: 'What the law can't find, the law can't take away.' ... We're moving all my worldly possessions to a safe place: from the house of Kosmos to the home of Penelope."

With childlike joy he ran to the window and looked out.

"Look outside at the morning sky, do you see! Another miracle! What happened to that terrible approaching storm? The moment we resolve to work for a noble goal, to let nothing block our path, then the storms get scared and run away, and the sky fills up with light! There are no obstacles for the man who follows his true heart."

He shoved a pancake into his mouth, chewed it slowly and appreciatively, then closed his eyes.

"How many times do I have to remind myself? If we would only listen to the heart's desires. ... Penelope!"

Lovingly the woman's voice returned his call.

"*Ela*, darling! What can I do for you?"

"Sit down here, eat something, and give me the joy of looking at your lovely loyal face."

Kosmos finished writing on the paper, folded it twice, then gave it to Penelope.

"And then, dearest Penelope, when you're all filled up with food and being watched, take Irene and get your house ready to receive my junk and books. Your junk and books, I should say. In case anyone inquires, this paper explains that ten years ago Kosmos sold all his possessions to Penelope: house, mule, snakes, dog, garbage truck, art, clothing, kitchenware, tools, and his whole universe of books."

From a small wood box he removed a large wad of paper money then placed it into Penelope's hands.

"Here's a thousand. It's all the cash I own. Take this for you and for Irene."

Looking forever into her love's eyes, Penelope stroked Kosmos's beard as she dropped the paper money into a ceramic bowl. She pulled off her shirt and her great breasts freed themselves and sprang to life.

"Giving everything to me, love? Why is it that the woman who has everything wants only one thing?"

Kosmos seized his woman in his arms, and as she laughed and laughed, he danced her around the room, singing another of his improvised love songs.

> "It's true,
>   that two,
>   can screw —
>   it's fun!
>   As in-
>   expen-
>   sively
>   as one!"

The laughing Penelope tugged the willing Kosmos to the waiting bedroom. He kissed her passionately and ran his hands along the smooth skin of her back. Before vanishing into the bedroom he glanced over his shoulder.

"Thoreau," said Kosmos. "I'm told that in your country there are hundreds of books about something called 'time management.' Let me tell you all you need to know about that subject. First, do what you love to do; then, do what you need to do. With that plan you will not be rich but you will be happy, and you can never go wrong."

In the neighboring town nearest to Dembacchae we found the humble house of Penelope. Made of white stone like so many on the coasts of Greece, the house stood one story tall, and contained three spacious and sparsely-furnished rooms. After a quick discussion, Penelope decided that one room would be the bedroom and kitchen for Penelope herself;

another, a guest room, for the guests, Irene's snakes, and the worldly possessions of Kosmos; and the third room would house bottles of wine, vats of olive oil, and Dante, Kosmos's spunky mule. By the end of the morning the three old trucks, four strong men, and two smart women had systematically moved all Kosmos's possessions — pets, art, clothing, kitchenware, thousands of books — to the rooms in Penelope's house.

The move proceeded with good cheer and great laughter. Here and everywhere I observed how the Greeks worked with lighthearted joy: there was far more joy in the work of the Greeks than in the play of the Bedlamericans, warped play which was rarely non-violent, cooperative, mentally nourishing, spontaneous.

One incident struck me as funny and curious. When Kosmos placed his arms around the statue of the Snake Goddess, he called to me for help.

"Hell and Hermes!" he shouted. "Thoreau, give me some hands with this ancient lady. Am I getting weaker or is the goddess gaining weight? Penelope's father made it, and gave it to me as a gift, and ten years ago when I set this statue by my doorway, I carried her across my shoulder all by myself. Now I can't even drag her across the room! Don't call it old age: I'm only fifty-five and I've got forty-five good years to go. Maybe this goddess is the same as every other woman. Getting her into your bedroom is always easy, but after the honeymoon, it's a pain-in-the-neck and lower to get her out."

Around noon, when the move had finished, and more food and drinks had been consumed, Rakis and Georgios said good-bye to us, so that Kosmos could spend his final Cretan moments with his family.

"There's one more thing to do," said Kosmos, as he looked up at the blank empty walls. He grabbed his artist's crayons then he set to work. Rapt and inspired in the creation, Kosmos began to reproduce, in sketches only, the same pictures on Penelope's guestroom walls that had appeared as paintings on the walls in his own house. Near the pictures he printed in large letters the words and poems which described his elusive paradise.

We watched him working silently until Kosmos broke the spell. Completing the last lines on the *Nymphs and Satyr* by Bouguereau, he examined his work and nodded his great head.

"Don't look at that picture too long, Thoreau. If you do, you might want to live like a god instead of like a mortal man. Or you might become a dreamer longing for a utopia, never satisfied with the miracle that always waits for us here and now."

"I'm already a dreamer, Kosmos," I answered. "But more than any dreams I love the moments in front of my eyes."

"You think that's true, my friend? Then why did you leave your country? There was a here-and-now there-and-then, wasn't there?"

Before I could think of a reply, Kosmos deftly sketched the *School of Athens* by Raphael, where the great philosopher Plato raises his finger to the skies to signify the gods, eternal forms, and humankind's loftiest ideals.

"What do you think?" Kosmos asked.

"I like everything except the title," said Penelope. "He should have called it: *Plato Orders A Beer.*"

At last, Kosmos faithfully reproduced the lines of the painting by Poussin. This touching picture shows three handsome shepherds and a shepherdess, standing in a scenic paradise of sky and hills, studying the inscription on a stone tomb. The words, conflicting with the idyllic scene behind them, remind these young persons that Death is everywhere.

Kosmos finished his sketch then turned and looked into his friends' eyes.

"I can tell you everything you need to know about death, Thoreau."

"What's that, Kosmos?"

"For as long as you can, avoid it."

He laughed his resounding laugh, then wiped his hands on the bottom of his shirt.

"Years ago I was visiting the grave of Nikos Kazantzakis, just outside of Herakleion. On a street nearby, an old woman approached me, carrying a straw basket filled with bottles and herbs."

"Balms!" she cried. "Balms for the poor! Every sickness can be healed!"

I stopped to chat with the old quack.

"You don't have an ointment to put back all your missing teeth!" I told the greedy huckstress. "Do you have a remedy for death?"

My hair stood up as the ancient woman reached out and gripped me with her cold and bony hand.

"Yes, you young fool," she said. "I have a remedy for death. But first pay me five hundred drachmas."

When I paid her she slapped her knee and laughed, and the laugh rang like a henhouse filled with cackling hens getting serviced by the rooster stud.

"What's the remedy for death?" I asked her.

She smiled her toothless smile, then stuffed my drachmas into her apron pockets.

"Here it is: While you are alive, live!"

I laughed at this tautological advice.

"But how should we live, Kosmos, and how can we live well? Is it better to be a female-loving Casanova or a mankind-loving Gandhi? Better to devote yourself to your own fulfillment or to help others? Better to enjoy the sensuous pleasures of the body or the sensible treasures of the mind?"

Kosmos touched my arm and grinned.

"Why do I need to choose, Thoreau? Here is the answer in one word: Experiment. Don't let the robot inside you take over. Don't live by the old habits. Question the obvious. Defy authority. Believe nothing except your own ideas. Break the old molds by concentrating your full and complete attention upon whatever you're doing right now. Let your intuitions be your guides. Try different things until you find the answers. Change is good."

I squirmed as I recalled the daring proposition about changing Penelope and Irene. I remembered and I hoped that Kosmos would forget. But Kosmos — watching how my face reflected the troubles in my mind — first laughed, then opened his arms and pulled us close to him: he tugged my arm, and then the arms of Penelope and Irene. In a small circle we stood together.

"And now let us resolve," he said, "that necessary business about changing women."

Penelope placed her arm around Irene as Kosmos looked tenderly at the young woman and began to speak.

"Irene, star of my heavens, listen to us and do not cry out until you hear everything we need to say. Penelope and I have decided that Thoreau will stay here, and live in this house, in this room, and take care of Penelope the way I took care of her each week. As for you, dear child, you will come with me to Athens and live with your Aunt Zoe, the sister of Penelope. Here you will attend the very best university in Greece."

Irene glanced perplexedly at her uncle Kosmos, then at her mother Penelope, then at her darling me. Kosmos continued to explain.

"Right now, Irene, Thoreau loves you, but he loves you for your beauty and your cheerfulness. That kind of love lasts a very short time. When you finish your education you will have a bright mind, and with that mind the man you love will love you not only for a week but for a lifetime. You will become a woman who is educated. Do you understand, dear child?"

Irene's eyes filled with tears.

"Educated like Aunt Beatrice?"

Kosmos nodded. Irene hugged me and then she shook with adolescent sobs.

"Uncle Kosmos, can your mule Dante come and live with me, too?"

Kosmos laughed.

"No, Irene, the mule will stay here with Penelope. But you can take Penelope's dog Bouboulina to be your companion at Aunt Zoe's house."

"And your little dog, Zorba," asked Irene, "can he come with us, too?"

When Kosmos nodded yes, Irene's crying instantly ceased. She jumped out of my arms then hugged the two little dogs, laughing and tickling them as they licked her tear-filled face.

Three times, with great vigor, Kosmos slapped my back.

"You're smiling, Thoreau. What did you think: that by changing women I meant that I would sleep with Irene and you with Penelope? I'm a hedonist not a pervert, don't forget that vital difference!"

He gripped my shoulder with his hand.

"Now listen carefully to the other important part of what I am proposing. Here in the house of Penelope, you, Thoreau, will have a room and everything you need. On Saturday mornings you will read to Penelope like I have done for the past twenty years. You will laugh and talk together; discuss the Kosmos situation; and with luck you'll have more success than I did in curing her bad habit of drinking too much on Saturday nights. You will take care of Penelope like a brother takes care of a sister. Treat her like a sister, and know that I have no objections to a little incest now and then, if the woman is agreeable, of course. Better when it happens from a friend than from a stranger or an enemy, don't you think?"

I shook my head and laughed at this lovable scamp. Kosmos laughed too, then carried on.

"Two months of your life is what I am asking. If I haven't returned at the end of the next two months, then I'll rot in that lousy jail like a heap of compost, and you can mark your calendar to visit me twenty years from now. If I don't come back, then take this tablecloth, erase the words and pictures on these walls, and forget me and forget my crazy dream of paradise. ... After two months you can stay or leave here as you choose. But from my point of view, you will be free from your commitment to take care of Penelope. Do you agree with all this, Thoreau? Only say yes if your whole heart agrees, and if you can do this for me with joy."

Instant and sincere came my reply.

"My whole heart agrees, Kosmos. I'll live here for the two months until you escape or are set free. I'll take care of Penelope like a sister and like a sister only. Our relationship will be purely platonic, one that transcends all physical desire, and frolics in the spiritual fields. Be assured that between us there will be nothing that you could call lewd, nude, frantic, romantic, erotic, exotic, unwholesome or obscene."

Now Kosmos spoke to each of us privately: first to me, then to Irene, then at last to his Penelope. And then he gathered us together for the last good-bye.

"And now," said Kosmos, "it's time for me to go alone. Alone now, or I will never find the strength to leave you. Tomorrow, Rakis will drive the three of you and the two dogs to Herakleion, and there you will deposit Irene onto the first boat for Piraeus. At the dock in Piraeus, I will meet Irene then take her to the home of Zoe. Both of us will begin new lives: Irene as a student, and me as a prisoner in Athens's finest jail. Tomorrow evening I will walk into the courthouse of Athens. They won't take me in, you see, I'll enter voluntarily. *Amor fati!* — love your fate! — what a difference it makes, that small change in the mind! But first, this afternoon I must go ahead, alone, to clean up some unfinished business and take a chance on a small adventure."

Penelope stuck her hands against her hips.

"A small adventure, he says! She's twenty and she's a young witch!"

Kosmos laughed and tenderly he stroked her cheek.

"She's lived more than a hundred years and she is old magic."

Penelope shook her fist.

"If she's older than thirty, then I'm the virgin goddess of Spring."

Singing the folk song 'Goodnight, Irene,' Kosmos deftly began to sketch a new picture on the wall. This one featured Kosmos sitting in his chair, reading to the naked Penelope, the woman listening intently, her eyes glowing as she watched the man who she adored.

"What shall I call this picture, about these happy mornings in paradise? Voltaire once wrote: 'Paradise is wherever I am.' I shall dedicate this picture to the one woman who never let me down, and call it: 'Penelope: Paradise is wherever you are.'"

Penelope laughed and cried at the same time. Kosmos slipped a backpack over his shoulders, hugged each one of us good-bye, glanced at his sketches on the walls, then strided out the doorway to the open road.

Lightning flashed like a last glimpse of a loved one; the thunderclouds cried out bursting into tears; and the rain poured down in barrelsful.

Kosmos looked up and laughed, then with a roaring voice he shouted to the stormy sky.

"But where is what I started for so long ago? ... And why is it yet unfound?"

Love does not dominate, it cultivates.

— Goethe

But then came another hunger
very deep, and ravening;
the very body body's crying out
with a hunger more frightening, more profound
than stomach or throat or even mind;
redder than death, more clamorous.
The hunger for the woman. Alas,
it is so deep a Moloch, ruthless and strong,
'tis like the unutterable name of the dread Lord,
not to be spoken aloud.
Yet there it is, the hunger which comes upon us,
which we must learn to satisfy with pure, real satisfaction;
or perish, there is no alternative.

— D.H. Lawrence, *Manifesto*

The intercourse of the sexes, I have dreamed, is incredibly beautiful, too fair to be remembered. I have had thoughts about it, but they are among the most fleeting and irrecoverable in my experience. It is strange that men will talk of miracles, revelation, inspiration, and the like, as things past, while love remains.

— Henry David Thoreau

We are very near to greatness:
one step and we are safe —
can we not take the leap?

— Ralph Waldo Emerson

3 1
PANZANO EXPLAINS THE CRANES

BACK AT AGIOS NIKOLODEONOS, THE BOAT sat motionless in the harbor, the sun climbed to its noon-time throne, the nuns knitted with crafty patience, and the passengers applauded the story they had laughed at and cried over with unsurpassable delight.

Panzano handed me a glass of cool water, and then nodded for me to follow him to a quiet place on the deck. He gazed at the glimmering sea like a lamb who had lost his shepherdess.

"Dolcezza, Dolcezza," he said, sighing. *"Mio nume! Mio tesoro!* My angel! My treasure! *Arriva in un momento quello che non acade in sette anni.* What does not happen in seven years, happens in an instant."

He stepped closer to me so that nobody could overhear.

"I heard them talking," he said, "the Mother-penguin and her eleven little birds. She told them: 'Do not wait to do good. *E sempre l'ora* — the right time is always now.' And then Dolcezza asked the Mother-bird what she thought about Panzano, and the old bat answered: 'He's a dreamer, a glutton, a bag of wind. He waits for roast larks to fly into his mouth.'"

With tears filling his eyes Panzano looked at me.

"She's ugly but she's right! I am *molto fumo è poco arrosto* — much smoke and little roast meat."

Panzano showed me items he had borrowed: a razor, a blade, and a dish of the cream that sits on the top of yogurt freshly made. He smeared the cream on the back of both hands, and then one hand shaved the other one.

"That hair there makes me look like a gorilla," he said.

After the shave he slicked back his hair with olive oil, and freshened his breath by chewing spearmint leaves.

"I have a plan," said Panzano. "First, I'll make the Mother-nun laugh so hard that she paints her peas, and then forgets her strict nunsense. After that, I'll confess to Dolcezza that I've lived like a mouse all my life, but if she will let me be in love with her, then I will learn to have courage like a man."

Panzano moved to the center of the deck and then drummed on his belly with his hands. Soon a large audience had gathered to hear his yarn.

"Some ladies have asked me while their cheeks blushed like rose petals: 'How many times can Thoreau *alzarsi in peni* — stand up and be counted — in one night?' ... That is a mystery but the secret of his energy is not. He is *vegeto,* vigorous, because he is *vegetariano,* a vegetarian. And except for emergencies when no other food is in reach, Panzano too — like the manatees, hippopotamuses, elephants and bulls — is an avid eater of plants. If you want to hear the story of how I came to be one, then hold on tight to whoever is standing beside you, or grab onto a life preserver. At the end of my confession, you will either laugh so much you will tumble over the sides of this boat — or you will throw me overboard."

When some persons in the crowd had clutched their neighbors, Panzano began to speak, illustrating the story with gestures from his arms and hands.

"In Rome last year I took a job as chauffeur and cook to a painter, an arrogant American, who had won some sort of prize that made him think he was higher than a Michelangelo and just slightly lower than a god. He had everything he needed but he could never be satisfied. His terrible temper was his master, and every day — whether they deserved it or not — he yelled at his hardworking staff. One morning he told me to prepare two cranes — yes, the birds — for an important dinner party. He bellowed that if the birds were overcooked or undercooked, or botched in any manner, then I would lose my job before I could say *'merde'.* Using a recipe from my grandmother's diary, I cooked the birds to perfection in a sauce of wine and pepper, with just the right amounts of the leaves of rosemary and sage."

Panzano shook his head and chuckled to himself.

"All might have been well — or at least it would have been different — if the savory aroma had not wafted through the window of the neighbor who lived across the street. That neighbor was standing there smiling when I answered the knock-knock on my kitchen door. She was the sexiest woman I had ever laid eyes on, and I assure you that the only thing I ever laid upon her were the gazes from my eyes. 'Whatever it is you are cooking, I must have some!' she demanded. I told her that that would be impossible, since I could not afford to lose my job. She offered me anything and everything if I would let her taste a substantial portion.

I refused politely once, twice, thrice. But every time I looked at her my knees rattled, my tummy quivered and my heart thump-thumped. At last, after dozens of debatings in my own mind — allured by her offers, dazzled by her promises, and tempted by her *tettas* — I agreed that one hour before dinner I would bring her morsels from those tender birds."

He sipped some water, raised his eyes to the clouds, shook his head, smiled to his listeners, and then resumed.

"Hoping for the best, I pulled off one leg from each of the cranes, and then I placed the birds on the serving plate on their sides, so that nobody would notice the missing parts. When I delivered the delicacy to the woman next door she snatched them then she slammed her door without a thanks. I rushed back to the kitchen and finished making the meal — soup, salad, appetizers and desserts — and served it to the painter and his guests. Before I could scratch my ear the door of the kitchen flew open with a slam, and the painter stood screaming at me, shaking his fists, demanding an account of the missing legs."

Panzano scratched his head.

"'Your honor,' I said — that's what I called him — 'haven't you ever seen photos of a crane? These birds have only one leg.'"

"He waved his fist at me. 'Tonight,' he said, 'your skin is saved because of my important guests. Tomorrow we will ride out to the country and we will count the legs of the cranes.'"

"I slept not at all that night. At midnight I knocked on the door of my attractive neighbor, but from the sounds of things she was entertaining another man. In the morning I drove the painter to that part of the world outside of Rome where the cranes lived. It was a lake and in that place the law claimed to protect the birds, but there was nobody to enforce the law, and nothing to prevent poachers from hunting as they pleased.

"'See there, your honor!' I shouted, in a voice filled with fake confidence. 'There's a flock of cranes with just one leg.'

"'Liar, cheater, fool!' he said to me. 'These birds have two legs but sleep on one. Watch this.'"

"The painter ran to the flock and shouted 'Wake up!'. The crane nearest to him lowered his hidden leg, stood for a moment on two legs, and then bent down and flew upward to a safe place across the lake.'

"The painter twisted my ear. 'Well, Panzano,' he shouted, 'it's clear that these birds have two legs. How are you going to explain this now?'

"'It is easily explained, your honor. You made a simple and honest mistake.'

"'What!' cried the painter. 'How do you mean?'"

Panzano interrupted his story — he now poured a gallon of olive oil on the boat's deck in front of him, explaining that this would protect him from anyone offended by his story's end. And then he told the finish.

"'Your honor, think back to last night at your dinner party. When the cooked bird was sitting on your table, did you shout "Wake up!" ?... If you would have shouted then as you did today, the other leg would have appeared like it did just now.'

"The painter stood for a moment and then he laughed so hard he cried. He slapped my back warmly, and then he told me that I could keep my job, for I was worth my weight in salt.

"On my next day off I drove out to that lake and watched the birds. They make a loud call, like a trumpet, that can be heard for miles across the countryside. When they mate, males and females alike leap and frolic high into the air, and they dance in strict and precise rhythms. I watched them for hours and hours, and it made me feel like a brother to these creatures. Then and there I promised that never again would I eat another bird, or fish, or animal. Watch these birds someday, the way they dance together, and you will understand."

The audience roared and cheered, and then one of the Greeks began playing the *bouzouki,* and another banged a drum. Twenty men and women rushed to form a circle and they danced the *geranos,* a crane dance from ancient times. After Theseus slayed the Minotaur in Crete — which saved the Athenian youth from being sacrificed in the labyrinth — the rescued boys and girls danced the crane dance to celebrate.

Panzano stepped forward to bow, and as he bent over he slipped on the just-oiled deck.

"He who sets a trap for others," he said, "often falls into that trap himself."

Dolcezza helped him to his feet, sat him down on the wooden crate, examined the old lumps on his head, checked for new ones, and then began washing his hair with a damp cloth and a bottle of liquid soap. Panzano sat smiling, staring at the young woman's eyes.

"Chi lava la testa all'asino, perde il sapone," he told her. "He who washes the head of an ass, loses both his soap and his labor."

The ship's assistant captain raised his left hand, his wristwatch gleamed, and he announced that the boat's departure would be delayed while they made necessary repairs. All passengers should remain on the boat until further news, he said.

Dolcezza scrubbed the soap lather from Panzano's hair. The Mother-nun and her ten charges continued to knit with the blue wool, which by now had taken the shape of a small stocking.

The passengers shouted "Thoreau! We want Thoreau!" and after accepting small gifts of yogurt and fruits — and notes from women asking when and where they could meet me alone — I continued relating my story to this incomparable audience.

3 2
YOU ARE DIFFERENT FROM OTHER MEN

"A SMART WOMAN lets her man believe that he is a lion, king of the jungle, when in reality he is the mouse lost in the maze, hunting for a chunk of cheese."

Kosmos had been gone for a scant two hours. Every minute of that time the weeping Penelope had been cleaning her house, talking to me about relationships as she wept and swept.

The storm died and the bright day blossomed once again. Penelope looked down at her table and then cried out a furious scream.

"Thoreau!" she shouted. "The thousand that Kosmos left me: I thought it would be his old stash of drachmas Greek. He left a thousand Euros, worth a hundred times as much! In prison, he'll need the money desperately, don't you think? ... Tomorrow I'll take Irene to the boat for Athens, she'll need today to get ready and to pack. Thoreau, do this for me, for him, will you? Catch up to Kosmos and return his cash."

So on a sunny October afternoon I left the house of Penelope, then walked up the wide dirt road toward Crete's north coast. I took the same road that Kosmos had taken, for I had guessed his destination: a certain house in Agios Nikolodeonos.

After less than two miles of walking I approached an old van which had broken down and stopped. The van's bumper sticker said: 'Freikörperkultur'. Sitting with her back against a tire was a young blonde-haired woman with murder-blue eyes, talking to herself in a loud voice, swearing about the perennial infamy of men.

The young beauty dressed in the simplest clothing and drove a dying vehicle: I could not figure out if she was really poor, or one of those rich people who enjoyed pretending to be. As I approached the woman my intuition explained three things: she had not been strong enough to remove the wheel to change the tire; she had been crying but her tears had nothing to do with her van breakdown; she would remember me and be gladdened to see me again.

"Karin!" I shouted. "You're still trying to figure out the difference between a pigeon and a dove? ... In your hard German language with mile-long words that string along like sausages, what were you just saying with so much rage?"

Karin raised her eyes and the instant she recognized my face her tanned cheeks blushed a tempting shade of red. When the sexy young woman stood up her loose T-shirt bounced alluringly, twisting my mind to wonder on her unbound breasts. She answered my question while looking at my eyes.

"What was I saying in German? If you knew you wouldn't want to know."

"Try me," I said.

Karin beamed, gesturing as she spoke.

"Men lie, men cheat on you, men never keep their promises. To call men slime is an insult to the slime! When I think about men I want to — how do you say it in English? — to eat backwards."

I threw my backpack into the back of the van then picked up a cross-shaped tire iron.

"Give me one chance to prove," I said, "that all your notions about men are right. But aren't you too young to hate men, Karin?"

She shook her head and laughed.

"A woman is never too young for that."

Karin examined her reflection in the mirror protruding from the door on the driver's side. She smoothed her hair with her hands then wiped the streaks of tears from her unhappy face.

"I hate men but I need them," the woman said. "I understand the problem but there's nothing that can be done to help."

In the future, given the opportunity, I would love to change this woman's opinion of my sex. For now, I loosened the hub nuts, removed the flat tire, replaced it with the spare. Minutes later we were riding together, bouncing up and down in the run-down van. Streams of tears gushed down the woman's tan-dark cheeks.

"My whole life is a mess!" the beauty blurted. She wiped her face with a handkerchief as new spurts of sniffles and tears flowed on.

Emotional first-aid is a step-by-step procedure: the first step is to allow the wounded patient to cry for a brief time before one intervenes. I wondered if a pretty young woman has trouble with relationships because most men would focus on her body: few men would want to see or to appreciate the real woman underneath. Yet at the same time I was thinking this, the woman's beauty distracted me. Her clothes were earthy, her body heavenly, her face celestial, her eyes gleamed like two blue stars. Woman's greatest loveliness is the enchanting magic that a happy spirit emanates. Yet Karin was so naturally beautiful that even dressed in misery and tears she looked divine.

After a good sobbing, Karin was able to speak. All the while she talked, she kept her gaze fixed on the road ahead.

"Do you mind if I smoke?" asked the woman.

"Yes, I mind. If I didn't mind, it would mean I didn't care about you at all. Poison yourself if you like. It's your body."

Karin blew smoke in my face then pricked me with a glance.

"It could be yours one day. ... Why didn't you visit me?"

Truth now, or truth later.

"I'm attracted only to women who don't smoke," I said.

Karin tossed her cigarette out the window, then threw out the entire pack of cigarettes. She drove to the shoulder of the road, stopped the van, then turned her head toward me. She stared at my face to try guess how I would receive the news she was about to tell.

"For days," she said, "I've been driving around to look for you."

Surprised but not speechless, I smiled. In the relentless rush for love, infatuation is the fool's gold. We are driven by a power that is both wiser and more ignorant than our rational selves. For love — or for what we think is love — men will stop at nothing and women are capable of anything. I empathized. With my whole love had I not been seeking Beatrice, and with my whole lust had I not been searching for that perfect body on the bike?

More tears filled the woman's gem-blue eyes. Had she been the ugliest crone in the universe, I would have melted at the tears: the fact that she was stunning increased my compassion many times. When I spoke now to Karin, my voice seethed and soothed with tenderness.

"What's wrong?" I asked. "Telling it doesn't always make it better, but holding it in always makes it worse."

The young woman looked into my eyes. She had already decided that she would tell me the moment I asked.

"We are lost," she said. "We no longer understand our lives. When we spend money the money spends us. We have all the time we need, and we do nothing all the time. We wander believing we're getting somewhere and we blunder and praise our mistakes. We are even more lonely when we are together than when we are alone. Nobody is honest anymore. Everybody's faking or hiding or running away. We don't care to help each other, and we can't remember how to help ourselves."

I understood. Every woman needed three things: to love, to be loved, and to be known as a unique individual: listened to, accepted, respected, appreciated. Between darkness and light, fear and courage, meaninglessness and true joy — love is the only bridge. When the bridge is burned then the poor self flounders, alone and hopeless and confused.

So many women, so much beauty, so much sadness, so much strength.

"Karin, is there something else that is upsetting you? ... Something more concrete and more personal than the postmodern swan song?"

Karin inhaled a deep breath before she confessed. Her eyes, staring at the stark Crete countryside, saw not the strong simplicity but the rocky solitude.

"Two weeks ago my brother-in-law put his hand on my leg then made a pass at me. I slapped his face, picked up a knife, then told him to run for his life. My sister walked in the door and saw me yelling at him. She threw him out, sent him back to Munich, then filed for a divorce. *Ach!* We rented a house on Crete to have a quiet vacation. What a vacation it's been! The three of us — my sister, her daughter and me — sit home all the time lonely and crying and cursing men. Her daughter, my niece, was such a happy child — for the past two weeks she has not smiled even one time."

It was the beginning of the new millennium, and the *Zeitgeist* was ripe with the hatred of the male species. Defending my gender would be defending the indefensible: there was not much that I could say. We made war, we mistreated our women, we misunderstood our children, we wasted our time and our lives farting around with money, computers, and sports. Most men were as mature as toddlers or as bland as gelatin. What could be done? All I could think to do was to try to be a good man — an exceptionally good man — in the midst of many senseless ones.

She cried for another minute, then wiped her eyes.

"I have present for you," said Karin. "You must protect your *schön* eyes."

From her hair she removed the expensive-looking pair of sunglasses, then handed them to me.

"Thanks," I said. "I'll remember you whenever the sun shines, which in Greece is more than three hundred days every year. Karin, tell me. How can I help you?"

She inched her trembling body closer.

"Just be a friend to us. I think you understand how to be a friend. You are different from other men: you listen. When I talk you look so deeply into my eyes. What are you thinking right now?"

"Karin, you don't like lies, but are you strong enough for honesty?"

"Try me," she said.

"I'm thinking that I can be your friend but I can't solve your problems, because nobody can help another person when it comes to the essential things. And I'm thinking that I like your openness. And I'm thinking that you have a perfect body — you must be a dancer — you are one of the most beautiful women I've ever seen."

Karin laughed.

"Thanks," she said. "I'm glad you find me beautiful. I spent a lot of time thinking about how I should look if I ever bumped into you again. It is possible to be a feminist and hate men in general, and still want to be beautiful for one man, and find one man you can believe in and care about."

For a few silent moments she gazed at me with undiminished hopes. She listened to her heart, then clutched my arm.

"My sister and I are living in Ag Nik. Will you come? ... My sister is despondent. Come and prove to her that even after marrying a hole-in-the-ass, Life goes on."

Self-revelation made this moment momentous! Brave enough to tell her wishes, the woman now waited breathlessly for the 'Yes' or 'No' to seal her fate. But what exactly was being offered here? In a flash I recalled Alexis Zorba's words: 'God has an enormous heart, but there is one sin he will not forgive: when a woman calls a man to her sister's bed, and he does not go.'

For me the only sin was insincerity. And so I instantly replied.

"Karin, I can't come right now. I need to meet someone in Agios Nikolodeonos. What are you doing later tonight?"

Karin jumped across the seat and kissed my left cheek.

"Tonight? Tonight! I'm making dinner for you at eight o'clock! Promise me you'll come!"

"I promise," I said.

"*Küss mich.* Kiss me. Promise with your lips."

Ever so lightly I kussed her impatient lips.

Karin jumped back into the driver's seat, removed the van keys from the ignition slot then dropped the keys down the neckhole at the top of her T-shirt. Pouting, she crossed her arms.

"You're lying!" she said. "That was not a *küss!* After I drop you off in Ag Nik I'll never see you again!"

My youth and love of angling tempted me to go a-fishin' for the keys. My glance roamed the regions of her bralessness, then jumped back to her blue-fire eyes. The woman was hurt, angry, disappointed; the moment could be saved thanks to the powers of my strong memory.

"Odos Ogygia epta," I said. "Seven Ogygia Street. You see, Karin, I've memorized the address you gave me when we last met. Doesn't that prove that I've been thinking about you, and planning to visit you? ... How many times do I need to promise before you believe what I say? I'll come tonight to see you. I'll pay for dinner with a check for a thousand laughs. Is your sister a woman? Then I'll have her holding her sides and laughing, too. Is your sister a nun? No problem. I once saw some graffiti etched onto the Sistine Chapel that said; 'The devil has his fun, even with a nun.'"

These promising words lit the woman's eyes.

"I will say to you," said Karin, "what my sister always says: 'My heart will be ground up like a sausage if you do not come.'"

At that moment I began to wonder about this question: What small percentage of what I thought I knew unquestionably was in fact, truly true?

"Karin, are you saying that you're in love with me?"

"Du bist ein Arschloch! In English that means: 'You are an ass!' Don't get your ego all inflatulated. I needed to love someone, and you were lucky enough to walk by at the right time. *Ach!* Men! Men are so predictable!"

The plan was made and agreed on: Karin would drop me off in Agios Nikolodeonos; I would take care of my business, and then I would meet her and her sister at their house at eight.

"It's not just for me," said Karin. "My sister has lost interest in life. And even from her work she gets no pleasure anymore."

I listened for the all-important meanings behind the all-misleading words.

"What kind of work does she do?"

Karin inserted the ignition key then turned the engine on. It spun and sputtered then at last started up with a clamoring growl. My question evaporated as a passing car, coming from the opposite direction, drove close to the van and Karin shouted swearwords at the driver in the German language slang.

"Are you half as tough as you talk?" I asked.

"Twice as tough. And my sister is three times as tough as I am. You can't imagine what you're in for tonight."

"Then I might need to learn the German language to defend myself. What does that bumper sticker mean?"

"*Freikörperkultur?*" she said. "Literally: 'Free body culture.' In my great grandmother's days that was a club in Germany. Men and women ran around and played games in the woods with little shame, less sex-guilt, and no clothes. Today there's an organization which is even more liberating: it's called WANDERBORE. My sister and I have been members for one month. It is organized by a superwoman named Beatrice Loverly. She is *Wunderbar!* She helps women to find themselves, free themselves, fulfill themselves. "

"Have you met her?"

"I have heard her speak three times, in London, in Frankfurt, and in Crete. Her talk was like listening to the best book in the world, a book written especially for me. If I could meet her, and spend some time with her, it would change my life forever."

I touched her arm.

"So not everything is bleak, Karin: that is one reason for hope and confidence. And there's probably some other good things in your life right now that you can hold on to."

She smiled.

"Yes, there is one thing. I have met the handsomest man in the world, and he is coming to bring us a new passion for life! ... But I don't want to poison him on the first date: do you have any allergies to foods? What would you like for dinner tonight?"

The Chinese proverb says that one joy scatters a thousand griefs. Karin had forgotten all her troubles. Humming and smiling, as she anticipated her evening with me her body shimmied in the promise of passion and her heart danced in the gilded clouds of dreams.

But I remembered Beatrice, and I slumped back in my seat and stared at the shrubby emptiness of the Cretan countryside. Beatrice Loverly was the kindest woman in the universe and I had made her miserable. One grief scatters a thousand joys. As Karin reached across the seat and squeezed my hand, I summoned all my will power to restrain myself from weeping like a fallen child.

Surrounded by seven snorting swine, I stood at the doorstep of the cottage of Hope. The door swung open, and when the old woman saw my face she shrieked with joy. Hope took my hand, led me to her bird cages, then opened their doors and released her four white doves. After shooing the curious swine away, the ancient woman pushed opened the door of her stone cottage and welcomed me inside.

The cottage looked unchanged. I remembered the iron cauldron, the wooden furniture, the candles, the hanging dried herbs, the mold-covered hunk of cheese, the owl and the snakes, the phallic horseradish root, and the makeshift bed where — on my last visit — I had eaten the apple of Sex and Foolishness. The spirit of the place reflected the very best gifts old age could give: simplicity, timelessness, benevolence, quiet joys, and peace.

Hope gathered together some scraps of food, placed them onto a plate at the table, then urged me to sit down.

I nodded to say thanks.

"Has Kosmos been here today?" I asked.

"Yes, my son, your brother Kosmos."

Hope pointed to the bed which looked like it had recently been slept in; then she pointed to the cottage's back door where a woman entered — the one who had carried the apple of Wisdom and Loneliness. Singing cheerily and combing her gray-streaked hair, she appeared just-loved and radiant. She left through the front door, skipping like a carefree young girl.

I placed my hand gently onto Hope's thin arm.

"Did Kosmos leave a message for me?"

Smiling, Hope pointed to the table where Kosmos had scrawled his note.

> Thoreau!
> My great soul alone can help me now.
> Take everything you've brought for me
> and give it all to Hope.
> —Meteoros Kosmosophos Polimegalokardiakosmos (Kosmos)

When I handed Hope the paper bills — the one thousand Euros — the old woman placed them into her pocket with hardly a glance at the cash. Four screams of joy came forth and four sisters arrived, each one bearing an apple in her lovely hand. With careful eyes, I examined the small apple of Joy and Innocence; the ripe-red apple of Sex and Foolishness; the golden-skinned apple of Wealth and Suffering; and the crisp-perfect apple of Love and Danger. I stared intently on this last apple, the one I most desired.

As Hope stirred the broth in her great cauldron, it sizzled and hissed as a windy bluster rushing through the crisp Fall leaves. A strange mist exuded from the brew.

"Whichever apple you choose, my son," said Hope, "you must eat everything: skin, pulp, seeds, stem, core."

I studied the faces of the smiling women, their smooth skin, their tantalizing fruits. So deep was my concentration that I hardly noticed the back door of the cottage when it blew open and slammed against the wall. In drifted Hope's sisters, Freedom and Destiny. Freedom held up a glass filled with clear liquid.

"Drink something, nephew," she said to me. "Only men who risk everything can break free."

But I remembered my mistake during the last visit, and I answered thank you no.

"Then eat something," Destiny suggested, placing a small cake on the tabletop. "Whichever road that chooses you, you'll need every portion of your strength."

I cut the dessert into eight even slices then devoured my piece of cake. The four tantalizing young women approached me, calling for me to choose, each one offering her smile, her apple and her charms. I reached out for the apple of Love and Danger. The room started spinning, the seven women laughed heartily, I staggered backwards toward the bed. The last words I heard before falling asleep were: 'Rethymnos Rum Cake'; and 'Too foolish for Love.'

Joyfully the hours vanished: first in a ravenous session of lovemaking with one of the enchanting sisters; next amidst a brilliant dream; last with a touching good-bye from Mother Hope. Before I left her cottage she embraced me, then looked into my eyes with a mother's incomparable love. Her parting gift — something large and soft — was stuffed inside a burlap sack which had been tied with a frazzled piece of string.

Feeling strong and fearless, inspired and renewed, I sensed a new adventure near.

Only an annoying shred of appleskin stuck between my teeth reminded me that I was not a god but a vulnerable young man.

33
THE VIRGIN AND THE GYPSIES

PERSONS, LIKE PLACES, have uncharted territories hidden deep inside themselves. And places, like persons, have secret spirits, personalities, and souls. Close to the town of Agios Nikolodeonos, my hidden campsite by the beach seemed to welcome my return. Still undiscovered by the unobservant masses, it had remained exactly the way I left it since my visit last. I unpacked my tent, secured the tent pegs under heavy rocks, then opened up the tent and stashed my backpack and Hope's gift inside. After counting my ready money — about a hundred bucks worth of dollars and Euros — I tucked the roll securely between my ankle and my sock.

It was early in the evening and the sun had just begun to fall into the sea. I listened for the sounds of passing vehicles, and when silence conquered sounds I climbed up the sandy slope to the road above. Walking on the road my mind wandered about my most recent adventures: Irene, Kosmos, Beatrice, Penelope, the apple-virgins in Hope's cottage, and Karin, the feisty beauty who would be feasting me tonight.

Lost in thought, I had been gazing at the distant mountains when a humming bicycle whooshed by me, then a small green apple hit the back of my head.

The bikress! Here! The voluptuous woman I had followed and dreamed about but always failed to catch and to make real! I shouted, she ignored me. I chased her, she pedaled faster away. One apple yes, but not one smile, not one word, not one backward glance. I dashed down the road toward the center of the town; by the time I arrived there I had lost her in the crowd of off-season tourists. Breathing deeply from the chase, I leaned up against the side of a kiosk, and then looked up at its wooden wall. I saw two posters there, the first one made me wonder and the second made me groan.

The first poster showed a large red circle with a diagonal red line running across it, and inside the circle lay a picture of a large open mouth, just about to swallow a black cat. The second poster featured words as well as pictures. It stated that ten women — "dangerous criminals who have rubbed many tourists" — were wanted by the Tourist Police. They had been arrested and then escaped from prison just before their trial.

It was suspected that they were now hiding in one of Crete's large port cities on the north coast — Chania, Rethymnon, Herakleion, Agios Nikolodeonos, or Sitia — where they would attempt to flee the island by boat or barge. A cash reward had been offered for information leading to their arrest.

The small pictures of the women were out of focus, but I immediately recognized the faces of Katerina the courageous, Thalia the fawn, Meli the spirit of loveliness, Romantza the wild beast. I pulled the poster off the wall, ripped it into small shreds, then dropped the pieces into the pocket of my pants.

I walked to my favorite food market. Because I was known and liked there, I was charged the same prices as the local Greeks. Although Karin had told me to bring nothing to the meal — not a condiment or a condom — I filled two large bags with breads, cheeses, olives, fruits, nuts, cakes, apple cider, teas. After paying in Euros and stuffing the change into my sock, I walked to the circular fountain in the center of the town.

Seven bells signaled one hour before eight o'clock. The rush hour had passed, the hawkers and the hookers and the crowds were gone, the streets emptied of vice and men. Because the evening felt too cool for outdoor dining, everyone had flocked to the indoor sections of the restaurants to gorge themselves on sumptuous appetizers and bumptious drinks. Along my walk between the food store and the marble fountain, I had found — then pulled down and ripped up — seven gypsy-posters more. Now I sat down on the fountain's chilly ledge. I looked out at the wild Crete sea and the red-gold clouds, and I pondered the poor gypsies' plight.

Peering through the geysering sprays of water, to the other side of the fountain, I spied a fat Bedlamerican tourist. Oblivious to the obvious, his head angled downward as he read from a trashy paperback. His body stood in glorious Greece as his mind escaped to a fabricated formula of fantasy. The tourist was approached by a bent-over shawl-covered woman holding a basket of flowers, and by a young-looking girl whose orange-red hair had been braided into long pigtails. The girl curtsied politely, then waved a flower at the tourist's face.

"Take my flower, meester! This lonely flower needs a strong man to keep her warm!"

It happened in one instant, as gracefully coordinated as a Russian ballet. First, the young-looking girl chattered distractingly and planted a rose into the buttonhole of the tourist's shirt. Then she stepped firmly on his foot, raised herself on her tip-toes, dipped her hand into his back pocket, slithered her body up against his body — and as he smiled from the pressure of her chest — she deftly slid his wallet out. Then, swiftly and imperceptibly, she kissed his cheek and dropped the wallet into the basket of the old crone. When the unaware tourist had strolled away, the old woman opened the wallet, pulled out the native cash, then tossed the wallet and everything inside it into the fountain's circular pool.

I placed my new sunglasses over my eyes, disguised my face with a stupid grin, then strolled around the fountain and walked past the old woman and the pig-tailed girl.

"Take my flower, meester!" she shouted again. "This lonely flower needs a strong man to keep her warm!"

She stuck the rose's stem through a rip near the collar of my T-shirt, but when she reached her fingers into my back pocket she could not find the cash-holder she craved.

"Meester," she said with a beguiling smile. "Where do you keep your money?"

"My money?" said I. "It was stolen by lecherous treacherous fugitive females who promised to love me till the stars stopped shining in the sky."

By this time the keen old woman had bent down to remove the contents of the bulge in my white sock. But I snatched her arm, then seized the wrist of the young-looking girl. As these two flim-flamming females tried to pull away, I tightened my grip and dragged them toward the round pool of the spraying fountain.

"Strong for an old lady and a child!" I said, in a cheerful voice. "Since you like wallets so much, let's go fishing for another one."

Then with great strength and greater gentleness I threw them both into the water, first the feisty girl who was not so young, then the old woman who was not so old. I jumped in and caught hold of their arms again, and we wrestled in the water, women swearing and man laughing until a siren from a police car shrieked louder and louder as it rushed our way. The hag and the child tugged frantically, but they could not escape my powerful hold. I spoke to the women in a mockingly-tender voice.

"'Forever! They said they would remember me forever!'"

The two prisoners stopped struggling to listen more intently.

"And do you know what I'll remember forever? The way I was skinned by ten gypsies, then belittled by a black banana peel!"

Old-woman Meli hugged me with her one free arm.

"Thoreau!" she shouted joyfully.

Pig-tailed Romantza gazed at me like a little girl who wanted daddy to buy her a bright-colored balloon.

"We didn't steal your things, Thoreau, we just borrowed them! We need you! Help us! Please! Oh, please!"

Were it not for the approaching police sirens I would have enjoyed pretending to be angry. Now there was not time to make jokes.

I pulled off my dark glasses and then, to calm them down, spoke in a tender voice.

"Where are Katerina and the others?"

Meli sighed.

"They are hiding in the mountains," she said. "The police are looking for us. We have no friends, no food, no chance to work. We are desperate. We can starve or we can sell our bodies or we can steal."

The sirens boomed louder, closer, more menacing. With two glances, one kind glance at each of them, I assured them that they could trust me as a brother and a friend. I led the women through an alleyway, out of the town, then back to my campsite near the beach. After we had gathered sticks to make a fire, I explained what needed to be done.

"First, we'll eat a good meal. In about thirty minutes, when it gets dark, you can go back to the mountains to join Katerina and the other girls. Then you can tell Katerina to bring everyone to the house of Penelope, in the town of Agia Souvlakis. The house of Penelope in the town of Agia Souvlakis. *Katalavehees?* Do you understand?"

Romantza did not understand.

"Who is this Penelope?" she shouted. "If she's your wife, I'll pull out all her hair and bite her boombarinas!"

Meli grabbed Romantza's arm.

"You will hug her like a sister, Romantza," Meli said. "I am sorry, Thoreau. Romantza is always thinking only of herself."

Sparks flared from Romantza's eyes.

"Meli is always telling me what to do!"

I unpacked and served the dinner and the three of us ate voraciously, consuming every scrap in both bags of the food. All through the meal, Meli sighed and stared with the tenderest affection, while Romantza gazed at me lustingly.

"Thoreau," Romantza said, clutching my arm. "You are from America so you are reech. How many houses do you have? How many cars? How many Euros? How many wifes?"

I laughed.

"Not all Americans are rich, Romantza. I have no house, no cars, no wifes — we say 'wives' — and not very many Euros."

Romantza shook her head.

"I don't believe you! But if it's true, Thoreau, then you're a gypsy, too!"

The peace of the fire, the sounds of the rushing sea, the laughing conversations, the lovely glances — dissipated all at once when we heard sirens blaring from cars of the Tourist Police.

"We can't go back tonight, Thoreau," Romantza said, moving her body even closer to me. "It's not safe for women to travel alone. It's dark at night, and Meli is afraid of the dark."

Meli wrapped her hands around my arm and squeezed the muscular biceps.

"Yes, Romantza dear," she said, "Meli is afraid of the dark, that's a good joke! But the fearless Romantza is not afraid of anything, so Romantza can go back tonight, alone."

Eight bells chimed from the tower of the tallest Ag Nik church. Ach! Karin, at this moment, would be cooking dinner and waiting for her promised guest. Again the ominous sirens blared. I looked at my two lively gypsies; I remembered Katerina and Thalia and the rest. What was their crime except that they were wild and poor? ... I shuddered at the thought that these wondrous women might spend years in jail. How could I now send Romantza and Meli away? Dressed like the old woman and the pig-tailed girl, they would be too-easily recognized. A better strategy would give them better chances to escape.

"Romantza, Meli, how many men did you scam today?"

"Only one or two," said Romantza.

"More like twenty-one or twenty-two," Meli said, pulling out a wad of Euros from a pocket in her dress.

I shook my head.

"Then you can't wear those outfits anymore. Romantza, my clothes are in a backpack in the tent. Go into the tent, take off that girl disguise, then put on something of mine — anything you want."

Romantza smiled happily, threw off her wig, then eagerly crawled into the tent. Wearing the clothes of the man she desired would give her a magical power over the man.

Meli lowered her old lady's shawl from her head to her shoulders, then unpinned her long dark hair.

"I know you like the hair long," she said.

Though she had lost a little weight from the stress of circumstances, she looked hardly less lovely than before.

"Are you married yet, Thoreau?"

"Not yet, Meli."

She smiled at that.

"There is something I want to ask you."

I was about to explain how I needed to leave soon to meet Karin, but before I could deliver those cold words I was melted by Meli's gaze.

"Ask me, Meli."

She took my hand and looked into my eyes, her face so close we breathed the same sweet breaths.

"You are not from our old poor world, Thoreau. You are from the new world, the fast world, the rich world. And even in that world you are special and important. You can sleep with real women, women who live in rich houses and wear nice dresses and take hot baths every day and cook food on a stove. Meli and Romantza and Katerina are worthless gypsies. Only the birds and the animals love us, and sometimes I think we are no different from the animals and birds in these rocky hills. Many nights I think we are nothing, we are the ashes in the fire, we are the shadows of the moonlight, we are the dust on the lonely road. ... Why don't you turn us in and take the reward? Why are you risking yourself for us? Why do you help us? Why do you care?"

The poorest of the poor and the richest of the rich, all have problems with their self-esteem. I bent down and kissed the woman's hand.

"You're a real woman, Meli. At least as good as any woman in a rich house and a nice dress."

She lowered her wondering eyes.

"Don't say those things, Thoreau! It might give me hope that I could live like a real woman one day. And then, the minute that hope died, I would be disappointed for all the other minutes in my gypsy life. Just tell me this. If you were sitting with a real woman tonight, what would it be like?"

Everything that touches us needs tenderness and Time! I wanted to read her the Dickens novel *Our Mutual Friend,* introduce her to Lizzie Hexam, and thusly let her see how social world's apart means nothing in the worlds of heart. I wanted to tell her how she was perfect, how her heart was the heart of a child, how the world had been cruel to her but she could always conquer it if she could stay sincere and kind.

Meli's face glowed with happiness as I placed my arm around her shoulders.

"What would I be doing with a real woman as you call her, Meli? ... We would eat something together, just like you and I ate tonight — though instead of fingers we might use forks and knives. Then we would talk, just like we're talking now. Then we might dance a little bit. And then I would ask the woman what she would like to do."

"She would like to kiss you," Meli said. "But she would not know if she should kiss you first, or she should wait for you to give the first kiss."

A laugh from inside the tent announced the popping out of Romantza, who emerged dressed in nothing but my long T-shirt.

"Look what I found!" she shouted. And she held up a just-opened package, the gift to me from old Mother Hope. It contained an enormous quantity — yards and yards — of excellent black cloth. Romantza had also found a dozen sewing needles, two pairs of scissors, and a huge spool of strong black thread.

I clapped my hands together: we now had the raw materials for the disguises they would need to travel safely through Crete.

"Do you know how to sew, Meli? Can you make widow's dresses?"

Meli laughed.

"Can I sew? Thoreau, you don't know gypsy women. A gypsy woman can do anything. If we do not learn, then we will not survive."

Romantza rushed to Meli, whispered something into her ear, then giggled and jumped up and down. Meli whispered something into Romantza's ear, then both women burst out laughing and fell into each other's arms.

"Promise you won't watch, Thoreau!" they said.

And I agreed, then turned my back to them while they began their skillful tailoring.

I sat with my back to the women and my front facing the fire, warmed by the flames and heated by the wild laughter of the gypsy maids. In thirty minutes they had finished their work.

"Turn around, Thoreau," said Meli. "Turn around and look at two old widows, who look like thousands of other old widows on Crete. In these disguises, nobody will recognize or notice us."

I turned around then stared.

"Oh ... my ... god! ... Those are not widow's costumes."

"We're not widows!" said Romantza.

"Not yet!" Meli added, as the two of them laughed and laughed.

The design was simple, ingenious, irresistible. Black cloth had been wrapped around each body — as tight fitting as another skin — beginning at the middle of the thighs, encircling the shapely buttocks and slim waists, then rising a few nips above the middle of the breasts. What held those dresses up? In one strapless stroke of elegance, the feminine body had been deified and the laws of gravity defied!

The women are ravishingly beautiful, the nightsky fills with stars, the hills resound with male cicadas humming their seductive songs.

"Do we look like the real women, Thoreau?" asked Meli.

"More real than the real," I said, transfixed at the beauty of the sights.

"Then dance with us!" shouted Meli. And into my arms they ran with joy.

Accompanied by the orchestra of insects, we danced around the campsite until Romantza sank her teeth into my chest with a kittenlike bite. I chased the two women down to the beach. The night's magic transformed us into three great puppies — playing, laughing and romping in the shallow water and the cool wet sand.

"Take this, Thoreau," said Romantza, handing me a strip of cloth attached to her dress.

"And this too, Thoreau," said Meli, giving me the same piece of hers. "Unwrap us, then wrap us up again!"

Meli had conquered shyness and grown bolder, and Romantza had no inhibitions to lose. I pulled on the strips of cloth and the two women spun around like figure-skaters. Soon the dresses had dissolved into two long strips of cloth which dangled in my hands. Working together, the two strong-willed women tackled me to the sand and then climbed on top of me, then pressed their faces close to my laughing face. Romantza — screaming like a hawk a-diving toward its prey — first ripped off my

T-shirt, then headed downward to remove my sand-covered pants.

Meli nibbled my earlobe, then sat up and brushed her fingertips against my lips and cheek.

"Thoreau," she whispered, her voice glazed with breathtaking desire. "I have one last question."

She kissed me with all of her gypsy fire and all of her womanly love.

"Will you marry me again, for one more night?"

I kissed the tears on her face.

"Meli," I replied. "I don't remember that we ever got divorced."

The next morning at dawn the sun appeared, lighting the road from Agios Nikolodeonos to the Dikte Mountains, where Zeus the god of gods was born. Here, under the beauty of the morning light, walking along this road, three plump widows dressed in mourning black were seen by many but observed by none.

Two hours of walking brought the three widows to a deserted monastery, where one of the women cooed like a pigeon, but no pigeon-woman responded to the call. Instead, a chill shivered our three spines as a deep male voice from behind us suddenly shouted then spoke.

"*Po, po, po!* What fine old widows do we have here! Two of them look like goddesses of love and fertility, and the one old widow in the middle has a donkey-sized penis and needs a shave! With more widows like these, all the *alter kockers* on Kreetee would stop twirling their worry beads and start strumming their *baglamas* and banging their wooden spoons!"

The two widows clutched and pressed against the middle one — that was me. But there was nothing to fear. The voice came from my old friend with the donkey, the tranquil man who loved olive trees. He would help us, I was sure.

"*Kalimera*, Thoreau!" said the old man. "To see your face makes me feel twenty-one again. I am the father of your dear friend, Kosmos. I have many names: Luck; Beauty-lover; and in Greek, '*Storeegeekotees*', which means, 'Tenderness'. But lately my friends have been calling me Father, or *Pateras*."

I shook the old man's calloused hand.

"Where," I asked, "are Katerina and the other women?"

"There was trouble last night," Pateras said. "A priest who wanted the reward money called for the police. The women — eight of them, I counted — had to leave fast to save themselves. Now they are waiting for these two widows near the cave of Dikte. If you like, I can take them there."

He placed his hand on my shoulder. I knew what he was thinking now, and disappointedly I sighed.

"And it would be better," I said, "less strange-looking and safer — if you go onward without me?"

Pateras nodded yes. I removed my black widow's outfit and all the padding, folded the cloth and stuffed it into the burlap sack, then placed the sack into Meli's hands. Then from my sock I pulled out a bunch of bills.

"Meli, Romantza, take this," I said. "It's all my money."

I split up the dollars and Euros into two even piles, then gave half to each of them.

"Give all the cash to Katerina. Do you remember what I told you last night? When it's safe for the ten of you to travel, where are we going to meet?"

Romantza squeezed my arm as she replied.

"In the town of Agia Souvlakis, at the house of a beetch named Penelope."

"A good plan, Thoreau," Pateras said. "That isolated house will be the safest place to hide."

The old man turned around so the women and I could say good-byes, and then he led his donkey along the small dirt path.

"It is best that we leave right away," he said.

"Thoreau," said Romantza, "Remember our deal. You promised that you would never forget me!"

"Not for a thousand years, Romantza. Or two thousand, at least."

She kissed me then bit my bottom lip.

"And you're so sure you won't forget me that you promised that if you ever see me again and you don't recognize me, then you'll make up for it by giving me one night with you alone!"

"I promised you those two things, Romantza, and I know you won't let me forget. And remember the two things you promised me: get along well with Meli, and stop stealing, because it's too dangerous."

Romantza shook her head to say that she agreed, then kissed me one more time, then turned around to follow the tail of the donkey and the kind old man.

Meli reached out to grasp my hand. We laughed together when I gave her the rose that the pig-tailed Romantza had stuffed into my shirt.

"I will never part with this," she said. "If I never see you again — "

I kissed her tenderly.

"Then give it to the man you love."

We stood staring at each other for one long moment.

"Go now," I whispered. And Meli walked down the path, slowly, looking back at me once, twice, three times with tears flowing from her star-bright eyes.

Where would I go now, after losing two more I'd loved? ... Back toward my campsite at Agios Nikolodeonos. During the two-hour walk I thought about how strangers can become friends, and friends can become as close as family. ... From the night of love and morning of loss, I was ravenously hungry, and I had nothing now to eat but the shred of appleskin which at last dislodged itself from between my teeth and gums. I removed it from my mouth, examined the golden shred, then chewed it up and swallowed the last bit.

I climbed down to my campsite by the beach. Waiting for me there I found two old women dressed in widow-black. Meli! Romantza! ... No, I was wrong by one-hundred forty years. The widows were Hope's sisters, Freedom and Destiny. They had brought me gifts: one bread and three wildflowers. After chatting for a few moments — they had added no rum to the bread, they promised! — they departed, advising me to quickly eat my bread. Destiny urged: "Whenever a man is hungry, the world is a terrifying place." And Freedom reminded me: "There is only one place and one time a man can fight for his liberation: this moment, and this place."

I bit into the loaf, chewed a few chews, then discovered it was filled with something too tough to swallow. There was money inside: two thousand Euros! I stuffed the money into my pocket; tomorrow I would mail it to Aunt Zoe in Athens, for Kosmos and Irene. I finished eating the bread just as the twelve noon bells rang out from a church in town.

The three flowers and the twelve bells made me remember what I had carelessly forgot.

"Karin!" I shouted.

Better sixteen hours late than never. Grasping the three flowers, I sprinted to the town, dashed though the winding stone-covered streets, glanced at street names and house numbers painted on the houses, then knock-knock-knocked with the golden knocker on the big front door. Across the top of the entrance lay a dried grapevine.

The door swung open, revealing an elegantly decorated living room, plush and luxurious far beyond the sparsely-furnished dwellings of the average natives of Crete. A five-year-old girl, not nearly as tall as my waist, came to the doorway dressed in a black costume like the wickedest witch of Oz.

The child took the three flowers from my hand.

"Karin!" she shouted, as she stared at me up and down. "The *scheisskopf* is here! The man with the big sex problems that Mama was going to fix. Should I ask him to come in, or should I close the door on his nose?"

34
WEALTH AND SUFFERING

FIRST DISTRACTION, then destruction. He who has no great love to go to is easily seduced.

Overlooking the whine-dark sea, in a posh second-floor bedroom, Thoreau lies in bed with a naked Karin cuddled on his left side, and a nude Gertrude snuggled on his right. Seven weeks had passed since he had parted from the wild gypsy women. Seven weeks ago he had stood on the threshold of the German sisters' front door, and swallowed the last golden-apple gob. For seven weeks he had two healthy women delighting in their own sensual pleasures, and devoted to his most fantastic whims.

Wisely, the Stoic philosophers taught the maxim: "Envy not this man, envy not any man." Sexual relationships are mousetraps: easy to get in, murder to get out. From the moment that Thoreau had neglected to hear his inner guiding-voice — and forgotten that this voice existed — he felt lost, trapped, empty, unhappy, and thoroughly confused.

Every morning at 8 a.m. bells from the unorthodox church clang eight times. Bells clang, women cling. Inside the elegant bedroom, an alarm-buzzer blares the three lovers awake. The Greek light, witness and abettor of so many miracles and monstrosities, helps to disentangle the three-backed beast.

Karin (or Gertrude) rises immediately and makes the breakfast while Gertrude (or Karin) makes fast love to Thoreau. The sexed screams of the woman are accompanied by the trio of sizzling sausages. Hanging everywhere in Germany — to remind the natives to stop working and have sex — these phalloid wursts resemble the German style of lustmaking. Sex and sausages are clean, mysterious, easy to make, and well done in a Munich minute.

At 8:10 precisely, the sated sister travels from bedroom to bathroom for a ten-minute ice-cold shower; she will then take over the cooking chores while her sister showers cold. Before departing from the perfect-bodied Thoreau, the woman whispers in the man's ear: *"Hat es dir gefallen?"*

At first he thought that the woman had been asking, "Did your hat fall off?", but his German language skills improved to get the real meaning: "Did you enjoy it?" ... His body enjoyed it while his mind rebelled. So Thoreau — who cannot lie to women and children — answers the question without answering, with kisses where words should have been.

The fat-filled breakfast — coffee, cream, sausages, seafood, cheeses, eggs, breads, jellies, cakes and a smorgasbord of aphrodisiacs — would be served precisely at 8:30 a.m. This gave Thoreau, every morning, twenty precious minutes to ponder his pitiful plight.

By any method of accounting, Thoreau had become a rich man. He lived in a rich house. He ate rich foods from china plates, he drank sweet drinks from crystal glasses. He had been dressed in expensive clothing, and undressed on a pillow-soft bed. Thoreau had lapped up the lips of luxury, sunned in the summa of sumptuousness, tiddlied the winks of idleness. He had no work, no debts, no deadlines, no responsibilities. He could have sex whenever he wanted — but he hardly wanted it at all. And because he was taking, buying, daydreaming, consuming — instead of giving, loving, learning, creating — his life became boring and soul-less and stale.

Why didn't he pack his backpack and walk out? ... In some ways, living free-from-poverty had been a paradise like basking on a perfect beach. And Thoreau gleaned that if he had been born with a modicum of money, then he might have learned how to be a serious artist instead of a lighthearted vagabond. Yet there was another, and far more powerful, invisible lock on the front door of his present life. The faces had changed but the story remained the same: both sisters were in love with him. If he left them now he would hurt them, crush them, perhaps destroy them. These lovely women would hate him, they would despise all men, and for the failure of this relationship they would immolate themselves in blames.

Thoreau liked the sisters, he admired them, he enjoyed their company — but Love, as he imagined it, would be a completely different thing. And that subtle difference — the starry space between the worlds of Like and Love — makes all the difference between mere satisfaction and wholehearted happiness.

Once every week he would try to face the situation, always with the same result ...

Thoreau: Good afternoon, Dr. Heissundkalt. I have a problem that I cannot solve alone. May we talk?

Gertrude: Take off your clothes and lie down on the couch.

Thoreau: Lately I have been unhappy.

Gertrude: When was the first time you remember feeling this way?

Thoreau: When I was eight years old, my father came home from work, threw his newspaper against the wall, and then yelled at my mother because dinner would not be ready on time.

Gertrude: Mr. Thoreau, do you know Oedipus?

Thoreau: Tell me about him.

Gertrude: He was a king who, unbeknownst to himself, killed his father then married his mother then had four children with her. Twenty years later he found out, and to avoid seeing his post-incestuous world, he put out his own eyes. The Oedipus complex, discovered by Sigmund Freud, is the desire of the male child to eliminate his rival father, and then to have sexual relations with his mother.

Thoreau: But could Freud have been mistaken, in assigning his own secret desires to the psyches of every man?

Gertrude: Freud is never mistaken.

Thoreau: Do you think that is my problem?

Gertrude: To answer that question could take years of penetrating analysis. Would you feel uncomfortable if I removed my dress?

Thoreau: Is that slip silk or Freudian?

The woman corrected her slip by removing it. She pressed her body onto the man's, and they psychoanalyzed no more on the couch that day.

One bell from the church announced that it was fifteen minutes past eight. Thoreau washed his hands, his face, his public parts. He stepped into a pair of comfortable shorts, and then he returned to the plush bed to sink into a stupor of contemplative broods.

The door of the bedroom eased open. For an instant, Thoreau imagined that the morning ritual would be broken by the whim-filled women, and Karin or Gertrude or both would slip back into bed for more fornicating fun. Instead, the five-year-old Nikola entered, wearing a white sun dress covered with yellow moons and stars. Attentively, the child carried a tray bearing a cup of hot Swiss cocoa topped with Austrian whipped cream. Nikola placed the tray with the steaming cup on top of a table, then she jumped up onto the bed.

"Mama said that the new maid is here, and she wants to start cleaning upstairs. And Mama said to tell you to put some clothes on your lazy and *wunderschön Klösse*."

Thoreau opened his constant companion — a German-English dictionary — then translated the *wunderschön Klösse* into "beautiful dumplings".

The child drew a picture for the man — a little girl riding on a tall white horse — then told him it was a gift for him to keep, and he thanked her and said he liked it very much. Nikola laughed as she watched the rays of kindness pouring from Thoreau's fatherly eyes. The child ran her hand across the man's whisker-stubbled cheek.

"Do you know what? ... Later today Mama will buy a big reading desk for you, and Aunt Karin will fill up the den with your favorite books. They said that since the minute you came to live with us they are the happiest women on Earth. And they said that they want you to stay and live with us for a million million years."

The child looked again into Thoreau's deep eyes, placed her small hand on his strong shoulder, then kissed his cheek.

"Why are you sad?" she asked.

Always, Thoreau had been amazed by children: by the deepness of their intuition, by the freshness of their ideas. Women are fooled by words and men are deceived by beauty, but from children nothing profound can be concealed.

Thoreau jumped off the bed, grasped the child, lifted her up skyward until her head touched almost to the ceiling. He smiled as she screamed with delight.

"Come down here, Nikola the Giant," said Thoreau, "and crush me with a mama-bear hug!"

"I can't come down!" Nikola shouted, between streams of shrieks, giggles and laughs.

Thoreau lowered her down then swiftly raised her up again.

"Come down, come down, and hug the clown!"

"I can't come down!" shouted the laughing, laughing, laughing child.

Into the bedroom stepped the new maid, carrying a bucket of sponges and a broom. Like the typical Greek widow, she had de-sexed herself inside a black loose-fitting dress. The dress neutralized the sinuous curves of her body, and a long black shawl hid her face and her man-killing hair. As the maid dusted the furniture, Gertrude, from the kitchen, shouted something in German to Nikola, her child.

"Mama said to give you the letters, Daddy," Nikola said, between her bursts of laughing. "The letters ... heeheehahaha ... on the ... haha-heeheehee ... tray."

Nikola kissed Thoreau's hand, then ran downstairs to help deliver the morning feast.

The letters! ... Instantly Thoreau knew that they would be momentous. Since his self-chosen captivity by Gertrude and Karin he had written to no one except Kosmos and Penelope. To Kosmos he had sent inspiring words from Kazantzakis. To Penelope he had written a long letter that first explained his current situation, and then asked three questions: "What do you need?" ... "Can I send money to you?" ... "Can I help you with anything else?"

Yes, the return addresses proved that the missives had been sent by Kosmos and Penelope. He opened the letter from Kosmos first. It was not a letter, but a picture. The colors, the simple lines, and the vitality between the lines all combined to bring that work of art to life, and to make it stick in his distracted mind. The picture comprised a large bird — it was a puffin — with black and white feathers and a flat brightly-colored beak. A red circle encircled the middle of the bird's leg, around the area of the knee joint. The picture had a title at the top: 'O Joy Seein' A Puffin Knee'.

And these words were calligraphied below the feet of the bird:

The whole secret is to be yourself, to be open, to be sincere.
Said the poet:

"Are not the joys of morning sweeter
 Than the joys of night?
 And are the vig'rous joys of youth
 Ashamed of the light?"

And now, to Penelope's letter. Thoreau ripped open the envelope, careful not to damage the stiff paper inside. The envelope carried no sentences of reproach or praise; it requested no money; it contained nothing at all except a photograph of Kosmos. On the back of the photo, Penelope had penciled these Odyssean words:

"Beautiful Calypso, don't be pissed off at me!
We both know that compared to you, my wife looks like a sack of olives! She is human and grows stale, you are divine and will remain young forever.
And yet, my whole heart breaks in waiting for the day that I will return home!"

Thoreau dropped the photograph. Tears fell from his eyes as he stared out at the sea and wondered about the essence of the human problem: Why is it so difficult for a man to open his own mind, to live heroically, to change and to improve his life?

And he looked at the light in the sky then answered his own question:

"Whoever lives a life smothered by material possessions becomes a coward, fearful of losing things, afraid of fresh experiences, terrified of all varieties of change. For as long as he values comfort above honesty his mind withers and his courage shrinks. He can never change his life because he is at war with his own mind. Goethe shouted, 'Remember to live!' — but what courage it takes, just to remember this simplest of all things."

His concentration on these ideas increased in intensity; his mind shuttled between the future and the past; his heart remembered the loveliest of beaches and a loving woman's face. The life he could imagine was perfect and beautiful, while the lives he observed were miserable and mean. The sea-view faded and the scene around him blurred behind his own sad tears.

How else can we explain why the far-seeing man failed to notice that the well-made maid had abandoned her bucket, flung her featherduster, noiselessly closed the bedroom door, and then feasted her famished eyes upon the powerful body of Thoreau?

35

DEU SEX MACHINA —
HOW THE BED MADE THE MAID

'Deus ex machina,' is said to mean
In New Latin, a 'god from a machine.'
Improbably, the god descends to save
The book, the plot, the hero from the grave.

TEARS SWELLED in Thoreau's bright eyes as the maid — maneuvering silently behind him — moved closer for the thrill. Her ten sharp finger-nails clasped around his head like a wreath of thorns. Her warm palms pressed firmly over his ears, just hard enough for him to hear, but not identify, her sultry voice. Her lips, blowing a hot sirocco of clove-breath, scorched the hairs on the back of his neck.

"Drink this," she whispered hoarsely, handing him the cocoa cup. "You will need the energy."

Thoreau drank deep, draining the cocoa and the cream-dollop in three long gulps. Deftly, like peeling a banana skin, the maid removed her dress. Uncostumed, this maid became a woman, and then the woman millimetered closer to the man.

"Have you found the difference," she asked, "between women from Greece and women from Germany?"

Thoreau tried to turn around to face the woman, but she held his head too firmly between her hands.

"The Greeks never ask what time it is," he answered. "The Germans — the women and the men — keep track of every minute of the day."

"What time is it?" the woman asked.

Thoreau peered out the window at the clock that topped the church.

"Three minutes to 8:30. In less than one hundred and eighty seconds, Gertrude and Karin will find you here on their sexpensive bed. They will combine the tools of the writer's trade — intuition, experience, observation, and imagination — and then assume the inevitable: that Thoreau tried to seduce the maid. There will be a mild scene."

The woman tied a bandanna around his head to cover up his eyes, then pressed her naked front against Thoreau's bare back. Disheartened, he had no strength to resist. They wrestled for few moments and at the end of the bout she had pinned him back-down against the bed. She placed the empty cocoa cup into his right hand.

"Here, take this," the woman commanded. "Smash this cup against the wall. It's a Greek thing. It means that you care nothing about those things that can be broken and replaced. Afterwards, you will feel better."

Half-heartedly, Thoreau tossed the cup and then listened as it bounced off the wall and dropped unbroken to the carpeted floor.

"Seven nights of sex makes one weak man," the woman said, as she massaged his forehead. "Thoreau, if you remember how, tell me nothing but the whole truth. When you wrote in your letter and asked if I needed anything, did you mean that?"

"Penelope!" shouted Thoreau. "Penelope!! Penelope!!!"

"Your guardian goddess," she said. "I love the way you punctuate me!"

Thoreau snatched the bandanna blindfold from his eyes and flung it at the woman's belly. Playfully, she pounded his chest with her fists.

"Thoreau, tell me which is right: Do mules have more brains than men, or do men have less brains than mules?"

Penelope, sitting on top of him, here! ... Thoreau smiled and recovered his calm self. In the presence of this wildly open woman he always felt entirely at ease. He wanted to hug her, to tell her how much he had missed her, how much her friendship meant to him. But before he could act, she spoke.

"Thoreau, stop thinking somewhere else and listen to what I am saying to you. I was talking about the stupid question in your letter. When a passionate woman lives alone without a man, what in the name of Hellas do you think she needs?"

A strong woman is able to live alone: she can be productive, caring, and creative despite her solitude But when a woman (or a man) is weak, then loneliness drives her (or him) into the doing of desperate things. How sad that so many beautiful women live without getting the gift of so-beautiful love.

"What does a passionate woman need, Penelope?" Thoreau asked, happy to be glancing at the light in her mischievous eyes. "A passionate woman needs a man to care for her, and a man to care for."

"Does that mean," she asked, "that a woman needs one man, or two?"

As Penelope laughed deeply, sensuously, Thoreau's head turned at the sight of the bedroom door moving open slowly, slowly, inch by inch. Penelope — who had been waiting for that moment — swooped down and wrapped her arms around Thoreau. Certain that his Reason would be defeated by her Passion, Thoreau protested nevertheless.

"Penelope! Get off me, stand up, put on your clothes. At least cover yourself with the bandanna. Remember the last time you meddled in my romantic life? You almost ruined me."

She hugged him tighter.

"I'll remember that, Thoreau, as soon as you remember that you promised Kosmos that you would live with me. He wanted us to take care of each other, so I would not lose hope while he was gone, and so you could find a center for your wandering life and mind."

"Penelope, please get up. You don't understand what's been happening here."

Tighter she squeezed her arms around him.

"Your letter said that you've been sleeping with two sisters: is that so hard to understand? In France it happens every day. They call that a *menagerie de trop.*"

Anxiously Thoreau's eyes glanced first at the slow-opening door, then up at the woman sitting on his stomach. Time still remained to rescue himself, if he could be cunning enough.

"The square man avoids the triangles of love. Penelope, keep your hands to yourself and listen to me — do not believe that you are not attractive and that I am not attracted to you. As our mutual friend might say: 'Penelope is built like a brick church-house, and touching her body charges me with spiritual thoughts. Her body tempts me to her temple, spires my desires, and rings my steeple bells.' ... Yet to me, Penelope, you will always be a big sister. While Kosmos is alive I could never betray him and seduce you."

Penelope shook her head to disagree; her long hair swept across Thoreau's muscular chest.

"While that selfish bastard is alive you won't sleep with me? Then let's pretend he's dead! I've written him a hundred letters, and he doesn't care enough to answer, not even once. Kosmos can take care of himself in jail, but you, Thoreau, how will you escape from your prison? You can't break out because your prison is inside your head. Will your whole miserable life be the life of a slave who wants to do the right thing, and an idiot who thinks the wrong things he should do are right?"

In a flash their eyes spoke profoundly to each other.

"A whole life lived in slavery?" asked Thoreau. "Freedom is everything. Almost everything."

"Good," said the passionate woman, "we are agreed. Now stop talking, pucker your lips, and open up your heart. And if you believe in the freedom that is made of actions — and not just the empty words — then kiss me!"

And she kissed him and kissed him and kissed.

The lascivious kiss was not quite consummated when Thoreau and Penelope heard the shouting of a high-pitched voice.

"Mama! Karin!" yelled Nikola, as she placed a fruit-laden tray onto the table beside the bed. "Bring up one extra cup and plate for the breakfast. Thoreau is playing kissy-kissy with our nice new maid!"

36
THOREAU'S BREAKFAST IN BED

TO BE CAUGHT *flagrante delicto* — caught in the act 'while the crime is blazing' — is the greatest challenge to the male creative mind. Caught red-hinded with their infidelities exposed, men find four ways to respond: deny, downplay, justify, confess.

Thoreau — in his young foolishness — had no fear of women: no fear of winning them, losing them, or drawing them into the orbit of his life. His sincerity would prompt him to tell the truth. And what truth would he tell? Penelope had hunted him, but Thoreau knew that he had been pleased to be her prey. Karin and Gertrude would leave him. He would lose the warmth of their bodies and the pleasures of their love.

'Lovers Turnover' is not a dessert at a New York diner; it is the perennial problem of women and men. Women would desert Thoreau; other women would replace them; these replacements would be replaced; and soon as the lust was lost these new lovers would be replaced again, again, again. How many women does a man need? If lust is the only goal, then ten thousand women are not enough. Lust is good; yet when a man grows past his adolescent phase he wants and needs far more than lust.

How many women would it would take to satisfy him? How many mistakes would first be made — how many failed experiments — before the great creative insights break through the ordinary mind?

"Thoreau!" yelled Gertrude from the hallway. "Tonight's dinner is my favorite, *Schmorgurken unterm Sahneberg* — stewed cucumbers under a mountain of cream."

Said Karin: "And your favorite, *Kartoffelpuffer mit Apfelmus* — potato pancakes with applesauce. And for dessert, *Schwarzwälder Kirschtorte* — Black Forest cherry cake."

The moment that Karin and Gertrude entered the bedroom, Thoreau hardly noticed that the two beauties were naked from the forehead down.

Terribly did their *Augen* flash. Karin and Gertrude stared at Thoreau and Penelope.

"*Sehr gemütlich!* How charming!" Gertrude said coolly.

"*Welches Ansehen!* What a sight!" Karin shouted. "*Das ist grauenhaft!* That is horrible!"

Glaring at Thoreau, Gertrude marched closer to the bed.

"In my professional life as a sexual therapist, Herr Thoreau, I have seen everything and heard more. I am trained to accept, without judgment, all varieties of erotic misbehavior, from vertiginous virginity to psychogenic detumescence. When a woman confesses that she is a nymphomaniac, I nod my head with sympathy; when a man leaves his wife to have intercourse with a barnyard chicken, I take notes and yawn. I am a doctor. I am rational. I am calm and detached as the injured retina of the third Buddhist eye. In one word: I am unshockable."

Penelope, sensing the storm after the calm, wrapped both her hands around the bulging biceps muscle of Thoreau's right arm. The German therapist gazed at and appraised her Greek rival like a jeweler studying a gem.

"*Sie ist so schön wie die Venus!* She is as beautiful as Venus!" said Gertrude, examining the full-bodied Penelope.

Gertrude dropped her breakfast tray. Her mouth fell open, and then out came a siren-loud scream that made the paintings tremble on the walls. Wailing again, she jumped onto the bed then desperately clutched her *übermensch* Thoreau.

"*Ich liebe dich!* I love you!" she cried.

Karin, immediately, let her food-filled tray crash to the carpet, then leaped at Thoreau shouting:

"*Ich bin verrückt nach dir!* I am crazy about you!"

Gertrude jerked Thoreau's left thigh. Karin tugged Thoreau's right leg. Penelope yanked Thoreau's left arm. Shouting, screaming, shrieking, swearing, the three women pulled Thoreau's body in three different directions. Jealousy was tearing him apart.

Thoreau grasped his powerful right hand around the wooden bedpost.

"Ladies," he said. "Is there something we need to talk about?"

Not one of the women wanted to talk. Thoreau watched them like an artist: Penelope's pendulous breasts; Gertrude's bicycle-built thighs; Karin's lithe body perfected by years of ballet. Even when they were angry they were beautiful. Like all men in trouble, he wondered if telling these women that they looked beautiful would help to get them calm.

Thoreau was not the lone observer of this centrifugal farce. As young Nikola watched the scene, her eyes filled with a child's wonder, openness, and curiosity. For the past seven weeks, Thoreau had delighted in laughing with her, and making her laugh and laugh.

"Nikola," he said. "All this exercise is making me very hungry."

And with his powerful right arm he pulled himself close to the tray of food that Nikola had placed on the table beside the bed. When his mouth opened to bite the bunch of grapes, the three women tugged him back.

Again Thoreau pulled himself closer to the grapes and opened his mouth to eat, but again the tugging women drew his body back from the unattainable fruits. The child's face lit up with joy as she laughed and laughed and laughed.

"I will help you," Nikola said. "You need one more hand."

Gripping a bowl of olive oil, she climbed up onto the bed then poured the oil along the bedpost.

"Nikola, no!" Thoreau said calmly. "If you grease that post, I won't be able to hold on."

Penelope yelled: "He promised! He's coming home with me!"

Karin cried out: "I loved him first!"

Gertrude shouted: "I cured him and now he is mine!"

The women pulled Thoreau's limbs with all their furied might. The olive oil trickled down the bedpost and the man's hand slid from the saving wood. Four bodies shouted as they tumbled off the bed onto the carpet, in one tangled heap of flesh.

37
WHAT THOREAU REMEMBERED THEN FORGOT

"IT IS SAFER," says the ancient proverb, "to be a meat bone tossed between a pack of dogs, than to be a man beloved by two women at once."

Thoreau lay sprawled on the plush carpet, gripped by three furious femmes: the clutching Karin, the grasping Gertrude, the pawing Penelope. Danger — especially dangerous women — focused the young man's attention and made his whole self fully alert. Strange-shaped shards of memories interconnected as a mystery unpuzzled itself. Thoreau thrilled at the swelling illuminations poised to burst from subconscious chaos into his mind's sweet light.

He remembered the old man who loved olive trees: his smile, his peacefulness, his hearty warmth expressing the most sublime abilities of human beings: to love, to give, to speak sincerely, and to be human kind.

He remembered — it happened a week ago — the 80-year-old old lady he met in a café: for thirty years she had saved pennies and nickels and dimes so she could visit Greece. But on her first day in Athens, an American tourist, pretending to change her dollars into Euros, robbed her of everything she owned. So Thoreau, after listening to her saga and realizing that he was rich, reached into his pocket and handed her enough money to live splendidly in Greece for a month at least.

He remembered his friend Kosmos, the vitality of Kosmos, how he lived fully in this world, yet searched never-endingly for his true paradise. His dream remained laughably quixotic and hopelessly unattainable, yet the man never lost his passion for that dream. His faith made that paradise feel so real, so close at hand. And the colorful picture of the bird with circled knee! A work of joy that could have been created only by a man who had discovered what his heart had been seeking for so long.

He remembered at last the eyes of Beatrice Loverly, the beautiful radiance in those eyes, the way she gazed at him that night too many weeks ago. And her voice, the voice that caressed him with so much vitality, and laughed with so much joy. Would they ever again walk together, watched by the starlight, on that quietly glorious segment of the beach? Would he ever again find one moment as magical as that?

Those four memories were about to meld into a new idea when Thoreau felt tug-tug-tuggings on his arm and legs. Penelope, Gertrude, and Karin continued their project of shrieking and shouting and swearing as they pulled Thoreau. The young man's concentration dissolved like cotton candy. The great solution — once focused like a moonbeam — scattered as the wind-blown sand.

With a jump and a thump and a ha-ha-ha, Nikola leaped from the bed and landed on Thoreau's strong chest.

"Mama! Karin! Don't hurt him!" the child cried out. "We were crying all the time and he brought us happiness!"

Silence. Six hands released Thoreau's three limbs. Ears perked up and eyes opened astonished as the silence broke beneath the telephone's discordant ring ring rings.

38
How Thoreau Explained
The Woman Naked In His Arms

THE TELEPHONE RANG and rang and rang, and nobody knew what to do except the child Nikola, who dashed across Thoreau's body then picked up the shimmering phone.

"Hello, *Halo, ela,*" the child said, in English, German, Greek. ... "It's for you, Thoreau."

When the man placed the earpiece to his ear he heard the most seductive voice chanting these most enchanting words:

"If a goddess steals a mortal man
   Himself he cannot help or save —
He can escape from her just when
   A stronger goddess takes him as her slave."

Thoreau pondered this poem for a moment, then grasped the meaning behind the words.

"Beatrice!" he shouted, thoroughly surprised. "Beatrice!"

"Am I interruptusing your coitus, darling?" the woman replied. "I could ring back in ten seconds, when you've finished up."

"Beatrice, I was just thinking about you!"

"Thinking about me while a trio of women dally in your arms! That's twice I've caught you naked with Penelope. Three times and it's a certified affair."

"She's not naked," Thoreau answered.

"Not naked!" said Beatrice skeptically. "What do you call a woman wearing nothing but a cheap perfume? Topless as a mermaid, bottomless as a barmaid, nude as a ninny, starkers as a nanny, bare as a frolicking nymph? Not even *dishabilled* in those thin thong things that thespians thwang between their thighs?"

"Penelope is not naked," said Thoreau, examining her clothesless body as he crafted his reply. "She is garmentally challenged."

Beatrice laughed.

"Darling," she said, "you do have a way with women and with words. But when it comes to actions — intelligent actions — you lack audacity. Pity poor Penelope. A woman will forgive every mistake that a man makes, except one thing. If she invites him to her bed and he refuses to go, then — depending on her self-esteem — she either doubts her beauty as a woman, or doubts his power as a man."

"Beatrice," said Thoreau, surprised how the mere sound of her voice could make him shiver. "There are some things I never had a chance to tell you."

"Dear sweet innocent Thoreau," she said. "Before you have a chance to say it, I know precisely what you want to say. It's harder for a man to hide his emotional feelings than it is for him to hide his sexual ones. A woman in love has a soul like a mirror; a man is love has a heart as clear as glass."

"Tell me, Beatrice," said Thoreau. "Do men and women love in different ways?"

Her voice, supremely sensuous, felt and sounded like her warm lips trembling on his ear.

"A woman is completely alive," she answered, "only when she loves. And everything between our loves is nothing, like the dark empty eternities between the stars. Know, dearest, that when a woman loves a man — when she loves him with her whole soul — her love is measureless in space and time. If he has been tender with her — tender in his actions and his words — she will love him and remember him for life. That infinite capacity for love is the heart of womanhood, the brilliant jewel of joy and agony in every woman's life. ... And how few men — how precious few! — prove to be worthy of a woman's glorious deep love."

Thoreau wondered if every woman loved like that, or if that depth of love in women was as rare as true creative genius among men. Beatrice spoke again.

"Now, darling, that I've warned you about falling into follies in the future, let me attempt to rescue you from this foolishness that funks your present life. Hand the telephone to Dr. Heissundkalt. Don't say goodbye; don't tell me something cakey-sweet that you feel now but won't feel one week from today. *Chaire*, dearest. Take the best care of yourself. Make your body strong and your heart stronger, so that when you meet just the right woman you will be just the right man."

Just then, Thoreau realized that he had been thinking about Beatrice, brooding about Beatrice, dreaming about Beatrice, for the past seven weeks. He wanted to tell her that, and tell her as a poet would express it — with such power that she remembers it, with such sincerity she believes it, with such beauty it delights her like a warm fire in the heart. But his own heart felt like jelly, and the poor words he almost found melted in his throat like peanut butter. Silently, Thoreau passed the telephone to Gert.

"Dr. Gertrude Heissundkalt, this is Beatrice Loverly. We met very briefly at the WANDERBORE conference in Crete."

"Ms. Loverly!"

"Call me Beatrice, Gertrude."

Smiling with admiration, Gertrude waved and whispered to Karin.

"It's Beatrice Loverly, from WANDERBORE!"

Karin's eyes lit up delighted and amazed. She rushed to her sister then pressed her ear against the phone.

"It is so thoughtful of you to call," said Gertrude.

"It's my pleasure," Beatrice replied. "The other day, one of our members rang me up. She informed me that your life lately has been filled with exceptional stress. Would you care to tell me about the situation, dear?"

A pause, a silence, and then Gertrude burst into tears.

"Beatrice," she said, sobbing as she spoke. "My husband had been fooling around with other women. At last, when he put his hands on my sister, I threw him out. I thought I could find strength in the spiritual peace of Greece, and in the intellectual challenge of my work. Yet when a woman shrinks her mind, closes her legs and shuts her fists, she can never take the gifts from the goddesses."

"And at the bottom of despair," said Beatrice, "a man betrayed you, the goddesses snubbed you, but a passion for your work rekindled your feminine flame! Take a slow deep breath, then tell me about it."

"One morning, my sister Karin came home and brought with her an interesting and problematic case. She told me that she had found a young man who had an overwhelming fear of women. He had lost interest in women, he could not become erotically aroused."

Karin blushed as she rolled her eyes, then shyly glanced at Thoreau, who stared at her with astonishment.

"Worst of all," Gertrude continued, "it appeared that he had a Santa

Claus sex life."

"A Santa Claus sex life?" asked Beatrice.

"Yes," said Gertrude. "He comes but once a year."

"I see," Beatrice replied. "And I assume that with great personal patience and professional skill, you worked to cure him of his sexual dysfunctions and fears?"

"That's right," Gertrude answered. "I studied some cases in Havelock Ellis, I formulated a plan of action, I enacted that plan in extensive sessions of therapy. And now I can say that the patient is completely cured. The change is between *Nacht und Tageslicht* — night and daylight. Before he came to me he was a wreck, but now in bed he performs like a car parked overnight in New York City."

"Like a car," asked Beatrice, "parked overnight in New York City?"

"Yes," purred Gertrude. "He is tireless."

"You put your whole heart into your work, didn't you Gertrude?"

"Yes, Beatrice. All my learning and experience were required to cure him. But then ... but then ... oh Beatrice, I am so ashamed!"

"You can tell me, dear sister," Beatrice said.

"Then I committed the greatest sin of therapists: I fell in love with my own patient! Oh, it is so wrong, it is so wrong. But I was so lonely and confused!"

More sobbing, but these were the tears of a confession that would heal the wound.

"Beatrice, there is one more thing. I almost cannot tell you, but I shall. ... With my sister I am sharing this man in bed!"

"Now, Gertrude," said Beatrice, "remember the words of our good Goethe: *Geteilte Freud' ist doppelt Freude* — 'A joy shared is a joy doubled.' ... Gertrude, are you ready to begin your new life?"

"I am ready."

"Good. Let's work together and get this problem solved. The first step is to forgive yourself. You were vulnerable, you made mistakes — some significant mistakes — and inside yourself you have been suffering because you want to be sincere. But the past is frozen — we can never change it — and now you must accept it then move ahead. You can't blame yourself completely: you were afraid of the future and you were lonely, and lonely women always fall into relationships with the wrong men."

"Yes, Beatrice," said Gertrude. "I see that and understand it now."

"And what woman on Earth," said Beatrice, "is immune to the charms of this marvelous young Casanova? ... His kind face and his two bright eyes could seduce a Medusa, and tempt even the most faithful wife. No woman can resist this man."

"What can I do now, Beatrice?" Gertrude asked. "My life is ruined and it's my fault. *Das alles kommt halt über jede Frau:* No woman can escape her fate."

"Gertrude," said Beatrice, "listen, dear. No woman can escape her fate until she first embraces it. You have made mistakes, and — because you are a smart woman — you can examine them, understand them, and then learn and grow. The secret of happiness is nothing more than this: Break the harmful old patterns, then choose to do the new good thing."

"What should I do?" Gertrude asked.

"Start now," said Beatrice, "by repeating a poem we learned at the conference. ... She who binds to herself to a boy ... "

Then Gertrude answered: "Does the winged life destroy."

Beatrice continued: "But she who kisses the boy as she flies ..."

"Lives in eternity's sunrise," Gertrude replied.

And then she breathed deeply and said: "Already, I feel so much better!"

"Of course you do, dear. The best medicine is truth. Now why don't you come to England to visit me for two weeks of talking, healing, and exercise? Bring your sister and your daughter, too. You won't be walled in: I have a cabin in the woods on a small lake, like that American writer, Henry David — lately I've never been able to remember his last name."

Gertrude explained the offer to her sister, who listened attentively. Karin became so excited at the notion that she jumped up and down on the bed as if it were a trampoline. The sisters hugged each other, grabbed the hand of Nikola, then ran out the bedroom door to pack their clothes. Karin ran back in, kissed a small kiss onto Thoreau's cheek, promised she would send a postcard, then scurried out through the doorway.

Thoreau sat stupefied. Was this Karin the same woman who last night swore to love him for as long as Germany had beer?

"Glück auf den Weg!" Thoreau shouted. "A pleasant journey to you!"

Penelope picked up the phone. She chatted and laughed with her friend Beatrice, then said good-bye with a promise that she would write soon.

"Well, Thoreau," said Penelope. "We're alone at last, and we have a nice soft bed. Shall we enjoy ourselves for a few hours, or should I sigh like the thousand virgins and get dressed?"

Thoreau threw the floored clothes at Penelope, and Penelope tossed a robe to the young man.

"You need a vice, Thoreau," the woman said. "You're too good, and this world gives too much trouble to the people who are good too much. If it wasn't for me and for Beatrice, you'd give up on this worldly world and retire to a goddamn monastery. *Pame:* Let's go! Pack all your books and things, say good-bye to this lazy bad-for-the-ass life, and then meet me outside on the doorstep."

"Where are we going?" Thoreau asked.

Penelope grabbed some food from the tray, then placed a motherly kiss on his forehead as she answered.

"Home."

3 9

Sunsets in Agia Souvlakis

Agia souvlakis is a tourist-fishing village on the south coast of Crete. Studied by anthropologists, the village might be viewed from four perspectives. High above, the rocky coastline and the quiet beaches stretch eastward many miles toward Paleohora, and westward two miles to Dembacchae. Moving closer, observe a few dozen white houses protruding from the hillsides like teeth from ninety-year-old gums. From the paved road higher above we cruise into the town-center — blink twice you've missed it — with a bank, a post office, a bakery, two cafés, two restaurants, one food store, a bus station, a half-star hotel, and a small church with a loud bell that rings weekly, on Sunday mornings at nine. Walk from the town-center towards the water and you reach the dock, made of a huge slab of concrete jutting into the sea. The dock collects painted boats, black-capped fisherman, orange fishnets in constant need of repair, and wooden crates filled with shimmering fresh-caught fish.

Agia Souvlakis is picturesque. Yet it was easy to discover how and why this small town had become immune to the mad plague of tourists who perennially invaded the most beautiful places in Greece. Here, in Souvlakis, the prices of everything that could be bought were suspiciously inflated, and the natives who sold them — unlike Greeks everywhere else — were uninterested, unfriendly, unwelcoming. In all of Souvlakis, there was not one place to buy fast-and-loose women or food. Credit cards and checks were not accepted; the bank opened for a mere one hour every weekday; and the lone grocery store sold food and wine only in the rare moments when the owner felt in the mood to unlock his doors. In Souvlakis, restaurants closed at sundown, and the "deesko" — as the local Greeks called their café with a music jukebox — bolted its doors at eight.

Many visitors commented unfavorably about the dockside public outhouse: it had no door, and it smelled like it would have defeated even

Heracles's labors to make it clean. But the greatest discourager of all was the half-star hotel, for everyone who stayed there agreed that its rating was far too high. Without heating or air-conditioning, the rooms felt too-chilly in the evenings and too-hot in the afternoons. Sleep was made impossible by either the olive pits that stuffed the mattresses, or the chickens squawking on the roof. Toilets were not quite level against the wooden floor, and their seats not quite attached to the ceramic bowls. And whenever a guest turned on the water tap there was a strong chance that a small fish or a string-like turd would emerge, and then — before it could be accurately identified — sink into a glass of brownish fluid, or slither down the rusty drain.

Attracted by the seaside scenic beauty, many tourists arrived on the morning bus. But repelled by the lack of comforts and luxuries — and the complete absence of television — most of these tourists departed after a few hours or a sleepless night, seeking Crete's northern cities for more excitement, louder music, flusher toilets, and cheaper booze.

Penelope tied a bunch of *scilla* flowers over her door — to bring good things to all who stayed there, and to promote fruitfulness, she explained. She took my hand then led me through the doorway of her home.

"Come in, Thoreau!" she said. "Come in, and be at home. You will like it here. It is quiet, but you can hear cicadas singing; it is simple, but the simplicity will bring you peace."

In this white sandstone house with blue doors and blue window shutters, everything felt earthy, invigorating, and bright. I examined again the familiar three rooms: the storage room for Kosmos's mule and supplies; the guest room now overpopulated with books and art; and the kitchen and bedroom where Penelope kept her wood stove, her cooking and eating table, and her small bed. The walls were still covered with sketches and words created by Kosmos, and onto these walls I added his latest inspired picture of the puffin bird.

On the kitchen table sat two basins: one filled with underwear in soapy water, the other brimming with green olives in olive oil and orange juice. Penelope stirred these olives; she placed two flowers into a vase; she opened her shutters to let more light pour in. Onto the table she placed a pitcher of pomegranate juice, nodded for me to help myself to a cup of the tart drink, and then began assembling ingredients to cook a meal.

"I'm going to welcome you with a dinner you'll never forget," she said. "A Cretan specialty: fava beans with onions, potatoes, tomatoes, spices and herbs."

She stopped her work for a moment to kiss my cheek.

"I'm so happy that you're here at last! Unpack your clothes and put your backpack under the bed."

Glancing lovingly at the young man, and lustingly at the bed, the woman added: "Maybe we should have dessert first, and dinner afterwards."

"Penelope," I said. "can we discuss something?"

"You are just like Kosmos!" she said, in a bittersweet tone. "The world is waiting desperately for you to act, and there is always something that you want to discuss. And what does it mean, this discuss-ting word? It means that you want to tell me not to do something that I want to do!"

"Penelope, I'm feeling — "

"What you are feeling at this moment, Thoreau, is called ancient Greek hospitality. Everything I have is yours: my house, my food, my heart, my body, and my bed."

She led me to the bed then sat down there, motioning for me to sit beside. I sat on the chair instead.

"Penelope," I said slowly. "I think that the best thing ... for both of us to do ... is to enjoy a platonic relationship."

"A play-tonic relationship!" she shouted. "Is that where you dress up like a leather purse and then tie me up? ... What the hell do you mean?"

"It's a very close and rewarding intellectual and spiritual friendship without any sexual contact. Like a brother and a sister, a bedless marriage of hearts and minds. A platonic friendship is a variety of love: Love from the neck up."

"Your neck up, or my neck?" she asked.

"Both necks up," I answered.

"Maybe it's not as bad as it sounds," the woman said. "There are a lot of things that I can do to you with both necks up."

I laughed, and before I could say more, Penelope spoke her mind.

"Listen, Thoreau: if you wait for the perfect woman then you'll never get involved in any good relationships, just like the artist who waits for the perfect moment of inspiration and never gets anything done."

To continue her persuasive argument, she bounced off the bed, leaped onto my lap, and then circled her arms around my neck and shoulders.

"Lovely face, great tits, good-hearted sincerity," she said. "The gods tell a man: 'In a woman you can have two out of three.'"

That remark made my lips smile, a smile that I attempted unsuccessfully to hide. Of the second and third qualities, Penelope had ample helpings. I wondered if I would ever find three out of three, and brains, too.

Penelope reached her fingers through a hole on the bottom of the wicker chair seat, then pinched my rump so hard it tingled like stings from a bee.

"Ouch! ...Penelope, I'm trying to think about Kosmos now."

"And I'm thinking about Kosmos every minute of every day," she said. "How will it help him if the both of us are miserable?

"Penelope — "

"Don't Penelope me, Thoreau! I'm sick and tired of being Penelopeed! Just shut up for a minute and listen with both ears. If we don't sleep together then people will talk. But if we do sleep together then the whole village will know it, and then the widows and wives and daughters will stay away from you, and all their jealous uncles and husbands and fathers will be your friends, instead of your suspicious rivals and bitter enemies. Under every rooftop is a sighing daughter and a lonely lusting wife. Trust me, Thoreau, it's too dangerous for a man to romp like Casanova in a small Greek town."

Penelope kissed my lips; I let her kiss me but I didn't kiss her back.

"Dammit, Thoreau, either you're a eunuch or you're made of wood! In all those years you Americans go to school, don't they teach you how to kiss right? ... Greece has a place for monks, it is called Mount Athos. What are you fighting this for? It will make our lives so much simpler. Like all men, you talk and talk about taking the road that nobody travels on, then you turn your back and walk the other way."

"Penelope," I said. "Please don't take offense. For a woman like you I'd scale mermaids and Mount Olympus, and vice versa. But we can't sleep together. My deeply ingrained morality will not let me make love with the girlfriend of my best friend."

Penelope jumped off my lap then watched my eyes light up as her curvy body shimmied and her dress cascaded down. Lust might have ensnared me, but I was rescued by a lucky accident. At that moment Kosmos's mule, Dante, ambled into the room. Unembarrassed by his swollen love-organ, he approached Penelope, nuzzled his nose against her posterior, then whinnied with yearning and joy.

Humor might break the tension and ease her disappointment.

"Penelope, if Dante lived in Bedlamerica right now his life would be easy. He would simply put a personal ad in one of those nervy meet-your-match websites: 'WHM (well-hung mule) seeks frisky female for fun, friendship, dating, serious relationship, and play. Religion not important. Photo appreciated; asses need not apply.'"

Penelope burst into tears.

"Men!" she shouted. "In this whole damn town there are two virile males, and the only one who wants me is a mule!"

We devoured Penelope's scrumptious dinner, and then we talked and laughed for hours and hours more. After receiving a playful pinch good-night, I sat down in the big chair where Kosmos would sit when on Saturday mornings he read to Penelope. Staring through an always-open window I watched the sky and wondered what the stars were thinking ...

Penelope! There was something remarkable about her that she'd been hiding from me: maybe our friendship would someday yield a clue ... Katerina, Romantza, Meli — they had not yet come for refuge to Penelope's house — I hoped that my gypsy friends were safe now, and that these wild women would find a way to make a living without becoming pretty prostitutes or petty thieves. ... The German women, Karin and Gertrude, had taught me a priceless lesson: the woman you're sleeping with may not be the woman you love. ... Irene, her childlike enthusiasm, and the rosy innocence of her first romantic crush ... Bliss, the unattainable woman on the bicycle, had a body and a face that knocked me down — and I followed her from fiery curiosity: inside this pure beauty, what were her passions and her dreams? ... Victoria, the shy librarian, who found courage to do what many strong men never dare: to risk everything and confess her love ... At last my thoughts played around with Beatrice Loverly: she had beauty, brains, sincerity, and all the kindness in the world. Without ignoring her own needs, she devoted her life to helping others. She loved, not in the daydream or the feelings only, but in action, by helping and by caring ...

The noise of footsteps snapped this string of reveries.

"Penelope," I said. "Are you taking a walk somewhere?"

Penelope placed her hand on my shoulder.

"To the place where all the old wealth is hiding," she said. "Three nights a week I do the work of cleaning — the bank, the restaurants, the cafés —

from midnight to six a.m."

"I'll help you," I said. "Then you'll be done in half the time."

In the darkness she stroked my cheek.

"Thoreau: Did you come all the way to Greece to mop floors and scrub toilets? ... No, you came to clean your heart. Your own work is more important. Tomorrow I'll show you a happy place in the mountains that the tourists haven't discovered yet. Goodnight, dear."

"Penelope?"

"*Ti?* What?"

"What's that perfume you're wearing?"

She laughed as she took my head between her hands, then pressed it against the section of her dress that lay above her heart.

"That is ammonia, my dear friend. The perfume of the working class."

She kissed my forehead. With her mop in one hand and bucket in the other, she left the house cheerfully, humming an old Greek melody.

The next evening, when I had gone out to find food to cook for dinner, I saw posters plastered all around the town. There were the do-not-eat-the-cats posters, which I left alone; and there were the reward-money-for-gypsies posters, which I ripped down as quickly as I could find.

Penelope had been right as usual: the Greek men here, seeing me as a threat to their daughters and sisters and wives, were not friendly and would not let me be their friend. The two exceptions were Rakis — who asked if I needed anything — and another friend of Kosmos, Georgios, who opened his brother's store so I could shop for groceries.

I returned home, my arms stuffed with bags of food. The kitchen had changed: it now contained a wooden table, crowded with burning candles and photographs of Kosmos. Penelope, kneeling in front of the table, sobbed as she wished aloud that Kosmos would be set free.

I touched her arm.

"Penelope," I said. "It's Friday and I know you miss your night with Kosmos. Let me read something to you, and maybe that will help."

She cheered up at this idea, and brought me a heavy anthology book-marked to the selection that she wanted to hear. It was a love-drama by the Roman playwright Pacuvius. Penelope lay down on the bed, I sat in a chair beside her, and then with fiery enthusiasm I began to read.

"The storm swells and the sea begins to shudder,
Darkness is doubled; and the tempest thickens
in the black of night; fire gleams vivid
Amid the clouds; the heavens with thunder shake;
Hail mixed with copious rain sudden descends
Precipitate; from all sides every blast
Breaks forth; fierce whirlwinds gather, and the flood
Boils with fresh ferocity."

We saw lightning flash and immediately heard thunder booming, and then a storm — even more fierce than the version described in the drama — suddenly attacked the town. The clouds gathered, the winds bellowed, the gulls cried out, the waves leaped up as if they would jump off the earth and snatch the distant moon. The sea raged lusty and impulsive as an Italian opera rife with lovesick gypsies. Penelope frantically screamed.

"Penelope, what's — "

"Thoreau! Help me! I'm afraid of nothing except thunderstorms! When I was a little girl — "

A blast of lightning-thunder rattled the house and Penelope screamed again.

"Hold me, Thoreau! It's the only way to calm me down. Get into bed with me or else I'll die of fright!"

I entered the bed then wrapped my arms around the woman; she snuggled up against me with a sly smile.

"Penelope," I said. "Are you really terrified of storms?"

She threw off the sash around her dress then kissed my lips.

"Thoreau," she whispered, "When I kiss you I hear bells."

I tried to stand up but she held me firm.

"Those bells are ringing from the church, Penelope."

A voice outside began to shout "The sheeps! The sheeps!"

Thunder and lightning cracked and blasted and Penelope kissed me again.

"Oh, goddesses!" she shouted. "I forgot! I forgot!"

I raised my head.

"Your pills or my condom?"

"The sheeps!" cried Penelope. "The fishing boats — the waves will smash them against the dock. They'll be destroyed!"

She jumped out of bed then grabbed two large flashlights from a drawer.

"*Grigora!* Quickly! Get your shoes on, Thoreau, and come with me!"

We arrived at the dock amidst darkness and chaos and anxious shouts. The wind was so strong at times I needed to hold on to something to keep from being blown to the ground. In the nearest café, the town's old mayor had organized a count and an accounting of the residents, to discover how many men were in danger, trapped in their fishing boats on the unrelenting sea. On the dock itself, Rakis stood, a true hero as he waved his arms to direct a dozen men. With the rain and the waves and the wind blowing wildly, Rakis pushed his weeping wife aside, and then he and the twelve men jumped into small wooden boats that rowed into the tempest to try to find their lost neighbors and friends. Wives and mothers of the missing were wailing and sobbing on the shoulders of those women whose husbands and sons were safe. There were no ambulances, no national guardsmen, no police, no rescue squads — only one lone doctor, an old man who shuffled into the café with his black bag, then sat down with a glass of *retsina* and his worry beads.

Ten men on the dock were tying ropes to the boats, trying to pull them up onto the dock before the waves could smash them to bits. These were not just boats for play: these were the fishing boats that made their livelihoods. Damaged boats might be repaired — losing weeks or months of precious work — but the boats that were destroyed could never be replaced.

"Thoreau," said Penelope, "this town is full of old geezers. They are strong from their work, but they are not young men, *katalavehees?* ... " She led me from the café to outside in the storm, where she gripped the shoulder of Kosmos's friend.

"Georgios," said Penelope. "You remember Thoreau, eh? He is strong like Rakis. Show him what to do."

Georgios tied a thick rope to a boat, then placed my hands around the rope.

"Wait until I signal," he said. "Then pull like a bull."

When he lowered his hand I pulled, with all my strength, and the boat jerked up from the water onto the concrete dock. Georgios shouted "Bravo!" and then "Come!". In this way we worked for three hours, alongside other old fishermen, to save whatever could be saved of the town's fleet of ninety boats.

Rakis and his men returned safely. They had found one man — half-drowned but still alive. Only one man had been reckless enough to fish that night. Everyone else had heeded the weather report — inside their throbbing arthritic joints — that told them for certain that a furious storm was near. Rakis carried the water-soaked man into the café. Minutes later there were shouts and cheers, and women screamed for joy, as the half-drowned man sat up, and the doctor raised his arm to say that all would soon be well.

The storm abated. Penelope placed her arm around me and we walked home. When we arrived there we found baskets of fruits and olives: the villagers had thanked me for my help. Penelope removed my clothes, rubbed my body dry with towels, served me a hot soup, tended the cuts and blisters on my hands, then rubbed my body with a soothing oil. She placed me on the bed, she stepped out of her dress, she wrapped her warm body around mine.

"Thoreau," she said. "I think I understand now what you were saying about being friends from the neck up. But I'm a woman, too, don't forget that."

"Only a dead man could forget that, Penelope. And one kiss from you might wake him from the under-kingdom of the dead."

She kissed me and she laughed.

"Let's make a bargain that makes us both satisfied," she said. "You will sleep with me in my bed. I will cook meals for you and clean your clothes. We can be friends only and have no sex together. But when I'm in the mood, I'll try to get you in the mood, too. And three times a week I get to pinch your ass."

"I'll sleep in the guest room," I said, "and share equally the cooking and cleaning. You can pinch me once a week."

"Twice a week," said Penelope. "And let's seal the bargain with a kiss."

"O.K., two pinches a week," I said. "Sealed with a hug and a handshake."

She kissed me for a passionate Meteoric minute. And then, thoroughly exhausted, inside each others arm we fell asleep.

On many evenings, after we'd eaten dinner together, Penelope and I would walk, holding hands, along the beach that stretched from Agia Souvlakis to Dembacchae. Midway, about one mile from each town, we reached Kosmos's favorite cove that he called *kaliparalea* — the place where Penelope and I first met. Here, every evening, we would stop for a few minutes, laugh about that wild encounter, admire the curving sand dunes that surrounded us, and then smile at the beauty of the Greek-light sky and the roaring sea. Continuing our walk, we passed the heart-breaking hotel: where Kosmos had been devoured by Ligeia, and where I had refused an invitation to spend a night with Beatrice. For that foolish decision, I told Penelope, I would never forgive myself.

Walking further, we arrived at the town of Dembacchae. As we weaved through the back streets we felt an excitement and a sadness brewing, and at last we rejoiced as we entered the still-uninhabited garden once owned by Kosmos. I watered the plants while Penelope filled a basket with fresh herbs. All the while we remembered the joy of our great friend. We left rejuvenated, enjoying the walk homeward along the quiet beach.

This ritual of visiting that garden continued for six straight nights, but on the seventh we did not complete our trip. As I turned the corner to enter the cove, I spied a pitiful, hilarious, quixotic sight.

A small tent had been pitched on the sand. Adjacent to the tent we saw a notebook; and near it, sat a water bottle made of stainless steel. Beside the water, book and tent lay a naked man. With his back against the sand he looked as helpless as a turtle stuck in a shell turned upside-down. One hand, two lips, both eyelids and a private part were the only body pieces that he could move.

Feebly, he waved a flag he had made from a tree branch and a red-yel-low-blue pair of superhero underwear. He was calling out for help, but in a voice so faint that he could not be heard unless you stood beside him. I approached the body, and Penelope followed, standing close behind me. The body was weak but the young man's lips babbled energetically.

"Water, and *Wasser, nero!*
Hello there and *yasu, halo.*
He's dying of sunstroke,
And thinking in one stroke
Of Emerson, Whitman, Thoreau."

"Do you need help?" Penelope stupidly asked.

The young man gazed at Penelope's figure and my face.

> "Have I died and to Olympian heaven gone?
> Or am I plunged to Hades where my thirst burns on?
> This must be paradise! The sunset's sacred show
> And a great god and goddess come to make it so."

"He's a poet, Thoreau!" shouted Penelope, grasping the young man's hand. "Treat him gently. Even when they're healthy, poets are sensitive souls. Kosmos says that poets are the un-knowledged legislators of the world."

Pensively, Penelope examined the poet's private part.

"Kosmos also told me," she said, "that poets are oversexed because they have the biggest pensées."

The poet eyed the curious Penelope, then answered:

> "*Pensée fait la grandeur de l'homme* — (blush pink!) —
> The greatness of man lies in his power to think."

I lifted the young man's head, placed the water bottle to his lips, and watched as the poet drank greedily, sucking at the bottle like a baby sucking at the breast. After drinking half the bottle's fluid the poet rhymed again.

> "A poet sound asleep he fell,
> Under the hot Greek sun.
> And when he woke with thirst from hell,
> He could not move or run.
> A lovely lass and a warty old hag,
> Passed by and thought him dead.
> But when they saw his rising flag —
> They screamed, they turned, they fled."

Penelope folded the poet's tent, stuffed it into the backpack that lay inside, then picked up the poet's book. I grasped the man and raised his body off the sand, then carried him in my arms toward the house of Penelope.

"My name is Penelope," she said. "And the brawny brainy hero who is holding you is named Odysseus Thoreau. Tell us how you wound up like this."

The keen-minded man gazed at his benefactress.

"All my money," he said "is now being managed by a pack of lovely gypsies."

"Gypsies!" shouted Penelope. And her eyes gazed at the far away.

"What is it, Penelope?" I asked.

"Fifteen years ago my father had an accident which broke his leg. He crawled to an old cabin with an old wood stove. While he slept the cabin caught on fire. My father's body would have burned to bones and ashes if it wasn't for a gypsy girl! She pulled him out of the burning cabin and saved his life. From breathing smoke she almost died, and her perfect face wound up covered with ugly burns. One week after we took her to the doctor, she ran away. She must have been fifteen or sixteen — what great courage she had! I saw her only once before the accident, and I never saw her again. ... Tell us the rest of your troubles, Poet, so we think less of our own."

The Poet drank more water and more, and then talked on.

"In the morning, just when I got off from the bus at Agia Souvlakis, ten women approached me and then begged me to give them food. They said they were starving, so I told them to take what they needed from my wallet and leave me the rest. They left me to rest. I was wondering how to help them when a police wagon, siren screaming, drove at eighty-miles-per-hour into town. The gypsy women scattered like birds when the cat walks by. They headed for Paleohora on Crete's west coast, but when the police questioned me, I told them that the women were going in the opposite direction, eastward toward Dembacchae."

"Good thinking, Poet!" shouted Penelope.

"So I came here to the beach to write a poem about their wild spirits. But I fell asleep under the Greek sun — that same ferocious sun that singed the wings of Icarus. And when I woke up I realized that I'd been knocked out by sun-poisoning. I could think clearly, but I could hardly move."

Penelope asked the poet his name, and he answered by pointing to a book she was carrying, and she read the title and author aloud.

"*The Oddity of U Lasses*, by Michael Seaport. ... Thoreau, his name is Seaport!"

All this made me laugh, as my intuition promised that this shipwrecked poet would prove to be a remarkable new friend. As I carried Seaport, Penelope sponged the poet's forehead with a damp cloth.

"We're taking you home, poet," she said. "We have water, we have food, we have a place for you to sleep where no sun will bake you like a Greek bread. My house is small, so in a few days, when you feel better, you can live at my father's house. You will pay us, but not with money or practical work. You will pay by helping me to understand the great poems about life and love. I have been trying to seduce Thoreau, so you must teach me everything about those poets who make a Romantic Movement."

Seaport and I laughed together, at the fact that the good-hearted Penelope did not yet grasp the distinction between the high poetry and the low.

"Penelope," said Seaport. "Beware of the doggerel. Here's a stanza from a real poem, a poem that has meaning and sincerity as well as snappy sound. It was written by a great thinker named Ralph Waldo Emerson. Listen and try to hear — and to feel — the difference between my nonsense and his sense."

And then passionately, with the utmost feeling, he recited:

> "Give all to love;
>   Obey thy heart;
>   Friends, kindred days,
>   Estate, good-fame,
>   Plans, credit and the Muse,
>   Nothing refuse."

Emerson's friend Carlyle once wrote: "Mankind's happiest hours are written on the blank pages of history."

Here, in this hardly-known village, for two-and-a-half months l lived some of my happiest hours. I walked every morning at sunrise, and with vigorous exercise I made my body flexible and strong. I discussed and praised and argued about the best literature with the wild-hearted poet Seaport. I ate dinner and talked with Penelope, my friend of friends. And politely I parried the advances of stray tourist women who fell in love with me the instant they glanced at my tanned torso and my sparkling-honest eyes.

When the half-gods go, the gods arrive. The days passed serenely; the days passed. On the sixth day of March all things changed for me.

We fear change, yet so often change is good. We fiddle with the preparations, we procrastinate, we make excuses, we forget to act or we forget to act sincere. And then, despite our tough resistance to the real, at the right moment the transformation comes.

At last his new life shouts to the man: "Welcome! I've been waiting for you! The door is open — always open wide — why do you keep on searching for the key?"

40
ARE NOT THE JOYS OF MORNING SWEETER ?

"WHACK! THWACK! Whack! Thwack! Whack! Thwack! Whack! Thwack!"

Every morning in Agia Souvlakis, moments before sunrise, the dawn's silence is geshmucked by fisherman, swinging then smashing the bodies of squids and octopuses against the concrete dock. This ritual accomplishes three significant ends. It tenderizes the sea-meat, so that the seafood-sellers can ask more money from the owners of the restaurants. It wakes those species of human workers whose livelihoods depend on early rising: the shepherd, the baker, the olive-oil maker. And it rouses the lovers-in-arms, so they can sneak back to their homes unnoticed, before the light.

At the sound of the first "whack!" I woke, sipped water from a hand-made mug, then jotted notes into my journal-book. Penelope came home, and I pretended to be asleep so I could observe her in the semi-darkness. Humming softly she approached me, kissed my forehead, then entered her bedroom and removed her clothes. She washed her face and body with a towel, she drank a cup of pomegranate juice, and then she fell onto the bed where she would sleep till noon.

Dawn's light pierced the windows of the small house. I tip-toed through the kitchen-bedroom to study Kosmos's drawings and writings on the walls. Better than strong coffee, these gleanings of love and paradise woke my mind; and the moment the mind opened I would begin the daily workout to keep my body strong. A simple regimen: walking, stretching, running for an hour on the beach, swimming in the chilly sea, lifting heavy rocks, dancing Greek dances on the sand. Usually, during and after these sunrise activities, I would feel nothing less than marvelous. But today the thrill of a strong body and the glow of the Greek light were not powerful enough to quell a crushing disappointment. Today, the sixth of March, I had promised myself this: I would snuff the candle of a sputtering love.

Every day for the past ten weeks I had written fiery letters to the woman — I wrote faithfully, without excuses, never missing a day. I told her that the sun rose every morning only to see her; that she was different from every other woman in the world; and that the stars in the night sky envied the dazzling beauty of her eyes. I was a fool, I said, for realizing too late how much I loved her. And always and forever I wanted her beside me to enchant my life.

These passionate outpours were answered in the most devastating manner: silence. As if she knew that silence was the one response that would discourage me. At last, frustration made me resolve to set a deadline. After this date — the fifth day of March — I would forgive her and then forget her. I would pull the Cupid's arrow from my heart, heal the wound by filling the hole with another woman, and then live for the pleasure of many women instead of the devotion to one.

Three times yesterday I had walked to the small post office to check for letters there. From the unattainable Beatrice Loverly I got not a letter, not a postcard, not a word. More relationships are killed by silence than by foolish words. If she had cared about me even one iota, then she might have written one sentence to explain: "I'm married, stop writing, good luck."

Early this morning a boy had come running and then delivered a postcard to me, and for a few exciting seconds I imagined that she had replied. My heart skyrocketed in a blaze of hope. But it was not a missive from her, it was my postcard to her — the last one, returned for the greatest obstacle to epistolary romances: insufficient postage.

What had I written to this woman I adored? ... A humble poem wherein all my love and heartbreak had been iambically compressed in the infinity of four brief lines.

> One night when you are sitting all alone,
> Wishing things so different than they are —
> Find courage by remembering the one
> Bright man who loves you from afar.

What a pity that Kosmos could not be here to advise! The Kosmos who had taught himself a method for surviving rejection. First he would let himself feel miserable for three days, all that while seeing nobody, and doing nothing but reading love novels and drinking juices and teas. Then he would sleep for ten hours straight. And finally he would wake wholeheartedly healed, eat an enormous meal, and then be eager to sing and to dance and to love anew.

Kosmos was gone. Yet I had made one close male friend over the past months: the poet Seaport. He could not heal the heartbreak, but he would listen attentively, ask incisive questions, sympathize with compassion, then quote from books whose authors had pondered the perennial problems and suffered the eternal aches. Most importantly — with his original mind and outrageous sense of humor — Seaport would make me laugh.

Along the main street in the center of town, I spotted my friend the poet, walking as he read, reading as he walked, oblivious to every surrounding sight and sound. He always dressed humbly: faded hiking pants with deep pockets, a T-shirt that said 'Socrates', a small backpack, and a toothbrush and a metal drinking cup dangling from O-rings attached to the pack. He was easy to spot and remember: on the back of his backpack he had tied the paperback book cover of the novel *Zorba The Greek*. He was wild about that book — he'd read it twenty times — and he had come to Greece to find the beach where the boss had meditated and Zorba himself had danced.

Now, lost in the deep forests of his book, the poet ambled into the *Café Lathera* — Café Cooked In Oil. I followed him inside. The cook was a lively woman, expert in her culinary art; the café itself was a large room spacious enough for a hundred diners or dancers or both. In the center of the café stood a marble-sculpted statue called 'The Fountain of Bad Judgment'. It depicted three naked goddesses — Hera, Aphrodite, Athena — each one taller than a man, guarded above by an infant with an arrow and a bow. Its name came from the story of Paris who could have received valuable rewards from Hera or Athena, but instead he chose beauty — and adultery — above all other gifts.

"*Parakalo, nero zesto,*" the poet said to the cook, as he held up his metal cup. "Please, hot water."

Seaport the poet sat down at a square wooden table. He reached into his shirt pocket, plucked a used tea-bag that had seen a dozen scalding battles, dropped the tea-bag into the water-filled cup, and then plunged his imagination into the faraway kingdoms of his book.

I smiled as I observed my bookish friend: Seaport studied the book's pages with the same passionate intensity that I would tender when I gazed into a woman's eyes. He looked like a writer: he had dark, medium-length hair; a wild beard; black studious-looking eyeglasses; and brown eyes that spent half their time glowing with laughter, and half agonizing at the sights of the world's distress. Thin but muscularly lean, his body was the body of a well-trained bicyclist or distance runner. He was smart, introverted, gentle, uncomfortable amidst the wrong people yet thoroughly at ease with Nature, children, and his friends. He loved to walk, and whenever he sat alone he would be scribbling notes from these walks into his journal-book. He was awkwardly shy with women but brilliantly bold with words.

"*Chaire* and *kalimera!* " I said, as I sat down beside my friend. "Having only tea today?"

Seaport emerged from his trance and looked up: our four eyes gleamed the glow of friendship and we slapped each other's shoulders with our hands.

"Tea is enough," he said. "I can cook better than any restaurant I can afford to eat in."

I flung a wad of Euros onto the tabletop.

"Today, my friend, I'm buying you a breakfast that would stuff Gargantua and Pantagruel. And for once don't argue with me about the money. It's a fair barter: you need the energy from the food, and I need your shovel-sharp mind to help me to bury a dying Love."

"You, having love problems?" Seaport said. "There's something here on the menu called the 'Lovesick Special'. ... Instead of eating your own heart out they give you the heart of an artichoke, and you wash it down with the hi-octane *rakee*. Avoid the freshly-whacked squid, a known aphrodisiac."

Already he had me smiling: soon we would talk seriously but the good humor made it easy to begin. He thanked me for the forthcoming breakfast, and promised to keep track of it as a loan he would repay. He jotted this note into his journal-book, then he slapped my shoulder once again.

"Do you know your own great secret, Thoreau?" said Seaport. "I understand it perfectly now. Waldo Emerson grasped it when he wrote: 'From a great heart secret magnetisms flow incessantly to draw great events.'"

At that moment a dozen tourist women, perfectly aged eighteen to thirty years, entered the café like a flock of geese. Giggling and chattering excitedly, they sat down around a large table, then looked up — red-cheeked and starry-eyed — as they smiled at my smiling face.

Seaport the poet examined the same face that the women were ogling at. Yet what he saw, beneath the supreme handsomeness, was the face of his friend tormented by sadness and lovesick grief.

"These women follow you," he told me, "because of 'the Thoreau effect.' They look into your eyes and see bright rainbows to their dreams."

Seaport waved his hand to catch the attention of the waitress, appraised her with one glance, then continued to talk to me.

"That woman! She's serving food in a small-town restaurant, when she should be modeling for the greatest sculptors on this earth! Whenever I'm near her I can't think and I can't write. How can a man concentrate on expressing life's greatest mysteries, when life's greatest mysteries destroy his concentration? ... She is a quintessential 4-B: beautiful, breasty, brainy, and bored. Doesn't looking at that body make you a-doodle-doo like the cock at dawn? ... Cheer up, Thoreau: forget about your one love lost. Ten thousand mermaids frolic in these warm Greek seas."

Despite despondency, I had begun to laugh. Seaport stared at the waitress for a fantasy-filled minute, sighing all the while.

"Did you know, Thoreau," he said," that your ancestor, Henry David — who people think was cold and ascetic — was a warm-blooded man, who had a brief but fruitful erotic relationship with a young woman in Concord? ... Henry David hid the clues — but not too carefully — all throughout his works. In his essay *Walking,* for example, he writes:

"'We hug the earth, — how rarely we mount!
Methinks we might elevate ourselves a little more.'"

The waitress gazed into a mirror, adjusted her hair, practiced a seductive smile, then approached our table. Seaport slapped me on the shoulder.

"Watch and learn, Thoreau, how my wit and erudition utterly fails to impress her. ... The Cretan air is redolent with sage!"

And then he shouted another gem from Emerson:

"A beautiful woman is a practical poet, taming her savage mate, planting tenderness, hope, and eloquence, in all whom she approaches."

The waitress, chewing bubblegum, sank Seaport's hopes with a disdainful glance, then shot me with a winning smile. She looked French, and she spoke English with a New York accent learned from watching too much American TV.

"What can I getcha, handsome? If it's not on the menu, just ask."

I ordered bread, cheeses, vegetables, fruits, puddings, cakes and two coffees *skétos,* without sugar. The waitress, skillfully balancing trays on her arms, returned quickly, then filled the table with excellent food.

"Thank you, dear," I said, touching the waitress's arm. Though meant to be a friendly touch it made her sigh and glow and blush. When she wrote the check for the meal, she added her name and hotel-room number on the back, then placed the check face down in front of me.

As I planned the most gentle way to decline this offer, the waitress who wanted my attention milked her opportunities.

"Would you like some cream in your coffee?" she asked.

I tried to say 'No, thank you,' in French, but my accent was atrocious, and this was a woman who wanted to hear 'yes'. Without using her hands she thrust her breasts forward, bended her body at the waist, then smiled charmingly as a stream of fresh cream poured down into the small coffee cup. Cream that had been stored in a silver pitcher nestled snugly between her breasts.

While the café-owner yelled to the waitress to stop flirting and to pay attention to the other customers, Seaport raised his hands and clapped.

"Bravo!" he sang out. "That moment was pour poetry! Not one word was wasted nor one drop spilled! Never again will I drink my coffee black. Thoreau, can you believe that for service like this there's no extra charge!"

Seaport attacked the food like a drift of hogs, a glint of goldfish, a colony of vultures, a solitude of poets, a swoon of teenaged girls.

"So tell me, Thoreau ... mmm, this is delicious. This heartbreaker of yours: What's her name? What's she like? Why are you sulking like the unemployed sheepdog, the morning after the wolf pack devoured his whole flock?"

"Beatrice Loverly," I said. "She's English, energetic, funny, compassionate, sexy, sensitive, smart. She is perfect — "

Seaport swallowed a gob of yogurt.

"If she were perfect, she'd be in love with you."

I tried to laugh. "Perfect except for that. For the past ten weeks I've written to her every day, but she hasn't answered even one of seventy letters."

He moved one fig and one breadloaf to one side of the table.

"You are a modern Cyrano de Bergerac!" Seaport exclaimed. "To the woman he loved he wrote two letters every day for one month. And each time, to send the letters, he had to run across a battlefield and risk his life. Ah, those letters from a poet in love! The pap of romance fiction pales beside the pulp of these enveloped figs!... Is this coincidence or synchronicity? Today, the sixth of March, is the birthday of the genuine Cyrano, not the fictional protagonist in the book."

Seaport stood up on top of his chair seat. He lengthened his nose by sticking a ripe fig onto the end of it, then brandished a long loaf of bread.

The dozen tourist-women burst into giggles; the Greek owner of the café threw a plate against the wall and cheered; the chesty waitress scurried behind me to hide.

"I will improvise a quatrain," Seaport shouted, "and on the final syllable ... strike home!"

> "There is a kingdom by the sea
> Between the sand and foam
> Where this sweet maid shall lie with me —
> If I could dare ... strike home!"

The poet jabbed the breadloaf into the waitress's curvaceous derrière. She screamed merrily then clutched her arms around me tight. Again, Seaport swung his doughy sword.

> "Dream, laugh, go lightly, solitary, free —
> With eyes that look straightforward, fearlessly!
> To work without one thought of fame or boon,
> To realize that journey to the moon!
> Never to write one line that does not spin
> Deep from the center of the heart within."

These mad antics lightened up the café's atmosphere. One of the dozen young women who had been admiring me now stepped forward with her camera to take my photograph.

"Is he a movie star?" she said to Seaport, as she pointed to me.

"He is a more than a movie star, my dear. He is a living hero. I am a dying poet. Thou art a lovely angel. What is your name?"

"Sophie Arnot," she replied. "Is he married or dating anybody seriously?"

"Sophie Arnot," said Seaport. "I have two questions for you. Arnot... Arnot ..."

> "Are not the joys of morning sweeter
>   Than the joys of night?
>   And are the vig'rous joys of youth
>   Ashamed of the light?"

I stopped laughing in the middle of a ha-ha-ha. That was the poem under Kosmos's drawing of the puffin bird!

"Seaport," I said. "Who wrote that verse?"

"Who else but William Blake?" Seaport replied. "The poet-visionary-genius so far ahead of his era that in his own lifetime he was thought to be insane. And the second stanza — "

"There's more?" I asked.

"There is a second part," said Seaport, "even more intriguing than the first. Blake wrote it between 1793 and 1799, when he was somewhere between the ages of thirty-six and forty-two."

> "Let age and sickness rob
>   The vineyards in the night;
>   But those who burn with vig'rous youth
>   Pluck fruits before the light."

Eureka, almost! Hearing these words, I walked to the round ledge that circled the Fountain of Bad Judgment, and I sat there silent and motionless, fist under chin, assuming the pose of *The Thinker*, that muscular statue by Rodin.

Young Sophie snapped my photograph.

"Is he O.K.?" she asked.

Seaport touched her arm and drew her closer.

"He is beyond O.K.," he said. "He has never been better. He is rapt in a satyrical satori, a miss-tickle illumination that shall transform his life. ... The last time I had one was when I lived in America as a starving poet. One morning I woke up and realized that if I could starve in a big city in America, then I could starve just as uncomfortably any place on earth.

So why not live in a warm and a beautiful place?

"I was willing and prepared to starve to learn to how to write like Emerson and Goethe. But for the past six months the art-loving tourists and the good-hearted Greeks have conspired to give me food. And in those streams of kindnesses I found what I needed most — what every modern artist needs the most but rarely realizes he needs — belief in the goodness of the heart of humankind."

As I continued to ponder the poem, Seaport continued to explain.

"Sophie, he is not married, his girlfriend just left him, he is lonely, he is sad, he is vulnerable, he desperately needs a new woman who will care for him and help him to forget."

This revelation made the young woman squeal with pure delight. She ran back to tell her companions, who likewise screamed for joy; then all the women rushed nosily and noisily to surround me as I sat. They stroked my hair like an idol, primitive or matinee. They squeezed my arm muscles and massaged my shoulders, then shot me with cameras that flashed in my eyes. All this commotion and attention disrupted my reflections and returned me to the present scene.

I hollered to Seaport in a voice just loud enough to trump the chatter of my annoying fans.

"Seaport," I said. "Suppose they made Utopia and nobody came? ... An idea grabbed me that is so wild I can hardly imagine it. ... Everything fits, except one thing. So many Greek youth, women and men, leave Crete to work, or to study at the University in Athens or Thessaloniki. ... What good is a paradise with only an apple and a snake?"

The door of the café burst open with such force that all chattering stopped. A white-haired woman walked though the doorway, and then pushed her way through the mob of younger devotees. Seaport studied her eyes, then sang out another pithy poem Whitmanesque.

> "Beautiful Women ...
> Women sit or move to and fro, some old, some young,
> The young are beautiful —
> but the old are more beautiful than the young."

The old woman pushed her way through the crowd, nodded when she saw me, then threw her arms around my legs as she wept with happiness.

"I prayed I would find you some day!" she cried out. "I had to thank you, and tell you the good news!"

Seaport raised his arms and shook his head.

"Great gods, Thoreau! Did you inseminate this poor old maid! ... I've heard of robbing the cradle, but this must be robbing the rocking chair!"

The white-haired woman slammed her guidebook against the shoulder of my facetious friend.

"You nasty man!" said the old woman to the young poet. "Don't think for a minute that he paid me to sleep with him! ... In Agios Nikolodeonos, he saved my life. I pinched pennies till tears dropped from Lincoln's eyes, just to save cash to take this trip — and then in Athens I was robbed of everything! I was broke and hungry and ready to leave Greece that evening, when this saintly young man gave me enough money to stay for a whole month more. I didn't come here for romance: I was an old fuddy-duddy who never fuddied with any duddy. But seven days later I met the man of my dreams! I am eighty years old, and for the first time in my life I know what love is!"

She kissed my cheek like a grandmother, wiped the slobbered spot with her handkerchief, then glanced toward the entrance of the café. An old man entered, limping of legs but lively of face, and sat down at an open table. The old woman rushed to the table to sit down across from the old man. Within seconds, they were holding hands, smiling and gazing into each other's eyes like shy teenagers on their first date. Miracle! — their white hair, their blotched skin, their artificial teeth, their sagging body parts — all the deformities of old age were made invisible by the all-forgiving eyes of Love.

"Seaport! Seaport!" I shouted. "Do you see that!"

I placed both hands on top of the shoulders of the waitress: she almost melted at the thrill.

"Beauty," I told her, as I took the hand of Seaport and joined their hands. "Do not ignore this good man. He will make you laugh, he will make you think, and he is the soul of kindness. Above all he is a poet, and a poet is a man of enormous size."

The full-bosomed waitress, a woman who would have run around the earth four times for one night with me, would not have trimmed a fingernail to increase the poet's happiness. Seaport released her hand.

"Enormous size?" he said. "What good is enormous size?

Dan meine Seufzer ... meine Seufzer ... werden en Nachtigallenchor ...

"And my sighs ... my sighs ... become a choir of nightingales."

Again, I stared at the old man and the old woman, as they gazed at each other with the utmost reverence. Wonderfully did my mind flash! In one instant I understood all.

I stuffed the Euros into Seaport's shirt pocket, then placed the check with the waitress's room number into the pages of his journal-book. There rose shouts of disappointment, murmurs of protest, and squeals of heartbreak as I walked out of the café.

Along the path to my destination I found then picked up four flat stones. With large strides and fiery determination, I dashed in the direction of the Souvlakis-Dembacchae beach.

41

PANZANO ARGUES WITH MOTHER-NUN
ABOUT THE WAY OF A WOMAN IN BED

BACK IN THE HARBOR of Agios Nikolodeonos, the boat's passengers concluded the chapter of my story with cheers, comments, laughter, and applause until the sweltering heat reminded us it was time for the Greek siesta. Children were placed in shady areas, blankets spread out on the boat's deck, and for the next two hours the passengers napped, or talked quietly, as the sun made an oven of the April afternoon.

Panzano, lying on the deck near me, talked ceaselessly about the beauty, virtues, and goodness of the nun called Dolcezza. He held up a foot-long carved-wood figure of a naked shepherdess.

"Look at this, Thoreau," he said. "This gift from Dolcezza, to me it means more than all the pasta in the world. As soon as the sun cools down I'm going to talk with Mother Watchdog, and get down on my knees and beg her for permission to visit Dolcezza at the nun factory. What should I call that Mother-monster? ... Maybe it doesn't matter what I call her: the snake will bite you whether you call him cobra or Mr. Cobra."

Panzano stood up, turned around, took one step forward, and then collided into Mother Whackanzakis, who had come to tell him a thing or two or three. Her palm poked his chest like she was knocking on the door of his heart, pounding impatiently for that door to open up and welcome her inside.

"What are your plans with my Dolcezza?" she asked, in her rapid-talking voice.

"I plan," said Panzano, "only three things. To make this young woman my love and my life and my wife."

Whackanzakis shook her hooded head.

"Dolcezza knows nothing at all about men. What do you know about women?"

"I know," said Panzano earnestly, "only what I've learned rowing on the canals of Venice, that magnificent city of water, art and love. *La donna deve avere quatro emme: matrona in strada, modesta in chiesa, massaia in casa è mattona in letto.* A woman must have four aspects: in the streets she must be self-contained, in church modest, in the house diligent, and in bed frenzied."

Mother Whackanzakis — who had been nodding in agreement through three-quarters of this epigram — shrieked like the whistle of a ship on fire.

"In the bedroom," she shouted, "it is not *mattona,* frenzied! It is *mattina* — morning. In the bedroom she should rise up early in the morning to pray and plan her long day's work."

Panzano stood his ground and shook his head.

"You are a hundred miles from the truth," he said. "The woman in the bedroom should be *mattona.*"

"Mattina!" screamed Mother Whackanzakis.

"Frenzied!" shouted Panzano.

"An early riser in the morning!" screeched the Mother-nun.

A crowd had gathered around these two antagonists to prevent violence and enjoy the argument. Mother-nun snatched the wood-carved shepherdess from Panzano's unsuspecting hands.

"Dolcezza is new to us," she said. "She did not know the rule that our nuns are not permitted to give or to receive presents from strange men. This figure was made from materials purchased with funds from the monastery treasury, and therefore it belongs to me."

Panzano placed his hand around the chest of the wooden shepherdess.

"That gift was given from the heart," he said. "And everything done from the heart is not only permitted, it is pure and good."

Panzano tugged on the wooden figurine, as Mother Whackanzakis tugged back. Back and forth they pulled, as they shouted at each other names that made the eleven nuns cover their ears with their hard-working hands.

"She is stronger than a bear!" said Panzano. He pulled a mighty pull, but the Mother-nun pulled back just as hard, and they continued this contest until the ship's assistant captain arrived to adjudicate.

Panzano sighed, then glanced at the assistant captain and the throng of observing passengers.

"I would like to tell you a story," he said, "about a woman who tugged on something that did not belong to her. It will explain why this Mothergrudger is fighting with so much tenacity."

The assistant captain, standing between Panzano and Mother Whackanzakis, grasped the wooden shepherdess and placed her in his jacket pocket, and then nodded for Panzano to begin.

"In a time not so long ago," Panzano said, "in a country not so far from here, a woman led a man into the city's courthouse and addressed the judge.

"'For a quarter of a century I have been a maiden!' she said. 'But this morning, as I was working in the fields, this man seized me, then forced me to give up what I have guarded all my life.'

"The judge asked the man to tell what happened, and he told a story as different as sugar is from salt. 'I'm a poor farmer,' the man began. 'At dawn today I loaded my mule and walked down the road to sell my vegetables at the market. A woman walking from the opposite direction — this woman beside me — waved at me, then lowered the top of her dress to show me her two melons a-swaying like ripe cantaloupes on vines. She grabbed my hand and led me to her olive grove, where we lay down and enjoyed each other for many a moan and a sigh. At noon I dressed and gave her some money, but she demanded more. Then she insisted that I accompany her to this courthouse, saying that if I didn't come along with her then she would go alone.'

"The judge asked if the only objective witness could speak, and when the farmer said that the mule could not, the judge asked the farmer to show how much money he had been carrying when he met the woman on the road. The man produced a leather pouch filled with silver coins. All together it was not a great deal of money, but to the farmer it was the savings of a lifetime, which he had planned to use to live on when he became too old to work.

"'Give this pouch,' ordered the judge, 'and everything it contains to the woman who claims that you have wronged her.' With a long face the farmer handed over the pouch. The woman clapped her hands, thanked the judge, then ran from the courtroom in great haste.

"'Now,' said the judge to the farmer, 'go and find that woman, and when you've found her, take back your purse, and use whatever force is necessary to accomplish this.' Off ran the farmer like a jackrabbit, and in thirty minutes he returned with the woman. The farmer tugged one side of his leather pouch, the woman clutched fiercely to the other side. The judge asked them to explain.

"'I was walking on the street,' the woman cried, 'when this man grabbed my pouch and tried to steal it from me!'

"'Is that what happened?' the judge asked the farmer.

"'Yes, that is true,' he replied. 'I pulled and tugged with all my strength, but she held on, and I could not succeed in tearing it away, nor could all my brothers and cousins put together have pried it from her arms.'

"Said the judge to the woman: 'Give that pouch back to the man.' And when she had done this, the judge said: 'Now, dear woman, leave this court and do not be seen in this town for twelve months, or the inside of our prison will see you for another twelve. If your story were true, then you could have defended your honor with at least as much tenaciousness as you fought to keep this man's purse of coins.'"

The boat's passengers laughed riotously at Panzano's story, but Mother Whackanzakis shouted and then reached out to grab Panzano's hair. The eleven nuns held her body, but her tongue wagged on and peppered poor Panzano with a potful of verbal abuse.

The ship's assistant captain had heard Panzano's parable and shook his head. Like the glutton who plucks out the meat chunks from the soup, or like the hasty reader who seeks only the juicy segments — he missed the best parts, and understood nothing at all. He awarded the wooden shepherdess to Mother Whackanzakis. And then he raised his left hand to quiet the passengers in order to report the latest news.

"The boat has been repaired," he said. "But now we are looking for the captain. Please wait on the boat until the next announcement."

Panzano had lost his wooden shepherdess; he was fighting to hold back his tears. Kind listeners in the crowd brought him breads, cheeses, and olives, which he formed into a sandwich as tall as his hand. He sat on the sandwich to compress it, then squeezed the huge tower of food into his gaping maw.

The nuns had just completed their knitting project: large stockings made from blue-dyed wool. Two nuns, Donnabella and Volutta, handed me a jar of honey as they glanced into my eyes. Holding hands, they giggled then scurried away. A passenger, a refined-looking woman from Athens, raised her hand.

"Please tell us, Mister Thoreau," she eagerly asked, "what you were looking for, and what you found on that beach in Crete."

Shouts from the other passengers agreed that the tale should now be told. And after a long drink of water and a deep breath, I continued to tell my story to two hundred glistening eyes.

42
THE LAST TEMPTATION OF PENELOPE

AT THIRTY MINUTES BEFORE midnight I threw on a black sweatshirt, pushed a flashlight into my pants pocket, then saddled my back with a small backpack. I glanced at Penelope. She had been writing a letter to Kosmos by candlelight, scratching her head, pausing frequently, laboring like a poet to transform her vast unfathomable feelings into the fewest and best words.

I placed a wine cork into her candle's flame, blew on the cork, then rubbed the burnt end against my skin to blacken my hands and face.

"Penelope," I said, "don't worry if I'm not in bed when you come home from work at the crack of dawn. Tell Kosmos I'm thinking about him. *Kaleeneekta*. Goodnight."

I walked outside, admiring the starry night. Seconds later, Penelope, her shoulders covered by a black shawl, ran to me then grasped my arm with sisterly affection.

"Who's the lucky woman?" she asked. "Is it that cream-filled French waitress at the cooked-in-oil café?"

We walked together for a few strides, and then I stopped.

"Penelope, it's not a woman. It's an adventure."

"Po, po, po!" she doubtfully replied. "When Kosmos talks about adventure he always means that there's a woman in the air. What do you mean, Thoreau?"

I thought that I would need to pause to collect my ideas, but the words flowed easily.

"You know that for twenty years, Kosmos has been dreaming of finding a paradise on Crete."

"Do I know it! He dreams of paradise and ignores Penelope."

"This morning, Penelope, I had an intuition that the paradise that Kosmos has been looking for is sitting on his favorite spot, the beautiful beach he calls his *kaliparalea*. And since a paradise found becomes a paradise lost — that's the paradox of paradise — this utopian community meets in the evenings after midnight, then breaks up at every dawn, before the light. What do you think?"

Penelope slapped my back as she laughed.

"Now I understand why you and Kosmos get along so well. You two imagine something impossible, then believe in it with more passion than something real."

"You'll be late for work if you come with me, Penelope."

"I'm coming," she said. "I want to see what nobody has seen before. And if there's nothing to see, then you'll need some shoulders to cry on. ... Or something soft underneath the shoulders."

Walking briskly, we reached the beach at Agia Souvlakis, turned east, walked one mile on the sand, then found the *kaliparalea,* the beautiful beach. Earlier in the day I had built a thigh-high stone wall here, and now Penelope and I stood at the wall, ready to crouch down behind it if anyone arrived.

Lovely evening! The sea dances against the beach sand as the night's stars sing silent songs that guide our tender souls toward the sublime.

"A fine paradise, Thoreau!" said Penelope. "Stars, sand, sea, silence and solitude — not one person around for miles."

"Patience, Penelope," I said. "Patience. You know that Zen saying: 'Until the Buddha comes, live as if the Buddha is here'. ... Ouch! Ouch!"

Penelope had pinched my bottom, two times. Now she wrapped her shawl around me and snuggled closer, like a spider spinning silk around a fly.

"Why did you bring me out here, alone, Thoreau?"

"Penelope, it's not — "

"You wanted to seduce me!"

"Penelope!" She clutched me tight.

"Opportunity knocks you up but once! Don't miss this chance, Thoreau. Come back home with me and let's enjoy each other. I'll show you a paradise, the only one you'll ever need!"

I knew the saying: 'Tact is the art of making a point without making an enemy.' ... Thanks to practice, I was as good as any man at refusing a woman who offered herself. The trick, I thought, was to refuse her without hurting her feelings or wounding her feminine pride. I was as good as any man at this — unfortunately, at this subtle art, all men are lousy.

"Penelope," I said calmly. "We have agreed to have a platonic relationship, from the neck upwards."

"I have thought about that, darling," answered Penelope. "Let's stand on our heads and then make love!"

"Penelope," I said. "There is a deep bond of affection between us. You bring out the best in me — "

"You bring out the beast in me!" she shouted. Furiously she kissed me and then she reached down to seize my manhood with her hand.

"It's like a rock! Come home and sex me up, Thoreau! That old buzzard Kosmos will never know about it!"

The aroma of a Greek restaurant suddenly stifled the fresh seashorey air. A deep voice, brash and good-humored, rushed across our ears like the waves of seafingers slapping the face of the sandy shore.

"Scratch him on the belly, Penelly," said the voice. "Those scratches would put a six-thousand year-old mummy in the mood for love."

I looked up. Penelope dropped the flashlight that had filled her grasping hand. Slowly, she turned around.

"Kosmos!" she shouted, as she ran to his open arms. "Kosmos, darling!"

She hugged him with all the power of a woman wild with love.

"Is this the dream of my dreams, or are we awake in each other's arms?"

"I am here, I am free, I am a man again," said Kosmos with a bold laugh. "Free to say that you, my faithful Penelope, look divine this evening under the starlight. Don't stare like you've never seen me before: buzz this old buzzard with a kiss."

The kiss lasted a full minute, and when Kosmos came up for air he glanced at me and smiled.

"It's good to see you, Thoreau! I knew you would be here tonight — every iota of my intuition told me so. Come closer, my boy, so I can see you better."

Kosmos and Penelope together embraced me like a son.

"What's wrong, Thoreau?" said Kosmos. "Here we are all together again — and on the doorstep of our paradise, too! Yet there's a spoonful of sadness stirred into your cup of joy. Tell me about it: it will make it easier to bear."

"Kosmos, it's a miracle to see you here! It's not a cup of joy, it's a barrel and a vat. But the sadness is a heartful, enough to make the whole world sad. I fell in love with the best and most beautiful woman on earth, and she fell out of love with me. I will never forget her, and I will never see her again."

A scent of spearmint spiced the atmosphere as a silken voice whispered sweetly from the darkness, above the gentle kissing of the sea.

"Men!" said the lovely voice. "Men are either too mellow, or too melodramatic. Men are helpless because they love women in their imaginations. Will men ever learn that real love means courage, responsibilities and deeds?"

"Beatrice!" shouted Penelope and Kosmos.

I stood stunned, astonished, thunderstruck.

Penelope ran to Beatrice, and the two women embraced, kissed cheeks, then began chatting and laughing uncontrollably.

"Thoreau, dearest," said Beatrice. "Penelope tells me that despite her best efforts, she was never able to seduce you. Have you lost all interest in lovemaking?"

As she stepped closer to me — her hips swaying with every step — the thousand thousand stars above seemed like they were spinning into brightly-colored swirls. Her flowing gown, made from a British flag, teased with a neckline that plunged all-the-way to the rope-belt around her slender waist. Her body was fit for a goddess: svelte, curvy, voluptuous. Her eyes captured my eyes. My heart had never felt as breathlessly alive as this: it had been plucked from my breast then dipped still-beating into the cold sea, awash in the most perfect sorrow and happiness.

"Beatrice," I murmured, softly, gently, reverently. "I lost interest in other women when I fell in love with you."

"Dearest," said Lady Loverly, "remember this. There are two kinds of women: the women who you chase after, and the women who chase after you. If you want to find happiness in love, slow down."

"Beatrice, I fell in love with you at the Meteora, the first moment I saw you."

"Young Thoreau. You never cared for me: you fell in love with the idea and the ideal of Love."

"Beatrice! I did love you and I do love you! And I will always love you! I swear it!"

The beautiful woman smiled more, and the smile made her more beautiful.

"It's a mere crush, darling, and it will pass with a little discomfort, like after-dinner gas. Do you know how I cured my infatuation for you? ... I began a new diet and exercise regimen devoted to the Roman saying, *mens sana in corpore sano*: a sound mind in the sexiest body on Earth. For hours every day I exercised; I ate the healthiest foods only; I threw myself into the heart of work. And work is what brings me to Crete to-night, in case you were wondering. WANDERBORE received a letter stating that there were ten gypsy women hiding on this island, fugitives from the law, without any resources, shelter, or friends."

My own words chilled me like crushed ice.

"And at last you're here in front of me, one heart away, and without your affection it is as lonely as if between us an Atlantic ocean lies."

Penelope grasped my forearm, then tried to tug me closer to Beatrice.

"Don't give up on her, Thoreau! Trust me: I know her like I know my own sister, like my own self! In ten million years she will never stop loving you!"

Kosmos shook his head.

"Hell, Thoreau, you're not a man anymore! One glance at that woman and you're all jelly and mush! Listen to me. Your chances of winning her are one in ten, but I guarantee that you will lose her if you act like a lovesick lamb. Begin the affair by worshiping the ground she walks on, and the woman will end the affair by grinding you into the mud beneath her pointed heels."

Penelope clutched me.

"Listen to the squawking of the cynical old bird! Ignore him, Thoreau! Do what your heart desires. Clasp your arms around her knees then tell her that you love her like you've never loved before!"

Kosmos placed his hand on Penelope's shoulder.

"You can't force someone to love you, Penelope: the love is there, or the love is not there and that's the end. Can't you see that she's finished with him, and wants to move on with her life?"

"They are perfect for each other!" Penelope shouted. "They are like Greek salad and olive oil."

"They are olive oil and water," said the man. "They will fight like that dog Kosmos and that cat Penelope!"

Penelope raised her right arm.

"You wouldn't know what love is," she shouted, "if it slapped you in the face!"

Kosmos grabbed her threatening hand. Now he was shouting, too.

"And you are an expert in the love-business of everybody else — except your own!"

Penelope raised her left arm, and when Kosmos grabbed it she shouted more.

"An expert? You think that you're an expert in the sex-business, but your love-organ wilts like a stalk of boiled celery! A couple of shakes is all it takes!"

The face of Kosmos turned radish-red.

"No man in Greece makes love like I make love!" he proudly said.

"Thank the goddesses for that!" Penelope yelled. "Or all the women in Greece would give up sex forever and become nuns!"

Beatrice stepped between the stir-crossed lovers, then calmly placed her left hand on Kosmos, and her right hand upon Penelope.

"My dear friends," she said. "Let us be silent so we may hear the whispers of the gods."

Silence instantly enchanted the evening air.

The four of us ducked behind my wall and then peered through the open cracks between the stones. We saw lights from the tips of wooden torches; we listened to soft footsteps pattering against the sand.

43
THE MIDNIGHT PLAYERS

As if the stars themselves descended to the Earth to taste its bitterest sorrows and sweetest joys, the night-scene was lit by slowly-moving torches burning bright. Heads covered by hoods and bodies by monk-black robes, a crowd assembled on the perfect beach. Silently they worked, spreading blankets on the sand, weighing down the blankets with crocks of food, building a campfire from driftwood, branches, and sticks. A torch tossed into the center of the teepee-shaped wood set the campfire blazing. The sixty-odd women and men removed their robes. Now dressed in loosely-fitting white chitons, they gathered in a circle around their leader, who first raised his right arm to get attention, and then spoke in a voice made of equal parts of strength, humor, and tenderness.

> "Love is all we have
> the only way that each
> can help the other."

They called their leader 'Pateras'. When Kosmos and I recognized this old man's voice and face, our first impulse was to rush out of hiding, and pummel him with questions and questions more. But Penelope, by squeezing our arms with her strong hands, kept her two men watching, silently and still.

Pateras placed his right hand over his heart.

"Love and be wise," he said, in his deep and resonating voice.

"Be wise and love," the crowd in unison replied.

"It looks like we're missing someones tonight," Pateras said. "If you're not here, raise your hand."

Some hands raised, some voices laughed, and then Pateras spoke again.

"Where is our oldest member, Chronos? ... And where is Hera, queen of our hive, the beautiful body who inspires us to be beautiful in our souls?"

When not one voice replied, Pateras began to sing.

"Penelopee, Penelopee ... as sweet as ripe canteloupee ..."

The eyes of astonished Kosmos gleamed and his jaw dropped open wide as Penelope stepped forward from behind the wall, out of the darkness into the circle of light.

"You're not dressed for play, Penelope," said Pateras. "And you're late tonight."

"I'm late?" said Penelope. "What time is it?"

The crowd murmured, but Pateras raised his hand and immediately the chattering ceased.

"Time for our greatest performance," the wise old man replied.

Working together, Pateras and Penelope first unscrolled a banner made from a white sheet that had been wrapped around two cane-shaped sticks of wood, and then they pressed the sticks into the sand, so that the banner became visible to all.

The Midnight Players —
A Troupe of Actors and Singers
Performing Classical Drama and Songs

A man dressed as a priest — shouting with an anger which had forgotten that the true gods are compassionate not cruel — shook his bony fist as he rushed toward the flickering campfire.

"Sinners! Sinners repent!" he shouted. "Let every one fly out of Sodom! Haste and escape for your lives! Look not behind you, escape to the mountains, lest you be consumed!"

Pateras patted the shoulders of the intolerant man.

"Priestos," said Pateras. "Men like you, who wake up every morning before the chickens, should not be carousing or reforming at this hour of the night. How can we help you?"

"I have heard a rumor," said the rasping voice of the god-terrifying old priest, "that the dramas you perform here, under the midnight sin, are festered with violence and immorality."

Pateras found a wooden crate for the old priest to sit on, then he patiently replied.

"And the stories in your own bible are nothing but peace and gentleness? ... Priestos, do not condemn us until you have watched us play. In our dramas, like all the performances in ancient Greece, the violence is never shown to the audience. Violent actions are always reported by minor characters or by messengers."

"The violence is never shown?" said Priestos. "Then that leaves more time for the immorality! Do you strip the gods naked, and poke their fun at the sacred temples of the goddesses?"

"Sit down here, Priestos," said Pateras. "Sit down and watch us play."

Pateras raised a Zeusian thunderbolt, forged from aluminum foil.

"Tonight," he said, "we will be performing a selection from *The Symposium*, by Plato. Is Appollodorus ready? ... Aristophanes? ... Agathon? ... Socrates? ... "

The actors and actresses scrambled to their places, and then the drama's narrator, Penelope, stepped to the forefront, holding a brightly-colored tropical bird. Penelope's acting voice was practiced, polished, and precise.

> "*Symposium,* tonight we play,
>   And after watching us rehearse.
>   This parrot has been heard to say:
>   Polly — "

"Polymorphously perverse!"

Out from the shadows jumped Kosmos, who had finished the rhyme with a notion of his own.

Kosmos approached his father Pateras, seized the foil-wrapped lightning bolt, tore it in half and then flung it to the sand.

"This is all lies, lies, lies!" shouted Kosmos. "This is not a troupe of actors, this is a community of highly-organized anarchy and love-free sex."

Pateras laughed, placed his hand onto his son's shoulder, and then spoke with the greatest calm.

"Kosmos, everywhere you look you see sexuality, even amidst a gathering of tired and retired old women and old men! Penelope here is forty years young — the youngest of our troupe — and the next youngest is ten years older than Penelope. What evidence makes you believe that we have gathered here for erotic escapades, and not for the education, the pleasures, and the self-awareness that are the rewards of practicing the creative arts?"

"Evidence?" said Kosmos. "My intuition is all the evidence I need!"

"Your Intuition?" Pateras replied. "Many men have followed their intuition where it led them to the greatest follies and atrocities."

"That is true, dear father," said Kosmos. "And it is also true that some men have followed their intuition to the stars. The great books, works of art and music, and scientific discoveries have all begun with intuition's magic spark."

Pateras smiled into his son's defiant eyes.

"And how have you and your intuition, Kosmos, learned at last to distinguish the artificial from the real?"

"In Athens, a while back, Father," said Kosmos, "I was strolling through the art museum, when my eyes were captured by a reproduction of Leonardo's painting, the *Mona Lisa*. Her five-hundred-year-old face intrigued me. Oh, the smile, the famous smile was perfect. But something about the painting bothered me, so every morning I came back to study it.

"Hundreds, yes thousands of people looked at that painting and didn't see the problem there. But I knew it, and I came back to look, day after day. I studied that enigmatic smile, I studied the full bosom, I studied those hands — the most beautifully drawn hands in all of Italian art."

"And what did you find, Kosmos?" asked Penelope.

"One dawn when I woke up, I grasped the answer. The smile was reproduced precisely, but what had made me squirm about that painted woman was her ordinary eyes. In the imitation painting in Athens, Mona Lisa's eyes stared straight ahead. In the real painting, the original, Mona's eyes are gazing to her left. One subtle difference that makes all the difference in the universe! One slight shift ... It's just as Dostoyevsky wrote: If we could simply open our hearts to the depths of human kindness, in mere minutes we could change this suffering Earth into a laughter-loving paradise."

"And from that great revelation in Athens," asked Pateras, "how did you come to return here?"

"In that moment, Father, I realized that though I had walked across this most beautiful section of the beach ten thousand times, I had never crossed these sands after the midnight hour. I had always been too busy at that time, between midnight and dawn, either reading, or painting a picture, or — too much of the time it was this — making love. How funny this hits me now: my obsession with sex prevented me from discovering the sexual utopia."

"Kosmos," said Pateras, "once again you are talking nonsense and smoke. When you speak from your own experience you are a genius, but every time you philosophize you sound like a raving idiot. Will you please sit down out of the way, next to Priestos, and allow us to continue with the joy of our play?"

Kosmos shook his head.

"Father, I will not sit down! I came here tonight to find bacchanalian revels of unbridled abandon. And until I see these wild sexploits, I will not move one dot on the Greek letter 'i'. I will stand rooted to this spot like an olive tree, like a granite mountain, like the stubbornest ass in Crete!"

44
THE WOOL FROM AN ASS

STARING AT THE FACE of Beatrice Loverly, I knew I had found my paradise at last. Her eyes glowed as she observed this great confrontation between Father and Son, Truth and Deception, Reality and Dreams. What did I want now? ... I wanted Beatrice to smile at me the same way she'd smiled during the very first moment when we'd met. Kissing her now, I reasoned, I might win her or lose her, but I would get her attention at the least. As I inched my face closer to her face, the perfect kiss was quashed. Beatrice raised her hand. Without turning her head to look at me, she pressed one finger gently against my lips.

The cicadas were singing now, the sea-waves slapped against the shore, the campfire crackled, bursts of godly laughter roared from the mouth of Pateras.

"Kosmos, you are seeking the perennial male fantasy: a cult of anarchy and sex. What you have found, my son, is a troupe of players who meet together in the wee hours of the mornings to perform. So if you insist on remaining here for eternity, then at least introduce us to your two friends."

When Beatrice and I stepped from behind the wall and walked toward Kosmos and Pateras, the crowd first murmured *"Xenos!"* and then greeted the beautiful woman and man with shouts of *"Yasu!"* and applause.

Pateras took the hand of Beatrice in his left hand, and held my hand with his right.

"You have heard the word *'xenos',"* said Pateras. That Greek word means 'stranger', and it means also 'guest'. It comes from our ancient tradition of greeting strangers with the most perfect hospitality. Please sit here and enjoy our performance."

Then he pressed my hand into the hand of Beatrice.

"I see here a man madly in love with a woman," Pateras said, "and a woman who — "

Penelope glanced at Pateras, and he changed his tone.

" — a woman who will reveal her own mind when she is ready to make it known. Kosmos, are you ready to get out of the way?"

Kosmos crossed his arms.

"The moon will fall into your lap, Father, before I move one millimeter from this spot."

"And you are so certain, my son, that all this is not a delusion of your romantic imagination that transforms grains of sand into a sacred worlds, wildflowers into Heavens, ordinary women into goddesses, and mice into miracles? ... Could it be, Kosmos, that the paradise you dream about finding is nothing more than what we Greeks call 'onew pokeh' — something that does not exist — wool from an ass?"

Six of the players ran and positioned themselves in front of the campfire. Three of them formed the body of a donkey, while the other three combed the donkey, and then searched the combs for the unattainable wool.

"Laugh at me if you must, Father" said Kosmos. "You can't change my mind, not with force, not with farce, not with reason, not with ridicule. Here I will stand until this beard grows as long as the waves and as white as the foam of the sea."

"Kosmos, do you doubt the words of your own true Father?"

"I doubt!"

"You think that a man who has practiced and perfected fifty-five years of flawless parenting — and has never told one falsehood to his son — would suddenly deceive him now?"

"I think!"

"You imagine that these exhausted, elderly and enfeebled senior citizens, some of them almost one hundred years old"— Pateras waved his hand at his troupe of players — "would have the energy and the desire to do more about sex than just talk and pretend?"

"I imagine!"

"You believe that there is more to this gathering than an innocent group of friends sharing their love of Greek literature and drama?"

"I believe!" shouted Kosmos.

"Do you know, Kosmos, what I must now say to cure you of this dear delusion?"

"Tell me, Father."

Once again, Pateras joined the hand of Beatrice with my hand, and as he spoke his deep voice sounded like the sea.

"Let those love now, who never loved before,
    And those who always loved, now love the more!"

A sea gull flew above and cried three times. Pateras looked into the eyes of Beatrice, then me, then Penelope, then his faithful son.

"Kosmos!"

"Father?"

"I say ... Welcome to Sextopias."

At this word the troupe shouted a resounding cheer, the musicians in the troupe played a lively Greek folk song, and the remaining men and women joined hands and danced — shouting, singing, and laughing — around the light-giving fire.

Kosmos watched with childlike eyes, shaking his head amazed.

"Even at the very end," he murmured, "I can hardly believe it myself."

Penelope kissed his forehead as tears streamed down the man's cheeks and fell softly on the worlds of sand.

45
WELCOME TO SEXTOPIAS

COOL NIGHT BREEZES caress the skin and make the senses quick. Music bursts from drums, wood flutes, lyres, *bouzoukis,* and the most moving instrument of all — the human voice. The fiery music makes them dance. Holding hands, the sixty-odd Sextopians — far more women than men — dance in a circle around the newcomers: around me, Beatrice, and Kosmos. One at a time, each of the dancers breaks from the dancing circle, approaches us smiling, and then welcomes us with handshakes, hugs, kisses, and warm words.

Like a child watching a circus clown, Kosmos stared wide-eyed and amazed. His face revealed his whole mind. Thousands of times he had sung and danced without thinking, but now he was thinking this: art and life were about to become one. What would happen, his wide-eyes wondered, if the joy of the dancer, the deep concentration of the painter, the passion of the musician, the truthfulness of the author — what would happen if these qualities were applied not to the arts that created things, but to human relationships and the arts of loving and being? ... Those cosmic eyes that dreamed of paradise now dripped with tears. Penelope, her hand filled with sprigs of furry sage leaves, wiped the teardrops and then kissed Kosmos on his ruddy cheeks.

My eyes, too, glanced gratefully at wondrous things: at the stars and the sea and the white beach sand; at the singing dancers; at the proud posture of Pateras; at the awe-filled eyes of Kosmos; at the stupendous bosom of Penelope. Yet these were fleeting glances, because my stares ascended to the radiant face of one wondrous woman: Beatrice Loverly. A woman of the world, her lovely face looked English, her red lips spoke seven European languages, her dark hair had been spun into silken French braids.

The gaze of Beatrice remained focused on the dancers as she watched me from the corner of her eye.

"These eyes of mine are not thy only Paradise," she said. "This is quite remarkable, isn't it, Thoreau?"

"What do you mean, Beatrice?"

"The way these people look at each other with so much joyfulness as they dance and sing."

Kosmos placed his rough hand on my shoulder, pulled me a few steps away from Beatrice, and then spoke with his usual self-confidence.

"Love is a murky paradox," he said, nodding at the woman I admired. "If you want to melt her, then ignore her completely and act like a block of ice."

A moment later Penelope stroked my shoulder, glanced at Beatrice, and then whispered into my ear.

"Love is a clear glass of water, there is nothing more honest than love. Give her attention, that's what every woman craves and needs! When you tell her how much you love her, she will fly into your arms and never leave."

We heard a roar of laughter, a throng of people shouting the Greek words *"Neh, neh, neh!"* — "Yes, yes, yes!" — and then a man and a woman approached us, one holding a measuring tape and another holding a scissors and a skein of white cotton cloth. First Kosmos was measured, then Beatrice and I were measured separately, and then — for some reason unknown to me — we were measured together standing back-to-back.

Our backs and the backs of our heads were touching, as the measuring tapes twined around my strong muscles and the woman's voluptuous curves.

"Beatrice," I said, "Should a man and a woman speak to each other with complete and unabashed honesty?"

"Of course they should, Thoreau," she replied. "But only if they are genuine friends. A man and a woman in love require a certain dash of deception to keep the love-fires burning."

Her lips brushing accidentally against my cheek knocked the words out of my mind — I forgot what I had planned to tell her. Instead of saying something simple and sincere, I mumbled a quote from the great philosopher Plato.

"Even stronger than geometry is the intense power of Eros."

Lady Loverly raised her ring finger, and the light from the campfire revealed her ring's glittering gem.

"Do you see this significant diamond, Mr. Thoreau? It was given to me many years ago by my rich and abominable husband. Somehow he seduced me into thinking that the things money can buy are more pow-erful than geometry and Love combined. My dear friend, I am very mar-ried and you are very indigent. Have you forgotten that you and I inhabit two vastly different worlds?"

Novels by Dickens dispelled my distinctions of class.

"We travel in different circles but we revolve around the same point. Beatrice, let's run away and live together like Percy and Mary, Lorenzo and Frieda, Henry and June."

She smiled at this idea, and then her voice scolded me like an older sis-ter, with just the right amount of compassion but too much good sense.

"Let us suppose for a moment," she said softly, "that Beatrice the realist and Thoreau the dreamer yield to a foolish impulse and agree to spend one year together, revolving and intersecting. How would we live? Are you one of those exploiting men who sits at home and lets his wife work two jobs to support them both — a man who lives by the sweat of his *Frau?*"

As Beatrice crushed my hopes with these hard words, Penelope grabbed her hand. The Sextopian men and women had separated into two dis-tinct circles. Penelope led Beatrice into the center of the women's circle, where they both were hidden by the ring of women singing and clapping hands around them. The women shouted wildly as the British-flag dress of Beatrice flew into the air, and seconds later Beatrice emerged wearing the white chiton — the loose-flowing toga-like gown — that the Sexto-pian tailors had made.

Likewise, amidst boisterous shouting, Kosmos and I were drawn into the center of the men's circle, where we both removed our clothes. As the men clapped and shouted sharp remarks, we dressed ourselves in the white chitons that fit us perfectly.

Pateras raised his hand. One of the Sextopians noticed this, and she ceased talking as she raised her hand, and soon another woman saw this woman's hand raised, and one by one all hands were raised, all legs stopped moving, and all mouths ceased to chatter and sing.

When silence descended, Pateras opened both arms to the starry night sky.

"Ye gods on Olympus!" he shouted. "Fill my hour so that I shall not say, whilst I have done this, 'Alas, an hour of my life is gone — '"

The Sextopians chanted back: "Alas, an hour of my life is gone!"

And then Pateras continued his prayer —

"But rather, 'Behold! I have lived an hour!'"

"Behold! I have lived an hour!" was shouted back louder than the waves.

A merry cheer resounded from the Sextopians, and then all eyes stared at their white-haired chief.

"I am called Pateras," he said.

Another cheer rose from the crowd, which Pateras quieted by raising his hand.

"Most of you already know the Casanova of Crete, my son, Kosmos."

Silence met this name, except for the sound of hissing onions sizzling in a frying pan.

"We have two guests more," said Pateras. "This goddess on my right is Beatrice Loverly."

Whistles and loud applause — especially loud from the Sextopian men — were changed to groans of disappointment when Priestos shouted:

"The wedding ring on that goddess's finger is bigger than my nose!"

Pateras laughed and shrugged his shoulders.

"She is married, and we may assume that her husband would like her to stay that way. ... Now please welcome our third guest this evening, standing on my left, a young Apollo who calls himself Thoreau."

Whistles and loud applause — especially from the Sextopian women — changed to loud laughter when some of the women shouted aloud to everyone what each mind was thinking all alone.

—"He's a fountain of youth — he makes old women feel twenty again!"

—"Thoreau, there's nothing like experience — I bet you've never made love with a woman who is seventy-five years young!"

—"He's long and thin and covered with skin!"

—"He is built like a statue!"

And at this, Beatrice Loverly made the crowd laugh more — and me as well — when she shouted:

"He is built like a statue, but statues have no heart!"

When the laughing and shouting died down, Pateras spoke again to his attentive audience.

"As you know, dear friends, we are what we have chosen to be: a school for sexuality and love. What is our business? To make a new world, a world where men and women can live in complete freedom and openness. It is dangerous work, this new-world making, and to survive in this business, you need to have iron balls. Unfortunately, mine are getting a little rusty."

Laughter rang all around again, and then Pateras spoke more.

"And what do we teach each other at this school? ... Sincerity, Passion, and Tenderness. No one who completes our courses would have the heart to harm a butterfly, to pull a gun trigger, to eat an animal, to deceive a friend or lover, to say one word untruthful or unkind."

Kosmos clutched my arm. With great emotion in his voice he spoke to me.

"Here, they are truly doing," he said, "what I have barely been able to dream."

Pateras now turned his warm glances toward Kosmos and Penelope.

"I have already told you," he said, "that in our beautiful Greek language, we have a word 'xenos' which means two things: stranger and guest. And we maintain a three-thousand-year-old tradition that lets every honest stranger on Greek soil be treated with unsurpassed hospitality. In the time of Homer, during the first moment that a stranger arrived he was not asked to tell the tales of his travels and his life at home. Don't think that those Homeric Greeks were not burning with curiosity, just like the Greek people today! No, our famous hospitality demanded that first, before the talking, the stranger-guest would be feasted with the tastiest foods. Here in our Sextopias, we have enhanced that old tradition: we eat before we talk, and before the eating, we enjoy that something which is even more essential than consuming food — "

An old man in the crowd — the one they had called Priestos — exploded with mirth, falling down onto the soft sand in fits of laughter.

Smiling as ever, Pateras now glanced at me and Beatrice Loverly.

"Sextopians are a community of Cupids," he said. "Whenever we see that Love is blind — that two persons who are perfectly matched for each other cannot realize that their intercourse should be more than friendly — then we play a game we have invented, a game we have named 'Back-to-back.' The object of the game is to escape from this thick cloth that we have measured with precision. You start by struggling furiously to get out. But in trying to get out, many couples have learned that it is much more fun — and mutually beneficial — to meet life with joyful acceptance, and to stay inside."

The Sextopians shouted, laughed and chattered, while Priestos continued his fit of hysterical laughing, rolling around in the sand.

"But first," said Pateras, nodding to Penelope, "we will need permission from one of our players."

Penelope gently grasped Beatrice's two hands, talked for half a min-ute, and then both women fell laughing into each other's arms. Beatrice nodded her head to Pateras, and then some friendly hands guided Bea-trice and me into the center of the circle of Sextopians, and positioned us standing back-to-back. One large white chiton — this one made of strong, thick cloth — was placed over our two heads, pressing our backs tightly together in a kind of girdle or straitjacket, a dress that fit so snugly we could hardly move.

Now Kosmos was led into the circle's center, and Penelope stood back-to-back behind him. But at the last instant Penelope stepped aside, and she was replaced by an old flame of Kosmos: a large woman named Lige-ia. The extra-large-sized chiton was pulled over the two of them, which pressed their backs together so closely and tightly that an olive pit could not have fit between.

"How do you play this game?" asked Kosmos.

"It's very simple," his father replied. "It's just like big business and big government: You make up the rules as you go along. And have no fear — we will not allow you to be hurt, either in your body or your soul. If a moment arrives when the sweet fun turns sour, then I will intervene and set you free."

"Penelope," Kosmos said, to the woman pressed behind him. "We can get out of this if we concentrate and work together."

From the start to the finish, the Sextopians enjoyed watching the game, and as one-by-one they realized that Kosmos had mistakenly believed that the woman on his back was Penelope — not the actual Ligeia — their mirthfulness knew no bounds.

The four-legged beast named Kosmos-Ligeia first lunged forward a few steps, then muddled backwards a few steps more, then stumbled as they swirled in a circle and staggered side-a-ways.

"If I can escape from my first two marriages," said Kosmos, "then there is nothing in the world that can hold me. Stay calm, Penelope, I have a slick idea."

The real Penelope had ducked down behind her friends. Kosmos now spoke to the Sextopian named Nikos, a neighbor in Dembacchae who had been helped by Kosmos many times. Nikos brought Kosmos a rect-angle-shaped can of olive oil.

"The humble olive," said Kosmos, "was a gift from the goddess Athena to the people of Greece, who were so grateful for that gift that they thanked the goddess by blessing our greatest city with her name. The wood from the olive tree makes ships for commerce and for war, while the olive branch symbolizes peace, and the fruit gives us the oil that makes Greek food divine. *Elaeeolado:* olive oil! ... This golden oil is good for everything. One bottle of olive oil can serve as your hair tonic, your skin moisturizer, your shaving cream. Add cider vinegar, and you have a salad dressing that doubles as a lotion to protect skin from the burning mid-day sun. When Socrates wanted to get clean, he covered his body with olive oil, then scraped the dirt off his skin with a stigil, a small tool made of wood or bone."

The bundled-together Kosmos-and-Ligeia stumbled too close to the campfire, and a handful of Sextopians shouted, then guided them to a safer place. Kosmos raised the can of olive oil in his right hand.

"Even these metal containers that hold the oil," he said, "are used in a hundred ways by the canny Greeks. Walk through any small town and you'll see the olive oil containers used as flower pots, watering cans, mufflers, antennas, trash cans, cooking stoves, chairs, chamber pots, and grain bowls for feeding the mules."

Kosmos raised his arms and then poured the entire canful of oil down his back, and down the broad back of Ligeia. Then with his mouth he grabbed his shirtsleeves — first the left, and then the right — and pulled his arms through the sleeves so that his arms were now pressed against his body under the shirt.

"Our mad-hero Herakles oiled himself before he wrestled that giant Anteus, so that the monstrous opponent could not crush him in his grip. And when the curiosity of Psyche urged her to take a peek at the sleeping Eros, it was an olive oil lamp that revealed his features to her, the same simple oil lamp that lights my nights for reading and for painting, and for seeing the body who sleeps beside me in my bed."

Kosmos, who made every task into a game, was enjoying this activity immensely, smiling like the quarter moon.

"Now, Penelope," he said to Ligeia, "just move your back and shoulders like a snake, back and forth like this."

After a few minutes of squirming, Kosmos managed to slide his body, so that he turned around and now found himself pressed against Ligeia, legs to legs, breast to breast and face to face.

Beatrice leaned her head toward me.

"These Greeks know how to have fun, don't they Thoreau! Do you think that you can wriggle around like Kosmos did, or would you like me to try?"

Kosmos jerked: Ligeia once more! Ligeia whose appearance always shocked him, like a man glancing in the mirror amazed at the size of his own paunch! He looked up to the night sky then shouted to the crowd.

"And if some cruel god destroys my ship again on the whine-dark sea, I shall endure it, because I have a patient mind. Already I have suffered many troubles in war and traveling, and this will be just one more."

Ligeia laughed as she continued Homer's tale.

"And as he spoke," she sang, "the sun sank and darkness came, and these two lay themselves down inside her pleasure-cave."

Wild cheers and applause followed when Ligeia leaned forward to kiss her partner, and then fell forward onto the sand on top of Kosmos. Priestos — after a nod from Pateras — opened his fishing knife, cut the entrapping cloth, and quickly released the woman and man.

The eyes of all turned toward the stuck-together Beatrice and me. Beatrice had succumbed to continual fits of giggles, yet between these outbursts she managed to speak.

"You know of course, Thoreau," the woman said, "that I was merely joking a few moments ago when I implied that you are heartless."

"There's truth in every good joke," I said. "Do you know what I've just realized? Tension in relationships is caused by uncertainty. Should we be lovers, should we be pen pals, should we be colleagues, should we meet once a month for tea? ... When I know the answer, then I can act with purpose and with poise. But the uncertainty stings me, injects me with a lethal venom known as worry, and makes me hesitate to choose a path. Who is the heartless man? He who takes no action when action must be taken. Shall we be friends, Beatrice, and enjoy the quiet pleasures of friendship? "

Beatrice's laughing stopped.

"But don't you see, Thoreau, that this uncertainty creates suspense, and this suspense is the whole secret of the electricity between a woman and a man? You never know if this marvelous woman is going to like you, or to hate you, or to plummet into love with you, or to trick you into her bed, or to flirt with your best friend, or to yawn from utter boredom while you make love with her, or to bite your ear and whisper that you are the most exciting man on Earth. Why settle for the safe harbor of

Friendship, when the Sirens taunt you to the unknown stormy seas of Love? Ten thousand psychiatric techniques all fail to change a personality, but Love transforms a person in one instant, and that is Love's great miracle and mystery."

"Beatrice, I'm a pauper and a dreamer, I have nothing but the clothes on my back — "

She tugged my chiton and laughed.

"And every time a woman smiles at you, even the little you have doesn't stay on for very long. Isn't that true, dear boy?"

"Trust me, Beatrice, about this: while you are married, I will be a devoted friend to you, but I will not pursue you in a manner that is sexual or romantic."

"You're giving up already?" she said, shaking her head. "Thoreau, dearest, when you forget me, do not forget this advice: 'Love and all good things are won by boldness and tenacity, there is no other way.'"

"I will never forget you, Bea. Will you seal our friendship by shaking my hand?"

"Thoreau, I am furious!"

"Angry at me, Beatrice? What did I —"

"So many women, so little time! Moments after you meet me at the Meteora you seduce a young American librarian —"

"Beatrice, I don't remember telling you about — "

"I heard it from Penelope, who heard it from Irene, who heard it from the widow Yentagabpolis, my dear. ... A week later you're following a blonde on a bicycle, and you wind up sleeping with the ten wildest women on Crete — "

"Believe me, Beatrice, that wasn't all my — "

"Next, with her mother watching, you make one less virgin in the world. A mere day after she leaves, you take advantage of two lonely German sisters —"

"Wait a second, Beatrice, I was trying to do something good —"

"And then there was that moonlit Matthew-Arnold evening when — after two hours of drooling all over my breasts and eating me up with your eyes — you insulted my sense and sensuality by refusing to spend the night with me in my hotel room!"

I shook my throbbing head.

"I wondered if — no, when — that stupendous blunder would come back to haunt me."

"Did I miss any of your exploits, dear boy? One needs a supercomputer and a seXML database to keep an accurate record of your erotic life."

"There were the two gypsies on the beach — "

"Oh yes, the merry widows. And tonight you bring poor innocent Penelope to an isolated beach — "

"Penelope is like a sister to me! For weeks I've been fighting her advances — "

"And finally, using the flimsiest excuse of all — my husband! — you want to be my — Oh! those two infuriating words! — my 'devoted friend!', and then you spit me out into the compost heap like ... like chewed up pomegranate seeds! From the first day we spoke to each other you knew that I was married, and suddenly that matters now!"

Before I could compose my mind and a reply, Beatrice slipped her arm through her sleeve, then pinched my bottom again and again, pinching so hard it made me shout and jump. Penelope placed, into Beatrice's free hand, a huge container of fresh Greek yogurt, which was then dumped on top of my head. Immediately, in a great show of female solidarity, six other Sextopian women passed various things to Beatrice — from seaweed to week-old soup — all of which were poured onto my shoulders, head, and hair.

The only escape was to fall forward, with Beatrice on my back, and begin doing push-ups. The Sextopians counted each one, and at push-up number sixty-eight Pateras knelt down beside me, made a small cut in the cloth-gown that joined me with Beatrice, and then ripped open the cloth to set us free.

When we stood up, Beatrice's two gorgeous eyes glared into my eyes with unquenchable anger. Pateras placed his hands on our shoulders and then spoke to us with the utmost cheerfulness.

"In my whole long life," he said, "I have never met a man and a woman who are more perfect for each other than you and you. Tonight you cannot see what this old man sees. But one day you will see it — let's hope that on that day it's not too late to save your relationship. Now let's take a break, let's drink something that will cool us down. And then my friends and I will show you how we amuse ourselves in this Sextopias. This next activity is unique. We call it: 'The Great Art Lesson.' You will like it, I am sure."

46
THE GREAT ART LESSON

TWO NAKED WOMEN were walking four abreast.

Bountiful Beatrice and pendulous Penelope, returning from their short swim, stepped from the cool sea-water onto the warm sand-beach of Sextopias. Talking and laughing — completely at ease with their nudity — they were soon surrounded by a dozen gray-haired widows chattering in Greek. These energetic ladies rubbed towels against the bodies of Beatrice and Penelope, combed and arranged their hair, then dressed the two beauties in the white chiton-gowns. And when the two women walked toward the center fire dressed in diaphanous clouds, they looked tall and statuesque, like two goddesses. Goddesses who come to whisper wisdom into the unlistening ears of men.

While staring at Beatrice and Penelope, I somehow noticed that four husky Greek men were assembling a platform made from wooden crates. Soon the entire population of Sextopias were sitting on the sand in a semi-circle around this improvised stage. The stage now felt the footsteps of Penelope, who smiled, then said "Good evening," and then unceremoniously removed her gown. At the first sight of her breasts — enormous, tanned, divinely shaped — the crowd cheered and clapped with boundless enthusiasm.

"Tonight, our model is Hera, who some of you know as Penelope," said Pateras. "And like every woman who reveals herself, she enchants us with her indescribable beauty and her inimitable grace."

Flowingly, Penelope moved her body into a seductive pose. The Sextopians sat silently and watched the wondrous woman — her face, breasts, hands, body, legs, and feet — with attention rapt and concentration profound. While music played, Pateras and Penelope improvised *mandinada* — dialogue songs.

"Beware of Art's benumbing charms!
After a night of joyous screams,
I grasped one live Medusa in my arms —
Is worth one thousand Helens in my dreams!"

"The Poet is a man like You;

He works, he plays, he dies.
But every thing he sees with Love! —
That's where the vital difference lies."

Kosmos rushed to the stage and stood in front of Penelope, as if he were attempting to protect her from the crowd's benevolent gaze.

"What kind of art lesson is this?" he cried out. "Where are the pencils? Where are the drawing pads?"

The Sextopians laughed; Kosmos looked up at Penelope then spoke.

"Did my heart love till now? foreswear it, sight! ...
For I ne'er saw true beauty till this night."

Kosmos turned, faced Penelope, then grasped her calloused hands between his two creative hands.

"Penelope, *matia mou,* my darling!" he said. "Why didn't you tell me?"

"Why didn't I tell you what?"

Kosmos kissed her hands.

"About this place, about my father, about your participation, about how beautiful you are, about this wild dimension of your personality?"

She freed her hands from his tender grip then placed them against her hips.

"Kosmos, I am following the advice you gave me, the advice you heard from your grandmother when she sat you on her knee."

"Pickled by my own advice!" he shouted. "What do you mean, Penelope?"

"You said: 'A lie you must never tell, the truth you don't always have to tell.'"

With both hands, Kosmos grasped his grey-white hair. For a moment he turned around to look at the audience — who were relishing this encounter like a good comic play — and then he stepped back and studied Penelope.

"What a piece of work a woman is!" he proclaimed, in his booming voice. "In tits, how like — "

But at this point the bawdy bard was silenced by boos and hissings from the crowd, who pelted him with kumquats, tomatoes, and grapes.

Pateras restored silence by stepping onto the stage and raising his hands.

"Kosmos, dear boy," he said, "a hundred times the Sextopians have reflected and debated about how to speak about the human body parts. You see, just like our ancient Greek ancestors, we unashamedly enjoy our naked sensuality. The nude body and the acts of sexual intercourse are healthy and humanizing, we believe. Yet we must avoid the blunders of the Romans, who were coarse and brutal in their sex activities. They reduced sex to mere animality, and forgot to include the divine elements of humor, awe, and intimacy."

Kosmos looked entirely perplexed.

"You go naked all the time here, and you make love like rabbits fed on carrots stuffed with aphrodisiacs — but you don't say the word ... " — and here he cupped both hands under his chest, and made a bouncing gesture with his hands.

Pateras laughed.

"We have a song, a song named 'What To Call Them?' ... "

Up from the audience jumped a dozen males, who leaped onto the stage and then knelt before Penelope, chanting "What to call them, what to call them ..."

And when Penelope nodded, the singers harmoniously sang:

"Breasts sound anatomical,
Tits too brassy crude
Boobs to childish, comical,
Knockers outright rude.

"Love pillows too gentle,
Udders too bovine.
Call me sentimental —
And just let me call them mine!"

The singers sprang up then patted the back of Kosmos, who smiled as if to say that he was just beginning to understand. Pateras approached his son.

"Kosmos, we have no censorship here. You can say anything you want to say. Of course, if your words are over-ripe with folly or disrespect, then — well, you have seen what the reaction might be. Go ahead and finish your poem about the piece of woman, please."

Kosmos, who had felt enough tomatoes and boos, stood for a moment helplessly, until Beatrice stepped onto the stage. The incomparable woman glanced at Penelope, and then she spoke an improvised poem of her own.

> "What a piece of work a woman is!
> How infinite in sensuality! how noble in forgiving men!
> In breasts and body how perfectly seductive!
> In words and deeds how unpredictable!
> In kindness how like the goddesses!
> In mystery how like the glowing eyes of night!
> The beauty of the Universe! the paragon of Love!"

As the crowd applauded, Beatrice and Penelope exchanged kisses on their cheeks. Pateras glanced at his son, then spoke to Kosmos and the Sextopians.

"Kosmos," he said, "as a painter you know that art is ninety percent seeing, and ten percent re-creating what you see. Here in Sextopias we are devoted to three arts: the arts of living and loving and making love. I have told you that we are concerned with education: education for life, the learning that is light years beyond what happens in the universities. Our learning is not for four or eight or twelve years: our learning begins at birth and does not end until the day you die. What is the foundation of every good education? It is this: learning how to see. How to look at every man, woman, child — and every living creature — with eyes of wonder and delight, and a heart flowing with joyful reverence."

"Like Walt Whitman," said Kosmos. "And like Homer, Cavafy, Wordsworth, and Goethe."

"Yes, we are learning how to see the way a poet sees," said the Father. "But those poets were solitary men, who wrote their visions to educate humankind, and to escape the agony of their loneliness. Here we have a community of women and men who are learning how to see so that we can be loving and creative not in art only, but in the day-to-day living of our lives."

Kosmos nodded, and Pateras spoke more.

"Seeing is essential, for every moment that we see with the heart, the joy of living is intensified."

As these words escaped the old man's lips, a deep resounding blast — from the blowing of a conch shell — burst the quiet peacefulness. The

Sextopians screamed and cheered; the wooden-crate stage was quickly disassembled; and more logs were added to the flickering fire. While Pateras, Kosmos, Penelope, Beatrice and I stood in the center of things, the Sextopians gathered into a large circle, clasped hands, and began to sing.

At the next trumpeting blow from the conch shell, the human circle split into two facing lines — one for the women, one for the men. With the merriest enthusiasm, all eyes now gazed at Pateras, and all faces glowed with the great anticipation that something marvelous would soon begin.

47
LORD MAKE ME CHASED

PENELOPE — SUDDENLY AWARE of her nakedness — raised her arms to drop a white chiton-gown over her mesmerizing body. With a sigh I turned my gaze away, and then I started counting heads.

Excluding tonight's new visitors — Beatrice, Kosmos, and me — I counted exactly sixty-four Sextopians: forty-three women and twenty-one men. A few stood nude completely; some were naked from the waist up; most of them wore the white chitons; only their leader, Pateras, remained dressed in ordinary clothes. His feet were bare, his legs concealed under loose-fitting work-pants, his chest covered by a blue denim-shirt with sleeves rolled up to the middle of the forearms. Thin yet muscular with perfect posture, he moved with marvelous agility, as if all his life he had been an athlete, a dancer, or a farmer swinging sickles in the fields. His white hair had been trimmed short; his mustache curled over his upper lip like wings; his clean-shaven cheeks glowed with a healthy tan. Smiling eyes and buoyant cheerfulness made his face appear far younger than its eighty years.

"Are we ready?" Pateras shouted to his friends.

"For this activity," said Ligeia, "we are always ready!"

More torches were lit to make the beach almost as light as day. Pateras raised his empty hands, as if he were about to blow into a horn. The Sextopians laughed, and then shouted the name, "Priestos, Priestos, Priestos!" In a moment Priestos stepped out from the line of men, mimed and gestured to indicate that his head was empty, and then ran to Pateras and handed him the conch shell. Raising the shell-horn to his lips, the radiant man paused, then lowered the shell.

"We have told our visitors," said Pateras, "that we are not a sex farm, we are an educational community. Our work is teaching the theory and practice of sexuality and love. But work is not everything; a whole life is made of six elements: Health, Love, Learning, Creating, Work, Play. How should mature adults play? We have not yet explained to this to our new guests. Our games — "

A very old voice from a very old woman — named Bedusa — interrupted the discourse of Pateras.

"When Marc Anthony returned from the wars," she said, "he had not seen Cleopatra for three years. Do you know the first words she spoke to him? ... She said: 'Honey, this is no time to talk!' ... Blow the conch shell, Pateras! I'm ninety-eight years old, I've got one foot in the grave, and the other foot in a dish of olive oil. Blow!"

Pateras joined the Sextopians in laughing at this good advice, and then he raised the shell again. This time he paused to admire it.

"Is this a work of nature or a work of art? ... Thoreau, my boy, take this shell and pass it around so everyone can see the details up close."

I stepped forward to take it from his hands, but Pateras winked at me, raised the shell to his puckering lips, and then blew a resounding blast. The Sextopians shouted and screamed.

"Penelope," Kosmos asked. "What do I do now?"

"You have two choices, Kosmos," replied Penelope. "You can stand there and be mobbed by sex-hungry women, or you can temporarily postpone your fate by running on the beach."

Ligeia and four white-haired women made a mad dash after Kosmos, and as I laughed at the sight I noticed that there were more than thirty gray-haired women running at me. Kosmos tugged my chiton and then we ran across the sand into the cool water.

Staring into the darkness, the Sextopian women gathered on the shoreline, waving their arms, calling for us to return. Pateras shouted something that made the people cheer, and then women and men threw their chitons into the air, and sang this poem in the cadence of a round:

"Lovely is the human body —
Why do we hide it under dress?
Beauty chases you each moment —
Why do you run after Ugliness?"

Penelope stepped into the water up to her knees.

"Kosmos! Thoreau!" she shouted. "Even in the sexual paradise there are boundaries and rules. Nobody is allowed to enter the water when we play this game. These women want to thrill you, not to kill you. Come back!"

The pristine beach glowed from the light of torches and a carefully-watched campfire. Kosmos and I — dripping with water and seaweed — returned from the safety of the sea, then walked on the sand to stand beside Pateras, Penelope, and Beatrice in the center of the semi-circle of Sextopians. Pateras placed one arm around my shoulder and the other arm around the shoulder of his son. He looked at us and laughed loudly, and he continued to laugh so hard that it took minutes to calm himself enough to speak.

"They told me," he said, looking at my face with fatherly affection, "that you two men were like rabbits. But I thought it was for the other reason, not because you like to run."

With admiration in their eyes, the women and men of Sextopias watched him, as if this night were a feast of a thousand thrilling possibilities, and Pateras would teach them how to enjoy it most efficiently and best.

"The secret of giving a good speech," Pateras said, "is the very same secret as the one for enjoying a good sexual encounter: Be sincere, be brief, be seated."

The youthful old man released me from his one-armed hug, the Sextopians applauded, and Pateras spoke on.

"As you can see, we do not believe in marriage before sex. We play love-games in order to practice and perfect our skills, so that when we discover our true love — the partner we want for life — we will be prepared to give her or him exquisite pleasure and happiness. Our three newcomers now know that it is not permitted to escape by running into the sea. Our other rule is just as simple: When a woman catches a man in these games, she may decide to keep him, or she may trade him to another woman who wants him more."

I raised my hand, a bad habit learned from a bad public-school education.

"What happens," I asked, "if the man does not want to make love with the woman who catches him?"

Beatrice flung something into my face — a pair of silk panties with red-colored letters that said:

WANDERBORE
Supporting Women In Technology
Invalid Password: Access Denied.

"Thoreau, my dear fool," replied Beatrice. "If you do not want to sleep with the woman who nabs you, you simply pray like Saint Augustine: 'Lord make me chased — but not yet.'"

Pateras laughed.

"We are a gynocracy — or a matriarchy, if you wish — a society ruled by the good judgment of women. When we men are caught and do not want to be, we accept the bittersweet gift with the utmost cheerfulness."

Pateras blew the conch shell, the men and women lined up in two lines, the shell-horn resounded once again — and amidst shouting and laughing like children, the women chased after the men. Men who were caught — sometimes by one woman, other times by two or three or four — were led by the hand to the 'base', a circle etched in the sand near the fire. When ten minutes had passed, all the men had been seized except for Pateras and Kosmos and me.

And then Pateras was snared by an attractive 50-year-old woman named Aspasia, who had a runner's body and aristocratic eyes. Kosmos stumbled over a watermelon and was grabbed by the cackling Ligeia. And when I turned rightwards to avoid a wall of women on my left, I ran straight into Penelope, who wrapped her arms around me and shouted:

"One-two-three, Love with me!"

A loud cheer from the women signaled that all men had been captured; and then the conch shell blew again.

"Now, dear women," said Pateras, "if you want to keep the man you are now holding, step to the right. All of you who might want to trade him in for another model — newer, sleeker, or more responsive — step to the left of me."

Ligeia led Kosmos to the right, to the no-trade area, and the instant Kosmos opened his mouth to complain, his father froze him with a glance.

"Kosmos, for once think twice before you speak. Here we are — think how rare it is! — sixty-seven persons who care for one another, each woman and each man on fire with the rapture of being alive! Kosmos, look at the beautiful hearts around you, peaceable and self-contained. Will you be the one rotten apple in our barrel of bliss? Is this moment a miracle, or is it not?"

"It is!" Kosmos replied, without a pause. "And this is not the place for expressing misery — we have the whole rest of the world for that!"

"Discover and then say something positive about your situation, Kosmos," his Father said.

Looking up and down the massive form of Ligeia, Kosmos smiled and shook his head.

"This is courage in man — to bear unflinchingly what heaven sends!"

"You can do better than that, Kosmos," his Father replied. "Say something complimentary about Ligeia's body. Look at her and see her for the first time."

Like Homer's hero Odysseus, Kosmos was a superb improviser, a man who "is never at a loss." He looked at the woman and nodded appreciatively, amazed at the sheer bulk of her.

"The spirit is willing but the flesh is bleak. Ligeia, your body ... your body ... your body is flabulous."

Ligeia laughed, then hugged Kosmos, then walked with him to the left side of Pateras, where she gave Kosmos to Beatrice, not as a trade but as a gift. Beatrice led Kosmos to the woman who loved him most — Penelope, of course — then glanced at me as she addressed her friend.

"Tell me, Nelly," said Beatrice to Penelope, "how is Thoreau in the sack?"

"I don't know, Beatrice, I've never sacked him," Penelope replied. "I do not think that he likes sex."

"That's too bad," Beatrice answered. "That's like keeping a Stradivarius violin in a museum locked inside a case of glass. With the right woman playing, imagine the music that body could make."

"I can only imagine it," said Penelope, stroking my cheek. "Beatrice," she said. "How would you like to trade the dreamboat Thoreau for a weather-beaten old frigate, Kosmos?"

"Boats always make me seasick," said Beatrice. "I love to swim, but no power on Earth could drag me onto a boat. But throw in a kilo of your fresh olive salad and it's a deal."

Like mindless commodities, the two men were immediately exchanged. Beatrice held my hand and smiled, and then she glanced at me with glowing eyes.

How beautiful she looked! And what breathtaking passion I felt for her, so much more than any poet could ever tell. And I wondered how the human heart was made, so glorious and strong that it could hold vast worlds of feelings, and yet so weak and foolish that it let a man fall hopelessly in love with a woman who cared nothing for him at all.

"Poor lovestruck boy," she said, squeezing my hand. "You'll get over me, darling, as soon as the next deep-cleavaged woman jogs along. Mr. Thoreau, your body language indicates that you are concealing your true thoughts from me. Do you think women like me are dangerous?"

"You, Beatrice? ... Nietzsche said that women are dangerous only from afar."

"Then move closer, dear, and worship me from anear."

When I stepped as close to the woman as a man should get without first checking if he was carrying a contraceptive device, she placed her hands onto my shoulders.

"Now dearest," said Beatrice, "answer this question for me. Should I tell you something that you want to hear, or should I tell you something that is good for you, something that will make you a happier and better man?"

"I want you to tell me what is good for me. I think."

"Bravo, Thoreau! That is the answer that separates men from boys. Now listen. For months I have wanted to explain to you how it felt when you refused to stay with me that night at Ligeia's hotel. And I've concluded that the disappointment and frustration is so far beyond the power of words, that only through actions can I make you understand."

"Beatrice, what do you mean?"

The conch shell resounded once again, and I heard the voice of Pateras announcing that this would be the very last opportunity for women to trade their male catches.

"I mean," Beatrice continued, "that revenge is a dish that is best served old. Enjoy your evening, dear."

With these words, Beatrice placed my hand into the hand of Bedusa, the oldest woman in Sextopias — and possibly everywhere else.

At once the furrowed face of this old woman looked familiar to me: she was either the great-grandmother who had sold me the withered vegetables in Dembacchae, or the mother of that dear old soul.

Bedusa clutched my arm.

"Praise the saints and the sisters and sinners, too!" she shouted. "This man can dock his dingy in my harbor anytime!"

"He's just a man," said Beatrice to Bedusa. "And like every man, you can trust him as far as you can Thoreau him."

Bedusa handed me a fistful of carob pods.

"Eat this," she said. "You will need the energy."

The Sextopian women had now gathered in circle around us. Bedusa grasped my chiton, then lowered it to the waist. The crowd laughed, and then listened as Beatrice recited a pertinent passage from Plato.

"Filled with compassion for humans who are born to work, the gods gave men frequent feasts to renew them from their weariness. And for companions in these feasts the gods gave mortals the nine Muses, and Apollo the Muses's guide, and Dionysus, the god of fertility and wine. By celebrating with these gods, men would renew themselves, swell with creative inspiration, and once again stand upright and erect."

Bedusa poured a small bottle of goat-milk cream into her hands, then rubbed the cream onto my chest. She smiled at me, with cracked lips and a toothless smile.

"First, I am going to rub this fresh cream everywhere on your body," the ancient woman said. "And after that, I will make love to you until we make a pound of butter from this cream!"

48
WILD NIGHTS! WILD NIGHTS!

THE NIGHT was young, but the woman was pushing ninety-nine.

The playful Sextopians — overjoyed that the love-chase had produced three happy couples — danced around me and Bedusa, Pateras and Aspasia, Kosmos and Penelope. The oldest woman glanced at Beatrice as she clutched my goat-cream-covered hand.

"You're in love with another woman, Mr. Thoreau," Bedusa said. "But after one hour with me, you will forget her like the rattlesnake forgets the mouse he swallowed yesterday."

Seeing the doubt in my eyes, Bedusa reached up, tugged my earlobe, and pulled my ear close to her mouth so she could whisper.

"It takes years of practice to master the art of anything: painting, music, dancing, making love. When young people sleep together, it's one-two-three good-night! Five minutes later and it's finished, they take a shower then they go to sleep. I will teach you patience, dear boy. Patience is the great secret of success in sex and love."

Bedusa sat down on a stump then placed a *santouri* — a dulcimer-like stringed instrument — onto her lap, then beat the strings with two padded hammers. As she sang Emily Dickinson's poem — adding a last-line of her own — her gaze looked far away into the star-blessed sky.

> "Wild Nights! Wild Nights! Were I with thee,
> Wild Nights should be our luxury!
> Futile the winds to a heart in port, —
> Done with the compass, done with the chart!
> Rowing in Eden! Ah! the sea!
> Might I but moor to-night in Thee! —
> Might Thy put more to-night in Me!"

The song was followed by applause and cheers, and then a gray-haired woman named Eponmowney shouted a question for Bedusa.

"Young men want to sleep with young women," she said. "And old men want to sleep with young women. So how can old women ever get to enjoy wild nights?"

This revelation caused the women of Sextopias to talk all at once, until Bedusa stepped forward and raised her bony arm.

"There is a goddess of love named Jelloey-ose," she said. "A goddess who directs the affairs of men and women who fall in love when they are far apart in age. And whenever an old woman sighs when she sees a handsome young man, this great goddess goes to the man when he is alone, just awaking from the deepest sleep. 'Bedusa is in love with you and wants to share your bed!' the goddess tells him. 'Take pity on her and go!' And the stupid man answers: 'Why should I spend the night with that ancient bag of bones?'"

As the Sextopians listened eagerly, Bedusa swallowed a gulp of yogurt-drink from a wooden cup, and then talked on.

"As soon as the man falls asleep again, the goddess visits him in a dream. She says, 'Look, you idiot! For once in your life think of the days ahead. In forty years you will be an old man, and that forty years shall pass like the flash of fireflies at night. And then each beautiful young woman who passes will torment you with her youthful beauty. Thinking about her you won't be able to eat or work or even sleep! Every time you reach out to grab her she'll slap you, or laugh at you, or run away! Your good looks won't move her, your knowledge and accomplishments will be nothing to her, even your money won't matter to the ones you want the most. You'll be existing, not living, like a ghost in Paradise — you'll see a thousand gorgeous women but they won't see you!'"

She plucked the strings of her instrument, and then glanced into the eyes of the fascinated men.

"And now the goddess whispers to the young man: 'But just sleep with Bedusa, this one night, and then I'll give you my magic blessing. And with my magic blessing, one of these young women will take pity on you — she'll look at the young heart beneath the wrinkled skin — and then she'll give you the greatest love-night of your life. And all you need to do to make this journey — from Hell to Paradise — is to sleep with Bedusa for one wild night!'"

This story made the crowd laugh loudly, and when the laughter lightened, Pateras raised his hand.

"Youth knows — " he shouted.

In one voice the Sextopians answered:

"And age can!"

"We all know," said Pateras, "that it is hard work to grow younger every day. The body rejuvenates by exercise, the mind renews itself by learning, the heart stays young by love. Before our three blessed couples find private places on the beach to couplelate, we must all stretch our muscles so they will be flexible and strong."

Pateras raised his arms and then bent down at the waist to touch his fingertips against his toes. Everyone imitated his gently-flowing movements. Bedusa reached up and grasped hold of my earlobe.

"If I bent down like that I would snap in half like a string bean," she said. "There was a time when I felt depressed about my old age. And then, thanks to this place, I understood that I could teach the younger women a thousand things."

The stretching exercises continued for a quarter of an hour, and then ended with four deep breaths. Pateras spoke again.

"One of our methods of sexual education is derived from the hetaera pattern of the ancient Greeks. In those days, it was natural to assume that a younger man would learn about sexuality from a woman who was older and more experienced. Where else could he learn? Not from the wives of other men, not from the innocent young girls. The Greek hetaeras were not prostitutes, they were women of learning and wisdom and grace."

Pateras made a gesture with both hands, like a choir conductor.

"Whenever you look at a woman or a man, ask yourself: 'Is this person a taker or a giver?' ... Look underneath their physical appearance, into the true beauty of the heart."

The Sextopians began singing — in a wonderful harmony — a song they called: *The True Beauty.*

"He that loves a rosy cheek,
   Or a coral lip admires
   Or from star-like eyes doth seek,
   Fuel to maintain his fires;
   As old Time makes these decay,
   So his flames must waste away.

"But a smooth and steadfast mind,
   Gentle thoughts, and calm desires,

Hearts with equal love combined,
Kindle never-dying fires:—
Where these are not, I despise,
Lovely cheeks or lips or eyes."

Penelope grasped Kosmos by his hair and then kissed him with the most delicious passion. With shy enthusiasm, Aspasia kissed Pateras. Bedusa, too short to reach my lips, was lifted up by Beatrice. But just before the kiss was kissed, a shout startled the Sextopians out of their carefree joy.

"*Xenos!*" the voice shouted, almost out of breath. "A stranger is coming!"

The Sextopians rushed to their rehearsed places. The nude members dressed quickly; other Sextopians set up the sign that said:

The *Kalee-Neekta* Players —
A Troupe of Actors and Singers
Performing Comedy and Light Songs

Two men and two women, dressed as clowns, performed cartwheels and acrobatic tricks. Pateras decorated my head and body in a white-haired wig and a moth-chewed blue robe; and to complete this old man's costume, a wooden walking stick. Penelope disguised the head of Bedusa with a blonde wig and a smiling mask from the Greek tragedies, and then dressed her body in a blue silk gown that covered every bit of skin from neck to ankle-bones.

At a silent signal from Pateras, six Sextopians danced around Bedusa and me; they threw flowers on our heads, and sang a daffy ditty as they danced.

"Pause, O Men — Retract thy claws
This fair young maid has entered — Men-o-pause.
Hark, you fools! Use eyes, use ears,
She has not seen that menopause — for fifty years!"

A stranger had entered the circle lit by the campfire, and in the moment of silence before the song's next verse, the stranger's voice cried out.

"Mother! Mother, what are you doing here!"

The singing abruptly stopped. All the women of Sextopias turned their heads, and all the Sextopians nervously examined the young face behind the astonished voice.

49
THE MAIDEN AND THE FLUTE

HOW QUICKLY FEAR changed to delight as we watched a lithe body skip fairy-like across the sand, and we recognized the pretty face who had discovered us: Irene! She ran past me into the hugging arms of her mother, Penelope, and her adopted Aunt Beatrice.

"Welcome back, darling," Penelope told her.

Kosmos hugged his one-and-only child.

"From that school in Athens," he asked, "did you come back to us as educated as a dictionary and as cultured as a cup of yogurt?"

Irene assumed the posture of a pedant behind a podium, then spoke with a mocking air.

"The Romantic Movement in literature," she said, "beginning in 1756 and ending in 1848, may be epitomized in Goethe's expression: 'Feeling is everything!'"

"That's marvelous, dear child," said Beatrice. "What a fine young woman you are! Now come here with me, there is a very wise old woman who wants to meet you."

Bedusa responded to the young woman as if, in Irene, she had found her long-lost granddaughter. They exchanged hugs and cheek-kisses and heart-deep words of praise, and then Irene pointed to the mortar and pestle on Bedusa's stump.

"What are you making, grandma?" asked Irene.

Sensing another story in the air, the Sextopians gathered around to listen to the talk between the woman old and the woman young.

"It's an old recipe, my dear, to protect young women from the long tentacles of lecherous older men. You see, when I was your age, there lived an all-powerful god named Zeus, who ruled all the other gods and goddesses because they feared his lightning-bolts. This Zeus, like most men, liked to chase the females of the species. Zeus had a son named Pan — although some people swear he was the son of Hermes — a pastoral god of fertility. Whenever we had a bad harvest, my grandmother would take old work clothes and straw, and sew together a stuffed Pan, and then beat him with an olive branch. 'Why didn't we get a good crop this year?' my grandmother shouted at the doll. 'Because of you, Pan, you loafer! You've got your father's love of woman and womanizing! Forget about the girls until your work is done!'"

Bedusa placed her hand on Irene's shoulder.

"The real god Pan — not the stuffed doll — spent his nights chasing women and falling in love with them, but they rejected him because of his ugliness. All those failures never discouraged him from chasing the wood nymphs through the forest and over the hills. The noise was keeping the gods awake at night, and Hera — wife of Zeus — was worried that one day Pan would seize hold of one of her innocent nymphs."

From an apron pocket, Bedusa pulled out a handful of black olives and dropped them into her mortar, and then crushed them with her pestle's quick and skillful strokes.

"So Hera commanded that Hermes should bring her the freshest and ripest olives on Crete, and moments later Hera made the olive oil by crushing these perfect olives between her mighty breasts. To her philandering husband she said: 'Take this oil, Zeus lazy-bones, and while Pan is sleeping, spread it on his hands. Then if he puts his fingers around the slender waist of a wood nymph, she will slide to safety.' Zeus took the oil, but as soon as he left cold Olympus and walked on the warm earth, his eyes noticed the lovely mortal woman Kalimastos, and instantly he fell in lust with her."

Bedusa cast a long glance at Thoreau, then winked at him, and then sprinkled some dried sage leaves into the mix.

"Nine months later Hera smelled the aroma of lamb burning — humans were sacrificing to the Olympians because one of the wood nymphs had become pregnant, and the father was the forest-god Pan.

"'Zeus!' shouted Hera. 'How could this be? What happened to my best breast-pressed olive oil?'

"'Ah!' said Zeus, slapping his hand onto his head. 'Forgive me, Hera darling, you know how men never can remember to do those little things. I forgot to grease the Pan!'"

The Sextopians laughed and cheered at the tale. Irene took hold of Bedusa's hand.

"In school in Athens," she said, "I wrote a poem about Pan, to explain why there can never be love without music, or music without love. The poem is called: *Pan's Passion Invents the Pipes.*"

"Tell us, child, tell your story!" Bedusa said.

Irene glanced through the crowd of Sextopians and found me, still disguised in a white-haired wig, ragged robe, and walking stick. She tugged my hand and led me to the center of the crowd. As she told her tale she played the role of the wood nymph, and I acted the part of Pan.

"Yes, the god Pan was an ugly creature," Irene began, "with the legs of a goat, and hooves instead of human feet. He protected the shepherds and the flocks, and he was always falling into a snare of love, and this time he fell for Syrinx, the most beautiful of all the nymphs."

And now in her thrilling soprano voice — a voice that had received some expert training since we heard her last — Irene sang her poem-tale.

"In Arcady, the great god Pan
  On goatlike legs and hooves,
  Chased Syrinx down and up the hills
  To make her feel his loves.

"Pan grabs the virgin's golden hair,
  To all the gods she pleads
  Her sisters, hearing helpless cries,
  Change Syrinx to grassy reeds.

"In foolish fits the forest god
  Shouts: 'Still you shall be mine!'
  He cuts the reeds in seven parts
  With beeswax they're combined.

"At once Pan grasps; 'I've killed my love!'
  He kissed the reeds, he sighed —
  The sigh blows through, sweet sounds appear —
  The pipes were born that night!

"'Though you can't join me in my bed
  Dear Syrinx, I can love you this way —
  Your sounds shall bring peace to my wandering mind,
  And our lips join whenever I play.'"

I remembered, months ago, the joy we had shared when I chased Irene across the Dembacchae beach. That too, was a paradise. There had so many paradises in my life, but always I recognized them too late, long after they had fled. And once lost — paradise, friendship, opportunity, love — could they ever again be found?

The Sextopians applauded and shouted "Bravo!" to the young story-teller, but Irene ignored the plaudits, took my hand, and then led me away from the crowd. On tiptoes she raised herself and kissed my lips. Stars glowing, sea roaring, cicadas singing — this night felt glorious.

"How are you, Irene?" I asked. And she replied:

"I feel like the night!"

Wonderful young woman! Irene, without losing her childlike innocence and joy, had returned from her journey with more confidence and poise.

"You're growing up very fast, Irene," I told her. "Thank you for that poem — it was vivid, concise, and expertly performed."

Irene laughed as her hand played with my hair.

"That's thanks to Aunt Beatrice," she said.

"Beatrice?"

"When I first arrived at school in Athens I was lonely, so Aunt Beatrice came to visit me. For one week she gave me lessons about how to speak, how to use my voice, and how to perform without shyness before an audience. Did you know that when Aunt Beatrice was my age she was a famous actress?"

"An actress!" I shouted. "Actresses are vain, airheaded and affected, and Beatrice is unpretentious, natural and genuine. Are you sure about that, Irene?"

"She performed throughout Europe, in serious dramas and comedies. Then she gave up her career to marry a millionaire old enough to be her grandfather, so that her brains and his money could change the world. Aunt Beatrice made me promise not to make that same mistake. She told me: 'When you fall in love, live under the same roof with the man for one year. If during the whole year he treats you like a goddess and if you're still in love when the year's up, then marry him before he gets away.'"

Irene smiled and then she hugged me with all her might. Her eyes glowed a skyful of goodness and curiosity and bright hope. Those pure eyes shined even brighter whenever they looked at me.

At a loud blast from the conch shell we unclasped and stepped apart. We heard shouts of *"Xenos!"* and "Not again!" and "Hurry!" as the Sextopians dashed in all directions to disguise their paradise.

50
MYSTICAL INSTRUMENTS OF PROPAGATION

THE WORD *"Xenos!"* has the same effect on the Sextopians as the word "Monster!" has on little children: it shivers them with curious chills and makes them shout and run. Scantly-clad seniors dashed in all directions, some grabbed their clothes, others picked up their instruments. The musicians among them began playing the liveliest music. Pateras stuck a sign into the sand.

> Circus of Souvlakis
> A Troupe of Actors and Singers
> Who Do Anything For A Laugh

Jugglers juggled three balls, four balls, five. Acrobats bounced hither and yon, via cartwheels and handsprings and forward rolls. Three Sextopian clowns balanced — on the tips of long poles — spinning bowls filled with wine. Male dancers danced like Russians — crossing arms and kicking their legs forward — encircled by the female dancers whirling in the style of a jazz-ballet. Singers topped with jester caps harmonized one of their favorite songs:

> What love! adventure! in each day!
> Each moment is a world of bliss!
> But not until we're old and gray —
> Do we so madly realize this!

Over the joyful music of this celebration we heard the growling din of an approaching motor — a startling contrast to the natural Sextopian soundscape. A vehicle that resembled a golf cart, with large tires designed for driving on the beach, rolled to a stop beside the campfire. Out of the cart stepped a white-mustached man, wearing no clothing except a black wool cap.

"Tiropitas!" shouted Pateras. "Our venerable Village Leader! Welcome!"

"Village Leader, or Village Idiot?" Tiropitas replied, as he embraced his friend. He yawned, he spit on the sand, he stretched his arms to the starry sky. "I have brought some very important news for you," he solemnly said.

The Sextopians gathered around him. Penelope told me that there was nothing to hide or fear: Tiropitas, a part-time member of this community, was everyone's trusted friend.

"I have brought very important news, but as soon as I arrived here I forgot what it is. Don't blame that on my age! I was a hundred and one years old last week, as you all know — it's not age that makes a man forget."

He spread his arms and ogled the females, as the Sextopians watched him and laughed.

"How can a man do any thinking," he said, "when there are so many beautiful women in the world? ... Oh, Saint Souvlakis look at me."

Tiropitas realized that he had forgotten to get dressed, and caught a towel flung to him by Priestos, then wrapped it around his waist.

"That's something I've always wondered about," he said. "Can someone be partially naked, or is nakedness always the whole goat?"

Some of the Sextopians came forward to shake the old man's hand, and as each one approached, he pretended to crane his neck and bite the air in front of the nose of his friend. Others Sextopians danced around Tiropitas as they improvised a welcome song.

> "Under the spreading olive trees
> The Village Leader stands
> With legs like chunks of feta cheese
> And arms like rubber bands.

> "Under the shady olive glades
> The Village Leader weeps —
> All night he chases Cretan maids
> All day he eats and sleeps."

"Tiropitas," said Pateras. "You're a hundred and one years old. How do you feel?"

"How do I feel?" he said, twirling his black worry-beads. "I feel like a *souvlaki* roasting on a spit! But don't worry about my health. I'm as tough as an olive tree — a good one can live and bear fruit for one thousand or fifteen hundred years."

"And what is the secret of your longevity?" said Pateras.

"My longevity ... Yes, they call me the donkey because — "

"I mean," Pateras interrupted, "How did you live and stay hearty for one-hundred and one years?"

"Oh, that business," Tiropitas said. "I have three rules for my health. One: Wake up early every morning, take a long walk, and then eat a good breakfast. Two: Every day of your life, make sex with a different young woman. And three: before you make sex, always examine the sexual organs of yourself and your partner. Or, as the folk proverb tells it: 'Look before you bleep.'"

"The news," said Pateras. "Try to remember that news."

"News?" Tiropitas replied. "I'm alive today, what could be more important news than that? My memory has never been too strong for things I didn't want to say or do. My first wife — may her soul rest and her body never rise! — every day would raise a frying pan at me and yell: 'Tiropitas, no man in history has ever said these words more times than you have said them: "I forgot". You would forget to bring your dingle-dongle if it wasn't attached to your groin!'"

"Your dingle-dongle?" Pateras asked.

"That's what she used to call it," Tiropitas replied. He waved his hands. "That reminds me of a story. Come closer, children. You should all hear this, remember it, and someday tell it to your kids — when they are old enough to wonder about these mysteries."

The Sextopians gathered, and one of them shouted: "What's the name of your story, Tiropitas? Is it a tall tale or is it true?"

"It is called: *Why Your Mystical Instruments of Propagation Are Never Long Enough.* ... Is it a tall tale? Very tall. Is it true? I know it, believe me, I was there."

Tiropitas scanned his audience; his eyes brightened when he looked at Beatrice and Thoreau.

"You there, Woman, and you there, Man. Fine specimens! You two come here and act in this story as I tell it. Don't be shy now, life's too short for that."

Tiropitas kissed my tanned cheek and Beatrice's red lips, and then began.

"Woman is the most beautiful of creatures. Man isn't so bad-looking, either. This tale is about the creation of the most neglected body-part of man. Do you imagine that even the gods could get it right the first time? ... No, it took three experiments to find out how to make a good man. The first two were failures. We — all the men standing here — are the third attempt."

Tiropitas twirled the corners of his white moustache.

"Yes, when the gods first made men, they made the man's dingle-dongle twelve inches long. Men then were like satyrs — every minute chasing women, or thinking about chasing them — those first men had an endless appetite for sex. Now and then these men would stop chasing the ladies for a few minutes, and get around to doing some productive work. But whenever they did, that protracted dingle-dongle would get in the way of things.

"One day the gods gathered and agreed: 'This is too much!' They put their heads together and after a lot of debating and arguments, they implemented man-experiment number two. This time they made that great twelve-inch dingle-dongle detachable. Yes, you could take it off, and then put it on again! That was great for wars: you could remove it before the battle, then fight without being vulnerable to kicks in the you-know-where."

Tiropitas fired a glance at Beatrice, and then at me.

"One day, a ravishing love-goddess glanced at the Earth and noticed the handsomest of mortal men — something like this one standing over here. She let down her hair, painted her lips red with pomegranate juice, and then put on a see-through dress. 'Meet me tonight in my sea-cave,' she said. 'My love-play will make you immortal, my kisses will make you divine. And my husband will make you into mincemeat. But don't worry, he's away on business tonight. Only once a year I get free for this, so don't be a minute late!'"

Tiropitas smiled at his audience.

"What happened next? ... The handsome man arrived on time, and the goddess kissed him with all her enthusiasm — "

The Sextopians applauded as Beatrice passionately kissed me. Tiropitas laughed, and then resumed.

"— but then the beautiful goddess screamed. She threw him out of her cave, flew straight up to Mount Olympus, and barged into the bedroom of her mother Hera, Queen of the goddesses.

"'You're home early, dear,' observed Hera. 'How was your night with that immortal mortal?'

"'That fool!' said the goddess, bursting into tears. 'He forgot to attach his dingle-dongle! He left it home!'"

Tiropitas grinned.

"That night, Hera made a sacred promise: this nonsense would never happen again. Goddesses deserved all the world's happiness, she believed. And think of the havoc they would wreak, if these all-powerful goddesses remained unsatisfied in sex! ... So the next day, man-experiment number two was scrapped, and number three was invented. The new man had been redesigned with a dingle-dongle attached permanently. There was no taking it off. And to solve the problem of getting in the way of everything, it was cut down to half the size."

The Sextopians greeted these last words with laughter, applause, and cheers. Pateras placed his hand on the old man's shoulder.

"That news, Tiropitas? Try to remember that important news."

"Give me a few minutes and I'll think of it," he said. "Until then, get back to doing whatever you were doing. Don't let me interfere."

Three women recalled quite well what they had been doing before Tiropitas arrived. After a few shouts from the eldest female Sextopian, the three couples met in the center — Bedusa and Thoreau, Penelope and Kosmos, Aspasia and Pateras. Pateras raised his hand.

"If you have read the great story, *Utopia,* by the courageous Thomas More, then you know that in More's kingdom, before two persons would be married, they would examine each other's naked bodies. Here we have a similar ritual, but only for the men. Men, now is the moment to reveal to your partner what we have been so foolishly taught to hide. Symbol of your vitality, glory of your manhood, pride of your prejudice, hero of your wildest exaggerations: your mystical instrument of propagation."

I stood bewildered while the Sextopians laughed at the old man's words and the young man's predicament. Pateras unbuttoned his shirt.

"Thoreau," he said. "Take off your clothes."

The three chosen men removed their clothing. I blushed but the women stared at me unblushingly. This crowd of Sextopian females oohed and ahhed as they gazed at the body that Mother Nature had given me, and I had exercised and cared for so well. Tiropitas studied me, and then he whistled and said:

"That was a sight to gladden the very gods."

Poor Bedusa! Her eyes opened wide as she raised her arm, and then she pointed her finger at my private parts. To prevent herself from shouting, she placed her hand over her own mouth. And finally when she had seen enough, she fainted and fell softly on the sand.

Friends loosened Bedusa's chiton, dabbed a wet cloth on her head, and then fanned her with great energy. From the crowd, one woman shouted:

"Pateras, tell us quickly. If Bedusa does not stand up, who gets Thoreau?"

Pateras nodded his head.

"Last year we had a similar problem," he said. "We agreed that the chaser — in this case, Bedusa — will lose her catch if, within the next five minutes, she does not stand up."

The women fanning Bedusa glanced at me, and then fanned the fallen woman much more slowly than before. An egg timer was produced that measured minutes, the salt trickled from the top part to the bottom, and the five minutes passed in a blink.

All at once the Sextopian women dashed in my direction. They shouted "1-2-3 Love with me!", and then grabbed and tugged my body like shoppers at a one-day-only sale.

Beatrice saved me by blowing the conch. The feeding frenzy ceased, all arms held me firmly, all eyes looked up at Beatrice.

"The Spartans," she said, "never asked 'How many are the enemy?' but always asked: 'Where are the enemy?' ... Thoreau never asks, 'How many women are there?' but always: 'Where are the women?'"

Pateras, shaking his head and laughing, addressed the crowd.

"When Love is temperate it is the sweetest thing, but save me from the other kind."

This quieted the Sextopians — it made them pause for a few moments to think. Pateras spoke again.

"Last year we discussed this situation," he began. He took the hand of Beatrice, walked with her through the wall of women, and joined her hand with mine. "And we decided by a unanimous vote that when a woman is unable to complete her tryst with the man she has chosen, then the man is returned to his previous capturer."

Pateras unstuck me from the clinging females. Taking me aside, he placed a conch shell in my hand. It was a large white shell streaked with golden-brown, it had a pearly bottom, and five horns sticking up from the top that resembled a rooster's coxcomb. The splendid shell looked as old as time, lovely as desire, powerful as love.

"I have two of these," said Pateras. "This one is for you, Thoreau. Give it to her, and don't be afraid to tell her how you feel. She might tell you to take the next mule to hell — women have told me that a hundred hundred times! ... Are you a real man? Then you'll be strong enough to hear that, to bear the unbearable pain of that. And then you will wish all good things for her, and then forget her and start your life anew."

The Sextopians began a spirited debate about changing their policy regarding who gets who when unexpected circumstances rise. Beatrice led me by the hand and walked with me twenty yards from this blathering crowd, to a quiet place on the beach.

I had wanted to behave toward her like a friend, but one look at her face and I felt breathlessly in love. Beatrice squeezed my hand.

"We're having so much fun here, aren't we darling! ... Oh dear, Thoreau, you're looking like the skinny fashion model who fell into the paper shredder: distressed. Shall we talk about it?"

"This shell is for you, Beatrice," I said. Slowly, I took a deep deep breath. "Remember that night when we walked from Kosmos's house along the beach. We were so happy together ... and then ..."

She took the shell with joy, and handed me a silken handkerchief.

"And then?" she asked.

"Then things fell apart like a stale baklava."

Cheerfully, Beatrice raised my hand and brushed her lips against the fingers.

"Can't we just follow Blake's advice," she asked, "and kiss the joy as it flies? We can be long-distance friends: we can lose each other's email addresses, and once every year we can exchange trite well-wishes on mass-produced greeting cards."

"Beatrice," I said. "Once your eyes glowed so brightly when you looked at me. Tell me why you won't let me love you now."

She placed her warm hand on my hand.

"It's the classic paradox, dearest, in the mathematics of Love. An immature man wants many women, and he wants each of those women to be devoted to him alone. When a boy is a boy and a teenager, he can fall in love with any number of girls. 'My darlings, my two and only!' he cries. Then one day — if he's lucky enough — he advances from youth to manhood. He puts away his toys, he chooses to live in the real world and not escape into the dream, he finds meaningful work that will help the world, and he commits himself to one woman — one. If I gave my heart to you again, Thoreau, I'd be the biggest fool on Earth. The instant you met someone YPWT, you would leave me cold."

"YPWT?" I asked.

Beatrice smiled.

"Younger, Prettier, Wittier, and Tittier."

"That's not true, Beatrice. I would be faithful to you. There was only one other woman who attracted me like this. She was — "

"The blonde on the bike with the cleavage as deep as Samaria gorge?"

"Yes, Beatrice, the blonde on the bike. But I don't think about her anymore. And when I do think about her, I remember that my brother used to wear a T-shirt that said: 'Tits aren't everything.'"

"Is he married, this brother of yours?"

Together, Beatrice and I turned our heads and peered at a strange sound shuffling in the semi-darkness. A strong feminine figure walked barefoot on the sand and approached the Sextopian campfire. For a moment I thought it might be Penelope. But when the woman moved out of the shadows to get a better view of the Sextopian debate, we saw the bicycle, the blonde hair, the superabundant chest, and the youthful face of the bikress — Bliss!

I cannot explain what prompted me to do what I did next. Without saying one word to Beatrice I turned my back on her, and then walked toward Bliss like a man enchanted by a magic spell. In the caves of my stupidity I heard — and misunderstood — echoes of the words of Pateras: "Forget her, and start your life anew." ... Rejected by Beatrice, my male ego could regain its blustering confidence if and only if I bedded Bliss.

As I walked I heard the voice of Beatrice sadly sing:

"All things must pass away, like mist, like tears, like dreams."

I never reached that gorgeous destination, the generous body of Bliss. Beatrice blew into the conch shell — hers had a slightly higher pitch than the shell of Pateras — and this sound was immediately recognized by the Sextopians as a signal meaning this: officially, and literally, Thoreau is "up for grabs".

Like a swarm of bees, the Sextopian women attacked me. I was captured by twenty hands, halfway between a woman I desired and the woman I loved.

Holding me, the Sextopian women walked me toward Pateras, knowing that Pateras would use his sound judgment to settle this territorial dispute. We passed by Beatrice, who had approached Bliss, and was now greeting her.

"Welcome, Sister," said Beatrice, and her smile glowed with genuine warmth. "This community is sympathetic to the plight of women everywhere. Here, for as long as you choose to stay, you will find food, shelter, safety, and good friends."

Near the campfire, the dozen female arms — arms that wound around me like an erotic Buddhist statue — were now disentangled by the skillful Pateras.

"You may not have noticed it, Thoreau," he said, loud enough for all to hear. "You were chased just now by all the women, and all the men, too. The men wanted to know your secret, and the women wanted to experience it."

Priestos ran forward, gave a friendly slap to Thoreau's shoulder, and then spoke to all the women and men.

"He is irresistible!" cried Priestos, his eyes twinkling. "I would give anything in the world to understand it!"

"Tell us!" shouted a chorus of Sextopian men. "Tell us how! Tell us now!"

Pateras raised his hands.

"Everywhere you go, Thoreau, women chase after you. They trust you like they trust their closest friend. One mere gaze into your eyes and women fall in love with you! And as soon as they fall in love they want to tumble into your bed! Yes, Thoreau, before we burst with curiosity, tell us, please. Steer our hearts between the Scylla of heartbreak, and the Charybdis of loneliness. Tell us the secret of your sexcess."

51
How Love is Lost

BY LATE AFTERNOON the banged-up boat had still not left the harbor of Agios Nikolodeonos, but not one of the passengers complained. The air had cooled, the ship's crew provided food and drinks, and by listening to the stories of my trials, travails, and troubles, the passengers happily forgot their own.

Panzano approached me with a lovesick sigh.

"Thoreau, help me," he said. "When I look at Dolcezza my eyes bulge like two boiled-hard eggs, my lips get dry as wheat germ, my stomach flips over like the pancake in the frying pan!"

I gripped his shoulder.

"I don't give advice, Panzano," I said. "I point out options, choices, and alternatives."

"Then please point out some ways to make her trip over my devotion then fall in love with me!" He seized my arm and held it tightly. "I'll give you all my gold teeth and be your dentured servant for seven years, if you'll tell me the secret of your sex appeal."

These words were overheard by an elderly woman, the boat's official gossip, and in minutes the word spread like a California wildfire. A long line of heartbroken women and lonely men gathered before me.

"I'm in love with the baker's wife," a man confessed. "Night and day I think about her, but the only way she'll talk to me is when I go into her shop and buy her breads and cakes. I have enough baked goods to feed a village, but not one kiss from her doughy lips!"

An attractive young woman approached me, turned her head to make certain there was no one listening, touched my hand, then spoke soft as the hum of a honeybee.

"Men whisper chocolate-covered words so they can take me to bed," she said. "Then after they've had what they wanted they leave without saying a word. Since men are pains, tell me how to see through men like window-glass, and how to weed the ten-thousand liars from the one true man!"

This touching tête-à-tête was interrupted by the crowd of passengers shuffling shyly toward us. They had sensed that, wherever I traveled, women fluttered and fell around me faster than the falling of October leaves. The lovesick men and women, gazing up into my tanned face, all desired to know how and why.

But how could I explain my good luck and my good heart? ... The woman breast-feeding her baby smiled into my eyes. A light-shaft of self-knowledge touched me. In a flash I grasped something new.

"You would like to hear the secrets of Love," I said to the listeners. "Many of you have told me that your love-lives need repairing; the first step for fixing anything is to understand how it works. The man who understands how love is lost will win the woman every time. And the woman who believes in Love will pick the one ripe pomegranate from the barrel of rotten fruit."

A mother in the audience instructed her daughter to bring me a glass of water and a hug; I took the water and then the embrace. When the crowd had finished laughing at the child's enthusiasm, I began the tale.

A King in ancient Crete fell in love with a peasant woman who let him court her for one month. Suddenly, without a word to explain why, she rejected him completely, and soon gave herself body and soul to the embraces of another man. Heartbroken and disillusioned, the King could find no peace in his mind, no virtues in any woman, no happiness in his entire kingdom. The King planned, plotted and pondered: should he kill the woman, or her lover, or himself? ... Not one of those violent solutions solved the problems of his heartache, and bringing back his lost love.

One evening, sitting down at the dinner table in his garden, the sad King drifted into anguished daydream. Suddenly he was roused from this bitter reverie by the braying of a donkey, who had just eaten the King's dinner, a cold cucumber soup. Moments later, an old man — the King's gardener and the donkey's owner — entered the garden, rolled up his sleeve, and then stuck his bare arm into the donkey's mouth.

"What are you doing, old fool?" the King asked.

The old man answered: "I am trying to get your dinner back, and then return this delcious food to you."

"That is impossible!" said the King.

Replied the gardener: "It is easier to pull soup from the stomach of a donkey, than it is to recover a love that is lost."

"Tell me," said the King, "for in a thousand eternities I could not guess.

What does every woman want?"

The poor man answered: "The three needs of the donkey are water, food, and rest. Any man who thusly nourishes his donkey will be beloved by that strange beast. The three needs of the woman are attention, acceptance, and affection. Any man who gives these to a woman will win her heart first, and the rest of her soon after that."

The King shouted: "How can I find love if I have none?"

With a long broom, the old man brushed the side of his loyal animal.

"Sire, see my donkey here," said the old man. "When we are traveling he is self-sufficient, he asks nothing at all from me. Before we begin our journeys, he drinks and eats large quantities of water and food. Because he has everything he needs inside himself, he is able to survive until we find an orchard or a stream. Had he started out empty, then he would have perished before reaching our destination. What can we learn from the donkey? He accomplishes his goal because he is self-sufficient, he has no needs. Regarding love: to find love everywhere in the world you must first carry it within yourself, or you will find nothing at all."

In the story the King recognized his own weakness. He raised his staff to hit the truth-speaking gardener, but then he lowered it without striking the old man.

"Since love is so difficult," said the King, "perhaps we should never love at all."

The old man shook his head to disagree.

"We are born to love and we must love," he said. "Love is a goddess dressed in golden olive oil: she is easy to find yet hard to hold. Whenever we find the love that is genuine, we must protect her so she stays with us for our entire lifetime of sunrises and sunsets."

Frustrated, the King drew his sword. His eyes flashed like red fire, and then he shouted furiously at the calm old man.

"Tell me now or I will cut off your head! How do we keep that genuine love from straying?"

From the saddlebag of his donkey, the gardener removed one jug of wine. Then he said to the King: "Put out your hands into the shape of a cup. Imagine that this wine is as sacred to you as your deepest love. Keep this essential liquid in your hands, and do not spill one precious drop."

The King sheathed his sword, cupped his hands securely, and then watched the gardener pour the wine into his cup-shaped hands. He pressed his hands tightly together to hold the fluid. Yet slowly, drop by drop, the liquid dripped down to the sand.

"Aha!" shouted the King. "Now I understand the answer! Love is never driven out, it slips away."

I slapped my hand against the shoulder of Panzano, who, while longing for Dolcezza, had been listening to the story with nods and sighs. Panzano's cheeks streamed with tears but the boat passengers sat silently. For an instant I wondered if my words had missed or touched the listeners' hearts. Before that wonder sprouted into doubt, the audience cheered the wildest cheer. A mass of men and women rushed forward to thank me, to hug me, and to shake my hand.

In the flurrying chaos the eleven lovely nuns got separated from their Mother-hen, and then politely walked amidst the pressed-together crowd. Quickly, Mother Whackanzakis pushed through the oblivious throng to gather her nuns together in one place.

Love — the god who wings us whenever we attempt the noblest deeds — made the love-struck Panzano even quicker than the nun. Saying, "Excuse me, I must find my one true love!" he shoved his immense body through the excited crowd.

"Dolcezza!" he said to the young nun. "You are ... you are ... better than lasagna with my grandmother's secret sauce! Every time I see you I want to jump up and down and sing!"

Soon afterwards, when the mob had settled down, the ship's assistant captain raised his left hand.

"Is the boat repaired?" someone shouted to him.

"The boat has been repaired," he said.

"And has the captain been located?" said another voice.

"Safe and sound, our captain has been been found," said the loyal assistant.

"Then will the boat be leaving now?" a third passenger yelled out.

"The captain, too much he has drinked," said the tired assistant. "The boat will not be departing at this time. Please remain on the boat until the next announcement. We expect some good news very soon."

The assistant captain looked up and stared at his bare left wrist. Mother Whackanzakis and her eleven nuns stood together; I watched as the Mother-nun waved her hands and spoke sharply to the youthful nuns.

Once more the friendly crowd on the boat's deck called out to me to tell them my adventures in the paradise of love.

52
BLISS WAS IT IN THAT DAWN TO BE ALIVE

"YOUR TROUBLES WITH WOMEN, my dear Thoreau, begin inside your lovely mind. Every pair of superabounding breasts titillates your wild desires to fructify. And then you allow your imagination to deceive you. Love is shy, lust is brash. Love is peaceful, lust is never satisfied. Love is always naked, lust wears alluring lingerie."

Standing at my side, Beatrice had been chiding me about my superficial attraction to the bedazzling blonde. A sudden silence broke the spell of looking at each other, and we glanced around to find Pateras, who had raised his hand to speak to the Sextopian audience.

"Thank you, Thoreau," he said, "for that intriguing tale. We will have great joy in discussing this at our breakfast, just before the sunrise. Where in Hades is Priestos? ... Will someone please add some fuel to our languishing campfire?"

Gasps and murmurs leaped from a dozen lips as Bliss approached the fire. The Sextopians — with their intense concentration on the world immediately before their eyes — had not noticed her presence before this. Bliss raised a heavy tree-branch over her head, swung it down with colossal force, and then smashed the branch against a rock. It cracked into two pieces, which she skillfully laid into the fire. Impressed by this feat of strength, the Sextopians surrounded her, staring at this Amazon woman with kindhearted curiosity.

Pateras gestured with his hand, signaling Priestos and Ligeia to bring four wooden bowls filled with fruits, bread, olives, yogurt, and nuts.

"Eat and enjoy this meal," said Pateras to Bliss, "and do not feel like a guest among us, but imagine that you have come home."

For months, all the while we were apart, I had been thinking of nothing but Beatrice. Now, as we were standing side-by-side, I forgot her like yesterday's lunch. Bliss stood up, tall and strong as Atalanta in the Greek myth. Braless Bliss dressed in nothing except cut-off denim shorts and a loose-fitting cotton T-shirt. She looked like a would-nymph luring me into the dark forest: a would-nymph, because one look at her and you are certain that she would.

As I stared at her body, I at once realized that I had not yet attained liberation or enlightenment, I had not mastered the Eastern secret of detachment, I had not freed myself from the traps of worldly desires. Bliss's body looked as perfect as a woman sketched by Doré, cartooned by Capp, painted by Boucher, sculpted by Rodin.

The eyes of the young woman glimmered with caution, as she debated whether to leave Sextopias or to remain. In a flash her intuition told her that this place would be safe. And now the essential question: Is it better to hide the true self and pretend to be mindlessly meek, or is this a situation where one dares reveal the deeps of the entire heart? ... Bliss exchanged friendly glances with Beatrice, and these glances told her everything.

Without words — using only body, face, hand gestures, and expressive eyes — Bliss told us that the people of her country lived in fear. There, a conservative government had restricted freedom and human rights. In order to protest those trends, and to raise awareness about the world's violence against children and women, she had left her country, she had taken a temporary vow of silence. In every city and town she visited, she had been nurtured by women and bothered by men. She traveled by bicycle, she lived outdoors, she slept under the stars. If she accepted food from us, then she would pay with work or with a song.

"Eat, now," said Pateras. "Later we will hear your music. Now you can rest, renew yourself, and listen as I describe our humble paradise."

The Sextopians gaped at Bliss, not only for her natural beauty, but at the way she devoured food with the velocity of a giant and the voracity of an animal half-starved. Pateras called for more food to be brought, and the moment that Bliss's bowls were filled, he began to speak.

"What are we doing here?" he asked. "We are making a place where women and men live in complete freedom; where we are awed and not ashamed that we are sexual beings; where all our creative powers can be unleashed. Here, by mining the mountain of our humanness, we have eliminated the four great obstacles to happiness: boredom, laziness, anxiety, fatigue —"

Strange sounds of a man snoring, reverberating like horse's snorts, interrupted this fine speech. Pateras sauntered to the source of the wood-sawing snores. With filial gentleness, he shook the shoulder of the snoozing centenarian.

"Tiropitas, wake up!" said Pateras.

The old man opened his eyes.

"I can't recall that news, Pateras," said the Village Leader, "but I have a riddle for you. What is long and thin, many women have seen it, it grows when I use it, it shrinks when I carry it around?"

Tiropitas laughed and then he shouted out the answer — "My umbrella!"

Pateras smiled and spoke on.

"Twenty years ago I took a walking trip through Crete, to figure out what to do with the next phase of my life. I was too young to die, too energetic to retire, too old to waste any time. What work should I take up now? Should I be a farmer, a merchant, a traveler, an artist, or a seducer of mothers and maids? ... 'Pateras, you fool!' to myself I said. 'Isn't it time to give up chasing after women? You have more fruitful fields to plow.' ... And after walking the whole day the answer found me: 'My work is to open minds.'"

Applause and cheers answered this remark; Pateras raised his hand for silence, and then spoke on.

"Luck followed me — not luck exactly, but the kind of amazing coincidences that happen whenever you listen to your inner impulses, and dare to do what they suggest. I found some people who were thinking my way: let's leave the old money-maddened world and start something honest and new! ... And so a small group of us founded Sextopias. We have now grown to a community of forty-three women and twenty-one men. To join us you must have no harmful habits, and one great skill: a skill in one of the arts or crafts, or some variety of useful work. Everyone here is at least fifty years old — Plato's age of wisdom — except for our newest member, Penelope. You see, we have been hiding ourselves — by meeting between midnight and dawn only, and by discouraging tourism to Agia Souvlakis. But I fear — we all fear — that soon we will be discovered and forced to flee. And so we agreed to take in Penelope, and to train a younger generation to carry on our joyful work."

Pateras had opened his heart to his friends and to this young stranger. Now he was moved by his own struggles, and thankful for the friends who would listen to the cries of his open heart. Here he paused, cocked his head, and focused all his attention on the song of the cicadas, chirping in the night.

"You know, don't you, about these creatures they call cicadas? ... They plant their eggs in the ground, and when the summer is finished the males sing wildly, knowing they must die. With the parents dead, the future of the species depends on these eggs that lay underground, unborn. That should teach us how our dear Mother Earth wants us to have faith in the future, faith in the dream of life."

Pateras listened more to the cicadas singing, so rapt with happiness that he closed his eyes then drifted in a meditative trance.

Aspasia, the woman who had captured him, rubbed his shoulders with her skilled hands. A lovely woman whose age was impossible to guess, her silk-white hair fell to her waist, and her slender body was not tall, but perfectly proportioned. Her young face, always smiling or about to smile, and her glowing hair, white as sunbeams in a forest glade, made this woman appear noctilucent — luminous at night — like some starry messenger radiant with inner light. After much struggle in her life she had learned to be a healer, a healer of body and soul. What is the secret of her power? As she speaks and listens, the words and silences massage you and you feel: "Here is a person who trusts me, who appreciates the person I now am, who believes in the person I will be." Breathing the pure air of this sacred trust, you come home to your self. The self that had been fragmented and weak grows whole and fills with energy.

Aspasia, still rubbing the shoulders of Pateras, brushed her white hair away from her forehead and face.

"I remember the first moment I fell in love with him," she said. "It was one week ago, when we first met. Pateras and I were sitting on the sand by the water, the moon was full, and I told him what I had never confessed to anyone: that I was terrified of death. He took my hand and answered that death is not our enemy, the real evil is dying. And the antidote to dying, he said, is to keep yourself healthy, and to renew your creativity so that every day of your life you are growing young. And then he told me about the goddess Eos, called Aurora, who fell in love with a young man Tithonus, and carried him back to her couch. Was this goddess blinded by the splendor of her own light? She wished her lover to have a long life, and she forgot that — remember this, wise women! — there are more important things than length."

When she paused, the Sextopians shouted, "Tell us the story, Aspasia!" — and then cheerfully she told.

"Tithonus was beloved by two immortal women, Persephone, Queen of the Underworld, and Eos, also called Dawn, the morning's Queen.

Eos came first; she seized Tithonus and brought him to her palace; she loved him with her rosy-fingers and her gold-streaked lips. The years rolled on happily, until one morning Eos realized that the honeymoon would end as soon as Tithonus grew old. So she begged Zeus to give her mortal lover the gift of eternal life. Zeus granted the request, but Dawn had forgot the most important thing: When you ask for the gift of eternal life, remember to demand eternal youth."

"It's difficult to think so early in the morning," said Aspasia. "Maybe that is the reason that Dawn forgot. But Tithonus grew older and older, and he did not die. His hair turned grey then white, his skin shriveled, his sexual prowess grew weak. Eos at last locked Tithonus in her bedroom, but he escaped, and made his way to a tiny island near the coast of the island that is now called Levkas, in the Ionian Sea. Nights there were cold, and he had only one white hair on his bald head. This single hair had grown so long that Tithonus was able to cover his entire head and body with it, and keep himself warm."

Aspasia looked up at her audience.

"Persephone never forgot him, though, and made certain that every day he received food and drink. And he repaid her — yes, this ancient man who suffered every moment, saved a queen from ravishment and disgrace."

Aspasia walked into the audience and returned holding the hand of her friend. "Ligeia," she said, "can tell us how."

53
WHY GREEK MEN HAVE SLENDER BUTTOCKS

As usual, Ligeia's enormous body was shaking with laughter. She glanced once at the slender Aspasia, she glanced twice at voluptuous Bliss. She slid her hands down the chiton that covered her gargantuan chest and hips.

"I was born in Crete," she said, "but as a teenager, I lived in Paris. When the French women would see a woman of my size, they would say: '*Il y a du beau monde.*' It means, 'There are a lot of people in there.'"

A fit of cackling burst from Ligeia, and the audience could do nothing but laugh along with this jolly soul. With new eyes I observed her: I understood that here was a woman with few inhibitions and many virtues. She was earthy, mirthy, and wise from experience. Always natural and at ease, standing in front of this audience was no different for her than kneading a bread in her kitchen, talking with neighbors and friends. She added common sense and balance to this community of dreamers, who might have otherwise neglected the basic necessities — such as eating and resting and working — in the mad pursuit of their golden dreams.

Kosmos, too, at the same time, had been struck with a novel idea. He tapped my shoulder.

"Thoreau, I just noticed something. Except for you, and Beatrice, and Penelope, and Aspasia, and the blonde Earth-goddess — everyone here is five years to forty years older than me. But each person in Sextopias looks so young! How can you explain that? ... It must be their good posture and good health, and their childlike cheerfulness. And the way they have conquered their fears, the fears that prevent women and men from saying what is inside them, and from doing what they love to do."

Ligeia began her story. Bliss, holding a wooden flute, accompanied the story with a song.

"The Greek philosopher Heraclitus, born in 540 B.C.E., in three words summed up the theory behind ancient tragedy and modern psychology: 'Character is destiny.' Who we are, our personality, determines our future and our fate. You know the legend of the most beautiful woman in history, Helen, the daughter of Leda and Zeus. She spurned her husband Menelaus, and let Paris carry her away. And that love-match set fire to the Greek army and started the ten-year Trojan war. Character is destiny. That was not the first time that Helen had been seized.

"When she was a young girl of ten or twelve years, she was abducted by the fifty-year-old Greek hero Theseus and his friend Pirithoüs. After the kidnapping, the two comrades cast lots, and Helen was won by Theseus, who planned to marry her when she reached the marrying age. They left Helen in the care of a trustworthy old woman, and then they sailed away and landed on a small rocky island in the Ionian Sea. On the black-sand beach they lit a fire and cooked their meal. 'And now, my friend,' said Theseus, 'let's steal a woman for you. Choose any woman in the world, married or not, and when the sun-god drives home his chariot at tomorrow's dusk, that woman will be in your bed.'

"Famous for his foolhardy courage, Theseus had fought in many battles and slain many men. But his heart shuddered when Pirithoüs replied: 'There is only one woman I desire. The Queen of the Underworld, Persephone.'

"Furiously, the East Winds blew. Theseus and Pirithoüs mistook this for a good omen; immediately they loaded their ship and sailed to seize their prize. This plot had been overheard by the aging Tithonus, who gnashed his gums.

'I've lived for two-hundred years,' he whispered. 'The sneeze of a cat could knock me down. What can an old man do?' ... And then the East Wind blew these words into his mind: 'When you were younger the world could be changed only by deception and brute force. Now what makes a difference is not force, but courage and ingenuity. You will never be too old for that.'

"Fifty seals swam close to the island, and then crawled on their shiny flippers onto the black sand. When they shed their skins, fifty naked maidens emerged, and danced on the beach beneath the moonlight. Tithonus seized one of the skins — which gave him complete power over its owner. Instead of ravishing the seal-maid as she expected and feared, he begged her to take a message to the husband of Persephone. She could not speak, so he gave this seal-maid a seashell-tray, and on the tray he placed a knife and covered it with a large stone. Quickly, the bare young maiden jumped into her seal-skin, kissed the old man's cheek, and then swam to deliver the news.

"Down in the Underworld, King Hades, husband of Persephone, understood the warning from Tithonus. He knew that before Theseus was born, the hero's father had placed two gifts for his son underneath a heavy boulder: shoes and a magic sword. So King Hades prepared a fitting welcome.

"'Sit down,' the king told Theseus and his friend. 'Sit down and stay awhile.'

"They sat down on two golden chairs. But they did not stand up. For these were the chairs of forgetfulness. When you sit there you forget everything. You forget your name, your homeland, your family, your past memories, your future goals. Poor Theseus and Pirithoüs! Their bodies did not move; their eyes stared blankly; their minds did not think or wonder or protest.

"For four years they sat there motionless. Four years, until at last the friend of Theseus, the powerful Heracles, came to attempt their rescue. Heracles could not move Pirithoüs at all. But he grasped Theseus, prayed to the gods, and then he pulled with all his strength. Heracles at last succeeded in pulling Theseus off the sticky chair of forgetfulness. But as he pulled, the world trembled with a sound like a thousand cicadas chirping: part of the buttocks of Theseus ripped off and stuck to the seat of the chair.

"And that is why all the Greek men, descendants of Theseus, have slender buttocks. We women chase you and try to grab you, but there's not much down there to grasp on to. Not much on the backside, and just a little twig on the front. Slippery men! Women want to love you and make love to you, but there's so little to hold on to, you always get away!"

The Sextopians laughed and applauded, the cicadas sang wildly, Ligeia and Aspasia embraced. After the applause, Priestos, Kosmos, and Penelope walked through the audience to hand out water, dried fruits, and nuts. Pateras had not moved from his spot; he had been listening simultaneously to Ligeia's story and the chorus of chirping insects.

And now the full-bodied Bliss stood up. She pointed to her tanned toned belly, and then by gesturing expressively she thanked her hosts for the abundant food. Bliss embraced Beatrice, and then Beatrice looked up at the Sextopians.

"We have a story to present," Beatrice said. "With my voice I shall tell the words, and with her body Bliss will show the characters. We will require a knife before we can begin."

Tiropitas, the Village Leader, had come to sit very close to Bliss, and two tears fell from his eyes as he examined her. He removed his wool cap, plucked the lone white hair from his bald head, and handed two gifts to Bliss: his last strand of head-hair, and one ripe pear. Bliss held the pear in her left hand, and then stretched the hair tightly between her teeth and her right hand. With two strokes she cut the pear into four slices. She placed one quarter into her pocket, then handed one piece to Tiropitas, and then tossed the two remaining pear quarters to Beatrice and Penelope.

"Ligeia told the truth," said Beatrice. "Greek men have small behinds. There are many stories to explain that, and some say it happened like this."

As Beatrice told the story, Bliss danced and mimed the story being told.

Athene, the wise and chaste goddess, was sitting on her throne at Mount Olympus, eating ambrosia and fruit. When she looked around for a knife to cut her fruit she could not find one, because all the knives and swords and weapons had been broken yesterday, when the Giants attacked Olympus and were defeated by the goddesses and gods. Athene flew to the workshop of Hephaestus, the god's blacksmith and crafts-man, who had made the first woman out of clay. Despite being ugly and lame, he was married to Aphrodite, and honored for his skills. Outside the workshop, Athene was surprised to see long lines — minor gods and goddesses, satyrs and nymphs — waiting to see the great inventor.

"Welcome, Athene," Hephaestus said. "Come to talk sense to the head of my love-crazy wife? I'm tired of being cuckolded every week, you know."

"That's a job for Hera," Athene tactfully replied. "I've come to ask: Why haven't you started to repair the shields and knives and swords?"

"When Zeus commands me," said Hephaestus, "then I am forced to obey. He asked me to make a substance that would be stickier than hya-cinth honey and stronger than centaur-hoof glue."

"And this new invention of yours," she said, glancing at the crowd out-side the workshop, "has proven to be popular, I see."

"I can't make it fast enough!" Hephaestus answered. "Zeus took the first gallon, and then Hera his wife flew off with a whole barrel, to glue

Zeus to his chair. My dear wife Aphrodite told me that she could make good use of it, but I didn't dare ask how or with whom. Oh, and Poseidon stole a fresh cup of my invention, and murmured as he left: 'Revenge is sticky.'"

Bad-tempered Poseidon waxed angry again: what wrought the sea god's wrath? An innocent young woman named Arnea, ordered to be put to death, had been flung into the sea. Her life was saved by purple-striped ducks, and her name then changed to Penelope. While the ducks pulled her through the water to the shore, Poseidon saw her body under the water, and not her face. But that body was lovely enough to make him fall in love with her, and he sent his servant serpent to fetch her to his water-bed. Penelope rejected his offer. She loved Odysseus, she said, and planned to marry him under the next full moon.

The wedding day came with great rejoicing, followed by the wedding night. In a cottage by the sea the newlyweds enjoyed each other, but while they slept, Poseidon himself rose from the waters and entered the cottage silently. "My wedding gift!" he said with glee. Onto the buttocks of Odysseus he poured the glue made by Hephaestus. And then he raised the groom and stuck his bottom to the bottom of the new bride.

In the morning, Odysseus and Penelope woke up and discovered that they were joined together, and nothing could unbind them. Strands of seaweed on the cottage floor were clues enough to tell them who had perpetrated this puerile prank. For one week, Odysseus and Penelope remained together stuck, backside to backside. Every time he reached out to grab his wife, they spun in circles, round and round, dancing cheek to cheek. Their desire for each other could not be satisfied. Penelope was patient, but Odysseus — whose name means, 'the Angry One' — had already begun to make a daring plan for their escape.

"Where are we going?" asked Penelope.

Odysseus did not answer directly. "For this insult," he said, "I will challenge the god of the sea."

They arrived at the island of Levkas — not far from Odysseus's home in Ithaca — and then they climbed the outermost white cliff, the one that Sappho would make famous by the flying leap that cured her love. With Penelope stuck behind him, Odysseus jumped off the edge. And surely they would have drowned, but Athene came to the rescue. She had grasped the one long hair of Tithonus, and stretched it out from the small island — where old Tithonus lay — all the way to the coast of

Levkas.

Had Athene been able to keep still, the leaping lovers would have fallen right in the middle of this hair, and been cut precisely. But Aphrodite sent her son Eros to shoot an arrow at Athene. The arrow grazed her arm; she sighed for a moment, and as she fell in love with Odysseus she pulled the hair just slightly to the right. "What a handsome man!" she said. "There are times I wish I were a goddess of love and desire, instead of the dispenser of conflict and peace."

Odysseus and Penelope fell on the hair and were sliced on their hind-quarters — separated at last! But like baloney at a quality delicatessen, the buttocks of Odysseus had been sliced thin. The newlyweds swam to the shore and then made love for two nights and days.

Odysseus survived the anger of Poseidon, and lived a long happy life with Penelope. And the aging Tithonus? ... Persephone asked the gods to pity him, and the gods agreed. Zeus transformed the old man into a young cicada. On warm nights you can hear him chirping his hate-songs and lovesongs about women: about the foolishness of Eos, about the faithfulness of Persephone.

The cicadas chirped louder and louder, and after a minute of silence from the audience, the Sextopians thanked Beatrice and Bliss with laughter, and then applause. From the world of his deep concentration, Pateras came back to us.

"Thank you, Ligeia and Beatrice and Bliss," he said, "for enriching us and amusing us with your stories. Tonight I have learned something important: We need the wisdom of the old folks to remind us what is essential — what in our culture must be preserved. And we need ideas from young persons, to show us what we never could imagine, and to lead us to new possibilities."

Kosmos, thinking of new possibilities, swaggered confidently toward Bliss.

"What nights we could have together!" he said.

He tried to place his arm around her shoulders but before he could complete the hug she grasped the arm and pulled it off her muscular shoulder. Kosmos, undiscouraged, now tried to impress the young beauty with brags about his sexpertise.

"Making love with me is the ultimate spiritual experience," he said.

Terribly did her eyes flash. As Bliss glared, the man explained:

"Yes, the ultimate spiritual experience. I will be in bliss, and you will be at one with the Kosmos."

A loud shout resounded from the Sextopian men. They surrounded Kosmos. Pateras told him why.

"Kosmos," said the father to the son. "Nothing could be simpler than the vision at the heart of our community: this is a place where women can be safe in every way: physically, artistically, emotionally. Here we permit no *kamakee*."

Kamakee! In the Greek dictionary the word means "hunting for fish with spears", but on the streets a new meaning has emerged. *Kamakee* is a sport practiced by vain Greek men; the object of the game is to seduce as many tourist women as they can.

The Sextopian men began pouring a gallon of molasses onto the head, bare arms, and chiton of Kosmos, and then covered these splotches of molasses with furry leaves of sage. At first, Kosmos accepted the treatment stoically, but then he turned to his father to gripe.

"I cannot believe my ears and eyes," Kosmos cried out. "Is this not Sextopias? Am I not permitted to enjoy and express a healthy interest in sex?"

The Sextopian women seemed peacefully delighted by this new conflict, but the Sextopian men shouted at Kosmos, until Pateras calmed and quieted the ruckus with one raise of his hand.

"This is Sextopias," said Pateras, "where every man has the right to his own opinions, no matter how ridiculous they are."

More shouting and arm-waving came from the Sextopian men. Some demanded that Kosmos should apologize; others wanted him banished for a night, for a week, for a month, or forevermore.

Pateras raised his hand, pointed to Kosmos, and then calmly spoke.

"We believe he has blundered. He thinks that what he has done is good and right. For this kind of disagreement there is one resolution, and only one."

Priestos rolled forward like a circus tumbler and then shouted to the crowd.

"Tell us, Pateras, tell us!"

The hand of Pateras fell gently on the shoulder of his son.

"Let him speak."

54
I Must! ... I Must! ...
I Must Increase My Lust!

ASPASIA AND LIGEIA BANGED on bongo drums, while the merry men of Sextopias — nude from the ankles up — formed a circle, as if they were about to dance. Instead, Priestos guided them through a series of pelvic exercises, where the men rotated their hips as they shouted together:

"I must! ... I must! ... I must increase my lust!"

Kosmos pulled me from the circle, with a face that pleaded for advice. He had a fondness for getting into trouble, and a genius for getting out of it.

"I've got more problems than Hamlet," he said. "For twenty years I dreamed of finding my paradise, Sextopias. And what happens when that beautiful moment arrives at last? I eat the apple of honesty, the Sextopians tar and feather me with molasses and sage leaves, and then they talk about throwing me out! ... Tell me, Thoreau, the solution to the degeneration gap: what can we do when two systems of morality collide? And how can I make these old folks understand my young ideas?"

"Kosmos," I said, "Beatrice once told me the one infallible technique for solving all problems in human relationships: 'Be respectful and be sincere.'"

Kosmos waved his hand.

"Be sincere? ... That's good advice for men like you, Thoreau — you're young and good-looking, and women help you because they love your eyes, not your ideas. And hundred-year-old codgers like Tiropitas can afford to be sincere: people care for him because he's half-a-step away from death, and they pity his helplessness. But men my age can't make friends or lovers with one smile: we live alone, we fight the world's madness that wants to crush our creative powers, we survive by cunning and ingenuity. Sincerity got me into this mess, and more sincerity will bury me up to my neck. ... I see it now: there's only one way out. Be bold! Be daring! Choose the road that takes the most audacity!"

His eyes sparkled as a plan caught fire in his vigorous mind.

"Learn from Odysseus: again and again and again, his wild stories saved his life, or persuaded someone to help him to sail closer to his blessed home. What strange powers lie in these simple sounds created by the human voice! Say some words and a beautiful woman kicks you, say slightly different words and she welcomes you into her bed! The right story at the right moment makes all the difference between a rupture and a rapture."

The Sextopian men finished their gyrating exercises, then they stretched their arms and legs. After drinking water and fresh juice, the men and women gathered in a semi-circle around the scheming body of Kosmos. With the utmost animation in his face, body, and hands, he began his spirited defense.

"Ah, women!" he said. "Sleeping and waking, I am thinking about women all the time. No saint has ever worshiped his god with the whole-hearted passion that I devote myself to the female of the species."

When he paused to take stock of his audience, the old Tiropitas stepped forward and spoke.

"We know what you're thinking, Kosmos," he said. "Every man's face is an open book. Be a poet, and tell your heart so crisply that I could write it on an almond shell. Then we will be able to remember it, talk about it, pass it on."

"I can say it in a poem, Tiropitas" said Kosmos. "A poem that I will sing for you. It is called: 'Men Think.'"

> "Your whims are as trite as a duchess,
>   Your heart is as sweet as the salts,
>   Yet your breasts are so lovely and luscious —
>   We'll forgive all your personal faults."

Women tittered, men stirred the molasses, Kosmos tried again. This time he sang a bawdy limerick.

> "A sexy Athenian hetaera
>   Described her bravura in bed terra:
>   'Each voluptuous night
>   When we blow out the light,
>   I remove all his clothing, et cetera.'"

The women laughed, the men grumbled, Kosmos bowed at the waist. Slowly and deliberately, he searched the audience for its most unpersuadable members. Each time he found a pair of doubting eyes — eyes that reflected a heart closed to him and his ideas — he peered into those eyes with a brave look that said: 'We know we disagree, now let's see if we can make a bridge.' His voice — whether he sang, spoke, or whispered — had music in it, always expressing far more than the words alone.

"I am sure, Sextopians, that you have heard it said: 'To understand all is to forgive all.' ... First try to understand me, and then you can forgive or condemn. Let me tell you how I came to believe the nonsense that I now believe."

The audience, made more sympathetic by the insight about understanding and forgiving, moved a few steps closer to Kosmos.

"When I was twenty-years old — when a youth has the strength of a man but the sense of a young boy — a spiritual crisis made me ache all over, body and soul. At that age I was roasting with desire. I fell in love with every young woman I met, but not one of them would have me. Not for a lover, not for a brother, not for a friend. How did I feel? Angry, frustrated, lonely, humiliated. My stomach burned like it was filled with rotten apples. What caused my problems? ... Women! Could I give up women? ... I tried, but then I realized that instead of thinking about women, I was spending all day and night thinking about how to give them up. In spite of those frumpy clothes in fashion thirty-five years ago, everywhere I turned I saw tantalizing bodies, heartbreaking faces, mind-muddling eyes."

The Sextopians were listening with complete attention. Penelope — who now grasped that Kosmos was about to leap from honest self-revelation to fantastic improvising — laughed and shook her head.

"One morning," said Kosmos, "when I was so desperate to solve my problem, I considered becoming a priest at Mount Athos — I got a letter in the mail from my Uncle Astayologos. It included a brochure with a photo of an 'uninhabited island' named Grabthos. 'Kosmos!' I said to myself. 'Peace and solitude! This is exactly what you need!' So I kissed my mother and father good-bye, packed my bag with just the bare necessities for survival, and then I walked from my home town to the coast. An old man rowed me across the waters; when we parted he kissed my hand and then swore an oath to Saint Souvlakis that he would come every week with supplies and food. As I took my first steps on the sands of Grabthos I experienced a world pristine, as silent as a dream. Here, I thought, I will solve all my confusions relating to the impenetrable world of sex."

Eager to hear the outcome, the Sextopian audience stepped even closer to Kosmos, while Penelope bit her tongue and did everything she could to keep herself from laughing out loud. Kosmos had lowered his voice a little, to add to the suspense.

"Yes, those first moments on the uninhabited island of Grabthos were so splendidly quiet, I imagined that I had been dropped onto another planet deep in space. Birds twittered unseen in the tree branches, the sea lapped the sandy shore, my own heart beat with excitement like a muffled drum. Suddenly the sound of running footsteps! ... 'What hungry animal will be sprinting from the forest?' I wondered. 'And will he devour me — and explain why this island is uninhabited! — or can he be made peaceable and tame?'"

Kosmos paused to sip some water from the cup provided by Penelope.

"Out of the woods a young Greek man appeared, running in my direction. Moments later, four young women, barely dressed, chased after the young man. Before my astonished jaw could fall open, from the opposite direction I saw a young man running after a pack of four women dressed like librarians. Waving my arms I shouted 'Stop!', and to my surprise the first man did stop, and ran in place before me.

"Under his nose I waved the deceitful brochure. 'This says,' I complained, 'that Grabthos is an uninhabited island!' The young man, dressed in a white lab coat, answered without blinking: 'Oh, that old thing. There is a slight mistake in that. It should say 'uninhibited island.' ... Before I could reply, he fled fearfully from the lovely women who pursued him with laughter and screams."

The Sextopians were smiling now, and Kosmos carried on.

"You see, this was an island dedicated to the study of non-human sexuality. A zany philanthropist had bought a beat-up boat, and then rebuilt it to look like an ark. He used this vessel to populate the island with almost every living creature that flies, and runs, and crawls, and swims, and slithers — at least one male and one female of each species. Researchers had been hired to observe and report their strange and extraordinary feats of sex. For eight wild weeks I lived on Grabthos Island. I studied the mating practices of hundreds of creatures: fish, insects, reptiles, birds, and animals. What I learned there about sex would fill a dozen encyclopedias!"

Tiropitas bit the air near Kosmos's ear, and then jumped into the tale.

"I know it, I have been there," the old man said. "I searched there for the river-loving big-mouthed mammals who stimulate writers, artists, dancers, and music-makers. The Hippopota-Muses."

Certain that his audience was thirsty for details, Kosmos paused to drink more water from the cup.

"Why do you think that the bull is pictured everywhere on the vases you find in Crete? ... Thousands of years ago, the entire ancient Minoan civilization on Crete worshiped the bull for its procreative powers. The potent male bull can ejaculate almost eighty times in six hours. And of all the animals in Greece, the bull has the longest panpipe: a phallus which measures thirty-six inches long. Twice as long as mine, my friends."

Priestos waved his hand.

"Kosmos, that's a lot of bull. Go on, I'm sure there's more."

Kosmos stretched out his hands like a measuring tape, as high as his head.

"The bulls are nothing compared to the elephants I have observed. The elephant organ is twice as big — its length is six feet! And hence his name 'pachyderm', which comes from two Greek words meaning 'thick skin.'"

"Bravo, Kosmos!" shouted Tiropitas.

That blessing from the venerated Village Leader gave Kosmos more than enough encouragement to carry on.

"Once — these eyes saw it and will swear it's true! — during the mating of two praying mantises, I watched with horror as the ungrateful female bit off the head of the male. And what do you think she did as the torso of that decapitated male-fool — thanks to a reflex action — continued to thrust into her and give her pleasure? ... Calmly she chewed up his head! ... And I named his remains, 'Kosmosaki' — little Kosmos!"

This story brought tears of laughter to the audience's eyes.

"It's funny," said Kosmos, "but don't miss the great truth hidden inside! Think, now. Does the male mantis know his fate beforehand, or does he suspect nothing? ... You can't imagine how that question tormented me. If he knew he was going to copulate and die in the same act, then is sex with a voracious female something so marvelous it's worth losing your head about? ... At least I now knew why the insect folded his forelegs and spent most of his life praying, or pretending to pray."

The Sextopians applauded, Kosmos nodded, and told on.

"Another day I learned how a male spider lures a female to his lair: he bribes her with the gift of a neatly-wrapped fly. But after the act of mating, he takes back his gift!"

Penelope shouted out, "Did you also name that stingy spider, Kosmosaki?"

Kosmos smiled.

"And one night I watched the method of another species of male spider: first he lulls his female partner to sleep by pressing rhythmically on the strands of his web. And then he mates with her while she sleeps."

Penelope's head-nod and gestures made the crowd laugh, and her words brought laughter more.

"Is it any wonder," she said, "why so many women seek sexual satisfaction outside the home?"

Kosmos stroked her hair.

"And after studying that spider, the next day I bought a *bouzouki,* and taught myself how to play. And then I devoted myself to practicing and perfecting the one art that wins the war between the sexes for both sides: the art of seduction."

Penelope kissed Kosmos and the Sextopians cheered.

"So now you see," he said, "how I became sexually lopsided. I tried to forget completely about women, but twisted by a wrench from the toolbox of Fate, I ended up thinking about women all the time!"

The tale-teller paced back and forth as the Sextopians discussed his story. At last Pateras raised his hand.

"Kosmos," said the father, "I've listened to your apology; I've heard comments about it from our community; I have been asked to ruminate on these ideas, and to elucidate to everyone where your ideas and my ideas diverge."

Pateras made himself taller by standing up on top of a wooden fish-crate.

"Lots of people mistakenly believe that all your psychological problems will be solved if you give free rein to your sexual impulses. Sexual freedom is one leg of the old goat, but to stand up erect he needs three legs more: sexual responsibility; the courage to be truthful; and the beautiful fire inside. We have heard Kosmos, king of *kamakee,* explain how he devotes himself to the double-pleasure of getting and then forgetting. What we practice here is the two-fold bliss of giving and forgiving. We are for sex, of course, but never sex alone. We live for the pure joy of deep and lasting relationships. Every Sextopian relationship is a coin with sex stamped on the tail side, and a head side inscribed with Love. And what have we Sextopians learned about love, that we would teach to every womanizing war-mongering man? ... Love does not dominate, it cultivates."

Kosmos was the first one to applaud these wise words, and then he raised his hand and spoke.

"Before you decide 'Kosmos stay', or 'Kosmos leave'," he said, "I have one more story to tell. In my own town, in Dembacchae, I am so far above the average man — in wit, in learning, in vision, in vitality — I am like a god. Here, in this community, I'm the kid wearing a dunce cap who sits in the corner of the class. Call me a fool, but don't throw me out for that! Remember: Every idiot needs a village, and every village needs an idiot. Think what a triumph it would be for your philosophy of optimism, if you could take an incorrigible chauvinist like me and then train him to be a whole man!"

"Tell us the one-more story you promised, Kosmos," said Tiropitas. "We don't need more philosophers here. We need clowns who can make us laugh."

Kosmos took a deep breath, winked at me, then spoke to the Sextopians.

"You recall, of course, that the Trojan War began when Helen cuc-adoo-dle-doo-kolded her husband Menelaus. She fled to Troy with Paris, a Trojan Prince. After ten years of bloody war, the Greeks beat the Trojans by pretending to be defeated. Troy surrendered, and Helen was taken home to Sparta, where her husband Menelaus stood waiting, his sword drawn, ready to kill her for her infidelity. When Helen was brought before her husband, the dramatists tell how she addressed him calmly, with a crafty speech. The gods, she said, crazed her with passion for another man, and who could resist the power of the gods? ... But what really happened is not the way they tell it in the books. Helen saved herself without words: when she met her husband, she smiled like heaven, and let her dress fall to the earth. And when that mortal man saw Helen's immortal face and divine body, he dropped his sword, embraced her, and made her his Queen again."

As Kosmos paused to let his moral penetrate, I heard the almost-silent sounds of bodies moving in a shadowy section of the Sextopian beach.

Kosmos added one more coda to his tale.

"Hundreds of years later, the power of Beauty struck again. This time the woman's name was Phyrne, a ravishing hetaera whose profession had made her famous and rich. Her perfect body had been the model for *Aphrodite*, the renowned statue sculpted by Praxiteles. But now Phyrne was charged with impiety, and about to be sentenced to death or banishment. After pleading to judges who were prejudiced against her, Phyrne's lawyer —who loved her passionately — found the best defense. He introduced new evidence: he opened her robe and displayed her body to the court. The judges reversed their earlier opinion, and now proclaimed that Phyrne was innocent."

Kosmos stood up tall then let his chiton fall, and displayed his body to his listeners.

"And therefore, fellow Sextopians, I pray that you, as well, will be so moved by the manly beauty of this body and its pleasure-giving instrument, that you will vote to let me stay."

After a brief silence, Penelope looked at Kosmos as she waved her hands.

"Where is the instrument?" she said.

Using his two hands like a girdle, he gripped the bottom of his belly and depressed his paunch.

"Ah! Here," he said, "is the paradox of becoming human. My father asks me to stir the stewpot of my sexploits by adding a pinch of Love. But how? ... You can't learn how to love until you find the right woman, and you can't find the right woman until you learn how to love."

Kosmos raised his right hand.

"During this heavenly night, if I have told you even one untruth, then may a Zeus-thrown thunderbolt strike my manhood! May the bastard-god Antieros make me never fall in love again! And may a horde of man-eating gypsies attack me and slander my good name!"

The centenarian Tiropitas stepped forward.

"That's it!" he shouted. "That's the important news I came to tell you!

"Tell us, Tiropitas," said Pateras. "Tell us, *parakalo*."

"The news! The news! Ten gypsies arrived at the house of Penelope! They pulled carrots from the garden and then ate these sweet roots as if they'd never tasted food before! And when I looked at these wild, ravenous women, I prayed to the ninety gods of Crete: 'Make me ten years younger and ten years stronger, so I can frolic in the flowers with these magnificent maids!' ... With a hopeful heart I waited for the miracle, but the miracle did not appear."

From near the cooking fire, Ligeia yelled: "What happened to the dinner I had simmering in the pot?" And then we heard Tiropitas's golf cart start then stall, and the sounds of a scuffle and shouts.

Two desperate women ran across the beach, smack into the naked Kosmos. He gripped one woman in each of his arms, and as their fists pummeled his broad back and shoulders, their tongues pounded him with streams of ancient curses and modern profanities.

5 5
A Gypsy Love Song

CALM AS A MOUNTAIN stood Kosmos, holding the waist of a wild woman in each of his brawny arms. The women, swearing and shouting, pummeled his back with their fists. Calmly and cheerfully he held on, with just the right amount of strength that would avoid hurting them and at the same time prevent their escape.

"Power," said Kosmos, "is like holding an egg in the palm of your hand. If you hold too tightly then you crush the egg, and if you hold too loosely then you drop the egg and it breaks."

The Sextopians, fearing the surprise invasion by more strangers, scrambled into their *"Xenos!"* drill. Six men and women dressed as court jesters encircled me and Beatrice, danced around us, and then sang a song they called *The Ultimate Question: Heaven, Reincarnation, or Hell?*

"The theories of life after death are a mess!
Though I've studied the latest reports,
On my deathbed I do not know how I should dress —
Is it white robes, or dog leash, or shorts?"

A conch shell blew to calm the chaos. Penelope and Bliss, with soothing words and gentle strength, separated the wild women from the arms of Kosmos. As the light from the fire flickered on their tanned faces I recognized my gypsy friends, Meli and Romantza.

Pateras spoke to the gypsy women in his deep calming voice.

"You can run away now," he said, "and hide like mice in a field of corn. Or you can stay with us and enjoy good food and music and the cheer of friends. We will help you, whichever road you choose."

The two gypsies raised their heads, their eyes brightened, their anger melted into relief.

"Father!" they shouted together.

It was clear to everyone who observed this reunion that Pateras was not the biological dad of the two gypsies. Months ago, when he walked them to safety in the mountains, he had earned their daughterly affection with his humor, his paternal care, his valuable advice.

Meli and Romantza hugged Pateras, then held his hand, and then chattered like children as they gazed at his protecting eyes.

"Priestos," shouted Pateras, "bring some food for our two friends, and for the friends of our friends. And bring me the biggest sack on this beach."

Greedily the famished women ate the food, and happily they laughed at the old man's humorous remarks. He raised an empty burlap sack.

"Sextopians!" shouted Pateras. "Is all life sacred and is every human being an important member of our family?"

"Yes!" shouted the Sextopians.

"Have we transcended the love of money and an obsessive attachment to things?"

"Yes! Yes!"

"For the betterment of our community, can we give up — for six months — the enjoyment of sexual delights?"

The Sextopians almost said yes, but quickly realized that Pateras had fooled them once again. They laughed and shouted "No! Never! Impossible!"

"That," said Pateras, "I am thrilled to hear. Now, let us help to lift the world off the shoulders of these courageous young women and their friends."

Eagerly, the Sextopians swarmed Pateras, and in minutes the sack that he had been holding overflowed with paper Euros. Romantza and Meli accepted the gift with tearful eyes. Bliss and Penelope and Beatrice joined the two gypsies, and the five women drank tea together, and talked excitedly.

Priestos cartwheeled across the sand. This body-in-motion signaled that now was the time of night when the Sextopians would divide themselves into small groups of two, three, four, five, or six. Each group would decide what they wanted to do together: some held hands and talked, others played games, some practiced a dramatic play, others sang songs or told stories near the fire.

While the Sextopians learned and played, Pateras strolled around the beach and spoke with anyone who needed the good sense of his talk. Sometimes he would tell jokes, sometimes he would say nothing and listen sympathetically, sometimes he would give praise, advice, encouragement. Pateras acted as a father, brother, psychiatrist, leader, matchmaker, and teacher all rolled into one.

"Nikos," he told a white-haired man. "Can't you see that Hagfa is in love with you? I could sing all 158 verses of the Greek National Anthem before some men make their moves. I know that you are shy as a chipmunk, but before loneliness drives her to Laertes, go and tell her everything you feel."

He advised a troubled woman: "Personal history repeats itself through our outer actions, until we transform the depths of our inner selves. If you're not happy, then your question should be: 'What actions am I going to take, today, to make certain that my tomorrows do not repeat my yesterdays?'"

When the cheerful energy in the small groups reached its peaks, Pateras blew the conch shell: now it was time again for an activity where everyone together would participate.

"What do we want to play now?" shouted Pateras. He knew the answer, but he loved how it gave them energy when he pretended not to know.

"Queen of the Hill!" shouted the Sextopians.

Pateras paused to examine their gleaming eyes, and then, slowly, he nodded 'Yes!'

The Sextopians cheered then set to work preparing for the game. Some players built a tall mound of sand. Other players made special headbands with blinders: whoever wore them could see only straight ahead. And some players ripped up bedsheets and cut them to make sashes from the strips of cloth.

The women chose Irene to be the first Queen. Her chiton was lowered to her waist, and her breasts were covered with a silken sash. Her role in the game was simple: she would stand on top of the sand hill and try to remain there for as long as she could. At the bottom of the hill, all the Sextopian women would dance around in circles, as they guarded her from the charging men.

The men would be dressed in headbands that partially covered their eyes and served as blinders, keeping their field of vision straight ahead. In addition, each man would also be adorned with nine strips of cloth tied in slip knots around his waist, arms and legs. The long strips of cloth, dangling down, would be easy for any woman to grab and untie.

Playing was simple. One at a time, the men would be called to dash up the sand hill to try to reach Irene. If the guarding women grabbed any one of the cloth-strips and pulled them off, then that man was considered captured: he was required to stop, and then to go to a quiet part of the beach with the woman who had seized his cloth. If the man somehow reached Irene, then he would try to pull off the sash that covered her breasts, before one of the women pulled off any of the nine cloth-strips that dangled from his body like seaweed strands.

With a wild shout the game began. Man after man was captured quickly by the laughing women guards. Before I could try, a warm hand seized my hand.

"Come with me, dear, there is something terrible and wonderful that I want to show you."

Beatrice took my hand then led me to a quiet section of the Sextopian beach. We knelt down close beside each other. By the light from a tall burning torch, we observed a small funnel-shaped hole in the beach-sand.

"This is what happens to a man," she whispered, "who falls in love with the wrong woman, and glides mindlessly into her lair."

A red ant — unaware of the immanent danger — crawled around the rim of the sand-pit, then fell along the slippery sides. Now sensing his predicament, he attempted to ascend the sandy slope to safety. Suddenly a spray of sand shot up from the pit's center; the ant lost his footing and slid down. Blink-quick, an insect hiding under the sand at the pit's bottom leaped out and wrapped its claws and jaws around the ant. First the predator sucked the life-juice from the poor victim, and then — when nothing remained except a hollow shell — she tossed the brittle corpse outside of the pit. Shoulders touching, Beatrice and I watched amazed as these ant lions — once, twice, thrice — devoured unsuspecting prey.

Meanwhile, back at the hill, all the men had been easily captured, and there would be a short break before selecting the next Queen. The Sextopians gathered around the gypsy women, Meli and Romantza, who stood up on the mound of sand. Pateras raised his hand.

"Our friends have told me that they want to say good-bye to us with an old gypsy melody," he said. "It is called *Camo-Gillie,* which means, *Love-Song.*"

Harmonizing divinely, Meli and Romantza sang two choruses, first in the gypsy-lingo, and then — just before Beatrice grasped my hand — in words that we could understand.

> *"Pawnie birks, My men-engni shall be;*
> *Yackors my dudes, Like ruppeney shine:*
> *Atch meery chi! Ma jal away:*
> *Perhaps I may not dick tute, kek komi —*
> *Perhaps I may not dick tute, kek komi.*

> "I'd choose as pillows for my head,
> Those snow-white breasts of thine;
> I'd use as lamps to light my bed,
> Your eyes like silver shine:
> O lovely maid, reject me not, Nor leave me in my pain:
> For it may never be my fate, To see thy face again —
> For it may never be my fate, To see thy face again."

Pateras gave some last instructions: Meli and Romantza would be led by Aspasia and Ligeia first to Penelope's house to gather the others, and then to Ligeia's hotel. The next morning Pateras and Penelope would meet them there, and with all minds working together they would plan the road ahead.

The Sextopians returned to their joys. A new Queen of the Hill was elected, and my heart skipped three beats as she released my hand and joined the game. The women surrounded Beatrice, and then her chiton was lowered and her great chest covered with a golden sash.

How those older men would have loved to reach her and procure the prize! Man after man tried to ascend the sandy hill, but far from his desired goal, each man was captured by a woman laughing with delight.

Only one man had a chance. The blinders were attached around my forehead, and the strips of cloth — usually nine in number — were doubled because of my youth and speed. Beatrice stood on the sandy hillock, smiling at me bright beams of encouragement.

The conch shell blew and the Sextopians shouted: "Go!"

I faked one step to the left, and then another step to the right — waves of women grabbed for me then fell — and then straight up the middle I dashed and stood before the Queen. I seized that swatch of cloth that covered her, but as I gripped she smiled at me so tenderly I paused, a prisoner of her eyes. What sweet power froze my hand? My hand felt stiff, but the remainder of me melted as she sang.

> "Gather my rosebuds, while ye may
> Banish those duds, who dare delay."

The flourishing hand of Beatrice swiped an agile jerk — swiftly she snatched one of my dangling cloth-strips so that its slip-knot fell untied. She waved the cloth-strip in the air above her head. The Queen was safe, the men groaned disappointedly, the women wildly cheered.

I knew that my next action would be against the rules. But I imagined that the test of every community is the way it handles thoughtful disobedience. I lifted Beatrice in my arms.

I held her in front of me — one arm under her back and the other arm under her bent knees — just like the night I had carried her back to her hotel. Beatrice laughed as she was swept into the air. Our joys were deeply felt but brief. To rescue their captured Queen, forty women rushed up the hill, tackled me vigorously, and then piled on top.

The conch shell blew and Pateras shouted something at the mob. Soon the Sextopian women climbed off my back and then brushed sand-grains off my chiton. I stood up and I looked around me. Beatrice looked radiant, beautiful beyond words. The Sextopians stood smiling and silent, as Pateras was about to remind me, cheerfully, the strict rules of the game.

After two snorts and a sniffle, all eyes turned from my face to the face of a man standing alone. Aglow in the languish of loneliness, the brave face of Kosmos quivered, and then burst into a chain of heart-rending sobs.

56
THE THREE SEXES

KOSMOS SOBBED like a child who'd lost his favorite toy. His cries were inarticulate to everyone — except Penelope.

"You love this place," said Penelope, after Kosmos emitted a beast-like moan.

Kosmos nodded, sobbed more, and then Penelope translated again.

"You want to stay here, learn our games, protect us from strangers, and help to build our community."

When Kosmos nodded that this was exactly right, the Sextopians laughed riotously at Penelope's ability to read the mind of her man.

Tiropitas, the old Village Leader, threw his arm around the broad-shouldered Kosmos.

"A woman crying is as common as a winter rain," he said. "Every day I see women crying, but I'm immune. It doesn't make me feel, it makes me think: 'How can I help her to stop?' ... But a man weeping is like a clown at the traveling circus, it's a rare event! Either it breaks my heart to see it, or it's the funniest thing on Earth."

Pateras raised his hand. When silence came he spoke to Kosmos and to everyone.

"In many ways, dear Kosmos, you are a perfect example of all that we despise in modern males. You think about two things only: art, and having sex. Create or procreate. You boast about your amorous conquests, you relish promiscuity, you worship 'the female of the species' because you fail to see each woman as an individual unique. Like a dog chasing its own tail, your life revolves around the quest for sexual pleasures without end. As if a woman needs a hound to hunt her, or a cocksure master to treat her as a slave! ... Here we think differently. A woman needs a relationship with a partner who treats her with honesty, respect, and complete equality."

With his heel, Pateras drew a line in the beach sand.

"Now we shall vote. If you approve of welcoming Kosmos into our community, then say 'yes' by stepping across this line."

Penelope was the first to cross the line, followed by Pateras himself.

"I don't understand this at all," said Kosmos. "You see my whole heart and my wild mind — and still you want me here?"

Pateras looked sincerely at his son.

"We are very strong," he said. "Your folly cannot hurt us because we understand it from the inside. At times, all of us here have squandered time and neglected to care for our health: Time and Health, the two most precious human gifts! We have been lost on the road of conformity; we have swallowed propaganda from the School for Selfishness. All of us have suffered like that poor hero in Apuleius's novel: we have wasted our lives so blatantly that the gods transformed us into a bleating ass. Live with us, Kosmos, and you will begin to 'Know thyself'. That new awareness will plant a seed of loving kindness. And that seed will change you, and open you to a new way of being and a new life."

Kosmos shook his head with gratitude, then gazed at his father with the utmost admiration and pride.

"My mother is harder than a rock," he murmured. "But my father is as tender as a child."

Bedusa stepped over the line in the sand, and then Tiropitas and Priestos followed. In less than one minute, all the remaining Sextopians charged across.

"I'm in!" Kosmos shouted, falling to his knees. "Dearest Penelope, I'm in!"

Tightly, Penelope hugged her exhilarated man.

"Kosmos," she said. "Take this. Here's how we welcome our new members. Wear this hat with these long ears sticking from the top. It comes from a story about King Midas: to punish Midas for his bad judgment, Apollo turned his ears into the ears of a donkey."

"I will wear it proudly!" Kosmos said. "And whenever a woman speaks I will try to let these ears remind me to listen, to listen with my whole self."

Bedusa stood up on a wooden crate.

"Penelope," she said. "Last night you promised that tonight you would tell us a story about Love."

Penelope drank water from a clear glass, then glanced at Kosmos.

"This is a tale about how and why two people have a passion for each other. My story, called *The Three Sexes,* has been told by Plato in the guise of Aristophanes. "

"Listen, men!" shouted. Tiropitas. "The story is about you!"

When the Sextopians had gathered close to Penelope she smiled, and then her sultry voice began to speak.

Long ago on this Greek soil there were not two sexes but three. It happened like this. When the god Hermes saw Ares and Aphrodite trapped under the net, he said: "I will give anything in Earth, Hades, or Olympus to be in Ares's place, stuck in that gorgeous woman's arms!" Aphrodite heard this compliment, then rewarded the flattery of Hermes by spending a night with him. The son born to them was named Hermaphroditus, who bathed every day in a fountain guarded by a nymph named Salmacis. Salmacis fell in love with Hermaphroditus; the foolish man rejected her offers of love. And so she threw herself into his arms, clasped him with all her might, and then begged the goddesses to make the two of them into one body. In one flashing thunderbolt, the goddesses granted her prayer.

So it came to pass that there were three sexes, the man-man, the woman-woman, and the woman-man. But they were not built like women and men today. Each human body had two heads and two faces, four eyes and four ears, four hands and four feet, and two mystical organs of propagation instead of our usual one. They could walk upright, or walk backwards or forwards, and when they wanted to move fast they ran at great speeds by rolling in a circle on their hands and feet, as easily as tumblers in a circus perform cartwheels. These humans were far more powerful than women and men today. Terrible was their might and strength, and the thoughts in their heads were great. The gods on Olympus worried that these humans would attack them, the way the Giants had once attacked.

"What can we do about these insolent creatures?" asked Ares. "We cannot let them continue as they are, arrogant and unrestrained."

"We can't kill them," Athena answered, "or else there would be nobody to worship us and make sacrifices."

There was much discussion about how to manage these three sexes of super-humans. At last, Zeus discovered a way. "I will cut these creatures in half," he said. "which will help the gods in two ways. It will increase the number of persons who can worship us, and it will diminish the power of each one. And what if, after that, they continue to challenge and to disrespect the gods? Then I will slice them again so they'll be thin as a strip of parchment, and need to hop along on one leg."

So Zeus used his thunderbolts to cut the humans in half, as easily as a strand of hair slices through a hard-boiled egg. Apollo healed these divided humans, then tied up the loose skin at the navel.

Zeus had thought far ahead, but there was one important consequence that he did not anticipate. After the slicing, the two halves longed to embrace each other. Those men who had once been man-man, sought other men; women who had been woman-woman looked for other women; and the hermaphrodites — the woman-man beings — looked for members of the opposite sex. And whenever one half would find the other half that she or he had been searching for, what wonder and amazement filled their souls!

So you see how the ancient desire for one another has been planted deep inside us, to reunite us with our original nature, to make one out of two, and to heal the state of humankind. Each of us is always searching for her or his other half. That is because human nature was originally one and we were a whole, and the desire and pursuit of the whole is called Love. And if we are friends with the god Love — if we understand his ways and stay at peace with him — then we will find our own true love. How rarely that happens in our present love-blind age!

Penelope's story brought clapping, laughter and sobs. The sobs burst from those men and women who had loved and lost, or never loved at all.

Irene, the loudest and saddest of the criers, wept on the shoulder of her grandfather, Pateras. He listened to her tale, let her cry a hundred tears, then gave her strength by speaking golden truisms and diamond truths.

Irene sniffled, wiped the tears from her face, and then stood up on the wooden crate and sang.

"Set has the moon and the Pleiades stars
    Silent the midnight sky
Venus embraces her roamin' Mars —
    Alone, alone I lie.

"O where is the man I dream about?
    Lying where tambourines played,
    by the sleepless kisses and swelling shouts
    of cute Egyptian maids?

"Or blessed on an isle where Love unfurls?
Where never a storm has blown
to frighten the heart of the good Greek girls —
I lie alone, alone ...
I lie alone, alone."

Calmer now, she stepped down from the crate. Without another word she kissed my cheek with the sweetest tenderness, and then she walked on the sandy beach towards the town of Agia Souvlakis. As I took a step to follow her, I bumped into Pateras. He threw his arm around my shoulders.

"Thoreau," he said. "Irene is going back to the house of Penelope. She came here for you, hoping you would love her and her only. Now she understands the way things are, and she is just beginning to accept them. Is she the one, Thoreau?"

"The one?" I asked. "How do you mean?"

"The one woman," said Pateras, "who you want to give your whole life to. If you desire to make the complete commitment to her — if you want Irene be your wife — then go to her now."

"Pateras, tell me. What if I'm not sure how I feel about her?"

He squeezed my shoulder with his hand.

"If you go now and sleep with her, then you will give her an illusion, an illusion that will hurt her the minute it explodes. If you stay here, then you will give her back her freedom, and let her heal."

57
How Do I Sex Thee? ...
Let Me Count the Ways

PATERAS LET ME ALONE to think about my feelings for Irene. He stood before the Sextopians with his hand raised, his lips filled with an enormous smile.

"Yesterday I was reading the *Kamasutra*. The book is a crockpot of outrageous superstitions and sensible advice. It gives a method for preventing the woman you love from marrying another man. Here is the recipe: first you crush dill weed, red arsenic and sulfur into a powder. Dry this powder seven times, then add honey to the mix."

He paused, held up the book, then read: "Mash this mixture with one pound of excrement from a monkey, and now pour this on the head of the woman you love. Then she will not be given in marriage to anyone else."

The Sextopians laughed, and when the laughter subsided Pateras asked what they would like to play. Together they shouted the name of another of their favorite games: 'How Do I Sex Thee?'

Pateras nodded; one wink after the nod, Priestos appeared. With one hand, he juggled two yellow-colored plastic balls, each one twelve inches across. Using a long strand of sticky tape — which first stuck to his left hand, then to his right, then to his forehead — Priestos stuck the two balls together to make one. Fondly, he caressed the yellow spheres.

"When I throw these breasts — "

"They are balls, Priestos, not breasts!" some of the women teased.

He wrinkled his face as he feigned disgust at the touching of the masculine globes. Before Priestos could review the rules of the game, Pateras blew a high-pitched note on the conch shell. The Sextopian men formed a circle and joined hands, and then the Sextopian women gathered close together inside the circle of men. Pateras blew the conch — this time with a deep pitch — and Priestos threw the ball into the air near the center of the circle of players.

As the ball fell toward the crowd, Priestos shouted:

"Sex thee ... number ... twenty-four!"

The Sextopians screamed as they ran in all directions, except for player number twenty-four, Tiropitas. When the Village Leader caught the ball, Priestos shouted "Stop!" and all the running players froze in place. Tiropitas took ten steps toward the nearest player; he threw the ball, which hit the leg of Bedusa. After Bedusa had been thusly selected, the Sextopian women scrambled to grab their choice of Sextopian men. Now all the couples met together near the campfire; Tiropitas and Bedusa stood in the center of the crowd. Sextopias had many more women than men, and the women without men now watched, knowing that the next round they would play.

The game that ensued reminded me of an erotic Tai Chi workout combined with a sexual ballet. Bedusa shouted the number of her choice ("Sixty-eight!") and then she and Tiropitas — followed by the other couples — moved their clothed bodies into sexual position number sixty-eight. In this variation, the man and woman lay on their sides, facing each other, hands entwined around the back of their partner's neck.

Penelope scratched my head behind the ear.

"We have catalogued, Thoreau," she said, "one-hundred and one different positions for making love. Some of us have memorized them all. But if we forget, we can observe the couple in the center, and then the memory comes back fast. This game is not for the sex of it, it is for mental exercise, and for keeping our bodies limber and flexible."

After a few seconds frozen in position sixty-eight, Bedusa shouted "Twenty-seven!" and position number twenty-seven — where the male and female bodies twisted around each other like a pair of chromosomes — was assumed by the giggling and groaning Sextopian players.

After much laughter, many positions and five minutes, all the salt-grains fell to the bottom of the egg-timer, and Pateras blew his conchshell horn. Tiropitas now held the balls-breasts in his hands; when he threw them into the air, the game began anew.

Six boisterous rounds were played. Then Pateras blew the conch shell three times, signaling the end. Water and juice were served, as the Sextopians talked with one another. Pateras approached me and took my hand.

"How could anyone not desire the friendship of a woman like this?" he said. "If I were ten years younger, I would climb Olympus, steal the thunderbolt of Zeus, and fight the three Fates to win this woman's love."

He led me to Beatrice, and placed our hands together, and the warmth of her hand warmed me everywhere.

"Beatrice," I said. "Do I have no chance at all with you until you are divorced?"

"Until I am divorced — or until you are married, dear Thoreau."

Pateras made a face at me that said: 'Go on, talk with her!' My silence made him sigh. He shook his head then raised his hand and spoke to the attentive crowd.

"In our Greek mythology," said Pateras, "Love is the oldest deity, born from Chaos, and not even the gods themselves are immune to the thrall of Love. Love is a power irresistible ... the greatest force in Nature ... a hot desire ... a raging madness ... a torment, an agony, a toothache in the soul. Why, then, do we need her and revere her? ... Love is the mother of all that is beautiful."

The Sextopians shouted their assent, and Pateras spoke more.

"When Love sets a man on fire, there is nothing that can help him. Whenever he sees his beloved he feels wild with rapture; when she is away he longs for her, he is painfully incomplete. A glimpse of her makes him divinely happy, while absence from her plunges him into the profoundest misery. Wisdom from the books cannot quench his desire, magic potions do not affect him, no travel and no change of scenery works to restore his calm."

Nikos — the old man who had fallen desperately in love with Hagfa but was too shy to reveal his love — approached Pateras and then addressed him.

"There is a woman," he said, "who — from sunrise to sunset to sunrise — fills up my mind like the summer sky in Spring. Is there no peace for me, Pateras? Is there no cure?"

"I am glad that you asked that question, my friend," said the cheerful Pateras. "Is there a remedy for the fantastic farce of Love?"

He eyed his friends, and then with a savvy smile he said:

"For every dote there is an antidote."

58
THE ONE AND ONLY CURE FOR LOVE

GRACEFUL ASPASIA returned to our Sextopian beach. Her face glowed young, her smile gave light, her silk-white hair streamed behind her like a bridal gown. Pateras glanced at her and sighed.

"How many men have felt this?" he asked, addressing the Sextopians. "Look at a woman for one moment, then instantly you're thunderstruck by Love."

Every man shouted that he had known that experience. One man, Nikos, glanced at Hagfa and then came forward to speak.

"This woman tears my heart from my body and carries it away with her!"

Aspasia asked Pateras's question to the women. They laughed and all agreed that the fast-acting arrows of Love had pierced them many times. Glancing at Pateras, Aspasia recited a slice of a poem by Heinrich Heine.

"If the flowers knew how deeply my heart is wounded,
    they would weep with me.
If the nightingales knew how sad I am,
    they would cheer me with their refreshing song.
If the golden stars knew my grief,
    they would come down from their heights
    to whisper consolation to me."

Moved by these winged words, Pateras let silence speak for a few moments before he spoke.

"When Love strikes, is there a cure? ... Eighteen-hundred years ago, a mysterious Greek author named Longus discovered a happy remedy for Love. You will not find his book so easily, because its theme — sexual education — is such a great taboo that it is still not taught in many public schools. Sadly, there are many cultures where love and knowledge are viewed as dangers from the devil instead of blessings from the gods. Nevertheless, we enjoy performing this tale as a lighthearted drama. It is called *Daphnis and Chloe: A Pastoral Romance of Innocent Love.*"

This statement was greeted with a cheer and then a flurry of activity. Aspasia opened the lid of a trunk that resembled a pirate's treasure chest, and then she threw costumes to grabbing hands. Priestos arranged torches to light up a large area that would be the stage. Penelope, the casting director, assigned Sextopians to play the parts of protagonists and the lesser roles: townspeople, sailors, goatherds, shepherds, cows, goats, and sheep.

"Priestos," she said, "you will play Philetas, the old wise man. Kosmos, you are Dorcon, the cowherd who wants to seduce the heroine. Beatrice, you are Chloe, an innocent shepherd girl. Thoreau will play Daphnis, the handsome young keeper of the goats."

With the deep voice of Pateras narrating, the skilled actors and actresses brought the words to life.

"This is a story about young lovers so naive that they did not understand how men and women fill each other with erotic joys. It begins and ends on the island called Lesbos. Here we glimpse the Golden Age: the sun shines almost every day, trees blossom then bear sweet fruit, red poppy flowers color the hillsides, goats are grazing and sheep are gamboling on the grassy fields amidst the olive groves. The main beach — "

Pateras was interrupted by a wave of laughter caused by Priestos, who had pretended to be a woolly sheep dropping money into a slot machine, just as Pateras had described the 'gambling' sheep.

"The main beach of the island remained unspoiled — in those days the gods guarded the sacred things — and the sea-waves licked the shore with the most enchanting moans. One day, as the mischievous Pan chased his lovely Nymphs across this beach, they heard unusual noises, and then ran to the fields to see. Some goats had strayed among a flock of sheep where they found sprigs of tasty nettles to devour. The bleating sheep and the missing goats brought the shepherdess Chloe and the goatherd Daphnis together for the first time.

"When Pan and the Nymphs saw that Daphnis was as handsome and good-hearted as Chloe was fair and kind, they begged the Love-god to inspire the two young persons with Love. The shepherdess and goatherd exchanged shy glances. Moments after meeting they played like children, running and chasing and throwing rotten apples at each other as they ran. When they rested under a tree, Daphnis played his panpipes, and Chloe made a wreath from branches, then twined it in his hair. Together they watched the bright sunset, and then each one returned to their father's home. But before separating, Chloe said good-bye to Daphnis with a gentle kiss, shy and innocent."

Beatrice, whose splendid acting had already mesmerized the Sextopians, now made them laugh by giving me — Daphnis — a kiss wild and passionate. Pateras shouted "Cut!", pretended to instruct Chloe, and then watched as Chloe's next kiss was delivered chastely, soft as an apple blossom.

"The next day, Daphnis and Chloe met again, and at noon Chloe fell asleep on the warm green grass. Daphnis watched her sleeping, and for the first time noticed how beautiful she looked. As he studied her, a chirping cicada jumped by, and then — in escaping from a swallow-bird flying close behind him — the cicada flew under the shirt above Chloe's bosom. Chloe screamed. Daphnis reached to seize the insect, sliding his hand over her breasts, and then placed the still-chirping insect into her hand. She took it and laughed, and then returned it to the safety of her bosom, and fell asleep again."

Now Kosmos appeared on the scene to play the part of Dorcon, dressed humorously as a dung-smeared cowherd with a crooked staff.

"Chloe's beauty stole many hearts. One of these belonged to Dorcon, a herder of cows, who was older than Daphnis, more experienced, and less honorable. Dorcon disguised himself under a wolfskin, and made himself look like a beast. He planned to scare Chloe, then ravish her. One sunny afternoon, Dorcon hid behind a bush on the path where Chloe always walked. Chloe approached, but before Dorcon could assault her, the sheepdogs picked up his scent and attacked him, biting him so badly that he had to flee to save his life.

"One week later, Dorcon and Daphnis were walking along the beach. They were surprised by pirates from Tyria, who seized the cows of Dorcon and the body of Daphnis. Dorcon was mortally wounded in the fight.

"Chloe heard shouts and ran to the beach, arriving just as the pirate ship had sailed. Dorcon, lying on the sand, called to Chloe, then handed her his pipe. 'Chloe, I am finished,' he said. 'But this pipe, which has outplayed all the cowherds on our island, will save the life of Daphnis, since I have trained the cows and oxen to come home, whenever they hear these songs. In return for this gift, kiss me, sweet Chloe, while I still live. And when I am dead weep a tear for me, and remember Dorcon whenever the cows come home.'

"Dorcon spoke his last words, received his last kiss, and then his soul passed on. As loudly as she could blow, Chloe blew into the pipe. The cows and oxen heard this stirring note, and without thinking twice — or even once — they ran to the edge and then leaped over the side of the boat. The stampede and the splashing waves made the boat capsize, and then the pirates — wearing their heavy swords and armor — sank to the bottom of the sea. But Daphnis, who wore almost nothing all the time, swam until he reached the horns of the oxen, and then let their swimming carry him to the safety of the shore.

"Chloe took the exhausted Daphnis to the cave of Nymphs. Here she washed him, and then for the first time she let him watch as she washed herself. Outside the cave, the sheep and the goats pranced joyfully to see that their mistress and master had returned. But Daphnis, for all his goodnatured cheerfulness, could not be merry. For he had seen Chloe naked, and that splendid beauty which had been hidden was now unveiled. His heart ached as though it were gnawed with a secret poison, and at times he huffed and puffed and could not breathe steadily, as if somebody had been chasing him over the hills. Watching Chloe wash herself seemed to him more dangerous and formidable than the pirates and the sea, since Daphnis was a wide-eyed country-boy, and yet unversed in the beatings and the thefts of Love.

"By now, you realize that Daphnis and Chloe were in love. They suffered unbearable pangs of longing every moment that they spent apart. Unaware of how to relieve their suffering, they sought advice from an old retired cowherd named Philetas, who lived in a cottage amidst a lush garden filled with pomegranates, apples, pears, grapes, and figs. Philetas gave them bowls of pomegranate juice sweetened with honey from his own hives, and then explained what they needed to know. He told them about his own youth, and how he met the timeless god of Love.

"Daphnis and Chloe were both hugely delighted to hear this, and they asked him: 'What is love? Is he a boy or is he a bird? And what can Love do? Tell us, old man, please!' And Philetas replied: 'Love, my children, is a god, a young youth and very fair, and winged to fly. And therefore he delights in youth, he follows beauty, he gives our fantasy her wings. His power is so vast, that the power of Zeus himself is not so great. He governs in the elements, rules the stars, and commands even the gods who are his peers with more sway than you have over your sheep and goats. All flowers are the work of Love. Those plants are his creations, and all true poems are sung when he laughs into your ears. Love makes the rivers flow and the winds blow. I knew a bull in love, who ran bellowing through the meadows as if he had been stung by a swarm of bees; and a he-goat so in love with a virgin she-goat that every day he followed her up and down through the woods and the grassy fields.'

"'And I myself, once young, fell in love with Amaryllis, and forgot to eat my meat and drink my drink, and never could enjoy a good night's sleep. My panting heart was very sad and anxious; my body shook with cold. I cried out often, as if I had been thwacked and paddled on my back and sides; and often I sat still and mute, like a corpse lain flat among the dead. I cast myself into the rivers as if my body had been on fire. I called on Pan to help me, since Pan himself had loved a fickle lass named Pitys. I praised Echo because whenever I spoke the dear name of Amaryllis, she repeated that name many times. I broke my pipes because though they could attract the cows, they could not bring Amaryllis to me. For there is no medicine for love, no meat or drink or charm, but the only balm is kissing and embracing and lying naked side-by-side.'

"So Daphnis and Chloe sat down under a shady tree hoping to cure their lovesickness. They tried kissing, but still the longing burned inside. 'There most be something that works better than kissing,' Daphnis said. They tried embracing, but that too, didn't quench the fire. At last they tried lying naked together, but they still couldn't figure out what went where. Daphnis burst into tears. He cried out: 'The sheep and the goats know more than I do about this impossible business of Love!'

"Chloe stroked his hair. 'I will always love you, Daphnis,' she said. 'And I swear that never will I kiss another young man. And you must swear to me that you will never kiss another woman.' "With tears stinging his eyes Daphnis replied: 'I will be faithful to you forever, Chloe. I swear it on this goat and sheep! If you ever leave me I will die of loneliness. And I promise that no other woman will ever kiss my lips.'

Now Penelope appeared on the stage, in the role of the farmer's wanton wife, dressed in nothing but three bunches of purple grapes dangling loosely from their vines. The audience watched her with their utmost attention, and then Pateras told more.

"Near the cave of Nymphs lived an old white-haired farmer with a young wife named Lycaenion, who wanted to make love with Daphnis. Straightaway she noticed that the lad was passionately devoted to Chloe, so she resolved to help the young couple, and at the same time satisfy her lustful desires. From behind a bush she had been watching Daphnis when he burst into tears: she had seen everything that the young couple did and didn't do. The next morning, Lycaenion strolled into the meadow where Daphnis and Chloe were talking, kissing, and eating — but mostly kissing. She told them that an eagle had swooped down and carried off her best goose, but it was so heavy that the eagle had taken it to the forest. She begged Daphnis to come and help her look for it, while Chloe stayed behind and tended his flock of goats. Daphnis agreed to help, and the wily woman led him deep into the forest, far away from Chloe.

"Lycaenion stripped off her clothing, and when Daphnis gandered at her body, he forgot completely about the stolen goose.

"'I had a dream last night,' Lycaenion said to Daphnis. 'The Nymphs told me that you and Chloe are in love with each other, yet you are very unhappy. Every day you see how the goats get relief, yet you can't just imitate the goats — human lovemaking lasts longer and gives far more pleasure. I can help you to cure your lovesickness. The Nymphs told me that I should teach you the art of making love.'

"When Daphnis heard these words he fell to his knees, and he begged Lycaenion to teach him all she knew. He offered her presents: milk and cheeses from his favorite she-goat, and even the she-goat, too. As soon as he learned his lessons, he said, he would run back to Chloe and teach her everything.

"Lycaenion began the lesson with these words: 'Kiss me,' she said, 'the same way that you kiss Chloe.'"

As Penelope-Lycaenion approached Thoreau-Daphnis to take the kiss, the conch shell suddenly sounded.

"That's the censor," said Beatrice.

"Let's take a break," Pateras announced. "The food is ready, and it can't wait for the drama's wedding feast. And let us thank our main actors and actresses — "

Applause filled the air, and when Beatrice came forward for her bow, the audience had so much enjoyed her performance that their cheers and clapping rang like a thunderstorm.

A swiftly-walking Ligeia emerged from the darkness, and handed Pateras a telegram. With hardly a glance, he dropped it into his shirt pocket.

But the moment after Aspasia joined them and took his hand, he retrieved the telegram and read it silently. Shaking his head, he crumpled the paper, and then tossed it into the raging campfire.

59
Sextopias Endangered

"Sophocles, when he had lived seventy years, declared that old age was a blessing. Why? Because old men and women lose their love-urges and virility, and are no longer slaves to that 'mad and furious master' called erotic love."

This remark from Pateras caused the love-charged Sextopians to roar with laughter. They believed the very opposite: when you live a healthy lifestyle, love and passion increases, not decreases, every day of your life. Priestos — so amused by the Sophoclean fallacy — fell down and rolled on the sand, holding his belly as he laughed.

Soon the sounds of sizzling onions hissed the frying pans, and the fresh sea-air surrendered to aromas floating in a spicy breeze. Sextopians carrying wooden trays appeared, laden with Mediterranean food — marvelously energizing food! The one-pot dish was called *sympetherio,* which means "relatives", and contained wheat berries, fava beans, chick peas, navy beans, lentils, scallions, onions, olive oil, dill, parsley, garlic, lemon juice, salt, spices and herbs. The food had been made with loving care, and made even more delicious by the garnish of dining with friends, outdoors beside the sea.

Pateras ate nothing but drank lots — fresh fruit juices, and a drink made of goat-milk yogurt and fruit.

"This perfect night is passing," he said, "and I have so much to tell you. Bring your food and come and sit beside me. Keep on eating and drinking while I talk."

Each Sextopian filled up a wooden bowl and then sat down on the sand near their beloved leader.

"Years ago," said Pateras, "I first conceived this place because the world was speeding away from all the good things I loved and valued. When I asked myself: 'What's causing most of the world's problems?' I found three culprits: violence, lousy education, and stupid men. And as quick as I understood the heart of the problem, I saw an answer: There should be a school for men where we could learn to understand and to express our feelings. All men will be idiots until we graduate with honors from that school."

The Sextopians — men as well as women — shouted that they agreed, and then Pateras, in his stirring voice, continued his true tale.

"How thirsty we are for wisdom and for happiness! How few men have the strength to be alone! And so this world is crammed with false paths, superficial answers, mail-order messiahs, easy roads to Paradise. Could our Sextopias be genuine, I wondered? ... We are not a cult: we don't take your money, we don't tell you what to think, you can enter and leave freely. Here there are no slaves, no masters, no well-paid priests — feigning expertise about the thoughts of gods — who smother you with guilt and fear. Come here, Thoreau, and stand beside me."

When I walked up to the man, he threw his arm around my shoulder.

"You think I am the leader of this place? ... I am not. We are all equal here. Each member of our community is an individual who makes her own decisions and thinks her own ideas. I am happy to serve as the co-ordinator, because all the others are smart enough to refuse the job. Now sit here beside me, and if you hear anything that you disagree with or do not understand, then jump up and down until I notice that you want to speak."

I sat down while Pateras raised his wooden cup and sipped more of his yogurt-fruit drink.

"In these wild times, is it possible to understand the difference between what is sexually liberated, and what is sexually depraved? ... In the time of Socrates there lived a philosopher Aristippus, who taught that 'pleasure is the greatest good.' In Athens he studied philosophy; in Corinth, in greater depth, he studied an enchanting courtesan named Lais. Asked about their relationship, he said: 'You reprove me because Lais doesn't love me, but why should I care about that? Wine and fish and olives have no love for me, and yet I enjoy them with pleasure.' ... What do you think about that, Thoreau?"

Before I could reply, he smiled and gave his answer.

"Sex without love? We don't prohibit that, and we don't deny that there are times it can be fun. But we do believe in a vastly sweeter and more nutritious nectar: lovemaking with love as the key ingredient."

I raised a hand; Pateras, amidst much laughter, grasped it then put it down.

"I know what you're thinking, Thoreau. Does all this mean that Pateras and the Sextopians believe that in sex everything is permitted? Or that everything is permitted as long as the lovers agree? ... No, we don't believe in that at all. We have seen — ten thousand times — how people make mistakes about what is good for them and what is not. We are very liberal here — "

At that understatement the Sextopians laughed heartily, and Pateras smiled.

"— yet there is one rule which all of us have agreed to live by. In personal and sexual relationships, 'Do Not Harm'. Everything is permitted except that. Sex and violence cannot sleep together in the same bed."

He reached into his pocket and retrieved a locket with an old photograph of his father, which he held up for all to see.

"My father often said: 'There are two unhappy men: the doer who acts without first dreaming, and the dreamer who never turns his dreams to deeds.' ... How can we travel from our world now, filled with ignorance and violence, to a better world, a sexual and romantic paradise where men and women revere one another, and express that reverence by treating everyone with tenderness, humor, sincerity, and mutual respect?"

Again I raised my hand and the Sextopians laughed as Pateras first seized my hand then put it down.

"There is only one hope for the future, and Aristotle knew it three thousand years ago: education. Not the education in the public schools and universities — no, that is mere instruction, and that hasn't worked at all! Those antiquated institutions are concerned with the knowledge that is either too useless or too practical: knowledge that makes money, makes weapons, or makes entertaining toys. What we need to do is to educate our imaginations, educate our character, educate our bodies and our hearts in the arts of ecstasy and love."

The Sextopians cheered at this idea, Penelope clapped vigorously. Tears rolled down the silky cheeks of Beatrice. Pateras waved his hands to quiet the applause.

"I have one more thing to tell you. But first, I would like you to find someone — anyone you like — and say what you would say if you knew that you might never see them again. Pretend that this will be the last night, the last moment, you can be together."

Penelope sought Kosmos, Nikos searched for Hagfa, Aspasia found Pateras. I looked for Beatrice; I could not find her anywhere amidst the mulling crowd. When I glanced at the sky I felt a tug-tug-tug on my left earlobe, and the next instant I found myself star-gazing at her brilliant eyes. Before she spoke I grasped her message, and my heart sank under the loveless sea.

"Soon, I'll be leaving, dear," she said calmly. "I need to return to England, to make certain that a certain man never does to any other woman what he did to me."

Beatrice kissed me as if she cared. Her whispers breezed into my ear.

"The same rule applies as much to love as literary style: less is more. What many women cannot give, one woman can."

The conch shell blew. I looked up to see Pateras holding his hand in the air.

"Now listen, everyone," said Pateras. "I need all your attention now. I have news which you will not like to hear. But you must hear. And you must understand."

Silence, silence absolute.

"Beauty is always in danger: beautiful women, beautiful loves, beautiful places, beautiful ideas. ... A short time ago I received a telegram from Judge Skleerokardos in Agios Nikolodeonos. The Judge denied my request to postpone development and new construction on Crete's South coast."

This news brought groans and moans and wails and agonizing shouts until Priestos hollered: "Pateras, what does this mean?"

The words of Pateras were clear, precise, and calm.

"It means that, every day, the towns of Souvlakis and Dembacchae will look a bit more like the sprawling metropolis of Athens. This beach, this home that is sacred to us, will soon be overrun with tourists, windsurfers, discoteks, restaurants, junk food, litter, beer, souvenirs, and stands that sell grilled meat."

More moans, groans and sobs burst from the audience, and when Pateras could not quiet them by raising his hand, he raised his conch shell and blew it with all his might.

"Listen," he said. "Our profound language has given us the wonderful word 'kairos'. It means: 'the critical moment, the right time for action.' This is our *kairos*. This is the chance we have to show the world how much Greek courage and cunning can do."

Murmurs rippled through the crowd as Pateras explained.

"For all these wonderful years we have made a paradise here, but there was one catch. We believed that we needed to keep it hidden. So we met at night only, we pretended to be goofy drama-players, and we situated our haven between two places so undeveloped, un-luxuried, and uninteresting that the tourists would never want to come. We have thrived here, it is true. But imagine how much more we could accomplish if we did not need to hide ourselves. If we could live and love and play and learn in complete freedom, in the beautiful light of the day."

As the Sextopians talked about this notion, Kosmos slapped me on the shoulder. He spoke softly yet resolutely.

"Good-bye, Thoreau. I've heard enough. Words tomorrow, deeds today. It's time to take the bulls by the balls."

Pateras stood up straight and strong like a statue by Phidias, and all eyes gazed into his fiery eyes.

"Our home is about to be demolished, that is a fact that cannot be undone. Will we weep like little children lost at the park? Or shall we stand up fearlessly and build another place?"

"Stand up, men!" shouted the hundred-and-one-year-old Tiropitas. "Spit on your sleeves, roll up your hands, and get to work!"

Priestos spoke again.

"You know our answer, Pateras. But the planet Venus is too hot and Mars too cold. Where in this endless galaxy can we go and live like the gods in the clouds, without the chains of the old world to drag us down?"

Pateras nodded.

"There is a pine forest near Agia Triada, where families of birds sing melodies that make your spirit fly. And on the south coast of Crete, we have our *Asterousia* mountains that sparkle like the stars. In the west, *Lefka Ori,* our White Mountains near the Samaria Gorge. And I know a village where ..."

Their hearts lightened with new hope. The place did not matter: they would seek sincerely and they would find the place. Wild cheers and a stampede ensued as all the Sextopians rushed for Pateras. They hugged the man, kissed his cheeks, thanked him with the simplest heartfelt words. And each woman and each man promised him they would be strong enough to start again.

Penelope stood up on a wooden crate, and soon drew attention from the crowd.

"Has anyone seen Kosmos?" she asked.

I told Penelope that I had last seen him immediately after Pateras explained his telegram. Aspasia rubbed the back of Penelope, reminded her to have faith in him, and then spoke to the community.

"There are lessons we must learn," Aspasia said, "from the blunders of other Utopian experiments. In America, in the middle of the 19th Century, some Transcendentalist philosophers conceived an ingenious Utopia that they would name 'Brook Farm'. It was the beginning of March, and they had just completed building a group of buildings to live and work in — they called these buildings their phalanstery. On the night that this great work was done they threw a party, but during this celebration all the buildings they had just completed caught fire and burned down to the ground. Imagine that heartbreak! Nothing but ashes smoldered from their golden dreams. Since they had borrowed oodles of money to finance this construction, they were now ruined. One year after the fatal fire, the community broke up."

The first fingers of dawn light had spread themselves over the horizon above the sea, and the clouds in the sky glimmered with priceless gold. Penelope squeezed my hand. She was telling me how she worried about "the impetuous fool", when a loud explosion shook the ground.

Priestos jumped up onto a wooden crate and then he shouted to his friends.

"A brazen clamor warns the city of tomorrow's doom! At last the armies clashed! And sounds of struggles quaked the gentle earth!"

We heard the church bells sounding, the same bells that had pealed for help when the storming waters threatened to destroy the boats. Pateras took charge again.

"Make a circle and join hands," he said. "And now let us sing, and hope that the goddess advises us with patient wisdom and not rash foolishness."

Holding hands, the Sextopians sang:

"Crete, my home, my beautiful island
Your dirt is gold, your sand is diamonds."

Although the music rang pleasant and becalming, this was not the time for me to sing. Without waiting for the next verse, I slipped free from the circle of entwined hands. As the dawn broke I ran along the beach toward Agia Souvlakis, hoping for good luck, fearing what I would find there, and wondering what I would do if it was found.

60
THE FOUNTAIN OF BAD JUDGMENT

WHAT IS OBSCENE? What words, art-works, behaviors should be censored and prohibited? ... In modern society, three sacred calves must never be molested: economic inequality, religion, sexuality. In the ancient world, sex was worshiped as a manifestation of the divine.

The word obscene derives from Greek words meaning "off stage". Greek dramas — though teeming with murders, incests, wars, rapes, poisonings, infanticides — never allow the audience to see the brutal actions. Sex is a liberating power. What harms us, the old Greeks believed, is viewing violence.

These thoughts ran with me as I dashed to find Kosmos at Agia Souvlakis. A grim surprise met me there: the once-peaceful town had aged a hundred years. Bulldozers and steam shovels rumbled down narrow streets just wide enough to let them through. Clouds of white dust drifted over the sidewalks, making walkers and workers look like ghosts. Jackhammers pounding through concrete rattled the windows, frightened the children, and shook up plates, cups, bric-a-brac and books.

In front of the Café Lathera a crowd had gathered, standing outside and peering through the windows and the door. Just outside that door a row of mourners squatted like vultures on a telephone wire. Elderly women dressed in black, these quick guides to the underworld were prepared to chant dirges, called *mirologues,* the instant that the near-death victim gasped his last.

Pushing through the crowd and stepping over the mourners, I walked into the café. The place was empty except for one foolhardy man. Kosmos stood in the center, singing at the top of his voice. He was standing in the middle of the Fountain of Bad Judgment, that marble sculpture comprised of three naked goddesses — Hera, Aphrodite, Athena — guarded above by an infant god of Love. Kosmos had saved two pairs of handcuffs from his jail experience in Athens, and with these he had chained himself to the statue of Aphrodite, his ankle to her ankle, his wrist to her wrist. As he spotted me his eyes gleamed brighter, he sang his Cavafy poem even louder, and his free hand waved at me to come near.

"Our most precious, our white youth,
    Oh, our white, our snow-white youth,
    Youth that is infinite, and yet so brief,
    embraces us like an angel's wings! ...
    It is always spent, always loving,
    it melts and falls among white horizons,
    lives and then dies forever."

The café door swung open and in stomped the friend of Kosmos, that Cretan giant named Rakis. With a metal file he began sawing away at the chains that connected the ankle of Kosmos to the ankle of the goddess of Love. After a few moments of this work, Rakis nodded at me, and then aimed his eyes at a pile of tools beside him. I picked up one of the files and rubbed it against the handcuffs near Kosmos's wrist. We had barely scratched this hard steel when the contractor of the construction project — a short middle-aged man, overdressed in a suit-jacket and wide tie — entered the café and approached the Promethean rebel.

"Kalimera, Kosmos," he said politely. "My job is to ask you to stop this nonsense. Unlock your handcuffs. Come with me to have a good breakfast."

"Good morning, Enthradis," Kosmos replied. "I must decline your generosity. My job is to protect the places and the people I love."

"What you cannot stop by law," said the glib man, "you should not attempt to stop by lawlessness."

Kosmos shook his head.

"There is a truthful fairy tale, my friend, that ends with this moral: Laws are devised by the rich to protect and increase their wealth and power."

"And you insist," said the wily contractor, "that grown men should be reading fairy tales?"

"We should read fairy tales," Kosmos replied, "until we are old enough and wise enough to share our power and our wealth."

"You should study the myths instead," said Enthradis, "and learn the fate of fools who imitate Prometheus."

The contractor waved his hand and three workers entered the café, the smallest one as tall and broad-shouldered as Rakis, and the biggest one at least one head taller than Kosmos's devoted friend. Rakis threw down his file and stood up, ready to fight them all.

"Rakis," said Kosmos, "do you want to help me, or do you want to hurt me so deeply that I will never be able to recover from the hurt? If you want to help me then remember our discussion about non-violence."

Rakis looked at Kosmos, recalled that dialogue, and then placed his hands behind his back. One of the workers, a plumber, climbed onto the fountain, then inserted his plumber's snake into the male organ of Cupid. When the plumber withdrew that long metal wire, the contractor waved his hands, and the three workers followed him out the café's door. A minute later, as Rakis and I continued filing to set the rebel free, a gush of water spouted, pouring down ceaselessly on the heads of Kosmos, Rakis, and me. It was water surely, yet it felt like runny mud and smelled like rotten eggs.

"It's funny, isn't it Thoreau?" said Kosmos. "An hour ago I lived in a paradise, naked and carefree, amidst lovely women and zany men. Now, for doing what my heart says is right, I will be arrested for civil disobedience. These villagers are like the sheep who thank their slaughterers! The same people who would not budge one centimeter when I rang the bells to warn them to save themselves, now gather outside in droves to watch me fall from grace."

He reached behind him and stroked the goddess's cold breast.

"I am united with Aphrodite, but I can't get any pleasure out of that because I am facing in the wrong direction. And to heap shame on the head of a man who already has troubles up to his neck, she delivers a liquid message from her son. Not showers of love and love's great happiness! Foul-smelling water sprays us from the penile organ of the god of Love."

For a few moments we enjoyed a lull from the ear-splitting clamor made by the stone-breaking machines. Kosmos seized that opportunity to shout to the crowd outside the café.

"Will Greece be an independent nation?" he yelled. "Or will we be a playground for the mindless rich? ... For three-thousand years the Greeks have fought for freedom. We survived the sieges of the Persians, the Romans, the Venetians, and the Turks. Yet the last invading armies may conquer us, since we welcome them with open legs and arms: the tourists!"

He placed his free hand on my arm.

"The human animal," said Kosmos, "is made to sing, to dance, to love. My father knows as much about this joy as anyone alive. But we need defiance, too, to save these sacred things. That's the one lesson my father can learn from me."

Sirens screamed in the distance, growing louder and closer, making me wonder if those sirens blared from a police wagon, a fire truck, or an ambulance. Kosmos laughed and squeezed my arm.

"Thoreau, don't you think that there must be a more effective way to save our global civilization from the injustices of big-corporation greed?"

"Kosmos," I said. "This isn't working at all. You'll be in jail and the town will be flattened anyway. There must be a better way."

We heard the loud crashes of nearby buildings getting knocked down to rubble and dust. The voyeuring villagers screamed — the huge claw of a steam shovel had just smashed through a window of our café. The café's lights dimmed, the floor trembled, and all the while reeking water from the marble Cupid streamed down on the head and shoulders of Kosmos. The fearless man closed his eyes.

"We need so little to be happy," he said. "Euripides, our rebellious playwright, wrote his ninety plays in a book-lined cave beside the sea. Think about the life inside these words, Thoreau."

Still, with his eyes closed, Kosmos sang:

"To be alive, to see the light!
 That alone is beautiful.
 To see the light, and to see the new grass leaves
 Or the grizzly faces of the stones."

Another loud crash knocked out a wall of the Café Lathera.

"Kosmos," I said. "Unlock yourself. It's time to go. There are better battles to fight."

The hand of Kosmos squeezed my arm.

"Don't say anything more, Thoreau," he said. "Not one word! Did you know that our ancient Greek ancestors believed that the human heart is as fragile as a Spring flower? They were so full of kindness and respect for life, that they could not let their dramas show acts of cruelty or violence. They told about them — never did they hide the truth! But these Greeks believed that the hardest events in life — the tragic moments when good men and women get no justice from the gods — should be always imagined and never seen."

61

WHAT HAPPENED ON THE BOAT
AT AGIOS NIKOLODEONOS

TWO SEA GULLS, scavenging for scraps of food, circled above the head of Mother Whackanzakis, then landed awkwardly onto the deck of the boat. When my story ended, the Mother-nun picked up the sides of her frock — to keep its bottom from getting dirty — then marched to the boat's assistant captain. Waving her hands, she complained loudly about the boat's delay, and demanded information about the future that could not be known.

Out of the Mother's sight, near the back of the boat where the lifeboats rested, Panzano and Dolcezza were standing together talking, the young man as nervous as a cube of gelatin, the young woman cool as an Italian ice.

"That necklace you're wearing," Panzano said anxiously, "is made of painted black-eyed peas: the Greeks call them 'gypsy beans'. Is that a gift from an admirer?"

"No, silly," answered Dolcezza. "Peas I have many, admirers none. At the nunnery we make jewelry and other trinkets, and we sell them to raise money for food and books. We sell IBCs, too. Do you know your IBCs?"

"You have one admirer," Panzano said. "One who knows his ILUs, but never heard of the IBCs."

Dolcezza reached into her pocket then smiled.

"Illuminated Bingo Cards," she said. "We cut the cards, then decorate them with drawings of scenes from the Queen Jane Bible, and legends of sinners and saints. Here, look at this."

Panzano examined a bingo card showing twenty-five numbered squares, adorned around the edges with colorful pictures of nuns, monks, candles, bells, wildflowers, and books. He praised the designs and the designer, then bought the card by handing Dolcezza all the money that the boat's passengers had tossed into the hat for him.

"No, that's much too much to give me for one card," said the happy

Dolcezza. "You can pay me one Euro, and here is your change."

"Thank you," said Panzano, as he placed the card back into her hand. "In love, just like in those old stories about paradise, all possessions belong to everyone. There is no difference between 'Thine' and 'Mine'. I take this card which belongs to me, and I give it as a gift to you. And now, since it is yours again, I will buy it from you for the one Euro you'll let me pay."

Dolcezza laughed as Panzano — many times — bought the card, gave it to her as a gift, and then bought the card again. They played this game until all Panzano's money had been transferred to the pockets of his favorite nun.

"Dolcezza," Panzano murmured. "The first time I looked at you my heart flew away with my head. *Come sei bella!* How beautiful you are! *Ti penso sempre!* I always think of you!"

A siren sounded from somewhere in the town. Dolcezza glanced at the paved sidewalk near the dock, then looked into Panzano's face and smiled.

"Close your eyes, Panzano," she said. "Close your eyes and open your hands."

Panzano obeyed, and soon felt his cheek blessed with the softest kiss. When he opened his eyes Dolcezza had vanished. His cheek tingled, and his left hand held a note that said:

> "When this boat leaves, Oh, tell me when?
> Then I shall kiss you once again."

As he ran to find her he collided chest to chest with the nun named Forza, who said to Panzano "Excuse me, sir", to which he replied, "My pleasure."

The distant siren blared a bit louder as the ship's assistant captain stood up on the wood crate he had placed in the center of the boat's deck. He had loosened his collar and removed his tie; he had forgotten to shave the beard-stubble dotting his cheeks and chin. Minutes after he'd raised his left hand, the chattering passengers ceased their gabbing and then swiveled their heads to hear the latest report.

"Our boat," he said in a tired voice, "is not yet ready to depart."

Mother Whackanzakis looked innocent as an angel whose heaven was a third helping of dessert. In her white-blue dress bulging with layers of flab, she sprang up and shouted at the harried first mate. Her voice sounded ever-so anxious for the boat to leave.

"Dark messenger," said Mother-nun, "who brings us news that always sounds the same. Tell us what the problem is."

With a shrug of his shoulders, the assistant captain removed his Cretan cap. Mother Whackanzakis now spoke to the impatient passengers.

"Greece charms us for four reasons," she began. "Its passionate people; its sublime sunshine and light; its incomparable food; and its humanizing inefficiency. It all started aeons ago. When the goddess Gaea decided to divide the world into countries, she first ripped up a thick layer of the Earth — as easily as you would pull off an orange peel — and then dropped this into a gigantic sieve. She shook the sieve and sprinkled some of the good soil all around the globe. Then she looked into the bottom of the sieve and saw that it was filled with rocks. She threw these rocks over her shoulder, and the country where the rocks landed she named Greece. ... And then — "

Waving his arms, Panzano jumped between the speaker and her audience. Dolcezza's note had excited him so greatly, that at first he babbled in Italian and forgot to translate into the *Inglese* that everyone grasped.

"*Gallina che schiamazza non fa uova. La verità è senza varietà. Le parole non empiono il corpo. Il ventre non si sazia di parole. Dal detto al fatto c'è un gran tratto. Altro è promettere, altro è mantenere. Il primo scudo è il più difficile a fare. Barba bagnata è mezza fatta!*"

When the assistant captain appeared dumbfounded, and the audience laughed and laughed, Panzano rendered his ideas into English crystalline.

"You cackle often, but never lay an egg. Truth needs not many words. Fine words butter no parsnips. Fair words fill not the belly. From words to deeds is a great space. It is one thing to promise and another to perform. The first step is the only difficulty. A good lather is half the shave!"

This strange sausage of sayings was snipped by Mother Whackanzakis, who grabbed Panzano's earlobe, then pulled him to a place where they could not be overheard.

"Panzano," she said, still tugging him by the ear. "If you make yourself as sweet as honey, then the flies will eat you up. Give me time enough and I could make you understand: *Il mondo è di chi se lo piglia*. The world belongs to the man who is bold!"

Sirens blared louder and closer to the boat. Mother Whackanzakis, after releasing the captive earlobe, quickly found three of her nuns, who began to sing a fragment from the vagabond melody by Sarasate, called *Zigeunerweisen*. The poignant song attracted the remainder of the nuns, who clapped hands and stomped feet un-nunlikely as they sang it to the end. Singing completed, the eleven nuns huddled in circle to listen while Mother-nun talked.

The boat's crew handed out cold drinks and desserts, and the crowd gathered around me with smiling faces and curious eyes.

"What happened," shouted a young woman, "after you escaped un-scathed in Agia Souvlakis from the Cooked-in-oil Café?"

I heard the question, I looked at the eager audience, yet I did not re-spond. The sirens were blaring louder and closer, and my sharp ears attempted to distinguish whether these screams were arriving to take prisoners or to give aid. The way the sea-foam taunted the sandy shore, a dazzling new idea teased the edges of my funconscious mind. As always, when my inner life caught fire, the world around seemed dull and lifeless as a faded photograph.

Recognizing my fit of concentration, seeing that I was in no mood to talk, Panzano stepped up beside me and sat me down on a wooden crate. He placed his finger on the cheek graced by Dolcezza's kiss; he took a deep breath and then looked up at the crowd.

"I can tell you the rest of Thoreau's story," he said. "After the accident of Kosmos in the café, Thoreau wandered for three weeks, looking for the tribe of gypsy women. Not for his own selfish pleasures, I swear it! — he wanted to give them money to escape to a new life. He searched all over Crete, looking for *patteran* — the Gypsy train — the grass, leaves, and branches that gypsies leave to show their companions the road they've traveled on."

Panzano glanced at the smiling Dolcezza, then told more.

"Alas, a lass! the isle of Crete has more than two-thousand caves! When Thoreau realized that he could not find the wild women, he re-turned to his place on the beach at Agios Nikolodeonos. Here he met me, Panzano — a paunch filled with a pinch of proverbs and a penchant for foolishness — after I had just been robbed by a horde of gypsies, on my first day in Crete. Thoreau had a night then a fight with a blonde beauty named Bliss, a fearless feminist who insisted on traveling around the world alone. This broke his heart because just as he failed to get the gypsy women safely off this island, he failed to keep his Bliss on Crete.

Two unscrupulous angels found him as he slept like a mummy on the sand, his spirit wounded and his body tuckered out. And as the two women forced their pleasures on this sleeping prince, it has never been more true that 'Bacio di bocca, spesso cuor non tocca' — which is to say, 'A kiss on the lips often does not reach the heart.' ... I, Panzano, resisted like a hero, but the two angels overpowered me by guile, then burned Thoreau's precious books and our cheap clothes. When Thoreau woke up he realized that by farce or force he should have stopped Bliss from her too-dangerous travel plans. So Thoreau wrapped up our dangling parts in glowing-yellow duct tape, which made him look like a laughter-loving god, and me like a three-hundred pound baby duck. Thoreau felt discouraged, on the morning of this first April day, but when the boat's whistle called, I cheered him up and urged him to seek adventures by running to catch this unsinkable ship."

Panzano placed his hands on his hips then laughed.

"And you see, it was not my courage alone, but my courage along with Thoreau's ingenuity that saved us! Thoreau had hidden our most valuable possessions under a rock so heavy that only the strongest men could make it move. Otherwise, I would have lost my passport — "

Panzano held up an empty piece of plastic that once contained the important little booklet. When he noticed that nothing sat inside it, he reached into a slit in his duct tape, then looked down at the deck, then cringed with horror at the fact that it was gone.

"My passport is missing!" he shouted.

"And my watch is stolen!" yelled the boat's assistant captain.

Other passengers cried out: "My jewelry! My wallet! My cash!"

Two police cars stopped with a screech on the concrete dock, then ten officers — the cream of the Tourist Police — hurriedly boarded the boat. The captain's assistant raised his hand.

"Carry on with your activities," he announced, "but do not leave the boat. The police will be searching the possessions of all the passengers. We apologize for any incontinence that this might cause."

Policemen mixed into the crowd to question and examine every passenger. As I watched this calm procedure, the tall nun named Donnabella tossed two blankets to me — "So this evening when the sun dies, you and your friend will not be cold," she said. Mother-nun clapped her hands, and then led her other ten nuns in a dance known as the zalangos. Donnabella, noticing how my eyes wondered at the dance, touched my arm then said: "The dance tells the story of the young women in the town of Suli, who chose to die rather than to live as slaves. In the dance, one at a time, a woman will separate herself from the circle of dancers. This reminds us of the women of Suli, who — to avoid being captured by Turkish invaders — one after another leaped over the steep cliffs of Zalongo with their children in their arms."

The nun named Forza grabbed the hand of Donnabella to bring her to the dance. But the chief of the police officers stopped her, then asked to look inside the blue-wool stocking she had knitted hours ago. Forza tossed the stocking to another nun, who tossed it to another, and at last the stocking flew into the chaste hands of Dolcezza.

A policeman snatched the stocking from her, reached inside, and then — to the gasps and shouts of the boat's passengers — pulled out then held up the assistant captain's wristwatch. The chief of police made a call on his phone, and then the remaining officers surrounded the friendless nuns.

Panzano's astounded face looked as white as the nun's robes. From the depths of his soul he cried out:

"*O occhi miee, occhi non già ma fonti!* ... Oh eyes of mine, not eyes but fountains now!"

Tears streamed from his face like a statue in the rain. He raised his hands to the evening sky.

"*Peggio di cosi si muore!* It could not be worse!"

More sirens blared, more vehicles topped with swirling lights drove on the paved street lined with restaurants that faced the dock. A policeman had grabbed the arm of Mother Whackanzakis, and she shook herself free, then strode to the police chief to explain that her girls were good. The chief grabbed her arm then yanked the woman toward a waiting police wagon.

"Stop," I said, stepping in front of the police chief to block his path. "She's a woman, treat her gently. And until she's had the chance to see a lawyer, to tell her side of the story, and to get a fair trial, she is as innocent as your mother or your sister or your wife."

It may have been that I underestimated the innocence of that policeman's female relations. Nevertheless, the savvy Greeks found a way to do their job without doing me harm. With a "Sorry, Mister Thoreau," a fishnet made from thick rope was dropped over my head and body, then tied to a post so that I could not move forward and interfere with the arrests.

At the same time, a policeman seized the arm of the young Dolcezza.

Panzano watched helplessly until he remembered her feminine kiss, and the man-making words of the Mother-nun. With a raging shout, he charged forward like a ram. Empowered by love, he knocked down policeman after policeman the way a bowling ball tumbles the ten pins.

It took six strong men to hold him and then wrestle him to the deck. After a fierce struggle, with his arms tied behind his back, he crawled from a swarm of officers and then stood up on his knees to shout his last words to his love.

"*Coraggio*, Dolcezza, courage!" Panzano yelled. "*Le do una mano fin dove posso!* I'll help you as much as I can!"

62
A Can of Worms Never Opens Itself

WHEN I STEPPED through the doorway of the courtroom I was relieved to see that the judge was a woman, between seventy-five and eighty years old. My relief turned to disbelief as I read her gold nameplate: Judge Skleerokardos. And then disbelief plunged into despair when I glanced at the wall above her seat. There sat a framed etching by Gustave Doré, depicting souls in hell, masses of men and women chained together as they climbed a mountain, without hope, prisoners of their past misdeeds. Carved above the drawing on a wooden plaque were the large-lettered words:

> *Quivi sospiri pianti ed alti guai*
> *Risonavan per l'aer senza stele!*

From reading Dante, I knew these Italian words would mean:

> 'Here sighs, and groans, and deep laments
> Resounded through the starless air!'

The courtroom was packed with defendants and their relatives, the first group waiting to be tried, and the second waiting to weep over the results. I found a seat beside Pateras, who squeezed my hand with fatherly warmth and encouragement.

"Pay attention to this judge, Thoreau. I know her as well as anyone, and I know her type. In her entire body there is not one unselfish bone. They have a dozen names for her here: some have said she is 'pathologically willful,' others call her 'the pit bull'. When she gets a notion in her head, a herd of wild bulls cannot drive it out. She's the one who denied our petition to prevent coastal development, and she presided over the case that sent Kosmos to the jail in Athens for twenty years. Maybe the third time with her will be luckier. What do you think?"

"Court is now in session," boomed the solemn voice of the bailiff. "All rise."

We stood up as the Judge climbed the steps to her padded seat, and we sat down when she banged her gavel three times against her desk. Turning her head slowly, she examined the faces in the courtroom.

"A can of worms," she said, "never opens itself."

Random titters at this canny remark brought her gavel crashing against the desk, and the instant she shouted "Silence!" there was silence absolute. The Judge placed a pillow on her desk then held up a black feather. She dropped the feather and it swayed down back and forth until it landed on the pillow without a sound.

"Did you hear that?" the Judge bellowed. "If you cannot hear the feather falling on the pillow case, then there is too much noise in my courtroom!"

She glared at the roomful of lawyers, defendants, reporters, and relatives.

"What do I mean when I say, 'A can of worms never opens itself'? ... I mean that this court accepts no excuses — no excuses! — for breaking the laws of this land. Every adult must be responsible for his or her own actions, and accept the consequences that those actions bring. My job is to uphold the law, in order to protect the law-abiding citizens from the lawless ones. ... Let us now hear the first case."

Pateras studied her two stern eyes that, long ago, had lost compassion's humanizing gleam. With his sharp elbow he jabbed my ribs.

"They say," he said, "that her backside is so hard it can cut diamonds. And that whenever a man stands in front of her, he feels like his two delicate olives are being hammered between her gavel and her desk."

"Is she any more compassionate towards women?" I asked.

"Towards women she is even worse," Pateras whispered. "She thinks that women are stronger than men, and therefore women should set examples for good conduct. And woe to the ones who do not."

An attorney in a white suit sheepishly approached the Judge's bench.

"Your honor," he said, "as you know, six months ago the teenaged boys on Crete began to imitate a bizarre fad started in Athens two years ago: they are eating cats. A victim of this irresistible peer pressure, my 16-year-old client — who has pleaded innocent — is accused of eating his neighbor's favorite pet."

"I do not see the defendant in the courtroom," said the Judge.

"Your Honor," the attorney meekly replied. "From eating the cat he is sick in the stomach — "

"Counselor!" shouted the Judge. "Your client will appear in this court by three p.m. today or I will send a cat that will eat him for lunch and you for dessert. Next case!"

Another suited attorney creeped before the bench.

"Your honor, my client is an American — "

"We will not hold that against him," said the Judge. "Unless he admits to it. Continue, counselor."

"He became involved in a wrestling match with the chef-owner of the best restaurant in Crete. My client simply said that he did not like the coffee — "

"Wait a moment, counselor," said the Judge, as she glanced at papers on her desk. "What were the defendant's exact words?"

"My client said — "

"Speak loudly enough for the whole courtroom to hear," said the Judge.

"My client said: 'This coffee is so weak, it is holding on to the sides of the cup.'"

Laughter tried to ring around the courtroom but three poundings from the gavel beat it back.

"I've been told," said the Judge, "that we have some of that coffee here today. Let me have a cup."

And after she had tasted half of it, she said, "This coffee is superb. In pronouncing my sentence, I want to emphasize two factors. Firstly, to insult our coffee — or our bread, our olive oil, our wine — is to insult the entire national character of the Greeks. Why? Because everything that we create is made with quality and pride. And secondly, we must protect our society from fools who have prejudices instead of artistic tastes, the self-deceivers who call themselves critics of food, culture, politics, or art. When these idiots gain power and prestige, then the worst things are praised as the best things, and the best things die from neglect. ... Now in this case, since there were no damages to the chef himself or to any property, I order that the defendant pay a sum of five-thousand Euros —"

The crowd murmured in shock at the announcement of this large sum, wondering how much more strongly the Judge would punish those who were convicted of a more serious offense.

" — five thousand Euros to be paid to our city's general fund. In addition, for the remainder of the defendant's vacation in Crete, he will be banned from entering all eating establishments. He is permitted to drink drinks and to eat food only from bottles and cans."

The Judge shuffled some papers on her desk.

"We have heard cases of eating and drinking," she said. "now we have a woman accused of being merry. Counselor may approach the bench."

"Your honor," said the lawyer. "My client, the defendant, owns a store on Sagapodia Avenue, where she sells kisses to lonely men. Her customers are separated from her by a wall, and she kisses their lips through a cut-out hole. We have provided proof that there is nothing more to it than that: no other body contact, I mean. We intend to defend our client with a simple and indisputable argument. Kissing is not harmful, and self-employment is not harmful, and therefore my client should be permitted to remain in business, without interference from the court."

"Counselor," said the Judge. "Please take the stand ... If I sprinkled a few drops of water on your head, would that hurt you?"

"Of course not, your honor."

"And if I dropped a handful of clay soil on your head?"

"No, your honor, that would not hurt at all."

"But suppose," said the Judge, "that I mixed that water and clay-soil, baked it in a high-temperature oven, and then dropped this brick onto your head. Would that hurt you?"

"Yes, but Your Honor — "

"My honor has nothing to do with it!" snapped Judge said. "It is the honor of your client and her clientele that I am concerned about. The kissing store will be closed immediately, and a fine of ten thousand Euros will be remanded to our town's treasury. Next case."

Pateras stood up and then approached the Judge.

"Judge Skleerokardos," he said. "My first client has been accused of obstructing justice. The Tourist Police were attempting to make arrests, and he — one man alone — knocked down ten officers before six more policemen wrestled him to the ground. I request that my client be rewarded one thousand Euros."

The Judge shook her head.

"And why does a man who breaks the law deserve to be rewarded?"

Pateras coolly replied.

"My client provided a valuable public service. He demonstrated that the town's police officers are in such poor physical condition that it takes more than a dozen of them to subdue one flabby tourist run amok."

"Your client may take the stand," said the Judge.

When Pateras looked towards the doors of the courtroom, the Judge said: "If your client does not appear then his bail money will be forfeited, his trial will be postponed, and he will remain incarcerated until that next trial."

After tense seconds, two wooden doors opened, followed by an out-of-breath Panzano running into the courtroom.

"Excuse me, Mrs. Judge," he said. "I am so sorry to be not on time. Tardiness runs in my family, like the revenge of Montezuma. My father always looks at me and says: 'Some men are born late, others achieve lateness, others have lateness thrust upon them.' And my mother tells me 'Panzano, you will be late for your own funeral.'"

"You just were," said the Judge. "Sit down on the witness stand then tell the court your name."

"I am Panzano Panettone."

"You have admitted," said the Judge, "that the charges against you are true?"

"I knocked down the policemen," Panzano said. "I was not thinking before I was doing. *Piu stupido di cosi si muore* — nobody could be more stupid than that."

"Can you explain your actions, Panzano?" the Judge asked.

"I was in love with a nun named Dolcezza, and the police were taking her away."

The Judge grimaced as she shook her head.

"What is the problem with this beast called Love, that countless crimes are perpetrated in her name? So many men, so many stuporous moments. ... Panzano, no matter how much you are in love, you are not permitted to defy the law. You had known the woman for how long?"

Laughter shook the courtroom after Panzano replied:

"For a long time, your honor. For almost twelve hours!"

The Judge's cold-stone eyes rolled upwards.

"It has been well-documented that testosterone impairs the functioning of the human brain. Do you still believe that those spasmodic glandular eruptions could constitute even the flimsiest shadow of genuine Love?"

Pateras translated that sentence by whispering into the ear of his client these simple words: 'Are you still in love with her?'

And then Panzano replied: "Last week she confessed to me that her name is not Dolcezza and she is not a nun. And I told her that I will love her forever, no matter what her name is and no matter what she has done."

Knowing what was coming, Pateras tried to slow down the avalanche.

"Judge Skleerokardos," he said, "I would like to remind the court that in the brief scuffle with Mr. Panettone, no officers were injured."

The Judge signed a paper then handed it to her clerk.

"Mr. Panettone, it is clear to me that you enjoy knocking things down. Therefore I order that you be sent to our town prison, where you will be provided with a hammer to knock down large chunks of stones. Based on your conduct during the first week, the length of your term in jail will be decided at a future time. Next case."

As he left the stand Panzano shouted: "If it will help Dolcezza I will knock down every mountain in Greece!"

Twelve women sat down in two rows of seats at the front of the courtroom, to the left of the Judge. Pateras spoke a few words to the women and then faced the Judge's bench.

"Judge Skleerokardos," he said, "I would like to introduce my twelve clients to the court. These first ten have been called Forza, Donnabella, Volutta, Scherza, Agevolezza, Impetuosamenta, Anima, Celerita, Bria, Voleggianda. They are not the nuns that they pretended to be. They are gypsies, by profession, and their real names are Katerina, Meli, Romantza, Thalia, Cinarella, Fenella, Floure, Kisaiya, Mizella and Narilla."

The gypsies had been cleaned and dressed in simple dresses, which made them look slender and poised and alert, like cats eager to escape the house.

"My next client, Mother Zitella Whackanzakis, is here before you because out of pity from her large heart, she tried to help these gypsies to escape. And my last client also befriended the gypsy women and tried to help them. As a nun she was known as Dolcezza, but in reality she is a student at the University in Athens. She is my granddaughter and her name is Irene."

Panzano applauded and the crowd in the courtroom buzzed until the gavel hammered three times against the desk. The Judge spoke.

"The ten defendants accused of robbery and fraud have agreed to make a full confession of their crimes, on the condition that all charges would be dropped against Mother Whackanzakis and Irene. To those terms the court agrees."

The Judge instructed Mother Whackanzakis and Irene to leave the defendants' seats but remain in the courtroom; and then she held up a booklet with many pages.

"Before me, I have a list of complaints against the ten defendants, a list as long as the Iliad. Pickpocketing. Shoplifting. Collecting money for nonexistent charities. Begging in public places. Kissing a man with two lips while snatching his wallet with one hand. Swiping breads and cheeses from bakeries and shops."

"Judge Skleerokardos," said Pateras. "Before pronouncing sentences, I would like the court to consider the defendants' youth and circumstances. Additionally I propose that since a term in confinement would be an excessive hardship on these women who have always lived in the outdoors, I will volunteer myself to serve their entire terms in jail. And I can guarantee that never again will they commit these crimes."

"Pateras," said the Judge. "You would like to guarantee that, but you cannot. It is impossible to blot out the stains of a criminal heart as easily as one wipes a blackboard with a sponge. The court denies your request. If there is no other evidence to present, then — for the safety of the citizens and the tourists of Crete — I will now recommend my sentence. One hundred years in total: for each one of the defendants, ten years in jail with no parole."

Wails and shouts from the courtroom, at the harshness of the punishment, quickly evaporated when the Judge banged her gavel and shouted:

"If we do not get silence immediately then I will clear this court!"

Silence. Heartlessly did her eyes flash.

"Ten years each, to begin — "

The heavy doors of the courtroom swung open and in walked a man in his mid-fifties, supported by a cane in his right hand, and a well-built woman on his left.

"I have come from Athens," he said, "thanks to the efforts of a young man named Panzano, who drove me to Piraeus and then paid my boat fare from there to here. I have something urgent to say about the problem of the gypsies."

The Judged shook her head.

"The evidence against them is overwhelming, and the defendants have admitted their guilt. It is too late."

"Is it ever too late," asked Kosmos, "to discover the whole truth, and to do what is good and right?"

There was a silent pause as the Judge weighed these words on the tipsy scales that balance Truth, Justice, and Efficiency. She looked behind her, on the wall, at the motto from Dante's hopeless hell. She sipped the last mouthful of cold coffee, and then drummed her fingers against her desk. At last, glancing at her gold watch — or gold locket — she shook her head and sighed.

"The court will hear you," said the Judge. "Take your seat on the witness stand."

63
THE TRIAL OF THE GYPSIES

THERE IS ONE PHOTOGRAPH of the American bard that Walt Whitman-lovers especially love. Not the tilted-hat standing-up photo from *Leaves of Grass;* not the white-haired sitting-down picture that shows him one stanza away from death. This supreme photograph gives us a man smiling joyfully, filled with the great secret of life. He is confidence without vanity, boldness without aggression, love without shame. Tenderly, the Poet looks into your eyes, speaks to you alone, and with the voice of a brother he whispers, "Walk with me, just a little ways, and you will understand."

Kosmos strolled through the doorway with this same Whitmanesque presence, power, and poise. Aided by Penelope and a cane, he walked slowly to the witness stand. He was wearing a suit and tie — alien garb for this earthy man — and his graying beard and hair flew wild around him as if the four winds were blowing in his face.

The Judge arranged her piles of notes.

"Take the stand, please," she said, "and let me instruct you regarding the testimony that you are about to give. We have already received written confessions that these ten defendants, living for the past eight months as gypsies, have been the scourge of Crete. They have stolen money, clothing, bicycles, jewelry, and food. In fact, we were unable to find an impartial jury for these gypsies, because every prospective juror had heard about their exploits, and told us that they would vote to lock them away for three lifetimes. Trust that I have not shed one tear to hear the defense attorney argue that these women are poor, innocent victims of an unjust society. This court does not believe in mercy, it believes in justice. Your testimony at this point is welcome as long as you contribute something new to the debate. Have I been clear?"

"Glass and women are always in danger," said Kosmos. "And your words have been clear as this water in my glass."

"Tell the court the name you were given at birth."

"Meteoros Kosmosophos Polimegalokardiakosmos."

"Do you," asked the Judge, "have tangible proof of your identity?"

"I am the only man in Greece who can pronounce my name. Please, dear Judge, call me Kosmos."

"Kosmos, then. What is your occupation?"

"My occupation? ... I have had dozens of different ones. Most recently I became an expert at uncovering lids from garbage cans, and then transporting the garbage to a dumping-station that I designed, where it could be sorted and composted or reused. That is the work I have done for money and for our environment. The real work I do is to uncover new ideas, then carry them into action."

"Have you ever been tried for a crime in the courts of Greece?"

Kosmos smiled at the familiar Judge.

"I think you know the answer to your own question, Judge, but there must be people sitting here who do not. I have been tried and convicted for two instances of bigamy and failing to pay alimony to support my wealthy wives. I had been sentenced to twenty years in prison, but after serving less than five months of my sentence, with a full pardon I was released."

"Can you tell the court what is your relationship to the ten defendants?"

Kosmos shook his head.

"That is the kind of question I always answer with silence and a smile."

The Judge banged her gavel twice.

"Kosmos," she said sternly. "Let me explain this to you in terms that are purely economic. The last man who gave a frivolous answer on this witness stand went home poorer by one thousand Euros. You are not the king in your kitchen, you are a jester in my court. What is your relationship to the ten defendants?"

"It is the same relationship," said Kosmos, "with these young women as with all beautiful young women: I will be a lover if they let me, a father if they need food and a place to sleep, a teacher if they want to learn about art and the great books, and a brother if they need a friend."

"And regarding these specific defendants," said the Judge, "which of those roles have you played?"

"None of them," said Kosmos. "In fact, I hardly know the defendants at all. I am here to help because the plight of these women has touched the lives of my father and my best friends."

Pateras stood up.

"Judge Skleerokardos," he said. "You made it a point to weaken Kosmos's credibility when you asked him to tell the court about his past conviction. It has been stated that he was sentenced to twenty years and was released in less than five months. In the interest of fairness, it would be useful to ask how he has been able to earn his freedom."

The Judge glanced at her watch.

"Pateras, you remind me of the camel who stuck his nose into a man's tent — a man who he had never met before. The camel asked if he could keep his nose there to keep it warm. The man said 'yes', and then the camel asked if he could stick his head inside to warm the head. The man said 'yes' again, then one thing led to another, and in less than an hour the camel was sitting warm inside the tent and the poor man was freezing, standing outside. ... Kosmos, you may tell the court how you managed to evade your twenty-year sentence."

"The whole story?" he asked.

The Judge nodded. "Just tell us the donuts and leave out the holes."

"To set the record straight," said Kosmos, "I was brought to trial, convicted, and sentenced so harshly because my wives hired the most expensive lawyer in Athens, a vile man who lives for money only and would sell his mother for a case of wine. My first day in prison I was issued a black-and-white striped uniform; I looked like a zebra, and I called myself 'Zebra the Greek'. ... Those first weeks in jail I gave lectures every night, and taught the prisoners how to manage their loneliness and isolation. We sang, we danced, we painted, we read Homer and Kazantzakis, we created things with our minds and hands. I had a good time, but then one day I woke up and remembered the motto of Andersen's nightingale: 'If I am not free I cannot sing, and if I cannot sing I die.'"

The listeners in the courtroom burst into applause, the Judge banged her gavel. Kosmos carried on.

"So I resolved to get my freedom back and never lose it again. I began reading books about the great escapes. There were a thousand examples of fearless defiance, but what about acceptance? I made a plan and made it work: I continued my program of helping my fellow prisoners to recreate their lives, to do what their education should have done: teach men to desire the things that are healthy and good for their bodies and their souls. And soon, the other prisoners and I were having so much fun every day, that all we needed to make paradise out of prison were some good women and some good meals."

Kosmos looked up at the Judge.

"Of course, the powers-that-be couldn't let that kind of merriment continue, because the whole point of prison is to be so unpleasant that it will be a deterrent to crime, not to be a vacation resort so enjoyable that people will commit crimes just to get in. So the prison psychiatrist was asked to solve the problem of 'the Zebra' as they called me. I was assigned to this psychiatrist, named Doctor Probleema, a man who I now admire, a man of absolute integrity. In every profession, ninety-nine percent of the members serve themselves, and one percent serve their clients. Doctor Probleema is one of the one percent. He started his career full of fire and optimism, but after six months he grew discouraged when his idealism collided with the bottomless stupidity of the real world. Well, one morning he called me into his office, asked me to lie down on the couch, and then he sat beside me holding a notepad and a pen.

"'You look exhausted,' I said to the Doctor.

"'Thank you,' he answered, 'I feel much worse than I look.'

"'Having problems that you care to talk about, Doctor Probleema?'

"'Wife is never happy with what I do at home, boss is never satisfied with what I do at work. Where can I relax?'

"'You can relax right here,' I said, standing up. 'Lie down for a minute.'

And after we had exchanged places I picked up his pen and notepad and then asked him: 'What is your biggest stress at work?'

"'In general,' he said, 'the worst thing is being assigned to projects that I do not believe in. Need an example? ... You, Kosmos, are the healthiest man in Athens, and my job is to 'cure' you and make you normal, by telling you how to diminish your natural rebellion and joy. ... But right now, my biggest headache of all is the cat problem. If I don't find a solution fast, then I can grab a shovel and bury my career plans in the nearest grave.'

"Smiling sympathetically, I said to the mind doctor: 'Tell me about it.'"

"'It started two years ago, when a report came to my office that hundreds of Greek teenagers were eating cold cats. Naturally, I thought it was a diet and nutrition report with a comical typographical error, and that the report should have said 'cold cuts'. So I didn't pay attention to it right away. But it was cats, the four-footed felines that these kids were eating. What had started as a fraternity joke caught on like the songs that top the charts. Next month, I have to speak at a conference about what's causing this crisis and what to do about it. Right now I know as much about the problem as that clock on the wall, and I can honestly say that nobody in my profession has learned anything in the two years since the problem first came to light. The more you forbid teenagers to do something, the more they want to do it. And the more that the problematic actions bother you, the less effective you can be with your response.'"

Kosmos sipped water, looked out at the faces in the courtroom, then glanced up at the Judge.

"So I said to that psychiatrist, 'Doctor Probleema, suppose I could solve this problem for you, tell you precisely why this has happened, and give you a plan of action for what needs to be done. Could you get me out of this prison for good?' ... The doctor laughed then said: 'Kosmos, you would not believe how easily that could be arranged.'

"We shook hands and I went to work. Was I discouraged because the professionals had failed to understand this catastrophe? ... Not at all. These big-name psychiatrists and professor-types spend their days and years sifting through dry papers and staring at lifeless computer screens. What do they know about real life? To them the human heart is not a mystery, it is a profitable enterprise. These people are the modern alchemists, and the only secret they've unlocked is the age-old trick about how to transmute leaden bullshit into paper gold. The world is not enriched by their efforts, but the gold runs like rivers into their bank accounts."

Kosmos smiled.

"You see, I've spent more than forty years — ever since I was a teenager myself — talking to people, telling stories to them, then listening to their problems and hopes, their disappointments and desires. Doctor Probleema signed a paper which allowed me to go outside the jail with him at any time. We went all over Athens — to the schools and homes and streets — and talked face-to-face with the troubled kids.

In one month of working like this I had the answer. I first gave the problem a name, so that we could identify it, and spin a discussion around it the way a spider weaves his web."

Kosmos's story had interested the listeners so much that they began talking quietly, until the Judge banged the gavel and then spoke.

"And what did you call it, Kosmos, this problem of teenagers eating the cats?"

The face of Kosmos now reminded me of the faces of those Greek sculptures before the Fifth Century B.C.E., a type which has been called 'the archaic smile'. Kosmos smiled with no teeth showing, and just the slightest upturn at both corners of the mouth.

"Dear Judge," said Kosmos, with eyes agleam. "what else could it be called? ... 'The *Ate-a-puss Complex.*'"

The courtroom exploded with laughter, which even the first three gavel-bangs could not calm down. Three more raps made it a bit quieter, and when nine times the Judge's gavel had circled then slammed against the desk, silence was at last restored. Kosmos, who had been raising his hands to help regain order, now looked at the face of the Judge.

"Those big-name psychiatrists laughed too, when they heard that complex name. But that is my strategy, you see: First I make you laugh, and then I tell you the deep truths that will change your life. Why were the teenagers eating cats? ... Tell me this: Why do kids today pierce their bodies and fill them with metal rings? Why do students leap to their deaths from the top of buildings at the Universities? Why do kids waste themselves by taking drugs and drinking too much alcohol? ...

"I can tell you the reasons for all this self-destructive behavior. We spoil our children with money and material things, but we do not love them enough, we do not give them the educational nourishment they need. Today's children are dying from the stress of modern culture. Their lives, like most adult lives, are boring and useless and fake. The way a plant needs water and sunlight and good soil, children need freedom and adventure and the arts. Instead, we throw them in front of televisions and computer screens — which dries up their bodies and brains, and makes them robots relentlessly programmed for one purpose: to buy.

"Until we give them back their childhoods — and until we adults set examples and show them how nobly and wisely real men and women can live — children will rebel and act out their desperation by doing the craziest things. Want to cure the *Ate-a-puss Complex?* This is what you must do: love the child, smash the televisions, knock down the shopping malls, show children the beauty of nature and the joyfulness of making art, read with them the best of the best books. Give children back their childhood, that sweet paradise that nourishes the child with real experiences, brave hopes, and tender dreams."

The hands of the listeners filled the courtroom with thunderous applause. Strangely, instead of bringing her gavel down, the Judge let the clapping continue until it sputtered then faded by itself.

"Kosmos," she said, "let us return to our wolves. How is all this pertinent to the case before us? For the past five months, these gypsies have comitted hundreds of thefts, frauds, swindles, and petty crimes."

Kosmos nodded.

"Judge, I cannot deny your facts," he said. "But I will take these facts outside into the open air, so that you can see them in a brave new light. You asked me: 'Kosmos, how is your story about the teenagers connected to the plight of the gypsy maids?' ... Here is the answer. This same cold-hearted culture that warps children is the culture that oppresses women and the underprivileged class."

Kosmos now pointed to the ten young women.

"These gypsy-women are accused of countless crimes, but they are guilty of one crime only. The one crime that our selfish society will not forgive: they are poor. They were starving to death, and as the old saying says: Hunger knows no laws. Judge, when I first sat down today you talked about your interest in justice. The murderers of justice are greed and nepotism. Have enough cash, or an Uncle who knows somebody important? Then anything goes. You get that high-paying job at the University or in City Hall. Your novel is published and grandiosely praised. You can be released from jail in an eyeblink, or be acquitted before you come to trial. Why are the poor persecuted for stealing a loaf of bread, when every day — with impunity and arrogance! — the rich steal millions and billions from the poor and from the working class? Can you tell me why, Judge?"

The Judge put on a pair of spectacles.

"There is a saying, Kosmos: 'The world is the curly tail of a dog — who can straighten it out?' ... We are not here to save the entire world. We are here to improve one small piece of it."

Kosmos stood up in the witness stand.

"We have the very same goal, Judge, so let's see if we can work out the details. Socrates stood trial on the trumped up charges of impiety — although he was always pious — and corrupting the youth of Athens — although he was one of the few men in Greek history who improved that city's youth. In the dialogue named *The Apology* he did not apologize! He told his accusers that when you punish a good man, you do evil to yourself. And that is my new idea to you: if you punish these innocent women for the crime of being poor, then you will hurt yourself, and hurt all the citizens of Crete."

"I do not understand," said the Judge, "how putting ten gypsies in jail will harm the citizens of Crete."

Kosmos scratched his head and then sat down.

"Let me explain this to you in terms that are purely economic. I assume that you know exactly how much it costs this town to keep one person in prison for one year."

Without hesitating, the Judge stated the amount. It was so large that the listeners in the courtroom all began talking at once.

"Now, Judge," said Kosmos, "since you have proposed a sentence of ten years each for the ten women, let's multiply that amount one hundred times. ... Is it better to use this large quantity of money to destroy ten lives, or better to use it for something that would improve the local community? ... We cannot let the defendants go free to steal from honest citizens, and we cannot put them in jail for the crime of attempting to save their own lives. There is still one good alternative."

"And that is?" asked the Judge.

Kosmos stood up, raised his arm, pointed to the roof above.

"Exile."

The crowd murmured, the gavel pounded, the Judge spoke.

"On the one hand," she said, "there is a precedent in Greek law for offering the choice of exile. ... On the other hand, 'Dreams without money are birds without wings'. ... When he was a boy, Leonardo da Vinci worked and earned money, and then he used his money to buy caged birds, so he could set them free. ... Nobody can enter a foreign country without money: they will not let you in, and even if you did get in, when you got there you could not legally work: you would be forced to starve or steal. Is your bank account as big as your heart, Kosmos?"

"I am a poor man, Judge. Right now I own nothing but my freedom and my daring mind. But there is someone sitting in this courtroom who might have both the willingness and the means."

Kosmos whispered into the Judge's ear, and then the Judge announced:

"This court will recess for ten minutes, then reconvene."

"Do not be shy, sister. Please tell the court your name."

"Mother Zitella Whackanzakis."

The Mother-nun looked even older now than when I had encountered her on the boat. Her body filled up the large white nun's frock; her face had so many wrinkles it was difficult to look at; and warty age spots blemished both her hands.

"Where do you work, Mother?"

"In Rome, at 'The Church of the Everlasting Bingo'. And at its branch office in Thessaloniki, in the 'Home for the Nearly Virtuous.'"

"How did you first meet the ten defendants?"

"I received a letter, from an organization named WANDERBORE, stating that there were ten gypsies who needed help. I journeyed to Crete in order to bring them to Thessaloniki, where they would be safe from the police."

The Judge looked into the eyes of the Mother-nun.

"Are you willing to accept the responsibility for managing these ten young women? I warn you to consider that these gypsies have lived nothing but vagabond lives. The wild grape seed does not often grow into a calm oak tree. Are you willing to take these women to another country, care for them as your own daughters, and support them there?"

"I am willing," said the Mother-nun.

"You are willing but are you able?" asked the Judge. "Do you have resources to finance not only their food and housing, but also the passports and visas and paperwork, and the outrageous fees that the attorneys will demand for the simple act of preparing these legal documents?"

"I do not have the money for this," said the Mother-nun.

Voices in the courtroom buzzed and then the Mother-nun spoke more.

"I have not enough money myself, but I know a man who has much more than he needs. He might be willing to pay the money, if I give him something that he wants."

The Judge scribbled a note on her writing pad.

"As I consider this request, I would now ask the defendants if they are willing to place themselves under the legal guardianship of Mother Whackanzakis."

Katerina jumped up.

"We are willing a million times!" she shouted. "If Mother Whackanzakis gets us out of this mess, we who preyed like tigers will graze like lambs. We will be good, I swear it! When she says 'Jump!' we will jump up to the moon, and when she hollers 'Stop!' then we will freeze in mid-air!"

The Judge motioned with her hand for Kosmos to step up to her bench beside her. She whispered into his ear.

"No, that would be impossible," Kosmos said. "I cannot do that."

The Judge banged her gavel twice.

"Then it will be my unfortunate duty to deny the request to —"

"*Perimeneteh!* Wait!" shouted Kosmos. "I agree to those slave-driving terms. I agree."

Flat onto the desk the Judge lay her gavel down.

"In that case, pending the proof of funding and necessary paperwork, I order that the legal guardianship of the ten gypsies be placed in the honest hands of Mother Whackanzakis. Funding for this project must be provided to this court within thirty days. Until then the defendants will continue to be guests of our county jail. I warn the defendants that if the promised funding does not appear in thirty days, or if their conduct is unsatisfactory, then without hesitation I will recommend the original sentence of ten years each."

"Might they do some community service work for a few hours a day during their jail time?" asked the Mother-nun.

"I will consider that request. This court is now adjourned until three p.m."

The Judge stood up and packed her papers into a black briefcase. Kosmos approached her.

"How are you, my dear Judge?" he said. "I didn't forget your birthday. Here is a card that I made myself."

"I will read it later," said the Judge. "I have time for one more story from you, Kosmos. Why are you limping and leaning on that cane?"

"It is nothing," he said. "I was doing some civil disobedience in Agia Souvlakis, when a wall fell down and broke my hip. The doctor promised that I will be dancing in less than a year, though for the rest of my life I will have some pain or discomfort there. It's good for me! That pain will never let me forget that in fifty-five years of living, there was one moment when I had the courage to stand up and fight for something that I loved with my whole heart."

The Judge opened her gold locket, and then kissed the fifty-year-old photograph.

"I trust, Kosmos, that you will also not forget your part of the bargain we made today?"

Kosmos, with great affection, squeezed the elderly woman's hand.

"I promise I will phone you one time every week, Mother dear."

6 4
POVERTY AND NAKEDNESS
DO NOT MATTER

AT PENELOPE'S HOUSE, IN AGIA SOUVLAKIS, Kosmos had asked me to
join his family and friends. The get-together would celebrate three mi-
raculous events: Kosmos's freedom, the trial of the gypsies, and what
he called 'shocking good news.' When everyone — Penelope, Irene, Pateras, Aspasia, Ligeia, Georgios, Rakis, the wife of Rakis, and I — had
gathered in the backyard garden and then undressed, Kosmos raised his
wine glass.

"There is a an old Cretan saying I want to share with you," he said.
"'Poverty and nakedness do not matter if you have a good wife.' Today,
for the first time in my life, I would like to discover if those words are
true."

With his arm around Penelope's shoulders, he gazed at her affectionately.

"Penelope, you are the Crete that Homer raved about: 'Ravisher of
eyes, bountiful and many-manned, with ninety cities gleaming twixt her
boundless hills.' ... Let these bare witnesses bear witness that on this day
I asked you to come live with me and be my wife."

Penelope finished the last bite of her pear, then tossed it over her shoulder into the pumpkin patch.

"No," she said. "I will not."

The face of Kosmos wrinkled with shock and disappointment.

"No?" shouted Kosmos. "There are two kinds of noes. Do you mean
the permanent 'no' that means never, the way the Spartans resolved to
die before they let the Persians pass? Or do you mean the temporary 'no'
that a woman says when she is flattered by the man's advances, but can't
quite decide how much she loves and how much she desires?"

Penelope stuck both hands onto her hips.

"Do you mean," she said, "the permanent husband, who is faithful
to his wife? Or the temporary husband, who dances with Selena while
thinking of Helena?"

Kosmos raised his hands to the sky.

"The Hindus have a theory that a man's past actions haunt him throughout his reincarnated lives. I don't know much about that. But I do know that what a man does in his past always runs up and catches him, just at the moment when he tries to transform himself into a nobler man."

"Kosmos," said Penelope. "A good marriage is both a pleasure and a business. For the business part to succeed, it needs a bit of money and a sound financial plan. If we were younger, then the money wouldn't matter: we could live on water and lust. This morning I sent nearly my whole savings to help the gypsies, in case that well-meaning Mother-nun fails to get the funding that she needs. Now I have nothing saved, and I refuse to be financially supported by any man."

"This news is wonderful, Penelope!" said Kosmos. "Yesterday afternoon, I asked Rakis to drive to Agios Nikolodeonos and take all my savings to the Mother-nun. Now we are poor, we can be poor together. We are lonely, we can be lonely together. We can't afford new clothes, we can be naked together. Kosmos and Penelope make the perfect match!"

Penelope shook her head and then Kosmos touched her arm gently.

"Don't do it for yourself, Penelope — do it for womankind. Marrying me takes one more rogue out of circulation. You'll be a hero to the women of the world."

Penelope laughed, still shaking her head.

"Between the two of us," she said, "we could not cough up ten Euros for the marriage license."

Kosmos reached for his pockets before he recalled that had no pockets and no pants — but even if he had been wearing pants, there would have been nothing in them to take out.

"Stay here, Penelope, I'll be back in thirty minutes and I'll ask to marry you again. What logic cannot conquer laughter can."

Grabbing his cane, Kosmos hobbled into Penelope's house, to the middle room where we had stored his furniture, books, and all the worldly possessions from his house in Dembacchae.

Pateras placed his hand on my shoulder then spoke in his deep voice.

"What an actress that woman is!" he said, laughing with a broad smile. "Don't worry about her, Thoreau — you'll soon see that Penelope is not as poor as she claims to be. I smell a wedding in the air this afternoon, and if they can survive together for the first three hours, then their marriage will last another fifty years. What about you, Thoreau — getting married this week? What are your plans?"

The old man's directness made me laugh.

"My plans, Pateras? ... To stay single for as long as possible. And to stay in Greece until my money dries up, or my tourist visa expires — whichever comes first."

Pateras smiled.

"When that money disappears, you should know that the experiment called Sextopias is still alive, and that you will be welcome there with open hearts, open arms, and open everything else. Aspasia and I are starting a new place near my home town. Ligeia is making something around Paleohora, and Priestos has a place near the Samaria Gorge. And that sweet couple Nikos and Hagfa — do you remember them? — have joined their lives, and found some land not far from Rethymnon. Don't tell Kosmos yet — his next wife will break the good news later today — Penelope has plans for a community on the Greek mainland. That will be five groups, and I am happy about that, but secretly my heart wishes that there could be six."

He squeezed my hand warmly, in such a way I wondered if he had just dropped a hint: I should consider becoming the founder of the sixth place.

"Pateras," I said. "Are you certain that this world is ready for the free expression of sexuality and love?"

"This world may never be ready," he said. "but it's the only world we have. In every age, a handful of enlightened individuals arise, and civilization never advances until these individuals seize the chance to think and to live freely, in their own way."

I looked at his eyes, and the hope that glowed there had scattered every shard of fear.

"What will you do if you're discovered by curious tourists or prying police?"

"We will protect our community," he said, "by living simply without many luxuries or things. In that way the people whose lives spin around possessing and possessions will have no interest in us at all. Even if they do seize our property or force us to stop expressing our passionate way of life, then we will find some way to carry on. Thoreau, do you know the dramas of Aeschylus? In one of these, two friends meet, and the first one asks: 'What's the news in Athens? Is it still unsacked?'And the second man, knowing that the city had been taken by invaders, replies profoundly: 'Yes, in its living men its foundation stands secure.' ... We are strong because we have the truth of the heart within us. Inside all living women and men, burning like the sun, is the dream of paradise and the all-powerful desire to give unselfish love."

Partings! Could this be the last time I would see the kind face of Pateras, the last time I could learn from his wisdom and experience? By looking at my face he read my mind, then answered these questions before I asked.

"There is a Greek tradition, Thoreau, that when an old man parts from a young man, he gives the young man two gifts: bread for his body, thoughts for his soul. You're a smart man, but many smart men get lured into the concrete jungle then lose their way. Don't shrivel up into one of those vain intellectual-types who spend forever arguing whether a zebra has black stripes on a white body, or white stripes on a body that's black. Look at the great persons in history and you'll see three common themes: they are men of action, they are men of non-violence, and their ideas and their actions are as one. The best technology today will be outmoded five years hence, but the best love stories will inspire us forever. Love is everything! Learning how to live better means learning how to change yourself, how to grow in love."

He placed a loaf of dark bread into my hands.

"And now I will tell you what I have learned in my eighty years of making mistakes with women. When I found Aspasia I knew I had learned something at last, but up till then I was as big a fool as any man. You may tell this secret to any woman you like, but never reveal it to another man."

Pateras whispered a perplexing passage into my curious ear. The moment Pateras had finished, Kosmos shouted that he needed me to help him with some work inside the house of Penelope.

"Take her feet, Thoreau, and help me move her. Am I getting weaker as I get older? This damn Snake Goddess feels heavier every time I pick her up."

After carrying the Snake Goddess to the middle of the room, we found the wooden statue of Priapus which had been smothered between heaps of clothing and boxes of books. Kosmos pulled out his art supplies, then cut two pieces of canvas to make two face-sized masks. He mixed some paints, then in mere minutes he painted one of the masks with the face of Penelope.

"Twenty years ago she looked like this, Thoreau," he said. "Why did it take me twenty years of wandering to realize how I need her in my life?"

He finished the mask of young Penelope, then pulled out a mirror and sketched his own face on the remaining mask. Clearly it was Kosmos, but a satyr-like Kosmos with slanted eyebrows and a sly grin.

"Not quite right ... Ah, your eyes! With your eyes here, my mask will be irresistible."

Kosmos, mixed some paints as he envisioned how he would capture the clear passion in my eyes. While he worked he talked about his life, and mine.

"We know how to love and play, Thoreau, but we haven't yet found our work. That's the only thing we need to be colossal men! If we stay this way, we won't be the worst men, and we won't be the best. We'll never hurt anybody, but we'll never do anything great."

"What about your art, Kosmos?" I asked.

"My art? Every artist needs three qualities: imagination, daring, and discipline. Of those first two qualities I have more than enough. But my lack of discipline makes me a babbler and a dabbler, instead of a serious artist who struggles to give form to his dreams. If only I had practiced my painting for one hour more every day, just one hour more! I could have been a professional artist, and made a living doing something I loved."

His hand wiped his eyes.

"For years I blamed lack of money for my failure: with money, I pretended, I would have had time to paint, time to study the master painters, time to perfect techniques and learn the open secrets from the best of the best. But money was never the real problem: I wanted to chase women more than I wanted to make masterpieces. No, I never had the discipline to be a real artist, and worse than that I never had the guts. Why didn't I put my heart on the canvas? I was afraid that nobody would understand me. And I thought that the censor-morons would call my work old-fashioned, or primitive, or Romantic, or idealistic or obscene. And they would have, that's for sure! But I should have painted whatever I wanted to paint, and then told them all to go to hell on the back of a galloping mule."

And now he spoke to me the way a father would have spoken to his son.

"You know, Thoreau, I've spent many weeks thinking about what I would say to you on our last day together."

"Our last day? I'll be back in Greece next year, Kosmos. Or at the latest, the year after that."

Kosmos shook his head.

"You say those words now, and that's what you believe. 'Keep the soup warm, darling, I'll be back!' That's what I've sworn to dozens of women when I've left their beds after a passionate night. I told them I'd be back next evening, but most of the time I never went back. What do you think, Thoreau: Are men slaves to the past, or are we free? In the mornings I believe that every man is free to shape this day into a thousand possibilities. But every night, as I compare what I accomplished to what I'd dreamed, I think that all our choices are made by two women: Fate and Luck."

Memories from long ago tugged him, his eyes reddened with tears, then he wiped his eyes and put the final brush strokes on the mask's eyes.

"You know what hurts me most, Thoreau? ... The way people exist without living. The way they cause their own suffering, suffering that nothing except their own brave actions can relieve. You know how I want to be remembered? As the man who advised: 'Don't wait!' ... Don't wait till tomorrow for the world to change — you can change the world right now by starting with your own sweet self."

He tied the masks onto the heads of the wooden statues, then asked me to help him to carry the statues outside to Penelope and the guests. When Penelope saw the two wooden figures — Priapus and the Snake Goddess with the faces of Kosmos and Penelope — she laughed wildly, and then she hugged Kosmos with all her might.

"Let's get married right this minute!" she said.

"I was thinking," replied Kosmos, "about setting the date for two summers from now."

"Right now or nevermore!" shouted Penelope.

The ancient village leader, Tiropitas, now ambled into the garden.

"They told me to come with a marriage license and join Penelope and Kosmos. I'm late because I didn't believe them — I thought they were playing pranks on an old man. Let's do this quick, before the both of you change your minds and I lose my ten Euros fee."

Tiropitas stepped between Penelope and Kosmos.

"This is a poem of Plato, called, 'I throw the apple.' Does anyone have an apple? ... There's not one apple left in all of Crete, eh? We'll use this pomegranate, then. Join hands, you two lovebirds, and repeat after me:

> "I throw the apple to you, take it free
> If you accept, then give me your virginity.
> If you decline to give, then take it anyway
> And think how quickly youth and beauty pass away."

Penelope threw the pomegranate to Kosmos; he caught it then bit it then threw it back to Penelope. She caught it, and then — after a funny-faced hesitation — Penelope took the bait with a bite.

"Now this is the time," Tiropitas said, "when the Village Leader gives you advice about how to conduct a marriage that is long-lasting and filled with joy. To the both of you I say: the secret of a long marriage is in this magic word: compromise. To the husband, I say: Never forget that your wife is a woman, and every woman is like a carob pod: no matter how hard is the outside shell, it is always tender inside. To the wife, I say: do not criticize your husband the way my first wife embarrassed me. She said: 'Tiropitas, you make love like termites.' I asked: 'Like termites, what do mean?' And she replied, 'Termites are boring in sex.'"

Tiropitas placed his right hand onto the top of the head of Kosmos, and at the same time touched Penelope with his left hand.

"By the powers infested in me," he said, "I declare that Penelope and Kosmos are now and forever wife and husband. May you be blessed as you have blessed your friends. I've learned one thing during my century of being alive. Real life, the life that matters, is a life with people — loving them, sharing joys and laughter, giving a helping hand, caring for another person's needs. Reach out to your family, friends and neighbors and you will never be lonely or alone."

Wife and husband kissed passionately as their family and friends looked on and cheered. Many teardrops streamed from the lovely eyes of their daughter Irene. The wedding kiss was followed by dancing and singing and eating until two hours before the sun set, when Penelope asked the guests to help them pack the garbage truck.

"We're going to the Meteora for a honeymoon," she said. "We will stay for two months so that Kosmos can walk naked in the mountains, to heal his swollen hip. And then we'll start a community with so much sex and love that the gods themselves, on nearby Olympus, will beg us to let them in to play!"

"With what money," asked a startled Kosmos, "are we going to do all this healing and community-making and honeymooning?"

Penelope nodded to her father-in-law, Pateras, and together they positioned the wooden statues — Priapus and the Snake Goddess — so that these two figures were engaged standing pressed together, face to face.

"Kosmos," said Penelope. "For twenty years the goddess and the god stood watching each other by your door. So close and yet so far. Don't you think, after all those years of looking at each other's eyes, that they would want to try the one cure for lovesickness?"

"Penelope," said Kosmos. "What the hell do you mean?"

Penelope laughed.

"Push on the backside of Priapus, darling," she said.

Kosmos pushed the wood statue forward, so that the wood pecker of Priapus lunged into the goddess's slit. We heard a loud smack and a louder click. And then the belly of the Snake Goddess dropped open. Out poured hundreds of paper bills and thousands of silver coins.

"Penelope! What is this treasure?" said Kosmos. "Did you hire those gypsies to help you rob the bank of Athens?"

"For the twenty years that I have been working, dearest, I always saved half of my money for the day I would be wed. And now half of this we will give to Irene for her education, and with the other half we will enjoy our honeymoon, and then work to make our paradise."

"But Penelope," said Kosmos. "I've told you five hundred times that from a woman I never take three things: guff, money or advice."

"You idiot!" she said, hugging him to her breast. "I am not only a woman now — I am your missing half, your partner for life, your best friend, your sensual lover, your support whenever you need me, and the one who depends on you to help me whenever I need help. I am your wife! And from your wife you take guff, money, and advice!"

Kosmos scratched his head, and then laughed, then spoke softly to himself.

"Leave Dembacchae-Souvlakis? ... Yes, it's time for that. But there's one last thing to take care of before we go." And then he shouted: "Rakis? ... Rakis!"

Rakis — who with one hand held a wine bottle, and with the other hand was lifting boxes and packages into Kosmos's truck — stopped working and embraced his great friend.

"It's all set, boss," said Rakis. "One man can't replace you, but I found six others, women and men, who will help me to take care of the old folks in this town, and pay attention to the teenagers, too. Tomorrow I'll borrow Tiropitas and Georgios, hammers and wood planks, and twenty energetic teens. In a week we'll build a village community center in Penelope's back yard. A place for young and old, where 'kids can be kids' — as you like to say."

Friends and family packed the garbage truck with everything needed for the next months' travels and adventures. When all the supplies and wedding gifts had been loaded and securely tied onto the truck, Penelope stepped into the driver's seat, Irene slid in beside her, and Kosmos opened up a map and then sat down in the front seat beside the door.

"Father," said Irene, beaming a smile at the man, "I will never forget your face when the coins fell out of the Snake Goddess! Who would have guessed that it held more surprises than the Trojan horse?"

A few tears filled his eyes as his hand brushed Irene's soft hair.

"There is a difference," said Kosmos. "Ours today was a delightful prize, but the one given to Troy — with Odysseus and the Greek soldiers hidden in its body — was a dangerous one. That explains the proverb: 'Beware of gifts bearing Greeks.'"

"That's not the way it goes, dear," said Penelope. "The proverb warns: 'Beware of Greeks bearing gifts.'"

The argument that erupted sounded louder than the revving engine of the truck. Pateras nodded, glanced at me, held up three fingers, and then pointed the fingers at the newlyweds. Instantly I recalled his words about this marriage's all-important first three hours. The rumbling truck began to move.

"Kosmos!" I shouted.

"*Ti,* Thoreau? What?"

"Where are you going?"

"To Herakleion, on the north coast, to put the truck on the ship for Piraeus. We'll drop off Irene in Athens on our way to the Meteora."

"Take me with you to the north coast, will you? I'm heading for Agios Nikolodeonos."

"We will take you anywhere you want to go. Squeeze in the front seat here and hold hands with my daughter — more beautiful than this Spring evening — the daughter who makes me the proudest and happiest father in the land of Greece."

Hours later, the garbage truck rolled to a stop in the center of the town of Ag Nik. The two women hugged me with tear-filled eyes, then spoke good-bye words that would have pierced the hardest stone.

Kosmos gripped my shoulders.

"Flourish, Thoreau. Never will I forget you! Have courage to go your own way. Once in a while you'll remember me: when some fanatic tries to smother your freedom or your truth; or when you hear the cicadas chirping on a perfect summer night; or when you smile at a magnificent woman, and she sees you but doesn't look back into your eyes. You can wonder about me but don't worry: I've found what I've been looking for. Even if the whole damn world moves indoors and people live like moles or like machines, Kosmos will be laughing and dancing under the stars."

I watched the truck vanish down the road. Lost in a world of thoughts, I walked with no attention to where I was going, letting my feet lead me on the way. Would I see these friends again, ever again? Would I remember — or forget, as Kosmos had hinted I might forget — how much those moments meant to me?

There was no need for speculation and no time for regrets. Shrieks as loud as sirens cut through the evening air. Death-chanters howled near a man or woman close to dying, hoping that the terrifying wails would chase old Death away. I looked up, realized where I was standing, then ran up a hillside to the source of the terrifying cries.

65
The Still Small Voice of Hope

Our world is changing at a dizzying velocity. Everything you know this morning is completely useless in another seven days. Yet here, on a hilltop on the isle of Crete, this century-old stone cottage remained the same. When I approached the doorway, four sitting women dressed in widowed-black — the death chanters — screamed, stood up, then scurried down the hillside. In the wooden cage beside the cottage, the lovely dove pressed her head between the wire bars, willing to give up everything if only she could be free.

I dropped my backpack, pushed opened the door then walked in. The six sleeping swine woke up and sniffed me, turned up their snouts, then shuffled out the doorway. I glanced around: despite the lack of light, everything looked familiar and felt like home. The enormous cauldron under the fireplace sat bubbling over a fire; dried herbs dangled from the ceiling; and the walls displayed pots, cooking utensils, and faded photographs. Flat on her back on the makeshift bed, eyes closed, lay the venerable woman, Hope.

"My son," she said, without opening her eyes. "I have been waiting for you to visit me. Many say that Hope is dying, while others chant that Hope is dead. What do you think?"

I kissed her wrinkled forehead. Her cheeks were furrowed like a plowed field, yet her whole face radiated joyfulness. She had filled her years with acts of giving. Rather than a lifetime of regrets and loneliness, her unending gifts of kindness had sown deep experiences and friendships, and had changed so many lives.

"What do I think about Hope?" I said. "As long as one person believes in her wholeheartedly, then she can never die."

The old woman opened her eyes and stood up. She yawned, stretched her arms up toward the ceiling, then walked outside to the dove cage. After talking to the dove in a language I could not understand, Hope opened the cage. Happily, the white bird flew out into the open air.

Back inside, she nodded at me, a nod that told me to grab a sharp knife from the wall. As I chopped the ingredients for her love-potion — onions, leeks, garlic, and aphrodisiacal herbs — the woman stirred the cauldron and sprinkled spices in.

I heard the sound of fluttering wings, and then I watched as a dark-haired woman, about my age, entered the cottage through the front door. With one hand she untied the ribbon behind her long silky hair and let it fall enticingly down, down to her waist. Despite the room's darkly-romantic light it was easy to make out her ripe beauty, her blossoming grace. With one arm she held a tray under her lovely breasts. Between the shimmering hills of that generous bosom, and on top of the wooden tray, a red delicious-looking apple sat temptingly.

"The apple of Love and Danger," said Mother Hope. "My great-grand-daughter has brought it for you, for you alone. Do you want the apple?"

Fearing it would disappear, I reached out to take it but Hope touched my arm, and held me back. She lit a candle then raised the candle near the tray.

"Look again," said Hope. "How many apples do you see?"

Now I saw clearly that two apples had been there all the time. To me they looked the same, exactly, and there was no way to tell them apart. Hope tugged my shirt at the shoulder, and when I bent down she talked in whispers in my ear.

"Two apples remain. One is the apple of Love and Danger, and that one is always fresh and good. The other apple has many names. Sweet it looks to everyone who desires it, but pure poison for anyone who tastes. It will not kill you if you eat it, but its venom will remain on your lips and heart, so that cruel words and deeds would wound the spirit of everyone you meet."

I understood: Love or destruction, there is no middle way. Men who do terrible deeds are reckless boys, ruined in childhood, who have never learned how to love.

"Tell me, Hope," I said. "How can I tell the difference between the two apples that look so much alike?"

Hope placed her arm around the shoulder of her ravishing great-granddaughter.

"Only she can teach you," said Hope. "Yes, she will teach you — if you make her happy in that bed tonight."

The sages swear that happiness comes from within, by your own efforts only. Without her own enlightenment, I could do nothing to make this apple-woman happy. Yet, as she looked at me and sighed, and her eyes gleamed with pure concupiscence, I resolved to do my best.

"And when I get the good apple at last, Mother Hope," I asked, "what should I do then?"

Mother-Hope wiped her hands on her white apron.

"Only a fool would eat it right away, do not do that! Before now your life has been carefree and comfortable, but when you bite this apple everything will change. With love you will find new dangers and new responsibilities. Eat this fruit when you are ready for the brave new life that Love bittersweetly brings."

I looked at the apples, and at the woman who held them on the tray beneath her breasts. Hope dipped a silver ladle into the cauldron, then poured two cups of soup, one for her great-granddaughter and one for me. The comely woman drank her love-broth in one long gulp.

"Drink this now, my son," said Hope. "Drink this then give this lonely woman the most joyful evening of her life."

I drank the warm liquid and my entire body warmed. Hope blew the candle out. The young woman placed her tray of apples onto the wooden table. Humming with excitement, she circled me inside her tender arms.

Early the next morning when dawn's sunlight sliced through the paneless windows, I watched the enchanting woman beside me. Her long hair spread over the pillow, her chest rose and fell like sea-waves, and her sleeping face beamed with ecstatic smiles. After dressing quickly, I kissed her red-ripe lips, and then I examined the kitchen table where both apples lay. Now it was easy to tell the difference between the good and the not-good fruit. So easy that I could not imagine how last night I could have been confused.

I stuffed the nourishing apple into my pocket, then I stepped outside to find Hope. She was busy burning trash on a red-brick grill.

"Can I help you, Mother?" I asked.

"Thank you, son," she said, tossing a pile of papers into the flames. "Do not help me now. This is the time to do your own work."

I lifted my backpack then swung it onto my shoulders.

"Is there anything at all that you need?" I asked.

"I need to help and to inspire others," she said. "That is the one and only thing. Take this silver coin and go to the fountain in the center of town. Give the coin to anyone who has more poverty than you."

"Hope," I said. "I've made so many mistakes. I've wasted so much time. It seems as if I've been close to finding what I needed, but whenever I get close I make the wrong choices, then take the wrong paths. And now that my friends are gone, I feel so far away from everything."

She held my hand between her two hands and she looked up at my eyes.

"Son, son," she said. "When the time is right — not a moment sooner — eat the apple of Love and Danger. Then you will know what you need for the new life. You've made wrong choices? It is never too late to change. No matter how far you've traveled on the wrong road, turn back."

We hugged good-bye and then I hiked down the hillside without looking back. I felt my pocket and found that the apple sat safely there. Remembering the silver coin, I walked to the fountain that sat in the center of the town.

I have always laughed at the way that difficult work becomes easy once you begin it. Conversely, the tasks you imagine will be easy often turn out to be laden with complexities and strife. Since I was carrying no other money, it would not be simple to give Hope's coin to a traveler who was richer in poverty than me.

66
THE POET'S QUEST FOR BLISS

"SHE WAS ALWAYS IN EXTREMES either crying or laughing — and so fierce when angered that she was the terror of men, women and children — for she had the strength of an Amazon with the temper of Medea. She was a fine animal — but quite untamable."

Sitting on a tree branch high over the fountain at Agios Nikolodeonos, I had been reading an anthology of love letters, this one by George Gordon, Lord Byron, about one of his mistresses in Italy. Handsome as a Greek god, Byron was beloved by all varieties of women everywhere. He despised injustices and defied conventions — social, political, and sexual. He exiled himself from England, wrote brilliant poems and letters, joined the Greek army to fight for freedom, then died of a fever in Greece at the age of thirty-six.

Byronic meditations were disturbed by a whirring hum, growing louder, like the chirping cicadas in love. A bicycle whizzed by along the street below. The bike — pedaled with marvelous agility by an athletic body and two bare feet — was ridden by that rare bird: the brazen braless-breasted Bliss.

A young man on foot chased behind the speeding bikress. He stopped at the fountain to shed his backpack, then followed her as she rode toward the restaurant-lined harbor in the heart of the town. In ten minutes he returned, huffing and puffing, looking as dejected as the giant Atlas after he had fumbled the world from the safety of his shoulders to the agony of his left foot.

Then the young man's face brightened, and he seemed to draw strength from a sublime idea. He raised his arms and shouted:

"Great goddess, Love! Make me your fool of fools and blind me with your splendid light! Keep my cholesterol low and my sperm count high! Lead me where you choose, but take me always through the roads of most intense experience! One chance! Give me one chance to meet this mobile maid!"

I dropped down beside him like Miss Muffet's spider, and hung from the tree branch with one arm.

"Hold, Poet! And remember the genius of youth: Courage increases possibilities."

"Thoreau!" said Seaport, with a smile. "I was just thinking about you!"

"It looked like you were thinking much more about that rolling blonde."

We embraced and I laughed out loud, overjoyed to meet my high-minded friend. Seaport gazed at the water far away.

"The beauty of women once more leads me astray," he said. "This morning started with a noble plan and a strict timetable to achieve my literary dreams. And then all plans scattered when I saw a heavenly vision, a nouveau mermaid half female and half machine! The voice of the singer Dante rose up from the forest of my spirit, and bade me to follow Woman to the wondrous who-knows-where! But I lost sight of her, and the guiding voice fell silent just when I needed it most."

"Before you followed your Bliss, Seaport, what were those noble plans?"

"I was going to the island of Melos," he said, "to search for the missing arms of the statue of Aphrodite. Have you seen them?"

"I never noticed that they were gone. ... Maybe this officer knows something."

A Tourist-Police officer approached us. As soon as he recognized me from the imbroglio on the boat he tipped his hat.

"*Kalimera,* Thoreau," he said. "We have been looking for you for many days. Can you wait here for a few moments. We have a pouch with money that belongs to you."

The policeman soon returned, asked me to sign a receipt, handed me my money pouch, and then explained. "On the last day of March," he said, "a woman named Bliss boarded the boat from Agios Nikolodeonos to the island of Rhodes. When asked how much money she was carrying she showed your money pouch, but insisted that it did not belong to her, and that she would not spend any part of it. But her own resources were not sufficient to buy the new visa to Marmaris on the coast of Turkey. Thus her entrance was refused, and she was sent back here on the first boat. She claims that she is now waiting for money from home. When that money arrives, the police chief will return her passport and then permit her to depart."

When the polite policeman had tipped his hat then left us alone, Seaport saw deeper than the facts.

"There are three kinds of travelers," he said. "High budget, low budget, and no budget. As a distinguished member of this third caste, I not only understand her problem, I empathize. Bliss is too proud to accept money from strangers, and she can't find decent-paying work. Forced to be so helpless and dependent, she must now be feeling downhearted, discouraged, demoralized, dispirited, dejected, and depressed."

"And by chasing after her," I asked, "you planned to provide her with moral and emotional support?"

He shook his head.

"I don't know why I followed her, Thoreau. For years I've suffered from kaligynophobia: fear of beautiful women. I have no eleutherophobia, peniaphobia, erotophobia, or phronemophobia — fear of freedom, poverty, sex, or thinking. But whenever I'm near women I desire, I get too panicky to talk. ... Join me for breakfast, will you?"

He untied the bandanna around his neck and then removed his last slice of bread. He tore that in two pieces, handed the larger half to me, and then held up a large plastic jar.

"Would you like some varmite with that?" he asked.

"Varmite? I've never made its acquaintance."

"It's a paste concocted out of brewer's yeast that looks like shoe polish, smells like roofing tar, and tastes like cat food in a can. I keep it for emergencies when there's nothing else to eat."

The stale bread scratched my throat as it was swallowed down.

"Seaport, when was the last time you've eaten a real meal?"

He scratched his head.

"I think it was the last time we met, in the Café Lathera, when you bought me a king's breakfast, and then ran from the café looking like the Moses who had just heard voices from the burning bush. That night I ventured to the hotel room of the waitress who so adroitly poured our cream. When her musclebound boyfriend answered the door, I unflappably pretended to be a traveling salesman selling penis-enlargement cream, and half of the island of Corfu. He didn't want the real estate, but he bought two large jars of moldy varmite."

I opened the large flap on his backpack then stuffed my pouch inside.

"Seaport," I said. "I wanted to give this money to Bliss, and she wouldn't take it. So now I want you to take it, along with this silver coin from a friend of mine named Hope. Better to have it and not need it, than need it and not have it. Romance ain't cheap. At minimum, you'll need to buy a good-quality bike."

Seaport removed the bills from the pouch, counted them, then rolled his eyes at the amount.

"I can't take this from you, Thoreau. We're friends, and more friendships are killed because of money than anything else."

"Take it as a loan, then," I said. "If I keep it now I'll spend it in Greece, and I'll have absolutely nothing when I get back home. If you take it now, you'll be helping me to do something I've never been able to do efficiently: plan my financial life."

He opened his notebook and wrote down the amount of the loan.

"Thanks, Thoreau. It's a deal — if you'll let me repay you with five percent interest, and if you'll let me buy breakfast for us both."

"I have a better idea," I said, as we clasped hands. "When the markets open, buy yogurt, fruit, nuts and bread — enough to stuff the gullets of six starving artists — then meet me at the public beach. We'll study the scenic beauty and have breakfast by the sea."

Seaport walked to the market, and I returned to my favorite camping place in that niche above the beach. Minutes later, Bliss rolled her bicycle along the sand, stopped for a moment to look at the sea, and then removed her shirt and like a ballerina spun around three times. Bare from the waist up, she swam far out from the shore. When she returned she made a cooking fire, and placed a pot with water over the flames. Now she faced the sea and began to stretch, in movements that looked at first like yoga, and later like ballet.

With admiration and confusion I stared at Bliss. She was a traveler, a dancer, a vegetarian, an independent spirit who loved nature and music and all living things. Despite her youth she had good sense and high ideals. She had left her country to discover what she could do to make the planet better, and to bring about a world with less violence, and a more equal distribution of the wealth. For months she had lived in Italy, in a community of women, to support endangered species, and to protest the human war against the natural world. We had talked little when we first met. Instead, we spent one long fiery night making love together, an amazing night, as only the strong supple bodies of two indefatigable athletes could spend.

Why then, had I refused to travel with the gorgeous Bliss? ... I did not know. Maybe because she was younger than me by five years, and I wanted the companionship that, without being stuffy, would be more intellectual, and share my devotion to books and writers and ideas. Maybe because with her I would have been a follower on her journey, not an equal partner on ours.

The last words that Pateras had whispered now came back to me.

"There are three kinds of foolish men," he'd said. "The man who thinks he can live alone; the man who gets involved with the wrong woman; and the man who doesn't recognize the right woman after she and he have talked together for one hour. You know, Thoreau, I'm more than eighty years old, and my heart still leaps like a young heart whenever I see how beautiful these women are! ... But beauty isn't everything! For every woman who tangles up your life, you must discover if she is your Calypso or your Penelope. Does she distract you and make you weak, or does she make you strong by helping you to do your own work? Too often, it's impossible to tell the difference until you're waist-deep in the relationship. And by that time it's much too late. Beauty has so much power over a man! The only chance to save yourself is to learn how to make this fine distinction between three species of women: the woman who is wrong for you, the woman who is almost right for you, and the woman who is exactly right."

I strolled down to the beach, ignoring the stares, hellos, and sighs from the barely-dressed women who were jogging by. Bliss was still facing the sea and stretching. Her sixth sense knew that I would find her here, and just as I approached her she gazed at the water and she began to sing.

"*O mangiar questa minestra o saltar questa finestra* — Either eat this soup or jump out this window."

"Remember me?" I said.

"Somewhat," Bliss replied.

"Are you mad at me for stuffing money into your bag?"

"I was mad when I found it. I'm not mad now."

"Do you still have the same plans," I asked, "for traveling around the world alone?"

"I'm leaving," she said, "as soon as a letter gets here." But the tone in her voice suggested that the letter might never arrive.

She stirred the rice in her pot, tossed in lentils and an onion, then covered the pot with a lid. I knelt down so that we would be speaking face to face.

"These days, in this world, it's not safe for a woman to travel alone."

"Then come along with me," she said. "There's plenty of room in my pack."

"Bliss, listen. I'd like to travel with you, but it's not the right time for me now."

"Men are so male!" she said. "When men don't want to do something, they never have the chops to say that they don't want to do it. They find any old excuse that will have them, then they hide underneath the skirt of that excuse."

On a sheet of notebook paper I scribbled my address.

"Will you write to me?" I asked.

Bliss took the paper and my pen, wrote the address of her parents' house, ripped the page then handed me a half. She stood up then hugged me with twice as much affection as I expected, and three times as much as I deserved.

"I might write," she said.

I could have argued more with her about her traveling plans, but what good would that have done? Reason rarely persuades: people do what they want to do, and then invent the reasons afterwards. I hugged the brave woman, and then walked back toward my campsite.

"Thoreau!" she shouted.

A flicker of hope filled me — maybe she had changed her mind.

"Thoreau, you forgot your pen."

"Bliss, I will never forget you. Keep the pen for good luck."

Seaport returned, arms laden with groceries, and found me on the beach. He arrived just as the first tourists were coming, carrying their beach umbrellas and blankets and sun-tan lotion and horrific modern novels and coolers crammed with icy drinks and artificial foods. A young woman wearing the latest-style bikini dropped her towel on the sand right beside us. She raised her sunglasses, then smiled at me with an enticing smile. Seaport examined the woman and then he sighed.

"It is a tribute to human inventiveness," he said. "that anyone can take one pair of shoelaces, tie them around their naked body, and turn them into a fashionable bathing suit."

The poet scanned the beach until his gaze stopped suddenly at a heart-breaking sight.

"Look, Thoreau! She's here! She is perfection! At last I have found Bliss!"

For a minute Seaport studied the woman like a book, and then he turned his gaze from the woman's body to my face.

"Thoreau," he said. "What did you mean about romance and a bike? I have as much chance of getting to know that voluptuous woman as a firefly stuck on a spider's web has the chance to survive past dinnertime."

"That's a good analogy," I said. "But your feeling is not a fact, it is the world seen through the dark distorting glasses of irrational fears. What does a man need to accomplish a difficult task? Four things: courage, money, luck, and ingenuity. Usually, if you have any two of these it's good enough. Let's admit that the task is impossible, and then let's decide what plan gives you the best chance to succeed."

Bliss stood up again and stretched. Watching this beauty in motion, Seaport turned green with longing, red with desire and white with fear.

"Even if she were wearing an astronaut's suit I wouldn't have the nerve to talk to her," he said. "But if she's topless like that, my nine muses would turn into nine mouses. I would not know what to say or where to put my eyes."

May the goddesses forgive us for stretching the elastic truths of love. Crossing my fingers, I laughed as I slapped the shoulder of my friend.

"Listen, Seaport. Let your eyes go wherever they want to go. As for what to say, let her do all the talking and you'll be all right. Did you know that she is a graduate student majoring in the 19th-Century American writers? And she once edited a savvy literary blog called 'Glorious Existence', based on the inspiring words of H. D. T."

He leaped into the air.

"She loves Emerson, Fuller, Whitman, Melville, and Thoreau!" he shouted. "Holy Aristophanes, she must be my missing half!"

I nodded.

"Seaport, sometimes a little chutzpah is all you need. Take all the breakfast food in these bags, then approach her as if you've been invited. Talk to her with Cyrano's *sang froid* behind a sword or pen. Tell her that you have a problem: you're stuck with too much perishable food. Ask her if she can help you to finish it off before it spoils."

"And after that?" he asked.

"After that, you plummet alone. Everything depends on your courage, sincerity, and ingenuity."

"Thanks, Thoreau," he said, gripping my hand with both his hands. "Either I'll never forget you for this, or I'll never forgive you."

"Probably both," I replied.

Bliss was now lying on her belly on a blanket on the sand, beside her pot of lentils which had begun to steam. Writing in a notebook, she would often raise her head to look at the water and the morning light. Seaport took three deep breaths then approached her, almost stumbling over his own feet. He opened up a large bandanna then placed it near her on the sand.

"Excuse me," said Seaport. "Is anyone sitting here? I seem to have misplaced my book of the complete essays of Ralph Waldo Emerson."

"Who?" Bliss replied.

Seaport unpacked his bag of yogurts, fruits, nuts, honey-filled pastries and breads.

"Ralph Waldo ... yeh. Well, my name is Michael Seaport," he said. "Here I have some extra yogurts and fruits. My friends aren't coming, and I need help with the work of eating this food before it spoils."

Bliss glared at Seaport and made his heart quake with a piercing smile.

"We've heard that line before," she said. "Another macho muchosmoocho American male on the make."

And Bliss returned to the writing in her notebook, and left the poet ignored.

Seaport later told me that he would have answered her the way a Zen master solves his koan: say nothing, just smile then devour the food. But Luck helped him, as Luck helps every man who tries his best. An old Greek man, dressed in a thick black suit, came wandering along the beach and stopped beside Seaport and Bliss.

"*Kalimera*," said the poet. And now, in his excellent Greek language, Seaport spoke to the old man, who knew some German but no English at all. "Would you like to join us for some breakfast?"

"No, thank you," the old man replied. "Just tell me, what are you cooking in that pot?"

"Try some," said Seaport.

Bliss watched, annoyed and amused, as Seaport dipped his spoon into the pot, then handed it to the old man, who took a sip.

"It could use more garlic," the old man said.

While Bliss chewed her lentil breakfast, Seaport talked with the old man. The Greek used his hands as he spoke, to show a man doing various kinds of work. At the end of the talk he smiled at Seaport, they heartily shook hands, and the Greek handed Seaport a scrap of paper with an address.

Bliss eyed the poet and then shook her wooden spoon.

"Nice of you to give away free samples of my breakfast!" she said. "What were you talking about?"

This would be the moment of nothing or everything. Seaport trembled like the sea.

"That man owns four restaurants and two hotels in town," he said. "He has just hired me for two weeks to work at a dozen different jobs: cooking, painting, schlepping barrels of wine, translating Greek to English, and doing any other work that his business might need. He offered a good salary and a bonus of three full meals every day."

"What did you say to that?" asked Bliss.

"I told him that you and I are married —"

"You what!" she shouted.

Seaport raised his hand.

"... and that it's not efficient to work alone. If he wanted to have two strong workers instead of one, then he could pay triple the salary he offered, and hire both of us."

That opened the emerald eyes of Bliss.

"What did he say to that?"

Seaport grabbed the wooden spoon, then ladled some spoonfuls of soup into his metal cup.

"Bliss, did anyone ever tell you, what goddesses rarely have seen — like Halkidiki olives, your eyes are amber-green?"

She stood up, grasped his shoulder with her hand, took a deep breath and then asked: "What did he say about the work?"

"He said that if we show up at his biggest restaurant tomorrow morning at eight, then we'll both be hired for the jobs."

With a great scream of joy, Bliss lunged her bouncing body into Seaport, crushing him in a passionately grateful hug. She lifted his poetlight body six inches off the ground, and then dropped him ever-so-gently onto the sand.

"You got jobs for us!" she shouted. "Decent-paying jobs! Bloody hell, I can't believe it's true!"

Her face brightened at this supreme good news, and now she snatched one of Seaport's yogurts from his hands. She pulled off the lid, tossed in some grapes, dipped her wooden spoon into the creamy delight, then ate voraciously.

"She vacuums up food like a poet!" Seaport said. "If you keep eating like that we'll have to change your name to Blintz."

"And from now on I'm gong to call you Soup-pot," she said, smiling.

"Soup-pot it is! Bliss, you remind me of Dervla Murphy. I've read every book she's written, and last year I wrote her a letter to thank her for her work."

Bliss's face brightened even more, and she sat herself so close to Seaport that their hips and shoulders touched. As she sliced a banana into her second yogurt, she smiled into his eyes.

"You know Dervla? She's my heroine!"

From the unimaginable joy of sitting so touchingly close to a young woman as beautiful as Bliss, the Poet looked as if he were about to faint. But at heart he was a brave man: he had determined to make himself a poet in an age too self-absorbed to grasp the worth of poetry; and for his whole adult life he had defied every trite convention and every false idea. Despite his inexperience with women, that morning he found his way. The laughing eyes of Bliss evoked his courage, and he relaxed and let his true self act and speak.

"In her book *A Travel Memoir To India*," said Seaport, "Dervla wrote that at the current rate it will be very soon when the human race eradicates all traces of natural beauty on our lovely Earth. Then we will look back on this current age the way people today look at the Ice Age: we will believe that it once existed, but we will not be able to imagine how terrible and beautiful it was."

Bliss smiled again at Seaport, then ripped a loaf of bread in half and stuffed a chunk into her mouth.

"Tell me more," she said.

Happy that two good persons had found each other, I left them alone on the beach. Luck brought them together, pluck dared them to reveal their true selves, and love would take care of the rest.

Months ago I'd told the lovely gypsy women that I recharged my energy with music, food, and love. Now I had none of these but there still remained my favorite method for renewal: a long walk in the lovely hills. I breathed the pure air; I picked sage leaves and carob pods; I smiled to a young child sitting by a stone well, crying all alone. I would saunter in the mountains the entire day, reflect about my love problems, and hopefully come back in the evening lightened by new solutions, new possibilities, and new ideas.

6 7
WHAT THOREAU WAS THINKING
WHEN HE WANDERED ALL ALONE

"O HOW I LAUGH when I think of my vague indefinite riches. No run on my bank can drain it, for wealth is not possession but enjoyment."

As I bit the first bite of Hope's crisp apple, those words by Henry David Thoreau filled me like a song. Henry David had learned that close contact with Nature released his good genius, filled him with raptures and ecstasies, revealed the transcendental link between the outer and the inner lives, and taught him what not even the best teachers could teach: how to live with simplicity, wisdom, and joy. For twenty-six months, Henry David lived in the middle of a forest, in a small cabin on the shores of Walden Pond. During that time, on many evenings he walked home to eat dinner with his mother and his aunt. He understood that the woods and the wilds were not places to permanently hide, but to renew our energy so that our work in the world could be faced with the purest integrity and the clearest minds.

The second tangy bite from the apple reduced its size to half. I saw two dark ravens circling overhead, then I walked to find a small gray bird lying on the ground on its side, breathing heavily, staring at me with a glazed eye. Cupping my hand, I tried to give the bird some water, but when I placed the water under her beak she shook her beak and did not open it to drink. Gently, I moved her out of the sun to a shady place. For a few minutes I watched her breathing. And when she breathed her last breath I stood up then walked on.

Hiking through these rocky hillsides, ablaze with brightly-colored flowers, I should have been radiantly happy. But the dark moods hunted after me, even under the glorious Greek light. What a contrast: these warm idyllic hills versus the turmoil of big-city streets! Earth and the cold-planet Mars are not as different as the best and the worst places on this Earth.

Six months ago I left my native city in Bedlamerica to discover how I could survive the whirlwind of that bizarre metropolitan world. Underneath the mask of culture and comfort, the great cities are gardens of troubles and grief. Crime spreads unabated; pollution rages unchecked; freedom is trampled; women are beaten or driven to despair; children miseducated, neglected, abused; animals are murdered as if they feel no pain; law is a conspiracy that strangulates the poor so that the rich qua-druplicate their wealth; millions of people starve and millions more slave hopelessly to make ends meet. There is no grace, no help to be had from the outside. These crises are praised as normal by our successful politi-cians, and thoroughly ignored by the big-name fabricators of our arts.

Genuine artists are never insensitive to the sufferings of humankind. Each day their voices cry: What can be done to light the chaos, and by this deep understanding make it more humane? ... Hawthorne, in his tale *Earth's Holocaust,* devised a specious scheme. All Earth's inhabitants decided that the world had become so overburdened with useless junk, they should eradicate the trumpery by burning everything superfluous in one great bonfire. The first things to be incinerated were yesterday's newspapers and magazines; then the robes and crowns of kings; then barrels of alcoholic beverages, until not one drop of drink could any-where be found. The blaze rose skyward as people threw in every gun in the world, then every cannon, musket and sword. Then all the pa-per money fanned the flames; followed by all the world's books; then at last all the material symbols of religion: crosses and priestly garb. Shorn of these obstacles to happiness — kings, weapons, money, faith — the masses expected a new world to appear. Yet one spectator knew better. When asked what the world had forgotten to throw into the fire, this mysterious stranger replies: "What but the human heart itself? ... And unless they hit upon some method of purifying that foul cavern ... it will be the old world yet."

For the world's violence, crassness, and distress I had no remedies. Love was too rare, truth was too difficult, education was too slow. But I was certain that the human heart was no foul cavern. I had met so many joyful children, tender women, and unselfish men — I would always be-lieve in the immense goodness of this heart.

From my pocket I retrieved Hope's apple to take the third juicy bite. The child in tears! I stopped for a moment, swallowed that apple chunk, then ran back over the last hill and found the child still crying by the well.

68
To Each Other
We Told Our Hearts

The child was called Sophia. She looked five years old; she was dressed plainly in a cotton dress; her amber hair swayed lightly like the stalks of grain. When upside-down I walked by her on my hands, she stopped crying; and when I tumbled down she laughed, then ran to help me up. Smiling, she grasped my hand. What great catastrophe had caused her tears? A boy in her class had unearthed a large slimy worm, and he chased the other girls while dangling the creature in his outstretched fingers as he ran. The girls ran away laughing and screaming, but the boy never chased after Sophia, he never chased her at all!

Holding my hand she led me to the wooden-shack schoolhouse which served children from the farms and tiny towns nearby. We met Paris, the school's caretaker, a slender but muscular man with a face like a fairy-tale gnome, and a nose as long as the handle of his knife. Outside the schoolhouse the worm-in-hand boy still chased the laughing girls, but now the school bell rang, and all the children dashed inside. Their teacher, dressed in humble clothes, appeared to own little money or resources. The school itself looked like it might tumble to the ground if you forgot to cover your mouth when you sneezed. Yet when Sophia said to me, "This is my school! This is my teacher!" her eyes glowed with joyfulness.

"What do you teach at this school?" I asked. "Science? Economics? Agriculture? Math?"

Helen, the young teacher with dark hair and the deepest eyes, was pure loveliness: gentle in manner, ample in bosom, slender in waist. Each time she spoke to me she clasped her hands together and lowered her entrancing eyes. *"Oh-shee,"* said Helen softly. "No. ... We teach this."

She picked up an accordion then played a lively melody. Instantly, the students — forty boys and girls aged 5 through 12 — leaped from their chairs, pushed the chairs to the edges of the room, assembled in a circle, clasped hands then began to dance. As they danced they looked at their teacher, and at the other students, with that same joy and tenderness that Sophia had emanated when she introduced me to this rare school in the lonely hills. When the dance ended, the children ate crackers and fruit, and then Helen pulled a random number from a box, and in that way one child was chosen to tell a tale. One of the older boys stepped forward then spoke with confidence.

"There were two brothers named Amphion and Zethus. Amphion loved philosophy and music and the arts; his brother Zethus despised the sciences, and loved to make war. Zethus teased his brother constantly, saying that all the time Amphion spent playing his lyre was wasted time, because it distracted him from the work of a man. One day, a god asked the brothers to build a city. Day after day, Zethus carried the heavy stones in a basket on his back. But when Amphion played his lyre his stones moved by themselves, and fit themselves into just the right places. And Amphion accomplished his work this way much faster and more skillfully than his brother who hated the arts."

I had taken off my shoes when I entered the schoolroom, stepped on the wood floor, and winced as a sharp splinter pierced my sock. Helen saw it happen. She filled a basin with water and herbs, then with as much care as any nurse could give, removed the splinter and washed and massaged my wounded foot. The goofy-looking caretaker entered, and the teacher Helen shyly smiled at me, then took his hand. With a gaze into his eyes she said: "This is my husband," and her voice trembled with thankfulness.

For two hours I worked helping Paris to haul wood and to repair a desk and broken chairs. After the work, Helen and Paris gave me a bowl of yogurt and their address; they questioned me about America; they begged me to come back and visit whenever I could. As soon as possible, I promised, I would send them a package for the children, filled with notebooks and crayons and pens.

The remainder of the day I walked, climbed, jogged, and sprinted through the flowering hills. When I returned to my campsite near the beach the sun was one hand above the horizon — in one hour the sun would dip into the sea. I made a fire, topped it with a pot of water, then tossed in the sage leaves and carob pods I'd gathered from the hills. A glance at a map proved that during the day's journey I had traveled about forty-five kilometers, or twenty-eight miles.

I remembered a night in Agia Souvlakis when Penelope and I were walking together under a bright full moon. As always, as friends do without reserve, to each other we told our hearts. Yet the sublime beauty of that night drew us closer than ever before. Penelope had asked me if she was foolish to chase after and wait for the non-committing Kosmos.

"Penelope," I said, "since you've asked me, I'll tell you: there's no need to worry that Kosmos will think less of you for confessing how much you love him. He knows, and he laughs at the fact, that Love makes a wise man into a fool, and makes a fool into a bigger one. Do you know the story of why Love is blind? ... Love and his friend named Folly were playing together, when Folly accidentally pushed Love into a tree. Love lost his sight. To punish Folly, Aphrodite decreed that Folly would forever do the work, like a seeing-eye dog, of taking Love wherever he desired to go. And that's why Love and Folly are always together, and why we're filled with foolishness whenever we're struck by the darts of Love."

Penelope laughed her hearty laugh, then squeezed my arm.

"Thoreau," she said. "It's my turn now to tell you something that you do not know. It is about Beatrice. She is the woman that every woman should want to be. There is nobody smarter, harder-working, or more caring about women and kids. She helps them to help themselves discover what they need. ... What's killing this world? Too many people taking without giving. Beatrice is the woman of the future: she takes nothing and gives everything. ... Don't think that she is looking for a man to worship her. She wants a man committed to something great, something far more significant than his own selfish pleasures. ... About you and Beatrice together, well, you know already what I think about that. You told me how Love is blind, and I can guarantee you that Love doesn't hear so well, either! Young men need to open up their ears and listen. It's what Zorba said to his beloved boss: 'You can knock forever on a deaf man's door.'"

This remembrance evaporated as the water boiled over the edges of the pot, then spilled into the fire to make it sizzle, hiss, and gasp. Suddenly I grasped what Penelope had been hinting at. Why had Beatrice not fallen for me the way a hundred other women fell?

To survive the clash against my country's superficial values, I had dropped out of things, practiced non-participation, dreamed not of facing challenges but of freedom and escape. I had lived for women and adventures, for walking and running in wild places, for books and brave ideas, for moments of being and joy. The rapture of being alive remained inside me: my inner fires would never be extinguished by the world's mean worries and worthless work.

Yet in the eyes of Beatrice I was immature. Light years beyond all selfish pleasures is the realm of Love. I had dabbled in the art of loving, but failed to master this essential art. I had driven my life recklessly, taken a wrong turn, and then missed the bridge that carries carefree young men to the awesome responsibilities of fully-human adulthood. And I had failed to realize that every man needs some kind of meaningful work. Work that protects and nourishes the persons and ideals he loves.

Hope always remains. If I could change, then Beatrice might change her mind about me. Had not the divine-looking Helen chosen that funny-faced woodcutter to be her husband for life? Love is blind, and Love blinds us by giving too much light.

Only one quarter of Hope's apple remained; I lay down on a blanket and then I popped the apple into my mouth to enjoy the last sweet bite. In one great flash of light at last I knew my heart. I loved Beatrice with my entire soul.

The spirit was willing, but the body too stiff and sore to leap up and dance like Scrooge on Christmas morn. Lying on the blanket, I promised myself this.

"Since love means action and not just dreams, tomorrow morning I will leave for England's green and pleasant land! I'll knock on Beatrice's door, throw ten dozen flowers on her head, then ask if we can talk about beginning a relationship. If she says 'no' then I'll leave quietly and forget her. And if she says 'yes' or 'maybe yes', then ... Just give me one chance, one good chance!"

I laughed then tried to stand, but everything below my shoulders — thighs, back, knees — ached like I had lost a wrestling match with Heracles. On my back I planned my route to England, and sipped more sage-carob tea.

The sunsetting sky filled up with gold-edged clouds. Noises from the road above my campsite broke this hopeful reverie. By the light from the gold-red sunset I could see a figure dressed in a white frock, slipping down the slope of sand like a mountain goat. What could this be but divine punishment for my outlandish courage to dream! I had been imagining the love of Beatrice Loverly, and now I was about to be assaulted by the terror of a sex-hating nun. With her flabby body and wrinkled face, Mother Whackanzakis charged at me, shouting in Greek and Italian, too fast for me to understand.

69
LOVE AND DANGER

AS MOTHER WHACKANZAKIS, the hunchbacked nun, charged at me like a mama grizzly bear (species *U. horribilis*), I thought of two ancient proverbs. The Chinese chanted: 'Of the thirty-six ways of avoiding danger, best is to run away.' The Russians rumbled, "When a mad dog runs at you, welcome him."

This repulsive woman filled me with no fear. A female Frankenstein's monster, she had a puritan mind that hated everything about sex, but a pure heart that helped every needy creature in distress. Her hands carried no sticks or stones; her words could not hurt me; and I imagined that she would stand over me and shout and wave her arms, until my soft answers and hard facts could turneth away her wrath.

Once again I had guessed wrongly, forgetting the first and last law: Never underestimate the intensity of a woman's passion. The flab-filled Mother pounced on top of me, then placed her knees on the ground around both sides of my hips. With a vengeance and her warty hands, she grabbed my wrists and pressed them against the soft sand.

"Hermes, messenger of Zeus," said her raspy voice, "stopped moving and looked around him with the greatest happiness. Then he entered Calypso's grotto. And she knew him the instant she saw him, because — even when they live far away — the gods know each other when they meet."

She pressed her knees against my arms, pinning them to the sand.

"You are the most promiscuous man I have ever seen!" she cried. "Even the mother with her large breasts feeding the baby, you were winking at!"

"I never even noticed," I replied, "the perfectly-shaped, rosy-nippled, Titianesquely-tinted beauty of that milking mother's mammoth breasts."

Curious about the fate of the gypsies, I wondered if the Mother-nun's appearance here meant that her efforts to help them had failed.

Suddenly this wonderful imposter raised her hands then plucked, from her two fingers, two pimply brown-colored lumps. She removed her yellow teeth, stripped off the her fuzzy mustache, then peeled off the wrinkled-skin mask above her face.

"Beatrice!" I shouted.

"Darling, I can't decide whether you look more dumbgasted than flabberfounded, or vice versa. Isn't it splendid the way Love either loosens the tongue, or Love ties the tongue in knots!"

"I've been stung by a Bea. Why didn't you tell me any of this?"

"Dear Thoreau," she said, "don't you recall that keen advice — about speaking and writing and wooing — from Monsieur Voltaire? The secret of being a bore is to tell everything. ... Darling, your chin needs shaving, your soul needs saving, and worst of all for this evening's activities, you are vastly overdressed."

She pulled off my T-shirt, dragged off my shorts, then sat up to admire the body revealed.

"Beatrice," I said. "This is getting very close to adultery."

She licked her luscious lips.

"Then make me immoral with a kiss."

Beatrice bent closer and as our nosetips touched, she placed her hand around my bared bottom.

"My Dover peach," she said. "Come to the window, sweet is the night air!"

Even covered by the nun's bulky garb she looked enchanting. I pulled off the white hood, I touched her face, my hand brushed her long dark hair. And I remembered the poem by Matthew Arnold that we had talked about, on that perfect October night when my arms carried her over the soft sand beneath the lover's moon.

> "Ah, love, let us be true
> To one another! for the world, which seems
> To lie before us like a land of dreams,
> So various, so beautiful, so new,
> Hath really neither joy, nor love, nor light, — "

To silence me politely she placed her finger on my lips, then spoke her own heartened version of the end of that poem of ultimate despair.

> "Until free sexuality and love we teach;
> And here we are as on a sparkling beach,
> Sweatingly fused for snuggles and delight,
> Where immanent arms re-clasp by night."

When she finished these words, Beatrice burst into tears. Her warm hands caressed my cheeks.

"I'm so happy with you!" she cried. "You give me courage, and strength, and hope for everything. The way you look at me, the way you speak to me — with so much tenderness! It calms me. It opens me. It lets me love you more and more and more a thousand times."

Quickly she recovered herself, the weeping wound down to sniffles, then at last she relaxed into a beauteous smile.

"Now darling, before we let things go too far—before we engage in one of those reckless sexual encounters that foments into a feckless emotional bond— there are two things I need to tell you. Firstly, we cannot commit adultery—"

Straightaway I ceased the kissing of her fingertips.

" — because yesterday I became officially divorced. Now secondly, in the process, I lost most of my money and property, and then donated what was left for the rescue of those ten brave but unfortunate young women who you know so well. So when I leave Greece I shall be as poor as a gypsy. Poorer, truly, with a daughter to care for, and the lioness's share of WANDERBORE."

Beatrice took a deep breath.

"So I would like to suggest, for the advancement of your literary career, that you consider finding a wealthy widow to support you and — "

With one passionate kiss I told her she was the only woman in the world for me.

"Beatrice, I'm coming."

"I know that, darling."

"I mean, I'm coming with you when you leave Greece."

"I knew that months ago, Thoreau."

"The two of us," I said, "working together, could accomplish the most amazing things!"

Beatrice smiled.

"Oh darling, you've just made me the happiest woman alive! Living together will be such a lark! ... But oh, my, look what we have here! I thought that it was only trials and adventures that changed a man and made him grow. You look like you're ready to frolic between my Dovery cliffs. Reach into my humps. ... Not those humps, dear, the ones in the back."

Sliding my hand into the back of her dress I tugged a string that released the pouch that had formed her artificial humps. Out tumbled a bottle of home-made massage oil, which clobbered me on the forehead. Next, a shower of letters and postcards fell down — all the letters I had written Beatrice — she told me later that she would never travel anywhere without those precious letters near. And at last, raining onto my face and chest, came a countless heap of condoms wrapped in foil. On the back of the condom wrapper I read the words: 'One size fits most"; and the front featured a cartoon picture of a smiling face, and a curvingly-stretched body enjoying a frenzied orgasm — the Love-goddess, Aphrodite.

"Wantonly I kissed his lips," said the smiling Beatrice, "because from this man I *want only* his passionate love." Then, with a clasp and a giggle, onto my manhood she dribbled the silk-smooth oil.

"Darling," she whispered. "Prepare yourself for a night you will never forget. I'm going to cover you with butter, and then make love to you until that butter turns to cream."

We laughed as we recounted my adventure with Bedusa. Then in the silence we gazed spellbound into each other's eyes.

"Beatrice, how did you find me tonight?"

She threw off her nun's dress.

"I had a hunch. ... And what about you, darling Thoreau? When did you realize what I knew the instant we met at the Meteora: that we would love each other, and make love with each other, and let nothing in this universe ever come between us, except a six-hundredth of a millimeter-thick latex prophylactic sheath?"

"That's a long story," I said. "I was attracted to you from the very first minute; when we dined at the house of Kosmos I admired you; and I've been in love with you for months. But it wasn't until a few moments ago when I loved you completely, with my whole soul. When I ate the two apples of Sex-and-Foolishness, and Wealth-and-Suffering, then I struggled so much because I could not live on the outside what my inner genius wanted me to do. Eating the apple of Love-and-Danger made me whole. I found the great Love — that's you, Beatrice — and as long as you want me I'll never let you go."

She kissed me to thank me for those words of confidence.

"What are you thinking now, darling, with your bright eyes so far away?"

As my mind relaxed my eyes came back to look at Beatrice.

"That at last I grasp Love. But the Danger that's supposed to come with Love, I don't understand that at all."

From just over the ridge of our campsite, along the road to Ag Nik, we heard a violin and a flute playing that poignant melody, "Gypsy Airs".

Beatrice sighed and then pondered for just a moment, and then her face grew bright. Lying close beside me she spoke with words that were gentle and strong.

"Man, we have not yet reached the end of our struggles: a risky, noble, and glorious task awaits us, and we must face it without delay."

The music came louder, and then — wearing nothing but a silk slip — Beatrice moved from beside me to a position sitting on top. She removed her panties then rubbed them against my chest.

"That music!" she cried. "It's so romantic here, so peaceful and so private. You know, dearest, that the ancient Greeks called the wedding night 'the night of secrets.' The bride and groom made love for the first time, while outside their bedroom their friends played music all through the night."

Now, strident police sirens clashed with the soothing music of the violin and flute. Suspecting trouble, I sat up on one elbow, then glanced around the campsite to search for my flung-away pants. Beatrice kissed my forehead as the sirens and the music both approached.

"Good evening, boss!" a voice shouted. *"O voi che siete due dentro ad un foco!* Oh you who are two in one fire!"

Panzano appeared, stood at the top of the ridge, and looked down on us with a broad smile. He held up his left hand that showed a silver ring, and then with his right hand he raised the hand of a young woman who stood beside him.

"We're engaged!" he shouted, with the thrill of a man in love for the very first time. "My bride is going back to school, and I'll go with her to Athens and look for work there."

He suddenly noticed that I was nude, and gingerly covered the eyes of the laughing Irene, his wife-to-be.

"We'll write to you as soon as we get settled in," he said. *"Arrivederci,* Thoreau! Good-bye!"

Beatrice sat up and sighed. "They're such a lovely couple," she said.

The sirens and violin music grew even bolder than before. And now, standing on the same spot where Panzano had stood, we saw the gypsy leader Katerina.

"Can you two wait about ten minutes," she yelled, "before you begin your performance? We've sold tickets to thirty bored tourists, for 'the greatest sex show on Earth.' The brochure says: 'Two beautiful people who love sex and do it expertly' ... Hey, in Amsterdam it's legal work, it happens every day."

Katerina read my face and spoke before I could shout.

"It's not to profit us, I swear it! Your gypsy friends have turned over a new fig leaf."

Katerina turned her head then shouted back: "Girls, who's getting the profits from this show?" ... and the gypsies in one voice replied: "Beatrice!" ... "And how much is she getting?" Katerina asked. And the gypsies shouted: "Everything!"

A canvas bag filled with bills and coins flew through the air then landed on the sand beside us. The sirens screamed until a man's voice, amplified via a loudspeaker, bellowed something about 'raising your hands.'

"*Plastra lesti!*" yelled Katerina, as she vanished behind the ridge.

We heard more police cars screeching to a halt; the sounds of a scuffle and shouts; car doors slamming shut; and then motors starting up and driving off.

"Oh, darling!" said Beatrice, caressing my cheek with her hand. "This afternoon I put them on the boat to Piraeus, and instructed them to meet us in Athens tomorrow night. I can't imagine what went wrong!"

Relationships are tested every day, in large things and in small. Whenever these crises come the woman learns what kind of man she's found: one that will give her scathing criticism, or one that will provide unconditional acceptance and support. Beatrice squeezed my hand.

"Darling, help me decide what to do now. I can't let those women stand alone against that gavel-banging judge. And I can't abandon you in this excited condition. My mother always told me that if you leave a man when he has three legs, then he'll walk away from you one-and-a-half times as fast."

One day I might explain how a man in that condition is neither willing nor able to walk at a faster pace. Now was a time not to explain but to act.

"Beatrice," I said, "you did promise that I would never forget this night. You'd better go and save the gypsies again, before all our good work is spoiled in a last minute of bad luck."

"But darling," said Beatrice, "you're so — "

"Go, love. I'll join you later, Beatrice — as soon as I plateau. Go, as fast as you can, and get those gypsies to any safe place off this island, before they steal all the sand in Crete. I'll meet you at the police station after I've found the tourists and returned their cash."

She kissed me quickly but tenderly, then slipped into her nun's dress, then climbed the ridge and waved good-bye. She vanished for a moment, then appeared again on the ridge and gazed down.

"Life-love," Beatrice said. "I believe that this rapidly-approaching swarm of marching people is that suckering of tourists coming to observe what they've bought tickets for."

She stared at me and giggled, then motioned with her hands.

"Dear, let's not have an eleventh prisoner to bail out. Pour that cold sage tea onto your extended warranty."

Beatrice blew me two kisses then ran. With the tea — and the help of some Bedusan reflections — I was lucky to get my umbrella quickly closed. Looking for my shorts I found the panties she'd left behind, and I read their red-lettered message.

"Hero, god,
  profound dissenter —
Gorgeous hunk of man,
  Here Enter!"

Exhausted and sore all over, I stood up like a ninety-year-old man. I rubbed my aching thighs, threw on the shorts and the T-shirt, then walked as quickly as possible towards the center of the town.

70
The Nude Life Begins

"Come here, darling and let me pleasure you," the woman said. "I am the lamp of Aladdin. Rub me and I shall grant you wishes three."

There is music that makes you vigorously dance; and there is music that makes you weep because it brings to mind the dreams you never dare forget. Yet there is no music more powerful, more sweet, more intoxicating than the voice of a beautiful woman who loves you, calling you to her bed.

She woke me with splendid kisses as the sun began to rise above the sea.

"I'm going to kiss you a thousand times," she whispered, "and each kiss will be more amorous than the lust."

Her strong and clever hands massaged the sorest muscles on my legs and thighs.

"The technique you are about to experience gives a man the most supreme excitement for the maximum amount of time. Close your eyes, and do not peek until you peak."

On my back on a blanket on the sand, I closed my eyes and stretched my body out.

"Thoreau, dearest, do you know that lovely Lawrence novel that had all England in a huff because the woman sleeps with her husband's groundskeeper?"

"I've seen it at book sales, Bea."

"The man has a name for his pleasure-organ. What do you call yours?"

"You can name it for me."

"'Let's call him 'Opportunity,' she said.

"Because he knocks but once?"

"Because he's ready at every moment. ... Ah, but now, resting so serenely, he has a sheepish look. I'll call him my little lamb."

Beatrice was silent, my eyes remained closed, and to pass the time I made up a nursery rhyme, less for the nursery and more for the nurse.

"Beatrice had a little lamb,
It hung around Thoreau.
And every time she fondled him,
The lamb was sure to grow."

I heard her moving around the campsite, and I assumed she was preparing for our daylong marathon of indescribable delights.

"Regarding society's sexual emancipation," I asked, "are we advancing or running away? ... Can adults talk freely about their sexual problems and needs, or is sex still shamed and hidden in the bulging pockets of the priests? ... Sexual energy, in the Greece of Pericles, was worshiped as a gift from the divine. What do you think, Beatrice? ... Beatrice?"

Nothing but the sound of waves. When I opened my eyes my clothes were dangling from a tree branch, and Beatrice was nowhere in sight.

Glancing at the beach I found her, one hundred yards away, posing as a mermaid on a rock. Staring at me with a smile half seductive, half defiant, half mischievous. When I ran to catch her she laughed then started running up the beach.

Chasing after her I recalled last night. I had apologized to the tourists (explaining that it been a college prank), returned all the money, and then ran to the police station. By the time I arrived there, Beatrice — dressed in a revealing gown — had made friends with the white-haired Police Chief, thanks to her beauty, her Greek-speaking, her charm, and a case of wine as a gift, far better than Kosmos's finest. The Chief took us all — the gypsy women, too! — to his favorite restaurant and treated us to a sumptuous meal. And then when dinner was done he arranged for his Lieutenant to escort the gypsy women to Athens via Piraeus by a private boat. From there they would be placed on the 'FunBun Bus' which traveled directly to the coast of France, where Prudence would take them to England, their new home. Bea and I had returned to the beachside campsite well after midnight, and fallen asleep instantly in each other's arms.

When I caught up to Beatrice we clasped hands and continued running side by side. The sun rose high enough to glare our eyes, so we turned around and sprinted back to the campsite, hands together, never letting go.

"No more games now, darling, I promise!" she said. "Get ready for 'the day of secrets."

She kissed me a kiss that lasted a minute-and-a-half.

"Mmmm," she cried. "Love me from my alpha to my omega darling, and don't forget my delta in between."

"Beatrice, that kiss almost knocked my socks off."

"Am I losing my power already? she asked. "Why almost?"

"Because my socks fell off when your robe slipped open five minutes ago."

That compliment was rewarded with another unforgettable kiss.

"Stretching before sex," she said, "is one of the great neglected secrets of top performance. Let's get flexible, darling, so we can twist and shout."

I began my routine of stretching exercises while Beatrice enjoyed her yoga stretches, moving her body — with the utmost agility and grace — into a dozen different postures. With breathtaking appreciation, I studied her beautiful form. In her silk kimono with arms and legs that slipped out as she moved, she teased me, she pleased me, she tantalized.

When Beatrice moved into the famous lotus position — a yoga posture sitting with the legs crossed and the body completely relaxed — she asked me to sit and face her, close enough for contact by the touching of our knees.

"Darling," she said. "I have an important question for you. You know that there are two flavors of enlightenment. In the first variety, the sage leaves the suffering masses of people, he climbs a mountaintop, builds a mansion there, and then spends the rest of his life living on royalties, acting as if the remainder of Earth's seven billion inhabitants do not exist. When the second species of enlightened person arrives at the top of that liberating mountain, she looks down to all the people in the valley and then she shouts: "How wonderful it is here! I will teach you how to liberate yourselves. Come!" ... Which variety is the right one for us, darling?"

"If we were sitting in a café and talking, Beatrice, I would probably say that that is such a profound question I will need days or weeks to choose the answer right. But here, now, so close to you, with our knees touching like this, I'm inspired as never before. It's clear that since all living creatures are connected, that the only compassionate and true path to happiness is the way of the enlightened being who attempts the impossible task of helping his fellow women and men."

"I'm thrilled to hear you say that, dearest!" Beatrice said. "Because the day after we get to America we are going to start a sanctuary for artists, rebels, mystic thinkers, outsiders, gypsies, and expatriates."

"A wild life sanctuary?" I asked.

"Exactly, dear," said Beatrice, rubbing my knee with her hand. "For men, we will show them living examples of how they can give up their silly games and toys, and become mature, tender and humane. For women, we will give them courage and resources to hold the world together until the men grow up."

"Beatrice," I said. "Pateras told me that he and his friends are planning five sexually-liberated communities in Crete and on the Greek mainland. How will ours be unique? What precisely will we promulgate and teach?"

She smiled and then the morning grew a hundred times more bright.

"The Seven Lively Sins of Sextopias!"

"Which are?"

Without a blink of hesitation she replied.

"Nakedness, Laughter, Lust, Sincerity, Touching, Lovemaking, and Love."

I shook my head.

"From Frisco to New York, that would attract every kook and pervert who thinks that sex unlimited will bring happiness to their troubled souls."

Beatrice nodded then squeezed my knees.

"And it will attract all the millions of good-hearted yet lonely men and women who are genuinely searching for the answers to the mysteries of sexuality and love."

"Wait a minute, Bea — did you say we were going to America?"

"For years, Thoreau, I've wanted to experience that great country."

"For years, Beatrice, I've wanted to escape it."

"Dearest," she said, "my younger sister has a house and a few acres in Ithaca."

"The Greek Island home of the hero of the *Odyssey?*"

"Not that one," Beatrice said. "I mean the counter-cultured small town in New York State. By now, my sister must have cured her nymphomania. In any case, we'll be welcome and happy there. ... You look like you have another question, dear."

"Who will teach the thrilling theory of those lively and virtuous sins?"

"We will, of course!" said Beatrice. "And first, starting today, we will practice them until we have them perfect. No matter how much effort that requires."

"I'm just starting to appreciate this idea," I said.

A red hummingbird — the first hummingbird I'd ever seen! — hovered halfway between our faces.

"A heart in mid-air!" cried Beatrice. "A love-bird come to bless us with his stimulating hum."

The magnificent creature sat in mid-air and watched us for a minute, then flew away. When the bird left us alone, Beatrice removed all her clothing, every button and stitch.

"Darling," she said, "the first lesson is Nakedness. When a woman takes off her clothes you see her body, but in essence she bares her soul. As she stands naked before him she looks into the man's eyes. If she sees his eyes filled with boundless appreciation at how beautiful she is, then in gratitude she gives him the most glorious sexing that she can give."

I stared at the woman in front of me.

"She's a woman, and she's a goddess, too," I said. "Eyes can wonder and admire what words cannot express. Her smooth skin. Her toned tanned legs. Her thighs like the bodies of two sleek swans. Her belly so flat, her hips so filled with hopes, her breasts so round deliciously. Perfect breasts that stand up firmly, tipped by pink cones and the rosiest buds. And her face, bright and red and glowing, is a sunrise every time she smiles."

With two tears falling from her two deep eyes, Beatrice brushed my forehead for the appetizer, kissed my lips for the main course, then nibbled on my earlobe for the dessert.

"Dear Thoreau," she said, with a sigh. "Now that we are emotionally closer than ever before, and about to merge as only one man and one woman can, there is something that I can no longer wait to confess."

A bolt of anxiety hammered me, but I went forth nevertheless.

"Whatever the problem is, Beatrice," I said, "together we'll see it through."

She looked at me seriously.

"I have the itch."

"Do we need to seek medical attention?" I said, nodding, trying to appear calm.

"Not that kind, dear. It's far worse than that, I'm afraid. I have the writing itch. Turn over and lay flat on your stomach. One of those French authors used the naked back of his mistress for a desk."

Flat on my belly I felt her notebook fall open on my back.

"I'll write about your amorous exploits in Crete, dear," she said. "Should it be in the vein of the 19th-Century novels, that end in marriage and prosperity? ... Or in the vain of the 20th-Century tomes, that conclude with dissipation and ennui? ... Or maybe à la the brainless bestsellers of our 21st Century, we could clash the big-zitted zombies against the virulent virgin vampires in a final boring battle on the Acropolis in Athens? ... Ah! It must be a *bildungsroman,* also called an *erziehungsroman* —"

"A dungs roman," I asked, "and a hungs roman?"

"A novel about a young hero's growth and education. *Tom Jones* and *Jean-Christophe* and *Wilhelm Meister* are my favorites. ... That reminds me, we'll need to measure you for the back-cover blurb. Turn over for just a second, dear. ... Thirty-one centimeters long — I wonder what that is in inches?"

"Divide by two point five four," I said.

"Aren't we a splendid team, dear? ... What should the title be?"

"How about: *Man Against Woman: A History of Lovemaking From the Slime to the Sublime?*"

She tapped a pencil against her head.

"Our title should include the words 'romance' and 'utopia'. Now let's find a pseudonym so we don't get pseud. Turn over onto your back, Thoreau."

Her left hand massaged me with the slippery oil, as her right hand scrawled notes into her book.

"How about B. L. Overly?" I asked.

"Darling, do you know the story of an author named Amadine Aurore Lucie Dupin Dudevant? .. She left her husband for a lover named George. She told him that she needed to invent a *nom de plume,* since in those days women writers were ignored and ridiculed. This lover wanted from her what men want from women, and when they walked together one morning, she kept chattering on and on so much — she was not an inexperienced woman, but she was so excited about her new career and freedom, and about her romance with this new great-looking man — that she just kept talking and didn't stop. What could he do? He asked her to put on a blindfold, then told her that her pen-name would be the first words she spoke when she took the blindfold off. He hired a carriage, and then drove them both to the most magnificent beach in France. And when she removed the blindfold, she looked out and she shouted:

"'George, sand!' ... And that became her famous name."

Now Beatrice stretched out on her back, and that gesture was the only invitation I required.

"Beatrice," I said. "I am now going to find your Thorogenous zones."

"That will be easy, darling. They are everywhere."

My hands raked her fleshy love-garden while Beatrice bit her lip.

"Mmmm darling," she said. What are you doing to me? I'm humming like that red bird ... Whatever it is don't stop. I've never felt like this before!"

With every passing moment she looked more like that writhing goddess on the condom wrapper.

"Beatrice, here's a T-shirt. Will you cover up your eyes? And the first thing you say when you remove this shirt will be the name of your novel's narrator and protagonist."

My lips enjoined her rosy lips, played there for a while, slid smoothly along her swanny neck, traveled lower — pausing to appreciate the scenic sites — and at last nibbled in gentle circles around the centers of her perfect breasts. The T-shirt fell from her eyes and the enraptured woman screamed.

"O, Thoreau!"

Beatrice opened one of the foil-wrapped condoms that featured the happy Aphrodite.

"Dear love," she said breathlessly, "we have only one-hundred-and-forty-four of these, not enough to last us through the week. Put this on now, will you, and make the world safe for femmocracy. Now tell me a story, dear, to keep my mind occupied the way my body will be. And tell me the story to prolong the pleasure for me, and to prove what the Greeks believed: that the woman's sex drive is tentuple stronger than the man's."

Carefully, I moved my body on top of her warm body, once again amazed how the strength of a woman can manage the weight of a man.

"A story? All right, Beatrice ... When Zeus decided to sleep with a svelte woman named Alcene, he wanted more time with her to practice his technique. So he ordered Apollo to prevent the sun from rising for seventy-two hours. And he commanded the moon-goddess that for the same amount of time she should keep the full moon shining bright. So Zeus made the night three times longer."

Her hands caressed me as she shouted:

"Make it ten times longer!"

By concentration? By love? By science? By prayer? By vitamins? By years of practicing abstruse techniques? ... I wondered if, and when, and how it would be done.

"Beatrice, my heart of hearts, let's be careful how we celebrate. Envious of my divine instrument, your perfect beauty, and our immortal pleasures — will the gods look down then venge us?"

Her fingers wrapped my sword inside a rubber sheath. Then I entered the castle in the splendid kingdom of Beatrice, and the woman screamed with the rapture that all words and art and music have forever tried to tell. As floods of passion swelled, with all her tenderness she kissed me, with all her joy she breathlessly cried out —

"Aphrodite will protect us, Love."

Ω

If you have built castles in the air,
your work need not be lost;
that is where they should be.
Now put the foundations under them.

—Henry David Thoreau
Walden (1854)

About the Author

Michael Pastore is a novelist, poet, non-fiction writer and independent publisher. He has written and edited more than 20 books, most of them currently available from his Zorba Press website. Pastore's lively articles, essays, and interviews — about love, literature, sustainable living, children and childhood, and humanizing technology — have appeared in more than two dozen print publications nationwide. An expert in many facets of literature, writing and publishing, he has been quoted in the prestigious *Times Literary Supplement* and in the *New York Times*.

Pastore lives in Ithaca (New York) with his library of more than 8,000 of the world's best books. About the importance of genuine literature, he says: "Why read? ... The best books give us timeless hours of joy, expand our empathy and imagination, corroborate our most sublime feelings, remind us of our past, bring hope to our future, caution us to live wisely, empassion us to seize the moment, show us ideals embodied in heroes and heroines, inspire us to be great lovers and rebels, give us courage to be our selves, challenge us to help others, and point the way to deeper meaning in our everyday lives."

About Zorba Press

Zorba Press is an independent publisher of books, multimedia books and audio books (forthcoming), and user-friendly ebooks in many formats. From the gorgeous gorges of Ithaca, New York, we publish the paperback books **The Zorba Anthology of Love Stories**; **The Ithaca Manual of Style**; the anthology **Zenlightenment!**

Currently, we offer about 30 titles — fiction and non-fiction. Our recent publications include **The Terrestrial Gospel of Nikos Kazantzakis** by Thanasis Maskaleris; **50 Benefits of Ebooks: A Thinking Person's Guide to the Digital Reading Revolution**; Michael Tobias's extraordinary novels, **The Adventures of Mr Marigold** and **Professor Parrot and the Secret of the Blue Cupboard;** and the comic novel by Michael Pastore: **Thoreau Bound: A Utopian Romance in the Isles of Greece.**

At Zorba Press, we practice what we call "Sustainable Publishing": publishing with a greater sense of awareness and responsibility. Sustainable Publishing is the attempt to bring to the work of publishing a healthy balance between four essential elements: Culture, Commerce, Technology (humanized), and the Environment.

Zorba's mission is to promote the innovative ideas and the daring books that inspire creativity, nourish children and childhood, point the way to a culture of non-violence, create a sustainable future, and nurture — for every living being — a new world of love and kindness, courage and freedom, sincerity and peace.

Visit Zorba Press at

www.ZorbaPress.com

22205539R00332

Made in the USA
San Bernardino, CA
24 June 2015